# FEAST OF DREAMS

✳ ✳ ✳

## A Novel of Geadhain

CHRISTIAN A. BROWN

ISBN: 0994014406
ISBN 13: 9780994014405 **(Forsythia Press)**
Library of Congress Control Number: 2015902430
Toronto, Ontario

*For Justin, Michelle, Barbara, Kimberly, and Sarah.*
*And Mom too—as always.*

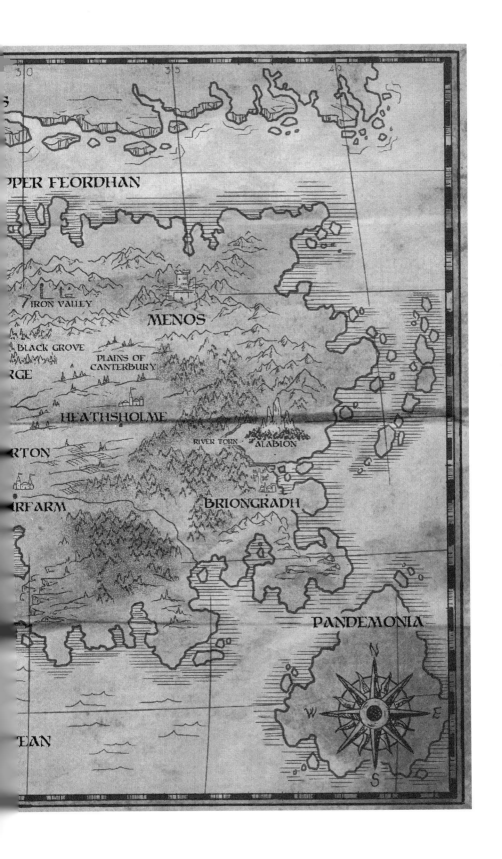

# CONTENTS

# ON GEADHAIN (GLOSSARY)

### I: Paragons, Wonders, and Horrors

***Brutus:*** The Sun King. Brutus is the second of the Immortal Kings and ruler of the Summerlands in southern Geadhain. Zioch, the City of Gold, shines like a gold star on the southern horizon and is the seat of his power. Brutus is the master of the wilderness and the hunt. His magik has dominion over the physical world and self. He is victim to the Black Queen's whispers and falls far from his nobility.

***Lilehum (Lila):*** Magnus's bride. Magnus sought her when learning to live as a man independent of his ageless brother. Through the sharing of blood and ancient vows—the *Fuilimean*—she is drawn into the mystery of the immortal brothers and imbued with a sliver of their magik. She is a sorceress and possibly eternal in her years. She is wise, kind, and comely without compare. However, she is ruthless if her kingdom or bloodmate is threatened.

***Magnus:*** The Immortal King of the North. Magnus is one of two guardians of the Waking World. The other is his brother, Brutus. The Everfair King— the colloquial name for Magnus—rules Eod, the City of Wonders. He is living magik itself; a sorcerer without compare; and the master of the forces of ice, thunder, Will, and intellect.

***Morigan:*** A young woman living a rather unremarkable life as the handmaiden to an elderly sorcerer, Thackery Thule. A world of wonder and horror engulfs her after a chance, perhaps fated, meeting with the Wolf. She learns she is an axis of magik, mystery, and Fate to the proceedings of Geadhain's Great War. In the darkest days that she and her companions must face, her heroism and oft-tested virtue will determine much of the world's salvation or ruin.

**Thackery Hadrian Thule (Whitehawk)**: An old sorcerer living in Eod. Thackery lives an unassuming life as a man of modest stature. However, he is a man with many skeletons in his closet. He has no known children or family, and he cares for Morigan as if she were his daughter. Morigan's grace will touch him, too, and he is drawn into the web of Fate she weaves.

**The Black Queen, Zionae** \\'Zē-ō-'nā\\: A shapeless, bodiless, monstrous entity without empathy who seeks to undo the Immortal Kings and the world's order. Her actions—those who perceive these things sense she is a she—are horrific and inexplicable.

**The Dreamstalker**: A vile presence that haunts and travels the waters of Dream as Morigan does. She is the Herald of the Black Queen, Zionae's voice in the physical world.

**The Lady of Luck, Charazance** \\'SHer-āh-zans\\: The Dreamer of serendipity, gambles, and games. Alastair is her vessel.

**The Sisters Three—Ealasyd** \\'Ēl-ə-sid\\, **Elemech** \\'El-ə-mek\\, and **Eean** \\'Ē-en\\: From youngest to eldest in appearance, they are Ealasyd, Elemech, and Eean. The Sisters Three are a trio of ageless witches who live in the woods of Alabion. They are known to hold sway over the destinies of men. They can be capricious, philanthropic, or woefully cruel. One must be careful when bartering with the Sisters Three for their wisdom. There is always a price.

**The Wanderer, Feyhazir** \\'Ph-āe-āh-'zi(ə)r\\: The Dreamer of mystery, seduction and desire.

**The Wolf, Caenith** \\'Kā-nith\\: A smith of Eod. His fearsome, raw exterior hides an animal and a dreadful wrath. Caenith is a conflicted creature—a beast, man, poet, lover, and killer. Caenith believes himself beyond salvation, and he passes the years making metal skins and claws for the slow-walkers of Geadhain while drowning himself in bitter remorse. He does not know it, but Morigan will pull him from his darkness and make him confront what is most black and wicked within him.

## II: Eod's Finest

***Adhamh (Adam):*** An exiled changeling of Briongrahd. Noble, loyal, and loving, his only hatred is for those like the White Wolf, who abuse and punish life. Humble Adam has a destiny beyond what he or others would ever expect.

***Beauregard Fischer:*** A waifish, lyrical young man lost in the Summerlands with his father. In his past and soul lies a great mystery. His cheek is marked with the birthmark of the one true northern star.

***Devlin Fischer:*** A seasoned hunter and Beauregard's father. He is as gruff and hairy as a bear.

***Dorvain:*** Master of the North Watch and Leonitis's brother. He is a brutish, gruff warrior tempered by the winds of the Northlands. He is dependable and unflappable. He is an oak of a man who will not bend to the winds of change or war.

***Erithitek*** \'Ār-ith-ə-'tek\: More commonly referred to as "Erik." He is the king's hammer. Erik was once an orphaned child of the Salt Forests and a member of the Kree tribe, but Magnus took him in. Erik now serves as his right hand.

***Galivad:*** Master of the East Watch. The youngest of Eod's watchmasters, he is seen by many as unfit for the post because of his pretty face, foppish manner, and cavalier airs. He laughs and sings to avoid the pain of remembering what he has lost.

***Jebidiah Rotbottom:*** A flamboyant spice merchant from Sorsetta. He sails the breadth of Geadhain in a garish, crimson vessel—the *Red Mary*. Currently, he uses different aliases, for reasons no doubt unscrupulous and suspect.

***Leonitis:*** The Lion. He is thusly named for his roar, grandeur, and courage. He is the Ninth Legion master of Eod (King Magnus's personal legion). Once Geadhain's Great War commences, he will play many roles from soldier to spy to hero. Leonitis's thread of destiny is long and woven through many Fates.

***Lowelia Larson (Lowe):*** The queen knows her as the Lady of Whispers. Lowelia seems a simple, high-standing palace servant, yet her doughy, pleasant demeanor conceals a shrewd mind and a vengeful secret.

**Maggie Halm:** Maggie is the granddaughter of Cordenzia, an infamous whoremistress who traded her power for freedom from the Iron City. Maggie runs an establishment called the Silk Purse in Taroch's Arm.

**Rowena:** She is Queen Lila's sword and Her Majesty's left hand. Rowena's tale was destined for a swift, bleak end until the queen intervened and saved Rowena's young life. Since that day, Rowena has revered Queen Lila as a mother and true savior.

**Tabitha Fischer:** The sole magistrate of Willowholme. She has assumed this role not by choice but through tragedy.

**Talwyn Blackmore:** The illegitimate son of Roland Blackmore (since deceased). Talwyn is a kind, brilliant scholar and inheritor of all the virtue that escaped his half brother, Augustus. Talwyn lives in Riverton. His thirst for knowledge often makes him cross boundaries of decorum.

### III: Menos's Darkest Souls

*Aadore Brennoch:* An Iron-born survivor. A woman whose strange lineage comes from the far, far East. Once a handmaiden to the Lady El, she will leave that meager station behind and rise into a woman of prominence and legend alongside her brother.

*Adelaide:* Mouse's childhood friend from the charterhouse. The girl's fate is the cause of much torment for Mouse.

*Alastair:* A mysterious figure who acts seemingly in his own interests. He greatly influences certain meetings and events. To all appearances, he is the Watchers' agent and Mouse's mentor. He almost certainly, though, serves another power or master.

*Beatrice of El:* Moreth's pale and ghastly wife. After a glance, a person can tell this ethereal woman is not wholly of this world.

*Curtis:* A young, athletic man with a shameful, criminal past trying to make a better life for himself in Menos. He is taken with Aadore, though will prove himself more than a doting suitor.

*Elineth:* Son of Elissandra.

*Elissandra:* The Mistress of Mysteries. She is an Iron Sage and the proprietress of Menos's Houses of Mystery—places where a wary master can consult oracles and seek augurs regarding his or her inevitable doom. While she is wicked, she is also bright with love for her children, and she fosters a hidden dream and hope no other Iron Sage would ever be so bold as to consider.

*Elsa Brennoch:* Mother to Aadore and Sean.

*Gloriatrix:* The Iron Queen and ruler of Menos. Gloriatrix single-handedly clawed her way to the top of Menos's black Crucible after her husband, Gabriel, lost first his right to chair on the Council of the Wise and then his life. Gloriatrix has never remarried and blames her brother, Thackery Thule, for Gabriel's death. With her family in shambles, power is the only thing to which she clings. Gloriatrix has ambitions far beyond Menos. She would rule the stars themselves if she could.

*Iarron (Ian):* An abandoned child, unnaturally calm and still, who was discovered by the Brennoch siblings, on Menos's darkest day—he is a star of hope to them.

*Kanatuk:* A tribesman of the Northlands who had been stolen from his home and placed into a lifetime of abhorrent slavery, serving as a vassal to the Broker. Morigan rescues him in Menos.

**Lord Augustus Blackmore:** Lord of Blackforge. A deviant power-monger with grotesque appetites.

**Moreth of El:** Master of the House of El and the Blood Pits of Menos. He traffics in people, gladiators, and death.

**Mouse:** More of a gray soul than a black one, Mouse is a woman without a firm flag planted on the map of morality. She knows well life's cruelty and how best to avoid it through self-sufficiency and indifference. As a girl, she escaped a rather unfortunate fate, and she has since risen to become a Voice of the Watchers—a shadowbroker of Geadhain. Mouse's real trial begins when she is thrust into peril with Morigan—at that time a stranger—and Mouse is forced to rethink everything she knows.

**Sangloris:** Elissandra's husband.

**Sean Brennoch:** Brother to Aadore. Once a soldier of the Ironguard, now a one-legged veteran. Sean wants no pity, however, and is more capable and clever than most other soldiers.

**Skar:** An ugly, ogreish mercenary whose heart is kinder than his looks. Fate sees his path cross with the Brennochs, and to them he will become a sword not for hire but bound to protect them through respect and duty.

**Sorren:** Gloriatrix's youngest child. Sorren is a nekromancer of incredible power who possesses the restraint and moods of a petulant, spoiled child. He shares a pained past with his (mostly) deceased brother, Vortigern.

**Tessariel:** Daughter of Elissandra.

**The Broker:** All the black rivers of sin in Menos come to one confluence: the Broker. Little is known about this man beyond the terror tales whispered to misbehaving children. The Broker has metal teeth, mad eyes, and a cadre of twisted servants whom he calls sons. He inhabits and controls the Iron City's underbelly.

**The Great Mother:** Her Faithful are multitudinous. Her elements and the shades of her divinity—Green, White, Blue—are prefixes to her many names.

**The Slave:** An unnamed vassal purchased in the Flesh Markets of Menos. A dangerous creature, more than a man. Although property, he later became a free man and substitute father to the Lord El. Together, the men traveled into the wilds of Pandemonia on a most dangerous safari.

**Vortigern:** Gloriatrix's second son. This pitiable soul lives in a state between light and dark and without memory of the errors that brought him to this walking death.

## IV: Lands and Landmarks

*Alabion:* The great woodland and the realm of the Sisters Three.

*Bainsbury:* A moderate-size township on the west bank of the Feordhan. Gavin Foss lords over it.

*Blackforge:* A city on the east bank of the Feordhan River. It was once famous for blacksmithing.

*Brackenmire:* The realm outside of Mor'Khul. It is a swampy but pleasant place.

*Carthac:* The City of Waves.

*Ceceltoth:* City of Stone.

*Eatoth:* City of Waterfalls.

*Ebon Vale:* The land around Taroch's Arm. It has fiefs, farmsteads, and large shale deposits.

*Eod:* The City of Wonders and kingdom of Magnus. Eod is a testament to the advances of technomagik and culture in Geadhain.

*Fairfarm:* The largest rural community in the East. With so many pastures, fields, and farms, this realm produces most of Central Geadhain's consumable resources.

*Heathsholme:* A small hamlet known for its fine ale.

*Intomitath:* City of Flames.

*Iron Valley:* One of the richest sources of feliron in Geadhain.

*Kor'Khul:* The great sand ocean surrounding Eod. These lands were once thought to be lush and verdant.

*Lake Tesh:* The blue jewel glittering under the willows of Willowholme.

*Menos:* The Iron City. It is hung always in a pall of gloom.

*Mor'Khul:* The green, rolling valleys of Brutus's realm. They are legendary for their beauty.

*Pandemonia:* The large island continent across the Cthonic Ocean and separated from most of Geadhain's other landmasses. Three Great Cities of immeasurable technomagikal power serve to bring order to this realm of chaos, a land where topography shifts and changes day by day from tundra to desert to lava field to wastes. Only these three Great Cities stand permanent in Pandemonia's constant flux.

*Plains of Canterbury:* Wide, sparse fields and gullies.

**Riverton:** A bustling, eclectic city of lighthearted criminals and troubadours. The city is found on the eastern shore of the Feordhan River, and it was built from the reconstituted wreckage of old hulls and whatever interesting bits floated down the great river.

**Sorsetta:** In the south and past the Sun King's lands. This is a city of contemplation and quiet enlightenment.

**Southreach:** A great ancient city built into a cleft in Kor'Khul.

**Taroch's Arm:** The resting place of a relic of the great warlord Taroch: his arm. The city is also a hub of great trade among all corners of Geadhain.

**The Black Grove:** The forest outside of Blackforge. It leads to the Plains of Canterbury.

**Willowholme:** A village located in Brackenmire and famed for its musicians and anglers.

**Zioch:** The City of Gold and kingdom of Brutus.

## V: Miscellaneous Mysteries

***Fuilimean:*** The Blood Promise. It is a trading of blood and vows and a spiritual binding between two willing participants. Magnus and Brutus did this first in the oldest ages. Depending on who partakes in the ritual, the results can be extraordinary.

***Technomagik:*** A hybrid science that blends raw power—often currents of magik—with mechanical engineering.

***The Faithful:*** Worshippers of the Green Mother. They exist in many cultures and forms, and the most sacred and spiritual of their kind, curators of the world's history known as Keepers, often lead them.

***The Watchers:*** The largest network of shadowbrokers in Central Geadhain.

# FOREWORD (A RECAP)

*Four Feasts till Darkness* is an expansive and complex work—even I lose track of things without my notes! It would be unreasonable, then, to expect perfect recall from my readers. To that end, I set one of my dear editors—Kyla—to scribbling down all the important bits of the story. Here you are: a refresher of the events of Geadhain's Great War leading up to *Feast of Dreams*.

—Christian

When first entering the world of Geadhain, we encounter a realm of magical smoke and metaphysical mirrors reflecting the darkest and lightest that its inhabitants have to offer. But as the pages of *Feast of Fates* turn, a deeper understanding of this mystical realm emerges, one that parallels the universalisms found in our own very real experiences in this world. It is a world unlike any other, where science and magic form a mysterious force known as technomagik. It is a land borne of a Green Mother earth, but ruled by the wills—both conscious and unconscious—of kings and queens that wreak havoc on their world. But there comes a time where even a mother must teach her children the hard way, even if it pains her. And so *Feast of Fates* sees the start of the Green Mother's tough love, depriving them of her protection for the anguish they have brought to her with their violence; it is the world's inhabitants alone who can save themselves.

Our story begins with the weavers of fate themselves, the Three Sisters—Eean, Elemech, and Ealasyd—who make their homes in the forests of Alabion. The Sisters represent life, death, and all its various contortions and permutations in the world. There, they both give birth to, and usher death upon, themselves and the world. With each renewal, they shape the twists and turns of our players' journeys, for better or worse. They represent destiny's infinite loop in a twisted sibling rivalry that will determine Geadhain's future. But even the Sisters of Fate cannot control the rumblings on destiny's horizon—the harbingers of destruction to come in the stormy and ethereal form of the Black Queen.

The scene shifts to the city of Eod—Geadhain's cosmopolitan metropolis. Nestled within Kor'Khul's oceans of sand, it is known as the City of Wonders for its host of technomagikal advancements and a skyline filled with flying carriages ferrying Eod's cultural and social elite. There we find Morigan, a young woman of character and strength who is traveling toward a destiny that was forged ages before her birth, and one that is intimately entwined in tapestries of the Three Sisters.

Morigan lives a simple life as a handmaiden until her world is thrown into tumult as she is drawn to the literal animal magnetism of Caenith, a wolf-man changeling whose initial gruff appearance belies his ancient origins and unimaginable power. The two are instantly bonded, each of them knowing that their attraction goes well beyond "love at first sight," and is more akin to having been written in Geadhain's starry skies. The two cannot deny what has been preordained, and the ripple effect of the Wolf and Fawn's union (as they come to know each other) as bloodmates begins to be felt throughout Geadhain. Their coming together stirs ancient powers of sight in Morigan, and inspires the beast in Caenith to reclaim its role in his life.

Morigan's nascent visions are a near-constant reminder that whenever there is joy, sorrow remains but a half step behind. She is witness to waves of destruction and death shadowing the realm, making their impending presence known not only to her but to all of Geadhain. In her mind's eye, she sees that just as we humans wage war against ourselves and the earth that has borne us all, so, too, does Geadhain face a battle against evil forged in blackness, smelted from the depths of all the worst the world has to offer.

Chief among Morigan's visions is the emergence from the pitch of the Black Queen.

This foul, black entity exerts her power chiefly by wielding the bodies of others like puppets. Morigan is forced to watch as the Black Queen overtakes Magnus's body to mete out a brutal attack on his wife. She is also witness to her use of the Sun King, Brutus, to wage war against his own people, pitting him against his brother in kingship and immortality, Magnus, the Everfair King. The incorporeal figure of the Black Queen has set the wheels firmly in motion to bring drought and death to the Green Mother's world.

A witness to Morigan's symbiosis is Thackery Thule, a sorcerer who guided her in her youth and through the painful loss of her mother. Thackery forms another piece of the puzzling group that will either pitch Geadhain forward into light or see it crumble before them into darkness. For years, Thackery's past was concealed from Morigan, but unwittingly, she begins to reveal tragedies long buried. His is a history filled with loss at the hands of those closest to him, the details of which will play out over the tapestry of time. He quickly realizes that Morigan's powers extend beyond simple fortune-teller's tricks; she may hold the key to Geadhain's future. In an effort to safeguard this knowledge, Thackery takes them to see Queen Lila. There, in the royal palace's Hall of Memories, Morigan reveals that the threat that Brutus poses to the queen, the kingdom, and the entire realm is also manifest in Lila's spouse, Magnus.

But the sudden emergence of Morigan's long-repressed powers has not gone unnoticed by other powers that be, and fear that she might pose a threat to the hierarchical order of Menos quickly makes her a target. In those moments where Caenith and Morigan are pledging their blood to each other, others are plotting to capture the Fawn and subjugate her before the Iron Queen of Menos, Gloriatrix, a woman so driven by grief at the loss of her husband that she has ruled her kingdom with a fist worthy of her title. Never content to do her own dirty work, she instructs her son, Sorren, to become a party to the destruction of Eod and capture of Morigan. He sets off a number of explosions that destabilize the city not only physically but also politically and socially, and Lila is struck with the realization of Eod's vulnerability. For Thackery, Sorren's indifference to inflicting pain comes as no surprise. As his uncle, the sorcerer was not only a witness to his past violence but a victim as well. As the mysteries of Thackery's past continue to be untangled, we learn that not only is Gloriatrix his sister, but his nephew was responsible for the death of his wife.

Before the dust can settle, Morigan is spirited away to Menos, a city that breeds its own brand of filth borne out of fear. She is to be held captive there until she is subjugated to the whims of Gloriatrix. But even with her newfound powers still in their infancy, the Fawn is a worthy match for her captors. So, too, is her new companion, Mouse, a member of Geadhain's underworld network of spies. This diminutive woman has been shaped by the mean streets of Menos, the ones paved with slavery, exploitation, violations, and hate. Mouse had done her time in the city and sought out a new face from a fleshcrafter, only to discover that there truly is no honor among thieves, landing her in the same captivity as Morigan. Like the city of Menos itself, Mouse's moral compass is one that, accordingly, wavers with the magnetic pull of the tides.

The unlikely pairing of these two women is a reminder of how difficult it can be to cut through the obscurities of a world where appearances are never quite as they seem. Our impulse to simply dismiss the "bad guys" is constantly challenged by being privy to perceptions of individuals both within and without the relationships of all our players. Good and evil are never as simple as they appear. Each player is "othered" by those in opposition. Good is never just good. Evil is never simply evil. Perception is everything.

Neither does "dead" always mean "dead." There are brokers and fleshcrafters who deal in the undead and nearly dead, and these manner of men are holding the women in wait for Gloriatrix's interrogation. But even the zombielike slaves of these nekromantic death dealers have deep within them a spark of humanity waiting to be lighted once again. For no one is this more true than Vortigern, the dead man whose shackles of catatonia are broken when Morigan's psychic bees pierce into his mind. Buried deep below his death mask is a past and present inextricably linked to the group. He was no random victim of Sorren's psychopathy—they were brothers. Vortigern's present death was the consequence of having once loved Sorren's wife and fathered a child with her, Fionna, the mighty Mouse who is now a witness to his deliverance from un-death.

But these women are not stunned into inaction by their newly gained knowledge, for the world of Fates is not one in which women are the meek observers of the world's affairs, passively allowing events to simply happen to them. And so their escape comes not at the hands of Thackery and Caenith, who have ventured into Menos's dangerous underworld to rescue them, but through the women's own ingenuity and intuitive powers. In the process of their escape, they rescue yet another prisoner, Kanatuk—once a malevolent, mind-thralled servant to Menos's underworld kingpin, the Broker. Although before being enslaved and brought to Menos, Kanatuk was a peaceful wanderer of the frozen North. Through Morigan's grace and natural proclivity toward reweaving broken souls, he is rescued from his darkness and restored of his past.

Elsewhere, in their efforts to rescue Morigan, Caenith and Thackery also encounter a young changeling girl being exploited at the hands of the seemingly insane Augustus and free her of the bonds of child bride-dom. A skin-walker without a skin, Macha is a sister of Alabion, and like her changeling brethren, she is possessed of visions of other worlds. Her dreams are ones that foreshadow the presence of an unknown, fanged warmother who has ushered an era of conflict and violence into their homeland. They form a troop of undeniable misfits that eventually makes its way out of Menos toward a destiny whose grandeur and importance is made increasingly clear through Morigan's visions and buzzing mind hive. She alone bears the full weight of those visions and the horrors that unfold within her mind's eye. Even the mental and spiritual link with her bloodmate do not fully spare her of that burden.

In an effort to secure what she believes is her rightful place in the halls of power, Gloriatrix has formed an alliance with Elissandra, a powerful sorceress and seer. She believes that the prophecies have foretold that when brother rises against brother, she will find her place in the resulting power vacuum. But even the Iron Queen is unaware that the powers that run deep in Morigan's veins also run in Elissandra's; we learn that they are both Daughters of the Moon, sisters in the providence of Alabion. And so Gloriatrix's plan to wage war against the immortals may be undermined and her suspicions of Elissandra warranted.

Meanwhile, King Magnus and his hand, Erithitek, have been leading the troops of Eod's Silver Watch forward toward Zioch, the City of Gold and host to Brutus's throne. Magnus begins to appreciate the scope of his brother's burgeoning depravity, unleashing terror and chaos upon his own people. It also becomes clear that there is every chance that his journey is one from which he might not return. He thus elicits a hard-won promise from Erithitek to return to Eod and keep safe his Queen Lila.

But not unlike the two women who use their strength and cunning to escape Menos, the queen that Magnus left behind is no manner of shrinking violet. Shaken by Morigan's prophetic revelations, she is no longer certain that the man she loved is as virtuous as she once believed, and whether the choices she made were truly guided by love or something more sinister. She sets out on a dangerous journey upon Erithitek's return, steeled to protect her people against any offensive from Gloriatrix. Yet love of husband and love of kingdom drive her to commit acts of terror against those who would threaten either, reminding us that each one of us believes we are "the good guys."

As Magnus continues the Watch's advance, he knows that his brother is lying in wait, hunting him. Once the two are face-to-face, Magnus comes to understand that just as Brutus has transformed his kingdom into a wasteland, so, too, have the feelings of fraternity they once shared been transformed into intense hatred. Empowered by the Black Queen, Brutus overtakes his brother in a firestorm of destruction. Lest mortals and immortals alike forget: even with all the accumulated powers of the world, complete control over one's ecosystem is always an illusion. Magnus's vanquishment by his brother shakes the foundations of Geadhain, and the land spews forth a natural disaster, a storm of frost and fire that sweeps the world from end to end, triggered by the outcome of the battle between brothers.

It is a battle that produces no winners, since it takes place in a realm where even the very concept of death is malleable. And death, or that which resembles it, is the destabilizing force it always is, bringing with it both chaos and clarity. Thus the Black Queen's reign of terror begins with the fall of Magnus and the rise of her corrupted avatar, Brutus, from the ashes of that climactic battle.

When the smoke clears, a world lies in ruin. The line between coincidence and fate is wholly blurred. And the Three Sisters reveal that they are adding a new sibling to their fold—one by the name of Morigan.

*—Lady Pale—*

*A quickening pall o'er eve doth glisten;*
*Twinkling sights, starry night,*
*In deepest of darks, do listen*
*For the slithering crawl,*
*The worm that gnaws.*
*Each bite, a letter of pain,*
*Spider to spine, blood to wine,*
*Be the sacraments of her name,*
*Which, while never spoke*
*But by madmen and damned,*
*Needn't be to invoke;*
*Or abjure her thin hand,*
*A sweep of her grace,*
*Gaunt beauty of her face,*
*And with the white lady*
*In ashes, you stand.*
*—Kericot, poet of Geadhain*

# PROLOGUE

"**O**h! It hurts! She's full of sprites today," said Elemech. She doubled over, and her face went white as the moon daubed on night's ebon canvas. She and her younger sister, Ealasyd, had been gazing out over the deep, green peaks of Albion when the kicking began. Elemech weathered her strain with a twisted face and was suddenly and feverishly sweating through her clothing—particularly below her swollen breasts and belly. Within her Eean kicked again. She was anxious to be born, and Elemech doubled over and huffed in pain.

"Sister!" cried Ealasyd, and she clutched at Elemech. "This is too much. We must take you inside, and I shall fetch blankets and comforts for you."

*No comforts this eve*, fretted Elemech.

Indeed, she would have no release from her worries tonight—not from the restlessness that had driven her out of a warm bed or from the agony of the soon-to-be-born's acrobatics in her womb. It was quiet in Alabion. The little hearts of the wood waited with bated breath, quailing in anticipation of Eean's return. The hush was profound, for any moment now Eean would push her way into the world. Beyond this, a deeper anxiety was felt out in the night. A fear. With a hand to her mouth and another upon her stomach, Elemech scrambled from her stone and backed away from the precipice's edge and away from the woods. A dawning truth was upon her, and its importance so took her that the abrupt and heavy wetness between her legs, the knotting of her womb, and the faraway calls and faint pulls of Ealasyd— who was leading her somewhere—faded to insignificance.

She cast her hidden senses out into the night; her intangible feelers whispered through the trees and fur and caressed a thousand creatures' bodies and minds at once as a breeze of sentience. These primitive souls and their fates she could sense: the bird a hunting cat was to eat within the hourglass, the wolf that was to end that cat, and the slow and silvery years that wolf would dodder through until peacefully dying in the darkness of his den. Tripe. None of it mattered. Where were the five beacons of possibility—Morigan, her savage lover, the old man, the dead man, and the one who named herself after a rodent? She knew they were in the woods, and yet somehow they were impossibly invisible to her. They were not dead, for she could feel the gnawing premonition of their importance as if she were some lesser being. Nonetheless, her talents simply could not find them. Unbelievable. How could this be? No creature, from the meekest to the mightiest, could escape a certain whiff of destiny.

When Ealasyd laid her older sister down upon the grasses, she knew they would not be returning to the cave for blankets and comforts. The birth was rudely happening here and now. The mucus that had washed over her small feet moments earlier and Elemech's wavering declared it. Elemech wouldn't be much use to her in this ordeal either, for the pain or some other catalyst had thrown her into a vision—or at least that was what she presumed Elemech's vacancy of expression meant. She gently asked what Elemech was seeing.

Elemech was surprisingly alert and glared at her. "Seeing?" she wheezed. "I'm not seeing anything." The truth sobered her and returned her to her body and its necessary labor. "Incredible," she whispered. "She's broken it."

"Broken? What's broken?" puffed Ealasyd. She was attempting to tent her sister's legs and not getting much in the way of cooperation from Elemech, who seemed immobilized or possessed.

"The order of things...Fate."

Ealasyd succeeded in hiking up her sister's robe and frowned at what she saw. It was quite red and unpleasant looking. "Oh my...oh dear. I think something down there is winking at me. Goodness. Sorry. Someone has broken Fate? That doesn't sound pleasant. Hopefully we can fix it, but right now you need to put your head down and get ready to push."

"You don't understand," panted Elemech. "Nothing can escape Fate. No creature can be free of the loom. What have we made in our desire to meddle? What have I..."

A scream throttled Elemech, and she was not able to speak through the shuddering pain. Eean was on her way and violently swimming down the red river of life. Perhaps her mother's grim intuition motivated her. Sparklers of light went off in Elemech's head; she felt herself tear, and her blood's warmth blanketed her thighs and the ground. In starry anguish she spun and spun, and she was lost in a torrent of images as red as her torment.

*A pale king is dangled by his ankle like a smelt by its tail above his giant brother's hungry, crocodile mouth. All the world is in flames behind them; a sunrise roars as if it is a wyrm—perhaps it is—and breathes fire and ash. She whirls in the searing cloud of death and is thrown over the ruins of three cities: one, where the whiteness still shines; another, darker than the soot that stains it; and a third, colorful but shattered and splattered with bodies. Great wonders of destruction are each of these places. She thinks this as she passes over them in her wind of consciousness. How many lives have been lost? She looks up, and for an instant she sees a star and then a face upon which it is drawn. It's a lad's face, and he is pretty and black of hair. He is important. He is a key of possibility.*

That was all she was given before returning to her grunting body. Nowhere in the maelstrom of visions did she see Morigan or any of the souls linked to her. They were all outside of Fate. The instrument had become the maestro. She could not see Morigan's destiny because it was beyond her. It was no longer hers or anyone's to know or touch. As the infant's head crowned, Ealasyd began to cry, and Elemech sobbed along with her—though not for the child's arrival but for Geadhain's fate.

# PART I

# I

# THE WEB OF FATES

F or days now, their company had been traveling the Untamed. *We're here to stop the greatest of all wars and to find the chink in the mad king's armor. For that, we need the wisdom of the Sisters Three. Epic shite, Mouse, so keep up your gallant front.* Of this she reminded herself repeatedly, as if her recitation of the cold facts would bring her more reason to tread this horrid domain. How many days they'd wandered, Mouse could not say—not that time mattered here beyond day's light and night's dark. Hourglasses were a modern convention for which this primeval land seemed to have no use. Mouse had numbed herself to many of the nuisances of the woods: the briars and their bloodthirsty barbs, the spongy lining of her boots that never dried in the loam and muck through which she slogged, the feel of a snake gliding over her while she fitfully slept, the throat rattles of animals as deep as wind instruments, or the frequent startles as something leathery, furry, or scaled cast a shadow upon her yet never attacked. They feared what sort of predators her dead father and the Wolf might prove to be. All these uncounted grievances Mouse had put aside for the sake of this mad quest to find the three oldest witches in Geadhain. This was a hero's journey. In her opinion, she shouldn't even be on it.

Still, in the end, despite every dread and torture she had escaped, including her own self-doubt, the bugs were testing her resolve. For if it wasn't a gnat nibbling at her, it was a spider falling onto her neck or another unseen thing scuttling under her clothing. Perhaps she had the sweetest blood of the company, or the insects could sense her natural terror of tiny, many-legged things. She awoke every morning scratching and frantic, and she ended her weary days in much the same way. No one else appeared similarly bothered.

From dawn to dusk, the Wolf boldly led them through the vast forest as if he owned it. Mouse learned from fireside chatter that he actually did or at least had once—as much as anyone could rule the Untamed. If they were thirsty, he sniffed out a babbling brook of sugary, crystal water from which to drink. If they sensed danger, he silenced it with a bark. At times, he darted off only to return with the carcass of a beast that had come too close to their company. In such moments, his bloodmate, Morigan, might kiss him, and Mouse would find a flower to distract herself or a gnat to swat. There was an animalism to their passion that made her uneasy. As travelers, the five never wanted for nourishment or worried about danger in even the thorniest and most hissing wealds they explored—not while a lord of Fang and Claw protected them.

When not defending herself from insects, Mouse would watch the woods in wonder. The grand, moss-bearded oaks were so old and imposing she could imagine them as dormant giants. They exuded a sense of watchfulness and wisdom. Amid these sleeping guardians, smaller tree species flourished without particular obedience to the rules of nature. Pines spread heavily at their tops like umbrellas instead of rising in coniferous shapes. There were birches with gray bark, knots, and holes ran straight through them. In these burrows, feral eyes often gleamed. All her life, Mouse had heard stories and henwives' gossip about the Untamed, but neither the eloquent poems nor the scariest or silliest rumors really captured the place's strangeness. Perhaps faery stories came nearest with their undertones of magik and otherworldly happenings. Aye, the magik of Alabion was undeniable. The glassy butterflies refracted sunlight, the winged lizards fluttered by her ear and whistled tunes as if they were flutes. The childlike dread that claimed her came from some of the larger shadows the Wolf growled at—ones even he deemed too much of a hassle to hunt. In such instances, she was reminded that death was only a misstep away. Many a time, her father's fast reflexes caught her from stumbling into a jagged rock made to split her daydreaming head, a hole that crumbled inward to be twice as deep as it appeared, or the coiled presence of a serpent that declared its poison with a rattle. She was more careful after these incidents. Nonetheless, the quietude of their travel lent itself to absentmindedness, for Morigan and the Wolf never spoke—not in words at least. She had learned they did so in currents of emotion and thought. All the trekking appeared to burden her great-uncle Thackery. He spoke only when addressed and then in a terse manner. Her father, Vortigern, was vigilant about her care and mistakes—though he, too, was quiet. He seemed as preoccupied as the rest with troubles or concerns he did not share.

At night, however, the fasting from conversation ended. The Wolf would find them a star-bright clearing in which to camp, and there they would light a fire and partake in food and chatter. Mouse came to look forward to these occasions, and throughout her daily toil, she would long for the fire's crackle, the Wolf's deep laugh, and the feel of her father's cold hand on her back. Somewhat against her will, camaraderie—an unwelcome stranger—had tiptoed into her heart.

## II

No sooner had they stopped that night than Caenith and Vortigern were on a hunt. They left Morigan to build the fire. Thackery's magik and capabilities for fire starting were as useful as wet matchsticks here in Alabion. No amount of grunting or concentration would summon his magik. Once Morigan had rubbed two sticks into a sputtering of flame, the three companions gathered about the fire. They smiled, spoke of nothing in particular, and passed around the waterskin Alastair had left them. Soon a chill crept into the woods, and the flames were a welcome friend to their pale cheeks. Settling into an easy silence, they looked about the tree-circled slab of limestone they had claimed and into the wispy forest shadows that seemed to curl like smoke. They listened to the woods for a sign of their fellows. Time fell away, the cold sharpened further, and the three huddled closer to the fire.

"Do you feel that?" Caenith's deep voice startled everyone except Morigan. "The claws of winter," he continued.

He had appeared from the murk with the dead man's shade behind him. He was in a loincloth, and fresh blood splashed his chest. Mouse leaped a bit at his ferociousness. With a crimson grin, he held up the crumpled body of a stag nearly his size. In a moment, the two joined the others at the fire. Vortigern had also been successful with his hunting. He dropped a pair of furry corpses and then went to his daughter, while Caenith settled in behind his bloodmate. The Wolf did not wipe off his paint of murder, and Morigan seemed unconcerned. Instead, she busied herself with their meal. She rolled up her sleeves, produced her elegant dagger, and started gutting what hadn't already been pulled from the carcasses. A silence settled over the company, and there was only the squelching of Morigan's butchery to hear.

"Perhaps a story," suggested Thackery.

During their evenings together, Caenith had revealed his propensity and talent for storytelling to those who did not know him as well as Morigan did. One of his stories was preferable to Morigan's bloody music.

"Hmm," pondered the Wolf. "A tale."

The Wolf began speaking, and they were all pulled into his spell. They nibbled on the meal quite absently once it had been distributed. Mouse was a master at escapism, and she found these tales especially captivating. After one blink, the Wolf's booming incantation had taken her from the campfire to the White Lake's shores. She learned there of the changeling Dymphana, of mortalkind's betrayal of her, and finally of the tragic end to her story—how the cruelty of man taught her and the other children of Alabion to hate.

"A bitter lesson," finished the Wolf, "and I can tell from your sour faces it is not one that has warmed your spirits." He smiled and wagged the half-eaten shank he was chewing on at his audience. "But it is an old lesson, a grievance from a bygone age—and as we can see from our fellowship here, it is a caution, not a law. The old and new can coexist. I am as old and stubborn as they come, and I have found a place in my heart for each of you in this pack."

"Pack?" said Mouse, and she smiled.

"A pack," stated the Wolf.

They finished off what portions of the meat they wanted, and then Caenith stomped out the fire so those who needed rest could have it. The bones of their meal were kept off to the side. When the deepest darkness came later, Caenith and Morigan would sneak away to bury the remains and murmur their thanks in the oldest tongue to the beasts' spirits. In Alabion, Caenith felt it necessary to observe every rusty custom he remembered. As much as these lands had once been his hunting grounds, they were a friend to him no more. Alabion was a stranger—possibly a wicked one—and there were cries and scents to the woods he did not recognize. He felt that honoring the old ways of the land might spare them from the Green Mother's capriciousness.

*Shall we?*

Morigan tugged Caenith out of his brooding when her suggestion did not stir him. Tireless Vortigern aside, the camp was now asleep, and the bloodmates gathered the bones and slipped into Alabion's tangles. Although Morigan would never be as acutely tuned to the physical world as her mate, she had adopted a shade of his wildness. She moved more quickly than she ever had as a woman and was even lighter than her mate, who crushed bracken and huffed at her heels. He was graceful only when he chose to be, which was not now. Sometimes he would lead, but tonight she found the place that called for the bones to rest. After a timeless race panting through darkness, splashing through ponds, and hiking moss-covered hillocks, she brought them to a copse of skinny, white trees that shone in the blackness of the woods. There they dug at the soil and leaves on the ground, laid the bones in a shallow grave, and gave thanks to their spirits. Morigan knelt, kissed her hand, and touched the soil afterward. It was not the gesture traditionally associated with the ritual: urination upon the site. Instead, this was an honor she had devised. The Wolf smiled when she was done.

*At first, I was afraid too much of the beast had entered you through me. I feared it would consume what was beautiful and pure in you. I was a fool to think anything could change you into a creature you would not wish to be. You are the rose of steel and fire that I crafted when first we met.*

Morigan heard his thoughts, turned to her handsome savage, and ran her fingers over his chest—still tacky with blood—and into his unkempt beard. He had the smell of a beast, but it wasn't unpleasant. She kissed him, and they tumbled for a while in a whirl of pearl and bronze and of strength and softness. *Enough*, she finally said to her grunting lover, who restrained the urge to nip and lick at her creamy skin. There were too many hazards here for them to consummate their love tonight. Morigan traced her fingers over Caenith's red, pouting lips and then picked a twig from his messy mane.

"Let's find you a spring and give you a wash and a shave, my Wolf," she said. "I might like you as a beast, but to the others you must be a fright in an already frightful place."

Off they raced like young pups, chasing and biting at each other. They were more carefree than they should have been and too assured in their fresh love and growing powers. Perhaps they were lax because the great, coiled viper of the land appeared to be sleeping, and they had forgotten that at any moment it could strike. If they had been nearer to the camp or a bit less focused on themselves, surely Caenith's ears would have perked to the greasy chattering and the silken rustle of unnatural movements in the woods. Alas, the Wolf was lost in sweeter distractions, and the strong west wind did not bear the faint but violent sounds of struggle their way. It swallowed them instead.

III

*"Adelaide," says Mouse.*

*She is about to ask her young friend what she is doing here, and then she dismisses the question as ridiculous. They are at the charterhouse playing cards and sitting upon creaking, worn bunks with threadbare sheets. Where else would they be? Out on the dismal streets of Menos? She can spot the grayness of the city through the window behind Adelaide's golden hair. Not out there. Not anywhere else. Only here. This is the only place to be.*

*Adelaide's pretty face is frowning. "Your move. Pay attention," she demands in an unusually authoritative voice.*

*Pay attention, thinks Mouse, and she stares at the colorful, lacquered cards arrayed in two rows between them on the mattress. Instantly, Mouse gravitates toward and grabs one of the cards. A king—pale, beautiful, and surrounded by an aura of power. He stands atop a crest of rock like a conqueror overseeing the battlefield. As strange as it is for Mouse's tiny mind, she feels as if she knows this figure or something important about him.*

"Is that your pick?" asks Adelaide. "The Everfair King takes two cards out of play and converts one more to his cause, or have you forgotten the rules?"

Three cards to choose, ponders Mouse. She glances at the line of fantastical creatures and places lined up before her. First, she picks a scarecrow that hangs ominously against the backdrop of a wasted, black field and a sky full of stars. He—the scarecrow is definitely male—has a hauntingly mortal face. However, he has eyes of pitch and a grim, yellow smile. He is happy, this scarecrow, even as he presides over the emptiness. She fancies him and feels as if he should have a name, but she cannot grasp what it could be.

Adelaide claps in her face. "Goodness, you're slow today, Mouse! Dumb as dear Bettifer, who eats her own hair. You, who are always telling me to hurry. Move along now before the other children return and sell us out for a second helping of that misery they call porridge. Two more cards. Go!"

Of course Adelaide is correct, and should their game and contraband be discovered, it will mean nothing but punishment. Mouse regretfully places the scarecrow facedown in a pile off to the side with the other discarded cards. Next she runs her hand over her choices and quickly settles upon the image of a bright sward, a radiant sun, and a flowing wind. All are rendered in bold lines. Mouse feels as if this could be a place—a real place somewhere—and when she closes her eyes, she can nearly feel the warmth, peace, and tickle of the summer breeze on her cheeks.

"The east wind?" says Adelaide. "The wind of change and sacrifice? The wind that chases the sun to its death each day? If you put that in the graveyard, you change the game's rules. No peace now. We keep at it until one of us has nothing. Are you sure? Do you understand? Attrition until death. You can't change your mind later. Just like the scarecrow, it's gone forever. Everything changes."

"I...I'm sure," replies Mouse, but she really isn't.

She's dithering when she shouldn't be. That is usually Adelaide's role. Gone forever. The warning echoes. Mouse shakes off the chill of it and looks for her third pick: the card she gets to keep. It's the one that will stay with her in the battle to come. The battle with Adelaide? she wonders, but her blood is boiling as if something more dire than this frivolous game is unfolding. Her fingers graze several cards—a pack of wolves, a beautiful ebon mare with a single silver horn, and a castle crumbled to its foundation and covered in ivy—before *freezing upon a card. Yes. This is it. This is the one she must have. What a queer relief this card painted in watercolors is. It's so soft while the other cards are bold. What is this picture other than plumes of gray mist or smoke? As she stares, she begins to make out the faintest outline of a shape: a scribble of a face, two slashes that could be suspicious eyes, and some bolder twists that could be the outline of arms and legs. As with cloud watching, though, what she sees fades to inconsistency, and she is not sure what she has seen until Adelaide whispers, "The Gray Man."*

*There is fear in Adelaide's voice. Mouse swallows the sudden lump in her throat. The mystery and fright of this card and the choice she has made are palpable to them.*

*"The trickster, the thief of secrets," Adelaide continues. Her voice is hushed. "He'll steal what you know and what you don't. He can't be trusted, and yet you've made your choice."*

*"I have?"—Adelaide nods—"I have," repeats Mouse.*

*The canny part of Mouse—the forgotten woman she is or was to be (why can't she remember?)—knows they are no longer discussing the stratagems of a simple game. These cards are not simply amusements. The cards have meaning. The unseen scarecrow she has buried in the graveyard calls to her. His face is so familiar, and his name dances on her tongue. Vor...Vorig...Vortig...*

*Adelaide studies her intently with a gaze that seems more knowing than it should be, considering she's a hapless child—always bumbling and in trouble.*

*"You've made your choice," says Adelaide quietly. "Now watch, and I shall show you the path."*

*With surprisingly deft hands, Adelaide sweeps up all the cards, shuffles them with a flourish, and pulls one off the top. Mouse recoils at the revealed picture. Even as a child, which she is starting to sense she is not, she has always hated these things. Spiders. And these ones are particularly repulsive. Around a dozen are cluttered into the frame, which is bordered in white, drawn lines of silk. Their bodies are lean with sleek, long abdomens, and they teeter on stilted legs like herons. Most revolting are their armored heads, spiked as the helmets of warriors and slashed with white markings that resemble war paint. Indeed, there is an anthropomorphic impression to the monsters, and even though they are mere representations, she can feel their deep-red clusters of eyes leering at her from under the armored crests. She quickly looks away.*

"No," says Adelaide. "You must be brave. Look at the card."

Mouse does as she is told. The spiders are eager to capture her with their stares, so she looks elsewhere within the picture—anywhere they cannot follow her. A glimmer of silver lost in the cobwebs like a rolled-up metal gnat provides this escape. She has to squint to make it out, as minuscule as it is.

"What is that glimmer?" she asks.

Adelaide applauds her discovery. "Good. Such a sharp eye you've always had, Mouse. It will serve you in the dark when you need to find what you have just seen—the first marker of Fate. A bread crumb for you to follow. However, there are three, as is always the way of things. I must show you the others before we part."

Marker of Fate? wonders Mouse. In flickers, her adult sensibilities are returning to her. The process stings. Each bit of memory drives like a spike into the back of her skull. She is aware she is in some manner of dream that is not quite a dream, and she is speaking with some manifestation of her old friend and someone or something else too. A guide, perhaps? She is starting to recall a place and people far from this dream whom she has left behind: Vortigern, Morigan, Caenith, and Thackery. She remembers enough of this other life, even though the recall is incomplete.

"The second marker," declares Adelaide. "Study it. Burn it into your thoughts. See the unseen."

Mouse concentrates on the new card Adelaide now holds between two of her fingers. Painted on the glossy surface is a slice of sunset scenery—a cartoonish crimson and orange sun setting over a stretch of woodland. Surely it is Alabion, judging from its tangles and density. A flock of white birds flutters to one side. Study it. See the unseen, she commands herself, and she begins to wonder what has startled the flock into flight. A growl in the woods? The passage of a predator? Something certainly has frightened the birds, but she can discern nothing more in the smears of black between the green trees. Perhaps it is not what spooks the birds that matters but where they are headed. She searches the landscape, which seems larger and more detailed than the confines of a card should be, and she notes a ripple of blue and gray—rapids on the east. Yes. This is to the east side of the woods. The birds will flee in that direction to or near a stream, and they will be safe from what hunts them.

"East," says Mouse. "They will fly east."

She knows this is the correct answer because Adelaide has folded the card away and is quickly flashing another in her face. "Well done. Now the last marker."

Mouse isn't clear what this is. It is a jumble of bones and serpentine strokes of darkness dotted with white marbles. Whatever the image is supposed to be, it roils her stomach with sadness—not sickness, though. The picture twirls inward and gives a sense of spiraling and constriction. She feels as if she could cast herself through the paper and fall to the very bottom of this abyss toward that pearl of gray shadows at the epicenter of the torrent. Wait. That isn't a pearl; it's a pinprick of light. An opening to a larger space. A place where there is music and the saddest song in all Geadhain sung by...

"Yes. Yes," says Adelaide, and the card disappears back in the deck with her prestidigitator's skill. "You have your signs—although I don't think you'll much like the journey on which they take you. Be brave. There is light after the dark. Always. Good luck to you, Mouse. Luck has ever watched your back, and you have a greater destiny than I ever did—I thought I was simply to die at the hands of that awful man. But it seems I have one last purpose and one last bit of joy, which is to say good-bye."

If this is a dream, the rules and realities are bent. It is like no other dream that has claimed Mouse. The clear, gold shimmer of her friend's tresses, the candied smell she always exuded, and the half-smile that never left her lips—all these poignant details are present and tangible. Mouse cries out for her long-lost and fallen friend, and the two fall into each other, embrace, and shed tears.

Memories are assaulting Mouse, and she sees Adelaide's corpse folded and broken in a closet in the charterhouse. She remembers sobbing and being unsure how to handle the naked, bruised body. She remembers how the brightness of Adelaide's eyes had faded to a dull, fishy gray. She remembers the sensation of something cracking inside her—a wall that let in the darkness and hate. Always suspicious and alert, she remembers one of the ironguards pulling her from the corpse and staring at the body afterward with a lip twitch and an eye tremble. Hunger. A lesser, more innocent mind would not have seen this as an admission of murder. Barry Grimsby was his name. She learned it and enshrined it in her skull. All the way into adulthood, she carried that name until she was able to take revenge on him and defile him with knives as he had done to any number of innocents. She pulls back.

"He's dead," she says with a wicked smile. "I ended him. Cut his balls off and fed them to him."

"I know," says Adelaide remorsefully. She is radiant to Mouse—a star one and true. "All that hate for me. I thank you for your vengeance, but I am sorry for how it has changed you."

"But how? How is it possible you are here?"

"I don't know. I know only that I was headed somewhere...yet I knew I couldn't leave. I wasn't sure why. Until now, at least. This is where I am supposed to be and what I am supposed to do. A voice...yes, a man's voice, I think. It led me back out of the grayness and to you, my dear Mouse. You have been lost for so long, but you're starting to find your way. There will be more sadness to come, and you'll stumble again. But I've given you a few more steps to take. I'm looking out for you this once."

Mouse does not care about any more of this mystery—only the miracle of it. She pulls her friend in again and squeezes with all her strength. She understands their intimacy is to end by her friend's sudden lightness and brightness.

"No. Please. A little longer," she pleads to the wisps of brilliance Adelaide has become.

Adelaide's voice fades like the last rays at dusk. "Remember the markers. Believe in what you see and feel. He will find you as he found me. But you must go. I wouldn't be a good friend if I kept you here any longer than was safe. Anger...danger...wake. Need to...wake...up. Don't think. Just kill."

Danger. Wake up. Don't think. Just kill.

As Adelaide vanishes into a golden mist, Mouse tumbles forward and scatters the cards. Her friend was right about many things. Mouse is a survivor and a quick study, and she knows she has to wake up. She pounds the mattress with her fists. Wake up! Wake up! Remember where you are supposed to be! The more she focuses herself and her Will, the more the world begins to shake and blur, and the greater that dreadful pain—the stabbing at the back of her neck—becomes. She reaches around to soothe the spot and feels something hard and wet attached to her. In disgust, she rips at it.

Mouse awoke and gulped for air, but her breaths drew in only cottony gobs that dissolved on her tongue like bitter, spoiled carnival candy. She spit them out and thrashed about. She discovered that the stuff completely enveloped her. Somewhere in her frenzy, she grasped what this entrapment was, yet she could spare no thought on it now—not when the situation was so dire, when she could sense a throbbing wound in her skull, and when she could sense a great, hissing darkness skittering around her cocoon. *Don't think. Kill.* She had specks before the shadow would do something unspeakable to her again and inject her with whatever toxin had lulled her into a coma. One of her gluey hands found a dagger—one of a pair of parting gifts from Alastair, her eternal protector—and suddenly the shadow was above her. She sliced down the silken bag in which she was trapped and slid out onto a rock floor.

Her surroundings came to Mouse in fragments as she stumbled to her feet. There were natural walls coated in ghostly webbing, tiny shadows balled up in ivory and strung around like festive ornaments, the fustiest of reeks, and a lanky shape draped over the deflated pile of strings she had escaped. She couldn't piece the nightmare together. However, she knew what was atop the string pile. As it rose from its web on long, slender limbs, she could see it clearly in the white-tinted darkness. It was an enormous arachnid twice her size at its full height. She saw a glint, a greasy sheen, reflecting off the ivory markings on its clacking, horned skull. She had a flash of the same chain of red eyes descending upon her in another time. There was hardly a moment to reflect, though, for the spider was coming for her. There was a fist of fear inside her gut, and she could not steady her knives. Praise the Kings, she still had them, though. *Only a spider. Only a spider,* she chanted as though that could shrink the creature or her horror. Then came the chattering. It crept into her ears like a spider all its own, and she knew this was but one of many monsters in the dark. It took everything she had not to scream.

IV

*Vortigern!*

The dead man heard Morigan's clarion call from within the blackness in which he swam. He awoke violently and suddenly. He shouted for his daughter and shrieked about so many red eyes. Caenith had to restrain him. When Vortigern had calmed enough and sworn not to dash madly into the woods to find his daughter, Caenith released him and allowed him to stand, pace, and anxiously scan the tree line while he rattled out his story.

"You know I don't sleep, so I saw enough of what happened. Fionna and Thackery were resting. You two had been gone for an hourglass or so. Then I heard the noises. Unwholesome sounds. The clacking of insect teeth like termites chewing wood." Vortigern glared up into the branches. "It was so quick. Even for me. Those things…"

*Morigan is no longer herself but resides in a different body of cold, gray flesh. Round, unfurling shadows slink out of the darkness like the tumblers of Eod on their cables of silk. She sees their eyes shimmering like rubies scattered on a jeweler's velvet cloth. Before she is horrified, this beauty mesmerizes her—the jewel eyes and the strange patterns on their barbed skulls. The casings are almost helmetlike. Now she understands the danger and leaps toward the sleeping and vulnerable pair nestled near the evening fire's coals. With her speed, she is at Vortigern's daughter in a speck. Suddenly, a weight clings to her. Thin and fantastically strong legs wrap around her like coils of barbed wire, and her warning scream is killed in her throat. A pressure balloons her head with whiteness, euphoria, and then a warm and welcome emptiness.*

"Are you listening, Morigan?"

Vortigern's tone was wrathful, for his daughter's safety was at stake, and the seer was merely daydreaming. Caenith could feel his bloodmate's absence and knew she was in that silvery limbo she often wandered to. *What did you see?* he asked.

*Spiders. I fell into Vortigern's memory.* They were near to one another, so she touched his chest and sent her stinging magik into the Wolf. He flinched as the wash of images ran through him. At once he knew the creatures—at least what they should be. The largest should have been no larger than his thumb. *Dream weavers,* he exclaimed. *I know this because the witches of these woods have long made pets of these creatures for their venom. Its properties can induce powerful states of otherworldly meditation and sleep. They are rare. However, these are not as the Green Mother created them. Their speed, size, and behavior are aberrations. They are communal, peaceful predators—carrion feeders off rotten flesh. Even as they kill, my Fawn, they will not eat their prey until it passes naturally within their webs. They feed on nothing bigger than the crickets their masters give them. I do not understand what I have seen.* The Wolf frowned.

*Carrion feeders? So Thackery and Mouse could be safe?*

*For the moment. Yes. Assuming any previous habits of these dream weavers hold true.*

Vortigern leaped before the silent pair. Their calm infuriated him. "Dammit! My daughter and uncle have been carried off to be consumed." He would not believe them dead. "By carnivorous bloody spiders! What are we going to do? We need to find them!"

"I'm sorry," said Morigan, and she took the dead man's cold hand. "We've been discussing it in our heads. I should have involved you—especially when your family, our pack, is at stake. Mouse and Thackery should be fine for a time. We shouldn't, though, test that presumption for too long."

"I shall find them," announced Caenith.

In a whirl of wind, the Wolf was behind Vortigern and sniffing at the ragged puncture marks running down Vortigern's nape. The wounds the dream weavers left would soon fill in like dimples in rubber—like all Vortigern's injuries. The dead man was too distraught to object to this oddness. Desperation blackened his dark eyes, and Morigan knew he would be sobbing if he could. She slipped into grief as well. What use were her powers if they warned her only when she came within sprinting distance of the doom? But could she really blame the magik and not its mistress's distraction? She was, after all, in control of her silver servants now. Therefore, if they were not attentive, it reflected her absentmindedness. She had been playing barber to her lover and indulging in kisses while her pack mates were made into meals. She was ashamed and with good cause. How naive to think Alabion, realm of ancient terror and myth, would allow them to traipse through its reaches without a challenge. By the time Caenith had finished his crude sniffing and tasting of Vortigern's flesh wounds, Morigan's gaze was just as black with contrition as the dead man's.

Vortigern's wounds gave Caenith's senses all he needed. The salty toxin could be tracked on the leaves of every tree and shrub between here and the earthy basin where the dream weavers made their nest. He could smell even the wet soil of that hollow and the spicy moss upon the rocks around the cave entrance. Furthermore, he understood why the dead man had been spared and what the presence of so many punctures meant. He was neither alive nor dead. He was without flesh to rot to the succulence the spiderlings would desire and without a pumping heart to distribute the poisons that might disable him. The dead man was not an appealing meal—more trouble than he was worth. However, the dream weaver's frenzied poking had managed to temporarily break something in his spine or brain, which explained his state when discovered. None of this information did the Wolf share beyond the slightest expression of bleak duty to his bloodmate. As he glided off toward the forest, he spoke in a trembling, angry voice to his companions. "Follow me fleetly. We are a pack, and when one is threatened, there will be blood for blood, as is the way."

The Wolf's call to action dispelled any lingering sadness. Morigan and Vortigern hurried after him as he tore through the woods in a rage. A lord of Fang and Claw was on the hunt.

V

Terror made Mouse's nerves sharper. She was faster and more perceptive than ever and too drunk on adrenaline to properly consider the nightmare she had entered. Fear's alchemy had dilated her pupils and infused her with grace. It allowed her to slip through the white veils that hung in abundance or to dance over the wreckage and signs of previous victims—knickknacks, bridles, bones, and clothing—as black shapes lunged at her. She had no idea where she was headed in this musty labyrinth and whether it was farther from or deeper into this madness. The destination was irrelevant and as unimportant as her mortification at being trapped in a lair of man-eating spiders. So much of Menos was inhospitable or polluted that she had rarely to face her entomophobia, except during encounters with oversize roaches immune to whatever poisons killed off lesser insects. She would have bathed in a stream of roaches and let them run over her face and into her ears and mouth if it meant not being here. Trading terrors was not in the cards, however, and the drive for survival seized her body. So, as nimble as the spiderlings were and as knowledgeable as they might be of their lair, Mouse was somehow more agile. It helped that the monsters weren't trying to end her. She vaguely grasped that they were only herding her. Now and then they darted close with their spitting faces and glistening prongs like tongues made of horn threatening to sting and entrance her anew. *Not a fuking chance,* she thought with a slash of her blades. She caught one of the horned organs and sliced it clean off the monster's white face. She grinned as it squealed and thrashed back into the darkness.

*One down. A dozen to go. I won't disappoint you, Adelaide. I shall live.* That promise gave Mouse a sense of purpose and sentiment—something other than fear to fuel her. As grim as the situation was, she needed a light in the dark, and she had found it in her dear, dead friend and the signs she had foretold.

Mouse sensed one of the spiderlings hissing above her, crawling on the ceiling, and she deftly sidestepped the net of its spindly legs as it dropped. A narrow escape. *How many more of those do I have left?* she wondered. For the passage she walked was constricting. The lattice of hanging threads was more densely entangling, and the floor was a quagmire of bones and webs. When she looked over her shoulder, she could see the glint of several clusters of crimson eyes. At this, her stomach sank. She was most likely not headed toward freedom but only deeper into the nest. She picked up her pace as much as the hazardous surroundings allowed and made a silent prayer to Adelaide, destiny, and anything that would see her out of this doom.

Then mercy spat on Mouse. Her foot struck something intractable, and she was flung into the gloom. Her daggers flew out of her hands and were gone. *At least I landed on a rubbery surface.* She shrieked when she realized what had broken her fall—dark, oily skin as quivering, soft, and cold as an eel's. Before the monster was able to react to the girl upon its back, Mouse had slipped off. She flailed in the dark for anything sharp to use as a weapon. Discovering a splintered femur at her feet, she gored the beast's soft under-side. Astonishingly, the spiderling didn't mount much of a resistance, except to coat her in its black blood and shrivel out a hiss. As it died, it curled up in a wet mess and rolled away from her.

Not a speck later, a groaning sound arose from the bloodied mound of webbing upon which she stood, and she nearly speared that too until reason flickered into her bloodlust. That was a mortal sound and not just any groan. She recognized it from her mornings this past week when her great-uncle would creak himself awake.

"Thackery?"

Desperate and hopeful, she clawed through the filaments using her bone as a spade. She looked for a limb, face, or sleeve to pull. The lethargic death of the spiderling made sense now. When she surprised it, it must have been feeding or poisoning or doing whatever vileness it did. Thackery was waking in earnest now that the needle in his head had been removed. *What disgusting ecology.* Mouse shuddered and gave no more mind to it, for she had spotted a gnarled, old hand. She grasped it, and it grasped back in shock. With much huffing and cursing, she pulled her gasping great-uncle from the heap, and he collapsed in her arms.

"Bethanny. Where...where did she go? She was here," he babbled.

Out in the silky darkness, the chattering echoed. Mouse knew the spiderlings would be upon them any instant. Mouse shook the man. "A dream. Whatever it was, it wasn't real. And you've awoken to a nightmare. Gather your wits and whatever magik you have, or we won't live to see another sunrise. I don't know where our companions are. I think Morigan and the Wolf wandered off, and I don't know whether my father would succumb to these monsters. I pray they are all looking for us!"

Slowly, Thackery was remembering. He clutched at Mouse's arm as his adjusting eyes noticed the deep shadows and flecks of ivory bone and threads and his ears took in the same susurrations Mouse heard. "By the Kings," he exclaimed as the depth of their danger dawned on him.

"Yes. They won't help us now either. It's only you, me, and this bone, which will only do so much good. We need a miracle or magik. I know you've had issues with your craft here in Alabion, but this would be a good occasion for it."

Their deaths were closing in. The chattering was nearer and frantic with anger. Mouse noticed the first movements in the dark and pulled her great-uncle to stand. She dragged him off the mound, and they waded through cobwebs and what was surely a carpet of skeletons from the way their legs were scraped. Mouse's back brushed against solid, cold stone. The tunnel had ended. There was nowhere else to flee.

"Thackery!" she pleaded.

Thackery was a spider more diabolical than those in this cavern, and he quickly accepted his predicament and started weaving in his mind for a solution. While he and the Wolf had never had a proper discourse on the eccentricities of sorcery in Alabion, what little had been exchanged between the two had been concise and meaningful. The Wolf rarely spoke in any other way.

As Thackery cast his mind back, something came to him. It was an exchange they'd had when the two had first set out for the Iron City to rescue Morigan. Caenith had spat in disdain upon the wonders of modern magik. "Sorcerers are what reap and never sow. That is why the Green Mother denies them their art—as you would call it—in Alabion. We of the East understand the sacrifice that every creation brings, magikal or otherwise. There is a scale. A balance to be maintained. For every act, a sacrifice. For every spell, a cost."

What must he sow? With what was he to water the garden? Not his sweat and frustration. He'd tried that already, and he couldn't even start the tinder for a fire. What was stronger than Will? What was the essence of sacrifice? "Of course," he muttered.

Thackery snatched the bone from his great-niece's grip, considered for a speck where he was going to harm himself, and carved the rough end of the bone across his palm. The wound was messy and the pain dazzling enough to blind him. Either the pain or the blood—or perhaps both—was enough to do what Will alone could not. An offering had been made to Mother Geadhain, and with it Thackery cast his wish to banish the darkness. It was a Will for a miracle, as Mouse had requested. The magik sprayed like a star's blood from his palm. It transitioned from red to silver to gold in a flash. A luminescent spatter hovered above the two companions, and Thackery's hand pulsed and throbbed with brilliance. Mouse was first blinded and then agape at the warmth and wonder of what her great-uncle had done. She did not know much about sorcery, yet his was beautiful, and it warmed her as much as summer itself.

This swell of light ate away at the darkness. No blessing was this to the companions, for the despair of their surroundings was exposed. Creamy mucus caked the walls, and the grinning skeletons and desiccated animals slept in silky bundles along the wall, floor, and ceiling. It was as if they stood in a massive charnel house that yawned on as far as the eye could see. The stink of fleshless decay—must, rust, and a sickly sweetness—tickled their noses. How many creatures and people had died here they could not count, for there were only bones, bones, and bones to see. Identifying one set from another was a task for the mad. Thackery cast aside his own bloody bone and bared his bleeding hand—a five-fingered star—to the spiderlings that had brought all this death. Not far from the companions, a handful of the monsters huddled and blinked their clusters of crimson eyes. *They're actually* blinking *against the brightness*, Mouse noted with revulsion. Thackery's light distorted their already monstrous proportions and man-like faces even further. The spiderlings clacked, spit, and scuttled backward into the sanctuary of shadows, and Mouse was spared any more disgust.

Unsure of how long this untested magik would last, Thackery pursued them, and Mouse followed. She locked onto the hand not bleeding light. She did not question what was happening or pay much heed to the death through which they raced. Twisting passageways appeared, and they chose not to enter the ones wherein shadows churned. Thackery forced himself into other passages and scared away whatever lurked there, and if the light he shone wavered, he squeezed his wounded hand into a fist for more blood, more pain, and more magik. Bravely, the old man shouted the names of his missing companions in case they too were lost in this horror. Moving and shouting through the maze they went, always hoping the next turn would take them out of the dark. While the spiderlings might have hidden themselves, they were never far outside the fringe of Thackery's golden glow. Mouse dreaded the cessation of that light, and she could tell from the sorcerer's pallor and the way his radiance flickered like a torch in the wind that this magik could not be sustained forever.

*Hold on, Thackery. This is not our end,* Mouse told herself as she clung to the notions of Fate and hope. She was only half convinced of her optimism when she saw the small sparkle of silver just ahead. The gleam was so different from the dull shine of corroded swords and buckles she'd spotted elsewhere. It caught Thackery's light and blinked at her as if a beacon. *A light in the darkness.* Exhilarated, she ran to it, grabbed whatever the small, chained piece of jewelry was, shoved it into her tunic, and hurried onward with Thackery close behind. He hadn't seen it. *She has blundered for a speck,* he thought. He was concentrating on his magik and pain, which had started to dwindle into an ache no matter how many times he dug his fingernails into his palm. *Damn the body's capacity for shock*, he cursed. He thoroughly understood the mechanisms of Alabion's magik now, and he regretted, though accepted, that he would have to stab himself with something else if his torch started to wane dangerously. He wondered whether he could handle another injury, for he was feeling leaden and light-headed. "Morigan!" he cried.

If anyone was to see or save them in this lightless pit, it would be the silver-eyed girl who could find anyone anywhere. When her sweet voice cut the dusty air, he cackled. He wasn't imagining things either, and Mouse cheered at the sound as well. Together, the pairs of voices rang through the tunnels, and the divided companions chased each other's songs. They cared not what monsters they disturbed. Soon the seekers met, and five weary souls stumbled into Thackery's light.

"Fionna!"

With his unnatural speed, the dead man was first to embrace his daughter, and quickly Morigan was upon Thackery. His glowing hand floundered free of the hug and cast strange patterns on the walls. A thicker, murderous slathering of black blood and spider bits coated the Wolf, and he kept his distance from the reunion. He nodded his respects. "I see you found your spark," he said.

Thackery grinned. "I did."

"Keep your torch lit. We are not free of danger yet," said the Wolf.

Evidently this was the end of their reunion, and the Wolf stormed out of the light. Again in the presence of the lord of Fang and Claw, the companions trembled no more, and they followed the path Caenith had taken into the nest. From here, any fool could have found the path to the exit. So much gore and so many ruined spiderling corpses—scattered about like balls of crumpled, black paper—littered the path, and it could not be missed. All three rescuers had contributed to the carnage. Morigan still clutched her black-lathed promise dagger, and black blood covered the dead man's arms to the elbow. Thackery could tell the gore-tarred Wolf had committed most of the murder. Knowing he was safe, aches and exhaustion finally came calling for Thackery. He allowed his light to sputter, and he leaned on Morigan and Mouse for support. His ankles were dragging and his eyes flickering when Alabion's earthy wind kissed his face.

Outside at last, the companions sat the old sorcerer upon a mossy seat and propped him up to look around. They were in a ravine made dark by heavy branches, and Thackery's magik had gone out. Any night here was daylight, though, compared to where they had just been, and Thackery spotted the silhouettes of many and varied boulders like the one on which he rested and the rippling shadow of a shallow stream that threaded between the rocks and trickled over his companions' feet. Quite close at hand and near enough to cause a shiver was a patch where the land bubbled, the water did not flow, and boulders framed a circle of darkness that descended into the earth. The sight of the nest enlivened the old man. He could hear the spiderlings in there. He was so accustomed now to their queer, clacking tongue he could detect it over the rustling leaves and trickling water. He clenched from his balls to his skull, which throbbed at the back. He began to remember the feel of something there—a hard, twisting object.

"One more task of you, element-breaker, before you rest," said Caenith. Thackery grunted a yes. "Burn it," barked the Wolf. "We cannot cure all the sicknesses of these woods, but these creatures should not be allowed to exist."

How dark and bloody this night had become. It was a lesson to those who tread without the proper fear Alabion deserved, and what occurred next shook none among the company. Thackery hopped to a stand, dug around in the wet soil for the sharpest stone he could find, and then drove it into his already wounded hand with a strength that bent him over like a willow in a rainstorm. No one helped him. Innately, they too respected the new and primal laws by which they now lived. Not the slightest objection or a single supportive hand was offered. The four witnesses merely watched with cold respect as Thackery screamed his magik to life. Flames and smoke suddenly jetted from the nest's mouth, and the spiderlings' sizzling shrieks were sweet hymns to the pack's ears. They at last went to the old man, who had passed out from his miracle working. The four whispered their thanks over his still body as if he were another spirit whose bones they owed worship for his sacrifice.

✳ ✳ ✳

VI

The company was quiet as dawn bled through the forest. Sleep had escaped all but Thackery. Contentedly, he snored on a bed of wildflowers in the clearing Caenith had found. Separate questions and worries consumed each of them. Even those who could speak to each other in their heads refrained from doing so. Vortigern sat near his daughter and brooded over her—often with a hand upon her—and he squinted into the woods for further dangers. Oblivious to this, Mouse lost herself playing with her find, which appeared to be an amulet. She held the object secretively, cupped it in her hands, and hid it even from her watchful father, and after what they'd all been through, he didn't want to press her about her discovery. If she had possessed her father's or the Wolf's senses, she would have noticed the pungency of the metal odor and the rust, iron, and blood on the object she fondled. From a distance, the bloodmates watched the others. Their company's fractured and sad nature displeased them. The Wolf and Morigan had not spoken in words all night. Their souls, though, had exchanged a flurry of hot, dark emotions that said what words could not.

*You mustn't blame yourself,* whispered Caenith finally.

*We mustn't be so careless,* Morigan responded, and she scowled. She slipped out of his arms and stood. *Even for you, a man to whom these woods should bow, that respect no more is given. We are all strangers and wanderers in this place. I have seen the charter of Alabion's justice now, and it is penned in blood. That is her language, law, currency, and price. I fear what that price will be for each of us. I can see now that none of us will escape this journey without a scar.*

The Wolf growled. *Where are you going?*

*That trinket Mouse holds. It calls to me.*

Behind her eyes, the silver swarm of magik that fed off the Fates of others buzzed for Morigan's attention. Magik twisted her sight with silver and pulled her toward Fionna and the necklace she toyed with in her lap. When Morigan came to her friend, the tow of destiny was so fierce she almost snatched the item from Mouse before remembering her manners. "May I see it?" she asked.

Warily, Mouse looked up at the seer. She felt reluctant to part with this treasure from her lost friend—even if she had no idea of its use or meaning. "I suppose. Don't do anything strange. It's important to me."

"I know."

As she and Mouse touched fingers in their trade, the bees stung her with prophecy.

*Such tasty memories the bees have found. The soul of a golden-haired girl and a lifelong friend lost in the Dreaming as Macha once was. She is here as a messenger.*

*For what? Morigan wonders.*

*Him, buzz the bees. The Gray Man. The Trickster. The Poet of the Stars. Time for her friend to go, and what sadness as she fades into the Great Mystery.*

*Then she sees Mouse spit forth from a white tomb. She is racing against her terror and from the monsters that pursue her. The bees find her bravery more delicious than her fear. Suddenly, she is with Thackery. Fear transforms into joy, and the warmth of his magik and sacrifice is all around her. Again they are running when she sees it—the light in the dark. She knows it is what Adelaide spoke of.*

"You've done it again!" huffed Mouse. "I can see it in your face. That expressionless vacancy—like a simpleton watching raindrops on a window. Ugh. You make it very difficult for a person to have any privacy, you know. Just give it back to me whenever you've done your weird work."

Morigan was fumbling for an apology when Mouse thrust the jewelry into her hand. With that, apologies vanished. Sparks dazzled her sight, and she was well and truly absent from the world.

*How incredibly fast the bees travel. Buckle up. Buckle down. We are taking you for a ride! the bees declare in their voiceless voices. She is not in control—just a dizzy passenger on this gallop through silver stretches of nothingness. The journey slams to a stop, and she is floating in the musty dark of the cavern where the amulet was found. She hovers over the slumbering shadow of a man wrapped in silks. Something wetly suckles in the space behind him. It's a dream weaver either feeding or poisoning, but* she is more interested in the glimmer of silver winking from the cocoon. Its details are crisp—a simple linked chain with a small, iron medallion. Intricate words adorn the amulet. They are as beautiful as art and from the same language Caenith used to engrave her dagger. Like her dagger, this amulet is a symbol of promise—a covenant—perhaps for love or perhaps for something greater still. She would pick at the threads of this mystery more if she had a moment, but the bees are again whipping her to motion. There! You saw it! Now see where it was!

More silver, shrieking emptiness. She would shriek too if she had a mouth, so perilous is this speed. Then the brakes slam on, and her vision wobbles to focus. There is a man dressed in tribal clothing, and he fishes in a wide, turbulent river using only his swift hands. Others in similar furs and tattooed skins are behind him and doing the same chore. She guesses these are his pack members, and her guesses are always right. Another guess tells her this is the living version of the man who will one day die in the cave with Mouse's amulet around his neck.

No. Not Mouse's. Not yet, say the bees.

What he has suddenly found in the water puzzles the man. It has been lost for ages beneath the stones and silt of the riverbed, and now the man holds up the shining object, the iron amulet, so his pack mates might see.

Enough! say the bees.

They are moving again so fast through the Dreaming's vagueness she feels as if pieces of herself could fly away like pollen in a breeze. When the mist parts, what she witnesses slaps her with the cruelest kind of sense. She knows what she sees is utterly true and free of lies. She is still in Alabion's woods, but she is in a place above the knotted bush and nearly as high as some of its oldest trees. She is familiar with too much of what she sees. There is a rough pile of stones still brown from fresh earth. They are built like a temple—a cairn like the one she and Thackery once made for her mother. Impossibly, her mother is here. Mifanwae takes Morigan's breath away with her stony beauty, which grief makes fiercer. Yes. This is the root of the sadness Mifanwae secretly bore and would not share.

For whom do you grieve? wonders Morigan. She doesn't wonder long, for the musk of man's sweat, the touch of a rough hand on a shoulder that isn't *hers, the sound of a hearty laugh, and brief memories of bearded smiles and hale flesh come to her. Mifanwae grieves for her lover and husband.*

*My father? she wonders. This is the only answer she will accept.*

*No, retort the bees.*

*This insult should stun Morigan, but it does not. Here in the Dreaming, she knows it is real. The gently murmuring babe that sleeps in a haversack on Mifanwae's back does not astound Morigan either. It is herself as a youngling. She has a few tufts of the same crimson hair as her mother.*

*Not your mother, chide the bees.*

*This sting would bleed, if she could bleed here.*

*Mifanwae speaks to her beloved's ghost and bids him to sleep well.* "Tagtae tobar, Aaown."

*In the speech of Alabion, the old words of the forest, the stranger Morigan has called her mother says good-bye to the lie she thought of as her father. Mifanwae kisses an iron amulet she clutches and then tucks it in her traveler's kirtle. It falls on its chain against her chest. When Mifanwae later flees from a snarling forest—yes, the trees are growling and reaching clawed branches for her—that kirtle and the chain it hides snag on a wooden finger. Fabric and chain are torn and regretfully left behind. Over decades the amulet tumbles and rolls from the cursed place where it dropped. In safer regions, animals and time shred the fabric around the amulet down to motes of dirt. They chew and play with the iron, which endures. It is unbreakable—eternal as the bond it represents. No matter where the rain and mud send the amulet, even as it is plopped into a lake, dragged along with the snails through mud, and taken on a dashing trip up and down the blue veins of Alabion for years, it never chips or loses its dark shine. One day it is found—first by a man fated for an early death and later by Mouse. All this Morigan sees in her Dream within a Dream.*

*There is no more to witness, and she cannot handle another cruel revelation. How merciful the bees have been in not showing her this before. Perhaps they could not or simply would not. Perhaps she would have broken from this truth and fallen before stepping on the road of destiny. She is strong now but tired, and she wishes to return to the realities and truths that love her—to Caenith and her pack.*

*Yes, Mistress, the bees hum, and she is carried off and away.*

She emerged into a circle of worried faces. Even Thackery was awake, and she wondered whether she had screamed at the start of her unstoppable ride. *Yes,* said her silver minions. Caenith was holding her. She must have fainted. His stare was less concerned than those of the others.

*Where did they take you?* he whispered in their secret language.

Morigan had to bite back tears. *Here...my mother. No. Not my mother. Mifanwae was here in Alabion.*

# II

# SCARS

## I

"My queen, it grows late."

Queen Lila was about to address the enormous man casting his silver-hued shadow over her as Rowena. But no. Her sword was gone and neck-deep in espionage with the master of the East Watch, and a hammer named Erik was her guardian these days. What sad eyes the man had, more black than blue—as morose as those of an owl perched over a graveyard. She could see them glinting from beneath his darkened visor. Rarely did she spot the hard, hidden handsomeness of the man—his black hair, broken but appealing face, and stubble crisscrossed in scars. Come to think of it, aside from the moment his naked, scorched self had abruptly manifested in a cindery puff within the Chamber of Echoes some weeks ago, she hadn't seen him without his helm. He was hiding then from the absence of his king or another private torment. She had been staring at him rather unabashedly for quite a spell. The sparkle of fiery colors off the immaculate polish of his pristine armor hypnotized her. His voice snapped her out of her trance. How quickly evening's shroud had fallen.

"Time has escaped us," commented the queen.

Erik gently led her from the bedside she attended. As they passed the hospice's cots and floor pallets, the hands and voices of the wounded reached for her. Erik watched the queen's remorseful looks and the aching way she touched the feet of certain sufferers or the backs of weeping kin. These days she was cold and ruthless in her judgments within the palace. She had become a steel queen to stand metal for mettle against the Iron Queen rising in the East. In these particular confines, however, where the faltering breath of the ailing made the air humid, and it was thick with the stench of eucalyptus poultices and incense to mask the rot magik would not heal, the queen's mask cracked or was simply cast off. Genuine pity replaced it. She had come here each day for the past fortnight since the storm of frostfire had struck Eod. "The day of ruin," the people called it—when first the skies were bare and then suddenly forked with red lightning, spitting shards of ice and arrows of flame to the earth. None of sound mind could have prepared for that wailing apocalypse. Thousands were killed instantly. They were boiled inside tarry craters the earthspeakers were still working to fill or entombed in buildings that could not hold against the storm's wrath. The injuries were uncountable, and they were still being reported. Those with only singed or frostbitten flesh dismissed the pettiness of their wounds and carried on with tourniquets and grimaces. Others had to be scraped from streets or, if mauled but living, extracted from rubble and taken to a growing encampment of emergency sites erected near the palace. Here was where the queen always found herself once the details of war, supply lines, allies, enemies, and stratagems had worn her patience to a snappy disinterest. Somehow in these miserable hospices, the queen seemed peaceful, albeit sad.

Time and again Erik made one-sided conversation as he guarded his new charge—he never managed to say these words. *You blame yourself for this or for my kingfather's fate. You see these sins as your own. You feel the weight and needs of this entire nation upon yourself, and what a terrible weight that must be to bear. You are not alone, though, my queen. As adrift as you might be, I am here. I shall be the rock you need. I have made a promise to the great man who speaks to us no more.*

The night he had appeared so rudely at her side, she held him and told him she could not sense the king anymore. The icy flame of Magnus's soul had gone as cold as a forgotten hearth.

"What does it mean? What does it all mean?" she'd sobbed.

She was without her lover and partner in eternity, and he was without his father. They were agonizingly alone. Only on that night did she cry for the king and never since—as far as Erik had witnessed. He and the queen did not speak of their grief again or further pursue the reality that the Immortal King—missing and utterly quiet in his queen's mind since the battle with his mad brother in Zioch—was quite possibly dead.

At the hospice exit, Queen Lila stopped so suddenly that Erik almost elbowed his liege. With what Erik perceived as a speck of wariness, she half glanced over her shoulder, and her gaze swelled wide with fear. She was staring at something behind them. Erik looked as well and reached a hand to his weapon. However, he saw nothing aside from the rows of squirming sufferers moving on their bloody, sweat-soaked cots like man-size maggots. What horrible times these were.

"Have you forgotten something?" he asked.

Queen Lila wished she could explain the hairs that prickled on her neck or the chill of Mother Winter's mouth that blew the humidity from the chamber, but no one else seemed to feel it. Most of all, she wanted to find a less hysterical explanation for the shadow—tall as a mountain, black, and somehow bright—that hovered in the corner of her eye. She would not turn around and look at it. She could not. She was afraid that if she opened her mouth, she would involuntarily scream. *What do you want, shadow? Why do you haunt me? Why do you come to me in dreams?*

"My queen?"

"No. I need nothing more," she answered curtly and moved ahead, trembling.

Caged in their separate silences, they drifted as unseen as spirits from the tented city, which was haunting with its ghostly globes and choir of whimpers. Inconspicuously, they came to a skycarriage near the barricades at the outskirts of the hospice grounds. They took the vehicle to the palace and arrived just as night drank the sky's last red light. Unquestioningly, the queen allowed her hammer to guide her, as she was still rather lost inside her thoughts and jumping at shadows. Erik noticed every small startle. Surely she was exhausted and hungry. Erik took her to the White Hearth, and soon the scent of food aroused her. She glanced down at the plate of warm meats, boiled potatoes, and pan-fried greens. She nibbled a bit and cast empty stares about the long table where she ate. The table was to be shared by a king, his queen, and their court, but today only Lila and her shadow of a guardian occupied it. Mater Lowelia wasn't about the White Hearth either, and without the woman's conviviality, there wasn't much to keep the queen's interest aside from the meal or the two pretty bards—one boy and one girl—laughing and plucking away beneath one of the tapestries. For a while their music appeared to engage the queen, but then she saw the young man place his hand upon the other's leg and the blush of sweet romance in the girl's cheeks. The queen's appetite was ruined. She got up from the table and walked away from her hardly touched meal. Erik followed. He was an invisible companion until they reached her chambers. Once there he opened the door for the queen and bowed his metal head. "Good night, Your Majesty. Sleep well."

There he was to remain posted at her portal like a mechanical knight. However, Lila had drunk her fill of the wine of secrets and silence and wanted not anther drop. Before her was the only person in Geadhain who could comprehend what and whom she had lost. "Come inside," she ordered.

The metal man shook his head. "Pardon? It is my duty to stand here while you sleep. Such is how I protected our king. I was his shadow, and so shall I be yours."

"You look after him no more." The queen's expression was icy as she said that, but then warmed a speck hence. "We must consider ourselves and what new rules there are to be. Come inside, Erithitek. I know your true name. Of course I do. Come inside, and we shall have a glass of spirits and talk of what it is we do not talk about."

With that, she turned from him and swept into her chamber. The hammer shuffled for a sand, cast glances up and down the bare corridor, slipped in, and shut the door behind him.

The queen's sanctum was a mirror image of his king's—a bed with netted hangings, a small landing of stairs to a starry balcony outside, two armchairs, and a mantel and fireplace he saw spark and burst with golden flames. As she turned from the mantel bearing two goblets, he saw in her eyes a flicker of the golden magik that had stoked fire from nothingness. She settled into one of the armchairs, took a sip from one cup, and held out the other for Erik to take. He hurried over, clanking, and he awkwardly removed his gauntlets and helm before he reached his queen.

"Behold. There is a man under all that metal. How refreshing." She smiled—the first he had seen since the frostfire—as he took his cup.

Erik felt his color rise. The queen's smile deepened at his embarrassment. He could never tell when she was being cruel or kind or how wavering that line was.

"Don't stand," she said. "You do enough of that. Have a seat."

The hammer removed his weapon and fit himself as best he could into the other armchair. It wasn't easy given his size and hefty armor. In the process, he spilled a bit of the crimson, syrupy drink he had been given, and the queen chuckled. After that, the pair settled into a somewhat awkward silence. The queen found some mystery or omen in the fire more entertaining than Erik's nerves, and his eye drifted to the twinkling stars seen through the flapping curtains nearby. The bitter liquor, which he felt he drank too quickly, flushed his chest and loosened the knots in his shoulders that duty had tied there. Erik never drank, but the queen's request had taken him so much by surprise he didn't mention that. Once or twice he caught himself staring at her fire-kissed curves. Although her pale, sensuous garments had been recently swapped for a highly virtuous, high-necked regal green frock, she could still seduce with her tumble of honey hair, her skin as sweet and inviting as caramel, her mouth-watering fragrance of mint, nutmeg, and brown sugar, and the sheer pull of her charisma, which could never be concealed. Transcendent beauty and grace clung to her no matter her mood or attire. Silhouetted in the flames, she now seemed more a painting or piece of art than a woman. *The Queen and Her Sorrow* or *Weeping Beauty*, Erik might call this work. He knew he was flirting with dishonorable thoughts that tickled his heart and loins. Yet the liquor was hot inside him, and his head was swimming quite pleasantly. She was exquisite. She was art. *Dammit. I am allowed to savor one moment.* After all he had suffered and with nothing but more war and mourning ahead, he deserved that.

"Magnus used to sit there," said the queen suddenly. She was staring at him, and he sobered in an instant. "I think he is dead," she added in a strangely calm voice. "The frostfire...Geadhain's own grief at the war between her most precious children. I believe that is what the storm was. The tears of our world. Magnus promised he would not leave me to haunt Geadhain—or perhaps I made that vow for him. And here I am. Here I am to remain forever." She paused, stared into the flames, and then turned to him as though emerging from a trance. "Forgive me for speaking so freely. I blame the spirits." She swished the liquid in her chalice. "However, only you and I can speak of these troubles. Only you understand what it was like to love Magnus. With everything. The whole of our hearts, lives, and souls. That is what it took to love him—to love a dream. Now that he is gone, we are left with vacancies about which only another as unfortunate as ourselves can commiserate."

Erik was drowning in the queen's words. Were anyone to know Magnus's fate, it would be the queen. She shared an uncanny bond with her blood-mate. Magnus dead? His kingfather gone from this world? He turned to the fire and allowed the hooks of abandonment to sink into his heart and pull him through pain, trembling rage, and then wrenching sadness. The queen silently watched him grieve. The various storms of his moods distorted and darkened his face. Quite a strong man he was to exhibit no more than that. A tear trembled on his lashes, but even that did not drop. The queen had done her grieving for now and did not weep either. That was why the king had chosen them—for their strengths of will. After a time Erik found the courage to turn from the fire and face the queen. Her golden eyes and words were waiting for him. "You harden as quickly as a smith's glowing sword plunged into water. I see why Magnus favored you as a son. I shall show Geadhain my own determination now. If I am to haunt our world, I shall do so as a ghost of vengeance."

"Vengeance?" said Erik.

A flash of memory returned to the queen then—a similar moment of valor and torment, when she had knelt before her bloodmate, and he had sworn himself to fury in her name. She would honor him with the same sac-rifice. She had spent the long, sleepless nights after waking from her terrors debating the worth of a life without Magnus. While she was too proud for suicide, she had many other deaths in mind. Why should one Immortal King be allowed to exist without punishment? Why should she debase herself or the proud children of Eod whom she and Magnus had raised by pleading for peace with Menos? For now that tales of Magnus's absence and defeat were rumbling up from the South, Menos's crowes were stretching their wings for flight. Soon black vessels would sweep over the city. Day after day in the Chamber of Echoes, her advisers had increasingly counseled for peace or prostrations toward the East. Finally, she took their counsel no more on matters of war.

"I am the queen. I am Eod's soul. I decide upon war or peace," she had declared one day so venomously that she was thereafter consulted only on civic trivialities.

Eod had a web of spymasters nearly as far-reaching as the Watchers—the Eyes of Eod they were called—and she had set these agents to work at once. Somewhere in the haze of her grief, she had found the prowling, slavering monster of anger and decided to fatten it with offerings. If the old powers—such as Magnus—were to pass into dust, then all the ancient orders should fall. In Erik she sensed an ally.

"In the South we have Brutus. Patrols seal his borders, and they claim soldier, spy, helpless wanderer, and foolish merchant alike. I believe that is how he was able to conceal the full scope of his evil, and it is evil he breeds in Zioch—a city no longer gold or filled with the harmonies of legendary minstrels but noisy with the churning of unholy machines and black with death's smog. Nothing good remains there to be saved. I have sent Eod's eyes to scout from above. The skies still are open, and they confirm the worst of what you and the battered returning legions have seen. Magnus did not defeat his brother—he merely delayed the realization of his ambitions. Brutus will soon create more of those hollow things you call Blackeyes, and I suspect I know from where. While the sages are still unraveling the horror of the alchemy that hollows out these people, we know enough of the ingredients. Brutus needs flesh and bone—*people*—and a large quantity of them to rebuild his army."

Erik's honor made him speak out of turn. "We must send word, Your Majesty, to—"

"Calm yourself, Hammer," replied the queen. "I am not so heartless or driven by hate that I would allow untold innocents to be murdered. I have dispatched another Eye to the regions of the South, which is where I believe Brutus will harvest his army. Sorsetta, the nation among the deep rivers and tall bluffs of the South, with its grand and placid populace and their abhorrence of war and violence, seems the most likely candidate for the slaughter. Waiting with the innocence of cattle for the summer feast, they are. However, the contemplatives among them practice some of our world's greatest martial disciplines. While they seem easy prey, they can fight back if pressed, and I am counting on them to entrench themselves in their mountain monasteries. The longer the Sorsettans hold Brutus at bay, the more time we have to dismantle Menos."

"Should we not do more than warn them? Surely we should send aid?"

The queen cast a withering glare his way. "We have our own people to worry about and our own tactics and deceptions to play."

He asked the more important question. "Dismantle Menos?"

"To the very black stones of its foundation."

"I don't...how..."

The queen waved away his stupefaction. "The past, Erithitek. All answers are in the past. Magnus was right to seek the Sisters Three, as is Thackery now to seek them on our behalf. However, Thackery's absence leaves us without a sorcerer for my task."

"What task?"

Before Erik's confusions could be addressed, there was a knock at the chamber door. More weapon than man, in a speck Erik was on his feet, his empty goblet was on the floor, and in his hand was the haft of the war hammer he'd left leaning on his chair.

"At ease," barked the queen. "Enter."

Lowelia Larson, mater of the White Hearth, came bustling into the room with her arms full of fabric. Her entire demeanor oozed suspicion from her pinched face to her possessive grip on the mysterious bundle she held. Erik noted that it was of too unusual a shape to be simple linens. Slipping in behind the mater was a man as proud and powerful as his name—Leonitis. The Ninth Legion master was unreadable beyond his frown.

"You are early," said the queen, and she stood. "Did you bring everything, Lowe?"

"Almost everything you asked for, Your Majesty," replied the mater.

She ran over to the bed and spilled her cargo. The queen followed, and the three conspirators hovered around while the queen picked through various items. Excluded, ignored, and increasingly frustrated, Erik stomped over to them. He saw a few articles of heavy clothing along with travelers' pouches, waterskins, a short sword, two hunting daggers, and leather wallets that held documents. The corner of one paper peeked out, and Erik saw official lettering scribed upon it. Folded up next to the supplies were two gowns. One was navy blue, and the other was the same emerald color as the queen's. The more he observed the assembled items—adventurers' gear and two dresses in the same modest style the queen had recently adopted and that appeared made for a woman a few measurements larger—the greater his unease.

"What is this, Your Highness?"

"Erithitek," said the queen, and she abruptly focused on him. She took his hand. The heat of her warm honey skin and the sparkle of her serpent stare paralyzed him. "I had not time to fully explain these circumstances to you before we were interrupted. I had hoped to ease you into the situation."

Not a stitch of what the queen was saying made sense—not the kind of sense Erik needed.

"You're not a stupid man," she continued. "Quite the opposite. The quiet ones are often the wisest, for they watch while others talk. I can see the threads being spun in your head. I too have been weaving. A tapestry of revenge." She smiled. It was beautiful and yet maleficent enough to send a chill through Erik. "I have not been unproductive with my grief. My king, your kingfather, would not wish the weakness of despair on me—not when we have so much to face. There is a red monster in the South and an iron one in the East. Menos is the greater threat until Brutus rebuilds, and I must strike at them when they think they are strongest."

"You're leaving," gasped Erik.

"Only for a time, and I shan't be missed. Lowe and Leonitis will see to that."

Officiously, the Ninth Legion master and the mater bowed, exposing their complicity in whatever plot the queen had furtively constructed. Suddenly, all the obvious signs he'd missed came flooding in. There had been late-night summons for Lowe to bring the queen tea for her restlessness. How long had those visits lasted? If he thought back, there had even been the nod she had given the Ninth Legion master this afternoon when they had met in the hallway. That lingering tip of the head and locking stare had been a look of meaning. In light of the conspiracy, the queen's frequent visits to the wretches at the hospices made magnitudes of sense as well. She was performing as much penance as she could while she could. Erik could not begin to guess how many more missives, whispers, and meetings had passed under his nose, by his ears, or before his eyes. Still, however much this great deception tore him, he was wrenched further by the sense of duty Magnus had left with him. It had been Magnus's dying wish for him to preserve this frightening and glorious woman, to take her all the way to Carthac if Brutus could not be stopped, and to protect her in whatever mad danger she chased. Ultimately, his purpose was not to question. He was Eod's instrument. He was a weapon, and a hammer should not ask its master why it was swung or question the innocence of the blood that wet its metal.

"Your silence is your agreement," muttered the queen with a cold respect.

Erithitek bent to a knee with the others. "I am yours to serve," he pledged.

The golden queen smiled again with malice. Whatever she had devised, it had been cultivated in darkness. However, Erik chose to believe it was for the benefit of Eod and not purely driven by revenge. He did not speak, as a sword would not speak, when she explained her plan to sneak from Eod and travel to Taroch's Arm, where she would use her powers to break the magikal seals on the tomb of the dead warlord Taroch and steal the titular relic itself. *Insane*, Erik thought before silencing that inner voice.

The question of how a queen would tiptoe out of her realm was shortly solved. Magik, she explained. A phantasm, as the exact metascience was termed, was a powerful and persistent optical, audio, and tactile illusion bound to an object through sorcery. This would serve as her feint. A master conjurer's distortion of reality was more powerful than the mirages conjured by trickster sorcerers and witches. A master phantasm would not shatter or be seen through if faced with disbelief, and as long as the talisman that trapped the enchantment remained whole, so too would the illusion. The illusion could encourage belief and build its resistance to a strong will by incorporating tactile elements—ones that worked through the viewer's subconscious to strengthen the spell's hold on his waking mind. *Elements such as the clothes made for a more rotund queen*, realized Erik, and he looked from Lowe to the garments laid upon the bed. He could not think up the equivalent for Leonitis until the queen ordered Erik to undress and change into the set of adventurer's clothing—tall boots, jerkin, leather pants, and a cloak. He complied without shyness, despite the stares the queen and Lowe gave his muscled body. A sword had no shame, and neither did he. Leonitis did not grow shy either when instructed to don Erik's old linens. Erik helped buckle him into the corset of armor. It was much tighter and heavier than the equipment Leonitis was used to wearing. Erik's hammer was no real treat to handle either, but the strengths of the men were similar, and Leonitis had the weapon up and strapped on his back after a single, clean swing. The legion master's old gear was then hurried into a sack and hidden under the bed to be disposed of later in secrecy. Lowelia's change was done as quickly as a stage actor's swap. No modesty was required. One dress went up over her shoulders, and the other shimmied down underneath it. She completed the act with a huff and a grin, and then she noticed she was enjoying herself a little too much.

The dastardly switch was complete. Erik thought this the kind of material fit for some farce involving a countess, a witch, and a lover or two—only this was for a game far deadlier and real. The queen then went over the details and final warnings.

"We are the only four in this world who understand the mission I undertake and the peril in which I must place myself. No one else can know. Trust no one else, as our house has ears that listen for their iron masters. Root those out while I am gone if you will, and show no mercy in their sentencing. For the time being we cannot risk the faintest ripple of more dissent and chaos in our kingdom, which is why this is the only path to take. It is a secret path and a liar's path, but virtue has no place in war. This is a dark time, and if not for ourselves, we must be strong for our missing king."

*Dead*, Erik silently corrected her. *Dead king. She has told them a lie. She was telling the truth to me at least.* Erik swallowed this betrayal without a sign.

"Thackery continues to hunt Alabion for the wisdom of the ages, and we are the only heroes of our kingdom to be found. We have been abandoned to our fate. We are not helpless, though. I shall never be helpless." Again a wrathfulness clouded her beauty. "From here on out, your wits and knowledge will be tested every sand of every hourglass. Do not disappoint me."

The three nodded to their queen.

"Come forth, you two," she beckoned to Lowe and Leonitis.

They were not at her side as Erik was—a habit he found impossible to break. The queen produced from a pocket two polished silver bands, each wide enough for a horse's hoof. Erik questioned how they had fit in her garment in the first place. She asked each person who was to be ensorcelled for a wrist. Leonitis pulled off his gauntlets and gloves, and the two extended their hands bravely through the hoops.

Lowe's courage faltered. "Will it hurt?" she asked.

"Not really," said the queen.

*Another lie.* Erik was becoming good at spotting them. She tended to soften in her features and voice while stiffening in her glare. Then came a gold flash from the queen's eyes and a pulse of great heat. For Erik the heat was pleasant from head to soul. It was as if he sat before a fire with a sheepdog at his feet. The fiery jolts of the queen's sorcery—anger's vicious energy—racked those subjected to the power directly. Had it lasted more than a speck, one or both of them certainly would have screamed. In their shock and the dazzle of light, neither noticed the silver circles shrink and sizzle deep as brands into their flesh. They were still visible but more akin to metal tattoos than jewelry. Lowe withdrew her hand with a whimper. She wasn't familiar with her own hand—slim and slightly brown—or the breasts to which she held it. Gone were the pleasantly fat, middle-aged woman and the groomed, brooding hulk of a warrior. In their steads were the perfect twins of the queen and her hammer. Their soft squeals or grunts of surprise only compounded their amazement. Their voices were no longer their own.

"This is good," assessed the queen, and then she slipped her slim, simple crown on Lowelia's head. "Those talismans will not come off, short of removing the hand."

With that nasty caveat, she threw off her dress and put on plain trousers, a blouse, boots, a muffler, and then a woolly, hooded cloak. Since Erik had turned from her nakedness and the others were still in awe of their new selves, no one noticed a thing until she snapped at them.

"We have a pittance of time for farewells," she said. "Especially with the four of us all standing together in one room. Imagine the surprise! Lowelia, keep those far-speaking stones I gave you on hand at all times, and pray you do not feel the warmth of one. I won't risk contact unless the stakes have become grave. More likely Rowena will make contact with a report on any suspicious activities in Blackforge. We must find the location of the Iron City's supplies in that region. Remember, you know me every bit as well as I know myself. You know my habits, wants, and needs, for you have attended to them for many years. I am confident you can play this role. Leonitis, just be brave and tall and silent, and no one will know the difference between you and my companion." She smiled warmly and genuinely and hugged them both. "Good luck." A frown spoiled her kindness when she spotted her companion. "Erithitek, put on your hood. Cover your face with your scarf. Discretion above all else."

Quick as that, the queen's switch had lashed again, and Erik fumbled to do as instructed while she snatched his arm and pulled him away. He waved to the second hammer. He had never really examined himself, but he was a handsome fellow. He supposed he was quite grim in the set of his face, though. He waved also to the second queen who stood next to his twin. Then he thought no more of those other selves, of tomb robbing, or of the frantic grief of the woman who led him. He thought not of her own words about leading them all down a path of lies—a path empty of virtue.

II

"Well," said the golden and beautiful Lowelia once they were alone. "Haven't we landed in the thick of it?"

"Indeed," replied Leonitis.

The legion master was still foggy about how he had been hoodwinked so. He had been back but an hourglass after weeks of exhaustive, wearying riding. He had barely stepped into the sanctuary of Eod—its embrace of flowers and sunshine and all things good—when the queen had asked for his report. A soldier through and through, he had splashed himself clean and gone to his superiors. The queen had been alone, though. No council had been present aside from the king's silent hammer, Erik, whom he had not seen since their dark parting. Dismissively, she had sent the hammer off on a serf's errand for food. In those fleeting moments of privacy, she had listened to his story but seemed already to know much of it. Then she had asked whether she could trust him. The queen could cast a spell and not only with her magik. Moreover, she had an innate magnetism, and he had been offering her his compliance before he knew for what.

After that, the details of her madcap plan had come to him through missives and whispers from the mater or in cryptic statements from the queen herself— which would have seemed nonsense to anyone else.

"Your boots are worn," the queen had said. "I can nearly see your feet. Go see the cobbler and perhaps the tailor after to mend your coat of arms. We are not a patchwork army of misfits but the army of Eod."

This had been a clever castigation—one that hid the queen's desire to have him measured for another man's armor and clothes. A great deal of the plan had been unknown until this evening when he saw the garments and forged identities laid out. Nonetheless, as the deception had unfolded, he still felt no doubt. The queen was as wily as she was beautiful. She had chosen well her false champion—a man without family aside from a grizzled brother in Eod's service. Each was an orphan, such as the queen tended to take in. Reaching back through the haze of time, his first clear memories of a woman were of the queen. Her soft hands had led him and his brother—so small then—into a sparkling garden and then set them free to run and play in the sunshine. He couldn't remember what came before that bright memory. It was something dark and slithering that did not want to be found. The memory hissed with a snake's warning whenever he poked about for it in his head. If the queen knew of this monster, she wasn't telling. "I found you in Carthac," she would say. "Two handsome sea princes washed up on the beach like snails. I picked you both up out of the sands, dusted you off, and brought you home with me to Eod. And here you shall stay and be happy and creep out of your shells one day to see and taste and know life."

It was a cryptic and empty biography. However, as a soldier, he had learned never to ask for more, and through discipline he had choked down any urge to investigate. His brother too was perfectly content in ignorance. As distant as the queen could be, she was mother enough for him, and the army made up for whatever other kin he and Dorvain needed. Perhaps that was why he so instantly leaped to her command—this woman whom he saw rolling by, a wave of beauty, once or twice a year.

"Still quite baffled by it all, I see," said Lowe.

She was striding about the chamber and practicing her queenly grace. Her twirls and sashays, though, were too exuberant and unrefined. She would have to work on being more reserved. Lowe recognized this and frowned at her shortcomings.

"I haven't gotten the hang of it," she said. "Deary mittens! Feels as if I'm wearing a pair of knickers that just isn't my own. Itching and pulling in all the wrong places."

"In time," he said.

*And shall I get the hang of this?* he wondered, and he flexed and stretched his unfamiliar flesh. That the queen had picked him as Erik's double was as crafty as all else she had arranged. He and Erik were within a knuckle of one another in size, with the hammer being taller and he being wider. Leonitis was rubbing the red welt that framed the silver band on his wrist. The smooth, dark hue of his stranger's skin so distracted him that Lowe had to repeat her question twice before he heard her.

"Why do you think she chose us?" asked Lowe.

He shrugged. "I am about the only man I can think of besides my brother who would fit the hammer's armor. You...well, you can make your own queenly garments to measure without making strange inquiries to a seamstress. Evidently, these guises aid in the convincingness of our illusions."

"That's all?"

"Our queen asks, and we obey. She has placed great trust in us. We are all she has."

There was more to it than that—any number of threads they could pull to unravel the mystery. Surely they each sensed isolation in these events. As alone as the queen was, so were they. However, what Leonitis said was the fundamental truth, and they both knew it. As orphans and outcasts united by their lack of ties to anything aside from Eod and that nation's mother, they would have done anything for the queen. It was possible the queen understood this. It was even likely she had used their absolute fealty to her advantage.

"We are indeed," agreed Lowe with a sigh. "Well, my hammer, I should settle in for the evening." Her enthusiasm was more muted now. Perhaps this was as a result of their conversation.

"I shall leave you then, Your Majesty." Leonitis bowed to her.

*Perhaps this could work after all,* he thought. After donning his helm and gauntlets, he took his post outside the queen's chamber. On his watch that night, he heard a few giggles from inside the chamber as Lowelia no doubt frolicked in the sheets and perfumes made for her mistress. Occasionally, a servant or Silver watchman strode down the echoing hallway he guarded. Not a soul tested the ruse, though. He gained confidence, first lifting his visor, and then removing his helm entirely. A couple hourglasses into his watch, he no more tensed at boots clacking and strangers approaching. He looked ahead, concentrated on the creep of ivy into white brick, and looked up at the little fascinating jewels of soft light that grew on the verdant mesh of the ceiling. This still amazed him after a lifetime in the palace. Suddenly, his brother's grizzled face—furred and rough as a bear's where his was sleek and comely as a lion's—appeared shouting before him.

"Half the palace is asleep, but this won't wait for morning! This is all I could gather for counsel at the moment."

Serious men gathered around Dorvain, master of the North Watch. Some were wizened. Others were hale. All had the same cold glint of wisdom and ruthlessness to their faces. Leonitis fumbled for his composure. "Gathered?" he said. "For what?"

Dorvain was canny and could feel something amiss, even if he couldn't put his finger on it. Luckily, he only sneered and dismissed the oddness. "No time for you to be leaning about like a dandy waiting for his lover. Stand up straight, man!" He whispered the next bit. "Dark news from the North. As if our troubles were not enough, it seems as if nearly all corners of the world wish to strike Eod at once. We must speak with the queen."

Dorvain did not wait for the gaping hammer to reply but shoved the man aside. His brow furrowed with that same sense of something amiss, but Dorvain saw nothing of the truth of his brother concealed in the illusion even as he touched it. Leonitis rushed after the man and the train of advisers and hoped the snoring, farting, inglorious woman flopped on the bed was ready to give the performance of the ages.

✳ ✳ ✳

III

Blackforge was a miserable place. During Rowena's journey east, the fiery pandemonium brought by the sage in his encounter with Master Blackmore had forced her and her companion to detour south to Riverton. Each morning she remembered that city's whimsy, and she ever longed for its off-kilter houses with their pipes, decks, and sloshing charm. She would stay in her moth-eaten blankets and hold on to that fantasy until the chill of Blackforge—the mist that bled through windowsills and under doors and stank of ash—at last crept beneath her blankets and forced her out of bed. Then she would rub her face and quickly find her socks, for the floor was as cold as a butcher's cellar. Afterward, she would wake Galivad, who somehow slept soundly in this squalor, and then try to rinse the daily film of grease from her face. However, the brown water that ran in the rusted pipes of the weather-beaten tavern where they were staying was as useful as mud. As time passed she was soon dirtier than she had ever been as a lizard-herding slave-girl of the Arhad.

Once up and about, she and Galivad would wander the ghastly town. It was depressing to imagine the original state of Blackforge's hovels now that they were pitted and singed from the storm of the Kings. That the locals said not much had changed made her feel only worse. Wherever she and her companion went in Blackforge, the cheerless, gaunt folk with their mopey brows and hunched postures made her angrier at her orders to be there. How could people live so near to Riverton's vibrancy and be so dull themselves? She was not a cruel person but a merciful one, and yet she found that trait wearing down as the days went by.

"What a sourpuss, my dear Merriweather," chimed Galivad.

He was teasing her with her false identity. They'd decided to keep the aliases they'd become accustomed to from their last bit of spycraft. On this and every other morning, the environs had failed to wither Galivad's radiant disposition. Persistent as a fungus, he had blossomed in this muck. He still whistled tunes when they were out and walking, and he happily greeted the specters that passed for people in the streets. Today they had not been out just yet. Before any adventuring, Rowena was first trying to finish the colorless slop on her plate—a gruel of oatmeal and some gamy, sour-smelling meat.

Rowena slid the dish away with a finger. "I think I've had my fill."

"Of just the meal, dear Merri, or..." Galivad fluttered his hand to indicate the somber room with slit windows, groaning benches, and long-faced patrons who sipped bitters or quietly bickered. One person laughed a cold and cruel laugh. Galivad resumed. "I come for the sweet mead and the enchanting music. I come to this harbor of sunshine to escape all that is dark in the world. I come for the culture."

He made her snicker—a happiness she had forgotten. Galivad stood and offered his hand. "Shall we, Merri?"

"Yes."

She held onto his pale, womanish, and incongruously large fingers more caressingly than a sister would, but she slid her hands into her pockets the instant they stepped out into a line of derelict log houses and a dreary day. As they slogged through muddy trails, they carried on blithe chatter as their alter egos. They poked about the streets, shops, and houses and kept their eyes and ears keen for suspicious happenings or whispers. One of the only helpful pieces of information they had sleuthed thus far was that the master himself had left Blackforge with a hunting party a week past. Their pallid informant had warned them not to celebrate, though, as an emissary from Menos would be en route to keep order in Master Blackmore's stead. They'd kept an eye out for said master in the meantime and continued to scout for other movements of the Iron City during the days.

If anyone asked about their purpose—though few had—they were rather practiced now at their false identities, and Galivad would spin out his most extravagant lies before Rowena could even introduce herself as his sister. They couldn't overtly be themselves except for those few hourglasses they were alone in the two-bunk apartment they rented. They lived in their roles, which offered a curious kind of relief. If there hadn't been a looming iron shadow in the East, and they had been in sunnier climes, Rowena might actually have enjoyed herself. Galivad was easy company, and perhaps his warmth had simply melted her chilly demeanor. The longer they chatted—in false skins or their own—the more the qualities in him that had once irritated her became ones she admired. He was a charming dandy with his dedication to personal grooming, snappy enunciation, and the way he sang both the bass and soprano parts of any song. Galivad did not appear to care for the conventions of being a man, much as she had once chosen to wear the uncomfortable armor of a male member of the Silver Watch, rather than one molded for her breast. One morning after bathing, Galivad had sat upon a stool and brushed his glistening hair, which was long, flowing, and of a sparkling golden beauty when wet. While untangling his locks, he had sung "The Handmaiden's Woes." That was one of Rowena's favorite songs about female servitude and subjugation, and she could not say whether it was man, woman, or spirit of Alabion who prettied itself before her. It did not matter. Galivad was simply beautiful—as beautiful as Queen Lila.

Rowena was thinking about Eod, Galivad, the queen, gender confusion, and, to a lesser degree, the one far-speaking stone their informant here had given them. ("Straight for the queen's own ear," the pale ghoul of a man had promised.) Then suddenly, she was rudely pulled off the main road into a cramped access between two buildings. Galivad did not explain himself but pulled her back with him into whatever gloom he could find and glared out at the street. His bright, brown eyes were like those of a frightened deer.

"What is it?" she whispered.

He threw her an agitated look and hissed, "There."

Rowena scanned the desolate marketplace fogged from the fall rains. She spotted tired vendors frowning at their patrons, and farther through the haze, she saw the picketed remains of the Blackmore longhouse, which was as black and jagged as a monster's claws. Apparently repairs had been abandoned, for the pulleys were untended today, as they had been every day since they had arrived. Logs lay piled about the ruins as if they were tinder ready for another great blaze. The figures were so black, they blended in against the charcoal backdrop—shadows smudged among cinders.

Ironguards.

There seemed to be a few of them. Rowena noted their faceless, body-hugging metal armor, which would have been almost rubbery in appearance if not for the barbs and rude angles that betrayed its hardness. Rifles were slung over their shoulders, and their barrels flickered with blue flame. The ironguards were the most obvious sign of a Menosian diplomat. Rowena then noticed a pair of iron masters. At a distance and with stalls and wagons between them, Rowena could catch only glimpses of the ironguards' charges. There was a gentleman. Indeed, she had the impression of genteel sensibilities from his tight carriage, ebony suit, bowler hat, and cane, which might have been inlaid with marble it shone so much. He was in the company of a woman who floated through the filth. Again, this was just an impression, and it was of lightness and an almost magikal step. How incredibly white she was—a bride to winter. From her hair to her lacy veil to her flowing dress, her eerie loveliness drew all attention, and even Rowena's breath. *Who is she?*

"Beatrice," hissed Galivad.

"Then that would be—"

"Moreth of El, her husband," spit Galivad.

Beatrice was the murderer of Galivad's mother. The mystery of Galivad's tragic childhood was a tale scratched in Rowena's skull at night—the insinuations of black magik and the untold quest of vengeance he'd committed himself to. Hate distorted Galivad's comely features. His lips snarled, and his eyes sparkled with murder.

"We have found our emissary," said Rowena.

"Yes," purred Galivad.

Right then and there, he might have charged out of the alley if Rowena hadn't placed a firm grip on his arm. Her passion as she spoke dismantled more of his anger. "Galivad, don't you see? More of the redheaded witch's miracles! If you can focus on your duty and not lose yourself to hate, you will see she has given us a gift. A twist of fate. A chance for revenge. But these are all threads of a larger cloth, and we cannot allow our carelessness to disrupt what is being woven. We must learn what Moreth is doing here, his intentions, and the ambitions of Menos that drive him. We must find the location of this war forge of which the smith spoke. Once we accomplish our tasks—once we have served our country and friends—then we may be selfish. We can seek justice for your mother. I promise to aid you in this."

For the moment, her reason leashed the animal of hate, and Galivad softened. "I wasn't going to do anything foolish," he said, and pouted.

*Yes. You were*, Rowena thought. His rage had been sudden and powerful. She was a dear friend to violence and had watched it transform her and countless others. Had she not restrained her friend, the situation would have become rather messy.

"I don't know why we're lurking in here anyway," complained Galivad, although it had been his idea. "They're on the move. We need to follow them."

With that, he dashed out into the street and nearly toppled a lad pulling a cart. Galivad cursed him for his slow, simple mind and stumpy limbs made for a donkey. Rowena raced after Galivad after stopping a speck to apologize to the dim youth. Her gruffness and size, though, only further scared him. There was no time to fix that properly, for the gray-cloaked rabbit that was Galivad skipped through the slippery paths ahead. She cursed the agile bastard and hoped she could catch him before he did anything regrettable.

IV

For diabolical masters of Menos, Moreth and his bride got up to suspiciously little throughout the day. At least that was Rowena's opinion. They strolled about in the rain like young lovers. The weather and the depressive air of Blackforge, however, did not dampen their pleasure in each other. Moreth was a consummate gentleman and lifted Beatrice's billowing skirt as she stepped over puddles. He pointed out landmarks for her with his polished black cane, and many times he simply stopped so he could whisper in Lady El's ear. These words always left her smiling and flushed. Rowena could tell Moreth was quite in love with his wife. *His evil wife*, she had to remind herself whenever one of Beatrice's musical giggles sounded through the glum clangs and moans of Blackforge. What was so appealing to Rowena turned the stomach of her companion, and every laugh of Beatrice resulted in a sneer from Galivad.

The lovers' itinerary was so commonplace that Rowena began to feel more like a criminal than they surely were. She and Galivad stalked the couple, hid behind corners, and if gazes turned in their direction, falsely busied themselves examining depressing objects at the nearest stand. The couple stopped to break a late-afternoon fast at a run-down alehouse that creaked and wobbled as though it might fall from a child's cough. Rowena discouraged Galivad from any reconnaissance inside. She didn't feel he could be trusted around the source of his hatred—not yet. Soon a cold and crisp night fell. They shivered outside the establishment in an alley within eyeshot of the eatery. Some moldering crates offered them moderate concealment but no comfort from the weather. From where they huddled, they could see the brown, lamplit shadows of Moreth and his wife through the tavern's grimy windows. Galivad was not in the mood for their usual colloquy. He had not spoken since that afternoon and was satisfied to sulk. After some deliberation, Rowena attempted to end the silence. "You told me a while back you had sought this woman before to avenge or learn about your mother's passing."

At first, Galivad did not reply and only trundled more into his cloak. "Yes," he said finally. She thought that was the end of the matter until Galivad suddenly turned to her, sapped, and slumped. "Coin can buy anything in Menos, and I shan't tell you what I did to earn my black crowns, but I had plenty. I had enough to learn of the last place where my mother performed and for whom that fatal performance was given. Beatrice. The servants in Menos are all sworn to secrecy, but they talk. The Watchers hear and sell every whisper in the Black City. I bought myself a position in El's estate so I could meet this murderer and epicure of mortal flesh. For it is said...it is said Beatrice dined on her."

Rowena gasped.

Galivad spit once quickly. "The El manor is in the Evernight Gardens, which you've probably never seen. I don't think you could have when we were in Menos. Too much was going on. But these houses...row after row of faery-tale mansions made for wicked witches and monsters. I still have nightmares of walking down that street for the first time."

He stumbled through the memory of that night and tried to describe for Rowena as best he could what he had not told anyone.

*No gardens here, he notes, in awe of what the Menosians consider beauty. It is the loveliness, he supposes, of a bloody sword held in the moonlight or the peacefulness of a corpse. Though the cathedral architecture—the parapets, twisting towers, hideous statues, and wrought-iron gables and gates—are distracting, he is only lightly intrigued. The black beast of vengeance has taken him this far through the meat markets, pleasure houses, and pits of blood. He's gone into bargains with one-eyed whores and sold himself to men and women who are seeking one with both his eyes. There is nothing he has not done to* feed his black beast. No service or sale of himself—for murder, sex, and darker trades—he has not embraced if it would mean he would be welcomed into the Evernight Gardens. Now the black beast is close to its meal, the witch and monster in mortal skin: Beatrice.

Galivad is admitted into the extravagant El estate. He does not recall arriving or ascending the grand courthouse-like steps. The dark mist of the dream in which he wanders hides much of what he does or has done. His memory is generous with forgetfulness for his sins. Some more moments blurrily pass. He has shown papers and paid imploring graces. Further conversations, meaningless introductions, and pandering occur. He is handed an apron and a pair of scissors. Yes. He recalls he is a beautician come to maintain Lady El's comeliness. The gleaming scissors understand why he is here, but he only begins to remember. They seem to snip the air of their own accord. As he is ushered into an opulent, draped, and overhung room where Lady Beatrice awaits, Galivad is smiling—a black but true smile of joy. It is an executioner's sadism at the snap of a spine.

Beatrice is disarming in all her whiteness. Even her hair and the pupils of her stare glitter with a frosty incandescence. Perhaps that is why she wears the veil he sees discarded on the dressing table behind her—to hide her winter light. He wonders how all that paleness will look once the hot blood from her throat drenches it. He has decided that is where he will slice her. It will be a deep, crimson smile across her neck. Awash with intent, his hands tremble as he comes to the white witch, and she turns, flips her exquisite mane of spider silk to the side, and tells him not to be nervous.

He is frozen.

No magik has stopped him. Neither has her unexpected courtesy. Instead, it is this smallest motion that claws at the meat in his chest—the way she tossed her long neck and the lopsided curve of her smile. These are movements he cannot forget. They are part of the cameo he has enshrined in his mind. These are his mother's gestures.

Galivad drops the scissors and backs away. Beatrice's eyes narrow. She seems shrewdly aware of his aims and then swells with a pity and warmth that shakes his core further. He stumbles into a run. Even today he remembers her stare and forgiveness. By what twisted right can she offer him mercy? All he has been given is another memory to add to the shrine and another pain to feed *the beast. He cannot kill Beatrice; he will not. For somehow, in the wickedest way imaginable, his mother lives on inside this woman.*

"She knew." Galivad sniffled; he had started crying some time into his tale. "A mistress of Menos with an assassin in her lair, and she let me go. Why? I have asked myself this a thousand times. Why spare me unless..." He shivered and shook his head. "I don't know what remains of my mother. Belle. I've never told you her name. She was as beautiful as a sunrise over Meadowvale. Beautiful to her soul. I saw a glimpse of her beauty inside that icy witch. I shall understand that essence and either reclaim it—if such a thing can be done—or put it to rest forever."

"Galivad," Rowena began.

While Galivad was baring his grief, the vigilant sword had abandoned her focus. This had been rather stupid of Rowena, for their targets had not only left the alehouse but were sauntering down the street together and mere strides away. Her companion's whimpering, along with their shadows in the alley, had piqued the attention of an ironguard in Moreth's entourage. The ironguard halted Moreth with a whisper, and rifles were pointed toward Rowena and Galivad. Rowena had the merest speck in which to act. Galivad noticed her wariness, and he started to turn. If he saw Moreth and Beatrice so close in this faltering state, Rowena knew he would not have the restraint to stall his hand from violence. Therefore, she did what felt right in that moment. She distracted a man the best way she knew how. She swept her surprised companion up, pinned him to the wall, and kissed him.

Galivad wriggled against her. He was uncertain for a spell before giving in to her hungry mouth. Surprisingly, Rowena enjoyed the tension of his lean flesh squirming against her own while a measly layer of cloth separated their bodies. Galivad's hardness too was rather immediate and impressive, and she wasn't a woman easily—or ever—impressed by the snakes in men's pants.

"It's just two lovers, Moreth. Leave them be," came a delicate woman's voice.

Recognizing Beatrice's voice, Galivad huffed into Rowena's mouth and writhed to free himself, but Rowena was as unrelenting as a stone coffin about him. To the master of El and his wife, they might as well have been wrestling in drunken passion. Moreth snorted at the lovers and then claimed his wife's porcelain hand. He kissed it tenderly and then leaned near to his wife and started whispering. Had Moreth's retinue not wandered over to investigate the alley, Rowena might never have heard his sibilant words and Beatrice's soft replies.

"The ironguards will take you to Fort Havok. I shall follow once I have arranged for more labor and materials here."

"How long will you be?"

"No more than a day. Perhaps two. It is a few days' trek due north."

"It is much safer to fly."

"Sh, my nightingale. I cannot fly with truefire. Think of the danger if the skies were angry. I would come down to the earth like a falling star with nothing for you to wish upon but my bones. By foot and cart with the element insulated in every comfort we can spare will be safest."

"I...yes. You are right. Be safe, my love."

The wicked master and his witch had another kiss and then shared some lewd promises as the party and its guards split apart. Since Rowena was not certain she was in the clear, she continued her frigid passion with Galivad. She counted to thirty. *Twenty-two. Twenty-three.* Before she could reach her goal, Galivad bit her and drew blood, and she released him as if he were a viper.

"What the fuk was that? How dare you!" he cursed.

"We got what we wanted," Rowena said and smiled.

"Yes. It seems *you* did."

Rowena let the man spit, stomp, and feel ashamed at his treatment. She wanted to comfort him—a strange urge for her, as he was not the queen. As she had said, though, they had what they needed—Fort Havok, a transport of unstable truefire, an Iron sage out in the open, and the many possibilities for mayhem those elements brought. The kiss hadn't been terrible either, she admitted.

V

In the pink shade of dusk that seeped through Menos's umbrella of smog, the gardens of the Blackbriar estate had a painterly sheen. Shapes were distorted with watery outlines in the glass through which Gloriatrix spied them. She was frowning, though she was relatively contented. Fate was bending in her favor. Operations at Fort Havok would be complete in another fortnight or so, and three great warships would soon rise out of a hidden bunker in a flock of darkness and bring wrath upon Eod. Gloriatrix decided she would be at the armada's head. She wanted to watch the end of Eod from the best seat in the house. That was the least she deserved, for she had been planning this black masterpiece with a maestro's precision— at much the same loss of fortune, years, and sanity a maestro often paid. For genius was costly. Retrofitting the crumbled hollows of Blackforge's mine into a clean, modern factory was no trifling affair. Preposterous sums of money had been spent on this construction. It was enough that every wretch in Menos could have eaten for generations. It was money of her own fortune, as well as crowns garnered through some rather creative accounting with the city coffers. The total cost in slaves and labor was surely obscene. The few collaborators she had in this gambit—Elissandra, Moreth, and Augustus—were to be applauded for their silence all this time. The riches she gave them weren't the sole source of their loyalty either. Undoubtedly, they also felt the surety of her vision and this war's righteousness. Were her zeal not enough of an inspiration, the forces amassed at Fort Havok would pulverize any doubt. She was eager to see her armada—all that metal and technomagik under her command. War between advanced cultures such as Eod and Menos should not involve prolonged, messy melees in trenches and on horseback. Whose ancient rules were those? Not hers. Such dated pomposity was for graying kings and warlords to flash their banners and measure their pricks and honor against one another. There was no honor in war. There was only victory. The rest was posturing. Geadhain had yet to see modern warfare as she envisioned it—as quick and cold as a bullet to the head. It was an absolute suppression of one's enemy. The world was not ready for the destruction she had prepared: the pits brimming with the smoking dead, the horizon of mushroom explosions, and the windy echo of Eod's desolation. Not even a sobbing ghost would be heard, let alone remembered, in the ash the city would become. That was why she would win. She knew the true cost of winning.

"Iron Queen," a foot soldier said, and roused her from her reverie.

Gloriatrix tucked away her evil vision and left her chamber in the company of two ironguards. She walked down the hallway, nearly paused before her son's bedroom, thought better of it, and continued. Her passion as a ruler overrode her instincts as a mother. Ever since the trouble in the Undercomb when Sorren's black magik had saved her, she was more appreciative of her son—though she would hesitate to call this affection. He had protected her in a moment of crisis, when true allegiances were tested. He'd chosen her life over his revenge. Was this love? She could not tell. It was not love as she understood the emotion: dark and painful. It was enough that she no longer feared her unhinged child. She'd even remained at the Blackbriar estate with him, and in the evenings when he decided to wake, they would share an awkward meal. *A mother-monster and her spawn,* she thought, and chuckled, for they chatted about such horrible things. However, she found herself increasingly at his bedside sharing a silver dinner platter and making gruesome conversation. Poor Sorren was unable to leave his bed. The servants had to wash him and change the bedding from under him. He really would not move, so there was nowhere else to dine if they were to do so together. An ennui had taken the pitiable, mad child—a sense that everything he wanted had trickled through his fingers like sand to the wind. She understood his regrets, and she knew how best to treat them: with disinterest. Sorren would have to learn how to manage his failure and draw power from it instead of allowing it to make him weak. A few times she sensed him learning this lesson as they discussed the horrors she had planned, and the shrillness in his voice would smooth to a captivated hoarseness. He would wax endearingly at her poetry of doom and the fields of corpses she would plant in Eod. Once, she imagined the windows actually veining in frost while he rhapsodized over the imminent carnage. *No. That can't have been real*, she told herself. She'd stuffed that memory into a dusty bin in her mind where she threw all the nuisances she didn't want to consider.

While she wandered in her head, the ironguards acted as her senses and kept her from tripping into the vases and other opulent relics that filled the estate. She was especially addled today. She entered the study. Curtains were pulled over the windows, and the bookcases framing the room stood like shadowy portals to nowhere. All this intensified the aura of mystery around her guest. Elissandra had already claimed the only throne-shaped chair in the room, and she sat poised, pale, and watchful as the Iron Queen made her entrance. A tufted settee was the only seat remaining, and Gloriatrix disappointedly took a seat there and dismissed the ironguards. The two women drank in the darkness for a spell.

"This will be our last meeting for a while," said Gloriatrix.

"Yes," replied Elissandra, who could have been smiling in the dark. "You were missed at the last council. I told them your son was ill. I believe the news heartened Septimus."

"I am certain it did." Gloriatrix snorted. "Undoubtedly, Horgot was beside himself as well, cooking up conspiracies and painting me in an unkind light. Did he ask about the treasury holdings again?"

"Indeed."

Somehow the swine had caught a whiff of the missing crowns she had diverted from their trade partners in the East. She had been so careful. Still, a decade of swindling left indelible if faint footprints. At the council meeting that followed the frostfire storm, there had been a slew of concerns more important than money to address. Horgot, though, had brought the matter up several times. She knew he would not let the issue die, which is why she had absented herself from the most recent meeting and would from the one tomorrow too. She could wait until Eod was a smoldering memory. Then no one would question her dictates or supremacy. First, the remaining pieces needed to be moved into place.

"Augustus?" she asked.

Elissandra was definitely smiling now. Gloriatrix could see the flash of it. "He was given his orders to pursue your sage, Thackery, and the young witch from Eod, Morigan. Moreth said Master Blackmore took to the assignment to hunt your treasonous brother with enthusiasm. I am told Master Blackmore is freakishly deformed—a monster, really. Moreth has seen enough disfigurement to make such an assessment. I don't know what use the young witch, this seer, will be to us now—not with events caught in ripples that will soon become waves."

"Not much use at all." Gloria folded her hands and leaned back. "I am mostly interested in her association with my Thackery. I'm sure Augustus will find a purpose for whomever he doesn't kill right away. Augustus's father was an incestuous lunatic. Nothing as time-honored as your traditions, Elissa. An illness of the mind and soul taints the whole of house Blackmore. Now he is a monster, I believe he will do his job well and violently. It was stressed that my brother is to be killed quickly and without torture, so it cannot be said I am not merciful."

She had decided this a while ago. Genocide was enough, and she would rather not see Thackery again or think of how his warning—as well as her son's magik—had saved her in the Undercomb. She preferred he die unseen and unheard and picked away to a dim memory by the carrion teeth and claws of Alabion's wildlife.

"The Untamed is dangerous beyond belief. Hopefully, Augustus is beast enough to succeed," said Elissandra cryptically.

"He is, and he will," declared Gloria. "Now, as you know I shall be leaving Menos in a few days to spearhead the operations in Fort Havok. In my stead you are the eyes and will of the First Chair."

Elissandra raised a finger. "Horgot has been persistent in demanding to know where so many of our soldiers are being sent. He says 'west' is not a sufficient answer. We should give him something on which to chew."

Gloriatrix wanted to say poison. It would be easy enough to get some skull-viper venom into his drink. Still, as with her brother's death, she simply couldn't be bothered to arrange the murder. The Iron Queen puffed. "We can't keep Fort Havok a secret forever. Tell the council I am overseeing the push west. From where is on a need-to-know basis. I don't need your second sight to foresee tremendous objections and displays of indignation at this statement. Allow them to scream at my ironfisted ways. I care not. It is better they learn their places and their uselessness in the motions of Menos now rather than later. If there are any voices that will not quiet, silence them. Permanently."

"Permanently?"

"In the ground."

The edict could not be misconstrued, and Elissandra bowed her head. Then her chin was up, and her silver eyes flickered like stars in the dark. "Did you feel that?" asked the ghostly woman.

Gloria glanced around. "Feel what?"

"A chill."

As the chill was mentioned, Gloria impulsively rubbed her shoulders and huffed a short breath. It was white.

"Argh!"

The cringing scream came from outside the study. It was from down the hallway, if Gloria had to guess. *Sorren.* She leaped off the settee and rushed from the chamber. Elissandra casually rose and drifted after her. Gloria's heart beat as fast as a hunted animal's. She began to run. She knew that sound. She'd caused it before. It was the particular pitch of fear men made as they died. Sorren was in mortal jeopardy. Too late, she realized she cared for him, her only child left in this world. She saw a sudden, searing value in that preciousness—the single drop of mortality remaining in her withered soul. The memory of running frenzied through Blackbriar's garden that day almost a century before and chasing that same shriek—higher and more desperate in its youth—was within her anew. As she flew into Sorren's chamber, the fever of anxiety swelled and trembled. She noticed the empty bed and the shattered window bleeding rain. Then the fever broke and took her down in a swoon. She gasped on the ground and heaved, and tears soon sizzled from her eyes. How it hurt her to cry. Long and muttering shadows surrounded her.

"Where is he? Where is my son?" she demanded.

A whiteness that was surely Elissandra breezed into the room and joined the circle of ironguards about the fallen Iron Queen.

"Gone," said the Mistress of Mysteries.

Although their breaths made pale twists in the air, and they all trembled from the cold, the others could not sense the depth of this chill—not as Elissandra could. From far beyond that insignificant space came the cold—past the sky, constellations, and spinning globes of dust and green, into a bosom of starless space, a tomb in the universe that echoed with whispers. Elissandra, who could hear these echoes, was at once cowed and reverent.

"Gone?" barked Gloriatrix. She stood, shoved away the people who tried to help her, and wiped her face roughly. Her hardness resurfaced. "Who took him?"

Elissandra glided toward the rumpled fabrics where Sorren had been resting. She felt drawn to Fate's hum there. "Took him? He was not taken." A pause. "He was claimed."

The sheets were in Elissandra's hands. Gloriatrix, that petty woman who thought Geadhain's reins were hers to hold, spit more words. *No. She is no ruler*, the Fates sang in their music of sparks and silver pins driven into Elissandra's brain. *We shall show you the true kings and queens. The great reckonings and shadows. The sleepers in the endless dark.* Elissandra could feel sweat as cold and wet as an arctic splash on her fingers. What was this cold? From what glacier had this residue come? Sorren? It could not be. For it was not a person who had been in this room but a shadow. *A shadow within Sorren rising at last*, she realized. Suddenly, she tasted dirt in her mouth, smelled rot all around, and heard a great, dry rustle of sand, bones, decaying parchment, dust, and scuttling things. These were sounds of death. With that, reality began to warp and whirl.

*She is in the room with Sorren and watching him as a spirit while he tosses on his four-poster bed. To the normal eye, he seems asleep but in the throes of a nightmare. She sees deeper and truer than those bare of gifts. She can sense the presence that will leave its mark on this place as a winter wind that seeps to the bone. Here and now it is worse—a cold from which even her spirit shivers.*

*"The chill of death," whisper her seekers—the holders of all truth.*

*These are manifestations of Will that a less adept daughter thinks of as bees. The cold presence has more shape in this realm, and the tentacles of shadow fascinate her. They are some deep-sea beast's limbs born of smoke and ice from the abyss of space and time. These tentacles wrap about Sorren and squeeze.*

*Sorren and this dark presence are arguing. The room echoes with their conflict, and she catches what she can of a language not even her seekers fully understand. For this is a tongue beyond words, and capturing this communication is akin to knowing the precise feelings behind a work of art or trying to grasp what the lightning bolt is expressing as it strikes a mountaintop. Elissandra cannot speak in emotion, which is how this entity communicates. However, as incomprehensible as the dialogue is to her, Sorren's small mind translates it to words—for the speaker's true weight and volume would shatter his head to pulp. The dark presence bids him to move, get up from his bed, and do what he is told. More images come to her—visions within visions. She sees the dreaded Black Star swallowing Geadhain's horizon. She watches a sword driven into her own gut and feels cascades of blood drain life from her. A horrible promise* of vengeance takes its place. Knowledge, power, and years beyond years for a host—Sorren agrees to it all. There is always a price with power, and the cost of drawing from this endless well of death and darkness is certainly Sorren's soul. At last Elissandra understands what she is witnessing. The taxman has come calling—or taxwoman. Sorren's pact is with a giver of creation and what mortal beings would equate with womanhood. This creator's works are black, grim, and horrific. Still, the other side of life is death. Both begin—and end—in pain and darkness. Rot is just as nourishing as blood. With unclouded perception, Elissandra knows that the two states are not so distinct. They are the same—different parts on a circle. In any case, the Mother of Bones to whom Sorren belongs will have her vessel. His time for play with her secrets is over.

No! he shrieks, and he wrestles against his master's clenching Will. I shall have my life! I shall have my revenge!

Such a petulant, spoiled thing Sorren is to the end, and that end is now. There are greater fates and grander wars than Sorren's beggarly grudge. It is so slight the Mother of Bones cannot conceive of its importance any more than a man can empathize with a fly's aspirations. The Mother of Bones simply takes what is hers. Sorren is screaming as the black tendrils constrict. This is the scream she and Gloria heard. Even as an ethereal thing, Elissandra is terrified. She understands that what gray, corrupted light Sorren has—what he thinks of as himself, his soul—is being snuffed out. What sits up in the murk and gazes at her is the Mother of Bones. It seems impossible in Elissandra's invisible state as a watcher in the past's dream.

Gazing upon Death's horror unmakes Elissandra. She tastes ash in a mouth she should not have, feels the sloppy churning of rotting organs in her belly, and perceives the nibbling of maggots under her intangible skin. Death glances away, for Elissandra is nothing but a speck on a beach to her. Death snaps its new neck and limbs and half-slithers, half-leaps from the bed as if its body were rubber. There is a flash of lightning, an omen to the world, and in an instant so fleeting Elissandra and her seekers cannot slow time enough to spot it, the window is broken, and there is only rain and wind screaming in from outside.

The seekers cry unfathomable names: Xalloreth, Erishkigal, Cthurimoch, the Great Reaper, and the End. The names do not stop spilling into Elissandra's head, for this being's manifestations are endless. Death walks Geadhain.

"Elissandra! Say something, you airy fool!" demanded Gloriatrix.

The seer had been hunched and clutching Sorren's sheets for sands and sands without making a peep. When Gloriatrix went to shake her, she noticed the woman was whiter than her standard pallor. She was so white, bloodless, and breathless she fell into Gloriatrix's arms. Elissandra's eyes were red from fear, and she glared at the Iron Queen.

"What did you see, Elissa?"

What could she possibly tell her? It would not serve her to tell Gloriatrix the awful truth. These secrets were power, and she would do better as their keeper than the Iron Queen. *The Mother of Bones,* Elissandra thought. *I saw a force from beyond time and space grind what remains of your son to dust and take his flesh. I saw a mystery in the Great Mystery. A Dreamer.*

*Yes! Yes!* agree the seekers.

*A Dreamer,* Elissandra thought, *who dreams of rot, ruin, and all things dark and dead. A Dreamer who is now in our world. I have no idea what I have seen, Gloria, and I fear this Mother of Bones is not the last of her kind we shall know.*

Elissandra found a touch of her poise as Gloriatrix sat with her on the bed's edge. "He...had a fit of some sort," lied Elissandra. "He became enraged and threw himself from the window."

Gloriatrix pinned her with a stare. "Is that all? We've checked the grounds, and there is no sign of him. No blood and certainly no body."

"Yes. That is all."

It was a lie, and the Iron Queen knew it.

# III

# ECHOES

I

"Here. You should have it," said Morigan to Mouse. "It belongs to you."

She held out the talisman Mouse had discovered in the dream weavers' nest. The ladies walked alone in the sweltering forest at a throwing distance from the others. They ignored the bugs that bit them and instead focused on the amulet's gleam as it rotated in the sun. The seer held it at arm's length.

"Wasn't it your mother's?" Mouse asked warily.

Mouse didn't actually want the thing anymore after overhearing Morigan and Caenith talking about it. They'd muttered names in a rare moment when they chatted as people should: aloud. She suspected they did that only when they spoke of truly important things, when words could be a comfort. This included dead parents.

"No. It was my father's," replied Morigan. Her pinched eyes and leery handling of the item suggested she wanted no part of it either.

"Surely you should keep heirlooms."

"No," said Morigan.

Mouse grimaced, and her forceful friend slipped the talisman about her neck. The metal fell somewhere between her small breasts, and its coldness shriveled them. No visions or otherwise unwarranted magik racked Mouse, and she relaxed her nerves after a speck. "What do you mean, it's mine?" she asked.

Morigan studied Mouse with a creased frown that could be taken for sadness. "I do not understand everything I'm shown or told. In fact, most of what I witness is just a terrible jumble from which I must sift any meaning. I know only that this once belonged to my father, and that now by right of finding and destiny, it is yours."

*A light in the dark. Her dead father's talisman. A voice that leads...to whom? To what?* Mouse realized she had unwittingly become quite tangled in Morigan's web. She wanted no leading part to play in all this, though. At best, she envisioned being a footnote to the seer's deeds. Fate, however, had decided differently, and here she was walking a land of legend with an arcane talisman. A ghost's words haunted her, and she was committed to a quest of her own. Mouse slumped a little in despair. Morigan and her silver servants picked up enough of this worry without pillaging her friend's head.

"You are not alone," whispered Morigan, and she hugged the woman. Mouse was trembling and felt thin enough under her cloak to break. "You are not alone," she repeated.

Caenith was suddenly shouting for them to keep up. He had become a taskmaster and herder since their previous separation and the danger it had brought. Mouse was quite done with affection too, and she politely elbowed her way out of her friend's arms and hurried after their pack leader. For a moment, Morigan hung back. She watched Mouse's willowy movements as she was caught in a shaft of sunlight. The pining sense of viewing a memento of the dead took Morigan. *I don't want to know,* she reprimanded her bees. They passionately buzzed with the heart-sinking sentiments of sorrow. They stilled at her command and held their truths for now, and she ran ahead.

II

What fickle moods the woods were having. A morning of summery, golden heat caused the company's living to stop and rinse the sweat from themselves in a cool river. However, an afternoon of fall breezes and dry, leaf-filled winds followed. Finally, in howled a night as cold as winter's herald. This had many of the companions clinging to their cloaks or to each other. Morigan stayed close to her mate. He was as warm as any fire. However, his emotions were less comforting—a blend of simmering unease and vigilance. He was still punishing himself for his companions' recent peril. She hoped his remorse would end soon.

Before long, the Wolf found shelter for his pack. It was a cubby of rock hidden in the shade of great trees and down a tumbling slope of moss and vines. He had to help his companions make the steep descent—especially the old, pale, huffing sorcerer. When they had settled into the cave, they scoured for tinder among the leaves, bones, and copiously shed fur that spoke of a previous animal occupant. Everyone was quiet and aching with fatigue and hunger brought on by their guide's tireless pace. Sullenly, they stared into the fire, and in time the Wolf returned from his hunt with some stringy beasts for them to cut up and eat. It was not an evening for stories and light chatter, and they chewed their meal silently and uneasily like soldiers on the eve of war. Sharp winds and streaks of rain whipped through the woods outside their shelter.

"Where are we going?" asked Mouse to break the thick silence.

The question was meant for the Wolf, and she directed her gaze across the sputtering flames and into his inscrutable gray stare. Before replying, the Wolf tilted his head to Morigan. She was sitting ladylike beside her kneeling savage lover, and she nodded at whatever was not said aloud. Mouse assumed they were sharing another private whisper. The habit was beginning to grate.

"To the Sisters Three," said the Wolf.

Mouse was annoyed and flicked away the rib she had finished gnawing. "Yes. That is the goal. That is why we are here. To meet these old witches and figure out why such terrible things have befallen Geadhain. But where, say, on a map are we headed? I had always assumed you, big man, being whatever you are—"

"Changeling," said Caenith.

"Lord of Fang and Claw," added his bloodmate.

"Right. Whatever you are. What each of you just said was basically nonsense. While we're at it, you two really need to stop talking as if we understand your strangeness. We don't. Nonetheless, where are we going? To a cave with a cauldron like in those wicked old faery stories? Or to a magik spring? A circle of ancient stones, perhaps? Where are these women? Specifics and an approximation of the time it will take to reach them would be nice."

Mouse's tone made Caenith consider how hard he had been driving these folk and how little had been mentioned of their journey. An apology was due. "Morigan and I can be distant. I see that. Please know that not one of you is far from our thoughts, even if our mouths speak less often than our hearts. We shall try to remedy that fault." Morigan nodded, and he continued. "Truth be told, I do not know the exact location of the Sisters Three. I know only where they are said to dwell. That's in Duvh Dorch." In his head, Caenith rolled the words around for a moment and tried to find an appropriate translation. "The Pitch Dark, I suppose."

Mouse was hardly delighted. She must have shivered, for her father's cold but welcome hands were pulling tight her cloak and rubbing her back.

"Rather spooky name," grunted Thackery.

The old man was bundled up next to the dead man and his daughter. His head peeked out of his dark clothing like a larva. Upon his cheeks and brow and beneath his eyes was a bruised sallowness, which Morigan dismissed as fatigue. She knew—from a small sting of her bees—she was wrong. Nonetheless, she gave Thackery a tender smile.

"Haunted," Caenith said. His eyes glinted, and his jaw set hard. "As dark a place as you will find in Alabion. The Pitch Dark is Alabion's heart—a knotted heart of trees, ancient laws, and the oldest magik. I have heard the stomps of the beasts that rule there and never thought to hunt any of them. Among my people are warnings of the monsters that should be left to sleep there—cautions that stretch back to before I was the lord of Pining Row. In the Pitch Dark, it is said that among the monsters are older mysteries still and ruins dedicated to tribes that lived before two-legs or four-legs claimed the woods. There are legends in Alabion too, and the Duvh Dorch is one of them."

"Sounds fuking lovely," mumbled Mouse. She was sorry she had asked.

"But more to your question," continued Caenith, "I would say we have another week or more until we reach the Pitch Dark. We are coming near to

Pining Row's woods, and there should be settlements where we can ease the burden of tired feet and backs."

"Settlements?" inquired Vortigern.

"The tribes of men and half-men who remained even after the land turned against them," said Caenith.

Morigan saw his explanation did nothing to reassure the company, and she continued to explain. "The Mistress of Mysteries called it the exile."

Having already shared this tale with her bloodmate, she now gave the company a short account of Elissandra's ranting before the Broker took her underground. She spoke of how the forests of Alabion had become a cruel habitat after the Everfair King had come and gone like a storm. Those scars never healed, and what had been bountiful became scarce. Centuries after, what had been scarce was gone. That was how Morigan, with her deeper senses, understood what she was told. She wore a penitent frown as she concluded her story.

"One of the faults of speaking so often in silence is that you forget there are others to whom you should be speaking. It seems this is to be a night of asking forgiveness, for I did not share these secrets with you three," she confessed.

On the other side of the fire, the dead man waved to her. "It's understandable. We haven't really stopped moving or had much of a chance to deliberate about our quest."

Thackery nodded, and Mouse frowned and squeezed out a thought. "What do you make of it, Caenith? You've lived in these woods. What do you remember?"

The Wolf scratched his beard and pondered. "I had not made the connection between the Everfair King passing through Alabion and the turning of the woods until Morigan and I spoke of this Elissandra, an outcast Daughter of the Moon. An exile. Yes, that would make sense. It is as my bloodmate supposed. It was faster than the turning of a season. Over a matter of days, food dried up, tribes found any pettiness to fight over, and even the animals became wily or violent when they were not before. Generations of this bitterness—for I can think of no better term—have changed the land into something dark. It's like a scorned lover whom jealousy and madness twisted. Monsters that should be spiders. Cries that only my or Vortigern's ears might hear from beasts I do not recognize. Back then, I wrestled with the reality that Alabion did not want me here. She did not want any creature here, and frankly, I did not want to stay."

"Is that why you left?" asked Mouse.

She noted the Wolf's bristly response to her rather innocent question. He growled, and rage and darkness creased his face. Such acrimony wasn't for her, however, but for whatever he remembered. "Aghna." He heaved the name like a stone.

He crept around Morigan, boxed her between his knees, and hung his head on her shoulder like a lonely dog. She stroked the sadness out of his black mane.

*A woman. How saucy*, thought Mouse, but she did not goad him with more inquiries.

Caenith continued in a speck. He was greatly sapped of his anger but for a flicker or snarl here and there. They were gone, however, as fast as the twists in the fire. Morigan had been wanting to hear this. Her bees yearned to taste his secret, and she slipped into his melancholy deeper than the others did. As the Wolf spoke, she let herself in through the doorway he had finally opened. Her silver magik guided her.

"Aghna," he repeated. "She saved me once."

*Two bodies slam into one another with a hardness greater than the slick rock they are upon. Their roaring passion shames the waterfall misting their bare arses. Morigan knows the glorious specimen of man and beast with his copper flesh and his huge hand that can cup two breasts as one. They are not her breasts, though. Not here. A hale warrior-woman of frost is fighting back at the great man atop her with commendable ferocity. What a beautiful creature she is—this other woman. Morigan reflects on this without envy. Aghna and Caenith are making love, if this tumble of bites with mouths that are sometimes snouts, the bloody kisses, and howling contortions as frightful as they are arousing fit within her definition of sex. As a watcher, though, she can feel the purity of emotion beneath the primal acts. She can see how their love glows around them in a halo of crimson hues.*

*She is not the one for him, comfort the bees in their buzzing voices. She is not you.*

*There is a silver ripple, and the lovers vanish. Morigan's bodiless energy appears before a gathering of white yews. They are ancient trees with trunks that split into hollows to nowhere. More trees surround her in a swell of dusty, white forest. Below, the woods echo with a soft clamor and clanging, and with her deepest senses, she catches memories—more than scents—of the peppery smoke and sweat of beings like Caenith. A village. Some people are singing in their canine manners, while others play flutes or beat drums. All this music is as long, drawn, and sad as the faces of its makers. All this comes from away and below. For now she focuses on a portal in the great yews—a gap of shadows she knows leads into the earth. Solemn, swarthy people appear beside the crack, and she breezes past them and down a dirt tunnel so black she wriggles in the dark like a sightless worm. However, she is never unsure of her aim. Caenith's sustained and unending growl is unambiguous. She would recognize it anywhere, even if sorrow does so soak the sound that it is hideous to hear—the whimpering of a dog with its leg inside a steel trap.*

*Ahead of her, the darkness bleeds with gray light, and she drifts into a deep cavern in the earth with a ceiling of root tips and walls woven of tuberous mesh. This is a dry place spiced with loamy smells and raining dust. It would make her sneeze if she had a nose. If she had arms, she would reach out for the man grumbling in the dark. He is nearly naked, her Wolf, as he is in the other world where he holds her. With all her painful knowing, she sees this is a symptom of his disdain for culture. It is the beginning of his degeneration into the beast who will one day slaughter people and gorge on blood in Menos's rings. Likewise for his growls and the way he claws, for his fingers will not stay quite mannish but are warped into half-talons. He growls and claws at the feet of the wrapped corpse that lies peacefully in the gloom. The cloth around Aghna's body, which this surely is, has been anointed with flowery oil far more pleasant than the chamber's must or the Wolf's unwashed musk. Morigan floats over and finds the state of the body intriguing. For days, the Wolf has grieved. Morigan can spot claw marks and torn roots from the times his feelings ran black. However, there is no gaseous and grotesque swelling under the sheet and no blotting of damp rot. There is only her body. It is paler than the white casings in which she sleeps and from which a hint of her original sweat still wafts. Aghna is dead but somehow frozen too. It is fitting for a woman of winter that whatever magik has been done to her suspends her in time. Now she is ageless, lifeless, and a statue to be remembered forever.*

*Not forever but foreverbloom, explain the bees, and they flash her mind's eye with images of a slick crimson flower like something made of melting wax and blood.*

*Why? wonders Morigan.*

*She wanted it this way, say the bees. Come and see.*

*There is a silver cloud of prescience—a Dream within a Dream. Morigan is taken through another tunnel in time and dropped into the swooning head of the white wolf. Tears blind her host's sight. She can make nothing out. Then she is tasting foreverbloom's burning nectar. It is as thick and sugary as molasses in her throat. In specks, it numbs her lips, deadens her limbs, and blots out her sight. Unfathomably, this act of self-murder brings no fear. There is only satisfaction.*

*This is how he will see me, thinks Aghna both bitterly and happily. How I shall be remembered. Not as a white wolf turned gray while his pelt shines as dark and beautiful as night. Please understand how I ache as I age. How my beauty and speed limp away from me each day. Look at me, Caenith. Look at me. Love and remember me as I am for all time. Find another to lead our pack. Someone whose heart is stronger than mine. A woman who can bear to leave this world without you.*

*Somewhere Aghna has left a note for him expressing these thoughts. He must have found it by now. Soon he will be there, and she hurries to arrange herself into a presentable, attractive corpse. Her veins already throb with ice. Just as she finishes her drink of death, she smells his raw, spicy sweat one last time before snow plugs her nose. How terribly he roars when he comes upon her cold body and sees the scattered foreverbloom petals and the rolling, emptied chalice upon the ground.*

*Caenith roars and roars. He lifts her up. She is as light as air itself and ready to blow away into the Great Mystery. She supposes Caenith is right as he weeps and calls her mad, but it was madness for her to love a creature who could not die. So madness is how their love should end. She feels a bite and a kiss somewhere on her flesh. That is enough for her to take with her as she goes.*

*The images vanish, and Morigan is again in the tomb beneath the yews. She understands now why Caenith left Alabion. She will leave this dark place and comfort him for it. She commands the bees to return her to the world.*

Returning to their circle, Morigan wondered just how much of his past Caenith had shared with their companions. Their somber expressions were enough of an answer. After a silence and a long listen to the rain that had not let up, Mouse walked around the fire, put her hand on Caenith's shoulder, and shook her head when she could not think of anything else to do or say. She was a stranger to romantic love, but the thought of aching for another's death for so long commanded her respect—particularly when that grief was carried in a man as hard as Caenith. She hustled back to her father and great-uncle after that, and as the fire crackled low, they could be seen tangled up together. Even Vortigern closed his eyes and feigned slumber. When it was quiet enough, the rain pattered low, and the coals were a red hiss. Morigan kissed the arms that had tightened some time ago around her. Caenith was surrounding her as if she too could be lost like Aghna. The beast of his emotions prowled in her stomach and made her sick with nerves.

*I saw her end herself, Caenith. She was...ill. You cannot burden yourself with her choice,* whispered Morigan.

*How can I not? It is my curse to watch the world die. To lose what I love.*

*Are you worried you will lose me?*

*No. Not to the passing of time, at least.*

In timid leaps or occasionally great bounds, as powers and mysteries burgeoned inside her, Morigan had come to peace with aspects of her strangeness. Death would not come to her by a wintering of years. The bees were sure of this, and so was she.

*Then there is nothing else to fear.*

*I almost lost you in Menos.*

*Yet here we are.*

*How can you be so brave?*

*How can you be so weak? Do you not have faith in me? In your strength? In our strength together?*

A cold but true appraisal had she served him, and the man inside Caenith smarted from the slap to his ego. The Wolf licked the hand itself. He surrendered and let the animal reassert itself within, and it chased away his doubts. Aghna was gone. He had honored her, but the dead should have no hold over the happiness of the living—not if they had truly loved one another in life.

As for Morigan, she was awash with the purring heat of a prideful beast inside her. Here was the lord of Fang and Claw whom she had wed. She was aware that this was how things would often be with Caenith. It was her duty to balance the duality of emotions and raw instinct in her bloodmate. At times she would need to be a kind ear for his mortality. Other times she must be a woman offering dripping meat or sensuality as an encouragement for him. What else were lovers and partners if not scales for each other? She was glad she had an eternity to play this game, for it was complicated, rewarding, and not something she believed she would ever tire of or master. Now she could sense his mood warming her stomach, breasts, and thighs, and his hands were soon making their way to those spots.

*I shall eat you soon*, promised the Wolf.

*Soon*, she promised back.

Into her head washed bleary images of stone pillars and an ancient altar. Snow sprinkled the scene. She pushed the prophecy away. She did not need a vision for every surprise in her life. She kissed and rolled with her savage lover until the dead man was undoubtedly aware of their frolicking. Even then it took much to settle Caenith. He finally stopped his pawing when Vortigern sat up and hissed a reprimand. "You will wake my daughter."

They would rest, the bloodmates decided. Morigan quickly drifted off with the beat of her lover's warm pulse thudding against her ear as she lay on his furry chest. That eve she had dreams bare of prophecy and clothing. Caenith was curled around her. At times he held her tightly, and at other times he was awake and still marveling at her magnificence. Never once that night, though, as the hunters of Alabion padded and sniffed around their small sanctuary, did he fear he would lose her.

III

They came upon the settlement suddenly—so suddenly, even the Wolf was surprised. Keen as he was to the dangers of birdcalls and rustling leaves, he had detected no such threat here. That was how the village had sneaked up on him. Without noise or vibrancy, civilization announced itself as Mouse stubbed her foot on a rise. When examined, it was found to ascend into the bush where it met with an odd, flat surface painted in moss. Mouse was not sure what locked her eye there. Perhaps it was the way the two planes met or how the shade fell so perfectly in a triangle between them.

"A wall!" she cried.

Her discovery drew her companions, and they thrust about in the hedges and weeds to find other signs of habitation. Caenith unearthed deep under the mulch bits of soft wood and a bone button turned orange from dirt and time. Afterward, as he rubbed his soiled fingers together and sniffed, he noticed a hickory tang of ash. A fire had occurred here many decades or even longer past, and he could taste the violence and metallic tang on his tongue. The Wolf could almost sense the skeletons around them now with brambles creeping through their sockets and mushrooms blooming in the bony flowerpots of their chests. As he stood and looked through the relatively flattened region of the wood they wandered, he spotted more rises and broken lines among the stunted trees, wildflowers, and shrubs. He knew these humps were all buildings reclaimed by nature. A large village this had been. He had more shivers of memory. They were not quite visions like Morigan's. However, ghostly echoes of voices, music, and laughter teased his ear. Phantom scents of spiced, sizzling fat had him licking his lips.

"Dead. All of them. I would say many hundreds or perhaps even a thousand people," he declared, and he dusted off his hands with indifference before striding on. "Stay close, my pack. Let us see what, if anything, remains that is worth finding."

Onward they slunk through the dead village. They were more aware now of the eroded shapes muffled in vegetation. A hump covered in posies could be a fallen roof, and a short cylinder of vines with nesting birds at its spout might have been a chimney. Beyond the whims and wars of people, life had persisted. It had pulled a great green sheet over the unsightly ugliness of what had occurred in this place. Even with the Wolf's warning, Thackery felt his guard slipping. It wasn't long before the place's calm serenity smoothed away his tension. It was as though this were a graveyard and garden in one. The flowers were sugary to his nose, and the smoky sunshine warmed his grinning cheeks. That sun skewered the branches, and in it butterflies kissed one another with their wings. For so long he had been fantastically tired from owning an aged body not equipped for this kind of endurance. The company's more leisurely exploring, then was of great relief to him. While they occupied themselves with theories regarding the ruins, he doddered along, drifted in mind and step, and paid scant attention to their talk. Perhaps it was this contemplative bliss that led his eyes to wander everywhere and nowhere until he noticed the rude, clear, claw marks. The five symmetrical grooves could be nothing else. They were rent in one fuzzed green wall they passed. Nonchalantly, he mentioned it to the others, and then he seated himself on a verdant ripple that embraced him like a chair and went back to sightseeing.

Caenith kicked through the underbrush and placed his hand on the markings as if he had made them. "These are the marks of a wolf," he said.

"A wolf?" asked Mouse.

"A changeling," he said, and frowned.

While four of them brooded in a small circle, Thackery fussed in his seat. It had suddenly become uncomfortable. Something sharp had passed through the mossy padding and was poking into his hips and back. He grabbed the arm of his makeshift armchair, and he was shocked and a tad horrified when the green skin peeled off and showed the whiteness of bone. It was a hand. Of course there would be skeletons, he told himself. This had been the site of many murders. He was calm and composed as he shuffled off the body, pointed this macabre tidbit out to the company, and hobbled on ahead. Caenith grumbled and hastened on to claim the lead.

Traveling through the dead village took longer than it might have, and Thackery's absentminded observations brought them many more distractions and delays. "Curious," he would mumble as he poked at things with his walking stick. He would say no more and amble off. However, he never went too far out of sight. They all noted Thackery's enhanced appreciation for life's many fine details, even those that slipped by Caenith's nose, eyes, and ears. Were the third and eldest Sister nearby, Eean and Thackery could have watched the world together as friends. They could have absorbed the glimmers of each bead of water dappling the trees, the hum of every dragonfly, or the grit of soil and leafy decay under their feet. As kindred souls, they could have shared in the simple wonders known only when one's life was trickling away. He was dying—slowly, gently walking the ashen road toward the dark sunset of death. On the old man wandered, his companions mostly following him instead of the Wolf.

How could they have missed the signs? Symptoms of the old man's ailing health were plainly evident—his degradation into near silence, his slowly mending hand, his shivering labors during their hikes, the peace of his slumbers, and his agitation upon waking every day. He was not grumpy; instead, he was dismayed that he could not continue on in the darkness of memory and ghosts where he had been. Caenith was angry he had not sensed this earlier, and the reality of the old man's imminent passing now thoroughly engrossed him. Vortigern noticed his uncle's sickliness as well. With his nonliving intuitions, he could feel death's hand reaching for the man. Many times Caenith caught the dead man casting weighty stares at Thackery's back. Morigan's bees were surely feeding a sad nectar to their mistress too. Although she kept silent, within the Wolf her star was flickering as temperamentally as the old man's health.

He tried to speak to her once. *Morigan, I have seen when an animal knows its time. When it soothes its mind, forgets its body's pain, and is taken with a wanderlust to find the softest place it can in which to lie and dream. Forever. I would not say days, but I do not think weeks would be an unreasonable—*

Morigan wanted none of her bloodmate's prose on death and shut him out of her mind with a stone wall of Will. Caenith did not know they could raise such barriers to each other, and he was as stunned as if he had physically walked into a wall. Regardless, her light continued its frantic shining in his chest, and he was able to overlook his hurt. Meanwhile, he refrained from barking at his companions as they ambled about the green dunes. Morigan walked with an arm slipped into Thackery's crooked elbow. Vortigern took his daughter's hand to console her for a grief she could not yet see coming.

Of all the company, only Mouse remained oblivious of Thackery's condition and its effects on the others. Therefore, she was the most useful in exploring their surroundings. She became quite accustomed to finding bones and less perturbed by the flash of whiteness. Occasionally, a skeleton was woven so seamlessly into a thicket it could have been a nekromancer's horticulture from Menos. *Kind of beautiful*, she thought.

Elsewhere, gaudy wreaths of bright yellow and orange were wrapped around the tarnished relics of chamber pots, or they served as colorful thrones from which chattering, furred princes presided. They came upon a stone path. *A constructed pattern. A road,* she thought. Along one side of it, Mouse found a curious burrow still warm from whatever creature had scurried out of it. Inside something shone metallically, and her magpie hands couldn't resist claiming it. Quick rifling brought her two treasures. The first was an ancient iron knife that would nicely replace the ones she'd lost. The second was a set of sandals. The buckles had drawn her eye. Like the knife, they were amazingly well preserved from any decay.

"Witchstitch," muttered Caenith, who had popped out of his gloomy cloud to see. "Made with feliron thread and leather dipped in...foreverbloom. As enduring as stone," he explained, as mystified as Mouse.

Even more mysterious was that the sandals seemed made for a man with enormous feet, and Mouse handed them over to her giant friend. He shrugged and put them on. Given the harmless relics they'd so far discovered, she assumed a settlement of humble folk had lived there. She debated who or what it was would kill such people. *Wolves,* she reminded herself, and she left alone whatever other treasures might be in the nest.

Around an hourglass disappeared in the forgotten village as they headed wherever the wind of Thackery blew them. After a time, nature wholly consumed the ruins. There were no more suspicious mounds, and Thackery became less interested in being a guide. They had reached a stream—a vein of a greater river that summoned the company with its burble. It had enough girth for a bank of large stones on which they could rest themselves. It had enough bounty that Caenith could wade into the stream and pluck out fish for them to eat. He swallowed as much as he wanted and then fed his pack by tossing ashore handfuls of flopping smelt bred as big as trout. A few of the company broke their fast. Distractedly, the women ate with little appreciation of the fresh, juicy meat. Even Mouse finally pondered the fitness of the pale, elderly man. He was nearly asleep while sitting up on his rock, and he had abstained from feeding himself.

"Something to eat?" offered Mouse, and she waved a fish at her great-uncle.

He dismissed her with a shake of his head that could have been a tremble. These filled his body.

"Are you cold?" persisted Mouse.

Thackery woke a little and gave her a pained smile. "No."

He gazed up to the sunlight and branches above him. His hundred lines were as deep as scars, and light softened his silhouette. Mouse was now as certain as the others about what was happening to him. A burning, unfamiliar tear escaped her eye, and she quickly wiped it off. Three of the company stood around the old man and watched his every nod. They wondered whether they should wake him if he started to nap, which it appeared he was doing anyway with his eyes open. Mostly, they played that game people play when they learn life has not as many sands for them or for another as they had hoped. In the ensuing quietude, Morigan thought of the father Thackery had been. Vortigern thought of his brave uncle. Mouse merely ached—a strange, uninvited squeezing of her chest. By the Kings, it hurt to care. Later, she would have to speak with the others privately. With their queer group—a sorcerer, witch, ageless wolfman, and walking dead man—surely this was not how Thackery was to die. There had to be a magik or miracle to keep him here longer. She knew life could be extended. She had witnessed the mortifying, patchwork extremes Menosians turned to for longevity. However, reason told her only the Immortal Kings (and the Wolf and possibly Morigan) could live forever. She did not want reason now, though, and her companions' stoic acquiescence was an irritation. This was especially true of the seer, whose authority on the future Mouse certainly did not want to hear. *Do not accept your end so peacefully, Thackery. Rage. Rage against it. We shall look for a scrap of youth, a curse, or a cure. In this age of miracles, with those we walk among, I see no reason why we should not steal a bit of their wonder.*

While the company held its vigil, Caenith was preoccupied. He had tasted a sourness in the river and a fishiness that had nothing to do with their meal. The river also spoke of darkness and a shape that swam and gobbled life. What was it? Caenith tried to form an image from the hints that came to him. Then he knew—the sourness, scales, and hunger. The Wolf had bitten this monster more than once and left it for dead. He had thrown it into the filth beneath Menos, and there it had glided along the currents to Alabion, which was where the Drowned River ran and where the Menosians flushed their filth.

They had to move. Quickly.

"Do not cross the stream," he barked and stomped out of the water.

This rudely broke his companions' solemnity, but they did not question him. In moments, they were moving down the shore and scanning for a crossing. Mostly, they were confused as to why they could not stride through the water, which was only waist-high on the Wolf. Catching up to her blood-mate, Morigan tore down her wall of silence and asked him what he was so concerned about. Little remained that the bride of a lord of Fang and Claw feared. His answer, however, had her stumbling into his arms.

*The Jabberwok. It lives, and it is here. If I tasted it, it could taste us too. It could find us, my Fawn.*

IV

"Augustus! Master Augustus!" cried the page.

Augustus Blackmore loathed the boyish sound of the man's voice. It was incongruous with the tall, well-muscled person from which it came. Talwyn appeared a speck later and poked his imposing head into the tent. His brow was as high and wide as that of a king of old—another reason for Augustus to hate the man. He parted the tent's fur flaps and let in the cold. This bothered Augustus less than the man's delicate hands. They were better suited for painting or thumbing texts than the duties of a soldier. *Not a callus on his palms or a scar on his kingly cheeks,* snorted Augustus, who had plenty of scabs. "What?" he spit.

"You...are needed. At once." Talwyn was shaking. "It's awful."

Augustus snorted again through the half of the nose he still possessed. He'd seen "awful." It appeared to be the magik of Alabion—a sorcery that conjured one horror after another. How long had they been here? Time had a certain evasiveness in this place. It hadn't been a year, though it might as well have been. In the days that felt like forever, they had lost at least twenty men and even all their felhounds—creatures without fear of death. That boldness, however, did no good against this forest's fangs and claws. This morning when they had done the head count, another three of their remaining thirty had wandered off to become nourishment for the mouths and roots of this cursed realm. *Don't leave the fires. Don't even leave your tents to piss or shite. Do it in a pot, and throw it out in the morning,* he had warned them. No one listened, though, or they were somehow beguiled. When the search parties went out in the safer shadows of day hunting for their missing comrades, the bodies were rarely found. What scraps they did unearth were insufficient to identify the owner. Judging by Talwyn's panty-wetting terror, though, one scouting party might actually have met with success.

"Brother, are you coming?" asked Talwyn.

A moment before, Augustus had been silent, tapping his lumpy chin and drifting in some thought or another. He was, however, at the entrance fast as a viper with a twist of Talwyn's feminine, auburn tresses—curled and luxurious—in the coil of his hand. Talwyn cried out. Master Blackmore's voice was exceptionally soft for the violence it whispered. "Never speak those words again, or I shall do worse than banish you to Riverton and let you gamble away your mongrel's life. Everything about you is so dainty and womanish. We are clearly not of the same breed or seed. I'd never seen such a fuking dandy until I met you. Remember, you are the bastard of my father's whore and not a claimant to the Blackmore name. If that whore had had any sense, she would have had an alchemist brew her a curative for her condition. She would have purged herself of the offal in her womb. I might still purge you myself when this journey is over. I have not decided what your fate will be when your usefulness is no more."

Content with the terror in his gasping half brother's face, Augustus released the man's hair and stormed over to fetch his scabbard and cloak from the roll where it lay. Talwyn collected himself, rubbed his scalp, and silently cursed his relative.

*I'm an ecologist, a linguist, and a well-respected scholar,* Talwyn thought. *Not a gambler, you imbecile. You would all be dead if I hadn't told you arseholes not to eat every sweet-looking berry that would have had you shitting blood. Or if I had kept to myself which fluffy animals had musk and secretions ready to incapacitate or poison. For even the softest creatures in Alabion are monsters. If I were a wicked man like you, I would withhold my knowledge and use its reservation as a death sentence. I could kill you, brother—half brother—without even dirtying my hands. The land would do it for me. Alas, I am not that man. But, oh, what sick justice there is in the world when a man like you has power and can speak to me and others as if we were lesser than your despicable self. However, at least there is some fairness too, as your outsides are now as hideous as your soul.*

The shock of his half brother's disfigurement had mostly faded to a greasy shudder now. It was not nearly as upsetting as when there had come a midnight knock on his door in Riverton, and a monster had stood in the dark outside with all that mottled flesh. The scalp had contained stubble in some places but had been bald everywhere else. There had been that half-snarl of a mouth and the cheesy knot of a ruined eyeball. The other still-perfect eye had shone with malevolence. *Good Kings*, he had thought. *At least have the sense to put a patch over it!* What a ghastly odor the man had exuded. Augustus had stunk as evil should—of meaty flesh and sin cooked in an oven to putrescent delight. The man was a genuine monster, inside and out.

Quickly, the monster finished dressing and was back upon Talwyn and breathing close. Talwyn sensed his half brother was coming into a dark acceptance of his freakishness and even reveling in it. Regardless, he would not give him the satisfaction of fear, and he swung open the flaps and behaved like a proper page—the designation Augustus had demanded he don for this journey. Talwyn bowed. "Master Blackmore."

Augustus pushed Talwyn out of the way and walked out into the chirruping, emerald shadows of Alabion. The master glared about his encampment. The tents were nearly swallowed in bracken that would not relent under boot or cloth, and the gray faces of the fur-clad warriors whom he had dragged so far from Blackforge turned to him. He had no idea what manner of misery beset the deployment of ironguards that Moreth had sent along or whether those people even felt misery at all. They were never spied without their masks. Once he emerged, the ironguards stood at attention with their rifles slung over shoulders and hands on the swords at their belts. Under their thorny visors, Augustus could hear them heavily breathing the humid air, so he knew they were living things and not wraiths. Only six had been sent. But they had fared better in these kingforsaken climes than any of his people had, and not one had been lost to Alabion's hunger. He motioned for the ironguards to follow him as he sneered at his bloodless half brother—as afraid as a woman after a bump in the night. "Show me this *awful* thing," he said.

*By the Kings, I hate you. Passionately and truly,* Talwyn said to himself as he pointed into the bushes. "Straight ahead. Not far you'll find a stream. I and a few others went to fetch water there this morn. That's when—"

Blackmore boxed his half brother's ear so hard it rang and swelled shut in a speck. "I said show me, page. I didn't ask for directions. I can make you deaf if that's what you'd like to be."

People laughed and clapped for the jester Talwyn as he stumbled. The ones who had been with him at the river and knew what waited there pitied him enough not to take humor in his pain. Talwyn recovered his poise, if not his pride, and went into the bush. He could hear his brother's breath—the huffing of a beast—and the soft swish of the metal men as they followed. Soon the rippling music of water rustled through the leaves. However, the burble did not drown out the dreadful crunching ahead. Was he only imagining that? It must have finished eating. He debated which monster was worse—the one at his rear or the one they were going to meet. He hadn't reached a conclusion before the thicket thinned and opened to a riverbank.

Involuntarily, Talwyn hugged himself and had to glance away from the hunched and scrawny thing at the shore. There was no escape from the carnage, though. The stones were as crimson as cinnamon candies, the grass was as red and matted as a painter's brush, the water was pink, and saturated boots, belts, and scraps of fur were scattered all over. Alabion's earthy sweetness could not suppress the shite, piss, and internal gases of bodies torn open—horror's fragrance. Talwyn thought he was about to be sick again. His last pool of vomit was but a breath away, and its acridity was teasing him into retching once more.

"What are you?" asked Augustus.

He was not disgusted so much as drawn to the monster. Augustus held up an arm to stall the rifles aimed at the creature. He was a man with slick hair dark as a raven's plumage. He was all sinew and wildness. He was definitely more, though, than his appearance. The face was striking and sharp. The metal teeth were especially glaring against all the blood as he turned and gave a pout of consideration to Augustus and his group.

"Well, I was hungry," said the Broker. "But not so much anymore. If I had known they were your sons, I wouldn't have made a meal of them." The Broker eyed Master Blackmore from toe to head. "I asked to speak to the slow-walker in charge, and I'm guessing that you are he. You're handsome. I like it. I like it all."

"He was *eating* them!" exclaimed Talwyn, and flung his arms open. "Our men. Mikael, Georg, Thomas. He was—"

A stare from the river monster silenced Talwyn. The Broker clucked and waved a finger. "They were bad sons. Smoking that weed that dulls the senses and laughing about titted pleasures and drink. I did you a favor. They're no good for hunting when the senses are dull. No good here, where the rule is eat or be eaten."

"Hunting?" said Augustus.

"Hunting," agreed the Broker. "The Iron Queen has left me with a task undone. I have blood and bones and a seer to bring her. And you—"

Suddenly, the river-monster slithered forward with its belly on the ground and its limbs as peaked as a lizard's. The ironguards jumped and nearly filled the air with fiery pellets. Talwyn recoiled, and Augustus held straight as a rod. The river monster closed the gap between him and the master and then sinuously rose. The naked, bloodied madman sniffed almost erotically about Augustus's chest, neck, and the mangling of scars on the right side of his face.

"A Wolf." The Broker grinned. "I can still smell his stink on you. He took away my family. All my sons. Gone. Flushed me down the toilet like a turd. He gave you your pretty scabs too. He and the element-breaker's flames. I hunt him also. We should hunt together. I like you. You do not hide what you are, and it is...beautiful."

"The Iron Queen? A Wolf?" Augustus thought aloud. "I do not know what you mean. However, I believe it has value. I too am hunting in these woods at the Iron Queen's behest and to reclaim my honor. I believe this could be providence. Come. We shall talk more at my camp."

The Broker shrugged and flashed a ragged, silver-fanged smile. Talwyn was delirious with horror—dizzy, nauseated, and cold all at once. A creeping grimace from his nightmarish half brother pushed Talwyn over the brink. The page slipped in his decorum and uttered the one phrase any kin surely felt he or she could speak when appealing to even the maddest member of his or her own blood. "Brother, please—"

That was as far as he got before Augustus struck him with a fist. As the blackness pulled him under, he heard the two monsters laughing together, and he struggled to swim lower and deeper. He hoped never to wake up.

# IV

# THE OPPOSITE OF LOVE

## I

Kor'Khul was majestic in its emptiness. A gauzy, rustling horizon enveloped the eye no matter where the hammer turned his head. He looked around as spellbound by the desolation as any novice wanderer would be. Kor'Khul had a somnolence to it, and as his senses rolled over the waves of sand without end, he sleepily blinked from the weight of heat and sweat upon him. The music of shuffling mounts, rolling wheels, and murmurs lulled him further. Often he wondered how their procession must look from above—the carts, wagons, and beasts of burden as small and black as a line of ants along a beach. An insignificant speck to whatever spirits watched from the sky. Perhaps Magnus studied him from a starry rest unseen behind the pastel-blue curtain that hid the universe. He wondered whether the queen thought of her bloodmate as regularly as he did. Did she ever consider whether Magnus would approve of this quest? When he glanced toward her, he did not believe she dwelled on either conflict, judging from her fierce scowl against the piercing sun.

She had yet to tell him where they were headed. In fact, she said so little and the desert pacified him so much, he was once dishonorable in his station—for a speck—and forgot she even rode beside him on the wagon. He felt it was a forgivable neglect, for she did not behave or appear much like the woman he knew. Earlier when they had emerged from the rat's nest of secret passages—ones he had never traversed before—and into a shaded lane of Eod, he thought the sudden thrust into daylight had played tricks with his vision. However, the tanned and brown-stared woman before him then and now was the queen, even if the golden shine of her skin and eyes had dulled. She had magiked her splendor away. He suspected this was another phantasm and symptomatic of how unscrupulous her nature had become. She did not offer him the same service and quickly explained, "No one would recognize your face because you are so rarely seen out of uniform."

From then on, she showed no qualms in lying her way into the caravan destined for Taroch's Arm or in presenting her falsified papers to the watchmen as the troupe rolled on through Eod's great gates. Throughout the days of their travel since, she had been quiet, aside from the most cursory response to a stranger when she was forced to talk. *Taroch's Arm for spice shopping,* she had replied. *Among other errands.*

The other errands troubled Erik whenever he considered them. However, he did not pester his queen for answers. Soon enough, he had found a far more compassionate companion in the whistling isolation around them.

At some time between noon and dusk, they were bumping along alone together at the rear of a wagon. They dangled their feet over the sands as if they were carefree children, and the queen finally addressed him. She spoke in an absent way as though speaking to herself and not to him. "All this life-lessness," she murmured. "The Arhad would tell you this was once a basin of life—a place of beauty and glades deeper than Alabion's ancient wells. I cannot see that as I look about into this sea of sand." She hesitated before saying her bloodmate's name. "Magnus...well, it was all sand when he found it thousands of years ago. So much for the Arhad and their legends. I think on the past too much, I fear. So deeply I am blinded to the future. I do not want to see beyond what I am to do. I do not want to consider..."

The desert ate her thoughts. Rather than chase her confession for a dark act Erik sensed she was planning, he was an obedient weapon and did not confront his queen. Her sniffling drew a glance from him, however, and when she started to weep outright, he sought to calm her with his big, awkward hands. She was losing control of her emotions and magik. Her tears were cutting through her disguise in lines and ripples of force that showed the shades and beauty of the woman the illusion hid. As he dabbed at her face and tried to calm her, she collapsed into him in a shuddering bundle—warm, needy, and deliciously perfumed. His heart raced down a strange, forbidden road. His compassion slipped out of its locker for an instant, and he was not a weapon but a man. "You must steady yourself," he urged. "Should we go back? I would not see you do whatever dark act this is—not if the mere thought of it brings you such deep remorse."

His suggestion only deepened her sobs. Folk behind the nearby flap would hear her in a speck. Again Erik beseeched the queen. He overstepped, but he knew nothing but the trembling woman in his arms—a woman he had last touched in a dreamy memory between life and death when she'd saved him from darkness. Perhaps now, he could save her. He spoke her name, as he had heard the king so commonly use it. He even used the same intonation, albeit in a deeper voice. "Lila, tell me your choice. What would you have us do?"

Her sobbing ended, and she sprang from his arms. Nevertheless, she had not cast herself free of him, and she clung to the large forearms of her hammer while staring at him in disbelief. For a speck, she had felt the presence of her bloodmate in him—a shadow of the man she had loved for a thousand years and even a hint of his wisdom. How disconcerting and at the same time validating this was for her. It was as if Magnus were speaking through his foster son.

Erik understood none of this. He knew only the queen's digging fingernails and the glare of her passion. He quite expected a slap or a reprimand rather than the soft, venomous whisper—as lethal as it was seductive—with which she responded. "You are a brave, good man. You are also clever in deducing the destruction I seek to bring. War is where we reveal the ugliest sides of ourselves. It's where we show our hate. I know you, Erithitek—how you challenge yourself to be better and bolder each day—and if we continue down this path together, I promise you will lose some or all of that virtue. Before we left Eod, I should have asked you—really asked you—about your willingness to let in the dark. Thus, I do so now. If you wish to leave, if you wish to preserve what the man who raised you treasured, then say as much.

I shall go on alone. I shall stain my virtue and no one else's. Speak now or nevermore. Suffer no guilt for your choice. It comes with my blessing."

One of her hands had released him. She was touching him as she spoke and holding his chin so their stares were trapped together. She was radiant and commanding, and he was under her serpent's spell. There was no answer save the one she wanted. "I shall not leave you," he said.

*He would do anything for me. Anything I asked,* she realized.

Erik would follow her into damnation, and she could see that conviction in his gaze and feel it in his flesh. His prickling beard stood like steel slivers under her fingertips. What a strange and silent comrade she had found. A sword, a hammer, or whatever she might term him, he was a weapon. He was a staff she could lean on when her weakness overcame her or a wrath she could unleash when it was time for blood.

She remembered bringing him back from the edge of the Great Mystery all those years ago. It was a memory now forged with new meaning. She was lost in the mire of wonders, regrets, and guilt that followed, and she could not take her hand off Erik's rough and warm skin. It was the opposite of Magnus's ice and smoothness, and yet it had many of the same aspects within. Gently, Erik pulled her hand away. The queen came back from wherever he had watched her go.

"When we arrive in Taroch's Arm," the queen said coldly, "I have arranged for a meeting with a Voice. He will provide us with what we need."

Erik nodded and turned away. He had received his orders and reaffirmed his loyalty to his queen. There was nothing left to do but spy on the desert and keep a hand ready for any harm that would come his mistress's way. Nonetheless, as steadfast as their resolve seemed, as much as he felt there was no more to talk about, he sensed the queen's attention on him more than once.

II

Wading through the sweaty crowds, it was easy for Erik to feel his descent into the sin the queen had prophesied. Vice was as thick in the air as the clouds of witchroot he coughed his way through while the queen dragged him down the streets of Taroch's Arm. It was good that he and the queen weren't prone to speaking, for he would not have heard more than a whisper over the barking hawkers, rattling coins, and cacophony of minstrels with their flutes, lutes, and foreigners' instruments. The spectacle might have been fun for any other person. For Erik, it was simply too loud. The city's architectural planning proved a welcome distraction. Vines grew on rows of boxy villas, and gracefully deteriorated buildings were sheltered along the great escarpment of salted rock—a more humble echo of the grandeur of Eod's palace. Cobblestoned bridges arched over a sunlight-sparkled swath of blue water. These glimmers of charm aside, the more they wandered, the greater the disparity between here and Eod. Every corner was besmirched where it should be white. Each citizen was rude and gruff instead of polite, and the place's inescapable noise and smoky reek generated a throbbing ache in his temples. He wondered how well the city had withstood the frost-fire storm and was hard-pressed to find signs of its having come and gone. He entertained one possibility with a chuckle: perhaps the city had simply concealed its scars with more revelry and filth.

While the queen moved single-mindedly to her purpose, Erik remained alert to the currents through which they swam. Danger loomed here, and not from the canny merchants and swindlers who lined the streets but from people wearing black cloaks and hoods with the embroidered image of a crimson hand on their backs. On these insignias, the fingers were more important than the hands. "Fingers" was the term given to the lawmen of the city's rulers. Erik tensed whenever he saw one of their kind spiriting away a miscreant—a pickpocket, a rowdy drunk, or a brawler. The two could be arrested if they weren't careful. All this risk could have been avoided if the queen had appealed to the Hand—the five-member council that governed Taroch's Arm—for the use of their relic. However, she seemed no longer in possession of the patience, diplomacy, and moderation necessary for these negotiations. She had become a sputtering fuse counting down to an explosion, and the best he could do was stay with her and limit the damage to her, her kingdom, and Eod's people. Lila's soul he would save too if possible.

Coaches were scarce in Taroch's Arm. They were seen only on the larger roads in the city and never on smaller streets. There was simply no room for them. Even with Erik and the queen's briskness and arrival at dawn, it took hourglasses to get to where they were going—not that she had told him their destination, only that they sought a Voice. At least he could tell that they were moving east toward the harbor and the white-tipped fury of the River Feordhan. Around midday, his taskmistress showed him a smidgen of kindness, and they stopped for a bite of stew and bread at one of the city's many taverns. The eatery was a quieter spot than most elsewhere in Taroch's Arm. It had a fenced-off patio higher than the street, plenty of sunshine, and clean gusts of the Feordhan's breath to invigorate him. They ate quickly, and after their server had cleared their plates, the queen clasped Erik's hands as if they were lovers, leaned in close with her honeyed scents and alarming beauty, and whispered, "Look up there. Atop the bluffs. That is where we shall go when night comes."

She was being inconspicuous and trying to speak free of eavesdropping on the crowded terrace, but he needed to wrest himself from her gaze to look to the great stone hill leaning over the city. If he squinted, he could see a scattering of pointy shapes across the flattest, highest plateau on the rock formation. What it was, he could not say.

"It's a graveyard," she continued in answer to his unspoken question, and she brushed her lips to his ear. "Taroch's crypt is there, and his remains—the part we need—are deeper within. We cannot force our way into the tomb without raising an alarm. The grounds are under constant patrol."

"Then how?"

The queen retreated. Some secret she kept amused her. A moment later, the server returned, and a sand after that, they were back out in the noisy street where no further questions could be asked or answered. Images of a daring, foolhardy climb to the peak of what was nearly a mountain bothered Erik throughout the afternoon, and when they reached the harbor, red and dimming with a murderous dusk, he was as solemn as the skyline. *Red sky at night. Drop anchor. Bunker tight.* It was from Carthac's seasmiths that he'd first learned of crimson clouds as an omen for storms. He saw the sailors along the piers pull tarps over their crates and cargo, and he noticed a port full of ships. Not a single mast was seen bobbing over the waves of the Feordhan. A little ways off, a gathering of Northmen stood by the water. They watched the waves smash against hulls, and pointed and cheered at the black twists forming in the sky. The Northmen caught his attention for a speck. Their bravura as they jeered about the weather was lovable. He couldn't say why, and he understood hardly anything of the North tribes, but he felt as if they would stand there even as lightning and rain assaulted them. They vanished as the queen took him down a side street with a florid and funny name— Corden? Corzenzia? He never got a good look, and he gave up on the name as they arrived at their meeting place—a tavern called the Silk Purse.

In they went. They passed a patio full of patrons complaining about the first pattering of rain. The folk appeared unwilling to relinquish their witchroot pipes, which evidently were not allowed within the clean, unfussy establishment Erik and the queen had entered. As was the order of business when dealing with the Watchers and their Voices, the seeker did not find them; they found the seeker. Erik made a pointless sweep of the room anyhow in case one of the stealthiest breeds of rogue had chosen to announce himself with gay colors and fanfare. No one stood out in the eclectic mingling of barbarians, sly, suited gents who might sell such barbarians in Menos, and the many shades of ruffians and brigands who hung about.

The bard was quite good and worthy of attention. He sat near the hearth, and his russet clothing seemed to flicker and flame like the nearby fire. This gave him the illusion of being a mirage. With his nimble, thin fingers, he plucked out a sad tune and sang in a hoarse, pleasing rasp. Despite his narrow, foxy face, his obvious talent, and the wiry handsomeness of his body— all things admirers would swoon over when being serenaded—he was nearly invisible as he sat on his stool and threaded his sly music through the room. He sent feet and fingers tapping almost without their owners realizing it. He sang an old war ballad—one of the last the king had rallied his troops with during a cool evening in Meadowvale.

The song scraped at the sore edges of Erik's heart, and he quickly turned to the bar and fetched a drink for himself and his companion. He got "a stiff one," as his comrades-in-arms called it. That was what he wanted, so he might again experience the hot relief of forgetfulness the queen's liquor had brought him on the night this had all begun. Afterward, he found the table the queen had claimed.

"Another drink?" she asked with an arched eyebrow.

Shy, he could think of no response. She pardoned him with a smile. "For you, something lighter," he said and passed her the second cup.

"Thank you."

The bard finished his song and many more while the rain carried on its own melody outside, and folk wanting shelter filled the tavern. As busy as the place became, elbows or requests to take the spare seats next to them did not trouble Erik and his queen. They were isolated within the vivacity. Perhaps they wore their secrets on their sleeves, for she sipped her wine with an elegance no illusion could repress.

She might as well have been in the White Hearth listening to the night's performers. She could not suppress the grace with which she caressed the lip of her wooden mug. It was as if it were a resplendent chalice, and she nodded her head in approval to the beat of the bard's sorrowful thrumming. (All his songs were sad, although he mouthed each with a smirk.) The night, the music, and the queen were hypnotic to Erik. Though he was always on guard and his hand was always on his sword hilt, he was loose in his manner. He was even free of that knot that seemed part of the meat between his shoulder blades—a knot of duty no fleshbinder or tonic would release. Alcohol appeared to be the remedy he had been missing all these years. There were also the smiles the golden woman across from him occasionally shone his way.

Magnus would be glad to see her happy. As his foster son, Erik was fulfilling his duty to the dead in being there, and he had never been surer that this was the road he was to walk—regardless of what sort of man he would become. When his drink was empty, he grabbed them another round and slipped further into comfort. A creeping quiet came with night's descent. The talented bard traded sets with a less talented trio—a harpist, a lutist, and a player of some twangy instrument—who Erik sensed were of no consequence.

Abruptly, a shadow fell over Erik and snapped him out of his musing.

"Enjoying the music?" asked the bard.

As suddenly as a ghost, the handsome man had materialized. As the man slithered into a seat, he held them rapt with his odd blue and green stare—an eye of each color, actually.

"We were," grunted Erik.

The bard projected a confident sarcasm. It was as if he were in on the most private joke in all Geadhain. It was a humor told in the lines near his mouth and eyes and even in the flirtatious and feminine but woodsy perfume he wore. As Erik assessed the threat, he decided the bard was a man crafted to confuse—down to his mismatching irises.

"You are the Voice," said the queen.

"I am." The bard grinned. "You may call me Alastair."

The queen found his candor unsettling. She could not think of the name of any other agent of the Watchers whom she had ever met.

"Come now," said Alastair, after reading her frown. "We are entering a new dawn. A new era. What is the point of pretense in a time so sick with its own uncertainty? We do not need to poison the punch more. Do we, Your Majesty?"

In Erik's boot was tucked a shorter blade in case he was down in a fight and without his sword. He had it out but under the table. He pressed its cold point into the man's ribs as soon as he finished the question.

"Good dog." Alastair's grin grew wide enough to swallow the room. "You are quite well trained. No messes on the rug for you. Now put that away. You must know the Hand's laws on bloodshed. If you aren't so educated, I need tell you only that the punishments are old and harsh and were made in a time before clemency or the Nine Laws entered our society. Eye for an eye. Tooth for a tooth. That sort of business. Kidney for a kidney in this case, I suppose. You'll probably be needing yours. I can always find another in Menos's fleshcrafting studios for a few crowns. Do put the knife down."

Masterfully, the queen withheld her astonishment, save for a chilly flicker that wrinkled her expression. She knew this stranger, although she could not remember how. This fact's absence was nagging, and she felt it was significant. Either way, gutting the fellow would not be prudent. She gave a nod to Erik, and like the dog he had been called, he obediently stowed away his weapon.

"How unusual of you, Voice," said the queen, and she leaned in on her elbows. "You share your name, and you come without a guise of mystery—not even a hood. I feel as if I know you or as if I should."

"Times are changing, my lady," replied Alastair. "Old reigns are falling. New orders rise to fill their vacancies. You might find that the kingdom you seek to preserve has already faded into history. This erosion of what we know has already occurred and will continue. My organization is no different. Change is as healthy as the season's coming. Rake the leaves, scatter the mulch, and after a long winter, the land will grow. I believe a push toward transparency and conviviality is due and much needed. If the Watchers must trade in secrets and lies, let us do so with flair.

"As for my name, it has traveled in circles you know. An old friend. A hand of yours that's missing. A rather interesting young woman. Accept that I treat you with such candor as a sign of trust. You won't find much of that these days. It's rarer than virtue or a falling star. I'm parched, though, after all that singing. Do pardon."

With that, he took Erik's drink for himself while telling the peevish warrior, through sips, how the man's blade was about as threatening as a butter knife and in desperate need of a whetstone.

The queen was as sharp as a soothsayer in reading the aims, desires, and drives of men. She had always been able to sense what troubled her blood-mate, and she even fathomed a glimmer of emotion for her in her hammer's eyes. Her astuteness, though, was ineffective when it came to this Voice. Alastair was a mystery through and through. He was sociable and charming, and yet there was a second layer to him—a wince behind his smile where some barbed knowledge he held pricked at him. He was as joyful as he was sad, and as playful as he was somber. Whatever secrets he bore, he did so alone, for she did not sense he was the sort to confide in others. As she pondered this stranger and how to handle him, she recalled exactly where she had heard of him. Although the far-speaking stone had been inconsistent—its magik had been warped by proximity to Alabion—a name had come through clear enough in Rowena's report.

"You!" she gasped, before hiding her excitement. "You're the one who helped them in Menos. Twice over! First Morigan and then my sword. Have you heard how Morigan and the sage fare? Have they reached the Sisters?"

"A fine question." Alastair raised his glass in a toast. "Let's pray they fare well. I'm no scouting hawk—merely a man. I have not heard of their progress through the woods. I do, though, have a mark on one—a witchneedle. What a darling lass to think she has found them all. I've stashed more witchneedles on her personage than pins in a pincushion." He laughed louder than discretion called for. "They're still moving, and at least one of them is still alive. I doubt we should worry about the not-really-a-smith or the one with the funny stare. So three out of five, then? Not bad. Gamblers' odds, for sure."

The queen chewed over this news. It wasn't worrying, but it wasn't satisfying either. *Good enough*, she decided. She had her own mission and its success to ensure. The war with Brutus could be strategized over later, and she would not need Thackery's advice from the Sisters until that juncture. Menos required its punishment before she dealt with the rabid king.

"I shall take that as good news," said the queen. "Now, the matter for which you were paid. Have you found a way in?"

"Such authority. What a clamp on your heart you must have to bother yourself with the affairs of your inferiors no more than you must. A queen of steel to lock swords with she-of-iron. I can see why you are who you are," Alastair said. "Upstairs, a room has been rented under the identities you assumed when reaching out to the Watchers. Shea or whatever you've decided to call yourself—"

"Siobhan," the queen stated.

"Lovely name. An old handmaiden of yours, I believe."

"Yes."

Alastair continued. "I have left what is needed in the nightstand. I shall leave the ascent of Taroch's Shadow—the mount, if you didn't know its name—to the two of you. There is a road leading to the necropolis—but you'll find many Fingers along the way. I recommend the north side. It has paths a mountain goat would climb and much darkness in which to hide. It will be a long trial best started at dusk. I doubt you have the time to make it tonight. The hourglass of the witch is nearly upon us."

"If we stay a moment longer, you might be right," said the queen.

She was up and on her feet then and sweeping away from the table. Alastair reached out and snatched her wrist as she passed. Severity darkened his fair-weather moodiness.

"You don't have to do this," he cautioned. "You should take a moment to rest."

What was he implying? What was this compulsion she saw in him? It was as hard as flint—a determination as strong as her ruthlessness and grief. It was as if he understood the full measure of her woe, her revenge, and the spiritual cost of it all. She was shaking with rage and fear that he saw so deeply into her.

"I shall finish this," she declared.

"Think," urged Alastair.

Erik stood for his queen and removed the man's grip from his charge.

"The Lady Siobhan has spoken," he said.

"What a faithful pup. Perhaps she will reward you with a treat one day. I wouldn't count on it, though," hissed Alastair.

He turned back to his drink. The queen had made up her mind, and he had other games to play. He polished off what remained in the cup, gestured for the trio of musicians to dismiss themselves, and returned to his stool for another set. Out of the corner of his eye, he saw the grim woman and her dog leave the Silk Purse a sand later. Surely what they needed from upstairs had been retrieved. In their honor, he strummed one of the gloomiest songs he knew: "The Rainmaker's Daughter." The song from the East was the musical tale of a love between a mortal and a river spirit that drove a wedge into each culture and ended in a war and eradicated both tribes. They held each other in the end, the mortal warrior and his aqueous lover. They had at least that moment of intimacy before the Great Mystery called them away. Mayhap the queen and her dog would partake in a similar bittersweet ending. However, as a rational man, he could see nothing for them but blood.

### III

The storm had passed, but the night was cold and slippery from the rain. Finding trails and handholds in the slick darkness was a deadly guessing game. Erik led the way, and he was almost glad of the danger. It gave him little opportunity to consider what they were doing—this skulduggery and sin. Penitence could come after. Once this and the other crimes they would undoubtedly accumulate were finished, he would take the queen away from her madness to heal—forcibly, if it came to that. Carthac seemed the obvious retreat, with its rocking shores and wind-sung melody of peace. While he was conflicted over his misplaced feelings for her, his vow to the kingfather had been hammered into an even stronger steel since Magnus's death. He would not fail Magnus's ghost. He resolved to take the queen to Carthac, and this flimsy fantasy whipped him onward up the black, winding trail of Taroch's Shadow.

Erik was the queen's hands through the climb, and he could sense how much she appreciated—and loathed—his assistance. When she slipped on a rock, his quickness would save her from a scrape, or worse. Her responses, however, were miserly smiles of gratitude shortly followed by commands to release her. "I'm fine," she said again and again. "Do let go."

Without him, she could have died in the ascent—falling to her death like a common woman. While she was a powerful sorceress, he did not believe she had the ability to translocate to the top of Taroch's Shadow, or she would have already done so—perhaps transporting herself right inside the tomb. Therefore, like it or not, she had to make this journey through grunt and sweat. She needed him when in her grief she wanted no one, and thus he bore her cruelty with patience.

Then on a crumbling ledge—wide enough to walk on but still precarious—he pulled the queen into him as the earth beneath her heels gave way to a shower of dust, and he held her as they watched the path behind them evaporate. She could have met her end then and there. Her heart beat strong through her clothing and against his ribs, conveying her terror. When words came, they were kinder and not just a demand to be freed. "Thank you, Erithitek. I...I would never have come this far without you."

"I shall not leave you," he said.

It was a soul-bound promise and not the first time she had heard it. The queen blushed, and he let her go. After that, she was not as biting with her tongue when he came to her rescue. She was, however, swifter with her escapes from his warmth, as there was a discomfort brewing from these contacts that she would not abide. If she stopped and stayed in his embrace, this child of her bloodmate, she might grieve with him as a mother would with her son. That might weaken her resolve to carry on, which she knew she must above all else. Fewer stumbles and deteriorating steps hindered them as they went higher, and the moonlight even gave them a faint glow by which to see. In due time, the smell of freshly ripped, raw earth became another beacon for them to follow, and with the brighter paths and thrill of nearing the crown of Taroch's Shadow, they hurried and soon hauled themselves onto a plateau.

Across the rutted ground, made more unsightly still by a grassy mange, was a graveyard of many markers. A towering fence tipped in gleaming points protected it. There would be no going over the barrier—not without great fuss or risk of injury. They would have to pass through it.

"I shall take care of this," announced the queen.

Quite finished with Erik's assistance, the queen decisively strode ahead. Erik followed behind and gave her space while she worked her magik near the fence. She grabbed two shafts of metal, one in each hand, and they began to glow like pokers left in the fire. He could spy her scowl even in the dimness. The queen's sorcery was hotter than he recalled, and its light was as gray as the moon's shine—not soothing and golden as he remembered. What did he know of magik to make such presumptions, though? Perhaps foolishly, he cast away the insight that her sorcery was somehow transforming along with her mood. Bitter magik or not, the metal responded as it should, and the queen silently teased the bars apart as if they were young saplings. The pair left the fence that way after slipping through the oval she had created. They would have to make their escape through the same portal.

Every graveyard created a sense of foreboding and had a lingering aura of death that could inspire sad poetry in daylight and terror come nightfall. Here, however, the eeriness was intensified. The harsh moon glared over their backs as though it disapproved of their skulking, and the wind was free, wild, and shrieking in their ears. It slapped at their faces. This was a sacred site—the resting place of both a hero and a monster. Somewhere among the stones—many so old the names were effaced—were Glavius's bones, and with the dead hero were the remains of the despot whose life and arm he had claimed. Erik chilled at the thought of what the queen would find inside Taroch's tomb. He felt concern and compassion for her, as she would have to go alone. He could not accompany her. Someone had to stand guard outside and ensure it was safe to leave the underground without discovery, and a sorcerer was needed within to break the wards on Taroch's tomb. They each, therefore, had a predetermined role for this mission.

The Voice had given them a key to the tomb—an implement similar to the cubic pegs and tumblers Menosians used for their feliron-bound prisoners.

The key felt slippery in his hand, and he fingered it nervously. Not a single part of her plan seemed reasonable or without danger.

An occasional flickering torch cast long and dancing shadows between the tombstones. Erik skirted these lights as well as certain men that prowled the night. In many folds of darkness walked people as stealthy as black cats—Fingers. At times, he saw them posed and still as grave markers. Had he been less tuned for battle, less gritty, or less paranoid, he might not have noticed the stationary ones. As it was, he was always able to pull the queen to the ground or to some other cover in time for them to evade detection. The queen no longer praised him for her safety—talking would only imperil them. Dawn was threatening their mission too. Their climb had taken hourglasses, and the night now had a shimmer of silver that would eventually become gray and then blue. Fortunately, Alastair had provided the location of Taroch's Rest, and they counted the graves and strange landmarks he had mentioned on the scroll wrapped around the key he'd left for them. They looked for a white vase, bright as a lantern and hard to miss, and a cobalt gravestone with a plaque so polished it would light the way. Luckily, they found each of the signs Alastair had described and came to Taroch's tomb with sands to spare before dawn was upon them.

Not much distinguished this place of rest from the other vaults laid in the earth they had passed. Mayhap such inconspicuousness was the point. The grass was less trodden, and there were no flowers about the flat, square slab. The two pressed their bellies to the earth and waited. Erik glanced into the fleeting darkness for figments that could be Fingers. He waited for those figments to wander off or reveal themselves as illusions. As soon as they were in the clear, he hauled up the queen, and they dashed for the crypt. There was no padlock, and only a large, smooth shield of stone set into the slab. With mounting tension, they pawed for a groove, a notch, or anything into which they could fit a key. Erik's finger fell into a square pit—if he had been a more excitable man, he would have cried out. Fetching the key hurriedly from his pocket, he pushed it into the pit. With a "click," the magik mechanism was activated, the stone atop the entrance rolled sideways like a rumbling wheel, and a stairway lay before them leading into darkness. Erik hurried the queen into the musty tomb.

Before proceeding, she conjured a charcoal sphere of light to guide her. It was the same somber shade of magik from before. It hung at her shoulder, this sad star, and its sorrowful mistress was like a ghost half faded into darkness. She turned back to glance at Erik. While the urge was great, he dared not meet her gaze. He snatched the key out of the tomb, the tomb's entrance rolled shut, and he watched until she vanished behind the plate. Afterward, he hid in the long grasses of the nearest knoll and hoped he would hear her knock when it came.

## IV

"Fine playing," said Maggie.

The Silk Purse's proprietor sat down at the table where the night's entertainment fiddled with his lute's strings. The bard glanced up and smiled at her with his eyes, although he kept on tinkering and tuning to the pitch of his voice. Maggie watched him for a spell. The man was mystifying. He was as distant as a dream one forgot and so far into himself, his music, or some secret obsession that she might as well have been elsewhere. He was certainly handsome, though, and in their short conversations today, he'd proven a capable and witty talker. She wanted a bit more of his talk.

"Will you be staying on another night?" she asked. "Before heading back to…"

She realized that in all their discussions, the man had never told her where he had come from—or where he was headed. Or much about himself at all. Even stranger, she couldn't pin down how she'd made his acquaintance. Had he come knocking at the tavern door yesterday? Had he smiled a dashing hello with a lute over his back and a promise to play for coin? That seemed right.

"Would you like me to stay?" he asked suddenly.

He grinned from ear to ear and displayed his offer of companionship as confidently as the fox he reminded her of strutting around the henhouse and picking its prey. She could see him evaluating her body—her full breasts, strong hips, thick, wind-tossed hair, and comely face. She was as chipped and beautiful as a sculptor's favorite piece. She wore her hardship plainly, but it had not dulled her beauty, and he seemed to appreciate her weathered self. As for the fox's proposal, Maggie was a sensible self-made woman without need for a man. Once or maybe twice a year, she took one to her bed, but she never asked him to stay or even to break a morning fast with her. Whatever her hesitations, when the fox smiled—fiery and daring—she lit up and felt as warm as a woman sinking into a bath. A decision was made. A little outside of herself, she slid his hand over hers. She reinforced her agreement by standing up from the table and leading him past her tired staff as they cleaned up the night's mess and rolled the drunks outside. The trip up the stairs and into her chambers was fuzzy. Suddenly, they were alone and kissing in the dark. He whispered of her beauty. "Like a cameo of Diasora," he declared.

She wondered who Diasora was while he plucked his fingers upon and within her as though she were his lute. They tumbled into chairs, onto the carpet, and onto the bed. She wasn't sure where they were half the time. She swallowed his hardness just as he ate and kissed the mouth between her thighs. Together they rolled and tumbled about in the dark and moaned in ecstasy. She rode him against the wall and swallowed his gasps as he spilled himself inside her. It was careless, and she should have known better. Apologetically and with a perverted grin, he cleaned out with his tongue what he had done, and passion carried her mind away again. Through the haze of their sex, she would remember his handsome smell—vanilla, subtle incense, and sweeter herbs such as marjoram. Sometimes he sang to her ears while playing the instrument of her body. She would most remember this—his passion and musicality.

When they finished, dawn had come. It cast its hard rays through the curtains and into their humid nest of sin. Maggie should have felt embarrassed or shamed even, but instead she snuggled into her lover's taut flesh while he continued caressing her breasts. Milk drops, the bard called them, for their pendulous whiteness and succulence. She chuckled as he said it. She would have slapped any other man who made nicknames for portions of her anatomy.

"Where will you go?" she asked.

She knew this was a fleeting encounter. Men as artistic at loving as he were called to greater passions than women.

Alastair kissed her breast. "Well, I shall stay in Taroch's Arm a while longer. I have another task to which I must attend. One more meeting after this." He sighed and looked off with his multicolored stare to count the ceiling's lines.

Maggie snuggled into him further until she realized what he'd admitted. "Wait! Meeting? Is that what this is? What is your aim?"

She leaped from the bed. Alastair went after her and backed her into a corner. He appeared stricken and white from regret. Rather brazenly, he kissed her so deeply she lost her breath. Although Maggie allowed it, she slapped him as soon as their lips parted. He grinned and rubbed his cheek. "What fire you have!" he said, adding sadly, "How much you remind me of a woman I once knew. Do understand. This is not how I had planned our parley. I am not ungrateful, though, for this turn of events. I would stay for a thousand kisses more if I could. However, my master is most demanding of my time."

"Master?" she exclaimed.

"You are fortunate, Maggie. Most serve masters and destinies from which we cannot break. You have made so much of yourself without the hands of others. Despairingly, I must ask this of you. It's a task you cannot refuse."

*I can, and I shall*, she thought. No man, not even a roguish wanderer, could boss her around. Then the fox whispered a secret and those familiar names to her: Thackery, Caenith, Rowena, and Galivad. By the time he was done, she had no resolve to argue. She had only an unwanted urgency to pack, make quick arrangements for the Silk Purse's managerial duties, and leave. She had no choice—not with so many lives at stake. While she busied herself about her apartment, the bard came to kiss her a final time, and they fell onto the bed. For all their grinding, they did not make love. Soon he stopped, studied her, and soaked in her beauty. Maggie closed her eyes. She would not watch him leave. When she was certain he had gone, she pulled her sturdiest boots from under her bed and put them on.

V

Without the hammer's guidance, the queen was an inelegant creature. She blundered along the narrow stone tunnel, and she would have been angry about her abrasions if her bloodmate's ghost had not haunted her. She'd last been down here with Magnus. In a sense, it was that trip's memories that had driven her to this undertaking. To think Magnus's expression of love would lead to this wickedness.

*"I want to show you Geadhain's wonders," he declares.*

*She has learned that Magnus is a man of promises, and he has yet to break one. She was rescued from her hideous marriage, and Magnus has pursued her ever since like no other man. He has allowed her to flower with knowledge in the humbling Court of Ideas. He has encouraged her to take trips with the watchmen and their flying beasts. No. They are machines of magik and science, she reminds herself. They go to the vast greenness of his brother's realm or into the snowy lands beyond Kor'Keth. She had not known there were lands outside the desert, that the world could be so grand, and that there were other colors besides the bone-white of sand. In days that feel like years from their fullness, she has seen waterfalls, wastelands, cities built of wrecked ships, and Carthac's majestic watchtowers that reach forever into the sky—all wonders that no woman, let alone an outcast bride of the Arhad, would ever see. Sometimes she goes without him on these journeys and with only a few men as her guards. On other occasions Magnus comes if she allows it. The decision is always hers. He appreciates her independence and never presumes he is welcome. As the days pass, though, she increasingly wants his cold presence near her. Lately, she has invited him on many private excursions, and to add to the excitement—and romance, she admits—he blindfolds her. The cloth is never tight and always to be removed at the slightest discomfort—much the same as his attendance.*

*She isn't sure where he has taken her today. She knows only that it doesn't smell the freshest. The pungency of dust and age remind her of the oldest sections of Eod's Court of Ideas. Had this been any other man or moment, she would have fled. She doesn't know whether escape is even possible, though, for he has magiked them here. She recalls them standing outside the busy city where they had shopped. He casts off the illusions they wore to hide themselves. He then points to the top of an awe-inspiring peak. It is not the cloudy heights of Kor'Keth, but it is unscalable still. As soon as he binds the silk over her sight and she has given consent, a tingling takes her every nerve. She shivers in places she did not know could shiver. A touch of his passion she feels. Like that, faster than the snap of her fingers, and with an instant of agony as if squeezed* through a telescope, they are no longer on the ground but in a dry, ancient place muffled in dust and spider webs. She feels these brush against her skin—though she can feel his cool hands clearing them as best he can from around her face as he leads her farther into the unknown.

While he guides her, his confident voice fills her ears and imagination with the history of what she is to see. "A warlord's tomb," he says. "Taroch's tomb. A mighty conjurer of lost arts and transmutation, he ruled the world through pecuniary crusades and physical warfare until his greed became tyrannical— worse than that of Menos's iron masters. At the height of Taroch's villainy, the Brother Kings came down upon him like a hammer of thunder."

She still doesn't quite comprehend the complexities of modern economies. Although she has learned the basics, when Magnus says this sorcerer's power allowed him to create unlimited currency or turn water into a fountain of gold or feliron, she is even more confused, albeit fascinated.

They arrive at wherever he is taking her, and his cold fingers remove her blindfold. After the darkness, she must blink and hold on to her guide in the dazzling chamber. For there are gems of every kind, and they are as large as fists and as small as pearls. They are embedded in the wall or clustered on high in branching arches of silver and gold. She has studied geodes with her tutors and learned of the strata within the earth, but this is such a glorious disarray of the natural order that she cries out in marvel. He holds her in the sparkling wonder, and she feels for the first time his strength and the trembling power contained within him. She feels it with a desire to feel more. However, Magnus always steps away before stepping too far, and he urges her to come forward. There is something she is too overwhelmed to spot in the chamber's dazzle—an ark of crystal. She cannot find another term for the boat-shaped treasure. It is a ship of diamonds crashed onto rocks of ice. As they climb up glimmering steps and onto what she thinks of as a deck, Magnus taps on the crystal floor with his foot. When she looks down, she sees a man startlingly well preserved and hold- ing something pulsing and golden. He is holding it to his chest like a dead war- rior laid with a blade. This weapon, though, is magik, and it is no simple sword. She cannot contain her delight. That is the arm of Taroch, Magnus explains.

She interrupts his tour to kiss him. History does not concern her. She has made a choice in this hallowed place to be with this not-quite man and his end- less mysteries.

Now she wept in the darkness as she remembered, but they were bitter tears and quickly lost in the thick whirl of dust surrounding her. "You asked me to wed you before you would take my virtue. You asked me here on this spot," croaked Lila.

Her voice brought her back to herself more than the scorching fury of her magik that shattered the encasement holding the dead soldier and ancient relic—more than the cinders and crystal fragments flying around her in a molten whirlwind as she unleashed her tortured magik. As the air calmed in the smoke-stained underground hollow, she remembered little of the destruction she had wrought. She could see it now, though—the beauty of Taroch's resting place ruined and Glavius's body finally burned and buried as the dead should be. Taroch's arm, a grotesque amputation with a sickly sheen of greenish-gold and vascular muscles still throbbing from a ghostly heart, called to its liberator's broken spirit. Surely this was a cursed thing. The queen's intentions, though, were not pure enough for them to be at odds. As she picked it out of the charcoal, its thumping made her smile. Had Erik or anyone seen her in that moment, grinning in the gruesome relic's fallow glow, she would have seemed wickeder than the blackest witch of Alabion.

## VI

"Flowerpot... Mr. Harkman's grave." Erik was recounting the various markers they would need to follow to find their exit when the grumbling from below rattled his bones. Perhaps it wasn't the sudden quaking of the land that had rallied the Fingers here to the graveyard. However, Erik pressed his body flat into the soil as their dark shapes suddenly moved about. The red sun and its cruel exposure made the task of hiding more difficult. Erik ventured to guess the quake had been the queen's work. She likely now had the relic and would soon be on her way. He had only to wait and listen for a knock on the stone plate just over the rise from where he hid. Would he even hear her? He poked his head up. It was a terrible idea. Several metal things whistled past his ear. They were too fast and small to be daggers and too large to be pellets. He rolled back into concealment. His heart was nearly in his mouth. He'd been noticed, and his position was no longer safe.

As Erik scurried to a showy monument with a marble guardian atop, more projectiles zinged at him. A few chinked the pedestal as he slipped behind its protection, and another pierced the thick leather satchel about his waist. He pulled the weapon out. It was closer to a long, thin, pointed bullet than an arrow. In a moment, he determined an automated crossbow or a similarly motorized propulsion device had fired these barbs. Another deadly trio of shots—launched faster than a person could throw—struck the statue's legs above and doused him in powder. These attacks were not warnings—they were meant to kill. Thus, when he saw a black shape lean out from a row of tombstones, he did not stall his hand or the dagger it found. The Finger did not delay either in brandishing whatever weapon glimmered in the sun. Erik's blade hit the attacker first. It was quick enough that the volley of metal spikes intended for him scattered into the sky. He raced to the downed and groaning man. Since he rarely missed and had no intention of adding murder to the charges they'd accumulated that day, he was pleased he had merely stabbed the shoulder of the rawhide-armored rogue. The Finger writhed and agonized over the steel stuck in his flesh. The huge man who was rudely upon him surprised the Finger. Erik eased the man's suffering with a punch to the skull and then rifled through his belongings.

Daylight was Erik's enemy, and he had mere specks to remove—and comprehend—the strange ballista strapped and buckled onto his attacker's hand and wrist. A cylindrical quiver ran the length of the forearm and then attached to a complicated leather truss with a pad in the center of what would be one's palm. While wrangling his hand into the contraption, Erik made a fist, and a needle shot out of a tiny hole in the end of the quiver. It nearly stapled his toe to the ground. At least he now knew how the weapon worked. He tossed off his cloak and threw on the one he had stripped from the drooling Finger. He hoped this would confuse his enemies and buy the queen time. He moved the body out of sight and dashed back to the knoll near Taroch's Rest. Dressed as a Finger, he was able to swagger confidently over to the two cloaked figures gathered outside the tomb. They were investigating markings in the dirt. He got within striking distance before either spotted the inconsistencies in his demeanor—his size, face, and the simple garb under his mantle. It was too late. In a speck, his hands turned to fists and sent one fellow dreaming. Then he choked the other fellow until his eyes rolled back. Erik punched him a few more times to ensure he would stay unconscious and then dragged both Fingers behind a large monument. *Messy. This is getting messy.* Without opening graves, he was running out of spots to hide the bodies, and the men he'd savaged would not remain still forever.

Erik returned to Taroch's Rest and fondled the key in his pocket while pacing the slab. Though the sun shone brightly, his sweat ran ice-cold. All through the grounds, he could hear activity—whispers and gusty rounds going off—as the Fingers swore and shot at shadows. Where was she? Even without a chronex, he felt over an hourglass had passed. Once the bells signaling calamity began to clang out in the city below, he knew they were out of time. He bent and cracked open the tomb. Amazingly, the queen stood there. She was blinking and covered in ash as though she'd rolled in a hearth. She clutched a grisly, luminous item in the roll of her cloak. He noticed a black fingernail. He said nothing as he hauled her out of the grave. They had what they'd come for, and they'd been discovered, so they left the key and yawning crypt door and ran.

Fingers were closing in—if not on them directly, then surely on the tomb. More shouts came from behind and echoed clearly over the huff of their breathing and stamping feet. Soon the shadows found their scent, and Erik and the queen began darting for shelter from a hail of metal spines. Erik fired off a round by clenching his hand and shooting blindly over his shoulder. He wasn't sure what he'd hit, but their pursuers slowed down, more cautious now. Unfortunately, in the frenzy he had missed a marker—the damned flowerpot or something else that would tell them where they should be heading. He saw the great fence in the distance, realized his mistake, and knew they were lost. *Oh well. Damned and onward.* They ran and crawled on hands and knees. At times, he shielded the queen as he shoved her ahead, and they stumbled toward the fence.

Suddenly, there was a blast of arctic air as if a doorway to the Long Winter had opened. They toppled. The fury rose in a screech, and they rolled helplessly on the ground. They were drowning in an icy sea. A frosty billow poured over the ground. It burned their skin like fire and turned their bones to icicles. They would have screamed if their throats hadn't been frozen. As the pair convulsed, they kissed the dirt and wept. A shadow passed over them. Frozen tears and agony prevented them from seeing who stood nearby. They would recall its voice, though—dry, elegant, and ambiguous in its sex. They would remember the visions and sensations that tore into them as it spoke, too. It brought fantasies of slithering, congealed rivers of blood, the rancid stink of buzzing tables heaped with mortal carcasses, flies tickling their faces, sweet and vinegary air, and the horror of their flesh melting away in rotten clumps. Death spoke to them.

**"Go east. Finish what you have started,"** Death commanded.

As if their horror were not sufficient, the coldness constricted them. Their eyes bulged, their lungs were squashed of air, and their sightless, battered bodies were flung here, there, and somewhere into a screeching storm. As abruptly as the nightmare had begun, it ended. The weight of a thousand stones was off them. Erik made a panicked examination of his body. His flesh was whole. There were no maggots in his mouth—only soil, which he spit out. Nearby, the queen groaned, and Erik rushed to her. She looked crumpled, and he gently rolled her over. In her vertiginous vision, she saw Erik's swarthy, scarred, and welcome face and the stark outline of Taroch's Shadow. An orange diamond of sun rising over his head bejeweled it. She squirmed out from under her guardian, and the two stayed on their knees in the sand.

Sand. They scanned their surroundings in awe. The bustle of Taroch's Arm lay many spans away. Its alarm was a din they strained to hear, and the cliff they'd climbed was hard to spot from where they sat. On the beach where they had landed, the Feordhan licked its salty, white tongue along the shore, and the world appeared fresh, bright, and empty of danger.

"Translocation," gasped the queen, and she hugged Taroch's severed arm for comfort.

If not the queen, then who had performed this great act of sorcery? Maybe "what" was a better question. In his life, he'd been grazed by the magik of several sorcerers, including an Immortal King and the once-golden, now-bitter queen. However, this power attested to his insignificance beyond Immortal Kings and twisted queens. Erik felt as small as a babe in that instant, and he shivered under sunshine that should have warmed him.

"It is right," said the queen. "I must finish what I have begun."

Using the dead warlord's arm as a crutch, the queen stood and strode down the beach. Erik watched her and hesitated for a speck. He was torn between the fright of having just been hurled by a force beyond comprehension and his obligation—and sick desire—to chase this mad woman who surely was headed for doom. Alas, he had made his vow to Magnus, and he dashed to catch up.

## VII

When he shut his eyes, Alistair could picture Maggie's exquisiteness. He smiled and thought about her delicate ears. They were so small, they would have fit better on a child. He was disappointed he could not nibble on them again. What a lovely evening it had been. How deeply she reminded him of *her*—the woman whose memories he kept in a chained box in his heart. Perhaps one day, with another twist of fate, he and Maggie might meet again. For now, though, he put Maggie and her wonder in that special place where he locked all his secrets.

Besides, he had another woman with whom to concern himself. That was the way he liked to think of his mistress. She had been grumbling that day and full of "get ups" and "go heres," which came as painful stabbings to his head. They weren't even really words—more like ravings or a stringed instrument being sawed back and forth. She was as powerfully insistent as a nauseating headache. When they spoke, it was closer to a conversation with oneself than actual discourse between two parties. Whatever complaints he might have about his mistress, however, she was wise, and their covenant gave him far too many gifts ever to criticize her—years a person should not live for and miracles from the realms men dreamed of only when gazing to the constellations at night. Thus he did whatever she bade, and when she'd told him it was time to leave that delightful nymph, Maggie, this morning, he had made haste without dallying. "Go to the warlord's tomb. See what Xalloreth desires," she had instructed.

First, he had the climbing of Taroch's Shadow to worry about. Still quite sore after his sessions with Ms. Halm, he found the thought of further athletics disagreeable. Perhaps he would roll the dice, invoke the powers of the entity that slept within him, and let her choose his next move. It was risky. Calling on his mistress's energy could take a toll in spirit and body and leave him out of sorts. He'd have shakes, fevers, and queasiness for days. Invoking her power didn't always work either. Sometimes he got his wish. Sometimes he threw up on his boots. A person could not predict what his mistress might do. Nevertheless, her fickleness and his flippant attitude toward life made for a marvelous pairing of vessel and entity. Another roll of the dice it would be, then. He really was too tender in places to bother with a hike.

Alastair stretched out his arms to embrace the morning and summoned her from within. When she came, it felt as if he would split and explode into a mist of blood. It was as if a vessel as papery as he could not cage the inferno that was his mistress. While she was a gentle host, her stirring was still an incomparable pain. He would call it religious—this sublime baptism in fire that dazzled his perception with starscapes, thunderous singing, patterns of light, and rolling waves of music. When the euphoria faded, he returned to his tingling body. He opened his eyes to see whether his wish had been granted.

He stood in the midst of a graveyard laid with sheets of white, wintry fog. He was confused, and considered where this was. The turn in weather surprised him. Then he sighed and knew what this meant. Wrapping himself tight in the perfumed cloak he'd stolen from Maggie's boudoir, he walked on. Praise be that his gamble had not decimated his body this time. In fact, he felt pleasantly trembling and warm from the magikal transit, which helped against the air's crispness. To his distaste, he noticed many open graves. Soil had been cast about scratched pits where the inhabitants had clawed their way out. The mist was sympathetic in hiding most of these shambling dead from Alastair, and they scattered from him as if he was as horrific to them as their tattered faces were to him. Pitiably, the Fingers of Taroch's Arm did not possess the same repellence, and he passed a handful of gutted, skinned, decapitated, and otherwise nibbled Fingers. The restless dead had subdued them. *Always with the cannibalism,* he thought, and sneered. Any time a nekromancer's pet got off its leash, it went immediately for warm, red meat. The livelier or younger the victim, the greater the spark of life, and thus the greater the taste. The blood-smeared tombstones and rotting shadows disgusted Alastair, although none of the horror frightened him. After wandering for a while, he grew tired of searching. He sat on a great limestone marker and shouted over the city's tolling alarm for the being he knew was also wandering here somewhere—Xalloreth. Death herself. It took only a few calls before his summons was answered.

"*Charazance*," came a hiss in the fog.

Bravely, Alastair replied. "Not the lady herself. Only the one in whom she sleeps."

"*A vessel? I would parley with my equal. Not some maggot.*"

With that, a tall, gaunt man dressed in disheveled satin pajamas staggered out of the mist. The man's dark hair was a picked boll of cotton with a dandruff of leaves and dirt. He held himself poorly. He was slack at the knees and elbows as though he were a puppet with loose strings. Alastair laughed at the state of him.

"Oh, Sorren. What a fright!" He clapped. "I'd say you deserve better, but you really deserve worse. You bargained with the wrong master."

In Sorren's sunken, sleepless eyes shone an agony Alastair had not imagined. That mortality quickly drowned under an inky darkness in his stare, and the master within Sorren spoke quietly. "*I should crush you to nothingness for your insolence. I am a Dreamer—a maker of the cosmos. I am Death. I am as old as the ghost of the farthest star in the sky. You will bow and weep and consume the ashes of your own flesh for speaking to me so rudely.*"

As the Dreamer of Death spoke, the dry grasses around her wilted to ash, flies and fecal rankness fouled the air, and even the stone Alastair sat on grew brittle and began to crack. He hopped off. Her threats were not intimidating. "You should save that power," clucked Alastair. "Otherwise, you will burn through your vessel as fast as a gambler's coin in a betting house. You should know better than to wake so strongly in his body. He will not last long enough for whatever you have planned, and finding suitable hosts can be rather inconvenient and time-consuming. We are special snowflakes—not too many of us around. You need us just as much as we need you."

His scolding had merit. Alastair took a few steps closer to the Dreamer and could see at least another decade on Sorren's body and a map of blue veins across his cheeks that were certainly fresh. The Dreamer considered this audacious thing before her and whether to smash or tolerate him. She decided on the latter. ***"Speak then, maggot."***

Alastair became uncharacteristically grave. "Charazance wishes you would not bully destiny. The more you force your weight, the greater the chance you will break the scale. She still believes the Daughter of Fate can end this war on her own, if only we help her and those drawn to her by serving as a guiding spirit and not a heavy hand. It was not wise to try to capture her through Sorren—that will only make the distinctions between enemy and friend unclear. We need clarity if the Black Queen is to be stopped."

***"Heavy hand? Weight? This world has seen nothing of my weight."***

The stone seat behind him shattered into dust, but he ignored it. "You need to leave mortals to make their own choices," Alastair implored the ghastly Dreamer. "Presenting opportunities and quandaries is what your kind is to do. Anything more and you become no better than the Black Queen, who would pervert life. Or the Sisters Three, whose meddling has caused such grief. You must see how their actions have broken the great order—perhaps irreparably. Consider what your terrible power will do to the delicacy of creation."

***"I shall deal with the Sisters,"*** thundered Death. ***"How dare you speak of meddling? I have witnessed your work here with Magnus's manling wife. You led her to the tomb. You knew what she would do."***

"We did not." Alastair sighed. "We gave her a choice, and we were hoping her love would win out over her hate. A gamble, which we seem to have lost."

***"You play your games of love, chance, and free will poorly. I shall show you how to craft mortals' Wills. I knew you would fail with the queen, for love is a poetry these creatures create to shield themselves from the truth of my coming. Remember, Charazance and her vessel, there is but one Will at the end—one keeper of the Great Mystery. I am Keminos. I am Erishkigal. I am Xalloreth. I am the nameless shadow of one thousand names. The reaper of all things. No matter your interference, the broken manling wife will serve me still. She will bring me an army, and I shall bring this world back to order with or without the Daughter of Fate. I shall rid this world of the sin of our mother. I shall drag the Black Queen***

*screaming into the abyss. If you will not join me in this war, you should sleep until it is over."*

Viciously, Sorren's liver-spotted claws shot at Alastair. Death had intended to grab and unmake Alastair in a manner most terrible. Alastair had been expecting this treachery; Charazance had rightly warned him her sister was not of a much better temperament than the monster that threatened Geadhain. He threw himself from Death's clutches in time. Scrabbling away from the cold, silvery darkness blooming around Death, Alastair took his one chance for escape. He rolled the dice. He knew that even in such a dire circumstance, his mistress would not be partial to him. He cackled as Charazance's energy crumpled his bones and fired him through a psychedelic chamber—a bullet that shot through space. The instant that bullet landed, he was brutally shoved back into a flesh mold, and every bit of him ached. He'd won the bet but gambled his last game for a while. With bleary eyes and a drunken head, he couldn't make out where Charazance had sent him. He felt wood under his hands, and he crawled along it until he bumped into more wood, and then he found blessed softness atop that. He hefted his body onto this cart, mattress, or sack of clothes and made a mental reminder to sweet-talk the owner of this resting place when he woke. Alastair fell asleep with his most charming smile and began to drool the speck he was under.

An hourglass later, the property's owner returned to her apartment and saw the knocked-over chairs and trail of disarray leading into her bedroom. She was certain she had been burgled. She wondered whether the thieves had been after the stash she had strapped under her bed for rainy days—a stash she had forgotten in the morning's hustle. As Maggie explored her ransacked chambers, she pointed her knife ahead of her. She found only one thief, and that was the man who had taken her dignity and the serenity of her life before running off elsewhere. He was back now and down for quite a stay from the look of it. She fetched a pail of water and a cloth for his ashen forehead and then sat on a stool by the bed. The valiant tasks she'd been charged with could wait awhile—certainly until he woke and told her what in the King's name was really going on.

# V

# A SEA OF TREES THAT EATS

I

Pining Row was named for the prominent howl of the wind through the pines there, and Caenith wagered it was only another day or so away. Beyond that were the Pitch Dark and the Sisters Three. When laid out with such simple goalposts, the journey felt simple. Mouse figured he was trying to cheer them up. She knew that before any celebration would come terror and possibly death. She regretted their quest while they slogged through cold water that stank of manure, while she spit out insects, and while they all became as wet as newborns with mud rather than blood. She was miserable and looked up often—they all did—through the web of branches for any sign of the sun in this wretchedness. The sun would not shine that day, though— just as it had not shone the day before, or any of the countless days they'd been trapped there.

She assumed incorrectly that the Wolf would be more charitable with rest, considering Thackery's state of health. Her great-uncle fared terribly in these climes, and in short order it became evident he simply would not be participating in travel any longer. At the first deep crossing, Thackery gave up without fanfare and just sat on a reedy bank, watched the white moths, and whistled back to the warbling black herons that stalked the stale waters.

Instead of reasoning with the fellow, the Wolf swooped the man up for a carry. Thackery didn't object, and since that time he had been cuddled and mostly asleep against the huge man.

At night they would camp on the driest ground the Wolf could sniff out for them—a scab of rock in the middle of nowhere or a bridge of slimy roots with a filthy hollow beneath in which they could rest. Once they'd settled, the Wolf would go off on his hunt. These days he hunted alone. Vortigern stayed behind, as he was alert to the shapes that sniffed the bog or the serpents that slithered down from aeries. After a dreadful, wearying slog, their first and only meal of the day was the corpse of one of the monstrous lizards that swam in the muck. The scowling Wolf hauled it to them. *A bit like chicken*, Mouse tried to convince herself—although she stomached the lie no better than the food.

On this day, they stopped for the evening upon an island of toadstools. After the Wolf left them, they began their glum routine. Vortigern paced around, and Mouse and Morigan conversed frowningly and hovered near Thackery. Tonight their morbid vigil was too much for Mouse.

"Is this it?" she whispered. "How he is to go? All that heroism and bravery, and we find him a quiet tree and bury him there?" Morigan did not reply, and Mouse grabbed her hand. "Don't ignore me. Can't you do something, Morigan? What you did with that girl, Macha? Can't you bring him back to us?"

Mouse's words cut Morigan deeply. She was a Daughter of Fate, a witch, and a miracle worker, and yet there was no magik she could summon to prevent Thackery's passing. Silently and for days, she'd bickered with Caenith over the old man's flickering health. The Wolf's philosophical stance about Thackery's mortality had become her first real annoyance with her bloodmate. *Seasons pass; leaves fall*, he'd conveyed to her. *Bones are ground into the dirt upon which we tread. Inevitably, all but those outside of time must return to nourish the earth. You must accept this, my Fawn. You must make peace with knowing that most of what you love is fleeting in this world, and you must stand aside and let it die.*

Morigan did not want to stand aside and let Thackery drift off like a brittle leaf down a stream. As someone who was likely ageless, she would have to accept she would witness the deaths of those she loved—but not

Thackery. No matter how she tried to imagine the world without him, she simply couldn't, and Mouse's pleas made her own struggle only more difficult.

"If I could slow this by any magik I had, I would," said Morigan, and her shoulders drooped. "Macha's soul was so very tired, yet her body was still young and full of life. I merely convinced her to stay in this world in flesh that would still have her. Thackery...his body does not want him anymore. It wants to return to the earth. It wants to die."

Mouse took the news poorly and threw down Morigan's hand. She glared off into the gurgling, black swamp.

"I wasn't finished," continued Morigan, and Mouse turned back to the seer. "I might not have the power or knowledge to fix him. I cannot cure a man of his age. Think, though, of where we are headed. Of the women who have miracles and magiks older than our Immortal Kings. If there is youth to be found, it would be from those who have cheated death. If we hurry, he might live long enough to see what they can do."

"How much time does he have?" asked Mouse. She knew Morigan had a sense of the sands of life.

Morigan glanced at her oldest friend. Thackery's deathly complexion made him glow in the dark. As Morigan reached out to touch him, she expected her hand to pass right through him. It came to his warm brow instead. *Good.* He would still be with them at least for a few days. It would be a week at best before he was cold and ready for the earth to consume him.

"I'd say a week—if we're lucky," she said.

"Plenty of time," declared Mouse optimistically.

While Morigan was not really convinced, there was a chance the ancient hags could save Thackery. Even just speaking of Thackery's death removed some of the dread surrounding it.

Chatter and even laughter lapped at the Wolf's heart as he came back to the camp. Even odder, Mouse applauded the night's catch instead of making faces at what she was forced to eat. After their meal, the ladies fell asleep next to Thackery. They held on to the old man tightly. Caenith and the dead man stayed up and watched the shadows.

A sourness that wasn't swamp bothered the Wolf. It was the Jabberwok's odor. The scent was faint and mingled with sweat and the barest hint of burning—a smell he could almost recognize. There was also the sound that was distant and only for his ears—a clatter of metal and shuffling feet.

## II

"What a queer place. I don't like it," said Mouse.

The company shared her unease. Some sands ago, the drudgery of swamp and the veil of flies and fog had pulled away, and finally they were aglow in sunshine. From that point onward, the ground hardened. The trees were still massive but no longer potted in a quagmire of bracken. Instead, they spread out on a green carpet. There wasn't an obstacle to be seen about the new forest, unless one considered a fluffy bush of wildflowers or an inviting seat of peat-cushioned stones an impediment. *Come. Lay down your tired head. Kick the boots off your weary feet,* the trees seemed to whisper in a clean, honeyed wind that caressed the leaves and appeased the senses. The wind whispered of safety and peace. Even Thackery was lured awake and weakly asked to be released from the Wolf so he might amble.

"No," said the Wolf.

The deceptiveness of this calm was readily apparent to him. It was too quiet. Not a birdcall or butterfly flutter could be detected. Only the grave had such stillness. Morigan sensed it as well. It was a false calm, as though she stood dumb and helpless in an empty room while creatures clawed and whispered on the other side of the walls.

"There is something wicked here," she warned.

Turning around wasn't an option—particularly with the pursuers Caenith had yet to tell his pack about. If he strained an ear, he could hear the people splashing in the muck and cursing. Looking left and right, he knew this section of woods ran on for a span or more. Again, this unfamiliar region of the land must have sprung up after his departure. It was another angry expression of Alabion's resentment for its children.

"I'd rather not go through the swamp again," said Mouse.

"I feel the same," agreed the Wolf. "We shall push on, but there will be no rest until we are through this weald." With his mouth hanging open, he huffed the air. He tasted the grit and freshness of pure, flowing water to the east. "Ban Beag. Small Lake. It feeds off the White Lake, and it should lie beyond this woodland. At least Ban Beag is untainted, as I remember, and still spiced with life. We should make it by—"

Morigan suddenly turned, ran, and chased some invisible thing through the trees. The Wolf was startled and shouted to her. When Morigan did not respond to the Wolf's calls, he tried in his mind, and once again received no answer. Then he was swiftly after her. Thackery mumbled about being bounced around so much, though did not quite wake. In a few bounds, the Wolf caught Morigan and roused her from her vision with a shake.

"My mother," Morigan gasped.

The word felt unsuited to Mifanwae now. It was Mifanwae she had seen—dressed in a blue kirtle with a baby trussed to her back. She was running backward—fleeing in reverse. Morigan caught her breath. "That woman. She ran through this stretch of Alabion. This is where she dropped the amulet Mouse found."

Morigan's pulse was still frantic. A shadow of cold sweat ran down her back. Vortigern and Mouse approached now, but as she turned to face them, her eyes were drawn instead to the forest behind them. What deep shadows the woods suddenly sheltered. Its trees were tall monoliths against the sunlight, which seemed paler than a moment ago. Could sunlight be gray? What odd characteristics she envisioned in the trees. She saw long oval lines with black dimples reminiscent of sunken faces and humongous boughs like webbed wings flapping rather than swaying in the wind. Although she was no tracker, she felt as if she should be able to tell from where she'd come. However, unless they'd come straight through a line of hedges, their passage had been grown over in specks. Was her fear deceiving her? She waved the company in close.

"My Wolf," she whispered, "are you seeing this too?"

From his wrinkled nose and bared teeth, she assumed he was. Caenith sensed the woods were moving in ways he could not quite see. A blink and the trees seemed tighter together and more looming. They oozed menace. Another moment lost in the blink of his eyes, and stones appeared next to him that hadn't been there a speck past.

*A weeping sky. A sea of trees that eats. What foolish hands and little feet.* The rhyme from Morigan's childhood storybook was maliciously whispered in her ear. The company pressed in on itself and gripped one another.

"Father...you...you're crushing my arm," stammered Mouse.

The dead man was perplexed. He held lightly his daughter's hand. Horror dawned on the companions. First they looked to Mouse and then to the pulsing, leechlike tuber that had slithered about her forearm. They all screamed or shouted at once. At that moment, a second prehensile root wriggled out from under the nearby rocks and was upon Mouse's foot. Faster even than the Wolf, Vortigern acted. He ripped the feeler from his daughter's arm and then tore the rest of it out of the ground. In the process, the rock flipped over and revealed a nest of coiled roots hissing like rattlesnakes. The dead man pulled his daughter away from the viperous pit. More of the hungry antennae spilled out and spread fast. The land made a vomiting heave as though a million more carnivorous things milled beneath.

"Go!" howled the Wolf, and he tossed his bloodmate over his shoulder and raced ahead with Thackery, still asleep to their danger, held tightly in his other arm.

The Wolf heard Mouse yelp as her father snatched her up too. Wherever the Wolf looked, the landscape shuddered. What faint guise it had worn over its evil was melting away or tired of concealing itself. Suddenly, the woods were keening. The wails were hungry noises for meat and blood and sounds trees should not make. The trees themselves were recast in horror. They were stretched and rubbery, and they always appeared impossibly fast in his path. He scraped his flesh on their thorny bark, and when he did, the trees drank in his blood and sickened him with their orgasmic squeals.

As for Morigan, she saw past the horror and into the truth of these woods. Eyes beamed like silver spotlights, bees went off like firecrackers in her head, and she reeled in revelations. For the whole world churned beneath the forest's thin green skin. One heavy step by Caenith, and he would fall right through into a gnawing abyss. She imagined the trees had faces, but they had more than that. They had souls—the spirits of animals and men whose bodies had been dragged into the soil and crushed to pulp. Their guts and essences had leaked out like fertilizer for this evil garden. *Caedentriae,* the bees whispered—although she was too lost in this Long Nightmare to care about their wisdom. Through the riot of screaming trees and the wailing and barking of the damned, one truth shone brightly for her. She swam toward it and clung to the raft of memory.

*Morigan is thrust into the vision so forcefully she needs a moment to find herself and realize the pale skin she inhabits is the King of Eod. He rasps weakly, and a strong woman holds him. Morigan consumes the king's past in an instant—his long, terrible hunt through these woods, his denial of his brother, and his fight to be a man. She sees how he has bled himself for magik— as Thackery did—in a land that otherwise denies his Will. He has lost much blood, and that is why he is so feeble. A mighty immortal with no more essence to squeeze from himself is now as helpless as a lamb.*

*The lamb lies in good, strong, wise hands. The eldest has found him. She who walks the wilds: Eean.*

*"Be still and quiet, little prince," says the Sister. "You have struggled enough. You will have your reward."*

*Morigan drifts out of the king's body, creeps up on the old witch's shoulder, and peers into her green glassy eyes.*

*"For everything, a price," warns Eean. "Love carries the steepest cost, and for the love you seek, it is an unfathomable cost. Your desire to be a man will break so many precious things, little prince. Magik cannot make love, but it can take it."*

*Like the child he is, he is selfish and blind to consequences. The king murmurs his agreement and then falls into the welcoming dark. He won't even remember this promise come daylight.*

*Love can be taken? Morigan wonders. From what? From whom? While the bargain and its penalties are not clear, she knows they are profound. She can see how such Blood Promises—forged from the wounded king's crimson droplets—have stained the land. For within these woods, with its frolicsome animals hiding in grass and its bushes of wildflowers and its long-faced trees, are the depraved counterparts of another wood in another age. Once the king's affirmation is made, this place will fester as a sore of that memory. Animal will feast on other animal, bird on nestling, and mother on cub until blood nourishes the land. When life is here no more, the trees themselves will come alive with this need to take, take, take what was stolen—love. This peaceful forest will become a blight on the land.*

*Elissandra is no madwoman, Morigan realizes. She knows the king took more than he had any right to.*

A glorious slap shattered Morigan's Dream. It was not the first, and it came from Caenith. He was immediately sorry but grateful something had finally worked. Morigan woke and leaped from the ground where she'd lain. She needed many breaths and calming words from the Wolf to know they were safe and in a new region of Alabion. Dark pines, open air, and a starry night surrounded her, and she heard the delight of laughter coming from nearby. As she turned, she saw a glimmering lake born from a bosom of rocks and penned-in trees. Not too far into the water, she noticed Mouse splashing and exclaiming over the joys of cleanliness as a guardian shadow watched nearby—Vortigern. Thackery snored at her feet. They had all survived. She sighed and looked back to her companions at the lake.

"Ban Beag. That must be the Small Lake. How did we get here?" she asked and leaned against the Wolf.

"I ran," muttered the Wolf, and he enveloped her in his strength. "We ran though the maw of Death. I still do not know what we ran from, however. That experience is another mystery in this place that should be so recognizable to me."

"No mystery. Only a nightmare," she said.

Morigan relaxed a little before telling him anything more. She suppressed the Wolf's inquisitiveness with a kiss and stopped him when he became greedy. Afterward, they brought their slumbering friend to the shore of Ban Beag, and they made him a comfortable bed of pine needles and ferns. Then the pair hopped into the water with an unabashedly naked Mouse. What a pleasure it was to have water on their skin again. While naked together, the keen Wolf did not fail to catch sight of the scars on Mouse's abdomen. He made no mention of them, though. They rinsed the travel grime out of their clothes, dressed in damp garments, and went to dry by a quickly stoked fire. The company relaxed to Small Lake's peaceful cricket-flutes. No one besides Morigan noticed the Wolf was gone until he returned with a dead, red thing. They were soon eating, and they woke Thackery for a handful of water, which he had no interest in. However, they forced him to drink. As the flames dimmed, they traded light stories around the fire and sang along to a few rusty tunes. Morigan hated to ruin the evening's agreeableness, so she saved her grim story until the heads around the fire were heavy. Only then did she talk of her dark vision in which the king and eldest of the Sisters Three had made a promise in blood. Only then did she explain how that covenant had warped the land.

The strong folk responded mostly with grunts. No one was truly aghast at the tale. It was not blood curses but Thackery's raspy breathing that kept them up through the night. Each gasp came between longer and longer pauses. Those who managed a hint of sleep woke early and without Caenith's prompting. Before the sun rose, the four were hiking into the steps of stone and pine beyond Ban Beag.

## III

The Broker sniffed the path ahead.

*Abomination*, Talwyn thought. He found everything about the creature disgusting—his hunch, the way he clenched his bony fingers as though receiving pleasure, and the scratch that was his voice. At least the creature had salvaged pants and boots from the people he'd slaughtered, though the clothes did nothing to make him seem mortal. It was like dressing up a wildcat. Talwyn conceded that the one and only saving grace of traveling with a monster was that it knew how to avoid other monsters. In short order, the freak assumed command, and with his tracking skills, not another soldier was lost for a while—except for one who disagreed with their new leader and was speedily dragged into the bushes to die an unimaginable, screaming death. That became the last objection any of Augustus's troops raised. For the moment, though, the madman had curbed his cannibalism and was making do with standard animal meat. Talwyn figured that could change with the flip of a coin, so he kept quiet and was a good little page. Being quiet was best. His botanical knowledge, the sole reason for his presence, seemed to be of no use. Amazingly, the monster knew each and every plant in this tremendous ecology and even where the vipers and flesh-eating swarms gathered. He waltzed the soldiers through the most dreadful swamp Talwyn prayed he would ever see, and he did so with a ghastly grin that reminded Talwyn of the snapping lizards that swam about them in the mud. Truly, not claw, tooth, or tangle of the woods bothered Augustus's troop for days. This was why the madman's pause was of concern. Here he'd stood for many sands now. He was sniffing, eating bits of dirt, and harking to ghostly sounds but not approaching the strange weald ahead that beckoned with twilit serenity. Talwyn and the rest of the shuffling warriors were getting anxious.

The Broker pointed into the trees. "The Wolf went that way."

"Then that is where our path lies," boomed Augustus. "Onward!"

"Hear that?" The Broker clicked his metal teeth. "No cheep-a-cheeps. No owls. Just death and despair."

Blunderingly, the advancing company of soldiers clattered to a halt and drew their weapons. Men bumped Talwyn to his knees.

"Oh. I never said to stop," the Broker said. He grinned as he jogged off into the gloom. "Clever Wolf thought he would lose us. We'll take too long if we go any other way. Stretch your legs like little doelings. Run as if the land has teeth, because I think it does. If you're lucky and fast, I'll see you on the other side!"

That was all the fair warning the company was given, and from Talwyn's lower vantage point, he watched a vine become a fatty, throbbing coil that slipped out of the grass and entwined a man's leg. He understood the danger. Then he was up, panting, and pumping his shrieking flesh through the absolute mania that suddenly enveloped the troop. The land was wailing. Unholy shapes writhed within trees as lightly glimpsed as insects within amber. Talwyn produced a blade and slashed at dark feelers that burst from nowhere. He was obliged to the madman, who moved as quickly as the blood pounding in his veins but slowly enough to be seen. Talwyn followed that laughing shadow. He felt as mad as the creature but knew it would be his salvation.

# VI

# THE FORGOTTEN

I

A pining wind joined the companions as they climbed the stone foothills surrounding Small Lake. The sun was out, but they felt no warmth. Mostly, the thick, mesmerizing shadows of the grand, tottering pines consumed them. The trees danced to this place's somber music. Mouse and her father hiked together a few paces behind their companions and appeared quite contained and content in their solitude. Morigan sensed their pleasure in each other's company in a more sensual way. It was like the delightful, creamy scent of freshly baked bread that filled her nose and set her stomach grumbling. Her Wolf's blood was changing her a little more each day. She pondered whether her temperance in turn affected her bloodmate. It didn't seem so, for he seemed agitated and grumpy. His mood felt like a slow-burning anger, as if he dwelt on ancient pain. Inside her, his beast howled and whimpered, and it was as sad as the sound of the wind. When they later reached a shelf of rock that offered a clear vista of lake, woods, and sky, he paused to speak to her in his mind.

*During a cold winter long ago, that lake is where the white wolf caught me...a lord of Fang and Claw. That is where I met Aghna*, said the Wolf.

*You loved her*, replied Morigan. *There is no shame in feeling sad.*

The Wolf took a long sigh. *I did love her with as much of myself as I could. However, I did not know the depths of commitment and passion until I met you. I did not know what it was like to need someone as vitally as breath or water. Aghna will always have a place with me as a stepping-stone to where I am now. I only wish...I wish she had not ended herself as she did. It was a shameful end and not worthy of her spirit.*

*She chose death, and we must respect that,* said Morigan.

Morigan felt a sudden tingle she couldn't explain. It didn't, though, seem a forewarning of danger. Thackery coughed, and she dismissed the premonition. At any other time, Caenith's gentle rocking of the old man in his arms would have been heartwarming. Alas, Thackery's lungs sounded clotted and wet, and a physician was unnecessary to declare the man as nearly dead. Thackery would likely not make it past Pining Row, let alone the Pitch Dark. Mouse hurried to her great-uncle's side. The coughing spell ended, and the old man drifted off.

"He needs rest, food, and a proper bed," stated Mouse matter-of-factly. "I don't see any other way for us to go on. I know you're concerned about the politics and intents of whatever tribes live here—if indeed there are folk here who haven't been eaten in the years you've been away, Caenith. None of that matters, though. We need to get to civilization—or whatever passes for it in these parts."

Darkening like a storm cloud, the Wolf gazed away from Mouse. Since the clawed ruins they'd discovered, he'd been dreading this inevitability—returning to his people to face the shame of his leaving. At least he would not do so alone. Morigan's love—her star in his chest, his second heartbeat, and even the gentle warmth expressed in the touch of her hand—gave him courage. She could read his soul and knew his every guilt, fear, and weakness. Together they would stand through his agonizing homecoming. After a great pause, the Wolf found his voice. "You might not see it, my friends, but there is a network of rivers that lead from Small Lake up into the foothills over yonder. If we follow those rivers higher into the rocks, we shall come to the Weeping Falls at the edge of the White Lake. In Alabion, there is no place richer with life. There the game is fat and eager to die. It practically falls into one's ready mouth. The lake's water is still sweet as honey, I'm sure. Above the Weeping Falls are the lands where my tribe once made its home—and where it might still."

As he spoke, his companions let their gazes wander over the basin. East of the cobalt ripple of Small Lake, the trees clustered tight as weeds. That deep darkness was a bit threatening. In that green-and-black tangle, they could spot dashes of gray—great steps like the ones they had hiked so far. These, though, ascended much higher into the slope of a valley. Atop that valley were a painter's dot of blue and a squiggle of shimmering light: a waterfall. Reaching that faraway point seemed a task suited for many days of travel. However, they had only one day if they wished to save their friend, and they would do their damnedest to meet that goal.

## II

Hard and fast they hiked. An impatient pause to empty their bladders became the biggest respite they gave themselves. No one spoke unless it was to ask how much farther to the falls. As friends, they shared a mission and a single focus: to forfend Death from taking their companion. The old man sensed the imminence of his passing. As he jostled along in the Wolf's arms, he made alert and delirious observations—commentary on the pines' majesty, the crunch of stone under their feet, and the whiff of spice and soil. In other moments, he waved to the deer, birds, and other creatures. Such senseless interaction was the mind's last glimmer of appreciation for life. Hourglasses later the company had climbed and descended the rolling hills around Small Lake and entered the thicker folds of woodland to the east.

The sun strained to reach them there, and they thought fleetingly of the claustrophobic regions braved before. Nevertheless, Caenith had yet to be wrong about his country, and the wildlife stayed plentiful and friendly, even sometimes dashing close—though not foolishly so—to the great hunter. On a hillock in the middle of nowhere, the trees fell away, and they came to a hidden rose garden. The place was heady with blackberry aromas, swarmed with golden butterflies, and caressed by twirling, flower-petal breezes. These petals were as soft on the wanderers' cheeks as the textiles of Eod's master spinners. In these moments, the company felt the wonder of Alabion's magik anew. There were reminders that this was no idyllic wilderness, however.

Once they passed a picked-clean, fly-crawling carcass, and often they heard the cries of caught prey.

They followed the streams that poured out of the mossy terrace of the land and used vines or green staircases built from the bedrock to go higher. When the sun chose to peek down at them, it was a challenger in their race. The sphere went from yellow to orange to red, and at each phase they would stop for a moment to look down the great incline they'd scaled and check their progress. After the third assessment, they learned their legs had carried them quite far over and up the rolling emerald tapestry. Ban Beag now appeared as a distant puddle. They hadn't much farther to go, and the rumble of the Weeping Falls urged them on. Darkness soon dropped upon them. The night's white moonlight, though, removed any hindrance. A witch's moon shone that night, and it recast the trails of water they charted into bright silver roads. Finally, the babbling stream they wandered intensified into a foaming channel, to which they gave a wide berth. Another excited stretch of travel later, they arrived at the Weeping Falls.

Alabion dazzled and awed with no care for its audience, and the Weeping Falls were too much to take in all at once. The river opened to a beach of pulverized granite, like the remains of a mountain. Water crashed from a hand of rock on high into a churning, misting maelstrom. Still, mineral spritz and fragrance lured the companions forward over slippery boulders so they might have a better look. Weeping seemed a misnomer for the obstreperous hiss of the falls—"Thundering Falls" or "King's Hammer Falls" would have been more apt. Caenith, even with his familiarity with the sight, was more awestruck than his fellows. The scent of fur, musk, and blood gusted from the heights of the waterfall. He stood quietly with the others on the lichen-and-mollusk-coated slab they'd found and surveyed the spectacle. Some sands later he passed Thackery into Vortigern's care and stripped off his clothes.

"Holy shite!" exclaimed Mouse. "Why are you nude? Are you going for a swim? Because that seems like a terrible idea."

"Not a swim." Caenith growled. "I smell wolves."

He hunched, howled, and shivered with uncanny magik. Mouse hadn't witnessed his transformation before. She'd seen only his huge shadow as it tussled with a monster in the Undercomb. However, she felt she knew well enough what he was. The twisting of bone and meat and the heaving, splitting, and swelling of his musculature into a massive, fanged shape thrice as large as the man it had been was not, however, a display for which any mettle or imagination could have prepared her. Mouse nearly vomited, but she swallowed the rising bile and let out a lunatic's giggle. Vortigern nearly dropped Thackery, who himself tossed a sleepy that-old-trick glance to Caenith as the metamorphosis ran its course. Caenith possessed a maw of daggers, an onion-and-pepper cologne unnervingly reminiscent of his mortal sweat, and rock-chipping claws. Mouse and her father were fine in a speck. They had to be, because the gigantic, huffing wolf was leaping from stone to stone. The Wolf stopped a few stones away, frowned with his cool gray eyes at the stragglers, and gave a bark for them to follow.

"Come on," said Morigan, and she picked up her bloodmate's belongings. "Do not fear him. It is still Caenith. We've seen stranger sights than him."

Morigan went on ahead. Another bone-rattling bark from the Wolf kicked Mouse into motion, and she and her father quickly bumbled forward. While the three cautiously navigated around the falls, the Wolf stayed ahead. He sniffed and tasted the night for information. He hadn't been in his other skin since Menos, and the power and freedom of his body exhilarated him—the wind in his fur, the explosion of fragrances, and the throbbing star of his bloodmate beating in tune with his massive heart. If granted freedom from all rules, he would hump, hunt, and run for season after season. He felt invincible and untouchable by the world. Again he was the lord of Fang and Claw—at last home with his mate and ready to rule. For all his ferocity, however, Morigan, his anchor to mortality, never left his consciousness.

Over the rocks and up the steep, damp thicket next to the Weeping Falls he took them. Come the deep of the night, they finished the climb and faced a calmly flowing channel. It was noisy only on the ledge it poured over. Down the channel, the water welled into what could only be the White Lake. It was grand and shimmering in the moonlight, with a silt beach sparkled in firebugs and the shadowed banks of a delta visible even so far away under the night's radiance. Other lights and threads of smoke lay past the luminous bugs and distant bank—a settlement hidden from much of the company's sight. The Wolf's memory produced a vision of the hidden realm. Thick forests would be there and a mountainous facade with caves therein. Those who lived between animals and men lit the lights the company had seen. These were the changelings. As the night was clean and clear, the Wolf could smell his people's sweat, and his ears prickled with their yelps and movements. The aspect of him that was man suffered a twinge of penitence and longing.

"Such beauty," whispered Morigan.

She crept up to the Wolf. He was frozen and thinking of his old home. She combed his fur and tried to soothe him. In a moment the Wolf padded down the shore. Thackery's mulched-fruit aroma blew in from behind and ruined the Wolf's contemplation, and the challenge to outpace Death was on again. Sand flew under his paws and at his pack's heels, and they raced toward the encouraging lights of civilization. By the time they had come to the channel's end, through tickling pussy willows and clouds of humming firebugs, Morigan was aware they were not alone. Shapes bounded along beside them. She could not see the shapes in the shadows of the forest, but their howls left her in no doubt as to what they were. Caenith barked happily and loudly back to them, and his elation pounded within her like a surf of fire. He was among his kind: the changelings had found him. The change-lings did not come near the company, and Caenith stayed his course on the shore. Soon Morigan caught hints of fur or the gleam of eyes in the shorter stretches of underbrush they passed. The changelings' accompaniment seemed a custom—the way riders would welcome home a king by blaring horns and raising swords aside his cavalry. This procession, though, used barks and howls. Morigan should have been put at ease by this reception, yet her bees stung her with caution. Was this concern over Thackery's life or a greater jeopardy? *One problem at a time*, she decided, and she ran with the speed required of a wolf's bloodmate. She assumed Vortigern would keep up, and Mouse was no slouch either.

Thus the White Lake flew past in starry streaks. Distance fell as dust behind them. Not long after, they were off the shore and weaving around trees, and she could hear the drums and see the fires the Wolf had sensed. Barking carolers heralded their coming, and the pack that escorted them appeared ahead in a wide clearing. Caenith and his company slowed. They were out of breath but not of wonder as they entered the changelings' realm.

The hickory-smoking hearths, the half-howled songs, and the chat-ter of old Ghaedic voices—while foreign to many of the company—were a gluttonous feast for their senses. This was especially true after their mostly solitary wandering. The lean wolves who had escorted them gently nuzzled them forward. The four drifted toward the magnificence and gulped in more and more of the uncanny city. First, there was the staggering monolith of a twist of yews that nearly blotted out the moon from the highest point of a towering dam of rock. Trees and their worming roots were all stripped of their greenness and continued down the small mountain that made the city. How bewildering it seemed, this fusion of nature and artisanship. It was so much like Caenith's weaponcraft. With her wolf-tinged sight, Morigan spotted runes and hieroglyphs carved into every conceivable skin and cranny of tree and stone. In place of tree leaves hung pelts, bones, banners, and other relics of the hunt. The city's many and mighty roots had been hewn up into patterned bridges or archways. None of this woodworking was gruesome to her. Wisely, she sensed this great pruning and carving was an expression of the pacts with nature the changelings honored. It was preservation more than cultivation. Morigan burned with the desire to know the million stories carved into all that wood. The tales were certainly more ancient than anything of the West. A multitude of pearly lights glowed all over the city and allowed her to gaze far and wide as they approached with their escort of wolves. The changelings then walked out of the caves hidden in the rootwork, arose from under bridges, and shuffled down in the well-trod dirt. The folk of the changeling city emerged to meet them.

They wore their savagery with unabashed pride. They dangled necklaces of teeth. Elegant coal inked markings around their eyes. They dressed, though barely, in skirts, kilts, or the occasional set of sandals. Men were bearded and braided or bald and naked. There was no uniformity to them other than their wildness, and most beat their chests and barked at the company. Mouse cringed from the barking and from a bare-breasted woman who was nursing a pup on one tit and a child on the other. Mouse stared with impropriety. A man unfurled from a drooling four-legged hump of fur, and she looked away. No matter where she cast her gaze, though, wolves stirred from the shadows and came to see the strangers. The barks and drums reached a furious crescendo. Mouse wanted it to stop—the heat, sweat, musk, slobbering half-formed faces, and pounding worse than the Weeping Falls.

Mouse and her companions neared a great ramp—as wide as a king's ascent to his throne—that led up into the city of stone and trees. Here they paused for a sand, and the pictographs drawn into the white wood distracted her. They were rather brilliantly drawn scenes of bones, blood, and murder. They depicted wolves eating deer and wolves eating men. She couldn't tell whether the next showed wolves eating or fuking each other. Then a glimmer caught her eye. *Finally something pretty*, she thought. It was one of the torches notched into the ramp. Mentally she started dissecting its crystal globe and the white firebug trapped or coaxed inside. She concentrated and successfully shut out most of the raucous howls, and then she realized the noise had ended. She looked around.

None of the changelings had left. However, the crowd stood silent. She believed that silence was reverence for the great black wolf who rested on his haunches at the head of her pack. *No. That's wrong*, she realized. For only some of the changelings' beady gazes dropped upon Caenith. The rest of the animal-folk looked somewhere near the top of the ramp that her position prevented her from seeing.

"What's going on?" she whispered.

Morigan and the Wolf remained silent. Still Mouse could read expressions as a seer read tea leaves, and if she had to peg Morigan's emotions, she would have said "horrified." Caenith's low grumble communicated the same feelings. What threat they sensed took only a moment to manifest. Clacking down the wooden path came a growling quartet of black changelings wearing their wolfish skins. A larger breed these were with cold marbles of violence for eyes, wagging tongues, and vibrating growls in their gullets. Chains were about the beasts' necks. Mouse would have thought this profane to a changeling, but then she saw they were vassals and willing servants of the woman who leashed them and strode out of the dark. She was nude except for a sash and a pelt of sable fur, which covered one breast and her womanhood. She was blindingly pale to the point of luminance. The ebon scrawling on her flesh and white mane of hair, which was bound in circles and falling braids, made her even more striking. Mouse knew she must be a queen, or whatever the equivalent was in Alabion. She looked away meekly but not before the woman's humiliating gaze caught her briefly and wilted her. She was a mouse to this huntress and devourer, and she should skitter away to find a hole before the changeling queen decided to make her into a snack. Mouse dug her chin into her chest and willed herself small and unseen. With her downturned head, she spotted those with knees kneeling and those with paws placing their snouts on the ground. Every changeling, it seemed, shared Mouse's fear and powerlessness.

She heard the old Ghaedic words the huntress growled in her smoky voice. She shivered as Caenith snarled and then whimpered back to the queen. Finally, Morigan hissed a name, and she understood. Aghna.

### III

Mouse had her first good sleep in months, and it was regrettable she could not luxuriate in the cozy furs piled atop her. Come that first flicker of consciousness, further sleep escaped her. As deep as she buried herself under the furs, she could not put to sleep the preceding night's memories: Caenith's incredible transformation, the race along a moonlit shore to a city crafted from dreams, all those glinting eyes and lights, and Aghna. The last thought ruined any restfulness, and she shook off the nightmare of the changeling queen's fierce, pale countenance as she rose into a cold morning. She rubbed her side and found her bearings in the dim cave they'd been ushered to last night. A lot was clearer now in the gray light. Nearby, Thackery slumbered in the second nest in this chamber. Initially, she had scoffed at the idea of sleeping in shallow holes. Even if pelts lined the dugouts, the whole concept felt foreign and too primitive for her sensibilities. It gave her the impression that she would climb into a grave and be buried—and perhaps then eaten by Aghna during the night. Last night she had been too tired to think of other arrangements, though, and had been dead to the world within moments of her father's helping her into her earthy bed. Now her father hovered at her great-uncle's bedside. He did busywork with a needle and thread while watching over Thackery.

"Here," Vortigern said, and his yellow teeth flashed like a bit of sunshine in the gloom.

He made his way over to her and extended a cloak she recognized as hers. Presumably, that was the reason she was so chilled. Vortigern wrapped the garment about her as he spoke. "These wolf folk are accommodating, if quiet and somewhat worrying to be around. They have wonderful artisans and tools. That needle and thread are like nothing in the West. I swear the needle did twice the work I put in. Anyway, my daughter, I thought your overcoat could use a proper washing and mending, and there we are." Her father's cold hands remained on her shoulders, and he clenched them. "Lenora...your mother, she taught me how. To sew. I only just remembered that not so long ago. It's strange waking up to this new life. Even though we still face death—and I am dead in a sense—I do not fear what is to come."

"I would like to hear about her. Lenora." Vortigern froze, and she felt his hands trembling. "Not now, Father. But one day."

Mouse touched his hand, thanked him for patching her clothes, and turned. They smiled awkwardly at each other.

"How is Thackery?" she asked.

"Better," said Vortigern, and he went back to the old man. He pointed to a tall, lidded pot and matching hammered-copper cup that had been placed upon the ground. "I was given teas with which to nourish him, and they seem to have brought some of his color back. His lungs don't sound as ghastly as before either."

Realistically, no tea—unless it was the Sisters' personal brew—would stop Death's hand when it came knocking. This one, though, did appear to have bought Thackery a few sands of time, and that was something. Mouse felt she should find the rest of her allies, since neither Morigan nor the Wolf was around. There weren't even any other nests for them to sleep in. She began to wonder what had happened to the bloodmates, or if that horrid Aghna had done something to them. She wouldn't put it past the white wolf. After living in Menos, Mouse could spot taint on a person as a ranger saw smoke signals, and Aghna's cloud was black.

"Did Morigan return?" she asked.

"No." Vortigern frowned. "Neither did Caenith. I presume one of the lovers saw to our well-being, since I did not ask for medicine for Thackery— it was simply delivered. Truth be told, I'm rather leery of walking around and asking about much. I don't think the changelings care for my...smell."

"Smell?" Mouse wrinkled her face in confusion. "I think you smell grand. Spicy. A bit like an old bachelor's smoking jacket. I'm not fussed about rustling a few bushes or prickling a few hides to find our friends, either, so I think I shall step out for a moment."

"Be safe," said Vortigern.

"Always."

A line of pictographs warned her of the outside world and distracted her as she lifted back the cave's hide curtains. In the morning gloom, without any candles or light, she had mistaken these carvings as notches and contours in the walls. Yet she could see now that on every surface was rendered a story—exquisite diagrams of wolves, trees, hunting parties, and carved swirls of blood. Something black as coal darkened the renditions, and the imagery ran in lengthy scrolls around the chamber with narratives beneath the pictures written in the changelings' slender, sticklike language. Countless tales and histories circled all the way to the ceiling, where a grand moon, clamped in the jaws of a mighty black wolf, reigned. A group of wild children with wild manes ran past Mouse and barked loudly. This startled her from her reverie. She dropped the curtain and walked out into a surly, clouded morning that bit her with icy teeth, even under her cloak. *Winter is finally on its way,* she thought.

Changelings either in two-legged or four-legged forms wandered about the winding causeway on which she stood. They did not heed her. In daylight they appeared less savage than at nighttime and were certainly quieter overall. Perhaps the lunar energies were less stirring. Every changeling, though, still displayed a paucity of mortal etiquette and mannerisms. Men and women were all as partially dressed as she remembered. There were more flashes of genitalia than at a Menosian peep show. She felt bigoted for even thinking it and meant no prejudice, but they smelled like animals. The musk was quite similar to that of dogs, with a dash of sweat and armpits thrown in. By comparison, Caenith smelled as perfumed as a dandy knight. As no one immediately leaped for her throat, she relaxed, pushed down her xenophobia, and reminded herself that these good people—however much beast was in them—had come to their assistance at a time most dire. She even smiled at an old wolf licking his chops at her, and he thumped his tail as she did. *Happiness or an appetite for my flesh?* She could not say. She didn't wait around to discover an answer and instead set off up the ramp to find her companions.

From behind the patchwork curtains of the many cubbies bored into the limestone wall at her side, she heard flutes, drumbeats, and syncopated voices that bounced between man sounds and dog howls. Unnerved at first, she soon became accustomed to their strange harmonies and even felt soothed by them. These folks' artistry was as ingrained in them as the desire to hunt, chase, and breed. She could see in their tranquil gatherings about the fire pits in certain dens how they swayed, gently bayed, and made music. She witnessed their sensitive genius in the etchings of the white wood balustrade she wandered alongside. She saw still more of their talents in the carefulness of the kneeling artisans along her path. They chiseled and caressed the wood or stone with the patient concentration of a master jeweler—or lover. These people were not any more savage than Caenith. Like her friend, the changelings were beings of two spirits—the savage and the cultured. Thinking of them as lesser beings would be to ignore the ages upon ages of untarnished history and beauty they had forged. Shortly into her travel, while feeling ashamed at her ignorant preconceptions, one of the artisans caught her staring at his work and gestured her over.

The artist was leaner and smoother than the hirsute giants of his kind. He had a trim face, many braids, and narrow, kohl-emboldened hazel eyes. They held a keen interest in her. In his other skin, Mouse imagined he would be a handsome brown wolf, and he wore patchwork pants and slippers stitched with tufts of that color. The artist appeared excited by her appreciation for his carvings in the limestone, and he tried to explain the eerie scene he currently worked on—a black forest with groupings of menacing stones. Mouse sensed a power being portrayed here from the lines and ripples coming off the rectangles. It was likely an ancient power, as with all else the changelings revered. Were those eyes watching her in the picture? She gasped. Blended into the scenery and carefully hidden among trees and rocks were great, lurking shadow beasts. The giant horrors possessed bird and mammal aspects such as wings, fur, claws and hooves. The mason laughed without disdain at her gasping and obvious fright. He stood, came close, tapped the monsters, and repeated *"anbuch."* She could not grasp his meaning. The artist was kind and persistent in educating her. Several times he placed his hand to his heart and then laid it upon the monsters in the wood. Mouse at least understood that perhaps what was shown here was not meant to scare. She then attempted her own communication with the mason and asked again and again where to find the bloodmates. She used their slowly articulated names, little walking figures with her fingers, and whatever other gestures she could devise to express herself. Eventually, the mason comprehended her or had something else in mind. He showed great enthusiasm, grabbed her hand in a stone-powdered fist, and pulled her away. He left his tools abandoned.

They moved up the ramps in the city of tree and stone and passed wonders in a whirl. As a pair, they were subjected to more attention than Mouse traveling alone had been. There were glares, grunts, and bared teeth in a couple of uncomfortable encounters, but her guide growled at the most persistent voyeurs. She sensed his helping her was taboo and planned to thank the man when she figured out how. Now and then, the artisan chatted and smiled at her, and her shrugs and idiotic grins appeared to amuse him. He seemed proud of his culture and eager for her to know it. Presumably, with the city's remoteness, guests were not regularly seen. Mouse had not even heard the place's name yet. She realized her fortune to have found a fellow thrilled by the prospect of strangers and not circumspect like his clan members.

The mason was a marvelous guide, despite her lack of full comprehension of everything he pointed out. He took her to the periphery of a circle of artisans who wove baskets with such ease and grace, it appeared to be magik. Once he picked up a castaway flute from the road, blew the dust from it, and played her a sprightly tune. Later he turned off the ascending road they were upon and into a warren that wound deep into the limestone. Inside, it was incredibly dark, and Mouse almost couldn't see at all. Eventually, they came to a glowing, smoky cavern. She arrived in a kitchen humid with toiling folk and boiling things, and her surroundings were quite indistinct through the haze of this unventilated space. Firebug lights glowed like lanterns on a foggy night, and many bodies bustled around a stone countertop hot with coals underneath. The culinarians were busy with a thousand chores. They hammered carcasses, tossed vegetables into crocks, washed, ran to and fro, filled urns from a natural spring font that flowed from the wall, and gathered fungi and spices from a garden next to that. The fragrance of buttery fats and salty things teased her belly into grumbling, and she noticed her guide staring at her stomach. *He must have brought me here to eat,* she thought. Mouse's host left her near the tunnel that had brought them there, and she listened to the clattering kitchen tunes while she waited.

A group of changelings rudely brushed by her and drove her shoulder into rock. She restrained herself from lashing out and merely muttered curses they wouldn't be able to translate. These new changelings were an unlikable bunch of louts. They immediately shouted to the serfs and slammed their hands on the countertop until their needs were heard and served. Meek and cowering before these people, the workers pleaded for what Mouse assumed was patience. They were quite different, these shriveling scullery folk. She suspected they weren't even wolves from their squirrel-pitched voices. If not wolves, then the workers were another breed of changeling that spoke the ancient tongue and chose—or were forced into—lives of servitude. Her face crinkled as she thought of Menos and its wicked order. Suddenly, she wanted to be elsewhere. As if summoned by her Will, Mouse's guide appeared to grant her desires. He bore offerings of a greasy animal shank and a waterskin. With urgency, a frown, and a strong grip, he pulled her from the kitchen. Mouse understood she shouldn't have witnessed whatever caste struggles had occurred back there. *All is not so well in the changelings' city. Can't say I'm surprised. I need to find the others. Safety is only ever an illusion.*

Soon out again into the gray day, a fairer dreariness than what they had left behind, Mouse sighed in relief. The artisan had a playful demeanor, and to amuse her he often stopped by the largest murals found on roots or wide stretches of limestone and animatedly recited his people's tales. She understood very little, and while this was clear to both, it never dampened his fervor.

While she was chewing on the seared, rare meat he'd given her, he shocked her with some strange behavior. He pounced in front of her and gnawed his way up the other end of the bone while it was still in her mouth. She'd seen other changelings wrestling with food in this manner, and she knew etiquette dictated she should growl and fight for the bone. However, she had no intention of doing that and surrendered her meat as soon as the game began. The artisan's pout revealed a momentary hurt, and then he continued on. He ate her meal, since she'd chosen not to fight for it.

Upward they climbed, using bridges and woven ladders to go higher. Mouse's burning legs suggested they'd been at this labor for hourglasses, though timekeeping here was as hopeless as elsewhere in Alabion. Around her, talented artists played hollow pipes that echoed like music in the wind, and wolfish choruses joined. Such harmonies contributed to a humming, numbing calm—a peace one might find in a monastery. Not that she would know much of holy places. Still, she could no more deny that a grand spirituality suffused the changelings and their city. The magik, if not rooted in sorcery or holiness, was simply innate and came from an attunement with the land. Caenith certainly had more than a bit of it. Steadily and at ease, she climbed and climbed. Her consciousness felt distant to the process, as if she were sleepwalking, and her guide's gravelly intonations guided her. It was such a gritty voice for such a slender man, and sometimes she drifted into slightly lewd thoughts when taken to gazing at the tattoo of a twining of holly and rose that appeared as if alive on his sinewy, moving back. On and on he preached. It was as if she wandered one of those fancied, sacred spaces with a blessed man. Perhaps through her continued acquaintance with hieroglyphs and images, she began to weave together a narrative. She was hopeless at deciphering the particulars, but she still figured out that the lordly beasts—the *anbuch*—were creatures of stature like the Kings. This made them either entities or parables of myth. She wondered where Caenith fit in this tapestry of legend as a changeling that did not age or die. *I need to hurry up and find that man and his mystery,* she thought.

Finally, they had crossed the last bridge in sight, and there were no more stories to tell. They ascended a trail chipped into the rock and barren of markings. They were nearly to the city's heights. It was so high the air thinned, and the city was sensed only as a murmur. Shadowy boughs clattered out a soft song above them. Their rattling came from the embellishments of bone and fabric ornaments that hung from the branches. *A little like wind chimes,* thought Mouse, *if one were to put wind chimes in a graveyard.* She hoped the whole forest didn't have those decorations. The sound would drive her mad.

Up here, her host's mood cooled. He stopped on the dusty track and shook his head in refusal. Then he pointed ahead to the path that went on for a while before winding in serpentine curves into the forest of rattling white yews. He spoke Caenith's name. Apparently, he had understood her intent this whole time.

"Well...thank you," she said. "I'm guessing Caenith is up the path." He nodded at the Wolf's name. "It was nice meeting you...uh..."

She realized she had no name for the fellow. It was probably a wasted endeavor, but she felt she should try to introduce herself. She didn't want to get into a long pantomime with the changeling to relay the origins of her nickname. All that was irrelevant anyway. She had a name given her by her mother, and she felt grateful enough to the changeling to share it. She tapped herself. "Fionna."

He mouthed the word and then repeated it. "Fee-ooh-nah." He tapped himself. "Adhamh."

Mouse struggled with rolling the *a*, *d*, and *h* together as eloquently as the mason had done and settled for "Adam." He shrugged, and they laughed quite gaily at their epiphany. Afterward, Mouse was blushing at her silliness. She waved a curt farewell and turned. The changeling—quite as fast as Caenith—suddenly pressed something into her hands. His closeness, heat, and sniffing along the side of her neck did not offend her. The mason was capturing her scent, and she caught a bit of his: stone, sweat, and wood oil. It was nicer than those of the other changelings and none of it unpleasant. In a speck, he stepped away. Rather warm and agitated, Mouse clutched the waterskin he'd given to her and turned back to the path.

"Fionna," she heard him mutter as she hurried away.

IV

Atop the changelings' city, Mouse balked with familiar dread. She had the sense of walking in a place of ancient, unexplainable power. She felt that clenching awe between terror and delight such as when she'd watched Caenith transform. Mystery steeped the grand white grove she wandered—this mystical forest that had flourished out of inhospitable rock. In this holy place, Mouse trod lightly. Perched white hunting birds cawed at her, and pale snakes slithered to a stop to raise their heads at her approach. She was being watched. Silent warnings these messengers conveyed that a horde of eyes, fangs, and beaks guarded this realm. Mouse had no doubt the whole of the land could rise against her or any other intruder. Although it was dark, yew needles fell upon her shoulders and drifted and illumed the forest like a blanket of snow, so it was not impossible for her to see a well-worn path. The trail appeared clear and easy to follow, and she took it. Walking through the woodland, she lost all doubts of Alabion's magik, age, and miracles. She felt certain that some-where in the cauldrons, mystic groves, and sacred fonts of Alabion they would find a few years to steal for Thackery. What else awaited them in the land of myth but wonders and magik? She asked the question of the beady-eyed crea-tures that spied on her. In the cottony silence, tiny paws, the bone whistles humming in trees, and the tinseling of foliage were all the ear could hear. She became tranquil and went wherever the trail decided to wend. She did not worry she would be lost. The woods soon delivered her to their heart. Trees opened in welcome, the path branched out into a clearing, and she came to the greatest yew—this realm's oldest roots. She gasped at the boggling scope of it. It was larger than any tree should be and seemingly as tall as the Crucible in Menos. This, though, was white and ethereal, whereas its twin was black and vile. The musical baubles strung high in the tree filled Mouse with wonder. These were unlike the bone chimes. They were curlicues of silver and glass that she knew would be ornately fashioned in runes and stories if she could she reach one. She was distracted and saw neither the black passages in the knotted tree's body nor her friend standing before them. She also missed the shaggy, bestial wolves that padded around the area. Then one growled at her.

"Come here. They won't harm you," promised Morigan.

The seer stood in a rain of white needles. She must have been motionless for quite a while to have accomplished her full, white camouflage. Mouse rushed to her companion. As they met, Mouse smiled in nervous relief, and she glanced at the circling shadows. Aghna's pets were off their leashes. Mouse wondered where the huntress and Caenith were.

"They are in there." Morigan pointed and indicated the openings in the yew—slits that whistled off to unknown places. "All night I've been waiting for Caenith to return. I am sorry I did not seek you out or send a message—although none of these folk could have spoken on my behalf."

Suddenly, the seer slumped, and Mouse helped her to the ground. They nestled there, and Morigan folded further into her friend. Although Mouse wasn't a good or even proficient consoler, she felt the weary defeat crushing her friend and surmised she'd probably been awake all night. Mouse gave Morigan a few pats and some stilted petting. After a sand of silence, she had had enough. "I shall go see what's what," Mouse declared, and she rose to her feet. In her opinion, life listened best when one kicked it in the child-bearing plums.

Morigan clung at her to stay. "No. I have given Caenith the privacy he is due for whatever he and Aghna must resolve. I've closed myself off to him and have only a small window in my heart through which I can still feel his spirit. I can't...I can't imagine what his mind is doing right now. Surely it's tearing him up to see his old love resurrected. He's in terrible pain, and I won't spoil him with my—"

"Anger?" suggested Mouse, and she felt a trifle angry herself.

"Not really." As if the softly prowling beasts in the area could hear them or were listening, Morigan whispered right into Mouse's ear. "Jealously or infidelity could never break what I have with Caenith. We share a closeness nothing can sunder. I am not angry. I am worried."

"Worried?"

"I can sense things, even when I don't want to." Morigan swallowed a lump. "Aghna is not herself—or perhaps not all she appears. She is slippery to my prying. All changelings seem to be. On some, this protection is armor against my abilities. Caenith was that way once. Now the *Fuilimean*, his trust in me, and my own strength have smashed all such obstacles. Aghna is a cipher, though. I cannot crack or even peek behind her armor. How is it that she lives? How can a woman end her life and then wake and walk again a thousand years later?"

"A woman, even a changeling, cannot," replied Mouse.

"Impossible," agreed Morigan, and she stole a quick hug. "I am so glad you are here, for I felt as if I were going mad. I sense a shadow in or around Aghna. It is as strong as what I have felt in my nightmares of the Kings—though perhaps not as wicked. That is not the end of my intuitions either. Somewhere out of sight, in caves and pens I sense but do not see, there are people whose natures are also slippery. Changelings perhaps, but despair fills these souls."

"Despair?" said Mouse.

Morigan nodded frantically. "Yes. There are people here who are kept against their wills. That is what I feel from the black emotions clouding this city. If I really concentrate, I can just barely hear them. They murmur as if through a stone wall. I feel their sadness but cannot make out their words."

Flexing her mental aptitude as a Thule, Mouse wove Morigan's words with a pattern of suspicion she'd been working on since her wanderings with Adam. She told her friend of the dingy scullery, its miserable workers, and their treatment. "We must remind ourselves, though, that these people are not quite people. They are animals too and surely have unfamiliar customs and laws—rules that might seem uncivilized or immoral. For all we know, vassalage could be no different here than in Menos."

"Yes." Morigan sighed. "You could be right. We shall ask Caenith just to be certain. I feel we have rushed into something blindly. We must keep an eye on Aghna."

"I agree."

For the time being, though, waiting was all they could do, and they submitted to it nervously. While Mouse had offered Morigan platitudes, she believed none of them. Streetwise and intimate with the Iron City's evils and with souls in general, Mouse knew Morigan's glimpse of Aghna, however superficial, was of great merit. Aghna was rotten or befouled in her heart. The changeling queen held the edgy look a Menosian master wore before doing something cruel to a slave. The company had witlessly run into the arms of civilization. Even the charms of her pleasantly scented Adam were all gifts with potential caveats. If they'd indeed entered a trap, they were fantastically outnumbered, spread thin, and separated from their strongest warrior.

While they waited for the Wolf to emerge from the haunting yew, Mouse and Morigan kept hands upon their daggers and traded the waterskin between them. They stayed alert like soldiers on the frontline of battle.

V

Caenith's separation from Morigan after a last, lingering kiss had left his heart an empty chamber. So he and Aghna could have their peace, Morigan had shut him out and erected a wall between them through which only dribbles of her light and feelings leaked. He had sensed her silver eyes watching, though, as he and the white wolf descended into the warren beneath the founding tree of Briongrahd: City of Fangs. Deeper and deeper they wandered to the hollow where Aghna's body had been laid to rest eons past. When they arrived in the tomb, it was untouched but for the torn, dried sheets in which her corpse had been swaddled. The Wolf expected an explanation. Instead, the white wolf had another game in mind.

"Earn your truth, mighty hunter," she teased. She sloughed off her clothes and stood naked before him. "If you catch me, I shall tell you."

"Everything," he demanded.

"If you catch me," she added with a sly malice that gave him pause.

They roared and ripped through their skins and into their second selves. Aghna was as swift as he remembered, and the lithe, white wolf was dashing down a black path while he still stumbled into claws and a four-legged crawl. Time could not diminish her scent, however, and even over the peaty fetor of his surroundings, he could track his far-gone prey around the underground's looping madness. He went upward to the woods where she'd escaped. He emerged snarling and caught a blink of her white hide in the heavy woodland ahead. With the limestone monolith of Briongrahd at his back, he raced into the trees. Time, as mortals knew it, did not exist when the wolf took control. Mainly, he existed in a lusty haze of sensory delights. Thus he drank in the trails of Aghna's smell along with all the wood's pine, musk, and mossy perfumes. He relished the fire in his lungs, the wind through his fur, the saliva on his gums, and especially the faint light of his bloodmate's star, which burned like an ember near his heart. The return to Morigan spurred him on. For her, he would run forever. So he raced all day until the woods were orange with dusk. Aghna was easy to track and careless with her tread. She snapped her way through bushes and even left the bodies of animals for him to find. Somehow she was stronger and quicker than any other creature the Wolf had hunted, and while he knew he would never catch her, he did not stop his pursuit. Aghna eventually tired of the game or finally wanted them to speak, and at last the white wolf lured him to the bank of a frenzied rapid—a stone channel raging with black water that could dash a man into porcelain bits. A plinth of rock with a teetering ledge fell over the rapid and seemed the perfect spot from which to survey the caliginous jungle on the opposite embankment. In three artful leaps, Aghna pranced up the rock face and waited for him at the top. By the time Caenith joined her, she wore her mortal skin, and the red light of a setting sun crowned her in gold and crimson. Although she was the woman he'd lost, his senses—old and inherited from Morigan—told him Aghna was more than she appeared.

"You did not catch me." She smiled.

"No. I did not," replied Caenith.

Aghna sat, and he sat beside her. Moving near to him, she sniffed his neck and chest, and he returned the customary greeting of one changeling to another. A curious scent lay buried under her sweet-sap fragrance—a tinge of rust and a lemony zest of violence. The Wolf did not care for that taste one bit. He drew a line when she took a nip at his neck—a sensual bite he would not reciprocate.

"Of course." Aghna snickered. "You are not mine anymore. You have sworn yourself to another. As have I."

"Who is this other?" The Wolf frowned.

"War," she said.

As she spoke the word, her passion was such he could not separate it from allegory. She spoke of being in love with war as if war was a man. If war was indeed a man, he'd tainted her with his kisses. Aghna stood, walked to the edge of the rock, and peered over the land with cold eyes as though she owned it. This was not the Aghna he'd left sleeping under the white grove but a woman aroused through power and ambition. She had changed, but still he did not fear her.

"War is coming to Geadhain," she continued. "The Black Queen is my quarry. A hunt to end all hunts."

Caenith scrambled to his feet. "What would you know of this?"

"More than you." Aghna sneered.

She reached out to him as he came upon her, and she drifted her fingers through his beard with a suggestion of desire. Then her hand held hard his chin. She was stronger than she should be. "War is all around us," she said. "We can hear it on the wind, taste its poison in our rivers, and feel its tremble in our soil. A war of men. The Iron City's evil. Man does not see the true threats—the Black Star and its queen who will come from above. They miss the treachery that has corrupted Alabion. A thousand years ago, the selfish king of the North took an irreplaceable element from these sacred lands. He took their love. Well, the Sisters stole it for him. No matter. All these injustices will face their trial in my court, and my hammer is one of fire and retribution. We have so little, and even now that is threatened. Iron and technomagik have pushed us to the brink, and even the brink now crumbles. No more, Wolf. I shall have Alabion's magik restored to her. I shall rise to the tide of the Black Queen and push back with a wave of fangs and claws. I shall make the world see Alabion for the glory that resides here. Our kind shall be reborn into legends and terror tales for the slow-walkers of Geadhain. We are not stories that shall fade to insignificance. We are the future."

A crimson aura and a reek of blood fumed from Aghna as she spoke. He could nearly see this red presence inking the air like blood in water. He snapped out of her clutches. Aghna was not the wise, entrancing wolf he'd once wed.

"You would meet war with war?" he said. "Such will end only in destruction."

"I am not the only one who shall bring the fist of judgment to the land." She grinned. It was all teeth and fury. "As old as you are, as much as you have seen, and as much as you think you know, little pup, there are forces older than this rock, the Sisters, or the stars themselves. All are coming home from their pits beyond this world—for a reckoning. Iron queens and middling kings are not what you should fear. The Dreamers and their conflict will cleanse this world as the forest fires reap rotting wealds."

Aghna was speaking lunacy—wars upon wars, the Sisters as enemies, and their own quest to stop the mad king a petty undertaking compared to a cosmic crusade. A reckoning. Caenith needed to understand, and he gripped Aghna and ordered her to confess. Terrible might she showed and slapped him off so fiercely he skidded backward on the stone. He growled, and she laughed. They leaped at each other and sprouted fangs to bite and claws to scrape. They tangled into a tumbleweed of rage, beast, and man. They rolled off the ledge, and noble Caenith stopped his scrapping. He held Aghna while the rocks ripped into his hide. They fell a hundred paces or more. In a rain of dust and grit, he hit hard earth and rolled into bushes and woodland. The impact threw them apart. He would have concerned himself for Aghna's well-being if her tone of ridicule hadn't penetrated his humming ears first.

"What a roar you still have. Your strength will be an asset in my army."

Caenith spit out some twigs and pounced to his haunches. Aghna was posed on a boulder. She crawled on it like a cat and appeared maddeningly unscathed, with only a trickle of blood around her mouth.

"Army? I have no duty to you or this city. You will never own me," spit the Wolf.

"Ignorant Wolf," growled Aghna. "By rights, Briongrahd belongs to its warmother, as there is no warfather to claim it. He cast off his people. He threw away his right. The forests are mine. The path to the Pitch Dark, the sacred heart of Alabion, is opened only to whom I wish. You forfeited any dominion and free passage when you left Alabion, even if you still think yourself a lord here. I demand an offering. A price. My price is the oldest currency. I want blood."

"Blood?" barked Caenith. "Death has left worms in your head. You are mad."

He sprang at Aghna and ended up only snarling on a rock. How was she so agile and strong? What black sorcery had transmogrified her mind and flesh and infused them with dark wisdom and power? He spun and saw her stride away. She leaned seductively on a tree.

"Death has left me strong," she said. "Strength is proven, and yours I know well. Less sharp than I remembered, but all blades can be honed again. I am wiser than to test it. Instead, we shall challenge the wills of those with whom you have made your new pack."

"Challenge?"

"I am no murderer," said Aghna.

He believed nothing she said. Now that she'd ended her ruse, she reeked of sin.

"I am a wolf of honor," she continued. "I could demand the entrails of one or all of your pack as payment for crossing my realm. I could demand even the sweet flesh of the woman—"

"Her name is Morigan, and you will not touch her!" roared the Wolf. With both fists, he pounded the nearby stone, and it exploded into shrapnel and powder.

"I would not," replied Aghna smoothly. "I could. It is my right. However, I would not. She is important, or so some believe. She has a role to play. Whether on her own or under a warmother's thumb is a different matter." Aghna rose and lazily stretched as though bored. "A gauntlet will decide whose fates belong to whom. I issue you a blood challenge. Choose your champion, and I shall choose mine. They will fight claw and tooth to the death. If my champion is triumphant, you and your pack shall be sworn to me. You will march in my war and howl as my warmaster. If your champion wins, I shall gift you passage beyond the River Torn. Either way, the blood debt is paid—from my pack or yours. Do you understand the terms of my offering?"

Caenith's outrage grumbled in his throat. Could he reason with her? No. The wildfire in her eyes would consume any reason. What choice did he have—other than slaying the white wolf here and now?

"Answer, or I shall claim the blood of them all and eat your Morigan while you watch in feliron chains," spit the huntress.

With the second threat on Morigan's life, ire seared away the Wolf's restraint. All the dark forces that slept outside of time itself might have empowered Aghna, but the Wolf knew himself stronger after their little wrestling match. If he could only grab her by the throat and crush her spine...

At the same time, Aghna understood what proficiencies she possessed over her old bloodmate. She'd always been faster in muscle and mind. Therefore, she caught his eye gleam and smelled his sweaty rush of murder. She foresaw his devolution into a half-man with fangs and rending claws. She flew away in a hissing wind specks before he smashed into the tree where she'd been leaning. There sounded a great crack, and then a cloud of leaves erupted as the trunk snapped. The wooden body fell, and the Wolf lost sight of Aghna.

From a distance she called out. "Make your choice, and do not come for me again unless you are sure you can end me." She paused and could be heard breathing excitedly. "If anyone is to end me, I would have it be you, Caenith. For the love we once had, I shall spare your pack until you arrive with your answer. Until then understand they are my prisoners and at my mercy."

She vanished, and the Wolf twisted and groaned into a beast and dashed west. Catching Aghna would prove a fool's quest. He wouldn't even try. He had to warn Morigan. He thrust his snarling Will against her mental barrier as recklessly as he threw his own flesh through the woods. Like a battering ram, his panic crumbled Morigan's resistance, and in specks he was screaming and howling. It was a bit of both, for it was hard to speak as a beast into her head.

Then he could hear her in his mind. She and Mouse were together, and they were running to the others. He bayed in joy. But the celebration turned out to be premature. In another sand, Morigan's dread and shouts staggered him.

*Wolves! They've surrounded us! We can't get—*

Her mind-whispering ended. Caenith hurled himself onward and told himself Aghna would not harm her. He would not entertain for even a speck the idea that the cursed warmother had broken her word.

## VI

The Broker threw his arm out as a line that should not be crossed. Behind him Augustus's bedraggled army—exhausted soldiers with mud-crusted armor and missing helmets, plates, and links—let out a sigh. The roaring Weeping Falls ate the sound. The natural spectacle could be seen in all its misty splendor through the trees.

"No farther," said the Broker. "Stay."

"Yes. We can camp here tonight," agreed Augustus, and he clapped his friend on the back.

While the two monsters whispered to one another, Talwyn and the rest of the soldiers started stamping down the underbrush for their tents. Pouting at the task and seeking distractions, Talwyn often spied on his half brother and the other monster. To Talwyn's dismay, the madman had assumed command in all but title. Augustus rode in the back of the proverbial carriage as a dutiful general to this crusade. Even more unfortunate, Talwyn knew, were the origins of Augustus's loyalty. The night after their escape from the nightmare weald, he'd brought his half brother the evening's game and caught the two men in Augustus's tent. They had been shirtless and touching the scars upon each other. Though he tried not to dwell on the matter, "caught" seemed the wrong word. There was an absence of guilt with their explorations. They had actually glared at him and shamed him as if he had pissed in a sacred chalice. Quite horrified, he'd hurried away, buried his head in his bedroll, and hoped to shut out the sick sighs that came from the adjoining tent. The surviving soldiers and four ironguards who'd escaped the hungry trees all knew of this affair by now, though not even the boldest would speak of it. Personally, Talwyn felt sickened to share any characteristics with his half brother—particularly his preference for beards and muscle over a woman's softness. Perhaps Augustus's tastes were for only the most depraved and debased relations, though, and not bound to a sex, for Talwyn was acquainted with chatter of Augustus's child bride back in Blackforge—all of it disgusting and likely true. Tonight he found the monster-men and their fraternity morbidly fascinating—more so for their whispers. Only Talwyn stood near enough to hear them.

"What are you staring at, fool?" snapped Augustus.

Talwyn leaped. "Nothing. Nothing at all, Master Blackmore."

Burying his nose back into his work, he paid no more attention to the two monsters. There was enough else to ponder. He dreamily played with an overheard word, *Bree-ohn-gradd*, while bumbling tentpoles and fabric into place. His distraction caused him to harm himself more than once. As soon as the camp had been erected, the men had a bitter meal in the gloom. The madman warned against large fires that night. More than he did any of the grisly meat in his mouth, Talwyn chewed on that word from earlier throughout supper. Around a campfire eerily glowing from dying coals, he counted the heads of those left. The number seemed to shrink each day—their new leader had only slowed and not stemmed the attrition of lives. During Talwyn's pursuit of varied academic degrees, he'd studied kept animals before. They were benign experiments on breeding and migration, and yet any time an animal was caged, no matter its species, it suffered from the same fever of desperation commonly announced by a watery, pleading gaze. Each of these men showed the same look. The deeper into Alabion the march went, the slimmer any hope of exit became. They would all die here, and the ones who did not show their despair had merely accepted their ends.

*I shan't die for Augustus*, swore Talwyn.

Why would he? He knew of an escape. Again that word seduced his thoughts—"Briongrahd." That was what the madman had hissed to Talwyn's half brother along with a caution they not pass too near. Any enemies of the madman were surely beings of better characters, and a wise person would take a chance with an uncertain death over its gruesome inevitability. *What's the worst they can be, these Briongrahdians? Cannibals?* He chuckled to himself.

Talwyn waited until the coals chilled to black and the night grew even darker. Only the rush of the falls and the hooting of hoarse owls ruled the senses. Talwyn had the liberty of a solitary bunking arrangement, as the rest of his tent mates were by now dead in the woods. Thus no one was awake to hear him creep outside. Still, he held his breath almost every step and cringed at the slightest crinkle of leaves under his boots. At one point he heard shuddering gasps coming from his half brother's shelter and was for once grateful for Augustus's revolting passion. It would keep him and the madman engaged. The ironguards did not see him. He could spot the blue flames coming off their weapons and thereby avoided them rather easily. In no time at all, the curtain of damp darkness and noisy cover of the Weeping Falls became a cloak in which he gleefully hid. Although he was alone and rushing off into danger, he could not deny his happiness at being free of his half brother. He wasn't a merciless man, so he tipped his hand back to the camp and wished them all quick and bloodless deaths. He had better hopes for himself in Briongrahd.

# VII

# STRANGE BEDFELLOWS

I

When Alastair awoke to the sun-gauzed vision of the Silk Purse's proprietress sitting next to him on the rather comfortable mattress he recalled throwing himself upon, his brain was still quite scrambled from his translocation. He fiddled with the idea he'd miraculously moved through space *and* time and arrived back at a moment before the queen of Eod had defiled Taroch's Rest. Maggie quashed this theory.

"Well now. The mutt found his way back to my bed." She snorted. "I thought you'd be on a ship to Sorsetta by now, after you helped those two villains with their theft. I saw you speaking with them. The man and woman who raided Taroch's Rest are described all over town. Mind telling me why I shouldn't summon the Fingers and have them haul you off for the crimes you've abetted?"

"Crimes?" Alastair muttered.

He groaned, and his head rang with bells of pain. It was difficult to reach into his bag of charms and lies, and he fell back on the pillow without pulling one out.

"You don't even deny it." Maggie grunted.

"I can't. It hurts. A tonic or something. Even a drink will do," he pleaded.

"Incredible! The gall!" she cried, and she strutted about in anger. "The Fingers will sort you out. I want no part of what you're peddling."

Alastair lurched onto an elbow to face her. He appeared as serious as he was pale. "Maggie, I cannot be responsible for your actions—or inactions for that matter. Whatever you choose to do with what I have told you must be your choice and yours alone. Hand me over to the Fingers if it means you make up your mind. Consequences will befall you either way."

"Enough with the threats and mysteries!" Maggie flew to Alastair and grabbed him. "I've had enough intrigue to last a lifetime. I don't need more. I have a life. I have a business. I—"

Alastair laid a finger on her lips. "Might you have a bucket?"

She dashed off and returned with a wastebasket in the nick of time. While he heaved, Maggie slapped away the notion of pitying the fellow who vomited until tears, snot, and crimson retch masked his handsomeness. Afterward, she emptied his sick, fed him some water, got a fresh washcloth to wipe him down, and settled him under the sheets again. For her caregiving, he flashed her a smile of thanks, and she had to bite herself from smiling back. Throughout most of the afternoon, he drifted in and out of a feverish void. When he was finally able to keep himself awake, Maggie questioned him once more. "Are you a shadowbroker, then?" she asked. "A merchant of the black market? I'm still not sure if you can be trusted simply because you know honorable men like Thackery and Caenith. I'd like to know with whom I shared my bed...who is still sharing it."

"I arrange meetings, yes," Alastair said with a sigh. "Not all are illicit."

"Only some?"

"Morality is a complex shade of gray. It can be darker or whiter based on how one perceives it," said Alastair. He pondered grayness and noted the dimming sunlight in the room. He became immediately frantic and tried to sit up. "What time is it Maggie? What day?"

"It's only a day after the morning you left," she replied. "The alarms have all gone out. However, the city is well patrolled if you're worried about escape."

Fortune was a finicky metascience. An unintended encounter. A door left open. A suggestion, casual or austere, that would plant the seed of possibility in another's mind. Who knew whether Maggie had already missed her window to help those struggling against the Black Queen? Alastair's being there was making her choice, the decision not to act, for her. At the moment, he felt trapped between entreating Maggie to move forward and remaining silent and becoming the reason for her abandoning her allies. Charazance would chastise him for influencing her great game. He might still be punished for this interference.

"On your feet," said Maggie suddenly. "I can see you're not ready to talk, but you've surely emptied yourself of enough wine or witchroot and slept enough to walk. And I have quite a ways to go."

"Pardon?" said Alastair.

Maggie threw off his blankets. "I'm not daft enough to leave you here, and you have many, many things to explain or from which you should—I hope—distance yourself."

She tossed his clothing at him. Until now he hadn't noticed she'd undressed him down to his skin. While slipping into his garments, he reached out with his spirit for the Dreamer within himself. He sought Charazance's blessing or disappointment toward this turn in fate and this unexpected choice that included traveling with Maggie. Dreamers were not subtle with their wants. They pummeled their desires into folk. Charazance's voice could break molars or bones. Now, however, she was suspiciously silent. The Dreamer seemed absolutely indifferent to Maggie's actions involving her vessel. Perhaps this twist intrigued the Dreamer. Possibly, it opened a new game of chances in which she could play. Alastair didn't care for the thought of being a piece—and not a scorekeeper—in the Dreamer's game.

"All dressed? Good." Maggie threw back her cloak to tap a dagger at her belt. "I can get us out of town, and if you try anything, I'll stick you. Or I'll scream enough murder the Fingers will take care of it for me."

"I would never hurt you," professed Alastair.

For him, this was distressingly true. Charazance had tied him to this woman. For the first time in his centuries of partnership with the Dreamer, he was at another's mercy. Alastair took a swallow of water for his sandy throat, took a breath to kill the tremor in his hands, and left the room steered by Maggie's hard gaze.

✳ ✳ ✳

## II

Leaving Taroch's Arm proved problematic for Maggie and her traveling companion. The evening streets were thin of traffic and light of rambunctiousness. There were fewer musicians and smoking drunkards and more persons chatting quietly indoors. A loose curfew was in effect. Swarthy Fingers on the streets were enforcing it and encircling suspicious or even ordinarily behaving folk—usually couples. Like a light going on, Maggie knew whom the Fingers sought. The female felon possessed an unmistakable beauty and heedlessness, and her male friend was equally memorable for his size and haunted, battered haleness like a gladiator's ghost. She'd noticed them in her crowded tavern and assumed from their body language, all hunched shoulders and nerves, that they were having an affair—especially after they went upstairs together. She had seen them leave not too long after, though. What had they done upstairs? What great game were they involved in? How high were the stakes? As a resident of Taroch's Arm, where shady deeds were the order of the day, and as the descendant of a master of Menos, Maggie knew a few things about subterfuge and vice. Although she couldn't decipher the mystery in full, Maggie felt that her duty, Thackery's recent quest to rescue his young friend in Menos, and even that couple's acts the other day were all interconnected.

Maggie wasn't an adventurer. To the contrary, she preferred the simplest life. Many workmates teased that she lived like a woman twice her forty years. Maybe so, but she owned a thriving business that practically ran itself and depended on no man for coin, comfort, or support of any other kind. Every so often, she might take in a show at one of the local theaters. She preferred operas or other bombastic performances. They were thrilling glimpses of lives and events she would never see. In the evenings, she indulged in a nightcap of peppermint tea and brandy and read a few passages from whatever novel she was reading that week. Her life was routine, schedule, and order. Some would surely classify her as boring: she would take monotony over excitement any day. Exciting folks tended to live short, unhappy lives. She avoided even the dive into domestic partnerships or pets—and the complications and needs those choices carried. They would offer disruption of her routine. Living in Taroch's Arm was all the thrill she could ever want. She was resentful of the man beside her. He appeared blithe about her escapade. She would say he was almost happy. He didn't try to run, either, which would have given her a reason to do the same. A couple of times he stopped to ask her how she felt. *How do I feel? As if you've shat up my life, you hurricane of a man.* Not once did she answer him.

In their respective states of grumpiness and gaiety, Maggie and Alastair hurried along and tried to find passage across the Feordhan from any of the boats along the pier. Passersby spoke of nothing but the burglary, murders, and grave violations. The story inflated in villainy with every recitation. The actions had caused the city to be locked down on all fronts. Though the warning bells no longer sounded from the tall towers shadowing the dock, the sense of crisis stayed sharply present. Ferries loomed at port as sad as dying giants. Their anchors were dropped, and their decks were bare. At best, a lonely sailor leaned over a balcony and dreamed of when he could once more be on the waves. Other ships were markedly barren too. Their captains and sailors were off drinking in one of the alehouses on the waterfront. Finding an occupied vessel willing to sneak across the Feordhan and possibly induce the Fingers' wrath felt a bit like a blind treasure hunt. Maggie told herself she should have left that morning as intended before the panic had settled into total suppression. If only she hadn't been delayed tending to a drunk, deviant man. Getting out of here would be a challenge.

"The *Red Mary*," she muttered, and her luck surprised her.

She was never lucky; she worked for everything that came to her. Her stare did not deceive her, though. Night couldn't dull the boldly crimson hull as garish as a set of painted lips against the cobalt horizon of water and sky. The *Red Mary* seemed to smile at her. If the *Red Mary* was at harbor, then Jebidiah had not fled south when the ship had returned for him yesterday. She assumed he would be sailing to another continent as soon as the vessel arrived. She remembered running back to her apartment that morn with the bells tolling cries of danger. Jebidiah had grabbed her by the arm. "Too hot!" he'd said. "Too many eyes will be falling on Taroch's Arm. I need out of this fire before it cooks me!"

She had then wished the merchant well.

*And here we are. Fates circling round and round.* Maggie sighed.

Alastair pointed to the ship. "Do you mean that harlot of a thing?"

"The *Red Mary*," she replied. "I know its owner. He might be able to assist us."

Alastair nodded, and his eyes sparkled at the idea of going aboard. Maggie puffed and hurried toward the vessel. Defiant of any curfew, a party of revelers had taken their merriment to the crates beneath the *Red Mary*'s shadow. They lounged, guzzled spirits, and made music with their voices and clapping hands there. These were sea tunes of wind, water, and valor. Maggie recognized a few of the singing, strapping fellows in their prim uniforms. A gentlemanly sailor with a groomed beard, a well-crafted face, and the broadest shoulders of the group recognized Maggie as she approached. "Miss Halm," he said and stood so he could bow.

"Captain Roberts," she replied.

As a sly and seaworthy man, Captain Roberts discerned Maggie was not there for festivities. The captain stepped away from the noisome bunch and took Maggie by an arm. He paid his respects to Alastair too with a tip of his head.

"I would have thought the *Red Mary* would be all the way down the Feordhan by now," said Maggie. She smiled. "Though I am glad it is not."

Captain Roberts returned an uneasy smile. "No. She is not. We did not make it out of the harbor before the Hand closed itself upon us. The waters are patrolled, and while our engines are grand enough that we could surely leave Taroch's Arm without punishment, returning would see that punishment come to pass—especially after all that has occurred here. Heading south on the Feordhan...it's funny you should mention it. It's also a source of grief."

"How so?" asked Alastair. He was suddenly intrigued.

The captain appeared reluctant to reply. "A blockade."

As they talked, they sauntered, and they were shortly next to a metal ramp that extruded from the vessel like a tongue. Captain Roberts elaborated no more on this blockade and led them into the *Red Mary*'s warm, carpeted passages. It seemed to Maggie to have red runners, although the little pink gaslights could have been coloring her observations. Bolted, wheel-handled doors lined the coppery walls. Most portals were sealed, and the trio wandered along passages until they arrived at one that was not. An inviting honey-colored light and string music spilled from the chamber, and they drifted over the threshold into a study replete with comforts—a wrought-steel fireplace beckoning with heat, bookshelves with gold-gilded spines and cartographers' instruments for display, a fatty, buttoned couch that demanded to be sprawled upon, and two teak-and-leather chairs embellished with lion's claws for feet. This pipe-smoking luxury would have suited any Menosian master. Such luxury, though, was for the thin, wispy fellow in a sateen robe who sipped bitters in a crystal tumbler while slouched in one of the room's small thrones. Alastair regarded him, and he seemed as miserable as a Menosian could be amid all this extravagance. As they entered, the man noticed who'd been brought into his presence, and he leaped, squealed, splashed his drink, and clutched at his housecoat. "Maggie!" Master Rotbottom cried.

He was quite inebriated. He slicked back his thinning hair and tried to find some grace. Then he invited Maggie and her friend to settle themselves.

"He's not my friend, Jebidiah," said Maggie.

Alastair ignored her qualifier. "A pleasure to meet you, Master Rotbottom," he said, and he extended his hand.

"Jebidiah, please," replied Rotbottom, and he took Alistair's hand in his own. "And the pleasure is mine. Mister..."

"Alastair."

"No surname?"

"I have yet to be claimed," said Alastair roguishly.

For a time their hands remained gripped, even though the shaking was long over. Jebidiah's blue eyes fluttered, and his cheeks clouded red. Maggie realized Alastair was charming the man. They ended their contact before her patience ran out. Alastair turned and winked at Maggie as he settled into the cushions.

"We've come to ask a favor," said Maggie.

"She has. Not I," Alastair interjected.

"Favor?" replied Jebidiah.

Maggie was irritated with Alastair, and she emphasized her independence in this venture. "*I* need to cross the Feordhan. Urgently."

Jebidiah swilled his liquor and winced. "That's unfortunate, my dear. After everything you have done, I wish I could repay you, but my hands are tied—or anchored, rather." Captain Roberts hovered behind his master and nodded. Jebidiah went on. "My lads and I would be sailing the sunny straits of Eros Del Sol this very moment. I would be anywhere but here. I'm already a wanted man in the East. Now the Summer Islands of Eros are barred beyond reach."

"Pardon?" interrupted Alastair.

Jebidiah began to explain and then waved the responsibility to his officer. He swished over to the decanters on his mantel to refill his glass. Captain Roberts proceeded to weave an unsettling yarn of the *Red Mary*'s misadventures after their last run on Maggie's behalf. Once Thackery and Caenith had been dropped in Blackforge, the captain had taken the vessel south and scouted for a path to the Summer Isles at the heel of the Feordhan, where it widened into the whirling Scarasace Sea. They were determined to make certain the channels were free of Menosian patrols before risking a trip with Rotbottom that could leave him captured and them without a master. Less than a week down the Feordhan, an obstruction in the river halted their progress. Captain Roberts was an eloquent man but fumbled with how to explain the horrific barrier that blocked the Feordhan. "This ramshackle dam of slag and spikes, of gears and slats of scorched metal. I'm sure it came straight from an unholy fire—perhaps the smoldering apertures that glowed all over the monument."

Water still passed through the loch of the damned, though the captain said it was black, vile, and plagued with dead fish. Captain Roberts had spun the *Red Mary* around immediately before the scouts shouted about movement—things with crimson stares and staves of flame—and warned the captain of the crisped hulls and masts of other ruined vessels amid the slag.

Rotbottom was back in his chair. "As you see," he said, "I shan't be going anywhere—at least nowhere I would like to. I can't take my lads into the desert. It'd be a waste of a ship, and sand really gets most everywhere you can imagine. Eod's best days are behind it anyway, I hear, what with the crowes all circling in from Menos and whatever evil Brutus has conjured in the South. I didn't want to believe it. With such scarcity of news, I would not have indulged in the rumor mills if my lads had not seen the dark loch themselves." Rotbottom pulled closed the robe's neck like a lady catching cold. "Word is spreading, though. Truth is leaking out—of terrible, terrible things.

Cannibalism and orgies drenched in blood. The sort of horrors you thought the civilized world would never witness. I've read some seedy romances in my day and seen my share of the flesh shows in Menos too. But it can't all be true. It can't. They say Magnus went to cure this madness in his brother, but where is the Everfair King now?"

Maggie was no stranger to the whispers. Missives and far-speaking stones were abuzz with stories of the King of Eod's absence and tales of the wickedness in Brutus's kingdom. Everyone knew of Menos's movements to one degree or another. Rotbottom read her frown.

"Escape is the smartest thing a person can do," he said. "I suppose I could sail all the way up the Feordhan into the savage winter of the North and possibly loop around to reach Carthac one day." He shivered. "What a terrible chill I get even thinking of it. I come from Sorsetta. Our coldest winter is a balmy spring. I'm not made like those hearty Northerners. I swear some of their mothers are oxen. No matter. I'm doing you a favor by not taking you east. You wouldn't want to be there. It would not be wise for me to dally anywhere within a span of Blackforge either. Recently Moreth—I obviously keep tabs on him—passed through the city of smiths." Rotbottom leaned toward his guests and licked his lips from the sweetness of a morsel of gossip. "They say the Iron Queen herself is due to visit there any day."

Iron queens, mad kings, and a missive she needed to deliver to persons undoubtedly engaged in cloak-and-dagger maneuvers with these powers. Suddenly, Maggie felt flushed from revelations, and they caused her to sink desolately into the furniture. How would she cross the Feordhan now? Why couldn't Alastair go meet these conspirators? A glance at the coy fellow, as wily as a fox, provided no answers. He would not make the decision. He would not commit to any choice beyond his presence. Beneath his passive involvement, she sensed purpose—but one that served only him.

Maggie's suspicions of him were true. He was a fox, but Alastair was a wise, watchful one. Adept at divining moods, he disappeared and reappeared with a tumbler of the brown liquor in which their host had been pickling himself. Maggie took the drink, and a few gulps of its burning, piny heat kneaded her muscles to softness. Alastair continued setting the mood. In a flash, he'd turned off the gramaphant—the hand-cranked machine that warbled static-filled music into the air. He plucked up a lute from somewhere in the room and was suddenly tapping his foot and crooning a song much lovelier than anything recorded. Maggie doubted he was even a bard, regardless of his facility with music. She suspected this talent was just another beguilement pulled from his bag of magik. The charade was pleasant, though, and the liquor was fine and soothing. Soon Maggie and the others were humming along, and each had a drink in hand. Even the abstemious and gentlemanly Captain Roberts had taken off his shirt—at Rotbottom's request and Alastair's provoking—and was dancing around the room like a sensuous ape. Fog clouded Maggie's brain, and she nearly forgot why she'd gone there. Nonetheless, Alastair's valorous songs left a film of importance in her mind—if not for her quest, then for their tales of other journeys long past. As the night and inebriation deepened, the music's solemnity transformed into heavy, epic tribal odes and song-stories of the North. He sang of wild, tusked, and furry monsters and scaly leviathans swimming under ice. He sang songs of the Northmen— their honor, ancient magiks, hunting, and harvesting of the frozen soil. Soon every bleary head was whirling with enthusiasm about the virtues of life won in nothingness or enthralled in imaginings of great lakes and trees sparkling with crystal beauty. Rotbottom and the captain appeared quite taken with the Northmen's passion, and they gathered around the bard to shout, slap chests, stomp feet, and sing so loudly that more of the *Red Mary*'s sailors came and joined in the fervor. At some kingforsaken, fuzzy hourglass, Jebidiah—in his undergarments and with his robe's belt tied about his head in a tribal band—demanded silence from his tribe of howling drunks. He announced they were to raise anchor and carve a new destiny in the North. Maggie thought she was certainly passed out and dreaming, but no. The shockingly sober Captain Roberts rallied his sailors. The crew was told to go full steam and carve through the patrols. "We'll have them in Blackforge before our drink wears off, and piss on Moreth if we see him! To freedom and life! To our new master, Jebidiah of the North!" the captain yelled.

Jebidiah bowed at his coronation, and Maggie felt abruptly sober. This was happening. The men formed a chain, hoisted up Alastair, and carried him from the room. The scrawny new master of the North, Jebidiah, goaded them onward.

They were gone in a speck, and their songs echoed through the metal ship. Maggie hardly had her bearings, and she came to her feet just as the *Red Mary* rumbled and then pitched ahead. It was surely carving through the water as Captain Roberts had declared. She dropped her glass, and it shattered among others the sailors had left behind. Sensibly, the furniture had been bolted to the floor, and she held on to the couch. Her head spun drunkenly as books flapped off the shelves like angry birds. For some sands, she endured the somersaulting ride, and then the vessel stabilized its speed. It hummed against the waves, and she collapsed but was no longer worried about being flung. *Blackforge? Did we break through the patrols? I can't believe this is happening.* Alastair's singing announced him before he appeared in the doorway. He was ruffled from being manhandled and rosy-cheeked with glee. Maggie did not know what to make of him or of the second chanting, huffing lunatic who followed his coattails: Jebidiah. Alastair finished his tune, and Jebidiah gave him a roaring ovation.

"More! More! *Un secondae!*" he cheered.

"I really must rest my voice and this twirling head," Alastair said apologetically. However, there seemed nothing tired about the man.

Maggie assumed mischief powered him as it would a trickster faery of the East. Alastair kicked aside broken glass and debris and made a trail to Maggie. He flung himself beside her and obtrusively laid his head in her lap. She was still too confounded by all this to react. *How did he do it?* she wondered, and she squinted at him as if to force him to reveal what magik he possessed.

"You are a fine man!" cried Jebidiah from the doorway in which he swayed. "As much an inspiration as the muses of Alabion! Only I hear they sometimes eat folk or make flutes out of their bones. I would rather you didn't. Eat me. Or perhaps..." Jebidiah caught himself pondering and was abruptly full of vigor. "I shall not cower but conquer! A whole world awaits the *Red Mary* and her sails. Well...we don't have sails, but 'engines' doesn't have the right oomph. I shall look marvelous in the furs and fashions of the North. I daresay I might take one of those wild dips into the icy currents the lads were talking about! Bear swims? Polar dives? Whatever they're called. I feel young again. Young and free. Thank you for this gift, bard."

"I merely laid out a destiny in song. Any choice of the *Red Mary*'s course is your own," said Alastair.

"Indeed it is!" grunted Rotbottom, and then his face greened. "My own... my own. Um. Excuse me, you two. I have an appointment with my lavatory and then my bed. Good night. Sleep well. We shall wake you before the cock crows. I expect more music for my breakfast."

Alistair waved to the old fellow bumbling down the hallway.

"How did you do it?" whispered Maggie.

He gazed up at Maggie from where he lay. Shadows softened her. To Alastair, she was more a cameo than a person and just as unusual and beautiful. Throughout his many years, he had rarely spent more than an evening with a woman, but there existed an honesty in her delicate lines, slightly sad eyes, and half-frowning pout that made him yearn to treat her with the candor her beauty demanded. He was so used to lying or bending the facts, and he knew she was mindful enough to slap him out of this bliss if he played his version of sincerity. For once he told the truth. "I only gave him a choice. No magik. No tricks. A bit of charm."

"Charm?"

He nodded.

"I can see that," she said and smiled while caught in his strange gaze of blue-green stars.

Perhaps it was the drink and her trust. He almost released the secrets that never left their cages. *I am a man who died many lifetimes ago. I have gambled, laughed, and masqueraded myself through the centuries. I have bedded more women than I could ever count—and a lad here and there, if we're being true. I've filled each ear with kisses and lies. Even the ear of one I once swooned for as much as you...For you, I would speak the truth. One secret for every taste of your lips or kiss on your pale neck.*

Alastair might have mumbled the last bit, for his hands were in her hair and pulling her close.

✳ ✳ ✳

## III

From nearly any vantage point on high—eagle's eye or skycarriage telescope—Fort Havok could not be spotted in the dark woods of Ebon Vale. Only the shrewdest senses would not be distracted by the beauty of the Feordhan crashing in the moonlight and would notice the rise in the forest—an unnatural scalp of bedrock amid all the green. A smart observer might wonder how this landmass had appeared there without any like formations nearby. That observer might then realize that shoreline creeping or any other act of wild nature hadn't crafted it, but that it was instead a creation of man. Indeed, Menosian hands had built this stone shell under which lay the remains of the vast, spiraling mines of Blackforge. As Gloriatrix flew over the landmass in her crowe and leered through the glass, she saw nothing of its previous incarnation. The impeccability of this camouflage did not impress her. It should be flawless, given the crowns and slaves spent. Since this was her first visit to Fort Havok, she likely wouldn't be impressed until she saw the armada within its interior. The sting of her missing son seemed to undermine this future pleasure too. Emotions wrinkled the Iron Queen's face to greater ugliness, and thoughts of construction and conquest washed away into the night.

Gloriatrix's son, Sorren, could not be found. Neither the Watchers nor her personal cadre of spies and assassins had found a clue, a whisper, or even a hair for the felhounds to track. Vapid, useless Elissandra claimed that Sorren had simply vanished and that "things would be as they would be." This was a poor excuse for failure and one for which she would have ordered any other woman strung up. As if these buffoons were not bungling enough, the Broker remained underground and missing. His network of abused, worshipful children appeared to have fallen apart as well. Horseshite, all of it. The grand incompetence exercised in trying to find a single missing boy infuriated her. This was how she thought of Sorren, she realized. To her, he was a child more than a man, and that barb in her chest drove itself deeper. Eod and Thackery were to blame for everything—Gabriel's death and the loss of her children. The City of Wonders and its allies had destroyed her family. So then would she take her tax of vengeance from these foes. They would suffer as she'd suffered.

Gloriatrix was trembling and sneering as the rock shield split down the middle, opened swiftly on technomagikal tracts, and swallowed her descending crowe. Although the night disappeared, she was not without starlight. Gray spheres twinkled in methodical, vertical rows all the way down the metal tunnel through which her craft drifted.

In time the passage expanded, and she noticed an iron-strutted cupola—gothic, ridged in thorns, and shining with more fallow lights. Next she saw the great and bustling bay beneath her. She strained to see the walkways and larger platforms below, but her line of sight constrained her. Scaffolding rolled upward and around the crowe as it slowly lowered itself, and she spotted behind the rigging humongous ebony ships. She corrected herself. Behemoths of their caliber should not be called ships. These vessels with their curved, raven's-beak hulls, bulging, wingless bodies, multitudinous vents that puffed steam, and prickling coats of weaponry were a new species of warship. They pulsed with dark, horrific life and shimmered with thousands of red lights that could be slit gazes. Their metal joints groaned. Engineers had not programmed them. They ran on protocols of their own with subtle, mechanized movements. Indeed, these colossi could not be considered anything other than alive. Smitten by these forces of nature, Gloriatrix stayed rapt to their shapes until they were hidden in smoke. She did not even notice when the crowe landed.

People came knocking at her cabin and then escorted her onto the cold walkway of Fort Havok. Outside, a wind of industrial tang and steely clangor prodded a smile from her lips. She had arrived in the tumult's center at an elevated metal stage that operated as a docking zone for several crowes besides hers. Stairways ran off the platform and onto the shipyard's floor. She saw many open chariots crisscrossing the area below upon tracks filled with ironguards and scholars. Woven amid these causeways were thinner lanes where slave chains of people and the reborn moaned together and lugged wagons. Lamplight, enslavement, and the presence of so much feliron gave Gloriatrix the impression she hadn't left Menos at all. Only the smoky air betrayed the illusion by being unquestionably cleaner and easier to breathe. Through the depressive haze, she once more spied the sleeping leviathans of this place. The three warships she had commissioned were beacons of red light in the gloom.

A design of their scale had never been attempted—not by the brightest or darkest of Menos's minds. The council she'd arranged for their creation wasted years and filthy sums of riches conceptualizing the warships and drafting the first schematic for a prototype. A season after that, they launched the original model of these sky lords, and it crashed ingloriously into the Feordhan. That would have spelled the end of any other woman's ambitions. Not hers, however. Following this failure, she trimmed the fat a little and culled the technomancers she arbitrarily decided to blame. In these sorts of scenarios, it never mattered who or why—only that any punishments were made publicly and with virtuosic brutality. She chose to have the men and women castrated while alive and choked by their entrails until dead. It went without saying that the surviving technomancers who were made to witness this debauchery worked twice as hard afterward. "Give them wings and cannons and wrath enough to blaze like the sun," she had demanded. "Or I shall defile your bodies and strangle you as your incompetence strangles me." After that, breakthroughs were made in staggering succession. Future prototypes became larger and progressively less unstable. More weapons and technomagikal engines were added until Gloriatrix, who was calculating but not a mechanically minded woman, lost sense of the science. Once the designs were finalized and the warships' production could begin in earnest, she decided upon a title for these bringers of doom: the Furies. A legend of Alabion had inspired her. The story told of a trio of witches who did terrible things on behalf of those bitterly wronged people who invoked their names. Her Fury, the one she would ride into the apocalypse, was called *Morgana*—the oldest avenger in the tale.

*Morgana crept into the cottage on footsteps of shadow and awoke the warrior with cold steel to his manhood.*

*"Celaine summoned me. She is the woman whose honor you stole as she bathed in the Weeping Falls. Tonight my sisters and I shall take what is most valued from you. Your seed, your progeny, your life," said the Fury.*

*With her sickle, Morgana sliced the scream from the warrior's throat and then quickly minced the life between his legs. She ate it before him and then passed his meats to the other hands in the room. The three laughed, and then they split the man open with their sickles and tore at the strings inside. When they had finished, they strung him up to the ceiling in a hangman's noose, so all would know their handiwork and his sin.*

Ages ago she'd first thumbed through the legends of the Furies and their inspirational vengeance in one of Elissandra's books while waiting for the tardy seer in her study. It was a story from a children's book of tales—or what passed for appropriateness for children in the East. Now the warship *Morgana* hovered in the clouds ahead. Her shining black coat of cannon feathers was a storm within a storm, and Gloriatrix shivered in admiration of her dream made manifest.

The ironguards led her off the landing zone, down steps, and onto a carriage set into the tracks. Everyone—ironguards, engineers, spectacled and scholarly dressed folk, and even slaves poked alert—saluted the Iron Queen's convoy as it wheeled past. She ignored it all, unless it was performed directly in the line of sight between her and the *Morgana*. Quite regrettably, she would not board the vessel that day. The welders and technomancers were still busy as ticks all over the warship. They sprayed sparks as they sealed the hull and tuned the cannons nestled in the *Morgana*'s feliron feathers. They were still unready to launch the Furies. She knew that, for the more ornately decorated ironguard—the iron lord with his silver-stenciled armor and twin matchlock pistols on his hips—rode next to her in the open chariot and graced her with a report. He also explained that the final payload of truefire had yet to arrive, and the Furies would have little fury without it. She was assured that Moreth had left Blackforge with the necessary minerals that morning, though, and his timing would not interfere with the schedule of events.

"I should hope not," she warned.

No more reports or conversations bothered her from then on, and soon the buzzing animation of the shipyard faded into hollow noise. The chariot veered into a clean metal tunnel of the mine. Steel plating and girders reinforced it. Here shafts intersected with other large shafts, and learned people and soldiers walked aside the dual rails. Tunnels, chariots, flatbed wagons loaded with oil barrels, and filthy slaves all flew past Gloriatrix in a cacophonous gust.

Finally, her carriage came to a stop. She disembarked and was escorted to the drawing room of her sanctum—a room of cold iron walls, dark furniture, ghastly portraits of gaunt masters, and tapestries embroidered with the traditional Menosian heraldry of a black gauntlet crushing a sun in its talons. The tapestry was a welcome relief from Eod's motif of a reaching hand. Here the hand was not afraid to grasp and claim the sun's power. *Neither am I*, she thought and grinned. She admired the heraldry as she went to a sideboard and fixed herself a glass of adder spit. She took her drink to one of the large velvet chairs in the room and choked back her poison for a while before she even noticed the woman sitting in the far corner. She was away from the lights and so still she might have been sleeping. It was her smell Gloriatrix noticed first—a waft of dried roses and nauseating sweetness.

"Who are you?" demanded the Iron Queen.

"Beatrice," answered the pale shadow.

The Iron Queen shrugged her ignorance. She couldn't place the name. The ironguards at the door hadn't filled the woman full of blue pellets, though, so she must not be an enemy.

"Moreth's wife," added Beatrice.

Chances were they'd met at a function, a slave auction, or some other irrelevant event. She seemed a lovely wraith of a woman, though, now Gloriatrix glanced over. She was even whiter than Elissandra and more youthful too. It was an uncanny youth, however, without the tautness and ghoulish cast that repeated fleshcrafting gave to the body—the fishy eyes and clownish mouths. Gloriatrix avoided cosmetic alteration as much as possible because of those particular consequences. She couldn't place an age or even a heritage on the woman, for her ears and eyebrows were high and pointed, her pupils were crystal slits, and her hair was translucent in its paleness.

"You're from the East," said Gloria.

"I...yes. I am." Beatrice nodded.

"You have the icy complexion of their witches," commented Gloriatrix, and she watched the reflections in her liquor. "Are you one of them?"

"No. I am not a witch," replied Beatrice.

*Well, what use are you? We're about to start a war, and the only women who should be here are those with bloodthirst and balls to spare.* Gloriatrix swallowed her thoughts with another sip. "You are quite far from home," she said.

"My home is with Moreth," countered Beatrice. "Wherever he wanders, I follow. He tends to every need a woman should have and many they should not. I feel I am disturbing you, Iron Queen. I can find peace in my chambers and leave you to your thoughts."

Beatrice rose, bowed, and glided to one of the doors leading out of the chamber. Either the adder spit or the woman's seductive rasp intrigued Gloriatrix, and she stopped the woman's exit. "No, no. Do stay." Gloriatrix smiled. "You don't seem such insipid company as one expects from a master's wife."

"You were a master's wife once," said Beatrice.

Gloriatrix blanched. She hated and then admired the woman. "So I was."

With a snap of her fingers, the Iron Queen summoned an ironguard to bring Beatrice's chair closer and to fetch more adder spit for them both. In a sand, they were comfy and quiet. They took small sips and made conversation with their elusive stares more than their tongues. Gloriatrix felt Beatrice was an utter mystery and an unearthed relic. The spider within her, the one that unraveled as well as wove, wanted to pick apart the threads of this woman.

"How did you meet the master of El?" she asked.

"The Forever Stones, far to the north of Eatoth," replied Beatrice with a wistful curl to her mouth.

"I'm not familiar with the place."

"You wouldn't be. Unless you traveled in the East and far from the cradle of what you know."

*East? How far east*, contemplated Gloriatrix. *Into the woods of Alabion, or past those legends and into the chaos beyond?* Past the deepest seas, the rocky steppes, boiling springs, blistering tundra winds, and wild forests all clashed with each other for dominance of the land. It was that impossible axis where all of Geadhain's Long Seasons existed at once. "Pandemonia," Gloriatrix said the word while thinking it.

"Yes," replied Beatrice.

"I didn't know anyone other than the basest savages lived there," snorted Gloriatrix.

"Not savages," replied Lady El. "Persons of deep spirituality and myth. Most travelers never live long enough or delve far enough to find civilization. In Pandemonia, there are great cities wrested from mud, stone, and vine—temples carved in glaciers and ancient crevasses. There is even one city built under a waterfall. What music Eatoth makes—an endless rainstorm on a tin roof. Not as inharmonious as you might think. Quite the opposite."

Tantalized by the woman's poetical waxing, Gloriatrix tipped her glass to her and urged her to continue.

"The sages of Pandemonia call themselves Keepers. That's what it would be in Ghaedic, anyway. They devote themselves to curating their realm as though all is sacred and to be enshrined. They believe all life on our world began in the East. Whatever cosmic seed landed on Geadhain, did so there. At least that is what their ancient wisdom teaches. It's a reason why the realm is so deformed and unwilling to settle into one shape."

"Intriguing," reflected Gloriatrix. However, she was unwilling to entertain the folklore of a land more mythic than Alabion. That was as old as anything needed to be. "Moreth traveled there, then? I did not know him to be such an intrepid man."

"Quite intrepid." Beatrice flushed with admiration for her husband. The emotion rose as a grayness in her cheeks. "He has made better use of his years than most, especially compared to masters who squander their vitality. He sailed down the Feordhan, all the way out to the Scarasace Sea, and across the ocean to reach Pandemonia. He docked there on who knows what shore—for the land is always changing. He braved the ultimate and unknown jungle for his sport."

"Sport?"

"He is a hunter, as are all the men in his family—except for his father, who frowned on the calling. You wouldn't think it, as gentlemanly as Moreth seems. In his soul flashes a sword of valor, though. He is as brave as any. More than the desire to kill drives a true hunter. He wishes to conquer fear, nature, and his own limits. Moreth is master of all these things, and he can dress up and play the part of a man too when it suits him."

Moreth's odd manners and honor suddenly shone with new sense to Gloriatrix. She understood how he could be so elegant and unflinching toward bloodshed without the sadistic infatuation some Menosians had for it. She saw why he allowed people to fight for freedom from the Blood Pits. They usually failed, but there was a chance still. Back in the era of the Charter for Freedom, she recalled how Moreth had been one of the bill's few supporters. *Rather illuminating facts and retrospectives*, thought Gloriatrix. *Although Beatrice still hasn't answered my simple question.*

"How did you meet Moreth?"

"Accidentally," muttered Beatrice. Gloriatrix remained silent and gazed at her expectantly. "I was...caught," said Beatrice.

"Caught?"

*A mark sizzles on her skin. The dark man and the stick of fire he carries left it there. He speaks her tongue with a broken accent, and she snarls at him. Her threat brings another puff of blue fire and a burning in her leg from something like a huge tick that burrows into her. She screams with the fury of the beast a shunned life has made her. She is the monster feared by all the tribes of Pandemonia. She leaps at the man. Even wounded, she is faster and stronger than any lithe, naked grappler. Even wounded, she feels she can kill him. He moves as twistingly as a sandstorm, though, and he has brought the hard end of his fire stick to her face before she can latch onto him.*

Gloriatrix snapped her fingers to break Beatrice's dreaminess. "Finish what you were saying. He caught you doing what?"

"Something I shouldn't have been," replied Beatrice. "There are times instinct drives the choices we make. It's not something we can control."

Gloriatrix sensed a suggestion of the unsaid there—a black serpent of murder that lurked under this exterior of pale loveliness. She thought for a moment the woman would lunge at her. She shook off the fancy.

"Then what?" she pressed.

"He forgave me," replied Beatrice. "He saw what I was and loved me for it. I did not believe such devotion existed in men. I returned with him when he completed his expedition, and we were wed on the anniversary of your coronation. The Crimson Spring. In the spirit of it, he showered me in red roses." She smiled and blushed again.

Gloriatrix grinned too. "I have always believed him to be a strong supporter of my rule. What you have told me, even if it was for the purpose of encouraging that belief, has only reaffirmed it."

"You need not look for machinations in me, my queen." Beatrice clanged glasses with her sitting partner. "I have no interest in politics. It is all quite distasteful to me. I prefer the sweat and blood of my husband's arenas. The essence of life is so visceral and thick in those spaces you could *drink* it."

Beatrice's eyes refracted light strangely. They dazzled like the crystal tumbler in her hand. Though Gloriatrix should have been reserved, she rather enjoyed this ferocity.

"A woman after my own heart," said Gloriatrix. She felt free and indecorous. "Why should men hold all the swords and mete out all the world's bloody justice? Women have more sense. The pride in their heads—and the meat between their legs—do not drive them."

"That meat is why the master of El spared me." Beatrice laughed, and the Iron Queen joined her. "I should not speak of my Moreth so. I do love him, and he is better than most of his species."

"Species?"

"Men."

Again they laughed. It was such unwholesome cackling, the attending ironguards shuffled and sweat. The ladies talked, drank, and spoke of all the foul things that would amuse a dictator and a bloodthirsty woman. A great while later, Beatrice excused herself. She cited a headache. It was a passable excuse, and Gloria didn't challenge it. The woman did seem drawn and struggling with pain. The Iron Queen would have guessed at more than a headache, though.

Gloriatrix indulged in more adder spit, which made its drinkers as venomous as its name, and she barked for reports to be brought to her. She mused for a moment on Sorren, his whereabouts, and his welfare. To her own surprise, she added that affection to her locker of unimportant fancies. She realized she was not lonely. She did not miss her sons and husband, and she was not regretful of any of the dark decisions made to this point. Now she had someone—not a friend but a fellow deviant—with whom to admire the genocide.

IV

Lowelia spent the day in meetings in the Chamber of Echoes pretending to be knowledgeable. Playing a queen, especially one as radical and opinionated as Lila, was no amateur performance. At every turn, her wits were tested. Authoritative, wise replies were expected of her—sometimes every hourglass. Her closeness to the queen had somewhat prepared her. She knew Lila's mannerisms and wit, and she practiced in her quarters or with Leonitis whenever she could. All in all, she'd crafted a convincing enough facsimile. Even in her most confident moments, though, she felt like a fraud. Each day, she grew more nervous and less comfortable with the deception, and she figured she would have to be caught eventually. Surely people could not be so clueless as to think nothing was amiss. These meetings with Eod's council of sages and watchmasters were the most nail-biting bits of theater she could endure. She was used to worrying over chambermaids and menus—not the pervasive, tactical threats over which the Council of Eod convened on what was becoming a daily basis. The real queen had chosen a terrible time to go on an adventure. Every realm in Central Geadhain and beyond was in turmoil.

The night of Lila's departure, Dorvain had irreverently burst into the royal chambers with a gathering of war marshals. After apologizing, he had bombarded Lowelia with reports of vanishing legions and deserted outposts beyond Kor'Keth. At the time, she had been snoring and dreaming of cakes—velvety, butter-chocolate cakes—and for an instant, she had had no clue about her surroundings. This confusion had never entirely left her. It was the cost of living a lie. She was terrified and a woman without an identity. Problems that would test even the real queen challenged her now. Missing legions and settlements. Murmurs of Menosians flocking in from the East. The whispers—so multitudinous they must bear some truth—of the butchery and madness taking place in Brutus's kingdom. What could she do? Should she be making any decisions, let alone decisions of such gravity she could damn thousands of lives? In one of these strategizing sessions, she feared she would simply fall apart and weep out a confession. Too often, she needed to coach herself back from these thoughts. *Get it together, you leaky bucket! It's just like being in class—even if you were never so good with learning. Listen, nod, take notes, and take in what you can. Leonitis can help you sort out the details after.*

Leonitis was a rock in these turbulent seas. She turned to him often. With Leonitis a watchmaster and not truly a royal's guard, he was a boon and a source of military insight to whom she could defer without causing suspicion. He made bearable the unbearable deceit. He was always ready with an "if I may" or "what Her Majesty means" when her tongue was too tangled for a reply, and he was impeccable in his performance. She sensed he wore his new responsibilities much more lightly than he had his old—for they were an escape from his brother's constant derision. As the story went, Leonitis was in absentia and recuperating from a rare, sudden, and violent Southern illness he'd contracted after the battle.

"Quarantined. Not even I can see him. Shites and shakes bad as the Rotbottom fever of old. A river coming out of each end. He is pure misery," said the queen one day, and others noted she had been unusually crass in that instance.

For a time, Leonitis's illness deferred many of the watchmasters' inquiries, and then the brotherly jabs resumed. "He shouldn't be resting. A real man would drag himself from bed! Put a diaper on him like the child he is, and get him to organizing his troops! How like my brother to disappear when bravery is demanded."

Brotherly love this might have been—the tough-as-steel kind. To Lowelia, though, it seemed like bullying. After only a short while, she could hardly stomach Dorvain's rudeness, and she imagined how unbearable a lifetime of such nit-picking would be. Leonitis, as the hammer, engaged in retorts and reminded Dorvain it was the Ninth Legion that had stood with King Magnus in Mor'Khul and his brother himself who had led the survivors to safety.

"A coward's exit," Dorvain had rebutted.

On and on they would distractingly bicker until Queen Lowe or another of the council called for an end to their arguments.

That day, neither Dorvain nor his secret brother engaged in their unfriendly parley. The topics of discussion were too grave. Gathered in the tinkling and dewy shadow of the white yew were the protectors of Eod. Sages and warmasters spread out around a stone table the earthspeakers had raised. Maps, charts, chalices, and mostly uneaten food littered the table. Present were twelve people: three watchmasters, six sages, Queen Lowelia, her hammer, and a thin, middle-aged, bespectacled fellow in gray, proper garb. He expressed his unease by pulling at his necktie or mopping his receding hairline with a handkerchief. Under his lenses, his eyes shifted uncomfortably. Just looking at the fellow made Lowe jittery, and she found his nervousness quite untoward, given his role as Eod's spymaster. Perhaps the news he bore that day accounted for his discomfort.

"The Iron Queen has left Menos," said the spymaster.

"She's taken wing," grumbled Dorvain.

"Which means..." Lowelia began.

She allowed the phrase to hang and hoped another would finish it. She wasn't entirely sure what it meant—only that it was dire. One of her advisers stood and answered. He was an old apple of a man as withered and small in his armor as a child playing dress-up. His name ever eluded her. *Gingin? Rinjin?* she thought. *No. Those sound like circus monkeys.*

"She's rallying then." Whatever-his-name shook his fist. "The Iron Queen has not left the Iron Wall in a century—maybe longer. If she's left Menos, it certainly isn't for sunning on the beaches of the Scarasace. She's ready to make her move."

"Against Eod," muttered Lowelia.

The meeting grew frantic with whispers and gestures. The voices got louder and piled tension and crazed fantasies of a burning Eod on top of Lowe's mountainous worry. A sharp pinch from Leonitis helped her to recall she was queen, and she brought the council to order with a clap. She pointed to the shifty man in gray.

"You there."

"Rasputhane, Your...Your Majesty," he said.

"Rasputhane, do your informants say where the Iron Queen has gone?"

"Not really," he said and shuffled his feet more. "Tracking the Iron Queen's itinerary is often a fruitless pursuit. We were lucky to learn she'd left the Iron City and luckier still to know she was heading west. I do know that no great flight of crowes has crossed the Feordhan. However, a steady migration of Menosian vessels has been observed in recent months—always northwest toward the teeth of Kor'Keth. Unless they are landing in the mountains or the Northlands, it is as if they vanish. From the sky, we have searched the area your sword reported as suspicious but found nothing worthy of alarm. There is a great deal of feliron lingering in that region, and the scrying and traditional technomagiks we rely on for such infiltrations do not work. We have been limited in investigating these regions on foot, as Master Blackmore does not open his lands to such exploration. We now know why.

He openly hangs the banner of Menos in his city. At last his loyalty has been made public."

Lowelia sighed. "Skycarriages are vanishing, and the Iron Queen has left her nest. And no word from Galivad or Rowena." The queen had informed her of these two and their mission and left a far-speaking stone in her possession. She waited and waited for it to grow warm with words. It never did. "We have further vanishings on our peaceful encroachments in the North. Brutus..." She said his name with a shudder. After hearing about the river blockade on the Feordhan and the atrocities Leonitis had suffered, which had yet to be revealed in full to the council, she dared not think too hard about the South. "Magnus, well, he can sort his brother out."

"Pardon?" exclaimed Dorvain.

Lowelia continued. "That is a matter between the Immortals. We should not concern ourselves with their war. We wouldn't tell the stars in the sky how to settle their feuds. We have earthly matters to attend to. As for your post, Dorvain, I would say to hold it—only, though, to Kor'Keth. Pull back your forces, abandon what outposts still stand, and use the mountains themselves as a second great wall for Eod. We cannot bother ourselves with Immortals or mysteries—not when Menos is swooping in."

Though her insight and disregard of the king—her supposed bloodmate—appeared callous, she addressed a warrior's circle. They knew war's mind-set and admired their queen for her ruling. Lowelia tapped into more wisdom than she could have thought.

"Swooping in," her hammer spoke. He axed the air with his hands. "Of course. There is only one way for Menos to strike. They could not cross the desert with any great force—not without much warning or attrition—and even their technomagiks would strain to break Eod's wall. They must drop from the clouds. A fleet of skycarriages. Death from above. That is how they intend to take our city."

Leonitis's deduction froze him, and a throbbing silence followed. People glanced to one another and then started sentences that never finished. Their impotence threw Lowelia into a fit of impatience, and she slapped the stone table. The sobering crack drew everyone's attention.

"Ideas?" she demanded. "Surely a council of watchmasters and wise men have some."

"I shall consult with my fellow sorcerers," declared the frailest among them, whose name remained a conundrum to Lowe. "If we have time, we could build an aegis perhaps. Reroute the magik of Eod's wall into the sky. Options. Many options. All is not lost. However, I must prepare at once. Do excuse me. We have not a single hourglass to spare."

A hasty bow, and he was off while chatting to himself. Lowelia threw a thank-you his way, although it trailed off in the absence of his name.

"Gorijen Cross," whispered Leonitis. "Master of the thunderstrike artillery and one of the mightiest sorcerers in our realm."

*Doesn't look it*, thought Lowelia—although she knew she wasn't much of a queen. Confidently, she rose in her stone chair and gazed at the rapt people around her. So dearly she'd been fussing about the imperfections in her impersonation that she hadn't done much to make it her own and to give a genuine performance. She realized this was the secret to any actor's influence. She was not and would never be Queen Lila. Fair graces and elegance were not gifts Geadhain had chosen to give her. However, she'd inherited prudence, an unbreakable work ethic, the back of a donkey, and hands that could scrub a floor as clean as glass. In war, it wasn't culture that was required, but an arbitrator, an organizer, and a woman who could throw herself in the mud and not complain about her dress. She was all of those things.

In that moment, self-assurance came to her. She decided to treat this scenario like any other messy kitchen with lazy chefs and gaping serfs who needed the good slaps their mothers should have given them. Orders no longer spoken with the queen's refinement came from her fast and furious. "Call on the reserves! Get the forges roaring and cranking out feliron bows! Fortify our parapets along the wall!"

Although she didn't know the ins and outs of what she requested, she didn't have to. These people before her were specialists.

In sands, the watchmasters and advisers were out of their seats, saluting, and tending to their new instructions. Once the table was empty, Lowe smiled her first smile since the queen had left her stranded in this body.

"Well done," said Leonitis.

"I think so too," she replied. "It got so tiring being someone else. I felt I was fading into the illusion, and you have no real strength as a ghost."

Leonitis clapped her shoulder. "You might have just saved us."

Thinking of the severity of her orders sapped her gleeful wind. She was suddenly rather spent. She glanced to her armored sentinel. "A bath and an early bed for this tired queen, and before that a nice bowl of heavy, rich stew from the White Hearth to bring on a dreamless sleep."

"Come, Your Majesty," Leonitis said, and he nodded.

He escorted her back to her chamber. In the course of their walk, weariness stole over her. The verdant braiding on the ceiling with its tiny beads of starlight made it feel like the deepest night, even though there was still another hourglass or two of day. Her exhaustion felt threefold when she reached her sanctuary, and she would have asked Leonitis to bear her to bed if not for the immodesty. She shuffled over to the queen's chair and fell into it. She was in a fluttering state, holding out for her stew, and not quite under the waters of Dream when the knocking came. Presumably, the food was being delivered. She called for Leonitis to receive the servant, but it was just a mumble.

"The queen is...you can't simply..."

A scuffling commotion pulled her awake and bug-eyed. She needed to confirm she was not dreaming—that the gray spymaster did indeed have a knife pressed in the gap under Leonitis's helm. The little man looked red and furious.

"Rasputhane! What are you doing?" she shouted.

"Careful. I'll be twice as loud as you," he hissed. "I'll summon every watchman in the palace if I don't get some answers! Now watch your tone, and don't get up."

"Answers?" She was not easily cowed, and rose. "I demand you unhand him!"

"I told you to sit!"

"I told you to unhand him!"

"Dammit!"

Evidently, Rasputhane had not thought his plan through. With the door slightly open, any passerby might see them. His hand trembled so terribly he might cut Leonitis or simply drop the weapon altogether. Despite being a hostage, Leonitis maintained perfect composure. As if waltzing with the spymaster, the big fellow took steps with his captor, did not reach for the hammer at his back, and stared through his ivory helm with a hypnotic focus. The spymaster sensed the man's deep gaze and turned to it for a speck. That finger-snap of time was what Leonitis needed, and like a beguiling cobra, he lashed out. In a slap and a glitter of steel, the dagger was gone. Next, a plated elbow to the delicate attacker's ribs left Rasputhane wheezing and curled on the floor. Still no mercy came from Leonitis. He dropped on the man like a cape of wrath, pressed on Rasputhane's back with his knees, and twisted the spymaster's arm.

"Scream and I'll break it right off," he warned.

Rasputhane obeyed, though he did make whimpering pleas that he not be killed. Lowelia dashed to the door, shut it, and joined her hammer. Leonitis started questioning the man, bending him a bit more if he didn't approve of his replies.

"Why did you attack us? Are you one of Menos's rats?"

"Menos? I'm no—"

Twist. "Don't lie!"

"Argh! I...I'm not lying! I would think you would know your own kind!" Twist. "Kings! Just snap it off already, you brute!"

"Wait," said Lowelia ere her hammer could act on the suggestion. "He thinks we're spies. We think he's a spy. Which he is—just not the sort either of us is worried about."

After considering her words, Leonitis grunted and came off the man. Immediately, Rasputhane scurried to the bed and clung to one of the posts. Although the spymaster's one arm hung limp, he found a little dignity, pushed his spectacles back into place on his snotty face, and glared at the two.

"If you're not spies or murderers, I'd like to know what you've done with the queen."

Lowelia and Leonitis held on to their silences. They were hopeful, as all naughty children are when caught, that silence would excuse them. How did he know? What did he know?

"It's very good," he continued. "The illusion. A phantasm woven by a master sorcerer. I had to see you a few times to be sure. Many look at me and think I'm a buffoon of a shadow master. I know what they whisper to themselves. A spy without finesse—about as inconspicuous as a drunken jester in a room of glass furniture. I have my own finesse. It's why the king chose me. I might not see you clearly through those disguises, but I know what I'm seeing isn't what I'm seeing."

"How?" gasped Lowelia, and she stuffed her hand over her mouth too late.

"Eastern blood, I figure. I don't know. I'm no witch or sorcerer. I can't read minds, but I can see lies."

Now that Lowelia examined the man, she noticed that his spectacles hid a queer glint of metal in his stare. It was reminiscent of Morigan but more subtle. For a while, she fiddled with telling the truth and cast glances to Leonitis, whose shrugs were not helpful. In the end, the secret was a weight she was so eager to shed that the whole preposterous tale flew from Lowelia in a manner of sands. Once she had finished, she sat on the bed beside Rasputhane.

"Matron Lowelia." He simultaneously chuckled and sighed.

"One and the same," she said. "I'm not away with a sick aunt as the gossips would tell you. I'll be keeping an eye on every one of those gossiping lasses and handing out demerits and praises later. Speaking of service, I called for my supper what feels like an hourglass ago. You just sort out the squiggles in your head, and I'll be right back." She stood and then slapped the man lightly on his cheek. "You're sworn into the secret circle now, but as a spymaster, even a bumbling one, I expect you to be good at keeping what shouldn't be shared."

Rasputhane nodded as she went to check on her meal. She cracked open the door, and she was glad to see at her feet a tray and a bowl billowing salty steam. Down the hall, a serving girl rushed away. She hailed the woman with thanks and glimpsed enough of a reaction to identify the blond girl as Euphenia from the White Hearth. Something about this bothered her, though. It wasn't until she was back inside with her tray and slurping at her meal that it hit her: Euphenia should not have been her server. Only a matron who wrote schedules and demanded military obedience from her women and lads would know that. A queen would never have noticed. When she and Leonitis had broken the afternoon fast earlier, she'd spotted Seritha and Harmony gossiping on their breaks and chatting away. They were on the service roster for this wing of the palace. Why, then, had Euphenia been sent? Had she chosen the duty?

The suspicion curdled the stew to poison. It was not real poison, as the queen's chamber had wards against any and all. However, toxins were assassins' tools. Spies dealt in subterfuge. She wondered what an eager serving wench might have overheard outside the queen's chambers on this of all nights. Where was Euphenia from? She scoured her memory. Riverton? Could it be farther east than that in the Iron City? These past weeks, she'd attuned herself to politics and intrigue, and she thought of every incident and encounter she'd had with the serving girl. She gasped upon remembering Euphenia had poured wine for Sage Thackery and the queen before any of this war or terror had started, and she locked in on the image until the serving girl was hovering with her eyes bulging wide—a nasty, hungry gargoyle of a thing famished for secrets.

Lost inside herself, Lowe had been gripping her spoon and dribbling broth on herself like a dullard. Leonitis went to her. "Are you all right?" he asked.

"I...I think so," she replied. She was trembling. "I think I found a spy." She looked up and appeared terrified. "She might have heard everything I just confessed."

## V

For the second time that day, the real queen would have been unsuitable for the task at hand. Only a matron familiar with the ancient palace and its snaking, hidden hallways—the ones taken for quick travel—could have followed Euphenia. The queen had her own secret passages and nooks within the palace, and Lowe also knew them well. Presuming Euphenia was a spy, she would seek an open space—for only certain areas lay unoppressed by the magiks that saturated Kor'Keth's natural density and added additional protection against sound, battery, and scrying. Nothing aside from one of the king's or queen's far-speaking stones would work within the palace, and Lowelia checked her supply and found every one accounted for. She assumed Magnus had not left his lying around. Thus, Euphenia would need to get to the harborage, training grounds, or gardens. Any place of free air to make a transmission to her masters in Menos. With three possible locations,

Eod's secret defenders split up, and each raced to an objective—praying he or she would be in time to halt Euphenia. If Euphenia was crafty enough to have found another way out, they were doomed. Lowe decided it was best not to think of such things.

Within sands of parting from the others at the queen's chamber, Lowe was well along the dim and earthy-smelling rock intestines of Kor'Keth. She was nearly to the King's Garden. After another five cracks in the darkness, which from the other side looked like crags in the rock face, she would be out of the catacombs and possibly ahead of the spy. She could only hope the others were faring as well. She was a woman used to hustling, but she was hardly in the spring of youth. She panted and ached. Lowe's shame, however, overshadowed all her pains. Euphenia—a little witch, a spy, and a leak. The girl was at least two of these things and had been under her care. Ignorance would not excuse the error if this girl contacted her Iron masters, and Lowe would not forgive herself for any damage already done. The kidnapping of the silver-eyed seer and the bombing in King's Crown. How culpable was Euphenia and, therefore, she herself in these and other acts of mayhem? She would have the girl answer that question, even if it meant flogging her for truth. Eod's inquisitors did not indulge in torture as did the Iron marshals, although they had ways to squeeze and bleed secrets. As she ran, the murderous shadow in her soul—the one that had once taken vengeance on her husband for their child's murder—possessed her.

She emerged from behind a screen of flowers grown around wire and into a grassy park chirping with noise and fluttering with breezes and crimson sunlight. Grand trees of myriad species abounded in an explosion of color, and they swayed their feathered, exotic branches like dancers in silks. So dense was the growth that past the small clearing, she could make out only pieces of the stone arch one would take to reach the gardens. She didn't spot Euphenia nearby. Two lovers, though, babbled and coddled each other, and they wandered down a path hedged in crystal roses. Since she'd stepped from an apparent nowhere, they did not see her, and she startled the pair as she ran to them. She identified the lass as a scullery maid, and one who should be on dinner duty at the moment rather than ambling through the King's Garden with a gangly beau hanging off her arm.

"Patricia, did you see Euphenia walking through here?" she asked furiously.

From whence the queen had suddenly come, how she knew the name of a serving girl who never tended to her, and why she asked for Euphenia were cause for confusion. When the scullery lass failed to respond, the queen slapped her, and she managed to yelp out a reply. Yes. She had seen Euphenia, coincidentally enough. "You just missed her, Your Majesty. She was in quite the hurry. I'm sorry."

Lowelia would have stayed to chastise the lass for missing work, but that was the lesser of the two evils with which she had to contend. Her whole chain of order was decaying and filled with spies and laziness. So many cuffs and demerit slips to be handed out when she returned to her post.

At the other end of the path stretched a wide courtyard of lacy verdure, golden orchids, and honeysuckle scents through which Lowelia tore. Guards stood beside the stone arch leading into the palace interior. They saluted their mad mistress, and when barked at, they pointed to the path where Euphenia had headed. Uncharacteristically for the queen, she picked up her skirts and ran. The soldiers made faces, but that didn't matter. She'd spotted Euphenia's blond head glimmering in the flash before dusk as it bobbed along under a hedgerow. *Caught you, little rat.* Lowelia ripped a long, partly crystalized branch from one of the king's exquisite bushes and then rounded a turn in the rustling maze. From here a road branched out to bloom-filled trails, and ahead it traveled to a brook and a faery-tale bridge made of silver, shimmering gossamer. The bridge hummed as Euphenia trod over it. This gave away her location in the splendor, and Lowelia knew precisely in what shadows to creep to stay unseen. Speedily and low, she slunk in the grasses and ducked behind the hyaline crests randomly scattered before the brook.

If Euphenia noticed an oddness, twist, or reflection in the glass rocks her stalker pressed against when she looked back, it was not enough to alarm her. The girl stopped on the path just over the bridge and fumbled in her pockets for the far-speaking stone. Clearly, she couldn't wait to share her news. She smiled and was bringing the translucent pebble to her mouth when a shadow came up over her shoulder.

Thwack! The first blow cracked the back of Euphenia's skull. Up and away the far-speaking pebble flew. It was never to be recovered among the many round diamonds in the water. Thwack! The second blow broke across the backs of Euphenia's knees. She tumbled, knocked her head on the silver railing, and fouled its beauty with blood. The attack had come too quickly for her to scream, and she managed only a gurgle of wrath as she slumped over.

Once the spy was downed with no sign of rising, Lowelia rolled her onto her back and tapped her face with the stick. She did not wake from peaceful oblivion immediately. It took many taps and finally a boot to the ribs to bring her back. She gasped, groaned, and clutched at the pain in her head and side. At first, the girl showed terror, and then fear begat hatred as realization took hold. *There you are*, thought Lowelia, and she recognized the detestation Menosians expressed for all who did not debase themselves as they did. In the afflicted, the emotion manifested as a sickness—a jaundice with a gleam in the eyes of lust and murder. Quite used to sneaky persons, Lowelia noticed the girl's hand slinking under her skirt, and she stomped on the girl's wrist before Euphenia could brandish the dagger she sought. Euphenia whimpered, and the weapon clattered to Lowe's feet.

"Why did you do it?" asked Lowe. Euphenia didn't reply, so Lowe lashed her cheek with the crystal stick. "Come now. We're past the point of shyness."

"We all must do what our country demands of us," hissed the traitor. "We are soldiers in the wars of our kings and queens, regardless of what we were or would choose to be: mothers, daughters, lovers, servers, spies, or matrons. Why do you lie to the people you are to protect? Should the honor-bound folk of the West not be beyond lies? How dare you look upon me with scorn when you are no better?"

"I am better," replied Lowe.

Euphenia gave a hideous grin. It was malignant and filled with blood. "Ha! You believe your duty is holier than mine? There is your weakness and Eod's folly. Each of you thinks you act in virtue when you simply kneel and yip like happy dogs to your Immortal master's commands. In the City of Iron, we know we are slaves, and we find pride in it. You cannot even see your subjugation. You are more deserving of pity than I."

Lowe drove her boot into the girl again. The red haze was misting over her, and she would not hear this girl's denigrations. When the traitor finished wheezing and coughing, Lowe continued her interrogation. "How many of you are here?" demanded Lowe.

"More rats than you can catch." The spy laughed. "I would be more worried about what I might say to your people than to my allies. What I might say to any ear that will bend my way about a queen who is nothing but a fat old woman filling shoes she has no right to wear. You can't protect this nation. You couldn't even protect your own child. Oh yes. I know about that. You're a failure and a lie—a lie that needs to be exposed. Nothing will stop me. You'll have to cut out my tongue to keep me from talking, and even then I'll write it down in blood and spit."

Euphenia should have stopped herself. Perhaps the beauteous illusion of Lila obscured the expression of the woman behind it. Still, as a spy and an interpreter of body language, Euphenia should have better read Lowe's glower and hunched posture. Being a gossip hound, Euphenia knew of the matron's secret temper and the rage that had deformed her infanticide-committing husband into a castrated cripple. Euphenia slid a razor into these wounds, as she was haughty from her perceived advantage. She believed the secrets she knew, which she had every inclination to spill eventually and strategically to leverage certain freedoms, ensured her value. She laughed too long and miscalculated her significance, though. All the bubbling, scalding rage that boiled under the matron's red skin suddenly erupted.

Lowelia grunted like a bull and released a flurry of fists that left Euphenia gargling blood and teeth. In a speck, Euphenia became so swollen and delirious that her mind did her the mercy of slipping into shock. Only dimly aware was the girl of the glint of the knife—her knife—as it was picked up. She was sedate when Lowe began her cutting. Euphenia felt the wrenching and sawing in her mouth, and she sensed the crunching and tugging at her hands as aspects of a nightmare rather than gruesome reality. However, that last amputation—some part of her hands—came with starbursts of pain that finally swallowed her in darkness.

Lowe remained far more composed than when she'd butchered her husband. She had not wandered outside herself. She stayed in control of her faculties throughout—even while shuddering with an anger that shook her slippery fingers as she carved. At least she had fingers; the same could not be said for Euphenia. Following the dotted splatters, she watched the spy's baby sausages floating in the creek below in a crimson cloud along with the piece of meat that was Euphenia's tongue. *Food for the fishes*, she thought. *No chance she'll be chattering or writing any notes to her friends now. Really, the girl should have known better than to give me ideas.*

Though some aspect of Lowe was aware of her dementedness, she felt no regret. She had protected her queen and country—her *children*—with the same zeal with which she had protected her dear Cecilia. Having crossed that line of dark reason twice now, she knew she would kill again if another of Menos's spies or another enemy were caught. She reflected on how war, anguish, and deception changed folk. They dredged up the darkest beasts in peoples' souls. Her beast was a monster and not as caged as she wanted to believe. As she looked around at the red scene and the mangled woman laid out as crudely as meat on a stone counter, she wondered when her beast would next escape. If it barked loudly enough, would she simply open the cage?

Quite calmly, Lowe looked around to see whether her actions had been noticed, and then she dragged Euphenia by her chewed hands under the bridge. She turned the girl's appallingly concave face, as puckered and red as a ravaged anus, down into the burbling riverbed. Whistling a funeral song, she held Euphenia's head underwater and watched the feeble thrashings of the still-living girl until her body stopped moving and stiffened. It had not been her plan—not that she quite had one—to murder Euphenia. She was up to her elbows in the mess now, though, and it had to be tidied. She planted the dagger inside Euphenia's garments and then rolled her body into the deeper waters. Impatiently, she waited for Euphenia's remains to sway down the channel into greedier currents that would ultimately tumble over the edge of the palace and deposit the body into a sewer-like grave. She prayed the corpse wouldn't beach itself somewhere else in the gardens, but she had no sands to worry over that. She had more mess to clean.

After folding her skirt for thickness and filling it with water, she rushed onto the bridge and doused the site of the murder. Several trips it took to wash the spot—although the threaded-metal construction of the bridge's planks abetted her act, and the redness fell through, leaving almost no residue. At the end, she was leaning against the railing, and birdsongs were in her ear. Her thin skirt was kissed pink as though by design or from dusk's deep hues. It was now nearly dry in the sweet breeze of the King's Gardens. The moment her blood began to slow, she heard chatter.

The two shy and hesitant lovers from before appeared on the path. They conferred before moving toward the bridge. Lowe used their indecision to examine herself and her surroundings hastily for any trace of Euphenia. Despite the carnage, the queen's illusion concealed the abrasions on her throbbing knuckles, and she noted no fingers or other mortal remains trapped in the bridge's silver lattice—except for a flutter of paper. She dipped and extracted it just as the lovers nervously walked by. She nodded at their respects and did not examine what lay crumpled in her hand until they had left.

It was a phantograph. The magikally rendered picture shivered as she bent it into a three-dimensional image seemingly popping off the square. The image was of a slightly younger or happier Euphenia resting in a wiry bed within a darkly painted hospice. She was smiling and holding a babe who looked as wet and exhausted as she did. *It must have been a taxing childbirth,* Lowe thought. That Lowe had left a child motherless drove the first needle of guilt into her chest. Such pain she banished, and she reminded herself of that mother's venom and wickedness—and by association, those of her child. Menosian cruelty was a hereditary illness, and kindness or love could not treat it. Only ruthlessness. She would keep the phantograph as a memento. The talisman would cast out whatever misgivings she might have in the war to come. That day, she'd learned there were few lines she would not cross—few moral rules she would not break to protect Eod. *Let Euphenia's death be another medal with which they can adorn my coat of valor or decorate my prison.*

Rasputhane and Leonitis needed to be told of her crime. Any punishments against her for Euphenia's murder, though, could be postponed until the queen returned and the rest of Eod's spies were brought to justice. She recalled the queen's whisper about this exact duty being done—perhaps not to her letter but in a much redder ink. Right now the city needed its queen; it needed a leader. Between her various trials and misadventures that afternoon, Lowelia soared with the conviction she could provide that leadership to the people.

Lowelia folded the phantograph away, took a long gaze down the creek, and then strode into the gardens. Those who passed her shrank as lesser folk did when meeting a queen. Perhaps, though, they did so more because of the narrowed, calculating gazes she gave, which terrified people for reasons they could not explain.

# VIII

# BLOOD FOR BLOOD

I

A s night deepened the shade of the cave where Morigan and her
company huddled together, they fought against their dread. They
shivered and somehow still managed to sweat. They paced and were restless like those driven mad by fever. They did not tread too close to their
prison's entrance. There the black and collared monsters, who earlier had
snapped Morigan and Mouse up by the scruffs of their cloaks, growled if
anyone neared. The monsters smelled atrocious to Mouse anyhow. She
wondered whether she would ever rid the beasts' stink from her nostrils.
Like the others, she missed the scent of their Wolf—clean, masculine, and
with a hint of wood and iron—and still more his body and spirit's inspirational warmth. For either Aghna had stolen him or he'd surrendered to
the white wolf. Either way, he had not returned to his company. At least
the changelings had taken his sandals and loincloth, which meant he had a
hint of dignity wherever he was.

Morigan could feel her bloodmate trapped in an indefinable prison. His
great raging animal made muted roars. Cast her mind about as she might,
the feliron-threaded stone of Briongrahd hindered her power, and her consciousness bounced around like a sloppily tossed ball. More often she found

herself in minds other than her bloodmate's—those of the blood-hungry wolfish overlords or the enslaved changelings, whose thoughts were as forsaken as her own. She experienced the captives' horror. She saw memories of a barking sea of wolves sweeping into peaceful villages and slumbering nests, rounding up their captives, and tearing out the throats of a hundred men, women, and children. These thoughtless murders were done to establish the penalty for dissension.

In these visions, the wolves often took the second skins of their captives—living or dead—and stitched them into patchwork garments for grisly warrior fashions. In the cruelest instances, the wolves placed feliron chains around prisoners' necks. The prisoners were allowed to keep their skins, but the captors trapped the changelings in their animal shapes and used them as wretched beasts of burden. These changeling slaves, two-legged and four-legged, now toiled inside the feliron mountain. In darkness, they ground their lives away. Their starved souls were granted only a few sands of sunlight before being herded back into the shadows to cook, serve, and churn out warmongering devices—diabolical wolf-headed battering rams, ladders, spiked collars, and metal harnesses wolves would wear into battle. Aghna was preparing for war—not one inside Alabion, where she already exerted supremacy, but with the realms of men.

Between grazing these slaves' memories, Morigan found her Wolf once or twice and managed a few precious words with him. The Wolf cautioned her about "choices" and "champions," and at one point he offered the unbroken warning "Aghna will come for one of you." Immediately, Morigan rose from where she'd been huddling in concentration and told her companions of the threat.

They were gathered about a pulsing firebug globe and trying to eat some of the perfunctorily cooked meat Mouse remembered Adam having given her earlier. Their fluttering stomachs rendered the meal indigestible, and they tossed their dinner to the dirt as Morigan went to join them.

"We've been through worse," said Thackery. He was suddenly awake.

If one boon had come from their misfortune, it was that the rest and herbs had done a great deal to recover Thackery's strength. Morigan no longer felt Death's bony hand reaching for him.

"We need a plan for when they come for us," she said.

"Why not just off the woman?" suggested Mouse.

They'd been left in possession of their weaponry, as if the wolves did not fear their metal. Perhaps they could use their daggers and fists.

"No. The wolves are too loyal to her," replied Morigan. "They could turn on us or go dangerously mad. I have seen what happens to a man as great as Caenith when his animal goes rabid, and many of these wolves have far less control. These people have great honor, even though Aghna has twisted them. We should not directly challenge their pride."

Mouse drove her fist into her palm. "All right. Another angle then. A good old-fashioned pasting. Beat her red and make her release us. We have our knives, and you still have your strength, Father. Let's not forget Morigan's powers. Great-Uncle Thackery, it might not be the smartest idea for you to use magik. I worry for the cost."

As a master spider himself, Thackery had already been spinning a strategy in his mind. He ushered the three close. "Don't worry about me, child. I'll cut myself again and call all my soul's wrath if I need to. However, I don't know how long we could keep the she-wolf captive to bargain for our freedom. Attacking her directly would likely bring us more bruises than results. I think Morigan might be the key here."

All stares went to the seer.

"Me?" replied Morigan.

Thackery tapped her nose with a finger. "At some point earlier on—when that darling Macha and the Northman were with us—I remember hearing you worked a few wonders back in Menos. Correct?"

Alabion's adventures tended to drown out everything that came before. Morigan hardly recalled the Iron City. He prodded her memory. "A sorcery of that strange kind you possess. You told me you cast a whole building to sleep."

"Yes!" exclaimed Mouse. "Do it again. The whole damned city."

Thackery and Vortigern nodded contentedly. Morigan hated to deflate their optimism, but what they were asking was not possible. "I don't think I can throw my power that far," she explained. "Even if I could, all this feliron and the nature of our enemies would protect them from the brunt of it. Changelings are slippery to magik. They are beings of two natures."

"I was getting too excited," said Mouse. "You are right, and that would be a great burden to place upon you. We're thinking too grand and elaborate. What if..." She lit up and lowered her voice. "What if you just got inside her? Like you did with Kanatuk! Find out what makes her such an awful wench and break it, or fix it, or spank it—whatever it is you do—even if you just scramble her skull and leave her drooling afterward. I can't say I give a shite about her welfare. She needs something horrible to happen to her, and you're just the one to do it."

Laying hands on Aghna and ripping apart her mind had a delicious flavor of revenge to Morigan, and she smiled darkly. "Yes. If I concentrated, I could break through her shell. I shall need to touch her, though, to have any hope of reading her secrets. Changelings are fast, and I feel she will be faster than most."

"I shall restrain her," offered Vortigern.

"Aghna will come," Caenith had warned. Indeed, the warmother would come, and the bees tingled and told her it would be soon. But Morigan would be ready to unmake her.

II

The company sensed Aghna's arrival by the rumbling drums and howling wolves outside their prison. They were quite prepared by then and as tight as wound steel springs. They would pounce on Aghna when she entered. That wind rushed out of their sails, though, when a man was shoved through the flaps and landed with an oomph in one of the sleeping holes. Over the threshold Aghna passed like an unwelcome breeze, and her hollow, charcoal gaze undid what courage remained after the surprise. She barked at everyone in the room but mostly at Morigan. It was as if Morigan were the alpha in command. Regrettably, Morigan struggled with Aghna's ancient Ghaedic and could pick up only bits of the she-wolf's ranting.

"She's asking whether I am one of your...pack?" huffed the tall man, and he picked himself up. Evidently, he was fluent enough in ancient Ghaedic but still a trifle unclear on the phrasing. "Please say yes, or she'll kill me."

Morigan knew the correct reply to that at least. "*Si.*"

"Thank you!" cried the man.

Aghna howled in triumph. They weren't sure why. "Who is he?" mouthed Mouse to Morigan, and the seer had started to shrug when the bees stung her with a name—Talwyn Blackmore.

Morigan said it aloud and stunned an already-reeling gathering.

"Blackmore," hissed Thackery.

Talwyn waved his hands to ward himself from Thackery's curled fists. "It's not what you think. I am not wholly related. I'm not a monster but a botanist. Well, a scholar of antiquities. A dabbler in many sciences, really. I...I fled! From my brother, that is, and his sickening lover. Only that turned out to be a bit of a frying-pan-to-fire scenario—"

Aghna roared for quiet. "*Sochae!*"

The five faced their captor. Quite clearly, she had planned something wicked, and they all felt it the way danger prickles any animal before it's attacked. Aghna barked her black demands to Talwyn. She knew he could interpret her better than the rest of the Western rabble. First she laughed at Morigan for her mongrel's use of the ancient tongue, which Talwyn reluctantly translated. Then she spoke in slithering tones, and Talwyn grew more hesitant still. When he did not immediately purge himself of words, she loomed suddenly before him. In the next speck, she strangled him high in the air. His feet dangled. Ere the appalled company could assist the poor man, Aghna threw him to Morigan's feet to gasp out her ultimatum.

"I...I don't quite understand," Talwyn said.

He coughed a bit, and Morigan helped him to his knees. As they touched, the cleanliness of his spirit moved her. He was a being as solitary and wise as a white owl of Alabion. She liked this gentle fellow right in that moment.

He continued quite shakily. "She wants you to choose. She says Caenith—I think I pronounced that correctly—she says he continues to offer himself, and that is no fair contest. The choice falls to you."

"Choice?" replied Morigan. "For what?"

"A champion," Talwyn said. "They will fight for our lives. She says for our service or our freedom. One of them...one of the champions must die as tribute. This is a battle to the death."

As proudly and grotesquely as a happy murderer, the warmother grinned as she watched the flicker of understanding enter each of her captives. It would be a blood tribute. One of their number was to kill or be killed, and they all looked so meek she was certain one of her wolves would not die. This had been the warmother's plan all along—to trap and goad them into servitude. It would be a slavery no less than that of the cowering changelings already enslaved. Mouse found her gloating contemptible.

"Fuk this," cursed Mouse.

She tipped her head to Vortigern. That was the sign, and she stomped her hard boot upon the lantern, which had been laid purposefully close to her feet. Its glass bauble and living light shattered. The chamber went instantly black, and it filled with scuffling noise. Aghna's arrogance had brought her into the cave without any other guardians, and that made her easy for Vortigern's gleaming, nocturnal gaze to find and his pale hands to seize in the darkness. They wrestled and clawed at each other. Vortigern grunted from the warmother's resistance. Aghna would not be held long, if at all. The dead man's wrestling was probably just an amusement for her. Morigan rushed to the movement of pearl and shadow. Caenith's agility flushed her body, and she grabbed whatever she could. For her first error of choice, she got a stinging elbow to her lip. Then she clawed at the next-lightest thing she could see—a fluff of white that turned out to be Aghna's hair. Vindictively Morigan pulled it, and Aghna gave a howl that would summon the wolves in one speck. A speck was all Morigan required, though. With her other hand—the one not tangled in hair—she scratched at Aghna's forehead. Nails scraped skin, and reality shredded.

*The bees are well trained and know where to travel. They sweep their mistress up and spin her in their silver comet through time and space to that one aching moment that means so much to the woman whose blood and skin is on their mistress's fingertips. Morigan arrives in pitch darkness, and the echoing is disorienting. She knows this vast emptiness of space and this silence; it is familiar to her, even though she needs an instant to assemble her thoughts. In this absolute forgetfulness, this gusty vacuum that sucks at personality and self—this death—she drifts. Once Vortigern wandered a similar eternity. However, this death has been longer than his was, and it is not as empty as she thought. On the inky currents, she can hear scratches of sound—a voice and a barely mumbled song. Whoever sings does so in that beautiful tongue of Caenith's, which is so ugly whenever Aghna speaks it. Morigan realizes, though, that it is the white wolf's spirit that makes this miserable tune, and that in death, Aghna is gentler. She is defeated. Aghna is forgotten, utterly and eternally, beneath the white yews.*

*Foreverbloom. Eternity. Blood and vows. In her great awareness, Morigan now understands. What a terrible curse, Morigan thinks. Through the forever-bloom and the soul-binding magik of the Fuilimean, Aghna has been given the permanence she wanted—the immortality the lack of which, she believes, has created the barrier between herself and Caenith. The gift, though, is not what the white wolf desired. It is not the complete immortality that graces Queen Lila but a mongrel's immortality. It is an eternal body and soul, but the forev-erbloom's poison broke the connection between flesh and spirit—it killed her incompletely. A coma is the nearest condition Morigan can think of. A coma, though, would simply cause one to waste away through years and malnutri-tion, but, the foreverbloom has prevented this mercy. The pitiable thing is not even a ghost.*

*From the long centuries of this imprisonment and deprivation from mor-tality, the white wolf's ghost has gone mad. Now all she does is circle the darkness and miserably sing like an imbecile wailing in the night. She cannot remember the ones she loved or the man for whom she cries. All her world is bugs, darkness, and dirt. It is an eternity entombed. Again and again, the ghost blows through the void to make music and art and share pain. Blood was spilled to bring Aghna here, even if it did not leave the body but cooled in dead veins. Blood magik trapped this shadow of a soul between the worlds. Aghna's eternal dance could be seen as a spell or an act of Will—one woven slowly over time that eventually grew into a vortex to pull in other matter or presences from beyond. Morigan understands even more then. She is only a little awed when this cry to the universe, this sacrifice, and this magik sum-mon one of those who sleep far outside the light of the stars. Just as with the nekromancer, Sorren, Aghna's death and tormented passion have called a creature who harks only to the deepest glories and despairs. No lesser emo-tions move a Dreamer.*

*Infusing the empty space behind Aghna's eyelids and filling it like blood into water comes a red, choking fog that reeks of sweat, shite, piss, iron, animal labor, and every conceivable stench of battle. As the entity manifests in this nothingness, the space thuds as loudly as a banged, gory drum, and* the eye in Morigan's mind wavers with fantasies of men being impaled, of men screaming under a shower of crimson viscera, and of a moon glistening ruby from a sheen of blood. These images almost arouse her, their passion is so hideously powerful. Then the Dreamer of War speaks to Aghna in the wordless rumble these entities use when expressing their wants. It's a lightning bolt of sentience that tears into the being of the watcher Morigan.

**"What unspent might you have, wolf. You are a waste of warrior's blood. Why weep when you can roar? You wish for strength. I shall give you the strength to conquer a thousand peoples. I shall give you teeth and claws unbreakable by the hardest metal. I shall give you years beyond years to hunt your bloodmate and chain him to your love. You should not cower in darkness but rule in fury. Wake yourself, great warrior. Be my hunter in the hunt of all hunts. Invite me into your heart. Say my name. The scream of those damned by steel. The snarl on the lips of the wolf. The glory of a chalice of blood warming your throat. I am war. Invite me into your heart, and we shall turn this world red."**

Morigan senses the ghost's sudden stillness and Aghna's contemplation over this offer. What insane fragment of Aghna still resides here and numbly sings of love and conquest is enough to make the choice, say the entity's name, and welcome it inside her slumbering, undead corpse. Morigan is in two places now—in the throbbing, crimson storm within the white wolf's head and above Aghna's frozen body in the chamber of dusty roots. Under the moldering caul that lies atop it, Aghna's face twitches. Her dead lips part and whisper. "Ra..." She coughs out a sound. "Guh..." A grunt follows. "Na..." Then a scream. "Rook!"

As Aghna finishes the Dreamer's name, the decrepit wrappings blow off her into ashes. Her eyes open and dazzle with bloody stars. Ragnarök, thinks Morigan. That name and its terror, these visions of scorched earth and orgies of battle where men and beasts gore each other and wash themselves in carnage—

Someone shook her, and her contact with Aghna was broken. The furs were torn off the cave's opening, and in the sparse evening light, Morigan saw shapes moving around her as she blundered into Talwyn's arms. Mouse screamed, and Thackery whimpered. A snarling wolf trapped those two against the far stone wall. Aghna was merely playing after all. She had the dead man's arms twisted in a knot behind his back. If he had been alive, he would have been in agony. Vortigern bared his yellow teeth and squirmed. Aghna spun to Morigan. In that instant, their intimacy still weakened the veil, and Morigan sensed the fire, fury, and clang, clash, and splash of blood in a smoldering, roaring aura around the warmother. She was too bright and foul to behold, and Morigan covered her eyes. The warmother barked once more, and then she was gone. Morigan looked too late to see her go and tried to charge ahead. Thackery restrained her. Aghna had taken her wolves—and Vortigern as well. Mouse slumped when she saw that her father was missing and then pounded the stone.

"What did she say!" shouted Mouse.

Slow and dazed, Talwyn answered. "She...has chosen a champion. The strongest one she could find. The pale one will be our warrior. He will fight to the death when the sun rises tomorrow."

III

After Aghna had claimed the champion for her enemies, she left the cave unguarded. Perhaps the warmother had decided their fate already and felt no need to pen them. Mouse's first urge was to race into the city and throttle every wolf until she was taken to her father—although surely that course of action would not end well. There would be no gladiatorial combat until the morning, and they had only a slight idea where Caenith and now Vortigern were being held. Morigan sensed only that it was somewhere above them in the white forest.

While the three gritty folk convened in a tight circle, Talwyn kept to himself. He felt not quite right about joining their circle. Unsure of what to do when the group broke apart and headed out into the city, he stood out of their way as they passed and shyly glanced to the floor. The silver-eyed witch—he had seen her eyes flash in the darkness when she'd grappled with the she-wolf—turned back to him.

"Are you coming?" she asked.

That was as good an invitation as any, and he dashed ahead. That evening in Briongrahd, a melody of wolf songs shivered the night along with

FEAST OF DREAMS

drumbeats so ardent the firebugs trembled in their glass prisons and cast long, wavering shadows. Excitement and music came from every cubby they passed and from the many maniacs slapping their bone-and-skin casks, howling, and dancing their way up Briongrahd's twisting paths. Finding Caenith and Vortigern would not be a challenge. The river flowed but one way—up into the white forest. Changelings and wolves made the river's currents, and hands and snouts shoved, nudged, and manhandled the travelers. Morigan supposed they should be grateful to Aghna in her munificence for not shackling them as she did the other unwilling denizens of Briongrahd. Truth be told, Morigan loathed the warmother, the promises and covenants she'd made, and the ugliness of a soul that would sell herself to a pitiless entity for a forsaken love—a love that could never be. Aghna deserved a single kindness, which was to be put into the grave.

While homicidal fantasies consumed Morigan, Mouse dwelled on a different darkness—one she was too terrified to share with anyone. Drawn from her memories and into hazy life from the pulsating, tribal trance of the night, she envisioned her golden-haired friend, Adelaide, and recalled the sadness of the girl as she'd said, "Are you sure? You can't change your mind later. Just like the scarecrow, it's gone forever." With all the running and chasing of Morigan's destiny, Mouse had neglected her own signs. The cast-aside figure—the one whose card she had placed into the graveyard of the macabre game she and Adelaide had played, which hadn't been a game at all. Adelaide's caution that once the scarecrow was gone, he was gone forever. The realization of that prophecy crippled Mouse. Either she faltered or Thackery sensed her horror, and he reached out to steady her while they climbed through the sweaty stream of changelings. He shoved others aside and pulled her to the less-crowded railing. "Careful, child," he said. "You have the look of someone about to throw herself into a sea of swords. Do not despair for your father. He has beaten death once, and he is the strongest among us."

"What if he is not strong enough?" said Mouse. She shouted to be heard and was unable to blind herself to the teeth, savagery, and dreadful music all around them.

"He is. He must be," replied Thackery. "We all fight for something. We should assume he does as well. If there is one thing that binds him to this

195

world, it is you, Fionna. He crossed death itself to find you. I would say there are few loves stronger and more tested. I would not worry about the trials of this vile huntress."

"I hope you are right," she said.

Then Thackery lost her to her torments and nearly to the crowd of wild-lings as she pulled ahead. She was determined to ascend the city. Mouse seemed to have a better idea of where to go than her companions. Thanks to her tunnel vision, she failed to notice the young chestnut wolf suddenly trotting along at her side. Never rushing ahead with his kin, the wolf barked and nipped at those who drove too close to her. If she had glanced down even for a moment, she would have recognized Adam's eyes, which never changed on a changeling.

Thackery kept up, as did Morigan with her steps of fire and anger. As she and her bloodmate neared each other, the animal in her veins woke further—although communication still suffered because of feliron inter-ference. She sensed he might even have been shackled in it. *I am sick of being chained, chased, and herded. Of being too weak for mighty foes. I shall become stronger. I shall become the strongest woman in Geadhain. I shall be a shield to my pack and a storm of death to my enemies*, she thought.

Bumbling along at the slowest pace came Talwyn. He pushed himself to keep up with the three determined strangers. He had an inkling that if he stayed with these queer strangers, he would be dashing from danger to danger often. That would be better than being trapped with his brother and a cannibal, though. At least these folk would not want to make a meal of him.

As passengers on the changeling river, the company quickly wended up Briongrahd, across the precipitous tract of zigzagging stone, and then into the white grove. Once there, the changeling horde spread out, barked, and ran into the pale trees, and the company banded together. Mouse now noticed the patient, tail-thumping creature at her side. She frowned at him. She was disdainful of all comforts at the moment, and thereafter, she reserved this undeserved scorn for the white grove—for the peace and holy silence of the woods had taken on sinister characteristics that night. Drums pounded, and the changelings moved as misty shadows between the white trees. The air was crisp and cutting with winter's knives, and somehow the cool moon felt bright and hot. It was either that or her nerves had her sweating. All appeared soft, surreal, and almost ethereal. Mouse felt as if the ghostly prophet Adelaide were near and repeatedly proclaiming Vortigern's end. Over in the trees, she could almost see Adelaide's whiteness dancing in the dark and whispering to her about death and covenants. Since regrouping, the company had not moved. Using a tender bite, Adam tugged on Mouse's cloak. Her feet were unwilling to progress.

Morigan and the rest perceived some trust between the creature and Mouse, and they did not shoo him away. They followed the pair into the white grove and kicked up clouds of yew needles. With the abundance of white flecks, they were only slightly mindful of the first true snowflake that tumbled amid the flurries. Where there was one, there were soon thousands. They clasped their cloaks and shivered from winter's true breath.

*Winter has come—the season of death*, thought Morigan. She had no idea from where the notion arose, but she could not cast it out of her head. She clung to the warmth of Caenith's fiery conviction more than to her garments. Grimly as those walking to their graves, the company went onward. They were unclear about their destination, and each mind was an echoing distance apart.

Adam proved a true and sympathetic guide. As a victim of the warmother's cruelty, he understood the threat of losing one's family and the great silence Fionna would face if her unusually dead father was no more. Every animal deserved the right to see its parent die and honor the passing. If this was Fionna's destiny, he would take her to face it. Adam led Mouse through the trees, changelings, and the circus of slapped drums and howls to a stone path so red from life's nourishment that it stank of metal. They had come to the road before the *Fuilfean*, the Ring of Blood.

Through the forest, the Ring of Blood rose as a carbuncle of horror. A gutting vision it made—the sudden hewing of the beautiful ivory trees. Their corpses were chopped further into a circle of pews. It was a crude coliseum from which the changelings could watch their sport. Already savages filled the seats. They acted without a scrap of civility, and Mouse would not deem them anything but slobbering wildmen that eve. Chanting and roaring made the company wince. Noise and chaos blinded their senses. Barking elders stamped in the pews; pups crawled, rolled, and bit each other below the stands, and madmen's drum music and spastic flute songs added a throbbing delirium to the noise.

On that dark eve, several thousand changelings had come, and more still slunk from all directions to attend the show. In awe of the assemblage, Morigan understood why Caenith had submitted himself, for her companions could not stand against an army. Morigan did not see her bloodmate, though she could feel him farther ahead and past the milling of bodies pouring into the coliseum. When the changelings noticed the company, a path through the throng was made. Neither the company nor its brown wolf lost courage. Full of pride and defiance, they strode into the heart of the Ring of Blood where their loved ones and champion awaited. Behind them the sea of wolves closed, and the high-pitched din lowered to a rumble.

*My Wolf.*

*My Fawn.*

Strides of distance and flutters of snow did not obscure the bloodmates from one another, and they could at last see and somewhat feel each other across the expanse. Soaring, turbulent emotions rode them—regrets and misjudgments of what had brought them to this moment. Morigan sensed a burning iron on her wrists as if she wore the same heavy chains as her bloodmate. The imprisonment was another insult to the Wolf's pride—he'd submitted to it in order to save their lives from the mad not-quite-woman who draped her frost-white hands over his flesh as though he were her pet. *She will have her due,* whispered Caenith, and he snapped at the fingers that caressed him. He drew blood and a hiss from the warmother. *In naming the dead man as our champion, Aghna has made the wisest choice for us. I knew she could not resist his strength. Do not forget, my Fawn, he fights for love of his daughter, and there is little that can sunder a love that pure.* As punishment for his rejection and for staring at Morigan, Aghna slapped the Wolf, and their mind-whispering went quiet.

*Fuking dog, I shall kill you myself,* grumbled Morigan with a hand on her promise dagger and a silver sparkle in her stare. Beneath her skin, the bees pricked at her. They were a swarm ready to be unleashed. Morigan wondered whether the power of the moon could be destructive. She had never wanted to call forth wrath more than she did at that moment.

Suddenly, Mouse's cry broke her spell, and she looked to see her companions running off—all of them—to a ring of bones outside the first circle of seats. There stood a pale, shirtless warrior marked in coal motifs and as frightful to behold as Aghna. He hugged Mouse and Thackery.

"Vortigern," muttered Morigan as she came upon them.

The dead man's hair was not in its proper tie but braided with bone tips. Of the two Thule brothers, Vortigern maintained a fitness his frail twin did not. Always engaged in hunting and sport, his taut flesh—usually hidden under his coat—made for a surprise. Muscles strained against the lines of stitches that crossed his seams and joints, and spiraling runes drawn by the changelings decorated his broad chest. Dimly lit, scrawled in mysteries, and forged of sinew and cold, gray flesh, he seemed like a man of stone and shadow. Morigan admitted he was a guardian and a fine champion. This bloody challenge, though, was an affront that should never have been. Once Thackery and Mouse had given the dead man room to breathe again, Morigan clasped his icy shoulder. She felt no tingle of dread run through her and presumed he would emerge unharmed.

"Good luck, my friend," said Morigan. "I am sorry this fate has fallen to you."

Vortigern smiled his yellow-toothed smile and drew her in for an embrace. He whispered to her, "It has been an honor knowing you, Morigan. You crossed death to unite me with my Fionna. If anything should happen, please use your gift to keep my daughter and Thackery safe and loved."

Vortigern left her shivering. She hadn't realized he was ready for farewells. Denying her another word, Vortigern stepped out of the ring of skulls, raised his arms, and roared with a feral tenor the spectators drank in like wine. The drums and barking renewed themselves. The clamor was too deafening for Morigan to shout after him.

"It's all right," said Mouse, and she pulled in Morigan's reaching arms. "He will come back to us. He promised me."

It was not the same vow he'd made to Morigan. Still, she managed to wring a little false enthusiasm from herself and returned a nod. The four—Talwyn included—drew together. Vortigern moved farther out into the Ring of Blood. From a circle of bones on the other side, the warmother celebrated the dead man's bravery with howls.

Behind the warmother and tethered to iron spikes were her slavering hounds. Aghna went to one of them, snatched up its chain, and led it into the ring. As it came forth, Morigan saw it was different. With her second sight, she recoiled from the agony emanating from the beast. What misery it endured in its knuckle-dragging, lumbering shape between a man and a wolf. Its shoulders had a mutated hump, one of its muscly arms dragged, and the other was a segmented canine's haunch that ended in a mangled ball from which claws jutted. Morigan found horror in its bald and ratlike tail and how it thrashed its head in pain and scraped at the iron circle around its neck as though choking. Aghna had done this. She'd bred a monster by seizing the transformation of a changeling at its most agonizing apex with the sealing magik of a feliron collar. The bees whispered this to her. The company shrank as the monster neared.

Upon seeing the dead man, the beast strained against Aghna's chain. It bulged with veins, sprayed saliva, and scrabbled forward. It was ungainly on its uneven limbs. The creature had one purpose: to kill. Vortigern wielded no weapon except for what power he'd returned with from death. Brave Vortigern did not retreat from the monster, and the company prayed his confidence would suffice. They knew that the consequences of his failure would be greater than the ravaging he would receive. Failure would mean the absolute end of their freedom and their complete subjugation. They would be no better off than that rabid changeling—if they were lucky. Vortigern had to win.

The drums beat madly while the spit-thick cries of the changeling horde raked the air. Aghna rattled her champion's chain. Suddenly, the drums and noise stopped.

"*Ta mae onorach!*" roared the warmother.

"'For her honor,' she says," Talwyn translated.

"She has no honor," spit Morigan.

Aghna dropped the chain. The trial in blood began.

Into the snowy background, the warmother faded, distancing herself from the conflict. Her monster seized that speck of independence, leaped forward, and attacked whatever was in front of him—as rabid things do. However, Vortigern hummed with the energies of one who lived between life and death in the silver space of the Dreaming. Since his resurrection, he had moved as a being of two worlds. He was a visitor to Geadhain and a phantom in the void. He sensed the outlines of the living as figures in a fog and could reach out and grasp them. However, in the otherworld—the gray realm superimposed over these smoky shadows of men and beasts—he saw clearly the colorful stains of things borne on souls. He saw auras of green fire for jealousy and roiling clouds of polluted black for hate. On occasion, he indulged in the brighter lights around others: his daughter, his uncle, or the bloodmates. To touch life or study the unseen, though, he was forced to slow his movements. So much of either world he could tear through in a storm.

When he'd wrestled with Aghna back in the cave, she had proved awkward to handle. The warmother had notes of the duality he possessed and thus slipped out of his hold. In the here and now, her beast claimed no such powers, and as frightful and fast as the monster appeared, it seemed quite slow to Vortigern—a rumbling, sloppy shadow. In the gray billows of the Dreaming, Vortigern stepped around the monster as gracefully as a lord romancing his lady in a ballroom. As its snout drove into the stone and missed him wildly, he wrestled the beast about its neck and squeezed with his unrestrained strength. He squeezed with all the might that crawling back from death had given him. A snap rang out so piercingly that it shattered the frenzy of the howling masses and killed their rancor, music, and black thirst.

"It can't be."

"Is that it?"

"What did he do?"

Questions and amazement flew from the company as they gaped at Vortigern, who now walked toward them. The slumped heap of the mutant wolf was behind him. While the companions laughed and ran to gather their champion, the changelings whimpered their confusion. Their miserable whines were untenable to the warmother. This had not been a battle but a slaughter. The slow-walkers and Caenith had deceived her. There would be no respect from her pack until she punished this insult.

Caenith shouted the danger as soon as he smelled the rankness of rage rising off Aghna's hide.

"No! Run!" he screamed.

CHRISTIAN A. BROWN

Feliron or not, the Wolf's chains would need the Sisters' or Magnus's enchantments to bind him now. His pack's challenger had fought in the Ring of Blood and justly won. *Damn Aghna for turning on her honor!* Caenith thought. He howled and ripped the chains and their anchors from the stone. He twisted the shackles around his wrists and crumbled the metal to flakes. Then he rushed forward across the snow-blurred and hauntingly silent field rank with the cloud of Aghna's fury. Now he could see it too, somehow—a crimson aura upon Aghna both of and not of this realm. It watered his sight like gazing into the sun. He leaped.

He was too late.

A grisly twist sounded in the Wolf's ears as Aghna manifested behind Vortigern. She thrust her hand between his shoulder blades and ripped out a black, dripping heart. Mouse shrieked, and Morigan, Thackery and Talwyn cried out in horror. Vortigern's endearing yellow grin branded itself upon Mouse's heart. She saw his dark, loving eyes so determined to protect her and so surprised at the tugging in his chest. Mouse had only a moment to capture the memory, and then Aghna splattered Vortigern's heart onto the stone and tore off his head from the stitches that attached it there. In her fury, the warmother ripped off the dead man's arms and one of his legs too before Caenith fell upon her. Mouse dropped at the same time as her teetering, decapitated father. She did not rise; she withered into a ball.

Morigan tripped over herself to reach her friend. She needed to shield her and weep with her. Thackery appeared in a gust of anger, pulled Morigan from his great-niece, and demanded that the seer go. It was a warning about Aghna's red radiance, which was no longer a metaphysical element and no longer something only for Morigan's uncanny eyes. Now all could see it. It was a scalding heat and a crystalline light that softened the snow into trickling streams. The Wolf grappled with this terrible heat like a man wrestling the sun, and soon the temperature would become unbearable—even for him. Would this horror take Caenith next? Would the death of Vortigern not be enough to sate the lust of Aghna and her unearthly parasite? Morigan's hatred and grief mingled with the Wolf's river of embattled courage. *Enough! Enough death! Enough madness!* Morigan screamed, or felt she did. She had degenerated into madness herself.

Hate conjured her Will, and she moved with the power of magik. She shivered and skipped into the silver space between life and death. She didn't see herself disappear, though Thackery and Talwyn did. They gasped as she flickered from here to there. In the Dreaming, Morigan witnessed the true, gaudy horror of Ragnarök, the Dreamer of War. With her heart, she felt him. He was warm and awful as a sunset of blood. He was a heat that drove every man and beast into a sweat of slaughter. With her sight, she beheld him as a whirling, crimson corona that sucked at her immaterial matter with the hunger of a hurricane. *Good*, she swore. Let him draw her to his seething core. That was where she wanted to be—at the heart of the Dreamer's connection to Aghna and this world. She would find and destroy it. As a banshee of silver radiance, Morigan screeched along the fiery, buffeting currents toward the brightest point of light she could see. Her bees led her where all else would not. She could not feel the fire that seared Caenith, for she had no flesh. She was a walker in the Dreaming. She was a watcher no more but a maker and an unmaker. Somewhere in the landscape of fire, she reached the eye of the inferno, where the waves parted around a clot of bloody brilliance. There lay the covenant Aghna and her host had made together. It was beating like a heart. She clenched and crushed that promise—that gob of red sentience and evil. She clenched it until it went into spasms and bled. *Die!* she Willed. She had never hated anything so purely.

A caterwauling explosion—a dazzle and rainbow of reds and golds— threw her from the Dreaming with smoke and ash upon her cloak. Caenith too was hurled some strides. Up in the coliseum rows, the changelings screeched, scattered, and protected their eyes from the inglorious dawn that had risen.

When the light sizzled away, the arena was cold and hollow. The snow came down heavily. It seemed eager to blanket the scorch marks that defiled the stone. A tremendous battle had been fought, and its victors had yet to stand and declare themselves. The Wolf crawled his way to Morigan and held her to him. Sisters' mercy, she was alive and startlingly whole, but she was filthy black as though she'd journeyed through a furnace. The Wolf knew what she had attempted. He knew she had sought to destroy Aghna's contract with a wicked, ancient force. Morigan—his brave, beautiful Fawn—had moved to another realm through a wrinkle in reality, and she had tried to stop that power at its source. It was another of her miracles—only not the one they needed to bring back their friend.

Haggard and seared in many places himself, the Wolf limped to his companions. Sage Thackery and some other fellow clung to Mouse. Aside from the Wolf, no one understood exactly what he or she had seen. A shy chestnut wolf tramped out of the curtain of snowfall and dropped a trophy at Mouse's side—a pale and patterned arm. As the screams at last tore out of Mouse, the animal ran off to fetch the rest of Vortigern's remains. Adam was quick with his foraging, and in a speck he had gathered every piece of their departed. Grief produced automatic responses, and Thackery understood they were to pack up the pieces of Vortigern. With the same silent agreement, Talwyn put aside whatever discomfort and shock he felt and offered his cloak as the receptacle. While the men shivered and worked to the music of Mouse's sobbing, Caenith watched the wolves. He growled at the ones moving through the drifting night—though not at Adam. That changeling bore Mouse's scent and the steely fragrance of honor. The Wolf would wait until later to tell the others he had seen a few two-legged changelings carry off their warmother. He wouldn't reveal yet that she was still possibly alive.

To the wolves and changelings who still hovered at the scene, he declared in the old tongue, "We are free of our debt through true honor, you sinful dogs. Enough blood has been paid for your warmother's disgraceful pride. She or any who follow us will stay dead. I shall wear their skins and eat the meat from their bellies while they scream."

Talwyn knew why the wolves kept away after that and vanished into the snow. Nothing save unrelenting horror had plagued him in Alabion, and while these folks did not buck that trend, he still felt an unexplainable pity for these noble, broken beings. It seemed as if their lives were made to suffer, and the Fates found torment such as this to darken their spirits even more. As men and women of the hardest steel, though, they persevered—including the weeping lass in the snow, who eventually picked herself up, threw on an iron mask, and asked him for his assistance in carrying her father's remains.

Soon after, the three of them started lugging the sagging satchel behind the soot-skinned giant and his sleeping mate, whom he carried in the crook of one huge arm. Certainly, the strangest of the strange were these two who were one. First and foremost, scientists were observers, and Talwyn saw a mystic synergy in their breathing and shared twitches. Their movements together formed the lines in a poem about unfathomable intimacy. *A heart that beats and bleeds and twists. A breath—your breath—upon my lips. Kiss the breath; consume the soul. I am you, and we are whole.* He recited the haunting poem to himself. Its origins were a mystery, though it was poignantly appropriate for the twin enigmas from which he could not keep his stare.

When the snow became bitter and blinding, the woman who'd lost her already dead father threw part of her cloak over Talwyn's shoulders—"because he was shivering." Not much of this made sense, but Talwyn tried to accept everything. He needed to stop then to bring a pause to their procession and weep for these indomitable heroes who could not find the grace—or weakness—to do it for themselves.

## IV

They walked on and on without direction through disorienting sheets of whiteness. Caenith led. Talwyn did not stop to grieve again. It seemed quite pointless in the company of a giant, a slumbering sorceress, ancient sorcerer and legendary rebel Thackery Thule—the same man who had scorned and scarred his brother—and a young woman as hard and cold as the winter that bit at them. A brown wolf too circled through the scarcely hinted trees ahead. It followed them, and Talwyn did not think it only a beast. *Here I am in the company of legends*, thought Talwyn. *Even this twice-dead man I carry has done deeds greater than I can imagine.* Thus, he refused to complain as his arms burned and his frostbitten feet dragged. Nary a whimper escaped him once they exited the protection of the white grove and scaled all the way down a snow-clotted slope of rock while roaring winds and clouds of ice blew at them like flocks of pecking birds.

At last the descent was over. They reached the cover of woodland. Geadhain applauded their trial by slowing the storm and cutting the cold with a murky light. Dawn had risen, though it was a somber one. It was quite apt for the task they had yet to complete—finding Vortigern's grave site.

The company wandered more erratically than when they followed Caenith's usual swath straight ahead, for he sought a particular spot and not a course to the Sisters Three. The snowfall eased to a gentle dusting, and only the swishing of their movements broke the numbing peace of the woods. Talwyn could not say how long they traveled after that. In the thick silence, he might as well have been asleep. When he stirred from himself, the company had entered a grove of birch trees. It was a frightful place, and he shivered at the sight of the ghastly trees with their peeling white bark and black-knotted trunks. They were always in pairs, these knots, like glaring witch's eyes. He suffered a second scare upon noting the taloned charcoal birds clinging to the branches of these trees. Without sound and with interest, the funerary creatures watched the company. They were staid as pallbearers, and they roosted on every tree Talwyn could see—most prominently on the large birch the giant led them toward. *Mourninghawks*, Talwyn thought. He felt he should classify the creatures for lack of a known genus. *Noun: a subspecies of diurnal bird of prey with broad, rounded wings and a long tail. They typically take prey by surprise, owing to their silence. Mourninghawks are magikal and communal creatures native to Alabion. They are not solitary watchers like Strigiformes but roost and travel in flights of "mourners." For predators, they are reserved—carrion feeders that do not chew and swallow their prey but feed off the emanations of their passing instead.*

"There," said Morigan.

She must have awoken earlier, the sleeping witch. Talwyn couldn't remember the moment or her being placed upon her feet. She went ahead of her mate and pointed to a pristine patch of snow at the base of the great birch. Even the omnipresent bushes eerily retreated there. *Bury him here*, the land whispered, and further guidance from Morigan was unnecessary. Caenith strode to the area and began to dig with his shovel-size hands. Almost none of this was unbelievable to Talwyn. Place enough strange things next to one another, and the fantastical starts to look normal. *He's wearing sandals and a scorched loincloth in the winter*, Talwyn thought, as he studied the Wolf. The man also emitted a delightful heat and a pleasing bestial cologne. He looked a creature made for physical power and ruling untamed realms. He would have to be large, savage, and warm to endure the wild. Being so close to the lord of the wild, Talwyn did not need the gracious comfort of the cape he shared with Mouse. That was another strange name he'd been introduced to in this bizarre and confounding dream. Throughout the whole of their trek, she'd shared the cape with him, as much as that might have slowed their escape from the savages of Briongrahd. The wolves, however, were unlikely to pursue them—not after the large man's threat. Nonetheless, his brother, Augustus, and that thing with the silver teeth could still find them, for these were the folk whom those monsters sought. As soon as they'd attended to the burial, he would tell the company of that hunt.

The giant and the chestnut wolf, who had come to help, finished their digging. Time seemed to pass in a blink. An earthy pit now awaited the remains, and Talwyn was eager to surrender them. Caenith washed his hands in the snow and came to assist him and Mouse in unwrapping their companion. There were no gasps at the quartered man. His other leg had finally detached itself. Mouse did, however, reach down and caress the gray, startled face, and then she brought it from the basket of limbs and kissed its forehead once, longingly.

Talwyn tended to keep himself removed from difficult situations. He observed things with tickles of curiosity and clinical detachment. As when Caenith had been digging, he drifted now into pondering the bloodless nature of the amputations and the shreds of dry visible muscles. In his formative years, for a bit of fun, he'd dabbled as an assistant to a nekromancer. However, he saw in these remains none of the telltale sutures or greasy rot that a remade would commonly have. On Vortigern, the stitches seemed cosmetically placed to symbolize his status as nonliving, without adding the unsightly elements of maggots and decay. There was also a startling lack of stink to the dead man's body. Rather a lovely cinnamon potpourri came from the remains. He was almost tempted to sew the dead man back up, stick his tarry heart in his chest, and see what would happen. Such desecration, though, would surely cause his new companions to shun him. Such absurdities softened for him the somberness of their actions—the reverent arranging of the corpse within the pit.

Like much of this dream, it ended before Talwyn knew it. Handfuls of soil and snow were tossed and gradually erased the twice-dead man from this world. While Caenith stomped and smoothed the grave, Mouse returned to Talwyn the cloak he'd lent to transport her father's remains. She slipped it upon him ere he could thank her. The dead man's pleasant smell wafted up through the collar.

Talwyn realized the ground was trembling. No—someone was singing a song so rumbling it made him tremble, and it stirred the mourninghawks to restless excitement and caws. It was music borne from the throat of the kneeling giant. He crept awed into the circle of mourners surrounding Caenith and the grave. He listened to the ancient Ghaedic ballad of deeds, warriors, and brave folk. He could imagine the Iron City, Blood Promises, and family lost and found through death. Talwyn noticed the hands that slipped into one another—old to young and giant to mate—when the song-story praised family and love. From Caenith's dirge, he learned more about these four than any interrogation would have granted. Their collective story seemed so sorrowful that he deemed them the most blessed—and cursed—folk in all Geadhain. They were cursed for the challenges they must face and blessed to have each other as swords and family. He stood in the company of heroes. He felt overcome and unfit to be present. Perhaps he would find the reason he'd chanced into their path—these beings that walked roads of fate and destiny most chilling to ponder. Perhaps he could chronicle their great saga so that others would hear and know with authenticity the strife that each step brought them as they fought whatever it was they fought. All the song-story spoke of was a dark and threatening evil—an eater of light. It was a force that required the intervention of the Sisters Three.

Although Talwyn lacked an adventurer's true passion and did best when he observed life through a clinical lens, his heart was now aflame. These subjects—no, these heroes—felt more intriguing than any academic recreation in his life. This was real. It was life, death, honor, and triumph. In a thousand experiments and lectures, he had not fathomed that a person's blood could pump so hard or inspirations fly so high as his did at that moment.

Talwyn's fantasies ended come a perfect and wolfish howl from Caenith—the lament's finale. Talwyn understood then what animal hid in Caenith's skin, and he was certain when the chestnut wolf bayed along. In time the duet whimpered out, and the Wolf stood and kicked more snow over the grave. He looked to Mouse for permission to move on.

"Does she still live?" asked Mouse.

Caenith curled a lip over his suddenly sharp teeth. He growled and nodded.

"I tried," said Morigan, and the words twisted her prettiness. "An old magik protects her. It's a pact with a creature not of this world. I nearly broke it, but I think I failed. I was not powerful enough. I am sorry."

Mouse walked to her friend, and they stared at each other. Talwyn hitched his breath in anticipation of violence or grief. After the pause, Mouse hugged her friend, and he heard her whisper promises frighteningly absent of anger.

"I'm going to kill her," vowed Mouse. "Death for death. I shall find a way."

"I understand," replied Morigan. "I shall help you. We shall find a way."

This was how heroes dealt with death, Talwyn discovered—with shocking equanimity. The dead were dead; the living would avenge them. Blood for blood and always forward. For they were moving through the woods again under the cries of the mourninghawks, which were clacking on their branches, fluttering their wings, and cheering the corpse in their garden. It was another blend of melancholy and beauty Talwyn fumbled to comprehend. A marvelously dark journey had begun, and he wondered where it would take him. Realistically, he expected it would end with him buried under a tree.

V

As they continued their trek through the day, Alabion's winter mellowed and no longer subjected them to harsh winds and flurries. Once they left the grove, life beyond the mourninghawks shuffled through the bushes and made artful dashes through the drifts. Many less hearty birds and lizards simply disappeared, although Morigan spotted an avian *v* flapping over them once, heading south.

Most of the company ached from cold, weariness, and emotion, and they needed a spot to lay their heads. Unstoppable Caenith was determined to reach the crossing to the Pitch Dark by nightfall. He did not outright stop their trek, but he provided an occasional respite. Amid the many unremarkable white humps of the land, he found a hidden bush, brushed the snow off, and unearthed brown, withered fruits. The delicacies tasted as sweet as prunes and were oddly warm. Though a botanist, Talwyn knew not the variety of this drupe, and he slipped away a pit for later dissection. The fruit sustained them a while longer. Eventually, however, after a great, careful trudge through snowbanks that concealed thorns, pitfalls, and holes under a veneer of innocent whiteness, the group's less hardy members began to stumble from fatigue. Caenith paused a moment, gruffly suggested they slake any thirst with snow, and then moved on. *Hold fast a little longer*, he thought after hearing the grumbles in their bellies. Real food would not come until he hunted, which would not be until they rested that evening.

By dusk, the Wolf and his pack had emerged from the trees and come into the shadow of the plinth of rock he'd tumbled from with Aghna. The others moved beyond him, wandered to the icy edge of the mighty rapids, and gaped at a crashing fury too powerful to succumb to any frost. However, the woodland that lay beyond the River Torn claimed all their awe. Even muffled in rime, the black oaks in the far forest gleamed. For a speck, the group thought it to be a trick of the mist. Across the river, the foliage steamed with vapors. It was damp and dark as a morass. They sensed the danger that awaited them on that far shore where the forest hooted and chattered with rainforest music—and a promise of unfamiliar terrors. Alabion was a mistress of many faces, and this was her most primal. They could scarcely look away from the dreary, moving shadows that could be snakes on every branch or from the swaying ice-barbed vines that hung ready as nooses for their necks. The Wolf announced that which needed no introduction. "The Pitch Dark," he said.

Talwyn watched Caenith as he spoke then to his bloodmate using only his eyes. He had seen Caenith do this before, and it seemed in every way to be speech. Then the big man vanished. It was almost a magik trick, and it left the five of them quite abandoned on the river's plummeting bank. Morigan and the chestnut wolf, who scampered off to the body of rock crowning the river, appeared to have shelter in mind. The four-legged creature won the race up the stone handholds and jagged ledges, and he leaped into a slit of darkness not quite at the top. For the rest of them, the climb took longer. However, the hidden aerie they discovered rewarded their efforts. A cleft ran straight above to the sky and let in the failing light and snow while keeping out the wind. Waiting for them in the dimness stood a nude young man with ebony ink sparkling across his skin. He appeared quite unashamed, but Talwyn gave him his cloak. He felt obligated to do anything he could for these folk. Adam donned the cloak from shoulder to hip and knotted it at the waist. He wore it like the long sashed garments of an ancient conqueror. The look suited him.

Until Caenith returned, much work remained to be done, and Morigan did not allow her company to sink into dreary lows. She swept their sanctuary with her cape and asked the others to gather sticks, leaves, and whatever else had blown there over the years to use for tinder. Soon a fire was lit, and the five basked in its smoky allure. Now that they'd stopped their trek, they felt extraordinarily tired and struggled to keep their heads from bobbing. Mouse fell asleep against Adam, and the changeling held her with an arm about her waist.

Morigan studied Adam. Though the enigmas in the flames seemed to mesmerize him, his every movement—from his puffing nostrils to his shivers when Mouse breathed upon his neck and chest—seemed to speak of his absorption in a different mystery. *He left his people to be here. They will never take him back*, Morigan thought. The bees buzzed about his devotion. Morigan sensed his loss of a parent or parents. His pain was nearly identical to Mouse's, and it had driven him to revile Aghna. Morigan's grapple with the Dreamer had changed her. It had awoken in her another layer of her power, and her mind flew across the flames and into Adam's head as smoothly as a song.

*"Work! Work! Work!" Aghna's hounds bark at him whenever they pass. In Briongrahd, the City of Fangs, the barking never ceases. He knows why he toils and why his fingers, cracked and aching, are condemned to chisel in stone the hunts and glories of his people for all time. His life is a counterfeit freedom and only slightly better than those of the seals, deer, bears, and owls who weep blindly in the rock. He pays for his family's sins. To kill another wolf would be inconceivable under the warmother's wicked code. To have them kill each other in the Ring of Blood, though, is not a crime for which she takes accountability. If the weak are not worthy to fight for the warmother's praise, then they are to be culled from the pack or diminished until meaningless.*

*His mother was weak by Aghna's assessment—though she was strong as the oldest oak to him. She was a woman of free thought and a spirit that would* not be chained. She was also old enough to remember the days before the white wolf reigned. She wanted to flee the warmother's tyranny with him and would have risked the West's dangers, so long as they could both escape. Often she spoke of the Western people's legends and their strange stone forests and flying metal birds. She did so with wonder and not fear. She told him the Western People had a smell, for she had met one once and chosen to let him live because of his scent. It was a scent of exotic oils, sweat, and the earthy turning of the leaves to autumn. It was the smell of the season of change.

He was very young when his mother died, and he only half recalls the flight she and the rest of her rebel pack made along the edge of White Lake. There were snarls and scuffles when they were caught and a howl of regret when his mother was forced to choose between her life and his. He remembers that burning moment too well. His mother chose death by leaping from the Weeping Falls. He was spared—but not from the shame and punishment that can be neither erased nor eased over time. Still, his mother's heterodoxies are his to nurse and honor forever. They pulse strongly alongside the pain. Never shall Aghna's brood strip those ideals from his soul. His father is an irrelevance to him—a meaningless gap in his mind that he smooths over like the stone under his hands. It was his father who betrayed them to Aghna, but he has since been erased. Aghna cast him into the Ring of Blood to fend for his pardon for wedding a traitor. Against one of her wild brood, his father fought and did not live. Perhaps the white wolf knows some justice after all.

While he chisels his stories, the young changeling reminisces about his mother. Sometimes he sneaks bits of her heresies into the wall-story of Briongrahd. No one checks his work or notices. Many do not care about the old stories now that Aghna rules. They want only odes to blood. So he scribbles here and there what he believes autumn would look like if she were a woman— red and powerful, borne on fierce winds, and foretelling of cold and new birth and all the miracles that come after. Not for the slightest speck does he neglect the flame of his mother's memory or fail to keep safe her wisdom.

Thus, when autumn comes in the winter, when the woman of fire appears in Briongrahd and rustles every burrow with her wind of change, he is ready to receive her. It is not this chaotic force that draws him the most, though. It is the dark two-legs that follows in her shadow. On the first night, he spotted her *from up high painted in the moon. He was pulled to her scent. She most deeply smells of the oils and fragrances of which his mother spoke. She is one he howls for and wishes to bite. She appears to him the next day as if she can smell him too, and the chase begins.*

Adam stared hard at Morigan. Did he sense her skulking in his soul? She felt for a speck like an intruder for her invasion. People's minds were not simply hers to pry into. She should remember that and stick to the fundamentals of companionship instead. She turned to Thackery beside her. He also observed the tender portrait of his great-niece and the changeling.

"How are you?" she asked. It was the simplest of questions but had countless connotations.

"I am angry," he said. "I am tired. I am still confused that it is he and not I who lies in the ground. I would not have stolen more time if I had known it would be at his expense. I do not think a man who could not die should pass before a man who should."

"You feel guilty?" muttered Morigan.

"How could I not?" Thackery kicked at the fire's edge. "Where is the fairness? And that witch, Aghna, breaking her word. After such a horrid bargain. If I had my power..."

Morigan gripped her friend. "Your power would not have stopped her. Mine barely did. She is no mere woman. She is..." Morigan reached for the word and grasped at the air with her hand. "A vessel. A host in which something else is kept. No—in which something sleeps. When it wakes, it is a nightmare. I have seen this thing. I have sensed it in others before. In Sorren. And something similar, only blacker, in the mad king."

"Sorren?"

"Yes."

They sighed. Morigan had been looking at the fire, and when she faced Thackery, her cheeks shimmered with tears. "If only I cared about these great worries more, but I don't. I really don't. I just miss Vortigern. I feel our fellowship is broken. Our wills, bravery, and purpose are all tarnished with his passing. I had a dream—a fool's dream—we would somehow one day all stand around a fire and celebrate our triumphs, our children, and our luck. He saved Mouse. He saved me. I could not save him. All this power, and I couldn't save him. I didn't even see his end. I'm a blind seer. Useless."

Morigan's sudden sobbing could have woken Mouse, although Mouse's face looked clenched, and she might not have been asleep. Thackery smothered Morigan in an embrace to contain her sorrow. He rocked her as he had done when she was young and still bewildered by her mother's parting or even by the notion that a person could be there and then not. It was a comfort for them both, this pattern of grief, and soon Morigan sniffled herself back into composure. Immediately, she spotted the quiet, observant man who had blended unnoticed into much of their procession today. She put a question to him more rudely than she intended. It was a twist of meaning her mood caused. "What are you doing here?" she asked.

Her harshness caught and pinned him, and Talwyn fumbled. "Me? I've sort of been going along with things. I actually don't quite know what's happening."

"You've seen what happens to those with whom we walk," said the seer. She seemed dark and threatening. "I would not blame you if you tried your luck in the woods alone."

Talwyn mustered his pluck. "No. I can't explain it, but I think I am supposed to be here."

"Oh, that." Mouse yawned and fluttered awake. "Destiny is a bitch. She cheats. Might as well tell us now so we know where to look. Pine or oak? Maybe a nice spruce with plenty of shade for the sparrows."

"Pardon?" said Talwyn.

Caenith's manifestation in a gust of wind upset the fire with sparks and stopped Mouse from gathering the details of Talwyn's burial preferences. While hunting, Morigan's heartache had stabbed the Wolf, and he'd messily killed the closest and fattest stags he could track and dragged them up the rock. Tonight they should not mourn, for death was not simply about the missing but the memory. They wouldn't worry about the wickedness to come or the darkness that pursued them. He could still smell the Jabberwok on the crisp, winter drafts somewhere west. Tonight, though, they would eat and rejoice in what it meant to breathe, sing, and live. Vortigern was finally at peace under the birches. He would have wanted them to toast his life as a hero and a father—however foreshortened both those roles had been.

Once the meat had been cooked and carved, they sat and ate together and spoke of the man absent from their campfire. Sometimes it was with tears, but much more often it was with laughter and smiles. For a dead fellow, his demeanor and actions had been so bright. When the fire went low, they let it die, and they fell feet to heads in a circle around the coals. Most dreamed of him that eve in flimsy echoes or profound visitations. As deeply as they slept and as close as they came to touching this illusion, when they stirred at sunrise, they watched his gauzy figure fade and knew he was gone.

# IX

# THE HUNGER

I

Hiding from the Blackeyes was no mean feat. When the warnings came, Beauregard and his father had been so tuned to the charcoal stink born on the once-pleasant breezes of the Summerlands and so raw with fear and starved for survival that their bodies had moved before their minds made any instruction. Thus, when the Blackeye war bands had descended upon the razed villages of Mor'Khul looking for any lingering life to feed their army, the pair had buried themselves in the gray silt of distant trenches and waited like quiet soldiers for their moment to move. Staying ahead of the Blackeyes and away from any settlements was the key to their survival. As dangerous as seeking civilization could be, though, the two men often rolled out the tired skin map of the Summerlands and plotted which village to journey to next. Certainly, this was a doomed endeavor, as they discovered come every new ruin they found. Still, however hopeless the chase, no other road lay ahead. On like damned desert spirits they marched for time uncounted. They would walk under the untamed wrath of the sun, breathe ash and despair, feel a rush of discovery, and finally come to the clenching realization that another village of soot and death awaited them. Some towns had been burned so terribly the ash rose to their waists. Not even a scorched bone could be found on the shores of these black lakes to reveal that people had once lived there.

In some quite-distant time—it felt less than a memory—Beauregard and his father could not have been more different. When measured physically against each other, they were truly night and day. Beauregard was tall and willowy. His black hair was the darkest thing about him, and he had little of it other than on his head. The rest of him was likewise fair for a fellow. His face was so porcelain and pretty that if he shaved his fine beard, he could convincingly play any woman's role on stage. Only his strong chin and deep gaze might collapse the illusion. On his cheek shone a darling and perfect red star. "The one true star of the North," his mom had called the birthmark. Now, though, grime covered it. The birthmark emphasized the boy's starry inclinations, for his head was always in the clouds. He chased dreams, songs, and poems. Meanwhile, his father was a bear in a man's skin. He was replete with fur, muscle, and even a roughness to his voice that made every word into a growl. Their aptitudes were no less divergent. Beauregard's nimbleness, wit, and romantic pursuits contrasted with his father's penchant for hunting and manly pursuits. In the misery of the Summerlands, however, old roles and attributes were effaced and rewritten. Both men were filthy and dark. Both were hard as rock in their stares and lean from starvation. They were more father and son than they'd ever been—two animals of a pack.

Beauregard acted as their storyteller and shaman. He was the one who wove the magik tales of the woman who awaited them in Willowholme: Tabitha Fischer. The woman had since been elevated to sainthood by their stricken souls—mother of one and wife of the other. If Beauregard represented the heart of their beast, then Devlin was its claws. He caught snakes, rats, and antlered cockroaches as large as cats. They were horrid meals, though nothing their hollow stomachs would refuse. A few times each day did the men speak, and then it was with whispers about Tabitha or where they were next headed. Speech was mostly an inconvenience. Their bodies developed fluency in the silent communication of nods, hand gestures, and the armpit reek of fear they would exude whenever either sensed a Blackeye.

When in hiding and stuck watching Blackeyes rake through the ash of villages—poking with their mangled pikes and glowing staves—the men did not question how these monsters came to be. They thought only of how soon they could leave their cover and run again. Before the Summerlands, they hadn't agreed on much as father and son. Even Beauregard's attendance with the scouting party that was to investigate the sudden droughts that had withered the land had become the source of many nights' arguments. After the scouting party had found the first desecrated village, Devlin had warned the scouts that they should return. Instead, the scouts had explored further and followed the trail of doom. One morning, the scouting party had awoken to a sunrise dark on the horizon from dust. Blackeyes rode crisped horses, and behind these black knights were a swarm of shambling manthings—each as hideous as a tarred bird jammed with knives. Father and son had found their commonality in that moment. Devlin had told his fellow hunters to run. The men were too stupid or brave to listen, it seemed. He and his son did not look back to see what became of them. However, thereafter their screams made for restless sleeps and wicked daydreams. Time was a lost convention. That could have been weeks, months, or years ago. Since then, the pair had dragged their bodies from one end of Mor'Khul to the other searching for a flicker of life. Even a scream of man or animal would do, as those had been silent awhile.

Their hearts told them to go north, but it was inaccessible. Each village in that direction was razed, and the Blackeye patrols seemed thickest to the north. Returning that way would be suicide or whatever passed for death in the Sun King's new order. Thus, Devlin continued leading them south, and he avoided the realm of smog and unspeakable grinding noises that was Mor'Keth in the center of Mor'Khul. Despite a glorious education in death and terror, Devlin failed to imagine what Brutus could have summoned in that crater of crimson rocks and endless smoke—that funnel of shadows that should have been a green and golden city. A king of monsters laired there now, judging by the sounds he heard. One night, they rested near Mor'Keth, and Devlin thrashed with dreams of fiery teeth gnawing at him and of a wet whisper that poured into his ear like magma and melted his insides while he screamed. After they traded shifts and rest, he discovered his son had had the same dream. Devlin needn't be a seer to know this was an omen—perhaps a brush with something ancient.

As they could not return to Willowholme or tread too close to Mor'Keth, they tried the fiefs on the west of the Feordhan. It took days of hiking, hunting foul foods, and scavenging licks of stale water from the dewy underside of rocks before they reached the grand river. The vision of the Feordhan's blue and salty presence snaking across the landscape stung them more than their hearts could bear. Not even the fingers of smoke dotting the river's bank discouraged them, and they hurried toward the fires. They were hopeful a battalion of the Sun King's enemies, even riflemen of the Iron City, had taken the embankment. Beauregard was keener of sight than his father, despite not being the hunter, and he saw something alarming. He grabbed his father's arm, and they skulked into a cluster of desiccated bushes. With their stillness and ashy cloaks, they concealed themselves like desert lizards. As they listened, they could hear the far-off clangs and sizzles of a forge. None of it, though, was the music of life. With sinking souls, they realized those encampments were not made for people but for monsters with inky stares.

"What are they building?" whispered Beauregard.

He meant the metal detritus cutting across the Feordhan's beauty in a black line. It could have been a congestion of logs or the start of a giant dam, but figures walked upon the blockage, and misshapen laborers added more strange bits to the construction—long and short poles and flapping pieces of thin metal that faintly glimmered in the sun. Therefore, he assumed it must be a structure of sorts. The sun had other places to be that day, and a dullness hung over the sky. However, they could still see the shadow of pollution spreading from the construction into the sapphire purity of the Feordhan. They coughed as a mouthful of scorched petrol blew their way.

"He's closing all passage along the river." Devlin grunted. "Brutus is locking his borders. Sorsetta it is, then. If the south is closed as well—"

"Sorsetta," said Beauregard.

They hurried away before being noticed. Alongside Tabitha, Sorsetta now became their candle of hope. Knowing Brutus was clamping down on his kingdom, they rested less and walked more each day. They ignored the pangs of pain, hunger, and thirst. The men concentrated on the toothy shadow to the south, a range of mountains they believed to be unsullied by Brutus's evil. As far as they walked, they still felt Sorsetta was farther—a mirage they would never reach. The delirium of malnutrition claimed Devlin first. A man as grand as Devlin being drained to a skeletal, hollow-cheeked wraith was dreadful for his son to watch. Beauregard's slenderness pardoned him more from deprivation. He needed less and thus functioned better. Rather soon, he found himself caring for his father. Beauregard became their eyes on the skyline, the listener for black hooves, and the hunter of scaly things to eat and squeeze for nourishing blood. When Devlin talked, he often rambled and never issued words of much sense. He did have moments, though, when he glimmered startlingly lucid, and he would praise the blueness of a sliver of sky or smile—he rarely smiled—as his son helped him along like a man of a hundred years.

Sometime into their eternity, the storm came to the Summerlands. Whatever magik Brutus had used to bring the great dryness had banished the rains and summoned the droughts and dust clouds of Kor'Khul. So when the raindrops fell onto the leathered foreheads of the two wanderers, they gaped with the wonder of men seeing a star descend. One drop became many, many joined into a cascade, and soon the two men were soaked and laughing. They could hardly spot each other for all the rain. Yet they had spent so long surviving that they did not trust any miracles. Instinctually, they knew to find shelter before crimson lightning ripped the clouds and before the rain went hard and cold as nails of ice. They cowered out the storm under a lean of rock that teetered and fell into the mud the speck the ebony clouds lifted. Again Beauregard acted on impulse and saved them. Neither could say what he had survived or what it meant. Never had they been shaken by such wrath or thrown so fast against a swallowing maw of lightning and hail.

The world changed thereafter, and they felt its transition as plain as the cold frost-speckled muck they wandered through. At least the storm had brought them water to drink and even a few dead animals to pick from muddy pools. They carved and ate these creatures raw before any rot began in the bodies, and for the next few days they possessed wind to their steps. Incredibly, the storm had driven away the Blackeyes. It was either that or the hordes had not pushed so far south. The men preferred to think the former.

A few sunsets and sunrises were all they needed to reach Sorsetta. They cried aloud and wept when the dirt festered with green—a color forgotten. Devlin hugged then kissed his weary son from cheek to cheek, and they carried on into the shyly unfurling grasslands. They bumped bodies and cheered like alehouse friends. Slowly, life reclaimed the desert, and the men's cheeks bloomed as red with contentment as the flowers swaying nearby. Sunshine, the first in ages, came out to celebrate their joy. Streams were about, and the two washed like beggars. They soaked the ash from their cloaks and drank more than their stomachs could hold. Afterward, they felt as grand as kings while they burped their way down the streams toward the steep, emerald hills where all water seemed to wend in a web. As they broke the tallest hill, they saw more steeps and valleys, and their spirits were cleansed in a waft of rich soil, manure, and woodsy smoke. It was life at last. Tiny huts and larger granges spread about the grassy highland. Shining tin, copper, and bronze roofs and the bold colors of the bricks of many dwellings teased the travelers with intimations of generosity. Ale, soft beds, and a hot meal would be ready for them. They had only to race down the hillside, knock on the nearest door, or shout to the closest person—a living, breathing woman in a yard of furry livestock—and they would have all their pleasures granted.

## II

The Sorsettans were legendary for their kindness to strangers. They were always ready with a meal and a smile. The owner of the first farmstead they encountered spotted them before they waved her down. A flurry of chatter and movement later, she had taken them to her busy house of many children and a woodworking husband. He stopped his whittling to heat baths and food for the strangers ere even asking their tale—a tale undoubtedly as haunted as the looks the travelers wore. Once the travelers were clean, they were fed a broth with hearty beans as succulent as sausage, and they sopped up the last in their bowls with stone oven–fresh bread. Quite full, they then settled around a hearth made of rainbow slate. Color could be seen as a rudiment in the Sorsettans' souls: it was evident in their glazed sienna pots filled with bouquets of red wildflowers, in the vividness of the soup—steeped with carrots and purple beets—they made for Devlin and his son, and in the twists of bright yarn they braided through their dark hair. The Sorsettans represented everything the Summerlands were no longer. The folk were so charitable and pure, Devlin could not hold himself from ruining their bliss. They must know of their danger. After dinner, he told the tale of what he and his son had lived through.

"The Summerlands are gone," he finished, and he pulled tight the crocheted blanket the kindly housemother had laid over his gaunt shoulders. He was often cold now that he was thin.

The housemother nodded. "We know."

"Brutus is mad," added Beauregard, and he reached for his father's hand as the assault of their long terror flashed into him. "He's killed them all. His people. His land even. I think he will come for Sorsetta next. Call it a premonition or simply a sense of what a dark force of nature the mad king is. You did not see the waste and hunger we have seen. You are not safe. Nothing is safe."

Sweetly and without terrible concern, the housemother sighed. She was a voluptuous woman bordering on chubby. That, though, could be understood, given the litter of children she'd pushed into the world. All seven gathered about her as she knitted by her pipe-smoking husband near the hearth. She nodded for one of her children to fetch the brightest red string from a basket. She finished hooking the new yarn and resumed her work before explaining herself to the travelers. "An emissary from Eod came after the storm," she said. "Praise his Everfairness or maybe the Green Mother herself, it did not smite us as it did other lands. The criers were along soon after to tell us what we earth tenders already knew. That a wound was done to Geadhain. That she bleeds and weeps. We were told to move high into Gorgonath, whose moutains and stone walls keep out the sea and guards the secrets of the deep. The Faithful grow rice on those fertile peaks and fish in the echoing grottos within Gorgonath that bleed from the Scarasace. We lucky countrypeople should have food for generations thanks to husbandry. That's all the Faithful really do—cultivate and keep. We've no one to fight with in a land so content with itself. Well, it seems that should soon change."

"Faithful?" inquired Beauregard. He was unacquainted with the term.

The housemother gave him a doting smile; he could have been one of her own young, she showed such love in the expression. "There is more to

life than conquest. There is much to be said for nurturing what you have—
the soil, the body, and the brotherhood and sisterhood of one another. The
greatest of those who contemplate these understandings live in Gorgonath.
Their very presence is a wind of peace that stirs all Sorsetta. They are ruled
not by the laws or rulers of people but by the voice of Geadhain and the truth
of her mysteries. To her, they are most devoted, and thus they are known as
the Faithful."

"Oh," said Beauregard, and he felt quite small.

"No shame in not knowing," said the housemother. "Staying ignorant
afterward is the real shame. You'll meet them soon enough, the Faithful. You
two are fortunate to have come along when you did. Tomorrow we and the
other homesteads will gather to kill what animals need be killed, pack up
what we need most—not a knickknack more—and then head to Gorgonath.
The providence of the Green Mother is what brought you here, so I reckon
that's the path you'll take as well."

Devlin coughed. "We hadn't...I mean, we must get back to Willowholme.
My wife. She is waiting."

"We all are," said the reticent housefather, and then he took a long puff of
his pipe and blew out wispy rings. "We are waiting for this scar on Geadhain
to heal. For the warring of the Kings to end. You won't get anywhere north
of here, my friend. As you've said, the Feordhan is blocked—quite foul, as
well, with oil and blackness—and you won't find a trustworthy oarsman
with whom you would want to cross it. You would have better luck seeing
whether there be person or fool in Gorgonath willing to test the Scarasace
with a vessel. Could take you on quite the voyage up to Carthac—if your sea
legs are worthy. Then you could crawl all the way down to Willowholme."
Done with his advice, he leaned back in his chair, crossed his arms thought-
fully, and puffed out more smoke circles.

"If that's the only way, we shall take it," announced Devlin.

His gruffness left the air buzzing with tension. Only for a speck did the
housemother allow the disharmony. Then she glanced to the younger of the
strangers with her gracefully slanted eyes. "Do you play?"

"Music?" replied Beauregard. "Probably not the songs you would know.
I'm a dabbler mostly. I pluck and croon while I work. Nothing more."

"I think you're something more," countered the housemother.

She whispered to her children, clapped, and sent them scurrying. They sought out empty pots and metal utensils to bang on. A tiny girl, who was almost faerylike in her lightness and air of mischief, appeared on Beauregard's lap with a flute. He didn't think it was intentional for her to have brought him this instrument—his favorite—but now he could not refuse so inevitable a performance. He took a few toots on the flute, blew out some dust, and coughed a bit. This was an amusement for the children. When ready, he did a quick scale of notes and then began an old tune from Willowholme, "The Breeze and the Barley."

Devlin had never actually heard his son perform. He had been too busy, distracted, or infuriated that his child wished to be a foppish stage-fool in a distant city rather than learn a man's responsibilities. Over the years, he'd deafened himself to the cries of "Papa" that Beauregard had made as a youngling and to the magikal sounds his son had conjured when he first started whistling, humming, and chirping tunes in his sparrow-sweet voice. Tabitha had adored her son's performances.

Now, as a captive man, far from his wife and too wasted of his great, burly strength even to lift his bag of bones from its seat, he finally heard his son's talent. Through nature's crafty magik, the lad had maintained the sharp pitch of his youngling voice, and in manhood he had come into the breathing and power of a horn blower. What kissed his listeners' ears was a songstress's soaring sounds sanded with husky annunciation. Devlin grasped this beauty fleetingly in verses sung between the melody that evoked memories of reeds, caressing winds, and freshwater. His son's fingers charmed from the flute the lilts of every grace of Willowholme. The children drummed and banged their pots, and their parents clapped whenever they were not as smitten as Devlin and could remember their hands and feet. Timidly, the eldest child asked the young man for another song once Beauregard finished the first. The children hushed themselves while waiting for an answer, as though their pleading for more might break this man of magikal glass.

So Beauregard wove his musical spell for a stretch longer. Stars drifted past the window, and the night darkened without his audience's knowledge. At length their bodies grasped the lateness, and they sagged tiredly when Beauregard put down his flute. A couple of children had drifted off to his tunes. The housemother tucked pillows under their heads and lay blankets over them. She then thanked Beauregard for his performance, piled him and his father with enough quilts to make them sweat, and left with her partner and a sleepy tail of young ones.

When the two were alone and Beauregard was hastening into a deep and clawing sleep, his father suddenly appeared beside him. Beauregard felt a shadow over his face and a strong grip upon his shoulder.

"If there is one thing alone I shall treasure in all this," said Devlin, his words trembling, "it is that I have come to know you as a man, a survivor, and a friend. You did not bend to madness or weakness as many in our ordeal would have. In the end, your wits and will delivered us from the desert of the Summerlands. I did not know you or seek to understand you until all we had was taken and I was forced to look upon the man you are. Forgive me, my son, if I ever made you feel alone or less than worthy of my respect."

Such sentiments Beauregard had waited his lifetime to hear. He reached to take his father's hand, squeezed it, and opened his eyes too late to catch the man before he returned to his chair. It was habit, so Beauregard stayed awake while his father slumped and snored. Then he realized there were no Blackeyes to guard against and no more nightmares for the moment, and he joined his father in the Dreaming.

### III

Morning woke them with a kind and golden hand to their cheeks, and the clattering of cheery folk graced their ears from drafty, unbolted windows. Beauregard and his father greeted each other with puckered grins. They'd slept, though they could have done so for hourglasses more, and were still haggard and footsore. Once they had splashed their faces and helped themselves to the crusts and cold broth left on the table, they joined the highland folk in preparations for travel. For people leaving their homes from the onslaught of evil, the Sorsettans were as gay and lively as circus folk. The housemother's holdings had drawn neighbors from far and wide. Beauregard noticed many caravans still meandering down the hills to reach this place. They wound over the green highlands like an earthworm of many colors. The housemother must be a luminary, felt Beauregard, to command such influence. Where these newcomers would park themselves could be seen as a problem, but the Sorsettans were accommodating and orderly with the host of oxen, mares, carts, and bustling families already present in the great yard. From what Beauregard saw, nary a toe suffered a stubbing, and no person got jostled in the rush. He assumed every Sorsettan possessed the same prudence and politeness as the housemother.

As he and his father stood still upon the doorstep, their sand of indecision ended as the housemother beckoned to them. They hurried to their grand hostess, and she gave them each tasks. Thereafter, father and son caught each other only in quick waves here and there throughout the day. To Beauregard, the housemother assigned the chore of packing and sorting clothing and commodities for the journey, all of which were laid across the green in a spectrum of glorious objects. Everything the Sorsettan highlanders owned was glazed, pigmented, and ornamented with natural symbolism. The lad handled each piece like a relic as he turned it over in his hands. That morning he cataloged many wondrous things: emerald-glazed cups made like cornstalks with yellow dabs around the rim, a woman's dress as red and soft as a rose with stitches shaped like thorns, and even books pressed on hemp and husk paper that were wholly handcrafted and bound. The connection of the Sorsettans to the land was humbling. Nothing seemed wasted. Neither technomagik nor industry manufactured anything that could not also be made from the elements and a bit of toil.

In short order, Beauregard's Northern sense of ownership was corrected when he tried organizing the wares into piles for the specific families who'd brought them. The housemother was darting about as busily as a hummingbird, and she poked her beak in to say, "No, my music maker. We take what we need as it is needed. It all returns to the Green Mother in the end. We are merely borrowing from her. Just pack it up and put it in." Which was exactly what he did, and he smiled at the seeming absence of covetousness in a modern society. How could people live without wants or greed? Give it an hourglass, and surely the darling children playing harmoniously over by the deteriorated stone fence or even the adults smiling at their sport would find cause to bicker. Contention was part of being a mortal. People came into the world screaming and covered in blood. From that moment on, they fought for air and existence. Then afterward, they fought against weather, age, and mostly each other. Warring—not courtesy—was in man's nature. Civility, scoffed the lad, was what man painted over the animalisms of himself. It was a pretense to conceal the truth that he was no better than a four-legged, fanged thing.

As he sorted, Beauregard kept his eyes on the frolicking children and his ears primed for arguments elsewhere. His subjects disappointed him with their calm voices and happy clucking. A mad king would soon be ravaging their land. From where did this foolhardy optimism come? "What she wills, she wills," was a proverb he heard tossed around with frequency. The "she" was Geadhain, he presumed. The phrase itself was an admission of submission to her unpredictability. The Sorsettans used the adage rather colloquially, be it for commentary on the weather or talk on the inevitable passing of an old relative, who himself sat in on the conversation and agreed. So often did Beauregard hear the words, it surprised him that these people considered fleeing to Gorgonath at all. Lying down in the fields, counting clouds, and waiting for the Blackeyes to harvest them seemed a more natural response from these pacifists. Of course, that would not be a natural end, he realized, and he chuckled at his creeping conversion to their wisdom. They weren't dullards after all—only folk who did not seek battle as a first resort. Perhaps an aloofness from the lust of the great kingdoms made them even greater warriors. He spent the rest of the morning absorbing more of the Sorsettans' truisms and growing increasingly curious about these Faithful who awaited them in Gorgonath.

While Beauregard contemplated philosophies, Devlin worked on more menial chores—the kind of work at which a person with cold steel to his or her gaze would excel. The housefather noticed his steel and took Devlin to an earthen byre where untended beasts milled about. Cut and bubbling right from the stone flesh of the land were troughs of spring water, and fat clover and wildflower patches with cloying honey scents further discouraged the cattle's migration. No cattle hound or even a stick to beat the animals that might get out of order did Devlin spot. There were plenty of children and youths brushing and coddling the animals as though they were pets. Devlin thought this strange. He puzzled over the lackadaisical attitude of the herd's keepers. He was dumbfounded as he walked into the barn with his guide and saw the dark crimson straw and neatly murdered cattle in rows along each side. *Tidy,* he thought of the carcasses that seemed to have fallen asleep like weary dogs with their knees folded under their briskets and their muzzles on the stone. Their throats must have been slit while they rested, and blood flowed toward a grate in the floor. Little stench of piss, shite, and sour animal musk—the smells of death—affronted Devlin. That made this the cleanest slaughterhouse he could imagine. It was almost pleasant with the bleed of golden sun coming through the tired shingles and the fresh, sugary breezes from the flowers outside. The housefather now handed him an apron and a long knife. Devlin noticed that other squatting butchers wore the same apron throughout the abattoir. Devlin equipped himself with the items. Even as a man who had killed and gutted a thousand meals in his day, he shuffled uncertainly.

"Go on," urged the housefather. "They haven't felt any pain."

Devlin held out his knife defensively. He was still unsure. Then he spotted pretty lacquered bowls by the bloodless heads of the dead, and he even sniffed the telltale chalkiness of *last night's milk*—a short-lasting, immobilizing poison—amid whatever concoction pooled inside. A soporific agent had been administered to the cattle prior to their end. Such an unusual practice for meat, to pamper it so. He felt at a loss and conflicted about this mercy.

The housefather stroked his white beard. "All lives are sacred, even those we must take. We don't do it often, if you remember the meals we've fed you. No need for meat when a potato and beans will fill you up right. We'll have our share to contribute to the rest of those who've come for shelter at Gorgonath. Curds and whey, we'll bring. But a strip of felsalted beef can last a person through the winter—can give him an inner fire against the cold and strength for war. So we must part with as many of our four-legged family as we can bear. The rest we'll set free, and we hope the Green Mother will guide them to sanctuary and then back here, once we are able to return. We've said prayers and given them milks, so they do not feel the knife. Most of that's already been done. You seem like a man who can tell the sharp end of a blade, though, so you'll excuse me for presuming you would not blanch when it comes to some blood and bones."

"Right," said Devlin.

"I'll leave you to it, then," said the housefather.

He looked as uncomfortable at having been made to speak for so long as Devlin was to assume his task. He hurried away. *Blood and bones*, thought the huntsman. He shrugged, found the nearest corpse, and began to whittle at it. The buzzing sunshine, whistles of his fellow workers, and flitting whispers of field and farm—bees, bells, and animal snorts—soon had him falling into a peaceful trance. Even the sawing and squirt of blood had a certain music to it, and it was not a grisly song. In this serenity, he found himself contemplating the tender treatment and life of the animal he carved. He thought of its wandering free through the bright highlands, never knowing the lash of a switch or bark of a dog. It had always had a mortal parent to feed, brush, and care for it. As he watched the blood flow, he butchered the animal with an unfamiliar delicacy. Once he closed one animal's clouded eyes. Later he tapped the pouting muzzle of another. Each was an action he did not realize he'd taken. Rising from this dreaminess after a while, he discovered himself outside the barn. He was washing the gore from his hands beside a curious and munching cow. Surrendering then, he smiled at the surreptitious magik of these people and their beliefs. After the redness of death had finished flushing down the crevasse, the cow lost interest in Devlin and dipped its head for a drink of the tainted water. The beast showed no fear or understanding of death, the red house behind it, or the butcher at its side. However Devlin tried, he could not explain the animal's tolerance or daftness or why he stood and stroked the soft beast for a spell.

He spent an hourglass with the herd and the tenders, learned the animals' names from the children, and waved to his far-off son whenever he could see his ebon locks gleaming. A time came when the tenders rounded up the cattle and led them to the tumbled barrier of the farmstead and then shooed them over the stones. Forlorn as children cast out into the wilderness, the beasts stared back at their friends and keepers. "What she wills, she wills," praised the tenders, and finally the cows remembered they were cows, and the herd began to shamble away. Devlin stopped himself from being drawn into remorse at the scene of their swishing hinds bobbing off into the fields. Holly, one of the cows he'd been introduced to, mooed up to the sun, and he turned from the irrationality and weepiness of his well wishes for her. A tin bell rang. Looking past the field and homestead, he saw the caravan curled like a lazy snake between the tufted bales, and he knew they were leaving.

*To Gorgonath and with haste,* he thought.

IV

To his great disappointment, though not to his surprise, Devlin learned the Sorsettans did not value speed. If the company had been any farther north, the food less savory, or the realm anything but an artist's vision of rock shelves potted in flowers, solitary sheep framed on hillocks, ribbons of ivory and blue skies, and quaint, abandoned farmsteads, he might have had cause to complain about their pace.

Winter was somewhere, however, Devlin couldn't feel the pinch of it on his skin in Sorsetta. He doubted they would get more than a few cold rains to shimmer the realm with dewy beauty and add mystique to its splendor with velvet blankets of mist come that season. On the bumping caravan, he and his son slept long hourglasses into the day and restored much of their stamina. Devlin began to reassume his husky shape and left his untrimmed beard to grow so wild that the children named him Big Bear. Beauregard would sing for his supper or any time someone asked him, which was quite often.

As father and son, they grew closer even than their shared struggle for survival had brought them. That battle against death had been won for now, and they could explore what it meant to befriend one another. Come a week, and Devlin asked for tunes from his boy. Come another, and Beauregard happily listened to stories of his father's hunts—accounts that had at other times been dreary. Now and then, they shared a moment when their Northern restlessness and penchant for worry kept them awake past the imperturbable slumbers of the Sorsettans. They would sit around the night's dead fire, look out over a quiet dale, and exchange conjectures about where Tabitha might be and whether she was sound. Always they assured themselves she was safe and happy, for to consider the contrary would be to take the meaning from their quest to return to her. They could not think of a life without that headstrong woman. Usually fretting turned to reminiscing, and they could then sleep happily. On more than one occasion, however, once his son had tucked himself into his bedroll, Devlin had stayed up to pace.

He would watch the handsome child sleep. *My child*, he would remind himself. In Mor'Khul, when death had come near, he'd nearly told the lad the whole and wretched truth. He was afraid he would die without the secrets ever being said. How could he say them now, though, after they'd come to know each other so deeply? He'd finally become the father Tabitha had wanted him to be. *I need no child. Our barrenness is a gift.* Once he had hissed that toxic verse to his wife following the bleeding and sorrow of her third miscarriage, which the medicine workers said would be her last ever. Stubbornly, he'd refused to apologize to her and went many weeks until the weight of his cruelty broke him to tears. For years thereafter, he'd worked toward penance. She forgave him in the end. A new road of penance and forgiveness would lie before him if he imparted his secrets to Beauregard. There was no telling how Beauregard would react. They might well shatter the boy's faith in him and in the woman he thought of as his mother. *She is his mother!* he shouted silently to the stars. She was more of a parent than that wanton woman—Kings rest her soul—who had been Tabitha's sister and surrogate.

Belle was a deviant. As a mother, she had been indefensible—too flighty and drawn to music or a pretty smile to be of any use to a boy. She had another, a boy, or so he had heard. Somewhere in Heathsholme. Devlin shook his head whenever he thought of where that lost child wandered the world. *What she wills, she wills*, he said to the stars on each night these desires to confess tormented him. Then he would bow to his son, his beautiful boy, whisper his gratitude, and kiss the small star on his cheek with a wish he need not ever know his true parents.

## V

Gorgonath declared itself as a great wonder of the world. That morning, Beauregard and his father had woken in one of the carriages, each moved by a change in the world. They had tossed off their sheets as excited as children on a festival morning. They had leaned past Eloa and Nithan—the housemother and housefather, who had finally given their names on the journey. They had slapped each other on the backs while grinning in awe. For sands or hourglasses, they stared at the twilight-shaded peaks that faded in the sunlight from shades of gray to blue. They stared at the rectangular towers of many windows and painted colors that stuck from the mountain like sticks of pastel. Crawling vines blended these domiciles into the rows of stone upon which they were built. Every line of the city was uneven. No ground had been leveled for progress. Paths went where they went, starting from a grand one at the base of a scraped flatland. Gorgonath, city of the Faithful, had an organic presence of sea curling behind the mountains, greenery heated in the sunshine, nature, and the harmony with the Green Mother the Sorsettans preached. It could have sprung from the exuberant imagination of a giant child. Indeed, a joyfulness permeated the construction. It was a vivacity the circling birds—not gulls but larger—caroled over the caravan.

As soon as the shadow of the Gorgonath's Ancient Wall had cooled them of the pleasant day's heat, Beauregard grew dark as well. He realized these gleeful folk had no idea what Brutus would do to them. Zioch and all the lush lands of Mor'Khul had once held the same bounty as this realm, and the Sun King had plowed it into ash. Beauregard shuddered from visions of what scab of a thing Sorsetta would become after the Sun King's passing.

"Father, we have to tell someone. These Faithful or whoever passes for ruler here should hear it. Brutus will erase the life from this place and everything pure and golden in this land. You know he will," whispered Beauregard.

It was not quietly enough, for Eloa passed the reins to her husband and joined them under the awning. "Bravery and nobility are rare, lad, and you seem to have them both." She pointed about the landscape. "The boats are on the lower roads, through the passages that wind out the back of Gorgonath. The Faithful, however, whom you would want to speak to, are up close to the sun and sky. As you might have noticed, our little band has been a lonely caterpillar this whole way. We're the farthest from Gorgonath and will surely be the last to pass into its gates. I don't think they'll keep the city open for long after we're in and accounted for. All I'll say is you might not have time to fulfill two wants—only one."

"Father?" implored Beauregard.

If the city was to come under martial lockdown, Eloa spoke wisely in that there would be few options to catch a vessel once that law was enacted. Devlin gazed up the brash facade and disoriented himself from the colors before even counting any streets. Even by carriage, if the Sorsettans relied on such things, the trip could take a day, and he had no money for transit. Did they rely on that too, or was a courtesy enough? They would almost surely miss escaping the city should they choose the road to the Faithful. Devlin tried bargaining with himself. He thought the Faithful must already know of the height of their peril. No people, he figured, could be so damned peaceful and clueless. Yet his son's expression glowed as fiercely from fear as Eloa's beamed complacency. The Sorsettans were not prepared for the genocidal king. They would wall themselves up and think themselves safe, and the mad king would melt this very mountain like a waxy plaything to a heap of running colors and screams. Devlin gritted his teeth. Had Eod given these people no proper warning? Was the North even aware? As he pondered these questions, he knew he would not deny Beauregard.

"We shall see the Faithful first," he agreed. "If they will hear us."

"They will," said Eloa. "They would never turn away a pilgrim."

"A pilgrim?" replied Devlin.

"What she wills, she wills," said Eloa. "If you two had been brought to our home a day later, you would have never found us. We do not believe in fate. The Green Mother provides, and we do with it as best we can. Sometimes that isn't a very good or glorious harvest at all. However, what we do with her gifts is largely our choice. You followed her whispers here, and I think you're hearing them still. That's a calling, lad—a summons that not even many of the Faithful have experienced, and they trap themselves in silence all their lives to hear her voice."

She returned to her husband. Devlin had the impression she'd aimed her wisdom mostly at his son—all that business regarding pilgrimages and callings. He chewed his lip over that and didn't notice the caravan roll through the grand stone gates or catch the grumble as they shut. If he had, such rumbling finality would have made him only more aware that they would neither catch a boat nor leave Gorgonath—not on that or any other distant day.

## VI

The caravan wheeled through the natural terrace beyond the gates and up the sole, slanted road. It finally stopped in a plaza of hundreds of deserted vehicles. The vivid buildings of the city were still quite a hike ahead. Beauregard stood for a moment within the tingling hum of the crowd. Then, after strapping himself down with an oxen's worth of gear, he keenly ran up the path. Many of the children swarmed along with him, while Eloa and the rest made no great fuss to race them to the top. Devlin frowned at the absence of guards or people of law. Someone must have operated the gates in the gully below, though, and the Sorsettans could not be so stupid as to have a city without soldiers. Such warriors were the Faithful, he believed, and he felt he would recognize one if he spotted him—or her. Still, their competency as fighters needed to be better than their patrolling, or they were all doomed.

Devlin caught up to Beauregard at the top of the climb. His son's gaggle of children had dispersed to Kings knew where, and nary a parent seemed more concerned than to weakly call for each in the crowd. A fair flow of folk strode about dressed as minstrels, albeit without the garishness. They were drenched in tasteful, complementary shades and colors. Most travelers headed away from the gates and along the thread of a wide and rolling road that went up and down and followed the ruggedness of the land. Others wandered off side paths through green archways and rustic doors. Some tended private gardens of straggly flowers and bushes that grew from stone. The lad slowed and dropped his packs to gawk at the olive-threaded architecture of the tower houses up close, and a speck later he interrupted an occupant with greetings, handshakes, and questions. None was treated as unwelcome, and they seemed reciprocated with earnest replies. Devlin had forgotten that other than a handful of disgruntled hunting trips into the Summerlands—where all the boy had done was complain—his son had never been outside Willowholme. Now Beauregard was seeing the world with a virgin's perspective and embracing his new lover. Devlin watched his son chat with one man and then wander over to two half-naked fellows kneeling in a circle of stones and ask them what they were doing. Couldn't the lad see the men meditated or prayed? Devlin hurried over and dragged the boy away before the contemplatives stirred.

"You can't go poking into everyone's business," scolded Devlin.

He couldn't maintain his glower, though, when the boy shook him off and raised his arms at the city's glory. "But it's beautiful!" cried Beauregard. "Like nothing I've ever seen! The salty air. The soothing calm. The quiet joy of these people. I want to see all of it, Father."

"You will," laughed Eloa, who had caught up to the pair. "But this is the last you'll see of us for a time. We have family here with whom we need to meet and settle in—distant family. However, there is no real breadth of clan or kind between Sorsettans. You'll see that yourself. Knock on any door, or ask any fellow to point you in the right direction. I wish you two well on your pilgrimage. I sense great promise in your journey."

"Great promise," concurred Nithan.

In a brief comradely farewell, the housefather slapped Devlin's back and then was off down the street and wrangling one of his errant brood. Eloa curtsied and left the two pilgrims. Forthwith, Devlin missed their companionship; the ancient city felt daunting without a guide. Beauregard, however, appeared unruffled. A grand exploration lay before him. He squinted against the light and pointed high up the mountain.

"We need to head up," Beauregard said, and walked on.

Devlin jogged to his son. "Why up?" he asked.

Beauregard turned his head. "Well, Eloa said we had to, for one. Furthermore, if I wanted to be close to the Green Mother, as close as a person can be to the sun, moon, sea, rocks, and sky, if I wanted a throne from which to see all her beauty, I would choose the highest point. From the mountaintops I could gaze down and ponder every green wrinkle and blue vein in her body."

Beauregard's wisdom calmed his father, and the older man followed along afterward without worry of being lost. Evidently, he had a guide. For a novice to wayfaring, Beauregard navigated like an aged adventurer. In this environment, he revealed skills of exploration and conversation as honed as Devlin's were for the hunt. In no time at all, Beauregard had adapted to the native elements of this society and suppressed sightseeing wonder for the custom of its silent civility. Exceptionally observant and keenly enthusiastic, Beauregard noticed every detail of this new realm. As they climbed the great road—always one path and ever winding up the mountain—Beauregard spoke to his father quietly and with a confidence that had Devlin admiring the boy even more.

"Look at how they all share in duties and wants," he said while they passed two neighbors, or possibly strangers, trading a bolt of fabric for a bag of grain.

Back at Eloa's homestead, they'd witnessed this behavior. It was no less engaging to see it in action throughout an entire city. Anywhere they went, the easy fellowship of the people could not be escaped. In Gorgonath, as Eloa had told them, no one was an outsider, and all were treated as kin. Drinks passed from one hand to another. It wasn't alcohol, as far as either man could tell. Half-eaten food was not thrown away but offered to another for consumption, or it was used in one of the many stone-and-soil gardens kept in the city. Labors too became a communal effort. The pair overheard the muttering of a couple of sweaty stonemasons strapped to the lofts of a tower like mountaineers. The workers planned to head over to the next tower once they had finished and then to as many more as they could patch up in the day. Beauregard knew this wasn't a civic duty—it was likely not even an assigned one. Rather, it was a meaningful obligation. The Sorsettans were famous for their weaving, exotic spices, and sea-born bounties of weeds and fish. However, one had to wonder where all the wealth from their industry went, for no commerce took place on the streets. Haggling did not exist: offers were made and accepted. It was as if "no" had been erased from the Sorsettan lexicon. Truly, the travelers did not see a single glimmer of currency, and they became certain coin was not a currency to these people. If treasure existed somewhere, it was kept in a dusty warehouse as a necessity for trade with other nations and was worthless in the city.

Abstinent from drink, sin, and greed, the Sorsettans represented an anachronism—a moral daydream of the modern age. They were a miracle in these times of war, technomagik, and violence—one not lost on Beauregard or his father. *This innocence must be preserved*, Beauregard fretted to himself. Horrible visions from Mor'Khul overcame him again and again. His steps went faster as the day warmed, until his father was puffing along behind him. "Slow down," Devlin called more than once.

Such reminders were welcome to Beauregard, and he would slow and ask a colorful passerby for a splash of water and a bit of refreshment. Nearly every time, the hospitality extended to an invitation into the sparse and tidy homes of these people, and he and his father stayed for longer than they realized. While there was never an expectation of recompense for the kindness, Beauregard repaid the charity with music when he could, which delighted these folk. As a nation of whispering, silent contemplatives, they rarely knew the pleasure of a hearty song. After three such visits, Beauregard and his father were back on the streets with smiles and full bellies. Day had dwindled, and the sun lay behind the charcoal mountains. It distorted the city with a veneer of orange and crimson as though aflame. "No more breaks," said Beauregard.

His father did not ask why. They both could see an end to their climb, and he felt eager to reach the white heights of the mountain. Up there, the snowless peaks were bleached from the sun and white as winter alps. Green spread along the rocks as well. It was stark against the paleness and outlined many slits and shaded bridges. A sanctum atop the city summoned them. From the pureness of its appearance, they could sense this to be the Faithful's home. Soon the houses vanished suddenly and were behind them, and they walked by themselves upon the great road. Like a gentle, invisible shepherd, wind pushed them onward in this exposed space. It was a pleasant companion on this lonely part of their journey. With the fiery light of dusk and an unfriendly breeze, they would have slid back into waking nightmares of Mor'Khul.

They arrived at the keep as night drew her black blanket over the sky. Torchlight fluttered from inside dark windows, and the stones of the fortress seemed hewn from shadows and awe as the building rose before them like a second mountain. How grand the citadel of the Faithful was up close. How mysterious its architecture, which was hard and cruel with Menosian curves, while spills of ivy softened it. They could certainly say it was ancient and of a time before what they knew even from lore. In his wonderment, it took a moment for Devlin to notice the gray figures still as statues and standing near. Only two people protected the square, sarcophagus-like entrance to the enclave of the Faithful. They appeared unarmed until the wind fluttered their obscuring, hooded cloaks slightly, and short metal staffs flashed beneath. They did not move as the father and his son approached the dusty landing.

"We are pilgrims," announced Beauregard. "We have come to speak to the wise. They must hear what we have seen in the Summerlands."

Perhaps a tweak of nerves made his voice tremble. Perhaps the silent guards and their Green Mother had already spoken of the travelers' coming. The men nodded, and one swept an arm to the dark tunnel he defended. Beauregard and his father went through the portal. The guards held their silence and offered no guidance on where his desired audience could be found. *A pilgrim will find the way*, thought Beauregard, and he followed his instincts, which had thus far led him well.

Willowholme seemed a lifetime apart from these sacred, softly echoing passages. The tunnel was so still, he could hear the scrape of his feet, the clatter of his belt, the hiss of the torches that lit the space, and every breath he and his father took. Beauregard noticed folk in the many small vestries they walked by. Many were motionless and of the same stone posturing as the two guarding the entrance. With their faces unseen, they could have been specters of worshippers long past.

Moving through a cloister of ornate rock balusters, earthy, grassy scents drew them to a twittering field of reeds. Gray-robed tenders waded amongst the crops. Even this work the Faithful performed in silence—at an unconventional hourglass no less. It amazed the young traveler how much he heard when the world was free of mortal brouhaha. Without that din, the swishing stalks, the splashing boots, and the whistles of whatever cricket and sparrowlike creatures inhabited the patch formed a harmony and language all their own. He regretted when they were away from the rice field and their own sounds dominated the silence once more.

Beauregard came to a cross in the passages, and he took the path that felt right to him—the left. He used the same inborn judgments when he found a flight of stairs and took those up and again when navigating the broader hallways with their arches and leafy carvings beyond. His seemingly indiscriminate choices brought them through many quiet and beautiful spaces. Mezzanines opened to cotton clouds and pitch skies. They found arcades where nearly undressed men and women traded blows with long staffs and whirling kicks. There they merely heard the thwack of impact and never a huff. They walked through long halls where the Faithful ate with wooden cutlery, and not a clatter sounded. Lastly they traveled through a great room wherein congregations of gray folk hummed a single, conjoined, skin-shivering note. That was the only utterance they'd heard in their wandering—Beauregard felt that silence, tranquility, and enlightenment through the deprivation of language made up the religion of these people.

Higher and higher they trod. They were trespassers in this realm but went unhindered. Beauregard should have been astonished at his leadership when they arrived at the first set of doors they'd encountered—huge metal ones built for deterrence. His heart pounded with expectancy over what lay past the doors of this antechamber. Another set of Faithful guardians in gray stood outside the portal, and without a word exchanged, they pulled open the grand fortified entrance.

Beauregard and his father walked into a hollow, warm, and golden space that smelled of lye. Beauregard estimated the number of candles in the room at somewhere in the hundreds. From stone alcoves and shelves, flames crackled and winked at the men. Their fire tips all pointed to the far end of the chamber where a tall window glowed with the crystalline starlight seen only when one is high above the land. By the window and pooled in a circle of moonlight was a simple bench of stone set upon a dais. Glimmering with whiteness, it seemed like the seat of a celestial being. In this instance, it was a queen who sat there and watched the men. *Can she be called a queen? Do the Faithful have such titles?* Beauregard wondered. Defining her as anything less would be unfitting for this dark-haired young woman. She was thin and bulkily dressed in an unflattering robe, with beautifully braided hair, a sharp face, and slanted, nearly black eyes. Her gaze held a glint of wisdom beyond her years. She reminded Beauregard of a hawk or an owl or a bit of each—hunter and sage—and he had a shiver of humility and fright as her watchfulness fell upon him. He guessed that she was his age, but she seemed a hundred years older.

As they approached, she relaxed her spell over the travelers and smiled. Still she did not speak. Her eyes, which seemed to hold them both at once, were so captivating they did not notice the scribbling she performed in her lap. Beauregard was, therefore, startled to have the slight hand and its fluttering paper suddenly thrust in his face. He didn't recall having approached the Faithful this closely, but apparently he had. The woman had given him a note, which he quickly read.

"My name is Amara. Welcome to the Silent Peaks, pilgrim."

Beauregard showed the writing to his father, and the two bowed.

"Thank you—" Beauregard began.

A gusty stomp ruffled the flames in the room. It was a puff more suited to the flapping of a grand sorcerer's cape. The Faithful appeared cross, but her frown soon faded to a lenient smile. Beauregard almost apologized for his indecency before he realized he should not speak. Along with another note, Amara handed him a tiny stack of bound sheaves and a quill to prevent another misstep. In the exchange, she reclaimed the first paper and burned it in one of the fat candles at her feet. She watched the smoke as though it held augurs, and Beauregard read her next message.

"We of the Silent Peaks have not spoken since we made the long journey from the Far East. That was before the king of the South claimed his land as our neighbor. Words can poison peace as much as bring it, and this place has known peace for longer than many of the stars have been in the sky."

Beauregard scrawled back a response. The feather seemed enchanted and was as smooth as an inky wheel on the page. His father was quite unequipped for the unconventionality of this dialogue, and he glanced around at the flames, out the window to the stars, and once even toward the black-pearl gaze of their hostess. Her stare could not be avoided if he simply looked in her direction. Eventually, he settled for peering over his son's back at what the lad was writing, and then he failed in that distraction too. Beauregard passed on the message.

"Your customs are beautiful, as are your people and lands. The hearts of Sorsetta took us in after what was an indescribable journey. I did not know folk could be so untainted by greed, sin, or vice. I feel obliged to protect those virtues from what we have seen in the Summerlands. I come bearing a warning."

Amara read his missive, burned it while contemplating a response, and then replied. She took her time for such a short statement.

"What have you seen, pilgrim? Nothing is indescribable. Tell me of the terror that blackens your soul."

Beauregard learned that transcribing his experiences rather than speaking them was a profound method of recollection. Briefly, he mulled over what first to tell the leader of the Faithful, who seemed able to sense the secrets he and his father carried and the memories neither wanted to retrieve. However, words to write proved easier to find than words to speak. His mouth did not need the courage to open itself, and his hand moved as a reflex of his mind. It was as instinctual as when his legs had carried him through burning sands and his fingers had scraped wet dirt from a dead land to suck what life could be scavenged in the Summerlands. Every darkness and fright from great to small with which the Summerlands had scarred him he wrote onto paper. Soon he'd produced pages of his account—inscriptions of his darkest innermost thoughts.

"At times I felt dead—or undying—and as if I walked between the worlds. You cannot understand such dryness—a tongue like a stone and skin that peels off you like a snake's does. It was a realm of fire and ash without end. Nothing lives there now and perhaps never will again. The only other creatures in that realm are reptiles and things that crawl and bite. The people are but ghostly caricatures to torment the living. Whatever souls they had are gone, and their bodies are but vessels for a red, endless flame. This fire would eat Geadhain. Brutus would do this to all of us—eat us and pillage what is green and bright. You can feel his hate and passion in the land—as hot as the sun that scales your flesh."

He wrote quickly and had no occasion to review his work. Amara plucked up each page as soon he had completed it. By the time he finished the last page of his account, she'd read, pondered, and burned his torments to cinders. Only his final words did Beauregard watch her contemplate with a taut, grim demeanor. She set his ultimate warning to the flame, played her fingers through the red moths it made, and then uttered a strange, soundless sigh. It was no more than a parting of her lips. She appeared young then and burdened. Following this small lapse in character, the hard will of a leader shook her, and she sat up sword-straight and began to write.

Nervously, Beauregard and his father awaited her wisdom. The boy trembled when he reached out to claim her note. Again her questions were short and to the point.

"Vessel? You speak like a poet and scholar of the Far East. Why did you say vessel?"

Had he? Beauregard forced himself to think. He must have used the term in reference to Brutus's horde. Vessels. Such was how the things had seemed to him; they were no more alive than puppets. They were empty shells filled with...Brutus, he assumed, or the mad king's rage and lust.

"That is what they were. Not people but shadows of people who did Brutus's will. No living thing, no matter how wicked, would ever become what they have become," he wrote.

Amara crumpled and burned his reply. Her body suddenly clenched in a spell of anger that only a scream could release, but she could do naught but flare her nostrils. A woman's moods were not foreign to these men, and they could sense the Faithful's need for privacy, whether or not she could.

"I am sure you have much to attend to for the people of Sorsetta," scribbled Beauregard. "We should leave you to peace and silence."

The Faithful snatched the paper, scanned it, and then hastily penned something under Beauregard's writing. She handed it back to him gently, though anger's redness still flourished in her cheeks.

"You will stay for the night—or longer, if you choose. Our lands are as open to you as they are to me. Thank you for the gifts of your journey and wisdom, as hard as it has been on you and your father. Show this note to the monks outside, and they will find you food and warmth for the night."

Thus ended their meeting with Amara, and she stood, went to the long window, and leaned out into the air and night. Devlin shrugged, jerked a thumb toward the exit, and then walked away. Beauregard felt less certain about abandoning their hostess. He could see she wrestled with monsters—ones conjured from what he'd told her. Leaving Amara would be only half responsible, for his confession had brought her harm. It was not his right to intervene further, though. Who was he but a hunter's son? What did he know of the agony of rule? He felt embarrassed and let the woman be.

Later, while tossing on his bed in the ascetic, moonlit room to which they were taken to rest for the evening, he thought of Amara—not as a young man typically thinks of a young woman but with empathy. He thought of the priestess's turned back and her study of the dark outside her sanctuary. He'd come to Gorgonath hopeful its leaders would hear and appreciate his tale. His wish had been more fully granted than he'd expected, for with his lyricism, he had portrayed a darkness that seemed inescapable—even for them. By describing an enemy that could not be fought, though, he might have crushed the very hope he'd meant to bring to Gorgonath.

## VII

Mornings often brought freshness, and Beauregard found a smile for his father as he threw off the sheets and stretched in the sunny room. His father looked tidy and trimmed from the washbowl, cloths, and hand mirror brought sometime that morning. Devlin stopped pacing and clapped his hands as the boy awoke. "Thought you would sleep for the whole season," he said.

"I could have," admitted Beauregard.

"Well, the whole monastery is hopping, lad," said Devlin. "Whatever you said to the young priestess—I assume that's what she is—lit a fire under their arses. I'm surprised you slept through all the noise."

"Noise?" said Beauregard, and he listened.

Now he could sense the activity—the clinks of metal, the scrape of objects dragged hastily over stone, and, startlingly, even some whispers. The hush of the ages had been broken. The monks of the Silent Peaks were speaking—however surreptitiously. Though Beauregard knew what he'd facilitated, he had to see it for himself. He left the stubble on his face, tossed on his wrinkled clothes, and went out into the hallway with his father. A line of hustling monks carrying staffs and heavy jangling leather bags nearly bowled the pair over. Caltrops spilled onto the stone from the impact. The pair mouthed apologies to the female monk they'd bumped, and they helped her place her sharp treasures back in their place. They quickly ducked back into their room as more gray-robed, grim-faced warriors flew past. These were people of peace and tranquility no more.

"I had it in mind to help, as we did with Eloa. I feel, though, that we might only get in the way," said Beauregard.

Devlin grunted. "Indeed."

They ate a breakfast of breads and smoked cheeses that had been left for them in a covered basket, and they listened to the hustle outside their chamber. They talked of their fortune and strange voyage together, and they again made prayers for Tabitha's safety. After a while, the sunlight streaming into the room became hot and stifling. It was too much a reminder of the Summerland's blasting heat, and the men grew restless.

"A fishing hole!" declared Devlin, and he leaped up from his bed. "What better way for a man to pass his time than with a rod in his hand? We are *Fischers* after all."

"I don't follow."

The spirited father hauled his son off his bed. "I doubt you noticed them last night, as single-minded as you were, but I saw two gents in the hall with rods, nets, and tackle, and Eloa did say these monks are known for their angling as well as their agriculture. Let's go find a fishing hole. An underlake or what have you. Bring your pad and quill too. I'm sure we'll be needing them."

Though he didn't quite share his father's enthusiasm, Beauregard followed along. Surely a fishing trip on the dawn of war was not a fitting use of one's hourglasses. Or was it? Would there be much time for simple amusements in the future? *What she wills, she wills,* he thought. The Green Mother certainly didn't have it in mind to stop them.

Out in the hallway, they saw a dazzle of metal poking from the top of a monk's pack. Although not a fishing rod, its sparkle tricked Devlin's mind into thinking it was. He forgot his manners and hailed the monk. The Faithful might at last be speaking but only for matters of necessity and not common parlance. Beauregard quickly scribbled while his father continued the ill graces by asking for forgiveness. In a speck, the confusion and errors were sorted. It was a rake, not a fishing rod, but the man wrote them directions for where they might find the underlake. Gorgonath's Tears, the monk called the place. *An unusual name,* thought Beauregard. Not much in Sorsetta seemed evocative of sadness. He was suddenly interested to see Gorgonath's Tears, and he was as excited as his unusually animated father. Reflecting on their trials and pleasures in that instant, Beauregard saw how deeply his father had changed. The cranky bear seemed less withdrawn, more open to joy, and even more loving. As dark as their ordeal had been, he felt thankful for this result. Finally, he had a father and a friend—two things absent for most of his life.

The monk's instructions were precise and led them back most of the way they'd come the last evening and then farther down the mountain. They passed through a whirl of activity as they went—sacks being hauled, secretive whispers made in shame behind hands, and regimented Faithful marching.

These people might have been farmers the day before, but now they wore belts bearing sickles that would cut throats and not harvests. The theater of war was starting. Its first stings were playing, and its dancers were arranging themselves. Beauregard tried not to lose himself to this gloomy distraction, which was easier once they reached the damp and torchlit reaches under the monastery. Fewer preparations appeared under way here.

"Don't think too much about it, lad," said his father wisely as if reading his son's thoughts. "We don't know what tomorrow will bring, and we should take every scrap of happiness we can. Just a few hourglasses to ourselves, I promise, and then we'll see whether we can be a bit of help to these people."

Devlin could not conceive how exactly they might help. He was a hunter—not a warrior. His son was a romantic. Neither was made for war. He doubted the boy could handle anything larger than a knife. *Yet here we are*, came the voice of truth. Each was being made into a warrior. They both had roles and responsibilities they would like to forget for the moment, it seemed.

Lost to their thoughts, they were quiet as they went lower into Gorgonath's gray flesh. Hardly another soul existed down there. However, there were vast, cool storehouses stocked with supplies. Into the racks and barrels of one such storehouse they delved and came out with poles and silver bait. If anyone had been around, they would have asked for permission. Instead, they left a note for everything they took, promising to bring back the items. They even helped themselves to a couple of waterskins of cider—without spirits, Devlin noted with regret—and some strips of felsalted pig they found in a second echoingly large storehouse later on. For each pilfering, they left another note and promise amid the now-vacant space on the shelf. The trek to Gorgonath's Tears turned out to be far longer than the monk's simple course had made it sound—to follow the widest path as far and low as it would go. They hiked until they needed a second to stop for cider and then another pause to find a place to make water. While they felt quite crass about having to piss in a pail and put a message on it, they laughed just as much at their misdeeds. Noon must have come and gone somewhere on high, and the tunnel was now quite earthy with starved, feeble torches and unusual gusts. It had a purgatorial quality that started to unnerve the two men. Whoever maintained the flames was evidently invisible. Perhaps a ghostly monk fluttered from torch to torch, for they still hadn't met another person in the underground.

Suddenly, the passage opened and teased them with sensations—puffs of salted wind, the echoing music of dripping water, and flickers of natural light. They hurried forward, and the pocket under the mountain into which they came embraced them with its beauty. They both thought it a grand spectacle. The stone ceiling was as riddled with holes as coral and pouring light. Ahead lay a crumbled beach, and rolling dark-blue waters—the blood of the sea. Beauregard had known this only from the Feordhan and had never seen it so pure. Out past the shady cove, through a crude, great arch, the Scarasace Sea rippled in a sapphire sheet. This further elated them with an ancient, briny perfume. Now at last Beauregard understood the name of the place—Gorgonath's Tears. Water condensed off the ridges atop the hollow and fell over the wanderers in a salty mist.

A beaten dock floated in the rocks and sand of the shore, and the men found it when their awe faded. They plopped themselves down on the rickety boards, took off their boots, and hung their feet in the water. All settled, they set their lines with bait and lures and cast them into the sea. For a spell, in the day's golden glory and with the wind sweeping through their hair, they were nothing more than two men on a dock enjoying a magnificent afternoon. They chatted in the smallest ways with short cheers for hefty catches or a pat on the other's back if he seemed to be drifting into moroseness. In any case, the seascape's beauty discouraged darkness from setting in. Soon the sun started to fade, and they realized they had passed most of the day with their leisure.

"One more cast," said Devlin. He knew their pleasure was at an end.

Beauregard smiled. "All right."

Their lures dunked into the sea, and they relaxed into the hunter's calm of waiting. Over the whooshing, dripping, and splashing echoes of the cavern, they did not sense Amara's approach. She was suddenly standing between the two. It was as if she too had been fishing the whole time. Devlin made a startled hiccup, and Beauregard turned in time to be handed a note.

"I was told to find you here. I would not have thought of such an activity today. My mind has been elsewhere."

Placing his rod into the dock's gaps, Beauregard scrambled to his feet and searched for his writing implements. Amara stopped him with a cold grip and a smile. She slipped him another message written in the specks he'd been fumbling.

"We're not in the Silent Peaks. Not quite. Please speak as you will. I have my vows, however."

"Thank you," replied Beauregard. "What brings you here, priestess?"

She held up a corrective finger and then quickly wrote something for Beauregard in the small pad she carried. "I am a Keeper—not a priestess," said Amara's note. "A tradition that comes from the Far East—from places and traditions that predate Western mysteries. We watch, listen, and learn all the Green Mother will share with us. To answer your question, though, I am here to thank you. I was not hospitable with my silence last night, and you and your father have helped me and the people of Sorsetta more than you could know. Far more than the realms we call allies."

Instead of burning her notes, Amara ripped them and cast their tatters off the dock. Beauregard gave her the one he had finished reading and asked, "Allies? I thought the Everfair King warned you of Brutus's coming."

Amara sneered, and it was alarming to see such an expression on her. She wrote extensively and angrily. "We were warned to be wary of our neighbor in the Summerlands. We were told he and the king of the North were settling a matter between their immortal selves, and any outlying lands could be caught in their conflict. We escaped most of that unholy storm by the Green Mother's grace. Still, our peacefulness can be a weakness. We do not always see or respond to malice. We can be a trusting sheep that does not know it is being fattened for the feast. We do not understand the drive to murder or harm life for sport. Eod's queen—not its king, whose fate I now question—warned us of a potential danger. Diplomatic safeguards were established so our people would not fall prey to the wild sorcery the Kings might conjure. We knew Brutus was angry. We did not know he was mad and owned by darkness. Your account, as personal and horrific as it was, has convinced me we are not safe merely shoring up our people in Gorgonath. Brutus will come. A monster like that is rabid and hungry and does not know how to stop. He will bring everything wrong in the world—all we fear and do not understand. I do not know why the queen would understate his threat

CHRISTIAN A. BROWN

when what you have described with your innocent pilgrim's heart is evil. Not a treatable malady. I know of no silence or magik that can cure so dark a soul. However, while Brutus might throw his wave of blood and fire upon us, he will find Gorgonath a wall he cannot break. That is why I thank you and the Green Mother, whose voice brought you to us. You two might have saved many hundreds of thousands of souls simply with your honor."

Amara knelt to both knees and laid her hands by Beauregard's feet. It was a prostration he'd noticed before in the monastery's quiet rooms for reflection, and his throat tightened from sentimentality. He had never thought of himself in any of the ways she had painted him. Devlin came over, read the Keeper's admission, and pulled her to her feet. Outside her sanctuary, the fading daylight stripped away her ponderous mantle of leadership and the impression of age, and she appeared quite young. She was as scared as the rest of them.

"We did what was right," said Devlin. "We'd do it again too. Nothing more should we say about that. We're here, and we wouldn't have spent the day on the docks, lovely as it was, if we had known how to help." He patted the Keeper's shoulder and then faced his son. "We want to be made use of. Right?"

"Yes," replied Beauregard sincerely.

Devlin knew he was conscripting them to war and most probably death. All that got lost in his impetuousness, though. A man had to learn, and he'd seen an edge to the lad in the Summerlands that could be the steel of a warrior if honed through fire and battle.

"I am glad," wrote Amara.

An abrupt and final burst of sunlight from the porous dome above sealed their fellowship and made them all bloodred. Night greedily ate the day, and shadows draped upon the three. Amara shredded the last of her written whispers and freed them like paper birds to the wind. They made a beautiful, tiny storm, and their patterns caused each of the three persons to ponder freedom and flight. Beauregard had forgotten to ask the Keeper why she destroyed her words. After now having seen it done so many times, though, he felt it another ritual of release to the world. She was returning substance to soil, ashes to ashes, and paper to dust. She made for a charming if odd creature, this Keeper—the girl who was forced into roles beyond her years

248

and who buckled under none of the pressure. Beauregard found her fascinating, although he felt not a spark of lust. They merely had a commonality of shared and secret traits, and he wanted to befriend her. Amara's subtle smile in the moment she caught him staring told him he'd already done so.

"Beau!" cried his father, who had gone to collect their gear. "Pick up your rod, lad! Before your catch gets away!"

Beauregard stirred and rushed to his fishing pole, which bent and strained like a branch tied with stones. He grabbed the rod before it snapped and braced himself at the dock's edge. Whatever he'd hooked was large, powerful, and frustratingly agile. It wove the line across the water. In a speck, he would be empty-handed and on his arse from a broken line. Devlin stepped beside him to help, but he quickly hissed his father away: this was his fight to win. Grinding his teeth in fury, Beauregard strained every lean muscle in his body, and when that final screaming pull ended, he was indeed on his arse. The line remained intact, though, and he was triumphant. He curdled his face, however, at his prize. *A fish?* he wondered, and he stared at the slimy, wriggling tentacular knot with its flecks of gold, crystals, stones, and weeds. The thing clashed with his senses. It was both beautiful and glittering, as well as oily and repulsive. He leaped back—and just in time too. The sturgeon-like head with needles for teeth suddenly lashed out from the mess. Beauregard and his father had been releasing their catches back into the sea that day. They had been fishing for sport and not for a meal. As wild and dangerous as it appeared, Beauregard didn't think he could, or wanted to, touch the creature long enough to set it free. Thus it flopped, rolled, weakened, and slowed. Its gills or other organs struggled for air. At a distance, the creature possessed a scintillating charm. Knit into its appendages was one extraordinary gemlike stone that could have been a slice of starlight. It flashed from white to silver and back again. He regretted that it would have to die. Amara roughly spun him from his deathwatch and stamped a note to his chest. She spun him around again and shoved him down the dock.

"Think she wants you to put it back, lad," his father said, and he chuckled. "Shame you turned away my help earlier. Teeth look sharp."

Amara's words gave Beauregard a wisp of courage. "A keeper fish! As rare a treasure of the sea as the deep minerals and stones off which they feed. They are the keepers of the Green Mother's salty blood, just as we are the tenders of her body. You cannot let it die. Do not fear it. They do not eat flesh—only rock and jewels of the deepest mines. This is a grand omen and a wonder, and you must welcome it."

He glanced back to the Keeper, and he could see her imploring him to press onward. It was best to do the duty quickly and hope she spoke true about the creature's appetites. He knelt and chanced his fingers by holding the now-docile beast's head and unhooking the lure from its snout. With a shade more bravery, he thrust his hands into the silky, wet coils of the creature and went to drop it back into the sea. The coils tightened, their spiky stones scraped into him, and he squealed. He was a speck from flailing and hurling the black burden off himself, but the slithering mass unspooled and drooped, and he gently laid the creature down into the blue skin of the sea. Queer as the idea seemed, he felt the creature looking at him with its dark glass eyes, which were mirrors of Amara's. Then its head flickered out of sight and into watery nothingness. He was proud of himself, and he waved to the strange and vanished visitor and bent to collect his rod and belongings.

The crystal he'd seen, the one of starlight, shone against the blackness of his wool cloak. While writhing on the dock, the keeper fish must have shed the precious object. This seemed unusual. From his brief contact with the creature, he'd noticed the stones were partially embedded and grown from inside its rubbery flesh. When he picked up the oddly shaped item, he saw it was as angular as a diamond blade tip. It immediately sent a shock through his body that shrank his scalp, testicles, and skin. He clenched his hand, which bled, and his teeth. As soon as he could, he dropped it, and the terrible clenching ended. *Magik*, he thought. He had never touched the stuff, but its presence now seemed as recognizable as any natural force. He didn't need lightning to strike him to approximate how it would feel. It would probably feel something like *that*. He pondered the stone's mystery and contemplated touching it again with his bleeding hand. He could sense the hum of it as his fingers neared.

The others rushed over, and Devlin frowned at the starry shard. Amara came up beside the young man and gasped. It was a genuine sound—not mimicry. She began to hastily jot her thoughts down with shaking hands, and she passed her words to Beauregard in a speck.

*"Ioncrach!"* he read. "A wonderstone in lesser tongues. The rarest mineral on Geadhain. It is said to have the power to grant miracles, break any magik, or cast out any evil. I have never seen one that large—only pebbles we have hoarded from our nets over the years or found washed in from the oldest reaches of the sea. They are said to have fallen from the sky, these relics, along with the Oldest when they graced our world."

"Oldest? Miracles?" exclaimed Beauregard.

A great mystery had been dropped into his lap. Amara undertook some hectic writing and soon shook another note at him.

"The Ones Who Sleep. The Oldest with bodies of stars and infinite Wills. Their very dreams, illusions of their sleeping minds, conjured the seas, lands, and man himself into being. They are what made our world and all we know: the Dreamers. They were here once, as real as you and I, and the *Ioncrach* are remnants of their wonder—pieces of possibility left behind once they abandoned us to dream again," she said.

This formed a pretty and unnerving faery tale to Beauregard, and it was not one he had ever been taught. Ancient beings wandering Geadhain? Fragments of their miracles? He was more reluctant than before to touch the shard.

"Take it!" the next note insisted.

A little against his will, he listened, wrapped the tingling shard in his cloak, and bundled it under his arm. Even with the layers separating his skin from the crystal, he still prickled from its magik. In his keeping was a power persons were not supposed to hold. It was a treasure for Immortal Kings or those who would usurp them, and he felt out of touch with himself and the wood beneath his feet. It was as if he could float off on the wind. *To the stars, where the Dreamers dream,* he mused. The astonishment of both his father and the Keeper did not assist in weighing down his airborne sense of reality. Finally, he clenched his fists and focused on the darkening cove. *Here be the world, the rocks, the sea, the wind, Father, and the pale young Keeper—even if I have a piece of the cosmos in my arms.*

"I'm fine," he said. "This has turned into quite an unusual day for two men who wanted only to catch a few fish." The wide-eyed Devlin nodded. "I don't suppose we could throw this at Brutus and his horde," proposed Beauregard gaily.

Amara's face stitched with a nasty wrinkle. She scribed her disapproval and held her words against the nose of each man to read. "*Ioncrach* is not a toy and nothing to joke about. Were you to throw about the *Ioncrach*, you could well level all Gorgonath and all Central Geadhain and leave the Sun King untouched and laughing. I do not know how to use it. I know only that in each instance, each finder and his or her miracle is unique and devastating in its own right. A wonderstone of that size is a cataclysm. In my awe, I broke a sacred trust in telling you our secrets—truths even the oldest and wisest might not know. For those are our roles and responsibilities as the untainted preservers and curators—the Keepers—of history. You must never tell another living being—not even your one-day wife or distant mother—that you hold such a relic. I trust you two will die with this promise and this power, even if it is never used. Can I trust you?"

"Yes," each man said in a dark and dire voice.

With a finger, she bade them pause while she wrote another message. Less aggressively, she passed it into Beauregard's grasp when it was complete. "The Green Mother has given you this extraordinary treasure to protect, Beauregard, and you must at all times think now of that burden. I know the strain of responsibility, and it can break bones as if it were the heaviest stone. You must be strong and no more a child. Today, the last of your youth is over."

She reclaimed her words, tore them into fragments, and ensured that the wind and sea devoured them. She then nodded for them all to leave. They silently traveled the underground, but from that sand and thereafter, Devlin struggled to understand his son's reserve and the darkness that stuck under the boy's eyes even as they walked past torches. The Keeper's words, the ones he hadn't seen, had altered the lad into a haunted figure that hugged his package of starlight greedily and scoured ahead for threats. Devlin should have been proud of this straight-backed, fearsome fellow, and he was. He felt saddened too, though. For with a parent's sense, he knew his son's innocence was no more.

## VIII

The pain, heat, and even hotter monster inside him—such was all Magnus's body knew. At times the writhing snake of vomit and broken glass in his belly would churn so hatefully he convulsed in tooth-chipping seizures. Then those empty-shelled men would come, pry open his mouth, and force him to drink more of whatever diabolical concoction his brother had devised to weaken him. The sticky black milk clotted his eyes, nose, and throat until he shrank to a mere freckle of wheezing consciousness. Then they would torture him. The Black Queen's children, the things with ebon and crimson stares, had no shortage of tortures. They would slide needles under his nails, flay strips of skin, place his testicles in vises of pins, and run burning brands against his softest parts until the room, already putrid with death and sweat's rankness, reeked further with the lardy fumes of his cooking meat. His tormentors didn't understand their victim enough to break him truly, though. Whatever was done to Magnus's body could not harm him in the fortress of his mind.

Again and again, deeper and longer, he retreated into the cold bastion of glittering ice that was his Will. There he sat in contemplation on a throne of frost, and he listened to the howls at his walls—his screams. Magnus, however, was numb from the coldness seeping through his back. Only occasionally did he rise from his throne and realize where he was with the fullness of his senses. In those moments, he looked through a window at his raw, horrific self, and he would grimace in pity—not for himself but for his lost and anguished brother. Then he would return to his seat so he might again embrace the chill of forgetfulness. There would, however, now and then come a moment when the screeching weather ended, and the glassy walls pulsed with warmth and the red light of a sun in this dark winter. The body Magnus dreamed of would suckle and drink something that made his spirit-self salivate. If he tasted this further, he would know iron and wine. This deliciousness of flavor could be only one thing—Brutus's blood.

During these moments, his brother whispered lunacies—confessions of a masochist and monster who lamented what he did and yet justified his barbarity. "I bleed you to love you," Brutus said. "Mother needs us. If you would only break. If you would simply let her in, let me in, we could be together. So strong you are. Such a beautiful statue of ice."

Brutus's whispers were a lover's promises, and more than once Magnus would quickly hurry from his window to the world as his brother surrendered to lust. Brutus clawed, touched, and penetrated his beaten cage of flesh in ways brothers never should. The fortress of Magnus's Will would rattle with his brother's grotesque passion then. It would shake from grunting storms and violently raining ice. Magnus gripped his throne and endured the tremors. The storm always passed with a grumble and more rage and often great blows in the physical world that shook Magnus's sanctuary and left his true body unthinkably red and ruined.

Soon—whatever soon meant in this eternity—Magnus simply stayed upon his winter throne and no longer cast his attentions to the outside. He did not heed the arrival of his brother's storm. Magnus did not need to see what was only a grisly cycle of sickness, rape and violence. So on his throne he remained. He sank lower into meditations and numbed himself colorless with cold. He did not think of Lila, Erik, or any outside this space. They weren't even memories anymore, as close as their bonds had been. There was but Magnus and the winter—the season of his birth and a truer mother than the black thing that wished for his submission. Slowly, Mother Winter bound, hardened, and tempered him to the same bitter, dark ice of his castle. At last he, the throne, and its element were one motionless, unshakable cold. At last he was prepared. A moment was all he needed. The faintest flutter of freedom or the smallest crack in his prison, and he would unleash his wrath. He would wash the world in ice.

He was ready.

IX

"Did you find her?"

With a babe on her tit and much of her mind elsewhere, Elemech had no idea why her golden sister tugged at her skirt and asked strange questions. She couldn't even remember why she'd agreed to go outside. For winter had come to Alabion as well, and her kirtle was unduly thin for a partially exposed woman sitting upon a rimy rock on a snow-salted plateau so chilly that none of their animal friends was about. *What a terrible day to head outdoors*, she thought and pouted. She would be grateful when her motherly capitulations wore off and she turned back into the sullen woman who watched Fates and deaths in the murk of her witch-water. The sorcery of motherhood tingled within her, though, and would continue for many more days. Kindly, she glanced to young Ealasyd. "Find whom?" she asked.

"Morigan!" exclaimed the youngest.

While forever forgetful, somehow Ealasyd clung to Morigan's name. It had yet to slip out of her head. Since the day of its telling, she had carved "Morigan" into the stones outside and inside the cave, named her favorite glow-moths after the Daughter of Fate, and even made a collection of little red-haired dolls—exclusively as toys. She would hiss at Elemech if she attempted to toss the dolls in her pool. In all their years upon years, Elemech had never seen Ealasyd hold such a memory. Surely this was a quality of the Daughter of Fate, this disruption of chains and patterns that were supposed to be unchangeable.

Elemech frowned. "Worry not about Morigan. She is on her way. Sooner than we shall be ready for her."

Ealasyd poked her elder playfully. "You still don't know, do you?"

"Know?"

"Where she is."

No. Elemech did not. The Daughter of Fate's power to control the weave of all things swelled stronger than ever. Elemech did not fear this power as much now. Some wisdom had crept into Elemech since her surprise. Besides, she could track Morigan by other means. If not through the girl's power directly, then she could do so indirectly, by the ripples of Fate she left behind. In the woods near the City of Fangs the other day, a flare of destiny as bright as a comet in the sky had woken Elemech from the half-sleep or drowsy meditation she was in. She had flown to her witchwater well and seen the near sundering of a Dreamer in its mortal flesh: an act that laughed at what she knew of cosmic rules. *She's broken it well and good. She's spit on the pages, burned up the book itself, and made her own rules.*

Elemech shivered and tucked away her breast so she might draw her shawl closed. Even if she had seen others in that vision—shadowy, blurred men and women of smoke who were Morigan and those she protected—the Daughter of Fate was the cause of this chaos. It could be no one else.

"Another two weeks, give or take," said Elemech, after mulling for some time in silence. "A bit longer with where they're headed now."

She trailed off glumly. Ealasyd knew her sister's expression. A secret was being kept and not shared. She didn't care for it. "Where are they headed now?" asked Ealasyd.

Reluctantly, Elemech answered. "The dark heart of our mother. Where all her wounds and nightmares live. In the Pitch Dark are the ones Mother made and forgot. All the lost, missing, lonely, and broken things. Everything wild, wicked, and dark. All her sins and sorrows. Your head is too tender to worry over what they might face."

"Monsters?" Ealasyd shuddered and looked around.

"Worse than monsters," warned Elemech.

Off to the darkest part of the woods, Ealasyd stared—to the boughs that not even the snow could whiten past gray and where the shadows seemed to slither. *What could be worse than monsters?* Ealasyd wondered in dread.

"Truths," muttered Elemech. "Shadows."

Huddling together, the pair watched the winter roar up in rage from the north and descend upon the Pitch Dark.

# PART II

# X

# THE PITCH DARK

### I

The company paused at the crossing. Normal folk such as Talwyn worried over the frightful risk posed by fording the hungry, frigid stream that cascaded about the Wolf's shins. Surely it would come up to Talwyn's hips. While this was the shallowest shore they'd found in their long morning hike up and down the River Torn, Talwyn had yet to step into the currents. He wasn't convinced the walking stick he clung to would hold, and he knew he would be far, far colder than Caenith once his toes touched the water. A dreadful fantasy played havoc in his mind—of his limbs seizing up, his stick breaking, and his body being swept off the distant drop in the river to frothing, dashing doom.

He could see by the severe faces of his fellows that these were mortal and personal bothers. Even the woman who'd lost her father only yesterday scowled at the woods with a fearless expression. However, dark designs lurked behind it. He wondered what ideas brewed in her head. He felt certain they meant nothing good. Behind her the old man and young changeling stood together as unreadable as Mouse. Talwyn's cloak had been returned to him, and Adam they'd since dressed in a beggarly diaper made of scraps torn from the company's garments. With his many tattoos, the changeling looked as wild as a warrior of old. Of all the heroes, though, he found the Wolf and his mate the most interesting. The large man strode carelessly and nearly naked in the cold with his head angled and his nostrils steaming the air. He often wandered between qualities of man and beast. He smelled other beasts he didn't like, judging by the wrinkle of his nose. Equally mesmerizing to Talwyn was the seer, who clutched at her savage mate as if she could see the same foes—not with those silver eyes of hers but with a different sight that could see farther and deeper. *What do they discuss?* he wondered, and he wished for an ear to their hidden voices.

*Aghna warned me*, whispered the Wolf to his mate.

An unpleasant flash of memory rippled into Morigan. She saw the white beast circling her chained Wolf and mocking him for his quest. "The Pitch Dark?" she had said. "You should leave the past in the past. You will not like what awaits you there should your champion prevail. I have seen the heart of Mother Geadhain, and it is black. Be wary of mothers, Caenith. They are never who we think."

It had been a vague, heavy threat. The bees hummed a warning. *Something awaits us here*, replied Morigan. *I can feel a pull. A calling, almost.*

The dark reaches of the woods tugged at her. The wind at her back seemed to push her into the water, and her skin prickled with the static of anticipation. A great fate lay beyond. It was a destiny that would change them. She felt that every step had been simply a climb to this moment, and she saw flashes of altars, pillars, and moons. As she dwelled on these premonitions, she heard howls and chanting, and once she saw three frightening figures in red. Still, nothing could truly rattle Morigan these days, and she would have stepped into the river's tides even if the bees had not thrust her body forward with the jolt of their desire. They wanted to see and feed off whatever glorious delights lay in the Pitch Dark.

*Sightseeing is over*, Talwyn thought, and he sighed as the seer moved ahead. He hoped his stick would hold. He stepped in, and the water felt as cold as a slipper of ice. None of the others cried out or even noticed his whimpering. As if his troubles were an amusement to the woods, the clouds suddenly twisted with grayness and belched a flurry of snow and wind. Still, he wore his freezing slippers, shut his mouth, and tried his very best to find some bravery. When they finally reached the other side and were muffled in the reaching shadows there, he knew it was too late to turn back.

## II

Morigan rose without the warm blanket of her Wolf's presence. How cold the Pitch Dark was compared with Alabion's other groves. She could sense with her wolfish senses the shivering of frosty despair, the menace of the clawed branches and their icy nails, and even the stinking threat of loam and ripped earth—the smell of an open grave. At some point during the night, the snow had let up, and while winter draped the land, much of it was gray, for the blackness of the Pitch Dark bled through any color. It was both winter and morning, and neither season nor daylight appeared to have sent the Pitch Dark's beasts into hibernation. All through the trees, hunters ruffled, huffed, and barked. Their musical exuberance was akin to that of a jungle at the height of its heat and fertility. She wondered which of these monsters her bloodmate hunted and when he would be back.

*I am not far, my Fawn. Only scouting,* came his whisper, which lit the flame of him that lived inside her. *You were so peaceful and beautiful, I could not bring myself to stir you.*

She smiled and walked to the pitiful campfire her companions encircled. With that horrible trick the memory plays on the living, she mistook the new man for Vortigern. However, his red hair and soft voice killed the illusion, and she pouted as she came upon the others. Thackery and Talwyn were chatting. The elder man sat on one of the timbers Caenith had hauled for their luxury, and he threw his cloak around Morigan as she came to him. "You look cold," he said.

She hugged the frail fellow tightly and wondered how the rest of the company was coping—especially Mouse. Since crossing the rapids, she'd been the last in their line and preferred her own company. Adam could not be seen and probably hunted with the Wolf. Last night Mouse had been cruel to the young changeling. She had shrugged off his touches and pushed away the food he offered. Morigan understood why he hunted and did not stay to be further spurned. Morigan wanted to reach out to her friend. She worried, though, that her empathy would only provoke Mouse's bitterness over the white wolf, Vortigern, and vows of vengeance. Nonetheless, she left Thackery to find Mouse. Her friend sat not far away on a different piece of timber, alone.

"Cards?" Morigan asked. She swept up her cloak and took the spot opposite Mouse with the fanned deck between them.

Mouse did not acknowledge her right away. "The Torn River. That must have been it," Mouse eventually muttered, and she tapped a glossy picture showing woodland with a blue vein winding between some rocks.

*The second marker*, buzzed the bees, and Morigan spun for a speck in a cyclone of prophecy. Flickering windows showed spiders and a golden-haired girl whispering. What a thoughtless friend she'd been to forget that destiny marked Mouse too. From about Mouse's neck, the cold iron chain that had once belonged to Morigan's father winked at the seer with light. *All these mysteries. The festering is coming to a head. None of us is safe.* Morigan shivered. She did not press her friend further, partly because she worried what Mouse might say.

After a while Mouse mumbled again. "The east wind. Wind of change and death. I wonder...where has it blown Adelaide? Where is the third?"

Mouse wasn't mad. Morigan didn't think she could be so easily damaged—not even by her father's traumatic death. A passion gripped her friend, however, that set her lips rambling. Chimes of prophecy tinkled within Morigan's head. Absently, Mouse's hand drifted to the amulet under her blouse and traced the metal. Then she began rather haphazardly to rifle the cards about on the log, even casting a few into the snow.

"A place so dark...where do you want me to go? A voice," she said faintly.

Mouse seized a card, and the seer had a glimmer of its picture—something gray and man-shaped—before visions again tore into her.

*A full moon. The holiest of moons. His moon. Tonight he will be called. On this eve, when the veil is as thin and shimmering as the membranes of a glass insect, when the stars all blink as though watchful, cosmic gazers, he will come. This vision whirls. It does not want to be seen, and it has some power to keep itself from Morigan. She has only fragments to grasp as they flutter past her consciousness.*

*A gleam of metal.*

*A sensation of warmth blossoming and then leaving the body. Someone is dying.*

*Blood. The sinful drip and drum of its music. The metal sweetness of it in her mouth as it flows and fountains from her over a cracked stone altar.*

*"Invite me into your soul," he says.*

*What voice is this? This sonorous song emerges as a hum and draws the eyelids closed and turns the limbs into lead. The tightness in her chest softens. She is heavy, wet, and dreaming herself to a death or somewhere else. Above her, the stars and moon are impossibly white and blinding.*

The dazzlement ended and left spots on Morigan's vision. Blind and desperate, she clutched her friend, whom she couldn't see. Mouse ripped herself free of Morigan. A moment ago, Mouse had felt the other's pins of magik inside her head and picking at some thought or fate.

"Please don't," pleaded Morigan.

Morigan, though, could not say what she asked the other to refuse. She could not glue together the chips of what she'd witnessed. In so close and raw a moment, she should have been radiating with intuition, yet the bees gave her nothing. A force shielded Mouse and her intent from Morigan. Even so, Morigan's gaze hung on the lump of iron swinging behind the fabric on her friend's breast. She felt the urge to tear off the talisman and wondered whether it was cursed. If not cursed, it was part of a terrible covenant that was damned all the same. A measure of what Mouse was thinking was plain enough to read without the bees—grief, anger, and a rashness born from each.

"Don't!" snapped Mouse. "Don't grab me again or get into my head! I've asked you not to do that before."

Mouse gathered up the demon deck and its scattered cards from the snow and went to sulk against a tree. *Honestly*, she seethed, *the gall of that woman.* She hadn't been thinking of anything risky aside from Adelaide's gloomy wisdom on markers and destiny. *Don't.* What a strange thing to say to one not planning anything devious—or not, at any rate, caught up in anything more subversive than her frequent musings on life's unfairness. She considered how she'd had to scrape and steal every bit of happiness, even after a beacon of Fate and wonders—Morigan—had entered her life. Dear Morigan was not enough to ward off the shadows that hunted Mouse. Any fate-reader could see that happiness was her bitter enemy. Love, family, and a father—forever she would be denied the fundamentals of mortal contentment. Glancing over to her withered great-uncle, she knew he barely hung on to this world. The Pale Lady would soon be along to collect on the short loan on life he'd taken. That bumbling scholar he parleyed with seemed no better off than Adelaide. He was a fool intended for death by tripping, bumbling, or comical carelessness. She imagined him putting on his boots with an adder inside or mistaking a corrosive, foaming solvent for his shaving cream. Doomed and dead was he. She supposed all of them were—even she. Mortals had to pay the price of running along with those who did not age. *We were never truly friends,* she thought scornfully, and she slid her gaze over to the seer who watched her. *We were just pets for you to keep. To remind you of the things you might miss when they vanish along with years and civilizations. Will you remember me in ten years, Morigan? Twenty? While you and the wolfman are still chasing each other's tails and sniffing each other's arses in one hundred years, I shall be forgotten.*

Without her father, her reason for being in these horrific woods, Mouse could find less of a cause to remain. She knew well enough that she was slipping into grief as if it were an iron shell that would protect her when a father and mother could not. While winter softly fell, her armor piled up as heavy as the snow on her shoulders. No matter the weight, a certain spark remained and would not be snuffed whenever thoughts of a yellow smile or the phantom spices of her father's cologne came to her. Love was eternal, it seemed. Damnable love. If the memory of her father would not die, why should he stay dead? Why should any of them be doomed?

During Mouse's rumination, the seer had not stopped watching her, and Mouse glared back brashly. She was uncertain of Morigan's motivations. *Damn you, Morigan, and fuk the Fates. I'm done playing kindly or playing along at all. I'll have everything I want. Even if I have to steal it.* Mouse held the stare of her friend or her enemy—whatever this twisted attachment was—until the other glanced away.

At that moment, Morigan knew that whatever she feared from Mouse had just begun. She only wished she knew how to stop her friend.

✳ ✳ ✳

III

Caenith and Adam rejoined them soon bearing a few stringy, unpalatable hares to eat. After their meal, during which everyone's tongues had seemed tied, the company set out into the Pitch Dark. They made fair headway and settled in for the night under a rocky frown over which a great oak had grown. Many remarked on how quiet the night was and how subdued the animals were compared with the day's cacophony. The Wolf surely knew something, and he silently scowled.

They set out early as gray and weary as the morning. Here the land glistened under an eternal winter twilight. It was more "silver dark" than pitch. They each thought glumly that they had likely not come to the blackest part. At least the glimmering frost and snow gave them light enough by which to see the ancient trees so grand they might have been the first of their kind.

The first disturbance came suddenly—a rumble of footsteps like small earthquakes and a roar like machine bellows. All but the Wolf shivered from surprise. He'd heard these noises of the greater beasts before. The Pitch Dark's true predators had scared the weaker carnivores into hiding.

"We are lesser here," he warned.

Every step thereafter was taken in caution. Without the dead man to share in the duty of protection, Caenith took each sleepless watch as his responsibility. He allowed the company to sleep a few winks—two hourglasses at most—before rousing them to move. Staying in one place for too long wasn't safe. The Wolf, though, would not say what they were not safe from, and they did not ask. They could hear the groan and snap of toppling trees that presaged the rumbling arrival of these hulking beasts, and they could feel the blasts of wind well enough to resist asking for specifics. Only Morigan, through her connection to the Wolf, had a sense of what prowled the Pitch Dark. She sensed blundering masses of fur and scale—things that might be bears if bears were horned and ten times the size. She saw grand monsters that swooped through the woods on leathery wings and wrapped their prey in an embrace of death. Sometimes her psychic ear heard the crunching and suckling of these horrors as they ate. Nature was out of order in this realm, or it was of an order so old that what was new appeared broken.

In the endless silver glow of the Pitch Dark, the company knew neither night nor day and neither rest nor peace. Less and less, they talked. None among them had an appetite for conversation. Talking could summon the lords that shivered the trees. Draped in silence, they crept along. At times it was so quiet only their cloudy breaths distinguished the six wanderers from specters. The rhythm of their travel set itself. There were no more fires. A fire was too dangerous an attraction. They had short sleeps—no more than gasps. Upon waking, they would receive from the Wolf a mangy, bloody, uncooked thing so that they might eat like feral beings. Afterward, they would dissolve a bit of snow on their tongues and use the same to wash the blood from their hands. They drank winter and washed in snow. At any given instant, a noise might come. Often it was one only harkened to by the Wolf, and they had to move faster. Onward into the snow they went. They hauled themselves over roots as large as city pipes and around these trees that were more pillar than object of nature. If they had not all been so hardened, they might have complained. Even Talwyn discovered a meek flame of courage—enough to keep him quiet and moving. The need for stealthy travel was a shame, as much of this extraordinary ecology demanded proper lingering study and discourse. Since he had no heat to warm himself, he kept the fires of his mind stoked instead by citing and cataloging the wonders he spied in the gloom.

*Illuminatus agisporus*, he termed the species of cap-headed and luminously blue fungi that infested several regions of the wood. The growths bled a warmth that melted the snow around them so that they might always be seen, and they wafted a caramel fragrance that enticed one near and made the mouth water. Theirs was a deadly allure, as Talwyn knew from the tiny animal skeletons curled like sleeping children around the mushrooms, and he never was fool enough to examine them closely. Once Mouse had been quite dreary and deeply dwelling on that same darkness he'd sensed before, and she nearly brushed against the fungi. The scholar had warned her politely, "Do mind the pretty toadstools. They're rather toxic."

Then the Wolf had barked punishingly. "Poison! Take heed of your tread!"

Mouse then muttered several expletives. Under the cold tension of the company, it appeared tempers were boiling. They would need rest and a fire through the night soon, or they would become as brittle and dangerous as the sheets of ice that fell from the trees without warning.

There would be no rest, though. The day-nights seemed darker, longer, and colder. Their necks grew as frozen as winter poles. They were strained and in constant pain from heeding the forest's calls. The silences were excruciating, and speech felt like a memory, even for the strange pair Talwyn had figured could chat in each other's heads. Indeed, the bloodmates seemed as pensive and self-absorbed as Mouse. Outside this trio of brooders, Thackery and the young changeling showed the fewest signs of despair. The old sage was alert and perhaps appreciative of the age and mystery of where they trod. He stared reverently at the oldest of trees and dallied longer than the others to hear the noises in the woods. Often Talwyn himself lagged but helped him along. They talked like brother monks in Sorsetta—with smiles of appreciation in their eyes, nods, or headshakes. Each man suffered from a weakness for scholarly intrigue, regardless of how inconvenient the timing. Talwyn wished he could have spoken with the old man more, for Thackery's blue gaze sparkled like a well of secrets, knowledge, and torments. He was a fascinating fellow, this outcast Thule, and when they had the chance, Talwyn would pick the man's mind for stories.

As for Adam, he appeared sweetly lost. Talwyn decided this was by choice, for the lad—either in man's skin or wolf's fur—never wandered far from the grim damsel of his affections. *Hopeless*, thought Talwyn. However, what did he really grasp of love—that ephemeral science that analysis could not conquer? Nothing at all. He certainly did not know about what bound many with whom he walked. He would record that fellowship most of all should he live to be these heroes' chronicler. Love was the thread between them that he most wanted to understand—for this power drove them to greatness and madness.

Somewhere in the yawning twilight, as the forest lulled in a beat of quiet between the roars and crashing, Morigan broke their silence. "Mifanwae," she said suddenly.

It was clear enough for all to hear, and she ran after a shadow none else could see.

*Morigan has not sensed herself leave the world. The cold trance of the journey or simply the closeness to Alabion's heart—and its magik—has her stepping through time without realization. No more is the snow, winter, or darkness of the wood. All is bright and ivory-wet in wonder of the moon. She* does not worry for her Wolf—not when the line of chanting folk has lured away her every sense. She knows they are worshippers, for they hum wordless melodies that are reverences of stone, tree, star, and especially moon. It is praise for the oldest forces, the spirits, and the energies of what men do not think have souls. "But they are souls," warn the bees unpleasantly. "Mighty souls." Droning among the worshippers' white-hooded number is a pitch that has been entrenched into memory. This is the voice that would sing Morigan's worries away when she was young.

"Mifanwae," she calls again.

The specters of the past do not answer, and she flies after them. In the Dreaming, she is a breeze, and she winds between the worshippers. Soon she floats beside her not-mother, Mifanwae, and almost-father, Aaown. At least that's the man's name as she recalls from Mifanwae's whisper over his cairn. She recognizes him, for there are no illusions or pretenses in this realm. She knows his smell of sweat and ferns, his gravely handsome face, his luxurious braids, and his roughly contoured naked body, which she can see clearly. She knows why Mifanwae loves him and why her mother (Not-mother, remind the bees) is silently seeping grief at whatever loss he marches toward. If death is the destination and Morigan has only this instant to understand him, then his eyes tell the tale of his years. It's one of commitment, love, and sacrifice. Yet Aaown is not fearful of any end. In fact, her almost-father glows with pride.

The worshippers hold lights and wend through the trees like a serpent of stars. A snake, she thinks, and dreams inside the Dream of a scaled beast devouring itself by the tail. It dawns on her that something will be consumed tonight. She can tell as much before the trees fan aside and a pale ruin rises from the entanglement. How long ago the trees were felled to make this place is as baffling to her as how old the stones of this ruin are. Timeless. The ruin feels older than a mountain or from a period when time had not yet been invented for man to count the minuscule moments until death. Mossy arches watch like eyes full of shadows and secrets to oblivion. The walls are cracked and bleeding ivy. They rise up like green-stained molars and are hungry for what is to come.

Sacrifice.

Morigan now floats at an altar. Aaown is ready. He has smiled and kissed his love one last time. She is the one to place the iron talisman upon him—the covenant. Mouse's new necklace. She is the one who whispers that she will *remember him after the Gray Man has emptied out his flesh. Morigan feels more anger than horror watching their last moments. Perhaps she has seen too much and is numb to pity. Perhaps she is still too upset from the lie of her parents to recognize how they suffered.*

*"Tagtae (Sleep)," says Mifanwae.*

*Aaown lies upon the altar and closes his eyes. Around him the chanting rises. It sways the air with power and calls to the ancient souls. Above Morigan the stars blink to darkness. She looks, and the moon swells and swallows her. Father, she thinks, of the moon or the man lying on the stone of sacrifice, as they are one and the same.*

Caenith growled and quickly made chase. He could sense Morigan an ocean's length away. She had performed that strange sorcery again where she stepped in and out of doors through which he could not follow. First, she had folded from sight along a silver seam of light and reappeared a few paces ahead, and he had easily caught up. As he reached her, she had winked from the world and back again a hundred paces away. After that, he had lost physical track of her. However, he still had her star in his chest to lead him and her fragrance that could never be lost, so he pursued those elements instead of the flickering passage she made through the wintry forest. While hunting her, the Wolf became reckless to the dangers of the Pitch Dark. However, his senses reported only an eerie peace. That was unusual but not of his concern, and it meant the others could keep up without worry. As the steam of the chase wore out of his lungs and his legs stopped pounding the land, he cooled and wondered where his Fawn's visions had taken him.

If this was a changeling city, he knew no other like it. He could not say what smiths in Alabion were responsible for its craft. While much of the ruin hid in great capes of snow, he saw the corners of enormous stones. They were ascetically bare as though a lazy mason had been at fault. However, not an edge appeared unsmoothed to his gaze, and his more-than-extraordinary senses could hear the ghostly scrape of a thousand sandy caresses on the masonry as it was coaxed into beautiful simplicity. The stone had been adored into this shape—not hewn. It smelled of the oldest soils from which it had been unearthed. *Where am I in this city forgotten in time?* Momentarily awestruck, he stumbled through the snowbanks that concealed benches, broken walls, and constructs of the ancient world. He wasn't a romantic for antiquity, though. He cared only for his Fawn, and soon his blundering brought him to her in the deepest dunes of the winter realm. The place could have been a temple from the chanting that echoed to his far-hearing ears. Songs had seeped into these stones through eons of worship.

The Wolf's warmth came over Morigan, who no longer shifted in and out of Dream. She was looking to the sky, where a milky haze of winter clouds covered the sun and gave it the luminance and majesty of a moon. Morigan stood at a mound that had been swept free of whiteness by her hands. Surrounding her and drifted with snow were five shattered, ancient pillars set around a stone table, which she had cleaned.

*What have you found?* he whispered.

*History*, she replied. *The past. This is where my story began.*

IV

Primeval magik infused the forgotten ruin and warded it against the horrible lurkers of the Pitch Dark. The winter had a silence here deeper than one would find in the echoing tundra beyond Kor'Keth. In the North, the wind and snow blended all senses into a buzzing whiteness. Morigan remembered that peaceful emptiness, even if those memories were not her own but harvested from the head of her friend, Kanatuk. Like her indigenous friend, she found contentment in the cold. She had the same sense of unity, reverence, and connection to life that Kanatuk's story-singing mother had sermonized to her tribe. This was a holy place. If sacrifices occurred on the gray altar here, they were of a sadness that should not be grieved but respected for its nobility. Aaown, her half-father, had made the decision to offer himself to the Gray Man. *He is my father, and yet he is not*, brooded Morigan. *He is the flesh but not the soul.* As she stood in the quiet winter and caressed the stone where Aaown's sacrifice had been made, she spiraled in circles of confusion the bees did not share. Morigan's inner quarrel was clear to Caenith, and it was not a battle he could win for her. When at last he heard their companions shuffling through the snow behind him, he turned and gave them a warning for silence. Then he backed away from his Fawn so she might contemplate alone.

The company made themselves useful and broke apart without instruction. They gathered frosty kindling and dug out a camp nearby beneath a grand, buried wall. It was sharply tipped at its top and reminded them of a mountain. Soon the heat of their first true fire in days had softened the landscape and revealed more of its strangeness. In the small orange bosom the company had created, winter retreated, bits of masonry exposed themselves under their rumps, and slippery windows along the gently melting wall showed them more of the surrounding history. Talwyn crawled on his hands and knees and dusted like an archaeologist to read the scratches upon the stone. Markings were not markings at all but thin lines of language. It was Ghaedic or a similar tongue.

"Can you read any of it?" asked Thackery, and he appeared beside the scholar.

"Not really," admitted Talwyn. "Not as well as I would like. It's Ghaedic. As you might know, though, there are as many subdialects and branches of that great tongue as there are mouths to speak it. Nuances exist to this text that are simply beyond my understanding." He tapped three lines that bisected each other like a six-pointed crossroad. "'Three' is repeated often. I would say it holds significance, certainly considering the ones we seek in these woods. But here we see three represented on two sides. So there is an opposition in meaning here, for they mean three I think, yet we see six. And these letters beside them...well, this is a uniquely pictorial language—more metaphor than consonants and vowels. Astonishingly plain, though. This rather pedestrian scribble next to it..." Many times, Talwyn swirled his shivering thumb around the spiny loop carved in the ancient stone.

Thackery realized the man was so engrossed, he didn't notice his blue fingernails or the cold.

"This," said Talwyn, "means death. But also life. Shadows and light. Dusk and dawn. Sleeping and waking. In fact, I can't tell what is referred to as *Dream*. Capitalized as if it's a place, not a state—the classification is used often throughout all I've seen. It's splendidly confusing, as every symbol seems to have two meanings. A definite dualism to the language of these... people. I would guess people, though you never know in Alabion."

"People," announced Morigan.

With her stealthy creep, she startled everyone at the campfire except the Wolf, who welcomed her into his arms like a throne of flesh. With the ponderous insight of a tired, defeated ruler, she stared at her company. Many sharp secrets cut her on the inside. She hated how much she knew—more than any person should be expected to bear.

"Worshippers of land and star," she said, and sighed. "Men and women who abided by the true laws of Geadhain. Not men or Immortal Kings, but the forces we cannot see. I don't know everything, and that at least is a small mercy. I have seen one of their rituals, though, where they tapped into a magik I can only call otherworldly. An odd turn of phrase coming from me, I know." She laughed. "Two of these worshippers were the ones responsible for my...creation. I hesitate to say birth."

"Mifanwae?" asked Thackery. "She was here? Your father too?"

"Yes." Morigan frowned. "But no. Neither was truly my kin. Not in body, anyway."

*They were merely servants to a cause,* she thought. *What is the "cause," then? What does that make me? How is a child made without proper parents? What was it that entered Aaown, and where did it take his flesh afterward? Am I even a woman or simply a construct—something made for a purpose other than life or free will?*

The bees were of no help. They had gone silent. Her perplexed companions weren't helpful either. Only the Wolf was her anchor in this madness. His whispers rose within her as red and hot as the flames into which she stared.

*Kill these doubts,* he scolded. *You are a wonder, and your birth should be no less of a miracle. Why does it surprise or disgust you that you are not a creature of slow-walking descent? What truth were you really expecting? A child of stars and magik is exactly the sort of flower I knew you were at first sight. Nothing else would explain how you captured and tamed me or the sweetness of your ancient scent. Do not dismiss the memories of the she-wolf who raised you, either. I can feel you walling off your love for her, and I shall not allow it.*

Morigan pulled away from the Wolf. *She was not my mother.*

*My nose never lies,* he said, and the iron circle of his arms proved quite inescapable for his Fawn. *You force me to listen when the beast has my mind, and now you will have my medicine, whether wanted or not. I smelled the sweat of her devotion to you. The kisses, stories, smiles, and songs. A smell as pure as what led me to her grave on that fated night can never come from trickery. I smelled a mother-wolf. She loved you more than any other parent would have. As guarded as you try to be with these matters, I have seen the flashes in your mind of the man she lost—the one you hold yourself from calling family too. If you consider the sacrifice of each of them and how she continued to care for you after that...I do not see how you could be angry with Mifanwae. From what I know, from the memories you have trickled to me, Aaown died. The scorching passion of your making consumed him as a flame would a moth. Whatever this oddity, think more on what it would be like to love an animal responsible for your mate's death. That's what Mifanwae did. I could not do such a thing. I would loathe that creature. I would snarl at it and punish it each day. Yet never did she treat you with unkindness as a smaller woman surely would have. You were her daughter in every important way.*

Morigan slumped and surrendered. *Yes. I know. Everything you say is right. However, I feel as if for every secret I learn, two truths go unanswered.*

*You will have your truths,* promised the Wolf. *The Sisters are not far now. I have never met a braver hunter, and I do not expect you will quail before them.*

*I shall not,* replied Morigan with fire.

She looked around at her companions and recognized they needed assurances as much as she did. They were not blessed to have Caenith in their heads and hearts. "I have most of the puzzle," she said, and they all looked to her. "I think the Sisters can complete what remains. When I know everything, I shall tell you everything. I promise. There is no sense in torturing ourselves with guesswork until then. I think we are all tired of wondering—I know I am. We should rest. We are safe in this place. We must prepare ourselves for the final push."

Mouse's bruised and puffy eyes told of utter fatigue, and she dropped herself to the ground. Adam became her bedding, and he tenderly lifted the sleeping woman and placed her alongside his body so she would not lie on the snow or stone. Thackery stayed in his huddle with the scholar, and they brushed off hieroglyphs and envisioned the shapes under the snow as excitedly as young boys on a treasure hunt. The Wolf remained with Morigan. Again he was the rock at her back—the constant, unmoving element in the cold. He stroked her hair and bled his hot whisky of emotions into her until she was drunk enough to flutter out of the world.

V

In their rush to the ruins, they had missed a meal, and Morigan stirred in the evening. Hunger pangs and the smell of cooking meat woke her. Caenith had sensed her hunger even while she rested. *Is there ever a need he does not tend to?* she thought, and smiled. The campfire was sputtering from dripping carcasses strung up over its flames. Rested, well fed, and warm, they were more awake and sociable than at any other time in the Pitch Dark—except for Mouse. She chewed her troubles as violently as she did the gristle between her teeth and felt like a stranger.

*Dangerous thoughts*, warned the bees.

Vengefully, Mouse glared at the seer and scared off any further intuitions. They left shortly after eating and burying the remains of their meal, and they were once more engulfed in the chattering twilight of the woods. A few sands away from the ruins and their protective warding, they heard the first crash through brittle, icy undergrowth by a creature of undoubted immensity. The company contracted into a familiar phalanx of fear. They hurried and did not stay to know what stalked the area. That night, the air possessed a stinging crispness that bit at their nostrils and made their panting unpleasant, and the snow was tightly packed and frozen solid in many places. They thought they'd shouldered the worst of Alabion's cruelty, but she showed them she always had new surprises in store. *No matter. We're almost there*, each believed in private. They sensed an escalation of events and a crossing into the final push. The punishments of the Pitch Dark lost a shade of their terror with an end to their race just on the horizon. No matter how they slipped and stumbled and no matter how the wind hissed at them or what horrors lumbered around, they had come this far and would not fail.

Around the gray misery of dawn, Caenith found them a rent and ancient log to curl up inside and allowed them a few hourglasses of sleep. It felt as if they had barely laid their heads onto each other—save for the Wolf, who never slept—when the clash of two titans in the woods chased them from their shelter. One of the monsters surely died, while the other roared with such might as to shake the trees and shower them in frost. Caenith became hesitant of taking breaks after that. A pause would only leave them too groggy to react, and he hadn't told his companions how often they had skirted close to the massive lords of the Pitch Dark.

The Wolf wanted to believe it was his protection that had kept his pack safe, but his instincts and understanding of the hunt informed him he was not leading so much as being led. All around them bellowed death's music, yet their path remained blessedly free of bloodshed. No beasts had crossed them, and he suspected they wouldn't so long as they did not err in stepping off that unseen road. The Wolf tested this theory once. He decided not to go east but chose a southern direction in which no cries of murder or musky alarms could be detected. Hardly a speck after crunching along the new route, a gargantuan shadow, which might have been a Menosian crowe—if they were flesh and bone and screeched like a steel train—flew over the company.

*Corvus maximus*! said Talwyn to himself, and he laughed madly at the flapping monster that roosted itself above them and shed black feathers as large as fans.

Looking through the branches, he spotted a gleam of eyes like ebon moons and talons that could crush a horse, before Caenith ushered them back the way they had come. The magnificent and massive bird did not follow them and merely cawed a warning to any who looked back.

*I am no more the master of this hunt*, growled Caenith to his bloodmate when they were again on the invisible road. *We are being herded somewhere.*

*Herded? Where? To the Sisters?*

Then Morigan could see what he sensed. It was a trail through the trees as clear as a road of ink laid over the snow—a black road and a vein to the heart of the Pitch Dark. Her impressions of what awaited them there brought the shiver of metal to her groin, the taste of iron—surely blood—to her mouth, and screams to her ears as the wind howled past. They journeyed toward a terrible darkness.

She stopped and pulled on the Wolf's arm. *Shouldn't we turn around? Or find another way? I sense only wickedness ahead.*

The Wolf snorted. *Wickedness ahead and wickedness behind. I smell it no matter where I might taste the wind. Better we meet who is summoning us with courage than weaken ourselves with fear or try to avoid it altogether. Either that, or we bring out our claws and try to conquer every monster in this wood. For I feel this power leashes them too, and they could be unleashed just as quickly.*

From somewhere not very far away, the king of crows prickled their spines with a cry. By then, the others stood beside their frowning leaders. Everyone understood this silent conversation. "Danger up ahead," said Caenith gravely.

Mouse was the first to respond. She shrugged and shouldered her way through and on ahead. Without any alternatives, they followed her. Caenith raced to place himself at the fore of any peril. Mouse kept on at his pace, seemingly undeterred by the Wolf's warning. It was not often that the Wolf felt pangs of mercy for another—particularly if that person was not his bloodmate. Yet he could smell the winey stain that hung about Mouse's person. It was the stench of grief. He understood grief, how to cultivate misery into an art, and the kind of suffering that could debilitate a soul for a thousand years. Mortals did not have the time he did—so much of Mouse's short life could be squandered missing the dead. Her soul was wounded, and if it was not healed of her sorrow, she would harden into a callous and ugly woman. He wanted her to stay the same woman Morigan and the dead man had helped her become.

"Mouse," he said. "I blame myself as well. For leading us to Briongrahd. For allowing Aghna to play her game. I believed in honor, which she did not have. I believed that your father could not die and that he was a perfect champion for that reason. I might as well have torn him apart with my own claws. This mistake and my remorse...they will remain with me for as long as there are stars in the sky." He grabbed Mouse. She stubbornly looked ahead. "Know this. Your father was a fellow wolf to me. I lost my hunting partner. No other two-legs I have known could run as fast as your father. I have no shadow to watch the pack with me at night. I shall not claim to know your loneliness or the depth of your loss, but please know I share it too in whatever small or great measure. We are all grieving and angry—even if our wounds are not as raw as yours."

"I wouldn't worry about me," she said, and she shrugged off his hand. "Those women are certainly a bigger problem."

For suddenly, three crimson-robed females had appeared in a clearing of woven black wicker trees. Neither the Wolf nor the seer had been prepared. This was a manifestation of magik, and Mouse, who'd been ignoring Caenith and glancing past his chatting head, had witnessed the trio pop into existence in a watery blink. As if the six companions had stepped through a sticky veil, a weight now clung to them. It was a heaviness of dread. Light squeezed through the thicket ahead and shimmered off the three women's scarlet clothing, turning them into red, ominous figures. The curved metal instruments they held in their hands could have been half-moons of blood.

Without wandering any nearer, the companions could not see much more. Branches and shadows inexplicably obscured even the Wolf's sight. Around them the Pitch Dark was silent. These women had shooed off any monsters to their lairs. The quiet air crackled startlingly when Thackery gasped. "The Sisters Three?"

*No*, buzzed the bees.

"No," said Morigan.

A little blood and witchery was a middling fright to the Daughter of Fate. She claimed her lover's hand and walked to meet the three certainly wicked women.

# XI

## THREE SHADOWS

I

With their sulfurous stench of ancient magik, the three red women were witches. That much the Wolf knew. The odor nauseated him well before the thicket broke, and the witches were revealed in full. Even then, they refused to be clearly captured by his eyes. It seemed they were only partially in the world. All about the humid space, moist from a grisly heat that had evaporated the snow, the Wolf saw the tools of their craft. An iron cauldron behind them stewed with a peppery-sweet red liquid. Withered, eyeless, knit-up animals swayed from the branches in spidery cocoons. Some of the desiccated dead were small, with bird, bug, or bat wings upon them—the mythic, nearly invisible tricksters no eyes could see, let alone track. *Faeries*, he remarked. Yet here the creatures were, pulled into this dark dream of a realm and rendered into hideous taxidermies. The pain of their ends was clearly visible on their twisted, dried-apple faces. Larger victims too were bound up in the webbed trees, and he spotted a few grand corpses—a many-horned bear, a monstrous lion with rusted scales—all withered to jerky and fossilized in white netting. Every one of these creatures had been drained of blood and life, and he knew by whom.

Silently and ravenously, the three red witches appraised the travelers. One caressed the blade of the sickle she held. The witches' mouths were as pink as their gazes. Their pale cheeks looked quite flushed, and only their tumbling silver hair implied age. The red witches were timeless, however. Any novice to evil and magik could tell they were not blushing maidens. What wickedness the Wolf did not see, he sensed as a shadow under their eyes and as a rancid, rotten fart that dispersed in the air. He imagined veins, wrinkles, and sores on their ceramic-smooth skin and brown, jagged teeth behind the perfection of their smiles. True ugliness could never hide—though these women concealed theirs masterfully.

"Malabeth," hissed the most diminutive of the three, "do look at what has wandered into our home. Lost whitehawks, sad dogs, and—oh my—big-balled bulls." She eyed Caenith's loincloth slyly. "We have not had such succulent sweetmeats for a winter's winter, and I could live off his for twice that."

"Delicious," agreed the fattest witch. "You've always had such a keen eye for good stock, Meag. The bull's entrails will make for savory sausage too. The bird and dog seem stringy and bland. That one—the skinny lambling—will hardly make enough juice for a beggar's broth. I shall fetch the spices while you figure out how best to squeeze the blood out of him."

After hooking her sickle into her braided belt, Malabeth waddled over to pick through dusty urns and wax-sealed jars scattered at the cauldron's base. She sought the herbs and foul things she needed to add zest to their meal. Meag, the first to speak, bent to a whetstone and began to whistle while grinding her sickle against it. Talwyn assumed the witches were sisters. He drew closer to the company and glanced to see if the others were as horrified as he was. They were hardly shaken. His companions challenged the terror with scowls and silence. He debated whether they understood the witches' threats, as even he, with all his linguistic mastery, could not always say for sure what words the red witches were actually using. Unless his eyes deceived him, the witches' mouths didn't sync to speech, and the voices, while distinct to each woman, carried an echo. *Let this be a nightmare*, he prayed. *A trick of the woods that will fall apart if I pinch myself.* He attempted that solution and ended up still in the same predicament but with a welt on his arm. His actions caught the attention

279

of the third sister, the tallest of the trio. She cast the longest shadow and had the huskiest voice.

She laughed at him. "There will be no waking from this Dream. Only a red sleep for you." She paused. "Although there is a feminine delicacy to you I think might sour the stew. What do you think? Malabeth? Meag?"

The red witches glanced up from their tasks. Meag tested her tongue against the blade of her weapon and did not wince as it ran with blood. Delightedly, she smacked her lips. "So wise, dear Morgana. That's why you are the eldest. Too sweet. He's far too sweet. He's never even sinned against one of us. Imagine that. I never thought I'd see the day. His meat would be like a bushel of sugar-root and would certainly ruin our feast."

The voluptuous witch sneered at the trembling scholar. "I suppose. I suppose. We could make a pudding or a pie with him—though neither of you cares for sweets."

"We do not," the others said.

"The salt of a man." Meag licked her sickle and wounded herself again.

"The sins in his sack," chimed in Malabeth.

"A dash of the love he never gave back," added Morgana.

"Delicious," they all cackled.

Morgana took a few billowing steps toward the company. She moved and furiously fluttered like a woman caught in a wind. She stood before her sisters, slashed her sickle at the company like a magistrate's gavel, and delivered her judgment. "The mouseling and the Daughter of Fate may leave, unless the ladies wish to join us in our repast. Tender, sweet manling, you are not welcome for our feast. Come back when you've fattened your manhood, and we shall welcome it to our table. None of the unchosen should stay, unless they are going to eat."

Since the company's arrival, Morigan had not been as silent and frozen with inaction as she appeared. In this flickering realm, which was neither here nor there but someplace near to Dream, she saw and understood plenty. These women were a terror and a nightmare on the land—a nightmare that had shattered its pot and now grew with a rambunctious, hideous Will. It was not quite a *Caedentriae*, a Long Nightmare, but another strain of that illness. It was a blackness and a wound in the forest—and, deeper still, in

Geadhain herself. Vibrations of destiny shuddered within her along with visions of Magnus, Lila, and three pale women—not as horrific as these but similarly ghastly—and promises of blood. Morigan had almost reached out and seized that truth when the red specter of the greatest witch came forward, and she dropped her focus.

"No further, Shadow," Morigan commanded.

Silver magik wreathed the seer's sight and hand, though she did not sense this.

"Shadow," grumbled Morgana. Then her voice thundered. "I shall show you darkness, child."

With that booming threat, the wind keened and tore the land with a flourish of leaves. The trees bent, and many of the bound corpses snapped free and whirled at the company. A few companions cowered. Still, no debris struck the seer or her friends. Suddenly, Morgana's sisters stood beside her, and the three witches' shadows rose behind them. The combined shadow the three cast loomed impossibly large. It was a monument to darkness, and it gusted with horrid cold like a wave of black ice that could fall and crush them.

Morigan shone brighter with light and braver with courage, and she stepped forward. She could not have said then whether she spoke in her head or through her mouth—or even what she was about to say. She channeled the omniscient wisdom of the in-between. Caenith felt her straddling realities. One foot was in Geadhain; the other was in Dream. He kept silent because he did not fear these red witches as much as he feared the greatness of his bloodmate, she who ruled cosmic empires. Awed and tingling with pride, he smiled as Morigan admonished these wicked creatures. "I nearly cast out a Dreamer," said Morigan. "I can cast out three shadows from Geadhain. Do not test me."

"We are no Dreamers," howled the three witches. "You cannot be rid of us without unmaking or remaking the woods. We shall remain until Geadhain has had her due."

"Her due?"

"What the Kings have each taken. What our shadows wrongly gave."

"That bargain was paid. Magnus's love has ended."

"His love has ended," the three witches said, and they grinned.

In that instant, they transformed into the warty, snarling, snaggle-toothed, hideous creatures they truly were, and the cold wind that slapped the company turned revolting. It crawled in their noses with the wormy putrescence of eons of vegetative and fleshy decay—the rot of Alabion. "The sickness does not stop when the rose at last dies. We shall remain for as long as the sins of the Kings can be remembered."

The silver seer took another step. "We must meet your shadows. We must meet with the Sisters Three."

"We are Three Sisters. We speak no lies. Give us your men and their delicious sins, and we shall tell you everything."

"Never."

Wrathfully, the shadow of the three witches bloomed high again, and Morigan's fanning light sliced back at the darkness. Impossible magik thrashed the world with hot and cold gales, disorienting twists of silver and black, and toppling upheavals. Mouse thought of Menos and of witnessing the city fall in upon itself. She flailed as if she stood there again. She reached for the Wolf—as all the others did—and clung onto his warm flesh. She had not felt scared—or much of anything—since her father had died. However, at that moment, with her heart behind her teeth, she was quite aware of life's frail thread.

Crash! With a thunderclap, the darkness ended, and the silver light flickered away. Once more all was calm and eerie in the grove. The catastrophe was a vanished imagining. Three red witches and a faintly luminescent seer could be seen standing near enough for parley. They appeared in accord—or at least they no longer seemed at odds with each other.

"Quite the shine." Morgana clapped.

"We rather like her," said Malabeth, and she clutched her pleasant paunch. "Think of the meats she could bring us with her power. Starling sweetmeat, even."

"Can it be done?" gasped Meag.

"She'll slay one—if not more," declared Malabeth. "She wears her crimson coming like a crown. A queen of blood."

"A queen of blood!" The witches nodded.

Over time, the company untangled themselves from the nest of limbs they'd made with the Wolf. They waited for more banter and for signs they were safe, yet the witches and their silver-eyed savior merely traded sly appraisals of each other. Unlike the rest of his fellows, the Wolf felt giddy with the sparkling light of his bloodmate's confidence. He was nearly drunk on her authority, and he knew the witches would not—perhaps could not—do them harm any longer. *Thank you, my Fawn. Conquest without violence is the hardest path*, he whispered. *I would not fancy being without my sweetmeats, either.*

Up ahead, Morigan smiled at that. Then she glared at the red witches. "Let us pass," she demanded.

"If you wish," Morgana said with a sigh.

Formally, the witches stood to one side and tipped their heads to the woods that lay past the steaming cauldron. Morigan motioned for her company to come forth. Horrid as cannibals, the vile women brandished their sickles and clacked their teeth at every man wandering by who wasn't Talwyn—though they never assaulted anyone. Thus the company continued unhindered and were almost to the edge of the thicket. They had pushed aside a thorny screen when Morgana and her sisters called out after one of them. "Mouseling, your lust for retribution glows with the fullness of a witch's moon. Such beautiful hate you water in your soul's garden. Should you wish to satisfy that darkness, to call upon the shadows and wrath of Geadhain, say our names but once with true and black desire. We shall come."

The others continued walking as though they had not heard. It was as though Mouse alone had heard the foul offer. What did the witches see in her? What could be so dark in her heart to make the sisters call her out?

Adam suddenly rustled through the opening to collect her, and she allowed him to take her through the bushes. He tenderly shielded her with his arms. Transitioning from the black grove to the darkness of the Pitch Dark gave the same relief as rising from a watery deep. More natural horrors replaced the pressure, fear, stink, and dizziness that had been constants in the red witches' realm. Mouse was actually happy to have her boots buried in snow and her feet already numbing. She was glad to hear once again the shuffling lords of the Pitch Dark. To amuse herself, she looked to where they had come from and snickered at the snowy conifers and soupy gloom that held no trace of a weald, a cauldron, or three red-robed women. *Damn this place. Either you're mad when you come, or you're mad when you leave. I'm not sure which I am just yet.*

"What were they?" asked Mouse, and she jogged up to Morigan.

Morigan stopped. "Witches. Spirits. Echoes of sin."

Talwyn let out the great shiver he had been holding in. "Sin? Whose sin?"

"King Magnus's," muttered Thackery. "His love for Lila has somehow conjured..." He withdrew the hand he was waving about in disgust.

*Good,* thought Morigan. Her companions were beginning to grasp the stakes of the wretched game they played. The less she had to explain, the better. Sharp Talwyn assisted her further and proved himself more capable than useless. "No. *Kings*," he said. "I heard them refer to both men clearly. I am rarely mistaken."

"Brutus was here as well? In Alabion?" exclaimed Thackery. "What did *he* do?"

Heavy silence stifled the fellowship. What heinous crime had the Sun King committed here? What had been so immoral as to summon or aid in the creation of the three red witches?

*We can show you,* suggested the bees.

*My Fawn?* asked Caenith.

Morigan slipped into a trance. Trees shivered themselves into spectral poles, and gray fog bled across her eyes. One path shone vividly through the murkiness—a golden trail left by mighty feet. It was a path Morigan felt she could race upon and use to reach anywhere in moments, for it was the passage of a fleet and powerful being. The footsteps made an old road from a thousand years ago or longer. With incredible restraint, she reeled herself in from the Dreaming and did not vanish from her companions. The urge to skip through space and time again, though, pulled her like a tide. "I see a path," she said. "I shall lead us."

She'd decided she would not leave them alone again, no matter how Fate demanded witness. After all, she had drawn these folk into her mysterious journey and made it their journey as well. She had a duty to bring them through Alabion's gauntlet—preferably whole. She'd vowed this to Vortigern; she would not fail him. As a witness to what the Kings could do when they did not heed the thunder and lightning of their storms, she swore never to be so careless with her actions.

Once more her gaze blazed into the wood like a silver spotlight, and her form softened and became cloudy. The five who followed her knew they were upon one of the hidden trails of destiny. Morigan flickered through obstacles that would trip her companions. Still, she never wandered too far away, and she managed to hold herself—or at least the image of her body—outside of the Dreaming. For an hourglass or a day, her silver ghost patiently bore them through the Pitch Dark. She was always ever so slightly ahead but never out of sight. So it was the company did witness with her the unveiling of the Fate she hunted when at last the great wall of pines suddenly fell into a tumbling ravine of green-shagged stone heads wearing caps and beards of snow. Perhaps these anthropomorphic wise men did breathe the wind to nudge the travelers down the slope and in a single direction—toward a sad, curved cave mouth.

*Here*, the bees whispered, and the company came to the mouth of rock and hanging icicles that protected them from winter. Luring warmth leaked from within. Around the company were bones scattered in the snowfall and farther down the black throat into which they stared. With the heat blew an animal's musk. Only a wolf or a pack of a hundred could create such a reek. Caenith and Adam growled and sniffed around the entrance. Neither changeling wished to proceed.

Mouse wasn't keen on entering a pit either, and a pit was where they'd come to. If she pulled out her cards, she wondered without genuine curiosity, would the one on top be the black, bone-strewn hole Adelaide had revealed? Could Fate be so vulgar? She reached not for her deck. She knew where she had to go. She wasn't afraid of Fate. She felt ready to throttle the bitch. Before anyone could debate the merits and strangeness of proceeding, Mouse strode into its darkness.

Morigan could see the Sun King's golden footsteps—which had led her there—bold as yellow paint, and she drifted into the cave as well. Most of the men chased the luminescent seer. She was their only torch in the dark, and they did not wait for the Wolf. He paced, grumbled, and barked. He called out to his bloodmate, who he felt was too deeply in the thrall of destiny to hear him. *What do you fear?* he growled to his lonesome self. *This lair? That scent?*

A monster awaited him and mayhap a truth just as violent. Chains of terror held the fearless Wolf on that spot. He might have stayed outside for much longer, but his bloodmate's whisper reached through the darkness and pulled him forward. It was a loving leash, but he went unwillingly. Her words did not soothe him. *Come, my Wolf. See who you are.*

# XII

# PURSUIT, SURRENDER, DESPAIR

I

Galivad and Rowena had been wandering Ebon Vale's shady woods for many days now. They were trying to stay far enough ahead of Moreth to plan a dreadful surprise for the sage, while at the same time attempting to locate the mysterious Fort Havok. Completing either of these undertakings would qualify as a success. Unfortunately, Galivad barely spoke to his comrade, and the two were more engaged in warfare with each other than with their foes. Since her forcible romancing of the man in Blackforge, Galivad had regarded her icily and replied only if she inquired about their tasks. She understood the expressions of scorned, used women, and his sulking countenance told her he'd suffered an affront. Really, though, she had no time to bother with a man's bruised pride—not when there were crowes to hide from every few sands. She was starving too in a realm of the wiliest game. Animals could be chased for sands simply to vanish.

The pair spent their travel in famished misery listening to the gassy burbles of their stomachs, eating filthy roots and berries, dodging crowes, and sneering at yet another rainstorm. Dear Kings, the weather was horrid. Rain fell as cold as shaved ice and still refused to become snow. When finally it did, winter came to wash the mud off their cloaks with a blessed whiteness.

Although they were people of Eod, folk of sun and sweat, they welcomed the weather, and, funnily enough, this chill at last changed the silence between them.

"Sounds like the same thing as yesterday. We need a plan," said Galivad one morning.

When he spoke they were walking along in a charcoal-clouded dawn. They kept close to the tree trunks and the rugs of untrodden pine needles, which made for untraceable steps. Thus far, their journey had consisted of a three-day hike outside the perimeter of Moreth's loud company. The Iron sage proved quite easy to follow and could be tracked from a span away without the need for a spyglass. Clues about his location arose either from the black spindles of his fires or the frequent shots of his rifle-happy people, who had surely slain half the local wildlife by now. Occasionally, one of the pair would sneak off to check on Moreth's progress and then return to the other with a curt assessment. Rowena had just done this. She had not expected a reply beyond Galivad's acknowledgment of her report.

"You're speaking again," she said.

"Seems I am."

"I am deeply sorry for our...misunderstanding."

Galivad snorted. "My misunderstanding. It was unfortunate. It will not happen again."

It was a cutting remark, and its nuance did not escape Rowena. They continued for a while until their temperaments eased and came in tune with the gentle, frosty weather. She stopped. "I am glad you have remembered your service to Eod," said Rowena. "We are allies and servants to the crown above all else. Now, I need your wits to help me with our problem. How do two pitiably bodied persons assault an Iron sage and his fully armed guard? If we do not capture him before he reaches Fort Havok, we might never learn his secrets."

Galivad favored the idea of skinning the man alive while his wife, Beatrice, watched and wailed. *Alive. Yes.* Galivad nodded to the woods. "We should take a closer look at the camp," he proposed. "Together."

Proclaiming their fellowship anew put a skip in Rowena's stride, and they set off for Moreth's encampment. It was rather early in the day, and Moreth's camp would still be rising. Moreth and his people moved at a crawl.

They broke long and often—not for reasons of laziness but because of their cargo's volatility. Truefire could not be unnecessarily jostled or experience even the vibrations of travel for very long without tempting destruction. Galivad mused that perhaps that was what he and Rowena should do—jostle the cargo. Darkly, he contemplated the fire shows and screams.

Using the land for cover, he and Rowena slowly crept ahead. They buried themselves in a bank of flocked bushes and peered out like timid deer. From there, they could survey the whole of Moreth's encampment as it came to life and began the day. Many of Moreth's riflemen were stretching awake as well as smoking witchroot, pissing, and rolling up their tents and bedrolls. With everyone up and about, Rowena easily counted every head of their number: sixteen. That didn't make for the greatest odds, but she'd certainly dealt with worse. However, the preening man in finery who sauntered around in the snow, chatted to his men, and smiled his greasy smile was worth at least six soldiers himself. Rasputhane's dossiers on Menos's twelve Iron sages (or eleven, rather, as one had met an untimely end in recent months) portrayed Moreth as an explosively violent man who could bring bloodshed as swiftly as a snakebite brought death. He would be the most challenging combatant of the retinue—particularly if they wanted to capture him alive.

Galivad noticed the sword's focus on the Iron sage. "We can't take on all of them. Not at once. Even a stallion such as you."

"Stallion?" Rowena laughed quietly.

"Indeed. Like our king's own, Brigada. The females of that breed should hardly be called mares when they are twice the might and fright of their mates."

Secretly, she felt pleased with the return of her companion's humor. Perhaps if his spiritedness continued, he would grace them with a song before battle. Who knew whether it would be the last occasion she would hear his ballads? If death were to be her destiny, she would drag many of Moreth's people with her into the black beyond.

As she contemplated death's variety, Rowena's roving eyes were drawn by hidden promise to the girded feliron cart with its thick tarp and the gently glowing cargo that lay beneath. Those phosphorescent rocks could decimate every person in the encampment. An advantage stared her in the face. However, she couldn't quite mold it into a strategy.

"The truefire," remarked Galivad. He was thinking similar thoughts. "It's no good, really. We could level half of Ebon Vale with that much. Hardly a triumph when it would leave us as dead as..." When he broke off, Rowena turned to him. He was smiling. "We don't need to kill them," he said excitedly. "All those soldiers."

"Go on," replied Rowena.

"They need only to *think* we are mad or determined enough to damn us all. I can play the role with its required flair." He touched Rowena's shoulder. "You will be the silent revolutionary. She who lights the fuse, so to speak. Or seems as if she might."

With much whispering and pointing to the camp, Galivad explained his rather crazed plan—a scheme to coerce the information from Moreth rather than confront him head-on. Rowena didn't care for the delicacies of manipulation. Brute strength worked best. In the end, though, his machinations won her over. She wondered where he had gotten his devious streak from, this mind that could well belong to an Iron sage. But those were contemplations for another day. Right now they needed to prepare. Moreth had promised his wicked wife four days of travel until they reunited, which left one to go. They would have to move on his forces tonight. Until then they would eat and take a wink of sleep if they could. They would need every drop of their reserves and more than a dash of luck if they were to survive the evening.

## II

Rowena took the second watch while Galivad enjoyed his hourglass of sleep. He was a tougher man than his frilly exterior let on, and for all their sore and road-hard arrangements together, she could not think of a time when he had whined. At worst, he made a song about it. His only serious upset came from seeing Moreth's pale wife. She regretted he might never have the chance to satisfy his revenge, as the odds of their disentangling themselves from the situation they were about to enter were piss-poor. *Sounds like a gibe from Master Dorvain*, she thought, and she chuckled. She reflected on the beastly watchmaster with all his burly muscle and bluster, and she felt a pang of sorrow at the thought she might never again see him—or the queen, or Lowelia, or the group of aspiring sword-maidens whom she had helped bumble through their swings of blades on the Twosday of each week. Indeed, she waxed fondly over every soul in Eod she could remember from its orphans to its leaders, even though she knew they might not notice her death. Heavy as a stone woman, she contemplated these folk for whom she suddenly longed.

Galivad's sleeping, cheerful beauty captured her anew. A man could not be lovelier. He was a gift that should be preserved and protected. The world would not weep for a stone woman. However, it would shine less brightly from the passing of a man of sunshine and songs. If such a balance were called upon, both of them need not die—only one. Deeply, she stared at him, and she lost herself to his golden curls and his twitching lips that seemed to smile and sing even while he slept. She considered kissing him but threw out the thought for its impropriety. *You are a sword. Not a woman. Not as others are. You are duty before lust. Honor before love. Never forget yourself, Rowena.*

"Ruining your face like that. Pity," said Galivad.

He startled her, snapping awake as he did, and she glanced away guiltily.

"What were you thinking of? It seems dreadful," he said, and he yawned.

"Nothing. Nothing dreadful, at least."

After a quick leap up, Galivad was fresh as a daisy and appeared ready to leave. Overhead, the skies roiled with dusk's violet ripples, and the windy start of a rumbling winter storm rustled the pines. If they did not hurry, their visibility would be entirely compromised. While they strode, Rowena watched furry creatures—more than usual were about—scurrying for their holes, and she crossed many hectic hoof and paw prints in the snow.

"I hadn't planned on the weather," complained Galivad. "Could be useful to veil our escape." Noises came to him. "There they are. Loud as dancing bulls. I don't think they've yet settled for the night. Around the back, Rowena, as we planned."

In their days of observation, they'd learned that four ironguards accompanied the truefire lode at all times during travel. Only when a camp was called and fires sparked would the guards relax. A few men would take to hunting. Others cracked open bottles of Menosian wine, and some soldiers despoiled the air with vulgar songs about the Iron City, which were cringeworthy to Rowena's ears after Galivad's voice. At this point, when the ironguards were lax and fattening themselves with pleasures, the truefire would be vulnerable. Sometimes a single ironguard stayed behind, leaned against the cargo, and smoked—until Moreth hissed at the fool to have some sense. Never in any of their scouting had the saboteurs seen more than two soldiers left behind. The fellows dozed in shifts, so there was only ever one man with whom to contend.

Tonight's patterns were no different, and she and her companion circled around Moreth's band. Soon the first damp flakes began to splatter out of the clouds, and Moreth's company stopped to make shelter against the storm. The saboteurs waited awhile, rubbed themselves to stave off stiffness, and panted nervously. When enough time had passed, they crept toward the encampment. No one would spot them under the snowy shroud that had fallen, and they sneaked around the perimeter. Finally, they hid themselves in their brownish cloaks against the bark of a tree near their target. With envy, they watched the eating and drinking louts. They were warm about their fires and as merry as a band of rogues. Rowena's anger rose at their fellowship. Wicked men should not be so happy.

When the feasting ended, a few fires were shoveled over, and ironguards wandered to their tents. Moreth stayed at the one remaining fire, leaned upon his cane, and peered off as if terribly stricken with worries. Naught but a lonely ironguard shivered at his post beside the truefire. The solitary soldier used the truefire's heat to warm his hands. He had left his black rifle propped against the nearest rest. Coincidentally, that was Rowena and Galivad's hiding tree, and they froze for a moment as he walked over. Their plan was going impeccably. They wouldn't even have to wrestle the man for his firearm. *Grab the rifle, subdue the guard, and threaten the cargo until Moreth submits all his secrets*, thought Rowena. *Simple.* How to flee without a thousand bullets strafing them afterward was the real conundrum. She would become a shield rather than a sword if it came to that. At least Galivad could return to Eod if he ran as fast as his litheness suggested.

Rowena's heart pounded to the beat of battle; she knew this was the moment. She debated all the strange and jumbled things a person does before a possible death. *What a pretty man you are, Galivad. I should have kissed you again and with meaning—not for a ruse. Do care for the queen if I cannot. Make a song to remember our odd, brave tale. I don't think I'll forget you, wherever the life after this takes me.*

*Rowena?* mouthed Galivad.

*Go*, she soundlessly replied.

Slowly, she slid out her sword. With the ironguard's back to her, she figured she could slice or bash him before he even gasped. She pointed for Galivad to slip around the other side of the tree. She took a step.

"Wait," came a woman's whisper.

She withered, and Galivad clenched. Both spun. A pair of shadows waited for them behind the next pine. They were crouched so low in the needles they could scarcely be spotted. Rowena caught no shine of steel, however, and inasmuch as she and Galivad were not yet killed, foes these might not be. Although Rowena couldn't be sure, she thought she might even know the voice that had called them. Galivad never forgot the tune of a lady's speech, and he recognized their caller. "Maggie?" he hissed.

One of the shadows, possibly the Silk Purse's proprietress, raised the customary finger for silence and frantically waved for them to come over. Keeping low, the two dashed across the snow and into the shadows to see why in the King's name a tavern keep had tracked them—or Moreth, which would be even queerer—all the way into the wilds of Ebon Vale. In a moment, the four were all hunkered together. The great pine acted as a conspirator's refuge, dimmed the sound, and separated them from the winter tempest outside. In there, it was brighter from all the whiteness whirling about the sanctuary, and Galivad instantly identified Maggie's companion. "You're the Voice," he said unpleasantly. "A Watcher's pet. What are you doing here? What are both of you doing here?"

Maggie elbowed the Voice so he might explain himself. Alastair looked down to the ground and did not allow himself to be compelled.

"He won't tell you," she huffed. "He's barely told me anything. He leads me across the Feordhan, and we chase the wildest goose without a bloody peep of anything resembling a reason. He's decided I'm the bearer in all this. The Watchers—or his damn self—can't be involved."

"Why is he here, then?" asked Rowena.

"I made him come along." Maggie tapped her waist. "Me, my knife, and a couple of threats that is."

Alastair humphed in disagreement with part of Maggie's statement. *I am here because of you. Because my master sees a gamble in lashing our fates together, although I do not. I am no easier with this arrangement than you are, my dear magnificent Maggie.*

"That hardly seems enough rope to tie this buttered weasel," accused Galivad. He remembered the man from Menos and Morigan's farewell campfire. The Voice seethed with suspicious intent and mystery. "We still don't understand why you're here, Maggie. Particularly now—in this of all places."

"He wanted me to find you," said Maggie. "He said we would. I never believed we would stumble across you as we did. I don't know the first thing about tracking. I just followed the stars north and hoped my prayers would be heard."

"Find us? Why?" asked Galivad, and he turned to the Voice.

Alastair ignored him entirely. He took to blowing cold breaths like smoke rings.

"Absurd! Isn't it absurd?" cursed Maggie as quietly as she could. "He's been like that this whole trip—as satisfied and smug as a cat that's gone and killed the canary, and I just haven't found the body yet. I can't be bothered with figuring out his bullshite. It has fallen on me, this duty, and I don't shy away from responsibility. I never have. Not when it involves that old sorcerer Whitehawk, the big man, and this war we're all falling into. I'm wise enough to know when it's time to play soldier. So I'll deliver the message this bloody idiot refuses to."

"Message?" asked Rowena.

"I'm only the bearer," Maggie warned.

Galivad reeled her onward with his hand. "Yes, yes. What is the message?"

"You can't..." Maggie struggled, and she wrung logic out of the illogical. "Well, he warned me you two were in pursuit of an Iron sage. Good, I thought. I hope they find him and end him. Only...he said you can't harm him. Not at all. Which I'm guessing is what you're here to do." Galivad paled. "If you harm him," Maggie continued, "you could very well harm Whitehawk... er, Thackery. And Caenith too. It is all such nonsense."

Rowena joined her companion in ghastly shock. How had this Voice found them? How could he know any shred of their intent or foresee the aftershock of events that had not yet even occurred? Was this magik? It had to be. If sorcery had not conjured this clutter of actions, whims, and synchronicity, then all that remained was...Fate.

"No," declared Rowena. She stretched her seams with muscle and anger, and then she seized the Voice's thin wrist. It was as delicate as Galivad's. "What seers of the Iron City paid you for your interference? I know the waffling loyalty of your order. Speak, you smug dog, or I shall gladly beat the answers from you. Is this some sort of game to you? Speak!"

She shook him like a naughty animal, and the Voice grunted in pain. Maggie quietly pitied the man. For all his glibness, she'd arrived at the conclusion that his secrets had crippled him. In the mornings of their travel, there were sleepy, vulnerable moments when he appeared ready to crack and wash her in the wave of his mysteries. That never happened, though. He always brushed away his feelings with smiles, gibes, and songs. At least the brown and frightfully mannish woman seemed to be shaking a few truth-leaves from his tightly tended garden.

"A game? Not to me. No," hissed Alastair. "My master, she is the one who enjoys games."

"Your master?" Rowena frowned and rattled him harder. "The Watchers? What stake do they have in this war?"

"Damn, woman!" swore Alastair. "With hands like those, Kings help the man whose prick you snap off in your steel trap. I can say no more. I shall not betray my loyalties. Do not ask me to."

"Loyalties," scoffed Rowena, and she threw his arm away.

Their scuffle left Alastair quite rattled. As he nursed his wrist, Galivad took a good hard look at him. It was his first proper study of the man unimpeded by shadows or his hood, which had slipped off with Rowena's attack. *What a slight fellow,* he thought. *Handsome—though thin of beard and as daintily featured as a theater lady who has drawn a red mustache on herself to play a man.* However unexplainable, he seemed familiar to Galivad, and not simply because of their last encounter. It was as if the Voice were indeed a famed stage performer. Galivad's study ended as the Voice covered himself anew. From out of the hooded dark, he gazed upon Galivad with his blue-and-green stare, which twinkled with a similar rumination.

"I'm going back to Moreth's camp," declared Rowena. "This nonsense has cost us time. We had no intent to kill Moreth anyway. I honestly don't see why it matters whether we do, though. Especially seeing as this Voice has orders we should not."

"I don't care what happens to the Iron sage," stressed Alastair. "My master, however, does."

"Then all the more reason to end Moreth," said Galivad. "Until you tell us who this master is, she is no more a friend to Eod than is the Iron sage."

Alastair tensed. Charazance stirred for the first time in days. Her shadow rose in him like a fever. Perhaps she wanted to remind her vessel of the hand that held the chain. Perhaps she was interested in watching him fumble. Either scenario was possible.

"Be careful whom you call an ally," whispered Alastair quite ominously. "We are moving into an era of ambiguities. One you call friend today might burn your house tomorrow. If the Kings, men, and other forces do not settle their three-pronged conflict, we might have no houses to burn down ourselves. You think in absolutes, but there are no such things. In the days to come, we shall see all alliances, beliefs, and loyalties tested. Many will be broken, and many will be made. We shall witness the unexplainable, the fantastic, and the dark. I do not know what else to tell you to ease an uncertainty that can only bloom. As for my place in this struggle, I am here to provide information and illuminate choices. I do not and shall never make those choices myself."

In that moment, he bespelled them with his passionate oration on the current of unrest that every living being in Geadhain had felt since the storm of the Kings. Rowena broke his hold while the others were still blankly staring. "A coward's way of pardoning himself from duty," she said.

Alastair was spared another insult or beating from the woman. However, the alternative was no better. Crack! Crack! Crack! Three blue pellets sizzled through their gathering. Whoever fired was so adept a marksman the first bullet snapped the scabbard off Rowena's belt, the second grazed Galivad's hand as he reached for his hilt, and the final puffed into the snow near Maggie's knee. It was intentional, as the shooter could certainly have popped off her kneecap. The brown, bulky lass wasn't entirely wrong in her evaluation of Alastair's character, and in that moment he considered grabbing Maggie and flipping a coin for Charazance's intervention. They could take a little leap from here to somewhere else—he did not care where. Alas, the Dreamer of Chance had returned to her sleep. This game was no longer interesting enough for her attention.

"Come out, my rabbits, or I'll make trophies of ears and fingers next," said a laughing man.

They knew it was Moreth. There could be no debate. They wallowed for a speck in their despair. Even gay Alastair could not summon a little whimsy for the situation. At last they shuffled out from under the pine with raised hands.

"What interesting and loud conversation," cooed Moreth.

He passed his firearm to one of the many ironguards who had encircled the tree, and then retrieved his cane from another fellow. Snow tumbled down in white waves, and the wind howled. It made the allies' capture all the more bitter.

"I hear better than most. Like an animal, my wife would say," said Moreth. "She would know, my Beatrice. I believe you will all meet her soon. She does delight in the torturer's craft. For I think it's best to let the Iron marshals burn, poke, and rape the secrets out of you. I feel you each have so many to share."

Moreth grinned as the ironguards came forth with pointed rifles and sacks for their heads. They muffled the companions in darkness. Maggie could not forget Moreth's smile—the tall teeth and hunger. It was all she could see in the blackness.

III

Other than Alastair, none of them had ever been in chains. The trickster's slavery was so old and dusty a memory he was shocked at how viciously the choking fear returned to him. Moreth's taunting narrative of what further delights awaited them at Fort Havok drove Alastair deeper into his panic. He could not be caught. He would never again be bound in chains. Charazance had promised him. What then was this betrayal? *You swore, Dreamer,* he shouted to the silent presence inside. *I could make my own destiny. I would be the House and not the Fool.* Moreth laughed. Alastair grasped this sound despite winter's whistling and his sacked head. It had the same timbre of malice that could have belonged to another master in another time. Alastair stumbled to his knees in the snow.

*The pillory is terribly made. Its wood is like sandpaper against his shins. It is as rickety and poor as the township in which it has been erected. Flies buzz in his ears and on his many scabs. He can almost hear their nauseating, wriggling breeding in the festering compost with which he has been splattered. If he were a strong man, he could shatter the wooden restraints, and if he were a brave man, he would strangle those who tried to stop him—strangle them with the nearby rope that will soon hold his head. He is not, however, a man of either quality but a laugher, lover, gambler, and thief. However, he has sung his last tune and conned his last con. None of his charms and wooing will save him—not when his mouth has been sewn shut to prevent his tongue's poison.*

*"Viper!" the crowd spits.*

*He tries to smile though his stitches and wink at the mob with his welted eyes. Both attempts bring him only tears and a hard, bullying laugh from some-one beside him.*

*"Weep!" shouts the magistrate, and the crowd hushes to hear its master. "Weep and remember your crimes as you carry them with you into the void hereafter."*

*While the man is a haze, Alastair can sense his corpulent shadow and the many little dazzles of light that bejewel him. A rogue, he thinks. I am the fox, but you are the wolf in sheep's clothing. Your people starve, but you haven't known a grumble in your belly in all your life. He realizes he should not have taken from the less fortunate. Scruples and hindsight, though, are rarely part of a vagabond's character. He would not have taken from these people, had he met this venal hog before. When he had encountered the magistrate, he had taken almost every precious thing the man owned—including the man's daugh-ter. It appears he is to answer for that next.*

*"For the crime of petty theft, you have been found guilty and have served punishment in the stocks for seven days."*

*Seven days? he thinks. That explains the reek of his soiled self. He squishes his buttocks and the shite in his pants and pushes out a fart for his captor, which only entertains himself.*

*"Repulsive," says the magistrate, and he waves his jeweled hand before his nose. "The world will be cleaner with your loss. For the crimes of larceny and*

rape, you are condemned to the hangman's noose. May the Kings take mercy on your soul. Do you have anything to say before you hang? Do you have any apologies for my virgin Georginia or for the others of Fairfarm you have wronged?"

His lips are cut open. Whoever his caregivers have been, they have been trickling him water and stuffing fingers of food through his laced mouth. His throat is so rusty, though, he can only croak at first. "Apologies?" he rasps after a time. "Indeed. I...am...sorry the Fairfarm drunkards are such simpletons they cannot win a basic game of cards. I am...sorry...you have not spotted your prick since you were a boy— if ever. I am, however, sorry most of all that your daughter told you that she is a virgin and that I raped her. Appetites such as hers do not come from chastity."

He is backhanded before he can finish the list of his regrets. He gives a gory grin to the peasantry. He will smile until the very end. Even when more punches come and he is spitting teeth, he grins once he has found his breath. The padlocks are opened, and he is dragged up rough stairs to the gallows. He bids the hangman hello, and the grand ogre of a man leans in close with his sour-onion stink to spit in his face. He blows him a kiss as the noose is tied, and he says a gleeful farewell to the fools of Fairfarm. He thinks he hears the ancient songs of his Romanisti people—a delusion, surely. Perhaps he will see his spurned ancestors soon. He embraces the twanging, folksome melody and hums what chords he remembers.

In a speck, the lever will be pulled, and his feet will drop. He has loosened his shoulders as he does when slipping out of restraints. Today, though, this is to guarantee his neck will snap quickly. For beyond the rabble, there is freedom—an adventure in the realms of shadow and mystery on the outskirts of life. Caught this once and never again, he thinks. He dreams of what gambits and scams he will play with the spirits. Will there be currency to steal, or will he be able to pilfer something greater? The conman does not see how brave he is in being truly free of the fear of death. He also does not see how bright his soul shines as the floor disappears under him. All he feels is an unexpected tinkle of amusement. It is as though a child is laughing far away. It is more like a hundred children actually, and the joyfulness grows and echoes. These are children with starry eyes and flesh that glows like the sun. He has hooked something with his brashness, his sacrificial death, and his unique soul that embraces chaos and chance. He has woken one of the ancient voices.

**"Not yet,"** Charazance says. **"Not when we could have such fun together...if you will agree to let me in."**

299

"Get up," insisted Maggie.

She heard Alastair whimper and fall, and then she groped for him in the cold. She had to get him standing before the ironguards did so in their manner. To her consternation, he wouldn't get out of the snow. She was a blind woman wrestling an uncooperative man. Now the ironguards were shouting and heading their way. She shook Alastair.

"Alastair!" she urged.

Suddenly, he reached for her, and a speck later, he stood. "Thank you," he said. "I fell."

*You did. In more ways than one*, thought Maggie. The sly fellow had descended into hopelessness, which she had not been aware he could feel. *No more chuckles when you realize you're as fuked as the rest of our lot. Kings be damned, Maggie. How did you end up here?*

"Move along," barked an ironguard.

They were poked back in line with the others.

*A firing line*, Galivad thought as he sensed his fellow prisoners rejoin the ranks. While preparing for his assassination of Beatrice in Menos, he'd witnessed many public executions. The ruling caste called the ironguards for punishment of the most minor acts—a person giving an offensive look to someone above his or her station, a child trespassing on a master's lawn, or a woman rejecting a man's advances. Usually, the guilty were imprisoned until amassed in large numbers. Then they were taken to a public square and arranged into a formation from shortest to tallest with their backs to a wall. There were no trials and no judges—although the nearest Iron marshal would be called in to determine fault. The justicars of the Iron City were far too bogged down with the riddles of which master had murdered whom or which bribes were the safest to take. They had no time for common crimes. Such was how Menos treated its citizen criminals. Galivad thought of its prisoners of war, and he dryly gulped. The Iron marshals would prepare a special red welcome for them, he was certain.

Rowena marched slightly ahead of Galivad. He sensed her warmth and her cloak's fluttering. It seemed she was always leading or shielding the pack. He regretted his treatment of her and thought of the sleepy silences when they had lain together. The reflections calmed him. When the torture began, he would recall his singing to her, the feel of her rough hand in a rare touch, or the pleasing contrariness of her square and somehow lovely face. She indeed had a stallion's broad beauty. *I might just have fallen in love with you*, he realized stupidly, and quite late.

Ahead of him, Rowena didn't dwell on old wounds and missed opportunities. She had once been *khek*—the shite of the Arhad's filthy beasts. Since that foul standing, she'd made herself into a sword for the queen's hand. She would not welcome death so openly. She strained and listened to Moreth's every gloating word. He was rather easy to attend to, for she was close, and in his arrogance he spoke plentifully and loudly. On he went about underground anchorages and three Furies that would ascend to the skies. Fuzzily, she remembered a legend of some sort on this topic. As Moreth had foretold it, Eod's end was already decided. "A shame," he whispered to his captive audience. However, Rowena struggled to project empathy onto the man. "All should have a fighting chance to live. There is no sport when death is so swift."

Moreth lapsed into quiet, and from then on Rowena had the howling winter as a companion. Even that screeching cold she did not allow to dull her only working sense. She listened for breaths, mutterings, or shifting branches. She listened for whatever could tell her where they were going and perhaps how to escape. In her head, she counted sands as best she could. After many hourglasses by her count, they stopped for a break. It was not a full period of rest, as Moreth seemed anxious to meet his goal. Soon they were moving once more at the plodding crawl determined by their cargo. At least they'd been given water, even if their blindfolds did remain. "To keep your strength up and your vocal cords lubricated for screams come your interrogations," promised Moreth, ruining the kindness. After wandering blindly for an eternity, Rowena and her companions eventually were halted in the middle of what was surely nowhere. However, intent on hearing as she was, she captured the whoosh and crash of waves. They were near water. The Feordhan was the likeliest landmark. The puff of pistons and axles and the grating slide of a gate into a dry, hot space followed. Where they next trod echoed as though they walked in a valley of steel, and the stomp of their heels rang like funeral chimes to their ends. Unwanted hands frisked them and stripped daggers, bags, and belts. Then they were loaded onto a metal platform that descended. A powerful wind ruffled them from bottom to top as if they traveled in an upright tube. Then they were ruffled again as a great object passed them in the shaft. *A vessel?* Rowena wondered. She craned her head around like a curious dog to take in all these clues.

"Watch yourself, Sword of the Queen. The railing is wicker thin, and the length of the fall would be considerable," warned Moreth. Rowena had stiffened as he named her. "Yes. I know who you are—and the dandy lad too. We have our eyes on your kingdom just as you have yours on Menos. As for the ginger fellow, he carries a Watcher's eye, but we've sailed beyond the port of care for what his masters will do to us for one dead Voice. Now, you..." Moreth's shoes and cane clacked their way to Maggie. "You are a bit of a puzzle. That engraved flint box you carried that my men found in your belongings. A family heirloom? I think it is. Genealogy is a hobby of mine. History as well. Cordenzia of House Kraedos. A bit of a rebel in our tales. Whitehawk squirreled her away somewhere—Taroch's Arm, if I recall. However, that was a poor man's lifetime ago. She would have family, and a heart such as hers would be full of sentiment. I would think her descendants would likely have inherited that weakness. To carry around napkins, baby blankets, and the knickknacks of those who are grown or gone. Was she a mother or grandmother?"

If she and Alastair ever had a chance to play cards, Maggie would prove an excellent challenge at Fates and Crowns. She had a faultless bluff—not even a twitch. Moreth wore a cologne, though, that smelled like a mixture of spruce and eucalyptus. It nearly caused her to sneeze and break her stonewalling.

"No matter." Moreth sighed. "The Iron marshals will flay the secrets out. I can wait to see whether I'm right. I usually am."

He walked away, and the lift continued its windy drop. They lowered into warm, noisy depths—an underworld of fire, smoke, and the screech of condemned metal souls. *An anchorage...Furies.* Rowena knew what was being built below, even if she could not see to gasp at the black, monstrous crowes because of her blindfold. *By the Kings, how many years has Menos been planning this war?* she wondered. Her terror deepened as she sensed the space widen into a cavern and the full clattering industry of the Menosian war machine welled over her in a billow of doom. There were clangs and shouts for truefire and oil. She heard obstreperous creaking, bashing, hammering, bolting, and the fizzle of sparks. Rowena was the last of her companions to hold out on her dread. She'd walled it behind her shivering courage this whole time. Mercy upon her, she could no longer maintain the delusion of hope against what they undoubtedly faced. The Iron Queen was more prepared for war than Eod ever was or would be. There was no sorcerer king in Eod who could throw back at this black might with his white magik.

She felt stupefied and sluggish when it came time to move. She was unaware the platform had finished its journey, and a rifle's end to the ribs brought her back to the nightmare. She bumbled into a busy causeway and detected whirring carts and grunting, sweaty slaves. *Kings, do these poor folk reek from toil, or are some of them dead?* She could not bear the sharp smacks and ensuing cries as lashes were brought upon the wretches, and she listened instead as the truefire shipment was signed for, assessed, and wheeled off. After that, Moreth dismissed many of his men with what seemed a customary cheer. "Drinks, pleasurefolk, and song!" he promised, and he sent them on their merry way. The remaining soldiers shoved the prisoners into a narrow cart made for tinned fish rather than people, and they hopped into another. With a lurch, the small train kicked into motion. It added another screech to the din as it moved along metal tracks. While it was terribly loud, the captives knew the anchorage's noise surely deafened what captors remained with them—perhaps even Moreth. Huddling close to one another, the company whispered their fears.

"I'm not ready to die," confessed Maggie.

"None of us are," said Alastair. He sounded impassioned, as if he actually cared. "I shan't let them hurt you, Maggie."

The tavern keep blushed under her hooding.

"I doubt you will have much to say regarding her treatment," said Galivad. "I don't see how we shall survive. I'm not giving up. I just—"

"You are giving up," hissed Rowena. "Listen for once! We must think and use all our cunning here."

"You think someone will come for us?" asked Maggie.

It was such heartwarming enthusiasm. Rowena hated to pulverize it. "No. We are alone—as alone as four persons can be. But I would say we have all wandered in shadows before. None as dark as this, perhaps, but shadow-walking still. A little hope. Hold on to that if nothing else. Or a promise or a dream. And tell these Iron masters *nothing*. The sooner you speak, the quicker you die. They will not keep any of us around once our tongues run out of betrayal."

It was a feeble plan, to be sure, but surely not as foolish as what had landed them there. Silence seemed to be their only weapon. By the time the double tram finally stopped, they were ready. Four strong and withholding souls stepped off the iron cart. Moreth, a highly keen observer, sensed the resolve in their puffed chests and proudly held shoulders. They would be difficult to break—but not impossible. He wondered which Iron marshal would be their inquisitor. He thought of asking Beatrice. He jumped as his wife called for him.

"I was just thinking of you, my love," he said.

"I must have felt the summons of your heart, for here I am," came the silky-sweet voice of his Iron mistress.

Galivad shuddered. Was he imagining that lilt again? No. It seemed quite real and quite like his mother.

"What are you doing here?" she continued, and her syrupy-sweet, cloying fragrance surrounded the four strangers while she examined them. "With these...creatures?"

"Prisoners from Eod," corrected Moreth.

"Oh. We're all simple clawed and angry things once the skin comes off," clucked the mistress of El.

She paused and hovered near Galivad, and he wished he could kill her with black magik. What a terrible occasion not to be a sorcerer. The sugar hint of her scent, though, smelled so much like Belle that the idea of murdering her repulsed him. In that moment, he loathed himself. Beatrice stunned him by ripping off his hood.

"Who is this?" she asked.

The suddenness of the light blinded him momentarily. The metal tunnel, the plated antechamber, and its gray lanterns became clear to him only gradually. Most of his attention, though, was fixed on Beatrice.

"Galivad, master of the East Watch," announced the Iron Queen.

She had appeared from an arch leading off the antechamber. Though he had never seen her, Galivad recognized the Iron Queen immediately. Who else could she be, this cold, lined woman who strode with absolute surety? In her plain velvet gown and unpolished iron jewelry, she seemed less grandiose than he had imagined she would be—she did not care for material conquests, apparently, only metaphysical ones. She wanted to rule souls and minds, and that was a more dangerous hunger than a desire for power. She made her way over and beheld him as if he were the fly in her pudding. Then she unhooded the other three prisoners and gave them an examination much the same.

"I brought them to you immediately," said Moreth, "to see what should be done. I caught them sneaking toward Fort Havok. Such lumbering quarry. Loud as pots and pans with a drunkard in the kitchen. Arguing when I found them. I believe they meant to interfere with my mission."

"How much do they know?" wondered a richly decorated Menosian with a rolling accent that was difficult to place. He was in a full set of armor of spikes and black curls—his face could not be seen. He stood next to the Iron Queen.

Gloriatrix turned to him and spoke with surprising courtesy. "Find out, Gustavius. Take them away."

"Yes," said the Iron lord. "At once."

The four prisoners sighed. Here came the moment—the great test of their endurance against evil. Each silently debated who would crack first and cry for the agony to end. As they were about to be pushed back onto the cart, a voice called out unexpectedly. "A moment," said Beatrice. "I shall interrogate the watchmaster."

Gloriatrix shrugged her approval. Moreth grinned at the thought of what red canvases his wife would paint with the watchmaster's flesh. Beatrice's crystal gaze seemed to paralyze Galivad, and he was roughly pulled away from the others.

Rowena was stricken and reached out for him. An ironguard butted his weapon into her temple and threw her into the cart with the others who were not to be Beatrice's playthings. Poor Galivad, her golden bard. He looked so lost, small, abandoned, and vulnerable. When the train pulled away and he vanished into darkness, the indomitable stone woman began to sob.

IV

"So that's the whole yarn," Lowelia said with a sigh.

Leonitis had never fully adjusted to his conspirator's dual personalities—how she could be queenly and articulate one moment and muttering "deary mittens" the next. Presently, she embodied the latter of her two identities. Leonitis and Lowe, together with the spymaster, were clustered in the sitting area of Her Majesty's chamber, and Lowelia had just finished confessing what she'd done to Menos's little rat, Euphenia. As a man of war, Leonitis could spot the rust of death upon the woman. It was under her fingernails and in the pinkness of her skirt. A knife's sparkle of madness lingered in her eyes. After her story, Rasputhane relaxed his death grip on the chair opposite the queen—the one where the king should sit—and looked beyond the room to the balcony, as if the stars could guide his troubled thoughts. Leonitis found cold stone a sobering comfort after these torrid events, and he'd knelt beside Lowelia throughout her confession. Now he came to his feet and stretched. "I think a drink is in order," he said.

"Definitely," agreed Rasputhane.

Leonitis retuned in a hurry with a glass of spirits for each. Lowelia did not take what he offered, and he stood over her as she wrung her hands white. "I'm sick of it. Just sick of all of it," she muttered. "All this lying and pretending. I don't know how much longer I can keep it up."

Rasputhane glared at her. "As long as you must."

"But I am a murderer."

The spymaster's spectacles slid down his nose, and his stare went frosty cold. "Stop being such a child. Do you think Eod is the holiest of holy nations? A sanctuary free of sin? How many murders do you think I have commissioned in my years here? More than your one and with much less reason. How many people do you think I have garroted myself? If my hands showed the blood in which they were washed, they would be crimson black. We do what must be done. In times of war, that is never pleasant. We are at war, Miss Larson. In a month, you might well look back on Euphenia's execution—which is what that was—with the grandest affection compared with what blood you are then wading through," Rasputhane said, and he tossed back his spirits.

*Quite a gulp for such a tiny man,* thought Leonitis.

"There will be no trial or charges of murder for you," Rasputhane continued. "No punishment other than what guilt you choose to carry. Toughen those shoulders, for they will have a hundred deaths or more to bear before this war is over."

However hard she tried, Lowelia could not find a retort for the fellow. She took the glass from Leonitis and followed the spymaster's example. A few burning swallows of brandy later, most of her regrets seemed scorched away.

"Since we're all partners in this affair, we should decide how to handle this infestation of rats," continued the spymaster. "A task that should have been seen to long ago—and with the ruthless enthusiasm you've shown today. Do pardon my disloyalty, but Magnus was...well, complacent when it came to the protection of Eod's information. Magnus valued knowledge. He saw it as his treasure. As we know, much is locked away in the Hall of Memories. He relied on the enchantments of the palace to block all the standard tricks of my trade such as poison or far-speaking. As far as I or anyone can attest, the palace's security has never been breached. Yet we are not invulnerable, and no secret is really ever safe. With Menos's shadow to be cast upon us any day now, we must ensure there are no more errors in our security. Everyone—our people, our military, and even our hidden agents—should be on the highest alert. Tension such as this keeps us prepared and makes for nervous informants in the enemy's camp. When the rats are anxious or feel they have an abundance to report, they scurry carelessly into traps."

"You are suggesting something," said Leonitis.

"I am," replied Rasputhane. "A decree that, in the absence of Magnus, only the queen herself can issue. Martial law. Curfews. A sealing of the palace, which should be done before the public announcement of war. We can delay these events no longer."

There it was. The gauntlet of reality had been thrown down, and it was every word Lowelia did not want to hear. Only the queen could make the announcement. She had not known this foolish ruse would bestow such obligations upon her. Her shoulders were already buckling before the spymaster added this burden. Rasputhane could see the woman shriveling from her responsibility, and he gave her another headmaster's glare. "Any other action would be devastating under the circumstances," he said. "The people must know to prepare their homes and families. They must learn to live in fear and readiness. I don't handle these sorts of things. I can, though, fetch the caller, who will pen a speech for you if language is not your forte. The announcements and rulings should be made in the morning. No later."

*This is my mess now—just as Euphenia was,* Lowelia thought. *The queen might not be here to help me, but I am not helpless. I've heard enough of her graceful speeches to plagiarize something. Remember those words.* She tuned out the men who were chatting nearby and reminisced about Her Majesty's eloquence.

"I shall craft the words for the people myself," declared Lowelia. She shocked the men with her calm—or the facade of it. "You are right. As the great Kericot did sing when the drums of war sounded and the dread Taroch pressed onward to Eod, 'We have crossed the Feordhan, and only one line remains to be drawn—victory or defeat.' And so the bard's wisdom echoes to this day. For a line has been drawn clearly between victory and defeat and slavery and free will. Come that red dawn, there will be people of Iron or people of light. Only one force will stand in the end." Speaking with such rhetorical force exhausted Lowelia. She faltered and smiled. "Or something like that. Longer, obviously, and as rousing as a war song. I shall sew out all the tatters myself. Sorry. I shouldn't have said tatters. I promise it will be a dashing speech."

Rasputhane clapped. "Well done. Needs work, as you say—quite a bit. I don't think, though, that the caller is in order. Another drink, however, is on the agenda to loosen the muse."

## V

It was Lowe's best performance yet.

Missives, far-speaking stones, and criers had been abuzz since before the darkness broke, and in an hourglass, their messages had called forth a crowd of thousands. "The queen calls for war!" the invitations all said—or a variation on that premise. "War with the Iron City! A stand against the Iron monsters!"

Lowelia had thought it best to be blunt with the people. For she knew how the common person liked to be addressed, which was not with duplicities and innuendos. Controlling the tone of the announcement was also important. Eod should seem like the aggressor and not a floundering, reactionary pacifist. Fearful people needed strong leaders. That was what Lowelia became that morning—a silver fist with which to grapple one of iron.

Though nearly every word she uttered had been earlier transcribed and well rehearsed, so imbued was she with passion that she might have been speaking directly from the heart. What improvisations she inserted into the speech flowed with the glorious melody of her fervor. She gave a thorough report on the state of the nation. She communicated their danger more brashly than a true royal ever would have. Time and again her council of advisers gasped at her candor.

She began, "Rumors are poison to our kingdom—a kingdom that has been nourished only on truth. Today I shall stamp out these false stories. I would see all whispers die so we might look to the black dawn together with our hearts and minds pure and united. You do not love without trust, and I need you to love yourselves and your kingdom, or we are doomed." She swept her arms wide while spitting out truth after truth. None who heard would ever forget her words. She continued, "My bloodmate, my love of one thousand years, now battles his mad brother in the South!" Later she declared, "Yes. Sage Thackery Thule, the man who wrote your freedoms with our king, was once a slave and master to Menos himself. Who better to grasp the bitter-sweet lessons of oppression than a man who cast aside the Iron City's dark traditions—his wealth, standing, and family too—so he might teach the world a better way? There are no traitors in Eod—only souls seeking sanctuary. We are the world's sanctuary and its hope. We are the star to guide the lost wanderers in the night, and what a dark night will soon descend."

Once she finished her address, the ocean of Eodians gathered in King's Crown was in a frenzy. Men stood on every cobble, women helped their gurgling infants pump fists to the heavens, and folk had turned carts into cluttered balconies from which they could chant the royals' names. From her terrace, the queen rained her people in smiles and roars for victory until she felt dizzy from looking down on so great a crowd.

Leonitis could not say for how long she had spoken. It seemed, though, to have passed in an instant. He wandered inside the palace with the queen and her trembling, amazed, and galvanized advisers. Among them only Rasputhane wore a smile. He was practically beaming. When he believed no one would see him, he gave Lowelia a wink. En masse they retreated to a small chamber for mediations—a place with sitting benches and misty fountains that had an essence of the Chamber of Echoes. What could the council say that she herself had not? What was there even left to discuss? All Eod's skeletons had been thrown out of their coffins now. One by one, the advisers gave respectful smiles and left the queen. Dorvain was last to go and more vocal than his peers. "I've never heard a leader speak with the kind of fire and forthrightness you did," he said. "That was a speech for the ages, Your Majesty—one I shall always remember. I do wish my damned brother had been here to see it. When he stops getting his diapers changed in whatever hospice you have him at, I shall tell him what he missed."

Lowelia nodded, and the watchmaster turned. He caught himself midstride. As he faced her again, he looked knotted from worry. "I mean not to press," he grumbled. "But is he well? It has been a few weeks now. Hasn't it? I might like to visit him, if I am not to stand with him in battle."

What a heartfelt and unexpected sentiment this was from the flinty fellow. Leonitis felt touched. "I regret that while he is improving, he still remains quite ill," said Leonitis. "I can ask his caregivers to pass on a message to him—if there is anything you would like to tell him."

*What a queer manner the hammer has*, Dorvain thought. There was a softness in the shoulders and stare that reminded him of those moments when he and Leo had laughed together after a drink or arm wrestling. It threw Dorvain into even more distracted a state. "No. I think...he's fine on his own, as you say. Excuse me. Your Majesty. Hammer. Spymaster."

He bowed to each, and then he practically had smoke gusting off his heels as he dashed out of the room.

"Funny man," commented Rasputhane.

"He is," agreed Leonitis, and he crossed his great arms. "But he is my brother."

The authority and purpose of her speech had not yet subsided within Lowelia. She said, "We are all brothers and sisters now. In war. Since the palace is under lock and key, I would like to see how prepared we are for the Iron storm. Rasputhane, you have full authority to hunt the rats in our house as you please. Hammer, take me to the battlements."

"Yes, Your Majesty," replied Leonitis, and he did not for a moment doubt it was his queen who commanded him.

VI

The work done thus far on Eod's defenses pleased Lowe. She commended the Silver Watch on its progress when she visited the troops that afternoon. The thunderstrike artillery had been relocated to the barracks atop the wall, as they would be the first to know about and respond to an aerial invasion. They were practicing throughout her visit, firing arrows of ivory lightning off into the desert and causing rumbles and sandstorms near the wall. "We are the world's hope!" shouted the soldiers as she passed them.

A circle of sorcerers was also present. They bound white flows of magik into the pointed parapets, and they didn't notice the queen at all. It was no matter. She noticed them and hoped they completed Eod's aerial shield soon. The conical silver roofs of the watchtowers they were enchanting would act as lighting rods for this great protective spell. Already, she saw a shimmer in the skies as though sheer white satin fluttered over the clouds. She hoped to see something more awe-inspiring when the magik was fully woven. *Let the Iron bastards know we are ready for them. Have them quake and worry for once.*

She did catch Gorijen Cross about—the diminutive sorcerer and leader of the thunderstrike artillery. He was exasperated and fussing over the sorcerers rechanneling Eod's enchantment into the heavens. They seemed to be chanting their incantations incorrectly, and Gorijen corrected them with slaps and shouts. Lowelia developed a kinship with the man then and there. Gorijen appeared far too occupied to deal with her, and she received a humble nod at her royal presence before he hurried back to his duties.

When her inspection of the wall ended, she took a skycarriage to each of the city's three gates for meetings with the technomagikal engineers. They reassured her of the barrier's impenetrability, despite some of its magik's being siphoned to the sky for protection. Who knew whether the Menosians would try to storm the gates when their crowes' wings were broken? As an added countermeasure, earthspeakers stood with their hands upon the wall and hummed. It was a subtle sorcery—an appeasing of the stone—to encourage it to a new, greater hardness. Stone was stubborn and took much time to enchant, so they would be there for many days. To test these measures, a few sorcerers in Cross's artillery stood by and unleashed their dazzling arrows against the fortification. From what she witnessed, nothing could scratch what Magnus's magik had raised. If all else were decimated, at least the white wall of Eod would remain as a memorial.

Down in the streets, the citizens hailed her entourage, and she learned that her maxim from above had been adopted below. "We are the world's hope!" cried everyone from the lowliest vagrant to the wealthiest master. As the day reddened to a close, they found they had spent as much time stopping to make visits of inspiration as tending to the duty for which they had set out. Weren't those visits a part of that greater duty, though? Hearts were Eod's weapons and as important as steel, sorcery, and great walls to strengthen. The people's empathy was all that separated them from the Iron masters. Without it, they would be an immoral technomagikal gargantua as obsessed by advancement as Menos. While Lowelia sowed bravery and hope, she wondered often what wicked fruits the real queen was growing in her garden.

"I shall unmake Menos to its very stones," Queen Lila had announced to the keepers of her secret. How did one unmake a city? Dark magik, realized Lowelia. Queen Lila thought to fight fire with fire. However, the flames of that wrath could well consume their maker. *What if I am stuck in this illusion forever?* she thought fearfully.

Just then, people cried her name and flung themselves toward her hovering skycarriage, and she accepted that life as a queen was hardly without its benefits. Nonetheless, she worried for Lila's safety and soul. Into her breast pocket, she'd placed the far-speaking stones—one of a pair for Rowena and a few from the queen. If ever their heat started, she would know. Each day, though, the stones stayed quiet, and the absence of news became cold news itself. The war could begin before Queen Lila ever succeeded in her gambit. She wished events would not unfold this way. Playing a queen, even convincing herself of that role, was a matter different from spearheading a nation through war. Would she have to ride Brigada or the queen's steed? She'd never been in a saddle before.

"You look tired and troubled," noted Leonitis as they rode through the sunset and toward the palace.

The day's circus of events was finally complete. *Deary mittens, my hounds are barking, and I would die to just kick these tortures a woman calls shoes right off.* That voice was silent inside the mater now, and Queen Lowelia had control of her mouth. "I am. It has been a very long day, my friend. We should have another toast this evening. It could be one of the last with this illusion of peace upon it."

They watched Eod flash by. Lamps blinked on in every window, and they could safely guess none would go out this evening. All of Eod stirred and lay awake for war. She had done her duty, and with an uncomfortable anticipation, she dreamed of what challenges she could test herself with the following day. The prospects of rule excited her. Sputtering sunlight warmed her through the glass of the portal she minded, and not at once did she sense heat by her breasts.

"Oh! The stone," she cried.

Except for Leonitis, the cabin was empty—not that she would have cared. While her companion gaped, she dug into her bustier like a whore looking for change. She finally pulled out the hottest far-speaking crystal she found. *Hot!* The damn thing burned as hot as a bead of fire. It seemed eager to talk. She needed a speck to remember the mechanism of its functionality and then brought the crystal up next to her ear. As simple as that, the message spilled out. It was a woman's deep voice that was not her queen's. Lowe could not respond before the stone's magik dried up and it cooled to a black, cold rock in her hand. What would she have said anyhow to this frantic whisperer?

"Who was that?" asked Leonitis.

"Rowena."

He waited and saw her expression travel from paleness to sickness. He moved across to take Lowelia's hands and squeeze them. "What did she want?" he asked.

She swallowed a little fear. "She's been captured. She's being held in a place called Fort Havok. North of Blackforge. I don't know how she managed a message to us. She has confirmed what we know, and that it is much worse than what we ourselves have imagined. There's an armada the likes of which we have never seen. The Iron Queen herself will fly. Rowena believes her flock of crowes will be upon us soon."

"How soon?"

"Any day now, war will descend on us. Queen Lila is missing. Our allies are captured. Magnus is gone. Who knows where my darling Morigan and

Thackery are off to? Nothing ever makes it out of Alabion except for tales to warn us of brutal endings. We are all that Eod and all those people beneath us have. We are the last and only defense against Menos."

She laughed, cold and smarting.

# XIII

## MOTHER-WOLF

### I

Since stepping into these cursed woods, this was the second time Mouse had been in a cave full of bones. When illuminated by the power radiating from her friend, the place wasn't so horrifying. Dust fuzzed the bones. They were obviously quite old, and the spiders and crawly things that made homes of the skulls were all small enough for Mouse to squish with her thumb—not like the red-eyed, white-faced lurkers from before. As they descended deeper into the cave, the trail of decay also thinned, as if whatever monster prowled these spaces had either grown lethargic or died. Mouse wondered what so unsettled the Wolf that he whined so queerly behind her. *Who cares? You have your own destiny to face. And a meeting with the Gray Man*, she ruminated.

Eventually, Talwyn asked the obvious. "What is this place?"

"*Pluach* (A den)," muttered Adam.

Somehow, the quiet lad had picked up a few of the essentials of slow-walker chatter. It was enough to know that a question was being posed about their new danger. Talwyn nearly inquired further when a scattering of black needles in the powdered floor piqued his curiosity. Dipping to a knee, he sifted out several long filaments. They were barbs almost, and it seemed the smaller bits were only pieces fractured from the larger. *Hairs*, he realized, *shed from a hide possessed of hard bristles as long as my forearm.* Once he had made the discovery, he threw the hairs back into the dirt and raced to the others. "A creature," he warned them. "Enormous. Larger than...I don't know what. But something is, or was, here."

"A wolf," mumbled Morigan. "Can you not see it?"

This was the first she had spoken, and her words echoed as if she had shouted. Caenith lingered at the rear of his pack and growled as she spoke. Suddenly, the light from within the seer's gaze shone brighter. It blazed away the shadows, lines, and even age of the cavern until it was smooth as an unblemished canvas. Upon that canvas, Morigan transcribed for the others what she had witnessed in the Dreaming. She shaped light and shadow into a kind of story of image and sound. The companions shuffled after Morigan through the tunnel of shimmering luminescence. They were uncertain of what was real and not. Phantom footsteps, scuffles, barks, chanting music, and fading laughs bounced around them, and they were strangely giddy from hearing these noises. They were as happy as the spirits must have been who had once made them. Only the Wolf remained aloof to Morigan's magik, and his growls became an irritating but easily disregarded buzz to the others in their wonderment.

Talwyn gasped at what he saw and heard. White shadows of stags and bears straddled rivers, and birds as grand as suns dawned over the treetops of Alabion. Could beasts be so huge? Could they communicate in cultured caws and growls or with a stomp of a mighty hoof or paw? Could they preside over tribes of sticklike people who bowed in their presence to the court of animal kings and queens? Could it be possible? He reached out to Thackery for his erudition as much as his support, and they wandered arm in arm. They pointed and exclaimed like two young scholars in a museum of breathtaking antiquities.

"Animal spirits?" proposed Talwyn.

"No. Living beasts," whispered Thackery.

"But the size!"

"I know. I know. Incredible."

"*Anbuch* (Ancients)," mumbled Adam.

The scholars' minds conjoined and appraised much. They saw patterns in the projected vision of these great animals and their ritual offerings.

However, what was being exchanged in the caves, glens, and aeries where the Ancients gathered, they could not quite understand at first. They could see altars where people lay and willingly bled themselves into bowls, and the great animals themselves opened wounds on their flesh and rained red showers over their faithful. Faithful. Yes. This was undeniably worship, and blood was the sacrament. They could smell the iron of it as fresh and earthy as if from an opened gut. A *Fuilimean*—or a nearly identical ritual—was being practiced not only from bloodmate to bloodmate but between entire communities and their majestic patrons. Morigan must not have been interested in many of these histories, because slowly the giant elk, bear, winged creature, and other lords vanished from the canvas of Dream. Only a creature of vast darkness remained. It was splashed across every wall. It raced, roared, or stood atop a throne of rock. She was the ruler of the woods—a giantess of black fur and teeth as white as the moon over her head. A wolf.

*"Mother-wolf," says Morigan respectfully.*

*In another time and place, she circles around the queen, who watches the forest. Mother-wolf is so enormous the stone under her claws cracks and threatens to bring her down in an avalanche. Down beneath the cliff, the campfires and shadows dance. Her tribe sings and barks for her gift. For they are all mostly the same now. Blood has bound fur to skin, paw to hand, and soul to soul. While she cannot shed her skin any more than the mountain might shed its eternal layers, she still bears the essence of all with whom she has shared herself. She now possesses their kindness and creativity—a temperance to steady her animal. She is proud of the music she hears rising from the woods. It reminds her of how strong her pack has grown from that single, simple moment.*

*The first of them was a child left or lost in the woods. She did not know by whom or why or even her name as a slow-walker. Names do not matter—only the essence of what drives the flesh does. She remembers the First's crawling rage and how even as a furless, clawless grub, the little thing attacked the snakes and bugs that came for her—as a wolf would do. Somewhere out in the woods, Mother-wolf heard her. Mother-wolf's ears never miss a sound. Then she stalked her. The First's angry, wormling cries and her fight against death intrigued the Mother-wolf. How long could a slow-walker child truly survive in Alabion's greatest hunting grounds, where she and all the elder beasts roamed? The child was doomed. If Mother-wolf didn't eat her, a bear,*

a cat, or Snake himself would—the real serpent, not his puny earthworm children. Mother-wolf came upon the First. Mother-wolf was ready to eat her
out of her misery, and then the tiny thing bared her fangs. The slow-walkers
called it a smile, but she had such useless, soft teeth. Mother-wolf did not eat
her but fed her with the milk of her blood, as she did for all her weak, lost, and
wounded children. For the First was not a little woman but wolf. What was
beneath the skin never lied. In time, the First's teeth grew hard and sharp, and
her hide was tough and hairy to the weather. She surprised Mother-wolf with
her nimble fingers and her new body that could run on four legs or two. For
Mother-wolf's blood had changed her.

Many seasons and hunts later, the First asked to seek out her people—the
pack she had lost. She wanted to tell them they need not fear the deepest dark
of Alabion. Mother-wolf did not know jealousy. It had not bled its way into
her just yet. She understood only that an animal must follow the wind of its
instincts, and thus she nudged the First from her lair.

Although the First left, she did one day return to Mother-wolf, and she
brought others who had learned of her change and communion. Mother-wolf
ate some who were unworthy and not truly wolves. With the rest, she shared
the red mystery of her blood. Over many more seasons of hunts and culling
those who disagreed with the new order, the divide that once separated the
oldest from the young races finally became indecipherable. It was too muddled
with fur, wings, fingers, and hearts to say who was beast and who was man. At
last, the woods were united in one mind and one soul.

Mother-wolf has done all this, and she is proud—a feeling she would have
never learned were it not for the First. She thinks of her nameless, long-dead
pup as she bites into her shoulder and brings the sacrament to her pack. They
raise a clamor beneath her. They lap their tongues in the crimson rain—clawing
and barking for every drop. Later, she will come for their bowls and offerings.
Like the other oldest, she has now learned how to take and not only give. She
acknowledges there are gifts and lessons—patience, kindness, and cunning—that
the two-legs have that can make her more powerful than any other animal of the
land. Her wound closes quickly. Her kind are never cut for long, and she blesses
her pack with a howl before turning to leave. She pauses, listens, and sniffs.

What is this beast that runs faster than her kin and rips through the snares
of Alabion as mightily as she does? His smell is as raw as fresh salt, soil, and the

*sweat between a man's thighs. She feels a tug to track this force of a being—this whirlwind that has entered Alabion. That lure is another two-leg sentiment that has insidiously entered her over time. She barks off the compulsion and desire and seeks her lair instead. If the beast wants her, he will track her, and he will see who is truly ruler of these lands.*

*Morigan!* the Wolf's mind-bark returned Morigan to the world. Her brightness dimmed, and the imagery on the cavern walls wafted to nothingness. Caenith sounded frenzied, and the beast in her stomach clawed for escape. He refused to join her and the others and hung back by himself. She wished she had the words to calm him. However, the truth he wanted would hurt him only more.

*Almost, my Wolf. We are nearly there.*

Morigan's awakening extinguished the torch of her magik, and the cave grew dark. A stubborn wind and gray light squeaked in from concealed cracks, so they were not left blind and fumbling. A feeling of pressure accompanied their journey, indicating they headed upward. They went higher into rock—a stone shelf, perhaps, if not a peak. The river of bones seemed to be drying up too. A few pebbles were accidentally kicked here and there and sent rattling like tin cups down a hallway. In time, their sweating began and their thighs complained of the gradual ascent, and there came the first signs they were not alone. Over the cavern's whistling, the sharpest ears heard a second, great wind—the rise and fall of bellows. They could not possibly be lungs. Yet the musky scent had offended the companions since they'd arrived, and it now smelled stingingly strong. It foretold of a great beast that lay out of sight in the darkness.

"Smells like...dog," whispered Talwyn.

He and Thackery wandered slowly together. Fear chained them close.

"Wolf," said Morigan.

Caenith brought up the rear and shoved his grumbling bulk past Thackery and Talwyn. He forced them to hasten their strides and catch up with the rest, who seemed determined to meet whatever fresh doom Alabion had conjured for them. The doom was bound to Caenith, they guessed, who had made it through Alabion's trials so marvelously untouched.

*At last your luck runs out, my large friend,* mulled Thackery. He prayed for the Wolf, even if he wasn't certain whom to pray to these days. The Kings had been relegated to lesser mysteries, considering all he had now seen. So he implored the spirits of old—the witches, giants, titans from the stars, and legends no one spoke of because they were too young to know anything of their own irrelevance. He asked those forces to guide them from here on out. Did they answer? The cavern did grow brighter and wider from a broken roof, and a refreshing gust of winter cooled the humidity of the place and dispelled a bit of the odor that flooded the passage. In the better lighting, though, Thackery saw claw marks in the stone—gouges as large as those a plowman would make with his tools.

*Have faith in her; believe in Morigan. She would not lead us to our deaths. She alone has guided us through so much*, thought Thackery. Casting a look to Morigan, he realized the burden she carried. Upon her back, she bore the stone of Vortigern's death, and yet she managed to walk without faltering. As he considered the young woman and how much she knew and was forced to endure, he yearned to tell her how strong she was and how grateful he was to her, this surrogate daughter of his. He was even thankful for this journey that would claim him sooner or later. Like many precious moments, though, this one passed in a speck.

"Do not raise your weapons or show fear," commanded Morigan.

A cavern suddenly appeared before them where the walls simply fell back and upward, and she strode into it. More light twisted down in thick, chalky lines about the enormous chamber, and the ground glistened with frost or dampness. They could not tell or did not want to understand what it was Morigan had left them to approach. The massive heap of gently heaving feathery blackness was in the middle of the space where no white beams were thrown to reveal anything more. Yet the heat that billowed from it, its pine, pepper, hound, and sweat odor, and the beast's shuddering breaths were all so familiar to Caenith that everyone followed his lead. *Bow*, the instinctual voice screamed in many of their heads. Bow and pray for your lives. Before them lay sleeping a true, ancient wolf—a ruler of the woods and a beast once worshipped in Alabion.

*Anbuch.*

Adam's mother had often sung of the forbearers of his race that had retreated, forgotten, within the Pitch Dark. All changelings knew these histories, and most regarded them as folklore. However, she'd impressed upon him the truth of the bonds and promises sworn between beast, land, and the ancient rulers. She'd told him these were not tales but the holiest of secrets. Adam, confronted by this miracle, fell to all fours, trembled, and laid his chin upon the ground. "*Anbuch*," he whispered.

Caenith did not succumb to supplication. Instead, he stumbled and throatily whined to the Ancient. Rumbling like a warship chugging into motion, the great heap shifted. The Ancient shuffled and rose and grew to improbable dimensions. The company members' imaginations seized hold of them, and they pondered black mountains, ebony moons, and other elemental forces—not a monster so monolithic it could no more be called a wolf. So great was her shape and so powerful her presence that as she yawned, showed her yellow fangs as big as fence posts, and washed them in her canine wind, their logic conflated fact and fiction and kept them sane in dreamy fantasy. The Ancient beheld them with her wrinkled stare—her eyes large and clear as full-length mirrors that captured their gaping reflections.

Through summer and winter, through sunshine and what hail eked into her lair, the Ancient had slept. She preferred dreams to the waking world, for in them Alabion flourished gloriously, her children roamed plentifully, and the woods stayed untainted by the sins of the Kings. A wolf's cry woke her from this impossible depth of dreams. It was a sound from which no mother could shield herself—the pleading of her son. She heard and smelled the other strangers in her den before she opened her great gray stare. They were not to be bothered, since they bore his scent. How deep and pure a match her gaze was for the pup that crawled forward. He was uncertain of whether he should be a man or beast. He was sure only of who she was. "*Mathair* (Mother)?" growled the Wolf.

Although the Ancient's whine shook snow from above and shivered the skins of the company with its power, none was afraid. They could detect the plaintiveness and the indelible love that did not need language to be understood. They could read their weeping companion—a man none could recall ever having spilled tears. They were tears only a child ever made for a parent. Talwyn knew the word the Wolf had said and the full strangeness of what transpired in the chamber. Now and forever, he would remember the black moon of a mother, the pale and unshaken seer standing in that shadow, and the kneeling, giant man with his howls of sorrowful joy. Those images would haunt him on bitter evenings and surface in his saddest times, for those three figures formed a testament to love that endured beyond time, reason, and barriers. They were bonds he hoped one day to know himself.

As the Ancient bent and began to groom Caenith with her pink sail of a tongue, the intimacy of that gesture broke the moment's spell, and all but Morigan left them alone. She lingered and shook her head as her bees drank in the entire ugly truth of her bloodmate's birth—the pain, joy, and horror. Then she too made her exit and choked back tears. The tale was not hers to tell—at least not to Caenith. His mother should be the one.

## II

Tunnels rambled off from the den, and after some exploration, the company found comfortable rocks arranged like rectangular couches. With a spot of light freshening the area from above, they chose to have their council there. They soon learned, though, that there wasn't much to say—not anything they could announce to the others that wouldn't add to the confusion.

"She...is his mother?" Mouse wrestled the thought out.

"Yes," replied Thackery.

"In the traditional or poetic sense?" asked Mouse.

"Both," replied Talwyn.

Indeed, no other explanation was plausible in this impossible debate. *An enormous, primeval being that could be the origin of all* Caenis lupus—*and possibly all changelings of similar breed—is the mother of our fearless guide through Alabion.* Talwyn chuckled at how ludicrous his life had become, and then he quickly hid his smile before the others spotted it and thought it indecent. They sat for a time and brooded so deeply that even as their arses numbed from the cold stone, they didn't bother to shift. Another thought boiled in the cauldron of the scholar's head. He couldn't halt his mouth from spitting it out. "If the...Old One or Ancient or what have you is Caenith's mother, who, then, would be his father?"

Thackery had an answer. In his head, his conversation with Queen Lila at the feast in his honor tortured him with its whispers. Digesting these thoughts gave him a stomachache, though he could not halt his mind from deeper postulations. *A man who does not age or die as the others of his race do. A man who is fiercer than any of his species, who can wear a wolf's skin, and who has the power of a hundred strongmen.* He thought briefly of Caenith's unflinching endurance and the absolute deprivation he overcame in their race to the Iron City. No changeling possessed such fortitude. He knew of only one man, a King, who did. The only wonder was how the seed had been sown. From his talks with Lila when she racked herself with tears, he knew the Kings could not bear offspring—not with mortal women and not even with those changed by their immortal blood, as she had been. Ostensibly, the same metascience should apply to the Ancient and those with whom she shared her sacraments—a power to change the flesh and create a unique creature with similar characteristics. However, it was not quite efficacious enough to bear a being as powerful as themselves. Thackery remembered a teaching from a shriveled schoolmarm he could barely recall beyond the nattering of her extremely aged mouth. That was no matter, for the ghostly teacher's knowledge had withstood the ravages of his old memory and still had much sense to offer. Two forces of equal magik were needed to produce an object—a being—equal to themselves. A being such as Caenith required an Immortal King and a...

"Thackery?" Talwyn was waiting for a reply.

"I don't know," said Thackery.

"You do," said Morigan.

Morigan startled the company. The seer had slipped among them lightly. Thackery wondered whether she'd again danced in and out of the otherworld. She appeared quite whole and without a suggestion of silver magik as she came to her companions and dropped herself onto the stone seat next to Thackery. How weary the poor girl looked—Thackery embraced her at once.

"This place," muttered Morigan. "There are too many pulls. Too many histories, spirits, and truths that want to be known. I do not know how much longer I can stay here without losing myself to all the whispers. I feel like a ship being tossed about in a storm."

"There, there," soothed Thackery.

Mouse found it hard to have sympathy for anyone. She had a duty to Adelaide and herself, and it didn't involve sitting around brooding over a twisted, furry family tree that wasn't hers to worry about. "Where's Caenith?" she asked.

"With his mother," replied Morigan.

What spiteful energy the bees fed Morigan as Mouse gazed at her. Mouse was angry—and with good cause. Even if they stood on unsteady footing with one another, Morigan would not insult her friend or any of the company by withholding secrets. Thackery already knew anyhow. She'd nibbled a few of his thoughts while wandering near him. It had been quite inadvertent, but so weak was the wall between Dream and reality that secrets blew about like pollen. "Gather round," Morigan said, and she sighed. "Stand up, make a circle, and join hands, please." The company shuffled about, and once they were organized, Morigan addressed them. "I won't keep these truths from you. I shall not hide his shame."

"Shame?" said Talwyn.

"The shame of his father," replied Morigan. "It is better if I show you."

Too late, Mouse realized what was about to happen. She couldn't have torn her hand from Adam's even if she had wanted to, for the volt of Morigan's magik clamped their grips together with impossible tightness. Again silver stars shone in the seer's eyes, and the companions and cave blurred to whiteness.

*A muscled shadow clings to the heights of one of Alabion's grandest trees. There he hangs by one hand and two feet. He's as comfortable as an ape while searching the green folds beneath him. Mouse assumes it is Caenith at first. His scent is different, though—more sweat and less spice and musk. He is larger still—nearly twice as thick and long as the brute she knows. Though he smells less like a wolf, he feels more like one thanks to these strange, all-knowing ideas she should not have. Only I'm not me—not really—but a phantom of a phantom of the seer, Mouse thinks. She sees the iron crusts in his beard and hears the screams of the animals he ate to make those red flakes. Now she knows this isn't Caenith, and her soul shivers from the strength he radiates as hot and feverish as a desert afternoon and more brilliant and bloody than the red globe that bleeds over Alabion. He is a king—the king of what rules the horizon. The King of the Sun.*

*Why are you here? In Alabion? Mouse wonders.*

*"Seeking, hunting, lonely," buzzes the queerest presence inside Mouse. It is as if she has eaten bees and guzzled effervescent cider.*

324

*The Sun King is hunting. He always hunts. He knows no greater way to exist aside from the rush and thrill of conquest and death—to race the golden horse of day and howl with the wolves of night. Never-ending life is a cycle of this chase, or so it was for years immemorial. Then his brother left him for a different cycle. Abandoned, he must now redefine himself. What meaning is there to be salvaged from endless life when he is told no longer to care for the creature for whom he has always cared? He remembers his brother's words, which he can never bring to mind without feeling rage. "We can be ourselves, Brutus. Real men. We can live and try to find love. Be fathers, rulers, husbands, and heroes."*

*Brutus does not know what any of those things are other than things his brother wants that he cannot provide. So he hunts. In hunting, there is simplicity—a chase and an end. None of what his brother has cast him aside for has any meaning here in the bloodiest hunting ground in Geadhain. The great beasts he once wrestled in ages of fire, ice, and sand—those paragons of scale, claw, wing, and fang—can still be found in this realm. They will be the family he has lost. At least they respect the one true order of life.*

*He sees something smashing aside trees and clouding dust in the land below, and he leaps. He grows claws and snarls to challenge it.*

*Mouse does not see whether he tangles with it for sport or the kill. She's willing to bet the latter. Dazzlingly, the bees toss a silver blindfold upon her. She is spun, the blindfold is removed, and suddenly, she is in another time and place. The Sun King is moving fast, and she moves as a wind at his back. There is so much speed that following him smears the land into a green, howling tunnel. She keeps up, however, thanks to the bees carrying her. In the eye of the storm of this baffling speed, she sees the King's great exertion, his incredible grace, and all the charisma he will one day pass to his son. How alike are the two men who are not quite men, from their bestial handsomeness to the same raw dedication to whatever they pursue. In this moment, the Sun King is engaged in the fiercest hunt. What he chases runs almost as fast as he does. Almost.*

*He catches the black-furred Ancient as she lumbers through a crossing. When they tumble into each other, they bowl over whole sections of woodland. They growl, bite, and try to judge who is superior to whom. She is different, this beast, from the land's other elders. She does not fight to kill but to play. When she has shaken him off, she does not run away or dash in for the kill. She waits* for him to charge her again. *This is a game to her, and as the sweat and blood upon the Sun King turn black in the night, he realizes he enjoys it. Their day of conflict has torn the woods, their bodies, and their fortitude. They have stumbled down a dell and nipped at each other all the way up a network of tunnels hardly wide enough for one of them. Finally, they flop themselves into more breathable space. He is tired and for once well and truly beaten. The Ancient senses this, and she nurses him as she would wounded kin—with her blood.*

*As the Sun King suckles, he cannot capture in words this exhilaration he feels. Words were always worthless tools. He enjoys this sense of a hunt without end, which offers somehow a new beginning. He bites himself a new wound— his have mostly healed—and feeds her too. She accepts, and the pressure of her fangs and weight upon him as she drinks brings him a specific heat—a scalding flutter in his heart, head, and loins. Who is this huntress? This spirit in the body of a beast? She is a creature so much like himself, but for the varieties of their skins. He could crawl inside her and feel the closeness of their souls—perhaps a greater intimacy than he had ever known with his brother. The Ancient stops her feeding and licks his great chest. She can tell what his passions are demanding. He is an animal too and makes no secret of his desire. They begin to roll and press into the other. They bite, drink, and lap.*

"Kings, Kings, Kings! He's going to shag the damned wolf!" exclaims Mouse. "I'd rather not see this. Show me anything else!"

*She is not the master of this vision, but that absentee hand steers the rivers of Dream away from this uncommon lust. Silver clouds bloom and storm about Mouse, and when they clear, it is to less torrid scenery. The Sun King and his new mate are atop the rock she frequents. Some time has passed—long enough to calm the restlessness of his wild nature and for him to learn what has changed the Ancient. He has learned how the blood and wisdom of men tempered her into something more than the grand animal she had always been. He watches the people below. They are her people and his people—their tribe of the new age. He thinks of his brother's words that he had never understood. For the first time in his life, he understands what it is to be a man, himself, and in love.*

*The Ancient knows the wanderlust that afflicts an unsettled animal, and she can see its frowning edge in her mate and feel it in his fingers. They claw instead of rake her fur. Her mate is thinking of the hunting grounds outside these woods. He is thinking of the pack he left. He will leave, and she will* not ask him to stay. Such is not the way of the wild, even if her instincts—the warmth, the nearness to his flesh, and the peace she feels when they tear meat or stay warm together—would have her shame her animal and plead for him to remain. Theirs is the strangest sort of love. Outside of Alabion and in the eyes of any other, they would be abominations. Here, however, they are perfect. If he is to leave her, he will not abandon her—not entirely. They both know what stirs within her. They can hear the second heartbeat that resides under her ribs.

"Holy sweet saint of fukery!" Mouse knows the truth by now. To see it realized, though, is a second and more startling shock.

The Sun King is pained and tells his mate he will return. He thanks her for showing him another way to live and explains that he goes to make a place where the world can embrace their child. It will be a realm of old laws and peace with the Green Mother. There the boy—for they can smell the sex of their child—will hunt, play, and live in freedom and without judgment or fear of his nature. Brutus's pale brother, from whom he has hidden himself and his feelings for however long this Dream has lasted, will help him build this sanctuary. He knows that much.

Will you tell him? asks the Ancient.

They are speaking but not in words or growls. They use another language that flows in beats of euphoria like a true love's caress, which Mouse has never known and yet understands.

In time, he says. We are to be men apart from each other. That is what he wanted—and what I have found with your help. I do not know how much he would even understand of our bliss or our child-to-be. I shall make him understand, though. You are not an animal; you are my love.

The Ancient nuzzles the King and takes one long whiff of his body. She muses on how these mortal sentiments can be barbed treasures to tear the heart simultaneously with yearning, sadness, and glee. They watch what will be their final sunset over Alabion together and hark to the songs of the Ancient's tribe, for this is a memory that neither should forget.

But he will, say the bees. The Black Queen will eat it right out of him.

After that, the bees are off and moving through time again. They deposit Mouse in a whirl some age from where she was. She is in the cave near where her real body stands. The Ancient has birthed her child. She grooms the naked thing while he chews on bones with teeth that should not fill a toddler's head.

*How very much like his father is he. His coppery hide and particularly the huge-
ness of his hands seem comical on his still-growing body. He has his mother's fur
too in a black mane upon his head. No child so young should have such locks. He
is an awkward thing—a creature who should not have been possible. However,
he will one day conquer these contrary characteristics and be the best of all the
strange elements he was given. Today, however, he is sloppy and odd. He cannot
protect himself without his great mother. Undeveloped in his perceptions, he is
unaware of the threat of a stranger entering their lair. His mother, however,
nudges him into a corner and hides him in the leftover skins of her kills.*

*Stinking magik coils up the tunnels of the Ancient's lair. The Ancient
paces while she waits for the witch and unleashes a snarl that casts rocks
from the ceiling as the blue-garbed woman steps into the chamber. Mouse
catches only a gash of green eyes and a pleased smile. It's a face as pretty as
it is hard, while the rest of her is swaddled away. She carries a wooden staff,
this witch, and she taps it on the stone floor. It causes an echo louder than
the Ancient's roar. It's magik, and it gets the Ancient's attention. Mouse—
or her Dreamwalker guide—knows this woman. She is the one who wanders
and collects the resonances of Fate. She is the eldest, if principles such as
age can be applied to immortals. She is a Sister of Three. Eean, the bees
declare.*

*She has come to make a bargain, but whatever Eean offers has the Ancient
stomping and snapping at the Sister. The witch remains unperturbed, even
while ruffled by snotty, tongue-lashing gales. She adjusts her kirtle and taps
her thunderous staff a few more times to show the Ancient what a real rain of
stones looks like. When the dust and posturing have settled from each party,
they have a quieter discourse of soft snarls and whispers. Somehow, these
conversations and their implications are shielded from Morigan and her fellow watchers. The Sisters Three are outside Fate and time, so a bend in the
rules is not unexpected. The outcome is understood regardless. The Ancient
howls at what is decided. She whimpers and coddles the creature she is to surrender—her curious pup, who has crawled out of the tent of skins to see what
his mother is fussing about. He is boldly unafraid of the witch and blindly
dumb to being given away. It wounds his mother's spirit to have him go into
the Sister's arms so willingly. However, that is his strength and the chaos of
the untamed wind he will be. He will blow where he wants. He will blow past*

*fear and always be free. The Ancient doubts the Sisters will keep him. Her mortal canniness knows these witches do not care for children. Her pup is being taken for a design different from simple rearing, but she must not keep him. He cannot stay.*

*When the Sister leaves, the Ancient howls again. She lets loose the pain she swore would not destroy her when her mate left. The sum of her loss is too great to weather, and the darkness of despair seizes her throat and strangles her into pitiful gasps. It is unworthy behavior for a queen of her kind, but she is unworthy of love. She never earned or deserved that gift anyhow. She was only a beast pretending to be a mortal. It is better that she forget and sleep. So she does.*

The circle broke, and it left them all gasping and throwing themselves away from each other. Thackery maintained more composure than anyone, as this was not his first trip as a passenger on Morigan's travels. Nothing she'd revealed truly surprised him. However, seeing a Sister in the meta-phorical, metaphysical flesh certainly left an impression not to be forgotten. *Eean. One of the legends has a name*, he thought. Without a doubt, the Sisters Three were the gnarled finger at the center of all these woven Fates. They had stolen Caenith to cast him as an orphan to Briongrahd. To what end, though? Seemingly, the Sisters Three had everything to answer for, and those answers had better be noble, given the extent of their deceptions. While the others were still recovering, he pulled Morigan close. "I am sorry," he whispered. "You should not have to witness these Fates. It is unfair how much these women, the Sisters, have thrown upon you."

She kissed the old man on his cheek, and he flushed from her affection. Then the now-recovered companions came forth with questions. Talwyn seemed possessed of a veritable diarrhea of the mouth. "Ancients...and that was a...a King! An Immortal. Brutus. The wild man, and now the mad. Caenith's father? Was I understanding that right? Incredible. Inconceivable conception. I mean...not the nicest way to come into the world. However, there was love, I think. Not the kind I'd pursue myself. All that biting, blood, and fur. Not my sort of dalliance. I'm sorry. I like a little fur—but not like that! I've said too much. Still, she isn't really an animal. A furry and wild woman, more like. So it's not totally a circus of horrors. Oh, pardon. I really should shut up. It's not a horror at all. I'm just...it's so very, very odd. But beautiful. Yes. I'll admit to that. I wish I had a quill and some parchment to write this all down. That magik you used—what was that? A sorcery of the House of Mysteries?"

"He is Brutus's son," Mouse said gloomily.

"Yes," agreed Morigan.

Mother-wolf and quandaries about what constituted bestiality notwithstanding, the identity of Caenith's father was the true storm cloud to these events. Therein lay the monster with which Caenith surely grappled. At the moment, Morigan sensed her Wolf was at peace. His beast paced happily behind her breastbone. However, when delight at meeting his mother ebbed, the horror at knowing his father would rile his spirit. She would face those torments with him. They had vowed never again to be alone. Sisters, Kings, and painful dreams wouldn't change that.

### III

Mother-wolf could not talk to her son with her mouth unfit for mortal sounds. However, the blood she and her cub had shared hundreds of years past was a secret language ready for them to use, and it held all the syntaxes of soul-speaking. A mother could never forget her child—not when a piece of him lay forever within her heart. For ages upon ages, she had clutched this fragment of Caenith while dreaming of earlier, better eras. She had nothing left of Brutus to hold on to. His roaring beast of flame had died to embers and then to ash so long ago. A shadow darker and older than eras of fire and ice had whispered to and then claimed him. She did not know his fate, but such painful emptiness felt like death. By slow-walker thinking, she would be known as a widow. Waking from a sleep of centuries to see her son and many other strange members of his pack felt so much like a dream, she was unsure she'd arisen. As her pup crawled toward her and cried for her, though, the piercing pitch of his pain could only be real. She knew her son had returned, and she kissed him as mothers do. Even if her tongue was as big as his back, making it seem more a lick than a kiss, the gesture remained unmistakably one of love.

Before he could ask or object to the memories cast into his mind, Mother-wolf showed him his father. It was part of why he'd come and part of what an animal and man must know. She spared him nothing.

Flowing into his mind came many scenes. First, there was the glory of a man wild and running through the woods and a brief flash of the same paragon rolling with his mother in warm musky pleasure. Later, they walked through a tribe of changelings who were inked in markings—folk who had disappeared into time and fantasy, as had the Ancients they praised. In these glimpses of history, Caenith knew the giant of bronze skin and animal fury to be Brutus. He recognized the face from his bloodmate's incursion into the Hall of Memories, where she'd found the Everfair King's buried, dark past.

Now he knew the secrets of his making and the fated, cursed link he and the Kings shared. Brutus was his father. Magnus, then, was his estranged uncle. As for himself, he was surely to be another thread woven into the Sisters' great loom. One of these witches he saw too in the flurry of memories, and she bartered with his mother for the property of her child. Once filled with the sickening truth, Caenith swallowed his rage. He decided he could delay his contemplation of the conniving Sisters and his murdering, mad, possessed father. At this moment, he lay with the mother he had never known he had. Their tale happened here and now, and it was the most important.

*Why*? he asked.

It was an expected question from an abandoned child. Was he not strong, brave, or simply good enough? The Wolf understood loneliness. He was a companion to loss. Feelings of inadequacy, though, he had no securities against. He wept and roared. He threw off his clothes, screamed into his furry skin, and bit at his mother for all the emptiness with which she'd left him. *I was never like them! An outcast among outcasts! I fought to be a creature of pride and honor with no hand or claw to guide me.*

Mother-wolf did not defend herself from her child's tantrum. His nails and fangs could only nick her steely hide. She allowed him his rage. When she felt it waning, she faced him, pushed him down, and laid their heads ear to ear. They breathed in each other's smell. They shivered. Their huge, thudding hearts were so close. They felt the body and spirit next to them, and all sorrows became a lifting fog on a crisp and glowing summer morn. However could they be unhappy in this moment?

*I am sorry for biting you, Mother*, grumbled the Wolf.

*I am sorry for surrendering you,* she said. *If I had not given you to the witch, though, she would not have delivered you to those of my sacrament. You would not have learned the ways of man. You would not have become so strong a wolf and so powerful a man as to find this pack of unusual hunters—one of whom is as much a mystery and miracle as you, my son.*

*She is. She is everything to me,* confessed the Wolf. *Nearly everything.*

They whined contentedly and nestled closer.

*Where will you go, my child?*

*We have hunted Fates this far, Mother. We have almost caught our quarry.*

*The witches?*

*Yes.*

Mother-wolf pondered his chase. Forgotten, evil presences still reigned in the Pitch Dark. She would protect him. *I shall take you to the witches, my child. You will fear nothing in these woods when I walk with you.*

*Now?*

*No. Not now. I should like to hear of the ages of my child's life I have missed—as much as you can tell me in this dove's flutter slow-walkers call time. I would keep you here whispering secrets to me for an eternity if I could. I would never let you go again.*

*Mother...*

Regrettably, they would not have forever. Before the Wolf and his pack resumed their trek, he told her what he could of his life with the changelings. He spoke of being friendless as a pup because he could not play with his peers without harming them terribly. He talked of how nature filled the void and became his companion and competitor too. Diving from the Weeping Falls or chasing the largest, fastest game in the woods—these were the trials and triumphs of his youth. He never had a mentor, and no one seemed to recall his parents. Those who might have known something of his strange deliverance deftly avoided contact or conversation. Soon, anyone who might have had any information had grown old and died—including the warfather of that age.

Because he was the strongest and the most enduring, he became the new warfather. He ruled his pack as no other in history ever had or would, for he was a warfather who would never bow—not even to death. To the wolves of Briongrahd, he became a permanence in an uncertain age when the smoke of change and technomagik spoke of revolution outside Alabion. Thankfully, such a clash between man and wolf never came. Menosians focused their resentment on the West instead. *We had such peace, Mother, for a time*, told the Wolf. *I found a taste of love too—although it was not the endless feast I have with Morigan.*

*An old name*, said Mother-wolf. She was pleased.

*Everything about her is a wonder from the past somehow resurrected and new in this age. I believe she is exactly that—a tie between new and old and between beings like you and the needs of men. When I am with her, I believe there can be harmony. For she has brought that to me. She has tamed the beast without leashing or lashing him, and she has taught me there are lessons even the oldest can learn from the fleeting races.*

Mother-wolf smiled with her grand, gray gaze. *I too was taught those lessons once, and they shaped me into what I am. My mate broadened these truths as a river forms a canyon after many ages. But he was more than a river. He tore up the land and reshaped it entirely. I would not change the weakness and tameness he brought to me either, my child. How it pleases me to see that one cares for you so. Do not lose that. Do not allow her to leave you—no matter how strong the instinct becomes. If you do, you might never chase her again.*

*You speak of the beast that is my father?* growled Caenith. At the mention of the Immortal, he felt ready to bite and claw once more.

Rising up, Mother-wolf groomed her child and brushed away his aggression as she chewed at the knots in his pelt. *We are all beasts. Men would look at me and see nothing else. Your father is as trapped and split in his nature as you are—perhaps more so, since he is confined in a body of two legs. You are able to choose your nature. He is not an evil man, though an evil is within him. In you, I have seen the memories of him, just as you have partaken in those of your father from me. I see and understand he now suffers as I have. I would ask you to find forgiveness and mercy for him when you find one another—however bloody that hunt will be.*

*When we find one another?* huffed Caenith.

*The weavers in these woods...the Sisters chose you for a reason. A destiny. Surely you know that.*

Caenith did know, and it clenched his every muscle to dwell upon it. With the gentlest of bites from her rending jaws, Mother-wolf relaxed those lumps in his flesh as well as those in his mane. Once he seemed thoroughly untangled, she touched her wet nose to his—a kiss. *I shall meet your mate now and take you and your pack to the edge of the Pitch Dark*, said Mother-wolf.

Caenith licked at his mother's face and ears and then padded away to shed his furry skin. The transformation took only a moment, and Mother-wolf indulged in the glistening, twisting miracle of her child—what she and Brutus had created with their love. She did not pray, for she knew the Green Mother did not grant wishes. Still, she did hope her next dream would not be so long. She hoped that when at last her eyes opened, it would be to her son and his great father rousing her with their bronze hands. Together. She would dream of that and nothing else.

IV

The black wolf and the giant who walked ahead of her—for he seemed taller now and surer in his carriage—filled the stone hallway suddenly. Only Morigan and Adam, who smelled them coming, were prepared for their arrival. The company had run out of astonishing things to discuss about the disclosure of Caenith's lineage. They stayed busy by being glum and unsociable. Now they all stood up to fumble out greetings. Morigan went to her bloodmate and kissed his cheek, and then she bowed to the Ancient. With her great, ruffling snout, Mother-wolf made a long examination of the woman. Rather satisfied with the inspection, she gave a gruff bark to signify her endorsement. Then Mother-wolf silkily moved her fantastic bulk past the bloodmates to conduct further sniffing and approval of the trembling company. Each remained rigidly still when it was his or her turn.

*She favors you.* Caenith smiled. It was all beard and white teeth and more wolfish than ever. *As if she could not. She will lead us from these dark woods.*

*You seem unshaken*, whispered Morigan to his soul.

*I am. We came to face your destiny. I now realize all of us face that same challenge. I know now why the Sisters wove our threads together.* He pulled Morigan against himself fiercely and with a passionate fire. He spoke while he kissed her. *They might play with Fates, but no magik can truly rule the heart. I should be pleased with their meddling, for without it I would never have found you.*

While neither wanted the kiss to stop, their companions shuffled and waited. Talwyn was asking the Ancient whether he could look into her ears to satisfy whatever dense and esoteric interest he was attempting to decipher. It would be best to stop him before Mother-wolf's tolerance was tested. As Morigan turned to look, the Wolf caught her and briefly pulled her to himself again. In Morigan's chest, the animal of fire roared.

*We are so close, you and I. In my heart and bones, I feel the tingling of your light. I want whatever nearness comes after this bliss. I want to press myself and my gratitude for every uncountable gift you have brought so tightly into you that we become one. One warmth and one soul. A season of fire and light.*

He kissed her neck. His beard tickled, and she shivered. Stars shone in the Wolf, and his heat burned through Morigan's flesh. They'd forgotten their intimacy for so long that tasting it was deadly. The others would see their passion in a speck, so they restrained themselves for the moment. They both agreed it was time to leave the Pitch Dark.

Mother-wolf felt them move. She was wistful at the animal pawing happening behind her, and she slipped by the company with a grace surprising for one of her magnitude. The return to the woods proved pleasant. Everyone—even quiet little Mouse—grew rather accustomed to the humongous guide. Mother-wolf's tactful nudges and warning barks saw them free of bumps and trips in the darker regions of the cavern. At one point, she caught Talwyn by his scruff and prevented him from stumbling off a deviously concealed broken edge and into a black unknown. After he realized he'd been snatched to be saved and not eaten, he praised Mother-wolf. Without a spider bite or bruise to be found, they soon exited the lair and walked back amid the dreary, clawing trees of the Pitch Dark. Night had nearly come, or dawn was just beginning—they could never properly tell. The denizens of the realm greeted them with a hungry clamor. The greatest of them was awake, though, and she walked with the travelers. The monsters in the woods burbled and barked in confusion, and shortly all fell quiet aside from the crunching of feet into hard snow.

Talwyn managed to fill the silence with blather about this plant or that— pieces of ecology their prior race for survival through the Pitch Dark had not afforded him the time to study. "Old! It's all so old!" he exclaimed often and with more gusto come every incantation. With great vigor, he talked of origin species and genera, about how the petals of such and such a flower had four folds when its modern incarnation had only three. "Three! Three! Don't you see?" he ranted like a madman who'd lost his favorite shiny bauble.

Not many of them really did see—not as he would have wanted. Wisdom did spread itself out through his excitement, though, and the company presumed that a variety of strains of life and fauna across Central Geadhain could be traced to roots here in Alabion. This wasn't much of a surprise compared with the shocking identity of Caenith's father, but it gave them thoughts to play with besides those of death, gloom, and war. They listened to his distracting prattle and allowed their minds and souls to breathe. Why should they not have a moment of escape and a pause from the chase and fear?

Eventually, the sun rose and proved it morning—not purgatorial grayness. This occurrence struck the company with its uniqueness because the hourglass could be plainly identified.

"By the Kings...daylight. I think we're nearly out of it," murmured Thackery.

Even Talwyn grew silent then.

At last they knew light and sunshine. Pure golden light fell through the canopy in slivers like a warm, welcome summer rain. They raised their faces to the light. Even with only a hint of brightness, the cold lost its sting, and their rosy cheeks went redder from smiles. They'd done it. They had braved the worst of Alabion, seen legends, and crossed paths with myths no mortal from East to West had known outside faery stories. Only the Sisters remained now.

V

Mother-wolf took them far into the realm beyond the Pitch Dark to a place so glimmering with beauty the Pitch Dark turned into a quickly fading nightmare. An old magik dwelled in these lands, yet it was one of gentler power than the twisted energy of the Pitch Dark. Winter-sagged, bearded trees surrounded them, and flocked bushes dusted them in a confetti of snow down a trail that seemed to open up before them. All was welcoming here, and many curious animals, their stares gleaming with coyness, looked at the travelers and chattered. Rabbits hopped across the path of Mother-wolf and were only slightly afraid for their lives. Some even braved sniffs at her great paws before dashing off. The same serenity brought tiny birds as pretty as gray-coated children to land on the arms of the company and sing them little songs. Through the wood, the air swept like a spirit of summer. From under the snow, a perfume of life persisted—peat, earth, and freshness so thick with honey they could taste it going down in cold gulps. In here, the Sisters' magik held a reign outside of time and proper seasons. Therefore, although it snowed, it never blustered, and nature seemed of only one kindly temperament. In many places, they found berry bushes the animals that refused to hibernate had nibbled on. Talwyn hastily vouched for the safety of the plants before sloppily devouring their fruits.

Given the calm pace of their amble, when Mother-wolf stopped walking somewhere in the drifting winter playground, it seemed sudden. Before them was a circular swath in the forest piled in white stones. *More ruins*, thought Morigan, and she could see the pale echoes of people from a past age drifting hither and thither. Under the frost there would be plenty of runic script for Talwyn to unearth, should the proclivity strike him. For they'd arrived at another settlement or site of worship for the folk who communed with the Green Mother and the moon. They were her people, Morigan supposed, seeing as two had been partners in her birth. She wondered who these mysterious nomads were and how they tied into Sisters, blood rites, and Immortals. She waited for the bees to sting her with truth, but the blasted things stayed silent and tame. Caenith unexpectedly came up with an answer. While the others had been tiptoeing about the ruins, he'd asked his mother of this place and its meaning.

*Mother calls them the quiet walkers*, he whispered to Morigan. *For they moved so slowly and calmly through the woods, it was as if they were hardly passing. She heard their chants sometimes. They called to powers as old as land and rock, and she never hunted them because of their respect for the ancient order. She says these places are sanctuaries. The Green Mother herself blessed them. We can rest here. She can smell our weariness.* Mother-wolf barked assertively, and Caenith chuckled. *She insists we regain our strength before seeing the Sisters.*

*I think she is wise,* concurred Morigan.

How her body groaned at the promise of a blazing fire and more than an hourglass of sleep! Was that a stream trapped under the glass of ice over yonder? She should ask her companions whether they wanted to rest, even though her mind was already made up.

"Shall we rest?" she asked.

Rather than reply, the company broke apart to snap off kindling from branches and dig out a fire pit. Morigan sensed the Wolf stepping away and felt the heat and scent of his mother leave them as well. Mother-wolf had brought them to a sanctuary, and she would not disturb them to say good-bye.

## VI

With his huge arms, Caenith encircled his mother about her shaggy neck and held her for some time. The mortal quality of the gesture amused and saddened her. She hadn't been held like that since Brutus. She spoke while he embraced her.

*Your father left to build a home for you that would tolerate your strangeness. Now I see it is we who are strange. We are the shadows of the past that do not know how to change. I have worried for how the world would reject you, and yet you have cast away the customs that do not suit you and honor the ones that do. We old ones are best left hiding in the dimness of myth and time. We would never find in the realms of man the pack or pride that you have.*

*Do not say so, Mother,* replied Caenith. *I shall find a place for you, as you wanted to for me. I can be the architect and guide of Geadhain's future. Morigan has shown me that the Sisters are not the only ones to wield Fate. The brave can too.*

*And you are brave, my son.*

*I shall make the world see you as I do.*

*Very well.*

Mother-wolf nudged herself out of his arms. They met stare to stare and said everything with their pained looks and last huffs of the other's scent. She smelled of the oldest trees under her coat, and he of iron, fur, sweat, and pine. When they dreamed or saw the woods thereafter, they would think of one another with a bit of torment from their mortal sides and a pang of restlessness from their animal leanings. However, never again would they not know or lose the memory of their kin. In a parting soul-whisper, Mother-wolf made her son swear something. It was the kind of dark promise to which silence was an assent. She tossed the thought to him as she slunk into the white forest. She did not wait or want to hear his reply. He could only imagine the wrenching misery it brought to his mother even to suggest it.

*When you find your father, even if he is still a wounded beast who cannot be cleansed of his illness, you must forgive him for succumbing to evil. If you must end him, tell him he was loved. I shall dream of you both.*

## VII

Whether Caenith, the great provider, was around for his duties or not, the companions were quite productive on their own. They welcomed the Wolf home with a sputtering fire. Some of the lazy hares that had survived Mother-wolf's passage had since lost their luck and lives to the hungry company, and Morigan was busy casting offal into the snow. Thackery whittled at sticks on which to roast the meat. Adam wore the blood of his crimes on his chin and chest and would have left it there for who knew how long if Mouse, in a scant instant of fondness, hadn't scooped up some snow with which to clean him. Expectedly, the scholar they'd been unable to shake or scare away with their doomed lives had engrossed himself in reading the script revealed during the excavation of their campfire. *A moment of peace at last*? wondered the Wolf. *Or the proverbial calm before the storm*?

*Come sit, my Wolf. Enjoy this pleasure,* suggested Morigan without glancing upon him. *What I would do for a comb or even a brush and some baker's soda to wash my teeth,* she mused to herself. Despite their rigorous, unkempt travel, though, she hadn't noticed any bad breath on herself, and she wondered whether immortals, of which she was apparently one, even worried about hygiene beyond the more noticeable stains. Perhaps their bodies were immune to illness and rot altogether. Caenith certainly didn't clean himself much for a man who smelled so pleasant. His teeth were white as porcelain tiles, and his breath tasted only of smoky liquor and passion whenever they kissed. How nice it was, Morigan realized, to ponder such stupid trivialities. She was thinking about his taste and kissing him and was dreamily lost to the flicking of her knife and the cutting of flesh when his warmth slipped around her.

*Did you say good-bye?* she asked him.

*Yes.* He sighed. *But not farewell. She says that my...father wanted to find a place for me. However, when I think of Brutus and all his sins we have witnessed, it is like believing the lion can be left to tend the lamb.*

*It's true, my Wolf,* replied Morigan. *You saw what I saw—how he loved her. They did not call it that, but a power that changes and tames what is dark in us can be no other force. Don't you see that he tried at least before the darkness took him? He wanted to build that home for his child, a place where conflicting things could live in harmony: man and machine, magik and science, nature and culture.*

*The Summerlands...Zioch.* The Wolf gasped loudly enough to startle the others before they realized they were not included in the conversation and went back to their own occupations.

*I have not seen them as they should be—only in echoes from you or the Kings,* said Morigan. *But that was the land of promise. Perhaps it was not quite the time for you to find your way there. Either the timing was off or the Black Queen stole him ere he could bring you to Zioch.*

*Now that dream is ash,* grumbled the Wolf.

*Ash makes for rich soil where trees can grow again. There is no stopping life—only missing the beauty of its constancy. No more tears. They are not becoming of you—unless you weep because you are happy, and then I suppose you may cry all you want. However, it still doesn't suit your handsome face.*

They smiled and carried on. The Wolf did not surrender his embrace. A bit later, he did have to leave her for but a moment, so he might pound a hole in the ice of the stream that twisted through the ruins. Thackery had been chipping at the spot with bumbling inefficiency prior to any assistance. Afterward, the Wolf returned to holding his bloodmate, drinking in her fragrance, and bestowing kisses and small bites. Mouse even discovered enough of her jaded humor to suggest they just go fuk already. Morigan felt the twitching rod of the Wolf's agreement against her back many times and grew hotter once the fire grew roaring. The Wolf could sail her from the stormy seas of lust to more calming waters, though, and once the eating and fellowship began, there were no lewd thoughts from him. Still, every caress and sultry rumble of his voice had a certain sensuality. That was his nature—predatory, prowling, and possessive. She didn't mind him hunting or claiming her. She had made the choice to be his all by herself.

That night, the company talked of many things—their aches, pains, and dreams of hot baths or any of the modern world's conveniences. They did not speak of Vortigern. However, there were pauses in the conviviality when eyes darkened and thoughts lingered. It was mostly light conversation until Talwyn's eyes and thoughts wandered over to the inscriptions rendered in the orange glow of the fire—inscriptions he'd been pried away from examining so he could eat. A bit haunted by his knowledge, he began to speak.

The writing in these ruins was extensive, more embellished in lore than the last, and richer with history. There were many allusions to grand religious pilgrimages here from everywhere across Geadhain. The pilgrims came to here from places where nature reigned the strongest—by oceans and rocks, in the peaks of mountains, or on tiny islands in the Scarasace Sea. These were mostly places of solitude and reflection.

"On the edge of the sea, there is a stone city with contemplative, kind souls," said the scholar. "In Sorsetta, the lands south of..." He nearly said "your father's kingdom" while glancing at the Wolf. "...the Summerlands," he finished. "The city of Gorgonath. It's not mentioned here specifically, but I know of those folk and their customs."

"Do you think they are kin to the white wanderers she described?" asked Thackery, and he pointed to Morigan, for she'd told them of the strange worshippers at the last site similar to this.

"Yes." Talwyn nodded. "The behaviors are too similar to dismiss a connection. Still, I'm rather at a loss to explain all this strangeness with myth, history, and the lady's visions."

"Lady?" Morigan laughed.

Talwyn was stone serious in his reply. "A lady for sure. A queen, even. How do you not see yourself in this light when even I can declare your royalty after knowing you for a sliver of time? I have not said this to any of you, but I am so very grateful I am here with myths, legends, and the terrors that must come with them. Anywhere but with my wretch of a brother. May the Kings rest his soul, but I do hope those red, horrific witches ate him balls first."

*A fine fellow for such a bookworm,* mind-whispered the Wolf, and they all snorted and chuckled at what was hopefully the late Augustus's expense. Talwyn was the first to stop laughing.

"You don't think they could have followed us this far, do you?" he asked.

The Wolf took a sniff. As far as he could tell, the winds were not soured by their enemies' scents. However, the Pitch Dark to the west efficiently suppressed the senses with its darkness. The Wolf doubted he would smell either Lord Blackmore or the Jabberwok. If the villains were witless enough to pursue them through Alabion's heart, though, the scholar was wise in judging them dead.

"I believe we are alone," said the Wolf.

With that, the companions sighed as one and were released from the terror they'd carried with them the breadth of the woods. There would be no more running or monsters—only three ancient and devious witches with whom to deal. Morigan could feel only the calm of destiny. It was as if there were no more pasts or dreams on which her bees could feast. All revelations lay ahead of them now. She would know of the white-robes who were her parents and the blackness that corrupted her bloodmate's father. She would hear the Sisters explain why they made men dance to their tune. There should be reasons for their manipulations—if such deviousness could even be justified. *You who play with hearts and souls and arrange us all as pieces upon a board. You three spiders in your great, reaching web. Tomorrow, the games end, the threads are snipped, and your tapestry is unwoven. Regardless of how and why I was made, you do not define life or purpose. I do. We do.*

Although she did not whisper the words to him, the Wolf sensed the ferocity of her threat. He nearly felt mercy for the three, knowing his mate was on the hunt.

## VIII

During her short, sweaty sleep, Mouse didn't dream of Adelaide, a scarecrow, a Gray Man, or a cave of bones. She dreamed not at all. The three trials were over. What now? She had tried reading the fire embers and listening to the wind for omens, but she was no seer. She possessed no powers except her mind and agility, and one day, time would consume those. Even Adam, whose body rose and fell in thudding warmth as he held her, had more means to defend himself and those he loved, whoever they might be. *Possibly me*, she realized, without wanting to commit any more of herself to the man. She threw off his grasp. He groaned but slept on. She stood and paced alongside the cooling ashes of the fire.

Love. She didn't need *that*. It had helped her father very little when the she-bitch tore him into pieces. She dearly wished Morigan's magik could have separated that woman from whatever energy she wielded. Better yet, she wished she could have destroyed the she-bitch herself. *How*? she wondered, and she stomped the earth. How could she have done what the seer could not? Power was only bested by greater might. What she needed was magik.

Until that instant, Mouse had not considered much of a plan for revenge. She and her companions sought the Sisters for wisdom, but why should it revolve entirely around Kings, doom, and prophecies? Meeting the three wisest women in Geadhain represented a singular opportunity. She could speak her heartfelt rage in the presence of the wise, and from what she'd learned of the Sisters, they never turned away a seeker. *Careful*, she warned herself. The Sisters Three, according to legend, oft gave gifts that left the recipient puzzled and unfulfilled. Mouse negotiated a bargain better than most, though. In many ways, the strongest weapon she owned was her tongue. Whatever the proceedings, she would leave with one thing. She wouldn't even have to steal it. Mouse returned to bed and rolled away from Adam's arm as he tried to welcome her back.

## IX

"Youngling! My darling! My sweet!" shouted Elemech.

Less than a day earlier had Eean learned how to walk. Inherently, she always remembered how to move her chubby legs, having done so a thousand times before. Now she scurried around as fast as a honey-coated badger in a bee's nest as she dodged the hands of her older sister. Exhausted yet determined, Elemech chased the tiny terror. She avoided the pitfalls of shattered clayware and tossed belongings left in Eean's wake. Their youngest sister's giggles and gleeful goading of this bad behavior made for a second thorn in Elemech's side. Elemech, though, possessed longer legs than the youngling did, and she soon cornered the naked child over by their shelf of odd wares—dried eyeballs, bat wings, paints, vials of putrid and glowing substances, and other ingredients for magik.

"Eean, stop now!" scolded Elemech. "And watch that shelf. You know better. Only your body has regressed—not your mind. Any more running, and you'll do harm you should not."

"It's not often I have someone to play with," said Ealasyd, who stopped her merrymaking and brought a ratty jumper for Eean to put on.

"Often enough," said Elemech. "Put some clothes on her, please. We should have visitors soon. We would not want them to think us savage."

"I can't help myself," muttered Eean. Her first words came out in a bullfrog's croak.

"She speaks!" the sisters cried.

"Yes, I do," replied Eean.

The three held each other fast and hard.

"I swear there are crickets in my legs, though," complained Eean from over her sister's shoulder. "I think they wish to run again. Being a child has as many urges as being a man surely does."

Elemech nearly wept with joy. "How good it is to have your counsel again, Sister. We've been through so much on our own."

"Come then," said Eean.

Taking each sister's hand, Eean led them to the benches at their stone table. When they were seated and she felt her legs wouldn't bolt on her again, she asked her sister to continue.

"They'll be here in a day or less," said Elemech. "I lost track of the one fellow with them—the brother of the beast from Blackforge. She has taken him into her spell now. He will not be seen anymore. After her long, long sleep, the Ancient has moved as well, so we can assume the Wolf now knows of his father."

Eean made little fists and tried to rest her chin upon them to evoke thoughtfulness. It was an awkward position, and it had her head slipping.

She gave up and set her hands beside her. *Poor Ealasyd, to be a dainty thing like this all the time.* She threw away her eccentric musings. *Focus.*

"Has Morigan learned everything?" asked Eean.

"More than we might have told her," said Elemech.

In the silence that followed, Ealasyd felt almost immediately bored. She went off to play with her crafts, and she sorted through the trail of mess left by her sister. She kept an ear open for any mention of Morigan that didn't involve the dreadful events over which Elemech and Eean so obsessed. Elemech grew whiter and whiter as the worries ate her from within.

"She was supposed to mend the wounds of Geadhain," whispered Elemech. "I think she will only hurt our mother more."

Eean sighed. "Sometimes a wound must be burned to be healed. We started this thread when the Kings failed to bring harmony. We meddled too forcefully with the loom, and in the end stalled nothing and brought sickness to Alabion. Brutus should have been our hope, but the Darkness found him. Perhaps it claimed him for this reason. Regardless, he is lost. If we try to change destiny with another act as great as Morigan's conception, we'll destroy the loom for certain. She is our last and only hope. We cannot abandon her now."

A tremble of anxiety ran through Elemech, but the older woman tried to hide it. Eean patted her cold, shaking hand. "She doesn't know everything. There is more for her to learn yet, for the journey will be what shapes her into a weapon against Zionae. The most difficult of secrets, however, she should hear from you. Ealasyd and I cannot share the mystery you hold. We cannot tell her what she and all living things yearn to know."

"I should not even care. Why is it I do?" exclaimed Elemech.

"Because she is not a tool," Eean said. "Dearest sister, in our remoteness from the world and with our gifts to see and know all, we are blind to the common laws of emotion. That does not mean we are above them. I eat the years of you two and have done so for so long that we, more often than otherwise, forget we are beings of nature—animals along with the rest. We are no safer from feelings than the woman who weeps for the unborn child that has bled from between her legs in the night. Your child has not been lost, though. She is not dead. Quite the contrary. And she is coming home.

Find in your heart some gladness for that, and it will make the breaking of secrets all the better."

Eean kissed her sister's knuckles and then pinched the woman on the cheek for some color. She needed to reach quite a ways, and the pinch left only a gray dimple. Since Elemech would not be stirred from her gloom and Eean's legs squealed their desire to bring havoc once more, the eldest sister left to do another lap around the caverns. Dark and sulking, Elemech sat in the shadows and thought of what she would tell her daughter.

# XIV

# A GAMBLE

I

In the Iron Crown, the chamber of rule atop the Crucible and a realm of false stars, vaulted glass ceilings, and vistas of black space, a heated meeting took place. Although technomagikal vents purified the air to an ammonia-tinged sterility untasted in the streets below, the room congealed from raised voices, sweat, and tension. Present were the nine masters not spearheading secret operations at Fort Havok. All gathered for a meeting of the Council of the Wise.

*Horgot is exceptionally repulsive today*, thought Elissandra. A sheen of grease bled into the silk of the man's collar, and that told her of the filth that oiled the crevasses in his bulk she could not so openly see. His fury brought quite a bit of spittle, and he had that thin white line of foam that gathered about one's lips when he or she simply wouldn't stop talking. He hadn't stopped for an hourglass now. A glance to her chronex confirmed the endlessness of his tirade.

"Enough!" she snapped. It was an unusual outburst, considering her languid temperament. "No. You may not see the Sixth Chair's scroll. No. I do not have any further information on the Iron Queen's movements. No. I do not know what has happened to all your ears in the Kingdom of Eod.

Even a stupid man, though, could guess they've been plugged. War is here, fool—happening even as we waste the afternoon listening to your boorish rambling. What is it you fear—an end to your miserable power? If you only knew the stakes, you would see how pitiful any claim to true rulership is. The Black Star is not far off, and the Kings have fallen or soon will. Maybe one. Maybe both. Dynasties are ready to disappear into the dust."

"Dynasties?" muttered Septimus, the young and pallid nekromancer on the council. Elissandra's words had charmed him with their air of doom. "Have you seen something? What will this war cost me...I mean us? Menos?"

"You mean *me*," retorted Elissandra.

She exercised little patience for this nonsense. Fiery nightmares ever tormented her sleep of late. They were dreams of destruction many scales worse than the storm of fire and ice—screaming waterfalls of the dying, explosions of earth, and a grinding that grated her ears even as she woke. It was as if the land digested all the ruin. She possessed a stomach for violence, but this was horrible to witness.

"War always has a price," she continued. "Usually, the victor pays the lesser dues. I should hope that would be Menos. I should hope you have faith in what we have begun. Together, I might add. A vote was cast. Let us not forget. All present were in favor. Do not lose your spines now—not when they must be rods of iron."

*Uppity bitch! I'll give you a rod. Right up your arse*, sneered Horgot to himself.

Elissandra threw him a glance of knives. "I heard that. Did you think I, of all people in this room, would not?"

Horgot reared back as if he had been insulted and tried to stuff some dignity back into the jiggling casing of his flesh. Watching him struggle for dignity was even more disgusting than seeing him huff and puff. After a century of playing the politics of men, and with dark changes and darker queens coming to season, Elissandra was not sure she could stand another of these trivial ceremonies in which people pretended to matter. If they had her insights about what the future only days or weeks from now would bring them, they might show some humility for once in their vainglorious lives. *All of you should die*, Elissandra thought, and she passed her stare around like a snake deciding where to strike next. *None spared. I long for* olden days of forests, songs, and moonlight. I did not see how much I hated the cage I have made for myself here until the Daughter of Fate showed me hope for something better. She will be the sword to cut the night, and you, black masters, should fall with black queens. Such is only just. Death. I wish every one of you dead. At least your flesh will finally find some use in feeding the gardens of tomorrow. For in a new world—my children's world—you are but rot and waste.

Elissandra's pondering of the Iron sages' ends provoked something within. Like a sultry lover, the powers of Fate invited Elissandra into the sheets of gray ether that welled in the world beyond and swept her mind away to show her the destinies of those in the Iron Crown. While the Iron sages might have seen a silver halo about the woman for a speck or felt unearthly prickles across their skin, they dismissed the abnormalities as Elissandra simply being herself. She would return in a moment, and until she did, they had other arguments to settle.

Elissandra remains in the room. However, a fog of charcoal flecked with silver has crept around the chairs and their seated figures. Nearest to her is Horgot, and she wavers between horror and glee at the state of him. He is as skinny as he has ever been. Half his body—one side's skull, shoulder, hip, and leg—is crushed paper-thin. The untouched side of him looks black with dust and bulbously puffed like a balloon not yet inflated. She is certain he is dead. Whatever weight has done this to him must have been no less than a building. Since she is a dweller in two states, the real and the not yet real, the swollen part of him still natters on about one grievance or another.

Once more, she hears the rumbling from her nightmares—a rainfall of stones and a percussionist's madness of tin sounds, screams, and eruptions. The land constricts and devours life. What is this? Another storm of magik? No. She can smell the chalk and iron dust blowing off the other disfigured, pulverized Iron sages. They are gabbing in their seats without any grasp of their doom. What balls up men like sheets of black paper? What topples buildings fortified with iron bones? Lo, is that dreadful crack and echoing groan the sound of the Iron Wall rent and falling? Only the Green Mother herself can summon such ruination. Only when the land howls from within and men wail downward into the black gullet of her grief—

"Kings be damned," Elissandra gasped.

"Oh. You've come back to us." Horgot snorted. "You can go away again if you like. You were not missed. In fact, I have arranged a repose for you. Gloriatrix too while she is off playing generalissima to our war."

He snapped, and the four riflemen flanking Elissandra's chair—the loyal ironguards of Gloria's personal detachment—spread out to points around the circle of Iron sages. The ironguards' rifles were cocked and loaded.

"How dare you! Never has blood been spilled in these halls! That is against all the time-honored rules and order of Menos!" shouted Jerrulus, the Tenth Chair.

Jerrulus enjoyed a simple life, for a master. He was proprietor of Menos's most profitable atelier and a man who never engaged directly in conflict. He preferred to sell poisons rather than use them. A sensible fellow, he abided neither Gloriatrix's intimidations nor Horgot's frequent spitting retorts. For the most part, he just sleepily watched his fellows argue as if he were a great wise turtle. Elissandra didn't mind the man, but she had not seen him in her vision of Menos's ruin a speck ago. Therefore, she wasn't surprised when the riflemen opened fire on him, and he danced in his seat to a red and spinning end. The gunfire knocked Jerrulus and his chair over into a smoldering heap. When enough smoke from his murder had cleared—but not the greasy, pan-fried stench of his death—Horgot addressed the remaining Iron sages. "Honor and rules. Humph." Horgot's chins trembled as he and the others chuckled. "All this talk of new orders between you and the Iron cunt, and neither of you ladies could see that such a shift was occurring under your upturned noses. A new order has been made—with fewer seats on the council than were previously required. Menos has suffered the manipulations, menstruations, and whims of ruling women for too long. It is time to return to the old ways of fist, sword, and prick."

Throughout, Elissandra remained silent and at ease. Her power would tell of her impending death as clearly as does the insight that visits the terminally ill in their last moments, informing them it is time. Thus, she felt no fear. She wasn't even bothered, except by Jerrulus's ghastly stink. The wretch must have shite himself when he died. The other Iron sages glared at her steadily. From their smugness, she knew they were all complicit in Horgot's coup. *You're all doomed. Have your pissing contest if you will. Soon enough, we'll be past the hourglass to declare a victor.*

"You might ask yourself why you are still living." Horgot smiled.

*I do not*, thought Elissandra. *I am living because you are not the one to end me. I have seen how you die, though, and I regret it will be so merciful and without great suffering. I do hope you soil yourself in terror like poor Jerrulus before Menos, the city you desire to rule so much, crushes you and your dreams.*

Horgot tapped his foot while waiting for an answer. She did not give it. "I see. Silence then. I did not think you to be so brave. No matter. Even if I underestimated you, we can hear all the details of Gloriatrix's plot from the Iron marshals. I know Moreth is involved, but we have not yet decided upon his punishment. First, we should hear how faithfully he has aligned himself with Gloriatrix. Did you think years of theft and deception could persist unnoticed in a society as mercenary as ours? Where every coin is caressed and counted and each master visits the fleshcrafter for a second set of eyes to watch the shadows at his back? I'll admit, she covered her tracks and fudged the ledgers quite expertly. Like these ironguards, though, there is no secret vault that money or persistence cannot breach. Not in Menos. Elissandra, you would spare us all a good deal of blood and bother if you would tell me now all you know."

"How generous an offer," replied Elissandra.

"But it is," said Horgot. "And you haven't heard the best of it, either. Cede your loyalty to Gloriatrix, and die a more noble death...well, a quicker one." He sought an item from one of the pouches at his belt. It was a farce to watch his fat hands fumble. Eventually, he found the small pearl of a far-speaking stone and held it up. "One peep to this, and I tell my ironguards, who should certainly have arrived at your estate by now, not to hollow your children with bullets."

"My children?" hissed Elissandra.

"Finally, some rage to you, Elissandra," jeered Horgot. "I thought you were all frost. I see the nerve has at last been struck. It's given you a nice color and made you prettier than you often are. Now for your decision. One death or three? Your answer will decide the outcome. Take a moment, and if you are wise, the next words out of your mouth will be a confession—the location of the Sixth Chair's scroll, the extent of Gloriatrix's ambitions beyond this war, and how many resources she has at her disposal. All are good places to begin. We'll let her finish wiping out Eod, or whatever she's designed, before I have one of my people hidden in Fort Havok scatter her brains on the deck of her warship. Yes. We know of that too. No doubt you thought me simply petty and irritating this morning. Really I was your greatest advocate in the trial of the Iron cunt—a trial in which you have now been declared guilty by association and conspiracy to commit...well, conspiracy. You had your chance to save yourself, and you chose to defend her until the end." Horgot noticed Elissandra clinging to the armrests of her chair. She was ready to leap. "I wouldn't try any magik either, or we'll skip the interrogation and go right to the execution."

Elissandra appeared frozen—almost as still as a woman drawn in watercolors. The Iron sages all observed that her form seemed to shiver. No doubt these were symptoms of the hysteria and grief that often consumed women.

"Speak, Elissandra," commanded Horgot. He was growing annoyed at her willfulness. "Speak, or I shall assume you have nothing to say and no desire to save your children."

Horgot brandished the far-speaking stone at the woman like a talisman that would compel her tongue to move. It worked, she spoke, and he grinned. However, it took a speck for him to realize that Elissandra's voice came from behind him and not from the woman at whom they all stared.

"You are all doomed," she said.

At all times, Elissandra carried a blade with her. It was small and hilted in onyx and fine silver. The lady's dagger was a tool without which no Menosian woman should walk the streets—or even the hallways of her own home. She declared her independence from Menos by jabbing the weapon into Septimus's throat and ripping him a necktie so deep the blade scraped the bone of his spine. There would be no fleshcrafting that, and he died even as the blood began to pour in earnest. *What fools*, she thought. *Declaring their treason so boldly!*

The Gray Man's children were serpent charmers of the soul, weavers of illusion, and benders of reality. Moments past, she'd left her shadow in her seat as lightly as a fart into the cushions and simply stepped out of the phantasm without anyone being the wiser. She'd then skipped around the seats to Horgot and his grinning minion, Septimus. From the speck Septimus had sat down that morning out of numerical order and next to his new master, she'd known the nekromancer to be nothing but fuel to the hog's aspirations of authority. Septimus's treachery alone was worthy of a knife. Nevertheless, the nekromancer was also the only person in the room who could challenge her with sorcery, which is why she chose the dagger for him first instead of Horgot. However, she'd wedged the weapon too deeply in his throat to extract it easily, and she had to think quickly.

Suddenly, the Iron sages were scrambling. Illusion no more held them. People turned, and the ones with rifles would soon shoot her dead without waiting for Horgot's order. A surge of motherly strength filled Elissandra. No one would touch Tessa or Eli. How dare the sages even tempt death by mentioning her children? Rampaging like a mother bear, she pushed over the heavy seat of Septimus—he who mindlessly gurgled and flailed as if to catch his life. She reached for Horgot's hand—the one that clasped the far-speaking stone. Horgot felt Elissandra coming and squealed. She wasn't coming to end him, though—only to grab the stone. He laughed a small triumph as she ripped his arm toward her. His fist and gargantuan tonnage held against her terrifying strength. Now the ironguards had spotted her in the scuffle. Bullets would be tearing her the instant any one of them could take a tidy shot. She must have seemed rather helpless wrestling a ponderous, immobile man with nowhere to go even if she won.

"Your choice," she said. "I'll take the hand with me."

Elissandra smiled a farewell and dropped. Horgot saw her claw downward with the hand not clutching his and tear at something that made a sure and audible rip.

Bang! Bang! Bang!

Bullets pierced the back of Horgot's tall chair, where Elissandra's head should have been. Contrary to what the Third Chair understood of physics, Elissandra continued to fall into the floor. She went down a fissure of cosmic lights that she'd opened like a zipper with her desperate swipe. She began to pull him forward. Horgot screamed. Then the void abruptly sealed itself, and the witch vanished. Horgot's face struck the solid stone of the chamber. He tried to stumble up, and it took only a speck of red blotting and slipping on the stones for him to notice the stub at the end of his forearm. At his wrist, the amputation was so clean it could have been done with one cleave of a butcher's knife. It had only just begun to bleed. After a moment of staring at his stump, he felt a fiery, startling surge of pain. It was so crippling that shock could not stop his spasms or clench his bladder with the tightness needed not to piss himself. Slopping around in urine and blood, the Third Chair mewled, ranted, and wept. "My hand! My fuking hand! That...that cunt! That fuking cunt! How did she? What were you shitesacks doing? Shoot her...why didn't you shoot her? Wah! My fuking hand! Kings be cursed, it hurts! Mm...mm...it fuking hurts! Stop staring at me, you damned mules! Call a fleshcrafter! Call the Iron marshals! I want my fuking hand back and that bitch's head upon a pike! Her children too! Carve them up in front of her! I'll mount the pale little shites on my wall! Go! Go! Go for fuk's sake!"

Quite a crimson exit the Mistress of Mysteries had made. The ironguards and sages needed many moments to react to the brutality—the toppled chairs, smoking and pooled corpses, and warm, dense fog of violence in the room. One woman had done most of this. Who knew what the Iron Queen herself would do if Horgot's assassins failed? What a glorious failure this was turning out to be after all the months of planning and all the seditious whispering preceding the moment meant to be her end. Elissandra's warning also gave the Iron sages a cold fire to huddle around, considering she would know their fates. "You are all doomed," she had said.

Perhaps they were. Septimus had surely chosen the wrong alliance. Currently, their new leader was without a vital piece of his anatomy and without an iota of the retribution they'd all sworn themselves to achieve. Perhaps the Iron Queen wasn't the menace they wanted to believe and was instead a stern mother to miscreant children. When left to their own devices, all that these men had brought down upon themselves was ruin—or, as Elissandra had foretold, doom.

II

The ironguards locked the three conspirators from Eod together in a dark and empty cell with no windows, no lights, and only a metal door. If the prisoners spoke even in whispers, the whole place echoed and cast their magnified fear back at them. Prior to their lockup, the Menosians had stripped them naked, inspected them like country fair cattle, and then gave them woolen shifts and slippers to wear. After their debasement, Rowena attempted to empower her companions with a speech on bravery, honor, and the value of integrity. The sound of a metal door screeching open cut her encouragement short. Several ironguards and a thin man in ebon finery entered. The latter carried a leather physician's bag, and he wore black goggles and rubber gloves. Although he was dressed like a physician, they knew he had not come to treat their maladies but to inflict them. They were in the company of an Iron marshal.

"I'd like to see you try to break me, Menosian dog," barked Rowena.

She spit on the floor and hit the glossy boots of the Iron marshal. The man nodded to one of the ironguards, who produced a handkerchief, knelt, and wiped his boot clean.

"I know what you're trying to do, sword—goad me into interrogating you first. How daring and kind. However, spitting on an Iron marshal or attempting such a juvenile psychological feint shows you are either fearless or not developed enough mentally to appreciate what I can do to you. Either way, you are right. You do seem too hard to break—as tough as a stone, really." The Iron marshal pointed to Maggie. She was huddled in the corner in Alastair's arms. "She should snap like a willow stem in the winter. Take her."

"No!" roared Alastair.

No flare of bravery would save Maggie—not from the rush of ironguards who flew forward, mercilessly bashed rib cages, and pressed hot iron barrels to the heads of those who resisted. Unlike her companions, Maggie did not defend herself. Her protectors watched her raise her hands and walk toward the Iron marshal.

"Please. I shall go," she said. "There is no need to hurt them."

The Iron marshal tilted his head to examine this curiously courageous subject. "Well, well. The quail has a bit of bite to her. I shall enjoy our time together. Miss Halm, I believe?" She did not reply. "Names are not a convention that belong where we are headed." The marshal smiled. His teeth were yellow and looked as if they belonged to a corpse. "We know only the songs of the knife, needle, and iron thread and the secrets I shall stitch and slit from you. Come along now. We shall only be in the next cell over. These rooms have wonderful acoustics, and I want your companions to hear the music we make together."

Alastair mumbled a threat, and a blunt strike to his mouth reprimanded him. Praise to Charazance his teeth stayed put, but his lips swelled at once. Maggie could stand no more. She shook her head and motioned for the Iron marshal to take her. Once Maggie had left with the torturer's entourage, Rowena hobbled over to Alastair, who would not rise out of misery or injury.

"That was so foolish of me," confessed Rowena. She was near to tears, and she held Alastair—an uncommon gesture for a woman such as her. "I could have bought us time. I only wanted to—"

"No," muttered Alastair. "Don't blame yourself."

He looked up. His eyes were watering, and he was plainly tormented. He could not bear to utter his truth aloud, though, and he pulled away from Rowena and cowered against the cold metal cell wall. *Charazance, why do you forsake me? Why have you fallen silent? I need a miracle. I need the oath you swore to me. I should not be here. Maggie should not be here.* An unfamiliar ripping at his heart occurred when he thought of the innkeeper's fate. *I have served you faithfully for many lifetimes. I have never pleaded with you as I am now. Please do not abandon me.*

In his chest, there came a flutter—static that indicated the slightest shift of his sleeping mistress. Charazance was listening but not offering aid. When Maggie's screams pierced the walls and rang in the metal box that held the two prisoners, Alastair—his guts dropping—knew this was exactly what Charazance wanted and where he was supposed to be.

III

After he'd been separated from the others, Galivad was hooded again and rudely pushed along for a while. As hopeless as his chances were, he plotted and readied himself for a moment to strike against the sweetly perfumed shadow of Beatrice, whom he could feel gliding behind him. However, as far as he took his imaginings into red scenes and screaming ends, his heart twisted at the thought of harming the woman. She even whistled once—an out-of-place and bright little tweet that could have come from a bird or a beauty who sang to winged ones from her window. *What have you done to her? How have you stripped her song, grace, and smell? What else have you taken from my mother? Is she even dead or just trapped inside you? I shall have my answers, you witch.*

Soon the echoing of metal tunnels dampened, and he entered a more welcoming chamber. Galivad could hear a fire crackling and smell the lemony polish of wooden furniture. These rich scents filled the chamber of a master. He was unhooded and found himself in a paneled sitting room with a grand hearth, high chairs, and long, tufted couches—exactly the luxury he'd anticipated. The hospitality of his torturer, however, continued to surprise him.

"Do leave us," said Beatrice to the ironguards in attendance.

The pair looked back and forth between themselves.

"My pardon, my lady," said one, and he made overtures with his hands. "I don't think the Lord Moreth—"

"You don't *think*," hissed Beatrice. "You do as you are told. My husband shall be here once he has finished meeting with the Iron Queen. I can fend for myself until then against one unarmed and bound prisoner. Stay, and I shall have a second interrogation afterward with two able-bodied young men and my favorite knives."

The ironguards babbled apologies and quickly left. Galivad waited for Beatrice to fetch her packet of knives, pliers, and needles, but she simply stood there. She faced the door and not him, which drove his anger into a rage.

"Get on with it! I know who you are and what you do to people. We're not here for a fuking chat," he said.

Beatrice waited a time before she replied. "Yes. I think you do know who I am," she said, and Galivad thought she sounded rather sad. "I know who you are as well...or were, before your position and status in Eod. I know your face as the one who came at my throat with scissors. Before that appointment, I knew you as a boy from Heathsholme. Frankly, we are here for a chat. I do not expect we have much time until my husband joins us. We should make the most of our sands."

Beatrice's compassion and candor slapped Galivad's face hard, and he fainted somewhat into the nearest couch. Beatrice came to his rescue and settled his back with cushions. With her so near, he might have tried to strangle her with his chains. He could not, however, since every sweep of her hands and each beatific smile looked exactly like Belle's. He had to know.

"Are you...is she in there? Inside of you?"

"Things are never so simple," she whispered, and looked down at her hands. "Life is never so kind."

Galivad waited, and he felt every beat of tension. At last, Beatrice looked up at him again with her large stare and a trembling pout so similar to his mother's that a lump wedged in his throat.

"I remember a cottage," she whispered. "Full of sunshine. It was as bright as a house of gold."

What she spoke of, Galivad recalled as well.

*As golden as the day is, his mother has more shine to her still. She stands in the dawn humming or lazily singing. She whirls about their modest stone kitchen like one of the magik beings of music and light that their night-time stories tell him live in the woods of Alabion. Most boys have a certain infatuation with their mothers. His, though, is a bond of unbreakable iron. For she must travel far and wide to work in order to pay for his tutors and this respectable, private stretch of land that a husbandless woman should not be of means enough to afford. So when he sees her, which isn't often, the memories he nurtures in her absence have enlarged her to such grandeur that her arrival is a festival, a circus, and a miracle in one. She makes their week—or month, if he is lucky—all the more amazing by performing and wooing him with talents. Schooling is suspended for her homecoming, for it is a great and lasting holiday. Every morning, he awakens to a song and a feast. Each afternoon, they take hikes over the rolling dales of their land. She brings her lute and strums for him the tales of the cities and realms she has seen outside the cozy green borders of Heathsholme. On some days, they might find a pool to swim in or a meadow in which to spend the hour-glasses counting butterflies.*

*Rarely do they play with toys, as she insists the world is the greatest tool of pleasure and leisure any man or woman needs. Still, he has a few wooden soldiers jumbled in his trunk, but they never see his hands while Belle is with him. Also within the chest are practice swords. These he and Belle use for theater shows in which they pretend to be warriors. "Not games," his mother tells him while offering subtle, actual instruction on swordplay—positioning, stance, and how to hold and swing a blade. "Theater is practice for life," she says.*

In the evenings, there are more songs and tales. She even teaches his small fingers how to pluck strings and, after puberty has done the worst of its business, how to steady his voice and conjure music from his throat.

"I love you, my little bard," she tells him.

As the days flee, his talent grows, his fingers are trained to agility, and his voice blossoms into a handsome sound.

"I love you too, Belle," he replies.

They share names as adults would. For he is not only her child—not when they are so close. They are best friends and confidants eternal. They are a pair of songbirds. One day, they will fly the world together—when he is older, wiser, and prepared for trials and vices. Until then, he waits, practices, and tries to be a deserving partner to her.

The summer is so splendid in Heathsholme that travelers journey and camp there just to see the fields of flowers. When it comes and goes without Belle's visit, he certainly does worry but not enough to bring him more than a few nights of tossing and turning. Then she misses the autumn storm of golden leaves in the orchards of Heathsholme. She was always sure to return for that, so that she might bake for him a cinnamon and apple treat. He has more sleepless nights than restful ones now. In the winter, the festival of Vallistheim comes and goes in a blaze of campfires and song. Belle does not return to celebrate with him. He watches the campfires and sings by himself. Soon after, his tutors stop coming. They apologize in letters and blame travel conditions, which were never unbearable in Heathsholme. A few are honest and tell him simply that they are not being paid. His mother is months behind on their wages. Similar letters, these officially stamped by the Council of East Arbor, arrive too. They instruct the owner of the house that they are owed taxes, which are beginning to accrue great sums of interest. To understand what this means, he goes through his books on fiefdoms and fealties to read all sorts of boring things that only shrivel his mood.

She will return. I know she will. He prays. He pleads.

Sometimes, he bundles up against the winter and stands at the end of their property's long road. He waits to see a shadow that will come his way while whistling to the stars. That shadow never arrives. In time, the firewood dwindles, and the coins Belle has left him for food run out. He takes his lute and his only real skill and goes to Heathsholme to earn a spot by a hearth. He hopes a *bit of broth and a day by the flames will take away the emptiness. It isn't the life he wants, but it is at least life. Belle would be disappointed to see him not standing on his own.*

*She will return. She will be proud of me. She will see I am ready.*

*One day, the mail carrier finds him at the tavern where he works. The man is sheepish and has his cap off and held to his chest as he presents Galivad with a letter bearing East Arbor's seal. It's in wax this time, as though very vital information is contained within. The mail carrier does not stay to watch him read the missive. He bows, apologizes, and wishes him the best. Young Galivad knows what the letter will reveal before it is opened. He felt the severing in his heart more than a season ago. Perhaps it had been in the spring after a dream of reaching for his mother while she fell down a dark, endless well. He is brave as he opens it and even stronger as he reads the rather brief, apologetic text that describes the unclaimed body of woman who died in Menos. The woman had taken months to identify because of the unusual state of her body—dried as a herb, surgically emptied of every known organ, and drained of all blood. The evisceration and exsanguination are explained more vividly than a sympathetic writer should have done and had obviously been the cause of much back and forth between the Menosians and the magisterial council of East Arbor.*

*Who cares? he thinks. Here it is. The cold truth. She is dead. Murdered.*

*He crumples up the letter and pitches it into the flames. At least he has a reason now to stop waiting for her and to see the world as they would have together. First, though, he will find the ones who have taken his truest friend from him and bring them pain.*

As he remembered, he could hear Beatrice's recollections snaking their way through his. She was speaking warmly about the pinch of cinnamon and salt she would add to her son's favorite pie—the pie Belle made—when Galivad interrupted her. "No more," he spit. "Stop it. Stop talking as if you were she. It's despicable."

"I suppose it is," muttered Beatrice. "Much of what I am is despicable, by the standards that people claim to be virtuous."

"What are you?"

With a shudder and a twist to her face, the traces of Belle left the Lady El. What stared at Galivad was icy and sharp like a snarling wolf made of frost. He noticed it only for a speck, and then the lady threw on a smoother facade. "They do not have a name for me in the West," she said. "Only stories of creatures that hunt at night for blood and fear the sun. None of that is wholly true. If my kind stays in darkness, it is not because we fear the sun's burn but because we loathe ourselves too much to be revealed in the day. I was like that once—a feral, hungry beast. I was everything untamed that my kind can become. Moreth tamed me. He found a better way for me to feed. My kind do not need the redness in your veins to sustain us—although that is the simplest way to quench the hollow pain with which we live in each moment of our long, long lives. It is a snack without the substance of a proper dinner." She licked her lips, winced, and placed a white hand upon her belly. Galivad saw her cravings and agony in that moment. "The greatest feasts, however, are ones of passion and inspiration—songs and sermons that rouse and rile hundreds. Or the thrill of two men carving each other up for glory before a crowd. Full-blooded feeling is what I need and what courses in those red, glorious rivers you fleshlings have."

Wistfully, she remembered biting Moreth once or twice while they made love, and she quivered at the memory of the taste. Such heat his blood brought in her loins, mouth, heart, and soul. It tasted of his bliss and devotion. When she came back to the present, Galivad had retreated down the cushions from her.

"I do not eat as I once did," she said with a shake of her head.

"But you...ate her? My mother?" accused Galivad.

"I did."

Stunningly, she made her admission plainly and without guilt. Galivad then realized fully with whom he was trapped. She was an animal, and he was a helpless meal should she need one.

"I could not control myself," said Beatrice.

She crawled down the couch toward him, leaned over his body sultrily, and sniffed at his chest, hair, and neck. All he could smell was her sweet and deadly fragrance. Galivad tried to wriggle away, yet she possessed another set of shackles—ones of ice. She used her freezing hands to restrain him. For a slight woman, she gripped with the strength of a drunken strongman. The beat of Galivad's heart had summoned Beatrice to him. Thud-thud, thud-thud, thud-thud. She could not ignore that music. Not ever. However, she was much better these days at resisting the urge to consume that juicy red fruit among the delicacies of organs and sauces of blood that lay inside mortals. Besides, she had not brought the watchmaster here to kill him.

She climbed off him and stood. She turned away, sighed, walked toward a credenza, and kept chatting to her guest while she looked within its shelves for whatever she sought.

"What happened with your mother, I regret. Truly. I pay my penance each day for that mistake. She was...special."

*I know, you witch,* he wanted to shout, but his terror stopped him.

"Ah!" Beatrice said, and she shut the cupboards and returned to her guest. She presented a fine mahogany lute to Galivad.

"It will be difficult to play with those irons on. I doubt, though, a talent like yours will be too terribly hindered." She smiled as if they were friends.

Galivad pushed the instrument away.

Beatrice's smile warped into a snarl. "Take it and play. I know you can charm pure bliss from this lute. I am hungry. I cannot tell you how my stomach aches with fires and sickness. If you were a woman, you might know the stabbing of the body's cycles or the tearing pain of childbirth. I have heard of such womanly agonies, and I know without a doubt they are nothing compared with what I suffer. I would take those pains and multiply them one hundredfold as a trade for this pain with which I live. I would dig into your body with my teeth and nails and feast on all the crimson sweetness of your flesh, but your mother's fondness is stalling my violence. Play and live. Play for her, if not for me, for I tell you truly she is not gone. Not all of her."

Suddenly, the Lady El threw the lute onto the couch, doubled over, and groaned. When her panting, white face glanced up, her eyes had split with serpentine black lines, and in her mouth clustered fangs—a whole maw of them like a lamprey's bite. Frightfully, the room flickered to dimness, and in the jet-black shadows she cast, Galivad discerned the image of unfurling, ragged wings upon the wall. He snatched the damn lute up and did not check for its harmony. He strummed whatever was most familiar to his frantic fingers, which happened to be the song about a girl trying to catch a racing star. It was the song he often sang to Rowena. Where was she now, the stone woman? Had the Iron marshals ended her? As he wove the tune, he thought of Rowena enduring torture elsewhere. He thought of the Lady El's horror, and all the terrors and regrets that still lay ahead. His fear and uncertainty only empowered his voice. They made it bolder, brighter, and as smashing as a hammer. With true passion, hope, and sorrow he sang, and he tapped into his mother's gift—a spellsong of music. Quite buried in himself, Galivad noticed the lady only when he finished his tune, fell from his fugue, and took a breath. Beatrice lay exhaustedly in a chair across the room. None of her monstrousness seemed to have lingered.

"Another," she said, and she shivered.

He nodded and picked the strings into one of Heathsholme's local ditties—"Barley, Wheat, and Chaff." She sighed and then tapped along with her hands and feet. After he had played that and a handful of folk tunes, she told him he could have a break. She even served him a glass of water and offered him a biscuit to chew on. Uneasily, he partook in her generosity.

"Beautiful. I am quite full now. Thank you," said Beatrice, but she sat distressingly close.

Galivad nodded and shifted away from her. Beatrice froze him with another unbreakable grip on his thigh. *Now comes the dessert!* he just about shrieked. Whatever horror he imagined, though, did not manifest in her manner, and Galivad felt only the warm shade of his mother's golden light.

"You have her magik," said Beatrice.

*Magik? What magik?*

"A light," whispered the Lady El, and her eyes twinkled as if she could see the invisible mysteries. "A touch of the faery or some other old power. There are mortals who have the most noble of lineages. They go through their ordinary lives without ever claiming the rights of that heritage. In Belle, however, that inheritance shone. She learned how to use her charms, even if she never knew of their ties to the old world. Do you think it was normal for birds to flock to a woman's call? For flowers to bloom so gaily in her garden simply because she sang to them? Childhood's innocence has not aggrandized those memories of yours—of ours. They are real." The lady's beautiful crystal stare glittered with stars of grief. "If I had been less of a monster...if I had met Moreth sooner, I would not have wanted to drink it all. Her starlight. I ruined her beauty. I could not stop myself from devouring her wonder. I hate what I have done. I hate what I am."

Galivad swallowed. In every fantasy of this woman's demise, he'd never thought he would pity her. He tried to crush the feeling, and still it sprang up again. It was as resistant as the spry rainbow flowers Belle's green hand had once conjured. Beatrice seemed so much like his mother. Hating her became impossible. Truly, he could not distinguish between the two women—his mother and the monster.

"You spoke of penance," he whispered.

"I did." Beatrice's tears fell. "A curse. A blessing perhaps. I did not ask for it, and I don't deserve such light in my heart. Nevertheless, what was good, mortal, and bright in her—what I *craved*—I have been given. I only wanted the taste of her light. By her magik, I think I have been given nearly everything. Every song and summer of her soul. Her memories. Her sons. I look at you, and I cannot tell that you were not born from my womb—a monster's womb that cannot bear children." Hysterically, she laughed. "I don't even know who I am most days! Am I a master's wife? A stalker in the night? The *leannan shide* that all children of Pandemonia fear? Or am I a carefree woman with a home, a road at her feet, and a soul that, however far she wanders, she never forgets? Still the hunger never stops. There is no respite in which to find an answer. What I must do to appease it disgusts me. For there is so little of true, soul-stirring beauty in the world. Without that, there is only blood and meat."

Galivad took the hand of this monster, his mother, whatever the Kings she might be—he could no more define the boundaries. *She took her in. Belle is alive, I suppose. A ghost inside a monster. I don't know whether I should love her, hate her, or kill her out of mercy.*

"There are days when I wish I could end myself," Beatrice murmured darkly as if echoing his thoughts. "However, it would take such an effort to put me in the ground—my pride and fortitude have foiled me, every time."

They shared a strange and shuddering comfort together, and they worked through layers of remorse and redemption too thick to penetrate fully. Still, it was enough to realize he did not despise her, and she did not want to eat him. Perhaps they even needed each other. *Can she be convinced to help my friends?* he wondered. *Or at least spare them from the darkest tortures?* Galivad mulled over his hate and the beast he'd bred in himself to confront this woman. He found the beast's bark to be empty and meritless. So much had been confessed, he would need time to sort through it. He needed to process how his mother could be dead and yet alive. Her enduring love for her sons...

"Wait!" he exclaimed. "You said 'sons.' As in more than one. I—"

"Beatrice?" A deep voice broke their union.

Instantly, the Lady El recoiled and leaped to her feet. At the door stood her husband. He had entered the room with an assassin's quiet.

"Moreth, darling, I didn't hear you return," she said as smoothly as she could in her shocked state.

Moreth was hardly fooled. "No. If you had, you would not be coddling an enemy of Menos and confessing to him the strangest secrets I have ever heard, which is saying much."

"Moreth, please. You do not understand—"

"No!" roared Moreth. "You do not understand. Had I been the Iron Queen or some toady of a footman even, your head would be rolling for treason. No trial. No inquiry. Only death! I love you, Beatrice, every terrible and beautiful stretch of your skin. I shall not see you throw our love into the fire for whatever"—he glared at Galivad—"*this* is."

"Nothing," muttered Beatrice. "This is nothing."

Both hearts—the captive's and the matricidal Beatrice's—sank in silence.

"Damned well better be nothing!" Moreth puffed, and then he adjusted his gentlemanly clothes, which were out of sorts after his explosion. "We shall discuss this in illuminating detail later, my dear. I shall send in the ironguards in a moment to collect our prisoner. Be grateful—wondrously grateful—I am a good enough hunter to have heard your...I don't care what it was...before they did. Gather your things." He found his love again for his infuriating wife and added, "Please."

"Gather my things? For what?" asked Beatrice.

Moreth considered and then dismissed the significance of the prisoner among them. The watchmaster would be dead before the day was through. "The Iron sages have revolted. The council is in disarray. Elissandra has warned us Horgot's assassins are in play. The sands of Fate demand we strike Eod now and secure rule. In hourglasses, the Furies fly to war."

IV

Maggie's music filled the echoing chamber of screams, and the Iron marshal conducted her like a virtuoso. Alastair cringed and drove his fists into his ears, but the sound could not be drowned out—no matter how desperately he tried. With so much suffering and all their miserable Fates, Charazance still did nothing. He wondered whether Charazance would show more than a sleepy indifference when it came his turn with the Iron marshal.

From elsewhere in the room, Rowena's strained grunting succeeded in disturbing his despair. It was as if she were birthing something. He looked to see what in blazes the woman could be doing. In the corner across from him, she was shitting. On the floor. Alastair needed a moment to absorb the information. All right. There was no chamber pot, since prisoners of Menos were given the barest of mortal necessities. He figured she had no choice. However, with her eyes puckered shut in concentration, she seemed to be forcing the exercise. She stopped grunting, and the farm-fresh smell of her results filled the tiny chamber.

"I had to," she explained. "Bear with me."

Right back into the maze of the bizarre went Alastair. He was thoroughly lost now, for the esteemed and noble sword of the queen turned to the pile of waste and began digging through it. She used both hands, no less—like a happy puppy who'd gone and lost a bone.

"Have you lost your fuking mind?" exclaimed Alastair.

"No. I've lost something else. Where...where is it?" mumbled Rowena.

The forage continued, and Maggie's screams at least took a pause, so Alastair need endure only one madness at a time. Rowena found something. *A brown pea? A peanut shell?* he wondered. Then she brought it to her mouth. *Don't. Don't you dare*, thought Alastair. What brittle ledge of sanity he stood on did not crumble, however, for she did not ingest her excrement. She spoke to it instead—a whisper he had no hope of hearing. He relaxed when he realized she had not turned into a crackpot and was instead using a far-speaking stone. Once she completed the communication, Rowena cast the object back into her feces and covered it up. Then she tore one cuff of her cheaply made prison pants and wiped her hands as well as she could. However, there was no real chance of removing the stink without soap and water. She left her soiled rag over the top of the mess, and he nearly chuckled. When she approached him, she wore her favored half-frown. He wasn't certain he could have been so efficient if handed the same dirty work.

"I swallowed it earlier," she explained. "As soon as we were captured. On the march out of the trees. I assumed we would be searched and all of our belongings taken. Menosian captors are deviously thorough, as you've seen. I am glad it passed through me in time. I think the anxiety helped. But that is neither here nor there."

"No. Rather brilliant. I would shake your hand, but...well..."

"Yes," agreed Rowena.

"Whom did you contact?" he whispered.

"The queen. I told her where we are—relatively—and what the Menosians are planning. Eod should have time to organize its defenses, if they haven't started already. My warning might have saved thousands."

Alastair slumped. "How gallant. I was hoping for a rescue."

"I doubt there will be one."

As if to crack down the mallet of judgment on Rowena's ruling, Maggie's screams came anew. However they might survive this, it would be without the aid of Eod—a nation that had its own destruction to prevent. What odds were those, though? Rowena slouched beside Alastair while she contemplated their outlook. In time, her shite began to fester in the cell, and it was a nauseating companion to their misery. Maggie's music went on and on.

Unexpectedly the wailing ended.

They heard heated discussions in the other room. Something was amiss, and they stood ere the ironguards barged into their cell. Rifles were pointed at them, and orders were barked to move. In the metal-paneled hallway outside, they met with the interrogator and Maggie. If the Iron marshal had not been so obviously interrupted—his pale complexion splotchy with anger—Maggie would have been in an even worse state. Even with that graceful escape, she looked halfway to death. She had bruised eyes, a bleeding, swollen mouth, lacerations, and blood on the strip of belly exposed while two ironguards held her by the armpits. Maggie lifted her head to her companions and burbled an unintelligible red-bubbled word.

Alastair had to be restrained from lunging at the Iron marshal. The ghastly surgeon slapped Alastair with a wet, rubber hand. It stung. The man had strength. "My appointment with Miss Halm has only just begun," warned the marshal. "I shall see how tightly a Voice keeps his secrets when we are alone together, Mr. Alastair. Yes. She told me your name. We shall have plenty of time aboard the *Morgana* to have our conversation. Each moment can feel like a year. I promise."

*The* Morgana, thought Rowena, and they were shoved into a march. She recalled the legend from Alabion of the three evil witches who mutilated in retribution. Right now she would have preferred those horrors to the ones Gloriatrix had conjured for them.

V

Tessariel was not so good at hiding. Sports and skulking were what the men of her family were made for. It was no wonder Elineth always won at hide-and-sneak. First he found in their room a panel she'd never known existed. This surprised her, as they had shared the same space for a decade. Before they slipped their pale selves into the hole behind the hidden panel, she and her brother made their beds so it would appear as if they had neither been there nor gone.

*You are quite a sneaky snake,* she mind-whispered into her brother's wispy white head once they'd completed the deed.

Eli smiled his thanks, pulled his sister in after him, and closed the panel behind them. It made a snap as it set. Between the untouched walls of the estate, spider webs flourished in abundance. These two were not children afraid of creepy-crawlies and shadows, however, for their mother had educated them on the darkness one should truly fear—men and the monsters of Alabion. Today, they only had to worry about the former. Mother had disturbed their afternoon of gloomy window-watching and restless reading with a mind-whisper that told them of danger. *Ironguards are coming to kill you. Hide yourselves, my lamblings, and do not come out until I have done what mothers do for their children.*

Their mother didn't need to worry about their part of the arrangement—staying alive. As they were bearers of the true blood of Alabion, resourcefulness and bravery were in their natures. Normal children made for such breakable playthings. They were babied creatures too much fawned over.

"Let's have a test of mettle and manliness," Tessa would propose to a young guest in a most distant, dusty wing of their great home, where no adults were around to interrupt them. "Go stand inside the closet for as long as you dare." Once the fool gave consent, she and Eli would lock the handle and leave the child there. Eventually, or sometimes suddenly, the child would realize this wasn't desired play. By then, though, she and Eli were off having the little silences and salons they enjoyed. If the child was lucky, a maid quickly discovered the missing young master all covered in snot and urine. When he or she was left unclaimed, she and Eli usually let the plaything out after a day or three or five. They certainly never let the creature die—that would have been cruel. Young masters never came to visit anymore. Even though she and her brother often bickered, they preferred each other's company to that of other children, who were simple, greedy, and weak. "Slow-born," their mother had named the Western species. Their mother was always right, and she had found the perfect moniker for those who did not have silver eyes and were as painful to watch as sleepy tortoises.

*Where...taking us?* asked Elineth.

Her brother's mind-whispering dangled at the bottom rung of his talents. It hung on by a finger with his aptitude for magik. Tessa was an intelligent girl, and she filled in the gaps in his pigeon tongue. *I don't know where Mother is taking us. Away, I would think.* While inside his head, she picked up an image of rich green trees and thick golden letters ornamented in curlicues —a storybook cover. *The Untamed? I hope so. That would be quite an adventure. Menos is so boring. And ugly. I never liked it here.*

*Ether oo I*, replied Elineth.

He meant "Neither do I," and she quietly giggled at how terrible he was with his gifts. The children kept this lightness of mood as they tiptoed through the dusty crawl space. Sisters Three be blessed they possessed such slim bodies, as these passages were tight. Dauntless, they did not scream when spiders and rats scuttled over them or when the bleeding light ran out from the old, leaky walls and they had to hold hands and feel boards or be lost. Perhaps they coughed a bit. Even that, though, they performed with subtlety. They needed to be stealthy now. They could hear heavy metal boots moving all over inside the house, and more than once, a rifle shot or a scream pierced the muffled dark. Still the children were not afraid. They were curious only about the death happening in their house. Many times they sighed as they identified the cries of certain staff members before the bullets silenced them. However, the children accepted that they could do nothing for these victims other than wish them swift journeys into the Great Mystery. Life was a woodland, and at the moment, if they wanted to live, they had to be the slyest foxes in the forest. The rest of the animals had to fend for themselves. A while later, the children reached a boxy bend that went around a rectangular shaft.

*Umbrater*, whispered Elineth.

This time, his sister couldn't interpret his gibberish. After he fiddled with a few planks and removed a metal sheet—so cautiously it did not wobble or make noise—she saw the flat seat and pulleys of a dumbwaiter within a dim cubby and at last understood.

*You want us to get in?* she asked.

He nodded. *Raferoom giz n acemen.*

*Raferoom? Acemen?* Tessariel circled his nonsense a few times to understand it. Listening to the drunken slurring of her Uncle Tidorus began to pay off. The safe room was in the basement. Of course. The room was concealed and warded and could protect them until their mother came. Elineth climbed deftly as a cat into the lift and then helped Tessariel into the cubby. Operating the lift by technomagikal force would cause a hum any nearby hunter would hear. That notion seemed too risky. They would descend by hand and sweat. They grabbed the iron-braided ropes that held the platform and pulled.

*We shall make it a game,* suggested Tessariel.

Surely this was the better way for the children to deal with the reinforced braid of iron and twine that split open their soft palms mere specks into the task—a better way to still their anxiety come every squeak or creak of the trolley. Their sluggish speed could have been another worry. Instead, they made it all part of the challenge—how much their burning hands and muscles could endure, how little of a rustle they could make, how patiently and carefully they could make their drop, and how fearless they could be with all these animals out to kill them.

An eternity hence, the children reached the basement. Being so white, they could see each other in the dark—especially their gleaming smiles.

They'd done it. They'd completed the longest stretch, though not the most dangerous. They still needed to run through the hunting grounds for the safety of their nest. Staying put presented one option. However, Tessariel's seekers gave her a sting of disapproval at this idea.

*We have to go*, she whispered. *It is not safe to remain here.*

Seldom did the seekers give her a generous warning of danger. Tessariel's budding premonitions were more along the lines of "watch out for that." Half the time, she tripped or struck herself regardless. With a warning like this, danger was a speck away. Elineth hurried and carelessly pried the dumb-waiter open from the inside. It made a metal cry they knew would summon the hounds. They were out in a moment, though. They scampered through a clay-scented basement arranged with grand shelves gray from dust. Floating eyes watched them from glass jars, claws waved from their encasements, and alchemical substances glowed with toxic radiance. It was undoubtedly a witch's underground store. This reminded Tessariel of her mother, and she called to her with magik while the two children hunched and ran. Mother did not reply.

*Rittle barther*, said Elineth.

*A little farther. Yes.* Tessariel remembered some of the hideous curiosities from their last trip to the safe room—a dried raven and a book she knew was bound in mortal skin. It had been a trip undertaken on the day the Kings had warred, or so the presses and criers had all claimed. *What became of them?* she wondered. *Could the immortal die?* She surely could, and she left that daydream for a less harrowing afternoon. Her brother came to a stop. They hunkered down by a pair of dust-painted pots and studied their final trial. Across a short dash of concrete stood a wall, and set within that was a black iron portcullis—the sort that could be found in front of a castle. They need not worry about the door's weight, as it would open upon command from either of them and from their father or mother as well. The shelves ended where they hid, and the stretch seemed an improbable distance to cover and have the time even to speak their names briskly to open the door. Elineth wouldn't risk it. The men of his blood were warriors, and he would be one today.

*Wait here*, he said.

Maybe his bravery finally made the mind-whisper smooth. Tessariel neither questioned him nor misunderstood his intentions. Elineth prepared himself and squeezed all the secret muscles his father had educated him about. He separated the sound of breath from the sound of the nigh inaudible currents that existed even in closed spaces. He tried to smell man sweat over the basement's powdery perfume. Upstairs, many of the noises had stopped, and that was unsettling. Nearby pinged a constant drip that made sifting through stimuli difficult for the immature hunter. He frowned, felt he'd done his best, and moved ahead. Tessariel gasped at his brazenness. All appeared well, though, and Elineth made the excruciating sprint to the door without being shot in the back. He leaned to the door to speak the command that would open it. "I am Elineth Donanach—"

"Yes. You are. Now stop what you are doing and turn around," barked an ironguard.

Elineth hissed and did not immediately respond until the second order came. At first, the blue fire of the ironguard's rifle glowed in the dark like a wicked eye, and Elineth could see nothing else. Then the soldier revealed himself by stepping into a pool of yellow light. From Elineth's perspective, everything beyond the man looked like the darkest of pitch. If he could not see his sister, then neither could the ironguard. The mercenary of Menos dropped his guard, lazily angled his rifle on his forearm, and took a hand off his weapon to flip up his visor and glance at Elineth. Elineth figured the soldier was rather sure of himself in this situation.

"Where is the other one? I was told the bounty was for two." Elineth held his tongue. "I could kill you first—though it might be nice for you to die together. I'm a kind man," said the ironguard.

"Excuse me, sir," tweeted a tiny songbird nearby.

The ironguard looked, as people are prone to do after a sweet sound. A ghostly girl stood by his knee, and she wore a toothy smile. She threw a liquid in his face. Tessariel assumed she'd grabbed a solvent, given the greenish color, effervescence, and witch hazel stink the concoction seeped even while corked. Since she was still learning her alchemy, forgiveness could be found if it didn't sear the fat right off his cheeks. It did, though. Splendidly. Tessariel dropped the vial and clapped at the results—the sizzling smoke, the bubbling molting of the man's face, and the matter that came off in clumps as he screamed and tried to paste his sliding nose and lips back together. The ironguard had tossed his rifle to save his unsalvageable face, and Elineth dashed and claimed the weapon as soon as it struck the concrete. For a while, he watched the ironguard wriggling pitiably on the floor. The man's iron helmet fused into the pink, fleshy peaks of his skeletal visage. His eyeballs ran as yellow as uncooked eggs, and his throat gurgled on chemicals and liquefied meat. It prevented him from mewling. Come the point of disinterest, Elineth stood atop the man with one foot on his prey's chest like a prize hunter. He aimed the rifle at the desecration of a face beneath him. "I'm a kind boy," he said, and smiled. "So I'll make this quick."

One shot settled the matter and sent much of the ironguard's rotten melon of a head about the floor. The children were satisfied with their sport. They'd won the game, and this chap had surely lost.

"Mother would be proud of you," he said, and he hugged his sister.

In their embrace, they did not see a shadow approach.

"Oh, she is, my lamblings!" cried Elissandra. "Of both of you! She is!"

Their mother folded them both within her arms. They were quite sticky and red—not white. Now Elineth knew why the footsteps upstairs had ended, and his sister's head filled with flashes of men twirling in ivory pillars of flame and her mother hacking with a sword amid great crimson sprays. They realized the deaths of others painted their mother. Yet they didn't care how her fingers marked them with bloodstains or how she smelled of murder and savage perspiration. She had found them. She patterned them in red kisses and then told them they must go. The children did not ask where. They followed their mother, who would never lead them astray or without love.

## VI

Constantly stepping into and out of Dream, particularly over such great spans, had taken its toll on Elissandra. She knew she had failed to warn Morigan, the Daughter of Fate, sufficiently of the dangers taught to all novice Dreamwalkers. Dancing in that gray river between worlds, a sorceress could easily lose herself—a memory, a name, or even something of the flesh itself. In today's instance, it was an earlobe, which she knew no fleshcrafting would ever regrow. That tissue and its spiritual attachment to the world had been destroyed. It would never be again. It was removed from the world.

Furthermore, the longer the journey, the stronger the currents that pulled at one's matter, and the higher the chance a piece of the traveler would be carried off into eternity. Bringing other travelers with you, especially ones untrained in the art such as her children, was a road to certain doom—quite similar to a botched translocation. None would arrive whole or where she intended. To escape Menos, Elissandra needed a more classic deception.

Assuming Horgot had ordered her execution on sight, all the city's gates would be informed to hold any suspicious women and children traveling together. She'd moved fast, though, and not all of the Iron Wall would be on deadly alert yet. She chose the Eastern Gate—a station notoriously lax owing to the unthreatening pastoral lands it bordered. Anything illicit in Menos, such as the poisons and assassins that masters wanted to sneak through unchecked, arrived in the city through the Eastern Gate. This was where Elissandra headed after casting disguises on herself and her children. By carriage, she arrived just as night waved a bloody purple hand over the sky. *Lovely*, she thought of her final Menosian sunset.

Some delays occurred at the gate. She noticed that younger women who traveled with others were being stopped, stripped of their hoods or fancy hats—causing much outrage—and inspected. The ironguards eventually waved them ahead, as they did the disheveled elderly woman and the two Ebon Vale stalkers—black and ruthless hunting cats—she kept penned in a large wheeled cage. The men thought it disturbing how those beasts watched them intelligently with their silver animal stares. If ever asked, the ironguards would not remember handling the papers on the old woman and her pets. They would not recall names or whether they'd held documents at all. They would remember nothing at all of the encounter.

Once at a respectable distance, with the Iron City a dim shadow at her back, Elissandra stopped by the gravel-and-boulder roadside to remove the razor she'd bound against her hand. She properly bandaged the deep wound. *Sisters and secrets of Alabion be blessed*, she praised. Bloodmagik and the essence of a mother's love had kept the phantasm going long and strong enough to slip under the grand enchantments at the gate. No one noticed the tiny drops of blood that appeared after she and her cats had moved on, and nobody suspected that the pruned expression of her wrinkled face was anything but the rigors of age. Outside the Iron Wall, she would be able to power her deceit without blood and pain until they at least found a place to lay their heads. In their cages, the Ebon Vale stalkers looked on concerned with their wide feline stares.

"You should not continue to pull us, Mother. Not with that hand," said the smaller of the two cats—Tessa.

"It is a terrible burden," agreed the larger animal.

"No burden is too great, and I shall not hear of it anymore until we are far, far from Menos," said Elissandra. She shivered finally from the pain.

"How far?" asked Tessa.

"Where?" asked the other cat.

Their mother felt it best not to reply. The lamblings had been through so much that day without clouding their poor heads with forecasts of destruction. From the deep well of motherhood and the desperation of her duty, Elissandra drew her strength. She stood, claimed the bar to haul the kennel, and resumed walking. They would stop in one of the hamlets many spans down the road that night, if she could keep going. Perhaps Fate would bless them with a caravan or carriage to catch. Before setting off on her next journey, she first had to find a safe harbor for her children. They could not come with her—they could not travel as fast as she needed to go—and that wounded her more than the darkness gathering in the clouds over Geadhain. She'd been granted a vision—a glimpse of the future—while swimming in Dream. Doom's drums pounded, and she had mere days to cross the Feordhan and stop Gloriatrix from razing Eod, the City of Wonders, which would soon be all that was left of Western civilization. She needed to stop the advance of the mad king and his Black Queen. First it had been Zioch—ruined from within. Soon it would be Menos and finally Eod. The three great bastions of life were falling, taken down by their makers and by madness. Elissandra thought the Black Queen must be smiling at the ease of civilization's disassembly. Gloriatrix and the Furies would be needed in the upcoming war, and Eod must not fall. A far-speaking stone was unlikely to sway Gloria from her cause, and Elissandra's seeming shift in loyalty would only make the woman shut her out. Regardless, she'd used the only far-speaking stone she could find in the day's commotion to warn Gloriatrix of Horgot's betrayal. Any other revelations would do damage to her credibility. She needed to force the Iron Queen's hand in person.

# XV

# THE SISTERS THREE

I

*Here we are in the soul of Alabion*, thought Talwyn, and he smiled. While their visit to the heart of the land had shown it black and full of illness, at least in this realm the spirit of Alabion strove to conquer its disease. For the first time he could remember since joining the company, he awoke without a startled gasp or an immediate worry about what would try to make a meal of him that day: witches, forest-hulks, or changelings. Alabion had a host of hungry mouths to feed. The others still slumbered about the campfire, which some thoughtful steward had kept lit. Snow had fallen, and it rested on his companions' heaving shoulders like second blankets. They looked clean and comfortable in the morning light—a perfect rendering of *Travelers in the Woods*. It was too bad Talwyn wasn't more than a terrible painter and didn't have fancy phantograph equipment with which to capture an image of the four. Full of ponderings, he scratched his beard—or rather his bare skin. He noticed then the smoothness of his jawline. The revelations came in pairs, for he'd miscounted the heads of his companions. The Wolf appeared to be missing, and Morigan slept next to Thackery.

"Good morning," boomed the Wolf from behind him.

"You startled me! You move like a white rabbit in the snow," said Talwyn.

He turned and saw the Wolf. He was squatting with his hands in the snow between his thighs—a position for four legs rather than two, but it wasn't out of place. Other aspects of the man, however, seemed quite different. Caenith was a hirsute fellow, and he wore his fur and kempt beard well. Sitting at the campfire, the scholar would now and then see Morigan grooming him with that graceful dagger of hers. She never managed to do more than tame his hair and keep his nails in check, though. Thus, Talwyn was astounded when he saw that the man's mane had been braided in many places and tipped with tiny bits of milky crystal. His face had been shaved to all but a fine, deliberate line of beard along his jaw.

"Your face!" exclaimed Talwyn.

"Yours as well." The Wolf snorted. "Faeries."

Talwyn checked himself. His locks seemed shorter, and he had lost the stink of travel. "They did this?"

"Bloody nuisances," spit the Wolf. "Pixies, probably. Damn things are obsessed with cleanliness. They move so fast and always when one sleeps. Even I cannot catch them. At least these are not the sort of faeries to take our clothing and shoes—although I would inspect what you value just in case. I would also not be surprised if they've gone and mended our garments in places only lovers should reach. They cleaned the scorch marks off my loincloth—from Aghna, if you recall. I shan't say what else they polished underneath." The Wolf shifted and played with one of his new braids. "I feel mighty fancy for my own skin."

"You look dashing. Like a king," exclaimed Talwyn.

The Wolf smote him with beauty—today more so than usual. Trimmed of his fur and wildness, he was revealed as the carved-granite paragon of masculinity one saw when the Wolf was not being such an animal. In his hottest fantasies, Talwyn could not have conjured a rawer, more sensual, more extraordinary male. And what was that cologne of sweat, metal, wood-oil, spice, and downy pelts the man constantly wafted? Realizing he'd stared a bit too long, Talwyn reddened. Morigan yawned, woke, and came to join them. Thus she rescued the scholar from drowning in embarrassment.

"He is right," she said.

The Wolf brought his hands from the snow. One claimed her waist, and the other touched her liquid-sunset hair, pink cheeks, and crimson lips. She looked as though she'd chewed on rose petals. Everything about her had been shined to radiance. She smelled so strongly of honeysuckle, summer wind, and all the sweet notes a wolf could chase that he was drunk on her presence in an instant.

*I forget how beautiful you are,* he whispered. *A snowflake of a woman. A diamond. I forget until you simply walk into my arms, and I am reminded. The pixies can be excused for their tricks, for they have somehow done the impossible and made you lovelier.*

*Men are not exempt from beauty or from being fawned over,* she replied, and caressed his ruly jaw. Not since Eod had she seen him so tidy. She smiled and remembered those days—that first race upon his warm, wolf wind and his leaving her breathless in the streets with a promise. *You are lovely too, my Wolf. Talwyn would certainly agree.*

*Sadly for him, there is only one fruit this wolf would eat. He is not it.*

Somewhere along the edges of reality from which they peered, the faeries happily chattered. Their work was validated, for the bloodmates kissed. Morigan sensed these watchers, even if she could not actually see the creatures. Apparently, the faery folk were wonders she couldn't simply reach out and tear open for inspection. A little magik and mystery to a woman who possessed too much of each.

The Wolf began to burn so hot the snow started melting, and indeed, he wanted to lay his bloodmate down on the stone and finish this oft-interrupted dance of theirs. However, they had friends who stirred and Sisters to meet. They cooled their passions.

Mouse reacted with the greatest alarm to the company's beautification—Thackery's patched cloak, Adam's washed and tied hair, and the magiking of his makeshift undergarment into a real sash and kilt. She also gasped at her sparkling nails and the puff of lavender oil that rose from her breasts.

"I feel...violated." She sneered. "Even if I'm all clean. Pixies, you say?"

"It's what Caenith said. Yes," replied Talwyn.

"I'll take red witches and monsters over tiny hands scrubbing every wrinkle and mole on my flesh," declared Mouse. She crossed her arms when she noticed the gentrified Wolf. "I can understand evil. However, this is just strange. I'd like to leave before they decide we're in need of something else."

"Agreed," said the Wolf.

The company set out. Although they had missed breakfast, an abundance of lightly frosted but ripe and delicious fruit hung from many bushes. The hungry among them gobbled up whatever crossed their path, and they savored Alabion's bounty. (The Wolf wasn't partial to fruit and had eaten a family of rabbits prior to Talwyn's spotting him. Caenith felt it was kinder to eat the whole litter than to leave the young without parents.) Out came the sun to play with their hair, and the wind ran as a soft, furred puppy between the legs of the travelers. In the woods, the birds and animals pranced as if this were not the season for sleeping. Once the company stopped as a pack of wolves—real wolves—ran alongside a herd of deer. If blood was to be spilled, the hunters and their prey would have fun together first.

"Unnatural," said the Wolf. His frown was a deep, growling crack.

They could not disagree. Nonetheless, an idyllic delight tickled their sensibilities and blurred what they witnessed with memories of the faery stories and legends they'd known since their earliest years. Swiftly, their scowling guide moved them along without further breaks for sightseeing. The Wolf had descended into a somber mood. His gray eyes held a cold distance and stared always ahead and up slightly. It was as though he viewed a clouded peak wrapped in lightning. In this uncanny realm of contrary seasons, the winter's swirling mist was warm and refreshing, and a while passed before the sun evaporated enough of this veil for the company to see what the Wolf saw. Sure enough, a crest of rock rose over the treetops so grand and sheer it announced itself as a primal twin to Eod's white palace. Sun shone atop the rocks in a crown of light, and there the rulers of the realm would be—the Sisters Three.

They ran.

II

"How do you propose we get up there?" asked Thackery.

As the eldest of the company in mortal terms, he felt rather winded after their youthful dash. The idea of climbing what was basically a mountain—this straight slab of rock with hardly a handhold—did not entice him. Talwyn did not believe he would do much better than the old man. "All the way up?" he squeaked.

"Just about," said the Wolf. "I see an aerie, and I hear women. Three of them speaking—although their tongue is strange."

All the company pondered except Mouse. Her mettle was only stronger since their sweaty run. She went forth, fit her hands and feet into whatever grooves would accept them, and started this great climb.

"Skirts up, ladies," she called out. "I have an appointment with three witches, and if you're not coming, I'm not waiting."

Morigan would not delay either. The Wolf looked to her. The golden butterfly of her light fluttering wildly in his chest drew him in, and he saw her face clenched in an iron-cast expression. The air rippled about her. She appeared ready to step in and out of the realms he could not enter.

*That power Elissandra spoke of. I can do it, my Wolf. Anytime I choose. It's no longer a reflex but something I can Will. I could dart up these rocks in two blinks or three.*

*Go, my Fawn. I can feel the pull of the Sisters as strong as the nights when my body wishes to throw off its skin and run under the milk of moonlight—*

Gone. She vanished in a twist of silver light while the Wolf still spoke. Talwyn did not ask about this mystery, as doing so would have made the giant man sulk more. No. The scholar dug up his courage, which lay in a shallower hole now whenever he went for it, and reached for cold stone.

### III

Morigan blinked, and for a speck she flew like a bird into gray clouds, a dazzle of sunshine, and rushing air. At the moment when she felt gravity's command, she blinked again and found herself standing on white-painted grass. Two steps it had taken her to reach the top. She kept her eyes shut for a moment—not from fear but from anticipation of this fated sand. Through the cold, hissing wind, she heard whispers. The Sisters' susurrations ran over her skin like beads of water—tremors of thought her mind would forge into words.

"Daughter of Fate," said one or all. "Welcome."

Morigan took a breath, wished her love to the Wolf who aided her pack, and confronted her destiny.

She stood on a slice of rock in a frozen garden. The place was so high and remote she could see all the green and white waves of Alabion until they shimmered off into the horizon. From that pinnacle, it was as if there existed no other world to be seen and nothing else of importance. She knew this was why the Sisters lived there.

A short distance away, three harmless-looking females watched Morigan. Each was pretty and all similar enough to be family. Two were golden-haired children dressed in threadbare, heavy garments and glowing with fairness and youth. Truly, they shone like fresh pearls. They bled inner light. They were nearly twins but for the harder cast to one's face. The tallest sister, who held the hands of the others, could have been a naiad of myth. She had a flowing jet of black hair, a frowning, pouting sadness to her beauty, and an enchantment and fluid grace to her carriage as if she might waver into mist. All possessed stares as green and far-reaching as Alabion's ocean of trees. All reined a thunder beneath their pale, ladylike facades. She knew that upon a whim, their delicate skins could fall away like dams of ash and release whatever roaring magik, power, and terror they kept walled inside.

"Eean, Ealasyd, Elemech," said Morigan.

Morigan nodded to each Sister as the bees stung their true names—the ones they shared only with each other—into her mind. This seemed the limit of what the bees would or could give her for now. The Sisters appeared warded from psychic dissection with an armor greater than Caenith's. Eyeing one another like predators, the two parties held a wary stance for a time. All were guarded and ready for battle.

Ealasyd was terrible at maintaining fronts. The very concept of not making friends never occurred to her. She ran to Morigan. "Sister! Sister Morigan!" cried Ealasyd.

She flung her arms around Morigan's legs. The gentlest touch, Morigan remembered, could hammer down the sturdiest walls. A bit of contact did weaken the golden witch's defenses, and Morigan had flashes of animal husbandry, doll making, and the river of a mind as sweet as milk and honey. Sheer innocence flowed through this small witch, however old and dreaded the legend might be. *She is the one who has no sorrow or sin. She is the virgin maker. The crafter of Fates. A soul so white it is not tainted or in judgment as it seeks the echoes of Fate. She is purity personified.*

"Come away!" hissed Elemech, who sensed Morigan's power slithering into Ealasyd. "Now!"

"I'd rather not," replied Ealasyd. "I'm as old as you I think. Who knows? Maybe older. I can make my own decisions. That is no way to welcome our lost family either. It's how you would treat an unwanted owl that won't stop hooting."

"Family?" said Morigan.

"Sister!" chimed Ealasyd, and she hugged Morigan again.

"Stop that!" demanded Elemech.

"I shall not!" refused Ealasyd, and she held tighter.

The second golden and young witch, Eean, stepped forth. Her voice was harsh and musical like a crack of lightning over a clear lake. "Look at us fighting like kingfishers over salmon. This is no way for us to behave. Or, as Ealasyd has said, to treat family. We haven't had a guest in many seasons and never one so special. We would do well to brush up on our manners. Morigan and her friends have crossed Geadhain to see us, and a little politeness is hardly an effort. Ealasyd, honor your sister's wishes, please. Morigan has much to understand, and we should not lay too many twigs upon her tender nest, lest we break the branch it rests upon."

Although full of pouts, Ealasyd complied and kicked her way back to her sisters. Elemech, the darkest Sister, gloated until Eean issued a second command. "Elemech, Morigan's companions will be along soon, and you should take these moments to explain the worst of what we must. I do not think you will find Brutus's son a patient listener. You know what I speak of, and this is your time many years delayed. A time to speak the truth."

Eean waved to Morigan. The gesture was heartfelt and with a weight to the shoulders that belonged on the oldest, droopiest tree. Then she took Ealasyd through a curtain of frosted ivy and into the shadows of a cave behind it. Morigan and Elemech stood alone, and neither wanted to talk. Brutus's son? Herself a Sister? The declarations clanged in Morigan's head, and each toll made her more furious and anxious. Across a length that seemed as grand as a stadium, the dark witch regarded Morigan with a fearful distaste. Finally and unpredictably, the cold woman warmed. She walked

toward Morigan. As the gap shrank footstep by footstep, Morigan's perceptions caught flakes of truth blown off the witch. *She is the one who sees. The
eternal and sad witness. Reader of the Fates. The Lady of Tears, for so much of
our lives are sorrow. She is my—*

"Mother?" exclaimed Morigan.

Abruptly, Elemech appeared before her. There was one way to tell
Morigan everything. It was the way souls like theirs best knew how. Elemech
grabbed her child's hands. The world shattered and fell into a gray, whirling
abyss.

*Where am I? wonders Morigan. The answer, though, slaps her in the face.
For she has not moved through space—only time. The season is different. It is
warmer and wet with moist heat. She still feels a bit bewildered and thinks she
hears her companions panting and hauling themselves over the cliff. When she
turns to look, she is wrong, and Caenith's shaggy head does not appear. She sees
the sinewy Aaown and soon after, a huffing Mifanwae. On the lea, the Sisters
are gathered, as they were when she met them. However, in this age Eean has
more years and is clearly the eldest.*

*Morigan feels a shadow in the corner of her sight and knows without turn-
ing to look that a second watcher stands with her: the spirit of Elemech.*

*"The Faithful. Followers of the oldest religion," this shade of Elemech tells
her. "True children of the Green Mother who hark back to the days before cultures, language, or progress. The vessel, Aaown, has offered himself for this
service."*

*"What service?" asks Morigan.*

*"You will see," promises Elemech.*

*Aaown comes forth. Morigan recalls when she last saw him—the ritual
when the moonlight drowned and hollowed him out. That radiance resides
within him now. Beautifully and mistily, he glows. Bright from within, his fingertips are like candles, and his veins are akin to cracks in a magma-filled crust.
Whatever light glows inside him must get out; it cannot be trapped. In less than
an hourglass, the light will destroy him. A person cannot swallow a star and
drink down the moon and expect to live. Not for long, anyhow. A Dreamer, she
realizes. Aaown has eaten a Dreamer, or perhaps it has eaten him.*

*"He had to surrender fully, which vessels never do," explains Elemech. She
is reading her child's thoughts, which drift in the air like a dandelion's cotton.*

"If a Dreamer manifests in a house of flesh, the deed to that body, the soul, still belongs to its mortal owner. A soul might be beaten and chained, but to cast it out is to cast out the Dreamer. This is the law of the pact. It's a partnership—albeit a horrid one—always and forever. However, if the soul chooses to leave, then that house is empty. It can be owned, if only for a blink in time, before the Dreamers' flames consume it. Aaown made this sacrifice and erased his very soul. Through all the histories I have seen, he is a singularly brave man for this act."

Sacrifice, thinks Morigan.

Mifanwae chokes on tears and reaches for her husband as he walks to the cold, dark, and beautiful witch. The Elemech of the past takes his hand, and they touch each other strangely. They are beings who have felt neither man nor woman quite like the other before. Force to force. Great power to power. Today, two stars will make love. Mifanwae cannot watch this second heartbreak. She has already lost Aaown once. Innocent Ealasyd is too young, and should also be spared. Wise Eean takes them into the forgetful darkness of the cave. Morigan understands that Mifanwae will stay in that cave. The faithful servant of the Green Mother will stay with the witches for a few seasons until the child is born. When Mifanwae leaves, she will take the child and her husband's ashes and iron talisman. They are all that will last after today. Mifanwae will bury that tiny vial of blackness under a cairn not far from here.

The Dreamer's passion is spectacular to behold. Truly, he is a star—or a galaxy—that rises in a mist of radiance as he lays his lover down. Even cold Elemech of the past smiles, sighs, and is wooed by his brilliance.

"Feyhazir," she moans, and then light and kisses smother her until she is unseen.

The lovers fade.

Long after the ghosts are gone, Morigan and the shade of her mother linger in the Dream. They are two bodiless shadows on a summer-bright cliff.

"Feyhazir," whispers Morigan. "Was that my father's name? The force that was inside Aaown?"

"One of them," says Elemech. "The Oldest have many names in many worlds. Some in tongues that tangle the mouth in loops. Some in music, tones, and sounds we could never make. That is what he is known as here on Geadhain.

*That is what the lonely widows would call him when he descended on moonlit nights into the bodies of able, willing vessels and stole into their cottages to seed his silver-eyed children. A Dreamer cannot make a true Immortal on his own, though, for the blood is never pure. A mortal womb is not sturdy enough to bear a genuine star."*

*Morigan laughs to think of herself thus. "Why make a star? Why contrive this birth?"*

*"It is true you are this child," says Elemech. "This star, this perfect creation, of which so few have ever been made in the ages of our world. We meddle, Morigan, and we often break things. Like a beaver that eats his own home, we cannot stop ourselves. Our attempt to bring happiness to the Kings and keep out the darkness failed. It left one of them mad and the forest stripped of love. There is always a price for magik—even ours. When we gave the Everfair King his love, it was taken from the land. We do not know how to bring that love back or how to exorcise the wicked shadows summoned by its loss. You have met them, these shadows, and they are the personified ugliness of our souls. They are our punishment. As the tenders, the daughters of the Green Mother, we cannot break the natural order. We cannot leave these woods to settle the affairs of men or rally mortal armies against the Black Queen—no matter how much we wish to give our aid. At times, the sorrow is so great, and these hands of mine are so useless to dry the eyes of all the world's weeping souls that I feel I would die if I could." She pauses for quite some time. "I have never told that to anyone," she says.*

*A tool, thinks Morigan. Secretly, she always felt this was the reason for her existence. She is a weapon in whatever war these women wage—a war that makes the notion of free will seem like a flighty indulgence among Dreamers, Sisters, and Kings. In that moment, Morigan feels reduced to such a small thing. Every shield of her dignity is rent and ruined. She questions everything she knows about life, feelings, actions, and love.*

*Morigan stops there, for even in this vision of the past, the prowling beast of her bloodmate growls some pride into her. Elemech's shade offers further comfort.*

*"I have watched every season and creature of this world," Elemech continues. "I know more than all the books and learned people of every age could teach. I cannot read your tale, though, Morigan. My...my daughter. I cannot*

*be sad for you because I do not know how your Fate will end. We did not plan for you and Brutus's son to unite as you did—allies against the darkness. We might have hoped for an alliance, but we could never have imagined one as deep as yours. We did not write every step, hear every wish, or conjure every fear you've ever had simply to sharpen you as our blade. I wish, though, I had at least participated in those trials and triumphs. I wish I could have been the mother you deserved, the mother Mifanwae became to you, and not a watchful, haunting shadow."*

"You mean that," says Morigan. *It is not a question, for the sunshine of Elemech's regret warms her as truly as any light. How achingly her mother regrets her mistake.*

"I do," replies Elemech.

*They stay in the Dream and are unwilling to leave this moment. They know the world they wake to will have only harshness for them, and they fear this one frail instant will never be found again.*

## IV

Carrying an old man and a dainty scholar up a cliff using one arm proved a bit of a test, even for the Wolf. Talwyn had been climbing, but he nearly slipped midway. Luckily for the scholar, the Wolf's hackles of premonition, which he noticed prickling more as of late, rose in time for a rescue. After that, Thackery and Talwyn made for an uncomfortable pair of burdens. Both gripped a boulder of a shoulder and peered down at the spinning, snowy abyss, and the Wolf cupped their bottoms on his forearm as if they were babes.

*Good Kings, is the Wolf ever hot,* Thackery groaned to himself. He remembered the first time he'd thought that. It had been while riding the Wolf in Kor'Khul. He laughed at the memory of that strangest voyage. *Never thought you would make it this far. Did you, old chap?* Before they had reached Briongrahd, he'd resigned himself to his end, and now he would balk and spit at Death if she came for him. Death must be a woman, he decided there and then. Just as their sex could bring life, women also held the power to take it. Certainly he'd seen enough women wield both light and darkness to make this a convincing argument.

He wondered what they would be like, these three witches. Could they really match the legend? Could they answer all the riddles of life? Could they tell a man how to live another decade if he wished? Aside from Adam, the fellow climbing the rocks like a spider, and Talwyn, who'd unwittingly been swept into all this, each had business with the Sisters.

When not contemplating his troubles or the ground and how far it had receded, Thackery watched his great-niece. For a slim woman, one not bursting with obvious strength and endurance, she ascended with great agility. Many times, the rough wind snatched her cloak and bent her like a willow in a storm. She barked at Adam if he tried to help her. However, when the worst winds buffeted, he held her to the rocks, regardless of her insistence on conquering the cliff alone.

*She is so terribly angry*, thought Thackery. He had also fed sorrow's gluttony through the years and knew well its appearance. A shadow hooded her gaze and set her lips into an unending pout. She suffered, and with Vortigern dead, he should be the one to treat her sadness. He was her caretaker now. *I must watch her, for angry, grieving people do rash, selfish things.*

Somehow, the Wolf sniffed his meditations. "We shall watch for her," he promised. "She and Morigan are sisters as much as two women can be. We are all one pack."

His thoughts had been hunted and eaten—that much Thackery knew. The Wolf appeared to be inheriting his mate's qualities. This didn't bother Thackery. On the contrary, he felt quite settled and cozy against the hot, churning slab that was his friend. Wolf, warrior king, lover of the ages, immortal, storyteller, and sleepless guardian were among his many designations. Thackery would have professed how very much he adored the Wolf, but presumably his friend knew that already. Had sniffed it out.

Before he even realized it, they'd reached the summit. There he drifted as if waking from a warm summer nap. They arrived on a shelf of green and frosted life. The Wolf set him down like a child learning to walk—held by his arms while his feet figured out the steps. Adam and Talwyn hung back behind the Wolf's protection. Ahead of them, Mouse slumped. She was huffing, pale, and momentarily beaten from the climb. She rested only a speck, though, and then stormed forward. Not far away an enigmatic woman—a twist of ivory loveliness with a flowing spiral of black hair—awaited them with Morigan. The two women faced one another and clasped hands. One might think they were praying. The Wolf knew they were not.

Morigan felt so distant from her bloodmate she could have been at the bottom of the Scarasace Sea. She swam in truth—a grand secret he could sense by how her light fluttered inside him. That woman she held. Surely she was one of the Three. Immediately, he noticed similarities between the Sister and the woman he kissed and longed for every day—her pronounced cheekbones, puffed and alluring mouth, and the full lashes of her gaze.

Her mother, he realized, and he nearly laughed. Morigan's designation as the Daughter of Fate was not a mere figure of speech or title of myth. She was exactly what those words meant—a child to the Fates.

Mouse stopped shy of interrupting the quiet pair and bowed to the ground. She displayed an unusual reverence. "Sister, we have come far and sacrificed much to meet you."

Morigan and the Sister kept silent.

Talwyn chanced a polite hello.

Still the statuesque pair did not stir.

"Up off your knees, little Mouse," called a husky voice.

Suddenly, two young, blond children wrapped in tattered winter stoles and wearing boots and mittens rustled out from a cave across the way. They too were undoubtedly Sisters. Before the company, the Sisters Three stood at last. Their hospitality and sprightliness seemed unusual for ancient witches. At once, the smaller of the golden twins rushed to the Wolf and poked his rocky thigh. "Who is this big fellow?" she asked. "As hard as a turtle shell!"

"Ealasyd, hands to oneself," said the other.

They spoke in a manner common to Alabion's witches. The sound was out of sync with the lips' movements, and the tone caused a buzzing between the ears. This was not quite speech. The second golden twin, the one with the matured timbre that belonged in a grandmother and not a child, hurried over to grab her younger sister. She pulled her back and then snapped her fingers several times at the two frozen women. Alarmingly, her snaps sounded like cracks of thunder. They made most everyone jump and pulled Morigan and her mother from their dreamy state. Once woken, the two women blinked and fumbled for a moment before finding their bearings.

"Elemech, Morigan's companions have arrived." Eean turned to the company and embraced the air in welcome. "They are as weary and creaky as old wood. Listen to the groans and complaints in their knees and knotted backs. We do not have much. However, we should find them comforts."

"Yes. Naturally," replied Elemech.

Of the three Sisters, she was the least inclined to kindness. In a ruffle of blue garments, she turned away from them and walked toward the cave. Morigan followed without acknowledging her fellows or even glancing back to the Wolf. Her indifference stabbed him.

"You seem so sad," cheeped Ealasyd, and she touched Mouse's shoulder. Mouse had still not risen. "We should play. That will cheer you up."

Without waiting for a response, Ealasyd tugged Mouse to her feet, and they followed Elemech and Morigan. The remaining company warily held their ground.

Eean smiled. "I don't think we've ever had a proper visit—only folk stopping by on the way to destinies elsewhere. No one ever wants to stay. I think, though, that all of you will have to for a spell. What an ache each of you bears. You will need time to mend—and kindness. Please come along. We are not like our shadows in the woods. I am sorry you had to meet them. I can promise you a stew better made than theirs. Come on. Hurry, or you might get lost in the dark or left in the cold."

It was perhaps an invocation, for suddenly the winter wind battered the four men. If the wind really chose to have a temper up here, it could blow one of them over the edge like a leaf. Heading indoors seemed a sensible proposition, even if hospitality came from an ageless witch in a child's body. Her mysterious smile was as sweet and exotic as candied ginger but suggested motivations beyond simple kindness. The remaining company headed off toward the lair of the Sisters Three. The Wolf walked last, and the eldest Sister trailed along beside him.

"We do not bow to Fates, and we owe you nothing," he growled low.

"We would never ask you to bow," replied Eean. "I do not think your back would bend that way."

"It does not."

"That is why the Black Queen should fear you and why we have placed such hope in you—and your bloodmate. You do not heed order but break it and remake it until the shape fits your desires. A smith you are truly, Caenith. A molder of chaos. Beautiful, untamed chaos—until it is in your hands. We would never want you to change. Or Morigan."

The Wolf digested her words as they passed through the stone mouth that had eaten his companions. "Good. Then we have no reason to be enemies." They walked on. "For now," he added.

V

Ealasyd's voice was a bright torch of song that took the travelers through an impossible darkness—these passages that circled and wove like a mad spider's nest. They would never have found the way otherwise—except the Wolf. He would have chased Morigan by her scent, which even the rankness of these tunnels could not obscure. Morigan remained quiet within him and did not want to share secrets. He sensed she was with her mother and prepared in his mind a picture of the two. They were sitting pensively and looked dour upon a rock together. They were back-to-back—touching but still apart. Such was the posturing of persons drawn and nonetheless resisting intimacy with one another.

A radiance pulsed in the tunnel. It was much different from and brighter than the patchwork lichen that sometimes lit the path, and the company entered a chamber. Everything appeared homier than they anticipated in the lair of three ancient hags—a puff of peppery incense, rugs knitted with beautiful whirls and ornamentation, a stone table, and three tidy pallets. There were the shelves, bench, and strewn tools of a crafter's corner. At a pool that cast crystal light onto the sparkling, fractured contours of the walls, Caenith found his bloodmate, and his picture of her and her mother was somewhat accurate. Mournful mother and daughter sat on opposite sides of the water. They studied ripples and patterns he could not see that bubbled forth from wherever that well drew its deep magik. While the company wandered about and took it all in, Ealasyd dragged Mouse over to the crafter's corner for play. The Wolf walked to the sad-faced women at their pool of secrets. Although he would have watched for however long it took Morigan to find him in her Dream, she spoke to him as he drew near. *I know you know.*

*What else makes sense? The Daughter of Fate must come from Fate her-self,* said the Wolf. *I see sadness, but I should see joy. At last you have your answer, and with that there should be peace.*

*I am a weapon.*

The Wolf moved behind his bloodmate and slipped his stone strength around her. *I have fangs and claws and a father who is the meaning of murder. We are more the same, you and I, than we ever fathomed. So alike I now know why we are so drawn to each other. Weapons can bring order and justice. We can be the judge and hammer for Geadhain—the sword to protect our pack. We can be greater than whatever these witches and Dreamers intended for us. The oldest one—*

*Eean,* said Morigan.

*She understands this. I would say she fears this—not in a dark and dread-ing manner, though, but as an elder who watches her son grow into frightful strength. I cannot smell a lie on her. I would have hunted you—no matter the years or circumstances that kept us apart. I believe that. I shall be man, lover, and weapon for you. Accept our truth, and be my blade too.*

Morigan grinned at his poetic summation of all life's tribulations. *I am. I shall.*

"What love," commented Elemech quietly.

She watched them mind-whisper to each other, squeeze close, and in a speck erase troubles that could plague people not as strong as them for a life-time. Elemech looked at the bloodmates as one being. They were as united as she and her sisters.

"Unbreakable," declared Morigan.

Caenith's bite followed. "How much of this did you three orchestrate?"

Elemech responded unflinchingly and even angrily. "Not as much as you would blame us for. Son of Brutus, I do not deny Eean took you from your mother. She had to. Would you ever have left the woods otherwise? Ever longed to see and hunt beyond these trees? We have tried so hard to help the wounded heal themselves. Long ago, we saw the two Kings wanting to be more than their great selves, and we knew desire could be a doorway to the Black Queen's suggestions. We decided to fulfill their wants ourselves. We lured Brutus here using the oldest scents on the faintest breezes. We hoped Brutus's love with the Ancient would ward him against the Black Queen's whispers. In reality, it was this love that weakened his bestial soul to suggestion. We are to blame for what he has become. Magnus came to us next—he sought us, let that be said. We showed him a woman who'd inherited the blood of the oldest clans. She was a true queen. Nothing less than that could hold his affections. For at least one thousand years, the Fates told me, their love would stand untested. We felt that a fair bargain for the forest's love. A thousand years of peace on Geadhain for a thousand years of suffering in Alabion. The Green Mother is without mercy, though, and you've seen that the suffering has not expired. You've seen what else it has spawned in the Pitch Dark. At the time, though, we thought ourselves clever. We had manipulated each king and hedged our bets for tomorrow with you, proud Wolf, and the uncertainty you bring. Alas, you fell into despair, and we watched our plans fall to dust. We needed our own child of chaos. Our own hope." She stared at her daughter, hard. "We saw another opportunity in Malificentus, who also came to us seeking. He sought an end to the Immortals, and considering how terribly we'd handled the Kings, we felt obligated to aid him—but not quite as he wanted. We did not want to end them. Unlike the Green Mother, we are not without mercy. Instead, we imparted a message to Malificentus. It was a warning in the trappings of a prophecy to rally the mortal armies to your side, Morigan. The call to battle never reached the ears and hands it should have. Our fault again for trusting the wrong hero. The message died in Alabion and remained here for centuries. Finally, our words made it past the woods and into the hands of Menos." She scowled. "But Menos would make war before it ever spurned its hubris and wished for peace. So that message was ultimately meaningless. Every one of our attempts to build allies against the Black Queen has failed."

Elemech's shame wore down her hardness. She wept, quietly, as she continued. "You can blame me for the decision to steer Fate rather than leaving the Green Mother's health to the whims of people whose minds change too often to be relied upon. We wanted a pure heart—a soldier who would feel the ache of the world as we do. A child who could feel the pain and horror of what we face. A child who could not be swayed by the weaknesses of man or infected by the Black Queen's tainted desires. We did not meddle beyond your making, though. Not past sending Mifanwae west and as far away from Menos and our mysteries as we could. We wanted you to know yourself before you knew us and our struggle. We did not know when you would return to us.

However, it was an inevitable journey. Your heart led you here. We did not know the heart-wounded son of Brutus had migrated to you as well."

"And when you learned this?" asked Morigan.

"We thought you should be introduced," confessed Elemech.

The bloodmates thought of a wind, an opened door, and a meeting on a hot day in Eod. Perhaps that wind had visited more than once. They dwelled not on it further.

"Whatever bonds and successes you have made together, we cannot claim as our own," whispered Elemech.

"My father?" Morigan asked. "These presences that come to our world to ruin and rule it?"

"Dreamers." Elemech uttered the word with impatience, as if her inquirer should understand. Yet Morigan did not. She could not stitch a sensible tale out of cosmic shadows that entered flesh, burned up bodies, incinerated souls, and made love to ancient witches. She could also not fathom anything of the darkest of the Dreamer's kind, who possessed desire only for ruin, rape, and doom. The Black Queen. Feyhazir. Ragnarök. Even the names of the Dreamers she knew sounded as though they came from a realm of nightmares.

"Tell me," demanded Morigan.

Elemech shook her head. "Telling is for those who cannot see as you and I do. I shall show you what we know."

Whatever magik suddenly crackled about the Wolf pulled him into a whirlwind, and Caenith held his bloodmate tightly. Strangely, there was no breeze. He hadn't even moved, and still a force wrenched his mind forward and sent it spinning into the swirling waters of Elemech's pool. He was hardly alone. In the corner, Mouse sewed a button on a doll-size coat, but she rudely dropped her crafts and stumbled like a sleepwalker to the whirling pool. Talwyn, Adam, and Thackery had been attending to Eean's fascinating stories of Alabion, which they all understood despite speaking different tongues. They also strode at once to the watery mirror that now dazzled with fingers of brightness. As one, the company gathered at the edge of the witch-water and fell.

*Into darkness. What is darkness without color or sound, though, other than an abyss? They are bodiless, with only the faintest consciousness in this* drowning deep. This is death—the great black untilled soil before life. It is a cold without a season and a temperature so low that even the minds of the travelers become dull with frostbite. Morigan has been here before, though not in so cold and vast a field with no whisper of spirit.

Then in the void, there is light. Two lights blinking on like eyes of fire.

"She is the First," say three echoing voices.

First what? the visitors wonder. For this ancient Dream is not a history, exactly. History cannot exist when there are no voices to record it. Perhaps this is an echo, then—a theatrical phantasmagoria of what might have been. The three voices affirm this thinking.

"'Zee,' the manlings would hum one very distant day from this darkness, as they watched the sun rise. Back when words were still crude and not shaped by the Everfair King's poetry. Back when all that men knew, lived by, and worshipped was the granting of another day and another light. Onae was the darkness they feared—a sum of all death and terror that their unshaped, uncultured selves could grasp. A light in the dark. Light and dark. Alpha and omega. She was the first."

"Zionae," whispers Morigan.

"Yes, Daughter," says one voice of the trio. It is stronger but with a tremble. "She was the great sleeper to Dream in the cradle of nothingness. First of stars."

More lights appear. In specks, the space dazzles as though every light in Eod has been flicked on at once. Those familiar with the city have pangs of homesickness, and then awe smashes that. The sea of lights courses and grows. Soon they are surrounded by more stars than any of the geniuses among them could count with even a hundred lives and all the technomagikal computations of the world at their disposal. Infinite stars. The festooning of lights does not seem to stop—only to swell. Watching the miracle makes the company feel giddy.

"But endless light was such a lonely Dream," continues their three-voiced spirit guide. "However, we should not ascribe the intentions of the divine to mortal agonies. So we do not know why she dreamed—only what. Next was rock."

Motes and star-jewels are all they see. Then, amid the cosmology, some glinting specks move or turn dark and become asteroids and boulders. Slowly, these masses coast along and soundlessly impact other lazy wreckages—glowing half-moons and flocks of floating rock. The watchers will never remember how long they hover in timelessness, for this is primal. They are basking in the dawn of life. A thousand or a million star trails and cosmic showers jumble past.

"Rock and light. Tears and wishes, we of smaller minds would think," say the Sisters.

The sweet young one adds, "I can think of no duller company. I would want friends or sisters with whom to play."

"Which is what she dreamed," declare the three voices.

Ethereal as they are, the travelers sense a pressure on their ghostly selves. There is some small, perceptible change in their vast surroundings. The stars seem brighter, and the patterns and movements of debris are less chaotic and more controlled. It's as if hands enormous beyond measure are arranging the disorder as a child might stack blocks. The universe has found or fractured itself into other egos and desires. Zionae is no longer alone.

Other Dreamers have entered the abyss. Whether they are children or broken pieces of the mirror that is the First, no sense can discern. These creators are unfathomable, invisible to the eye, and unknown to the mortal senses or imagination. They exist as phantom sensations that can be compared only with the thrill of music, the pulse of an orgasm, the chill of terror, or the clenching of hunger. They are here although nowhere seen, these Dreamers, and they are the company Zionae has created or sought.

The stream of time blurs and roars by at maddening speeds, and the travelers see these colossal, playful Wills give meaning and shape to the chaos. Planetoids stop their drifting and park their hulking bows at what cannot be random ports. The disarray of stars is plucked and placed into prettier formations—a celestial language. Colors are suddenly dabbed onto a canvas that has so far been an uninspired black, brown, gray, and white. Stars are painted orange, red, or pink. Some are stretched and flared into suns. Other constellations are given lines a sky-watcher could interpret as the bones of creatures not yet dreamed. The universe is the Dreamers' playground, and it does not seem to end. It rolls outward in a meadow of rainbow and black mist and is ever expanding. It is alive.

"Fire, water, wind, and soil," say the Sisters. "Such were the passions and instruments of these artists. They made wondrous works—everything we know. We are not the only Dreams here on Geadhain, though we were the first."

*With that, the nearest hump of rock in the sea of eternity undergoes a metamorphosis. Fantastically, the planetoid transforms into a red and fiery-veined chrysalis. Then it is a cocoon of white and then dry and dusty skin. Finally, it sheds those brown scales for a body of blue and green. Stability has been found—an equilibrium of liquid and solid where further Dreams, grander and more complex creations, might thrive. Time has slowed now for a while and possibly forever. They watch the orb gently twirl on an invisible string. They cannot take their eyes off its beauty.*

*"Geadhain," murmur the Sisters reverentially.*

Quite gently the Dream faded, and the travelers slipped back into their bodies beside the pool, which was now dull and still. On the opposite side of the pool, Eean and Ealasyd stood by their sitting sister. No one remembered his or her steps before the vision. Many of their heads felt adrift with heavenly lights and dazzling memories. What had they seen? A miracle? The past? No. They realized it was not the past—only a phantograph conjured by the Sisters and one that continued to resonate. Man had been created—dreamed from nothingness—in a time no being or historian could remember. Ancient people crawled from caves to greet the dawn, the Zee, and they feared the dark, the Onae, until however many eons had come and gone. The digestion of this staggering myth would have to wait, for the Sisters had more to share.

"Geadhain is the greatest Dream," said Eean. "The Deepest Root in the tree of stars. After her birth, she was stretched and fattened on the Dreams and milk of her makers, and then the Dreamers left. To other rocks. To dream new stars and miracles."

"They grew up," pouted Ealasyd. "I wish I could do the same."

"Hush now, dear sister." Eean patted the young one's head.

"Why have the Dreamers returned, then?" asked Thackery.

"The Deepest Root," muttered Morigan.

Elemech smiled at the Daughter of Fate for knowing the truth. "You certainly have my insights—and many more I have not given you. What happens in Geadhain, happens throughout all that the Dreamers have dreamed. If you cut the roots, the tree of stars will die."

"And Zionae," began Thackery.

"Wants to cut the roots," hissed Elemech.

A spell of silence and doom was cast over the company. Finally, the men and women of this mysterious war—they who would be its heroes or failed generals—grasped the threat and severity of their mission. Inquisitive Talwyn was more interested in facts than vague apocalypses, and he had questions. Too many, but he settled on one. "This Zionae," he started. He was still thinking. "This...maker. Mother of Light and Darkness. Why would she destroy her own creation?"

The two eldest Sisters sighed, while Ealasyd found crawling on the wall a larva that successfully bid for her attention. She wandered away.

"We cannot say," replied Elemech.

Mouse spoke up. "But you're..."

"What?" Elemech laughed. It was a harsh scratch. "Omniscient? All-powerful? That's nearly true, little Mouse. We have more wisdom and magik than any woman or man should be given. Still, we are flesh and blood and bound by the rules of the physical world—and even more rules than those. Even the Green Mother, while you might not consider her so, is a living being. Therefore, she is a creature likewise trapped by certain limitations. She can grieve; she can be wounded. She can dream wonderful miracles and children of her own." The two eldest sisters shared a long stare before glancing back to the company. "The Green Mother was also young once, with a soft mind that dribbled memories as our Ealasyd's does. We can see only what the Green Mother has seen. We can remember only as much as she can remember, and while that tale is a scroll that might seem never-ending once unfurled, it does peter out. Those ages, the ones her memory does not reach, are where Kings and Dreamers had their births and reigns."

*Magnus and Brutus are older than these women.* In the private hallways Morigan shared with the Wolf, she gasped. *I don't think the Everfair King—or anyone really—suspected as shocking a truth. Magnus saw them as his elders, yet they are as unwise to certain truths as he is. My Wolf, the Sisters have not seen the starry hands that laid the two infants in this world or heard the voices of those makers. They do not know what we do.*

"We do not leave these woods," said Eean. "The deepest truths are hidden away like gold in a mountain. They must be sought out in the dark and toiled away for until found. We could not take on that search, and it is not our place to intervene beyond a shift in the winds of destiny anyway. To do so would be to go against the Green Mother and all we are. Nature must take its course toward bounty or ruin. While we might bless—or curse—men with what they desire, we are not acting for ourselves but for their destinies. Fates forged by their hands. If those hands are to raze the field and not till it...what she wills, she wills."

Eean looked to the Wolf. "Son of Brutus, we asked your mother to choose. We did not take you." Then she turned to Morigan. "Daughter of my sister, every wind was merely an opportunity. Every choice to seek us was your own." Lastly, she addressed the company and looked from Thackery to Mouse. "To the other seekers of our winds, those who have challenged the Green Mother's gauntlet, we would offer the same choices. Know, though, we are never to blame for how far or unexpectedly those winds will blow."

Morigan was impatient with this allegory. She had come for truths. The Wolf felt her star flare in rage. "What is the choice before us?" Morigan demanded. "What is it face? What are the true natures of our enemy and this war?"

"Darkness," said Elemech, and she glowed with gloom. "Absolute night upon the world. Love has become hate. The great Dreamer devours her creation. We have only another few cycles of the moon before Zionae's star—the closest a fleshling will ever come to seeing her glory manifested and but a shadow of what she represents—is above all Geadhain. The Dreamer's power in that moment and her reach between the veils will be strong enough to shatter all barriers between spirit and flesh."

"What will she do?" whispered Thackery.

Elemech spoke as if all hope was already lost. "She will consume her sons. Utterly. Maybe one and likely both. Perhaps she fears their unity and seeks to defile their brotherhood, since their combined force is a reckoning beyond measure. Together, the Kings rule all the elements and passions of our world. They are living Dreamers. If she enters them, she will enter the world not as a spirit but as a Dreamer unchained and unbound by rules. She will go into realms in which Dreamers cannot walk. Should that happen, no wind of destiny will alter the fate she will bring. I have seen this end—an ocean of shadows. Feasting, lusting, madness, and hunger. The snake that eats itself eternally. Oroborax. The whole of Geadhain devoured by her disease. I have watched maggots nibble on valleys of corpses. I have seen a rape every sand for a thousand ages." Somehow Elemech's mood went grimmer, and her bitterness chilled them. "Yet I have known nothing as unholy as what she will bring."

Morigan glided on the currents of her mother's words.

*Beneath her span forests—horrible, black, and wiry as pubic hair. They have the same greasy reek that copulation after copulation in an unventilated pit would produce. Every river bubbles and heaves with blackness and smells as would a gully of vomit and oil. As Morigan flies from pole to pole of Geadhain, she notices no corner where Zionae's rot hasn't set in. No plant, creature, or even insect is spared. What has not yet eaten itself or another still prowls the pubic groves and wallows in the earth's sores, which bleed tarry pus. So little can even Morigan's silver eyes glean through the sooty, crackling thunderheads all around her that cough red and gray matter as if dying from consumption. The colorless thing—neither sun nor moon—that hides behind the miasma illuminates only suggestions of atrocity. Her unforgiving senses bring her visions of what is unseen—the tortured mutations that wander below. There are tendrils, spines, wriggling genitalia like spitting tails, and bleating holes that could be anuses, ears, or mouths. All the world is in love with horror. All animals and men mingle into a soup of despair. She knows that some of the shuddering atrocities roiling under her were once men or women.*

*When the tribes of horror are not hunting, feasting, or fuking corpses and each other, the tormented look and wail to the moon-sun. They cry from the hunger that will chew them from the inside out. They cry for the Dreams in the tree of stars still untouched by their taint. Not forever, though. Not even for very long. Soon the hunger will finish its meal of Geadhain, and the fat stars will beckon to the hungry waiting to join the feast.*

Morigan fell back into her flesh, and the vision fizzled. Zionae would ruin Geadhain with her madness, but she would also devour all the Dreams and miracles ever made.

"No," gasped Morigan.

"Now you have seen it too," said Elemech. "We are a drop in the pond, but we are the ripple to become the wave."

What burst from Thackery sounded like heresy and treason—a betrayal of all he knew. "The Kings." He shook his head and was unwilling to part with the thought. "If she wants to use them as her vessels...if they are her entry to this world and the means through which all these wicked events will be enacted...could we? Should we? What if we could stop any harm before it began?"

He meant murder.

"One cannot destroy what is not wholly of this world," said Eean. "No element on Geadhain could burn hot enough or drown deep enough to end the Kings. Breaking the bond between a Dreamer and its vessel is impossible for a mortal."

"That is half a lie," said the Wolf. He could smell the Sisters' plot and remembered too what his bloodmate had done to Aghna. "Morigan is not of this world, and I am not either. Not really."

"The act could kill even you," said Eean. "But yes. You are capable of it. Morigan as well."

A great silence fell.

Elemech and Eean revealed no guilt the Wolf could sniff or sense, which was understandable for witches who entertained the notion of a child's murdering his parent.

"That is one path," said Eean. "One way the wind could blow."

"What is the other?" asked Morigan.

Elemech showed some vitality and even a bit of a smile. "In the east, Zionae once fell."

"What do you mean?" asked Talwyn quietly.

Elemech became inflamed with emotion. "I mean *fell*, scholar. A piece of her matter. The great celestial body that Geadhain witnessed once in its primordial age, and that it will see again in all its glory as the Black Star when the sand of our doom drops in the hourglass. That is what fell. A fragment of the divine. Imagine an aspect of creation herself crashing down to our world. Because it was so long ago, the Green Mother cannot remember it. However, she remembers the strike and still bears the scar of Zionae's descent into the *Claeobhan*."

*The Cradle,* thought Caenith, Adam, and Talwyn from what they could construe of the Ghaedic word.

Elemech continued. "I am not able to follow this ancient memory and find this forgotten myth. You are, my daughter. If you were to discover any physical piece of what Zionae left behind in this world, you could see into her heart—into the heart of the great Dreamer herself. Perhaps then you would find the cause of her illness or, at the very least, what weaknesses such a seemingly invulnerable foe might have. Only if you take this journey and you know and possess this truth can you hope to confront her and live."

Thackery felt faint, and Talwyn was there to break his swoon. The others were livid. Their options were to kill the Immortal Kings, unleash catastrophe, and possibly kill two of their company in the process or to seek out a strange and unfathomable place where the Mother of Creation had once landed, lived, or walked and confront her. *What awful choices*, thought Talwyn. *Only doomed, mad persons would pursue them.* He supposed he was one of those damned, wandering souls now. The company sighed. Their mission had not ended; it might never end—at least not in the way they wanted. They sensed the Sisters waiting for an answer—except Ealasyd, who remained cooing to her crawling friend on the wall.

"I have no answer," said Morigan. She stood, and the Wolf rose too. "This is not my choice to make without counsel and agreement from every voice that would have its say. I am not the only life, fate, or weapon in this war. Each soul must speak and choose for itself."

Two Sisters nodded and held their tongues. Neither was surprised when Morigan led the others into the outer caverns. Surely these Fated souls would not hold their meeting in the presence of meddlesome witches who could be blamed for a thousand wrongs.

What a shame Morigan did not catch the pained and hopeful gazes the Sisters cast after her. With her insights, Morigan would have seen the three as nothing more wicked than old, weary souls who worried for Geadhain's future—women who punished themselves for every life, leaf, or hope that had been destroyed.

VI

Morigan easily guided the company through the limestone labyrinth. While wandering the tunnels, no one spoke. Once out on the lea again and exposed to winter's bluster, they huddled about the one great rock on the summit, which evoked the prominence of a stone table around which kings and

"I shall see this through," muttered Mouse. "Father told me to remain. I n hear him inside whenever I listen."

She trailed off, and Adam cupped her shoulder in compassion. First stincts urged him to bite her. However, he suspected even a small nip ould not bring her the intended optimism but earn him a slap.

"I shall stay with you until the sadness has left your spirit," he said.

Mouse gasped, and heads turned. Normally, Adam contented himself th silence. He believed in speaking only when he had something impor- nt to say. What Adam had failed to tell the company was that, since com- g to this mystic place, he could clearly understand the witches and their lf-mind, half-mouth language and his companions' words. This magik d not weakened when away from the Sisters themselves but seemed fused into the very stones of this peak. Perhaps he should have used his ice earlier, though, for Mouse stared at him with unaffected surprise and asure.

"My word!" exclaimed Thackery.

"Hardly a shock," said Talwyn, and he tapped his chin. "Some kind of nd-magik has affected us since we came here. I cannot even tell whether is talking as an Easterner or a Westerner, although what he is saying cer- nly sounds proper."

"Yes. This is a nice gift," said Adam. "I shall make good use of your ears ile I have them. We have a hunt before us, as you would agree, mighty olf. She is a deadly prey. I think killing this Dreamer's pack, these Kings, ll not do. We must kill the mother herself."

"Yes," Caenith agreed. "If we can preserve the Kings, we should do Even Brutus. The Kings are bound to nature and the forces beyond. stroying them could bring upon Geadhain judgment from both realms. nae, however, is a disease. She must be thrown out of their bodies and s world. We must learn what makes her weak and how to harm her. Then must destroy her."

Against the dusk, the company shone as bright and focused as a blade heathed. An agreement had been forged.

"East then?" asked Thackery.

"East," said Mouse.

"I have said where I shall go," said Adam.

leaders would broker peace or war. There they began to spea
much to share. She placed her hands upon the stone and gla
to face. "Another quest," she spit, "or we kill the very people
world together? We all watched the storm together, and we're
tain Magnus is dead. They certainly didn't speak as if he were
happen if we *really* destroyed those men? And that's assuming
even possible."

"We would be trading one calamity for another." Thacke
he looked as elderly as he was. "The wiser Sister, Eean, implie
ing the Kings could be done—though it could kill the killer. V
anyone to an end like that. I don't care whether I sound selfisk
be both those things. I have earned that right. I don't care wha
feited as a result. We must act always with love and honor. W
the lives of each other and those we are sworn to protect, or
achieve will be hollow."

Every member of the gathering smiled at his wisdom. St
for answers to unanswerable questions. How far would they k
How many would be standing in a week's time? In a year's
hard character, though, they did not dwell on the qualms c
and lose themselves in the bog of how to flee from this dut
the cleanest path through the mire. As Morigan had anticipa
companions would abandon the world to doom. They would
and that gave her a rush of glory.

*Brave and noble, each of them*, whispered the Wolf. *I hav
dream of a cottage, although I think a cave would be better. I
songs and live out our days in pleasure and with family. I shall
with you once our long walk has ended.*

Morigan picked up the great bronze hand that alway
upon her, kissed it, and then placed it back on her waist. She
her dream with the company—at least the essence of it.

"I have not heard a single person declare he or she will
that warms my heart. I do not think I would reach the enc
otherwise," she confessed.

"Leaving?" Thackery puffed. "Dear child, I could never
Talwyn shone with a bit of cheer. "This is far too intere

"East," concurred Talwyn. "Still, we should ask the old dames where 'east' is, as that is quite a lot of ground to cover."

"One more journey," said Morigan, and she wanted to promise them it would be the last.

## VII

Savory, saliva-inducing aromas were enough to lure the company back through the caverns without much help from the seer. When they arrived at the witches' grotto, the wolves charged in like muddy hounds ruining a feast, which was what had been prepared for the company. The stone table had been tidied of its ritualistic fetishes and laid with a splendid scarlet-and-gold embroidered runner. The resplendence was secondary to the bowls of peeled and sweetly steaming fruit glazed with honey, pinesap, and mint. There were roasted hares and hogs, although there was no great hearth in sight. Platters of buttered potatoes and heaps of boiled greens seduced the stomach with wafts of ginger and cinnamon. Few of the travelers had attended so magnificent a meal, and even the Wolf forgot his predisposition toward meat and hungered to try everything on the table. They restrained their appetites, though, suspicious of the three witches who sat waiting for them upon the benches before the feast.

"We have had our council," said Morigan.

"We know," replied Eean. "Now the questions, curses, and what have you can wait a spell while you nourish your bodies and souls. Food is the oldest and simplest medicine. It can cure the ills of heart and mind. We cannot do much for you—not as much as we would like. We can, though, make sure you are strong, rested, and ready for the challenges you have chosen."

Elemech rose, bowed, and said, "Please."

The cold one's gentleness became the wind to break the willow, and the company rushed to find seats, grab cups of heated golden lager, and fill their plates with food. Morigan settled in next to her mother, and Caenith was across from her at the table. The Wolf had chosen this spot at the table strategically so that he might watch Morigan and Elemech interact—their glances that slipped to each other, their almost-touching hands, and the similarities in their mannerisms. In certain ways, however, they could not be more different. Morigan was all light, and Elemech was darkness—a shroud worn over her soul from all the visions and doom she had witnessed. Even Elemech's happiness seemed pained to the Wolf. It was as though her smiles came from the reflex of an ache and not from something pleasant. The Wolf pitied the dark Sister and swore he would never allow Morigan to lose her hope and become like her mother.

"Too much worry and not enough eating for such a large man," whispered Eean from the seat beside him. "Half this feast is really for you."

He nibbled a bit, but his hunger was strangely absent. After a pause, he turned to Eean. Her sage presence encouraged trust, and he spoke freely. "I would protect my Fawn from every evil in herself and the world. I would rip out my heart and squeeze from it my blood to show her the depth of my passion. Still, I do not know that my devotion will be enough to keep her whole and unchanged from the purity I love."

Eean's emerald eyes sparkled. "You see only one side of darkness. As an animal, you think too thickly in blood. She has already changed. She is no longer pure by that standard you carry. However, she is more whole than ever. My sisters and I have seen many, many loves, son of Brutus. Princes with milkmaids. Changelings beloved by hunters. Your father and the Ancient. The Everfair King and his Blood Promise with the daughter of the Arhad. Indeed, we would age a hundred years if I told you of all the epic loves and star-crossed tales we have seen. For every grandiose love epic, though, the end is predictable—loss, tragedy, or the kinder decay of age. What we have never witnessed, in all of man's history, is what you two weave with your souls. A new music. A dangerous song. You should not be afraid of change when that force has taken the two of you so far together in distance and in heart. I see your love, and it is a circle from summer to winter. It's a caterpillar that casts off cocoon after cocoon, to be only more beautiful and dazzling than it was before. I think you are trembling before your next step. Do not tremble, Wolf, but roar and leap."

*Leap?* he thought. What did she read within him?

Eean pulled down his mighty shoulder with her child's hand, which felt gnarled and ancient for a speck, and she murmured into his ear. "There is a place."

Eean's words buzzed and burned into him, and suddenly Morigan felt his beast excitedly pacing her chest. She could neither hear nor otherwise perceive what he and Eean discussed. When the Sister finished claiming his ear, he smiled at his bloodmate. He was sharp, handsome, and slightly frightening. Afterward, he began to eat ravenously.

Thackery squandered the pleasure of this meal by brooding over his two charges—Mouse and Morigan. How could he protect either woman with this ramshackle body of his? He'd proclaimed his commitment to be their caretaker, but even considering another journey brought his pulse racing to an unhealthy pace. Alabion had not claimed him. Through a grace he thought impossible, he had made it to the Sisters. Where the feet of the company went next, he would need to be twice as lucky to have the same fortune. He sighed.

"What is it, son of Thule?" whispered Eean.

She was so small that the Wolf's shadow on her other side obscured her to invisibility, and Thackery had forgotten she sat between them.

"Age." He laughed. "You seem young, but I can tell you are the oldest. Only age would display such wisdom. Only age could look at the knots and wrinkles of this old face and read it as worry."

"Indeed," croaked the tiny witch.

They shared a snort and a chuckle.

"I am worried," he admitted. The sweet-barley mead stoked the fires of conversation. "I have appointed myself as their guardian—Fionna and Morigan—and yet I need stewardship. I had to be carried this far, and I mean that quite as it sounds. It was mostly in a man's arms. Caenith can protect them better than I shall ever be able to. I suppose I should hand the responsibility to him fully and sit on the bench as the elderly do...waiting for a gentle end and being proud of the young."

"A sad end to a glorious life," muttered Eean.

"It is the end that is before me—an unfussy grave in whatever fell land Zionae's relics lie. Not a bench for me, I'm afraid. That would be too common a passing."

"An unworthy end. You surrender to the Pale Lady too easily. Think of what you could still accomplish."

Thackery turned to the witch. She appeared at once lined and decrepit and fair and golden. Did she know the question he wanted to ask? Her gaze was green and encompassing as all the mystery of Alabion. It said yes.

"There is a place," she said quietly.

Talwyn watched Eean chatting to the two fellows and was amused at how she cannily split her time between them. They never noticed. Being quite heavy from the drink, he heard none of what was said. From the range of emotions the men expressed, though, he assumed she'd said something of tremendous weight. Talwyn tried to drink away the strangeness, and it worked. Certainly owing to magik, the spirits and food never dwindled, regardless of how gluttonously the company guzzled and gorged. For a feast of magik, it felt as filling as bread and barley, and soon the companions leaned on their elbows, pushed away their plates, and cautiously sipped their drinks so as not to tempt any bile. They could not recall a moment when they'd been so fat and satisfied. Ealasyd shortly tired of the chatter. It had been mostly talk of the company's journey thus far, and it had too much blood, violence, and sadness in it for her taste. Macha sounded like a good playmate, though, and it was a shame they had not brought her with them. Ealasyd dwelled on playmates and supposed the sulky lady, Mouse, would do for companionship this evening.

"You're all too wet-headed to leave tonight," said Ealasyd, and she stood and stretched. "Elemech had me make up some beds for you, though we'll see who actually sleeps in them."

It was an odd comment, but perhaps the youngest Sister was more of a prophet than they believed. The Wolf leaped up from the table—not in the least drunk—and dashed over to collect his bloodmate. They seemed in a hurry to leave. They made pardons and vanished in a wind.

"Let's get back to our crafts," cheeped Ealasyd, and she looked to Mouse. "I'm feeling inspired." With that, she dragged Mouse away from the table.

Meanwhile, Thackery and Eean spoke in the coyest of stares and then excused themselves as well. Around then, Talwyn noticed the heaped pallets the youngest witch had mentioned and took a bit of a stumble to reach them. He fell onto the mattress like a sloppy lover and was snoring as soon as he laid his head down. Only Adam and Elemech remained at the table.

"Well," said Elemech, and she drummed her fingers on the stone. "It appears the evening is at an end."

She stood and turned. Adam caught her with a request. "Wait. You grant wishes, do you not?"

"I do not make bargains. Eean has the gifts and patience for that work," said Elemech, and she dwelled on the choices Eean had offered the heroes that night.

"A small bit of magik," he pleaded, but she began to walk to her pool. "Please," he begged.

Tiredly, she waved for the changeling to follow. She would hear his appeal, and if it was worthy, she would reveal a choice to change his destiny.

## VIII

Worms glowed on the limestone walls. Thackery knew he headed somewhere far beneath. Within the Sisters' abode sprawled more tunnels than one could ever map, and Eean had taken his hand. To drop it would leave him stranded and yelling in the dark. Thackery pushed his heart and lungs further than an old codger wisely should, but his excitement would not be dimmed. Could what Eean promised be true? Though Thackery had studied the permutations of magik, from its blackest spells to its whitest charms, he was aware of no magik on Geadhain that could do what Eean had offered—the power to turn back the sands of time. History was rife with the failure of sorcerers who had tried to distill, steal, or conjure the essence of youth, and never had their manipulations borne any lasting fruit. Perhaps the error of these sorcerers and madmen had been that they sought a process, a catalyst, or a power and never a place. Indeed, as the eldest Sister had whispered to him earlier that eve, a place—a literal fountain of youth—was where this unfathomable mystery resided. Anticipation sped the sense of travel, and it felt as if he'd only just stepped away from the feast when the caverns illumed with watery shimmers. The font of youth lay nearby.

"Come," said Eean.

The chamber they came to was a ragged hollow. It was rank with salty mildew and dripping and echoing like ice melting in a metal room—not what he would have expected from a place of such power. What dew fell upon Thackery tasted sugary rather than stale and spit-worthy. Rather often, he found himself licking the droplets that trickled near his lips. The activity took away from the embarrassment of his fumbling—he was cuts and bruises all over—as they navigated toward the far edge of the chamber where water shone and beckoned. "There is a place," Eean had whispered at the dinner table, "where magik can be drunk and years can be washed away. Enough that an old man could again become young. Enough that a hero could see his journey to the end and perhaps to a happiness in the pages yet to be written."

It was a chance to be with his daughters and live again. Such a choice was no choice at all. He'd begged her to take him to this mystery, whatever the price, as soon as possible. Any cost seemed fair for the opportunity to remain with his family. The darkest days were still to come. To leave his girls now would be abandonment, and he'd already lost a family once. The otherworld, including the spirits of his dear wife, Bethanny, and daughter, Theadora, could wait. Morigan and Fionna needed peace in this world before he contemplated leaving it for the next. A desperate affection consumed the old man, and in a haze he arrived before the pool.

From where he stood, the waters looked ordinary and unlike Elemech's scrying pool. A ring of flat stones rose around the dark, liquid oval and was perhaps the only unnatural element of the scene—squat and made for sitting. A sense of indeterminable age radiated there. It was concealed behind a brittle, cracked wall of perception about as adequately as was the apparently young girl with her timeless eyes and ancient carriage. She took his hands to help him kneel. Eean then did the same, and they settled for a moment. Suddenly, Eean held a curved, cruel-looking knife.

"The years must come from somewhere. Otherwise, the order is broken," she said.

Eean clenched the blade in her palm, pulled the knife along it, and cut open her hand. She placed the instrument down and swished her hand in the water. More sweet condensation pattered down on Thackery's face and ran into his lips. He thought he tasted a hint of iron in the droplets.

"Make the most of your years, Thule," said Eean. "People are rarely granted second chances—not like this. We bestow upon thee the highest gift the Green Mother can give. She expects true greatness in return."

"I shall be a weapon, warrior, and conqueror in her name," pledged Thackery.

"Close your eyes, warrior," commanded Eean.

Thus she anointed Thackery. Upon his face, Eean ran markings of blood and water like war paint. She cupped her hands, squeezed her wound, and fed him the blood oath. She made him remove his clothing, and she decorated his chest with more red runes and secrets that tingled his flesh. Lastly, she ordered him to wash himself free of his pain. Her demand became clear when he stepped into the shriveling iciness of the pool. His body seized, and the fullness of his life entered him. The warmth of his kisses with Bethanny. The grotesque feel of the wet rubber of his family's skins clutched in his hands. Sorren's grimace and laughter. Young Gloriatrix calling for him in the smoke of Menos's desolation. One of Mifanwae's songs sung as she swept his tower. Had that been her first day working as his handmaiden? It must have been, since he was still trussed up in casts from his fall and feeling helpless. Then a hundred conversations with little Morigan—always asking questions, which even an irritable man like himself always found the time to answer. Then the Wolf's musk and a rush of his regard for the man. All his existence fought for recall at once, and the frenzy of the memory storm ripped his guts and throat like a vomit of razors and fire as it poured through him and out into the cavern as a scream. A howl, really. Eean hadn't told Thackery of the agony, but it would not have stopped him. For the magik of time, the reversal of years, was a shedding of more than wrinkles and spots. It was a shedding of the past—a cleansing by fire. It was birth, and that was never painless. While Thackery howled and howled, Eean swayed and sang ancient verses in harmony with his horrific music.

In time, the agonies and memories dribbled to whimpers. In one last haggard heave, the pain disappeared from Thackery's body. He collapsed against the rocks and wept, even though the torment had ceased.

"Rise, warrior. You have been reborn," said Eean.

Her shadow and a white and slender foot came near him. Thackery looked past his forearms—lean, youthful, and tanned—to see the miracle worker, and he laughed and wept a little more at the grim beauty staring upon him. He saw her icy skin, ripe breasts, hard curves, and flowing black, gray-streaked hair. Children's clothing hung in a tattered circlet about her waist and neck.

"Do not forget your oath," she said with some force.

"Never."

## IX

"What is that?" wondered Mouse.

Fastidiously as an enslaved charwoman and for ages now, Mouse toiled in a corpse yard of creepy wooden dolls with broken smiles and missing eyes. She pricked herself while stitching tiny coats for the horrible things. One of the figurines, quite drowning in dolls save for his head, winked at her in the light. She dropped her doll to investigate. From out of the mess Ealasyd called her "works in progress," Mouse took a pale, lean, and handsome-angled figurine. She played with his flopping limbs. He was missing hair she knew should be black. He had no yellow smile, either. He was unfinished, but the onyx beads that were his eyes seemed a perfect match for her father's. The doll was missing only a few details and a proper gentleman's suit to make the simulacrum flawless. Mouse nearly muttered Vortigern's name, but Ealasyd spoke first.

"Oh," said the Sister, and she shuffled over. "I tried and tried, but I couldn't find the right shade of yellow for his smile. A lovely smile, if a little creepy—like flowers blooming in a cemetery. I tried daffodil, marigold, toadflax, and silver wattle. I had my poor sister search the woods for what must have been a year. I'm terrible with time, though, so it might have been ten or eighty. Still no luck. It just wasn't right. And if it isn't right, it can't be made."

"An off-white, an aged ivory, is what you are looking for," said Mouse.

In a snap, Ealasyd sprang to motion and rummaged through tiny pots on the paint-splotched, untidy shelf above the one where the dolls spilled out. While she searched, she mumbled to herself. "Periwinkle...midnight...where are all my spring sunshines and grays? Hmm...pigeon, dusk, bone. Oh, that's a nice one. Not quite. Not quite. Ah-ha!"

At last, Ealasyd claimed a pigment, snatched a brush from the shelf, and then took the doll from Mouse. With her hands rather full, she returned to her workbench. In a daring act of balance, she used one foot to kick off whatever was there so she might sit.

"Tusk," declared the Sister when she'd settled. "Right under my nose the whole time."

She broke the wax of her small container, sucked on the end of her paintbrush, and pushed it into the pigment. In a moment, she started painting. "Pins and horsehair," she said. "This should not take long."

Mouse had gotten used to requests. She stood and tried to find the items Ealasyd desired on the highest—and easily the messiest—shelf of the crafter's cupboard. There had been no cataloging or attempt at order. Nonetheless, she found the pins without too much of a fuss. The hair, though, could lie in any number of unmarked sachets. She opened each like a grisly name-day gift and was rewarded with dried spiders, maggot husks, withered chunks of scaly meat, quills, feathers, rabbit paws, rat feet, or any horror a little ghoul would appreciate. Eventually, Mouse discovered something black and as soft as horsehair should be. She went to Ealasyd. By then, the young Sister had completed her painting. Even with such a simple task, she'd managed to deface her fingers and lips with stains. She showed a paint-filled, yellowish smile to Mouse, and it clenched Mouse's heart. Without a doubt, Ealasyd had used the correct color.

"I'll need your help," said Ealasyd, and she patted a spot beside herself.

Once they sat hip to hip, Mouse passed over the horsehair strands. She held some of them while Ealasyd braided the rest into a cultured mane. She should tie it with a ribbon, if Ealasyd kept such an item. Mouse wondered what had happened to her father's ribbon, and she searched herself futilely for the object. Of course, it was lost and blowing through Alabion. Some animal probably had it in its nest. Come the turn of seasons, it would be wet and decayed—much the same as her father. Mouse could not continue making the doll once the memories and pain had her in their grip.

"I still need help." Ealasyd frowned and waved the incomplete hairpiece at her pouting assistant.

"No. I'm sorry. I am finished." Mouse stood.

"Don't you want to know his story?"

"I know his story. It is over. It has ended."

"A story is only ever over once we close the book. There is no ending until then," said the witch innocently.

Mouse could sense a shape and pattern in Ealasyd's words. What did the Sister mean about an ending? Mouse required the bench again. Her anger fizzled away. In Ealasyd's presence, one couldn't stay angry for long, and Mouse spilled out her pain.

"I failed. I did not have the power to stand against Aghna—or any of the evils we've faced," she said.

"Is that what you want? Power?"

Mouse thought. Deep down, power was what she craved. It would be an end to being at the mercy of people or Fate. With might, she could have destroyed the white wolf herself or protected her father. She wanted never to feel not strong enough again.

"Yes," she said.

Ealasyd's gaze gleamed, and her voice shed its honey and sweetness. "Are you sure? Power never leaves its wielder unchanged."

"Yes," repeated Mouse.

Mouse sensed a stirring within the Sister—an ancient shadow. She should have feared the grand presence with whom she suddenly bartered, but it was too late to recant. She'd beseeched the Sisters. She'd asked for Fate's intervention. With great strength, Ealasyd pulled Mouse down and fed a whisper into her ear. Once the secret had passed, the grand shadow lifted from Ealasyd, and she seemed again a cheery and simple witch. Afterward, Mouse could not stay to help Ealasyd complete her doll. She could not sit still with the secret, a worm of fire, gnawing at her nerves. She could hardly keep from running. She asked, almost demanded, that Ealasyd guide her outside. Ealasyd shrugged, sighed, rose, and led them into the dark maze beyond her home.

No one save Elemech saw them leave, and she only shook her head.

## X

"There is a place where the first oaths in Alabion were sworn," the Sister had said. "Any oath forged there will live as long as the Green Mother stays green. We have seen the chieftains of the old world make peace after the longest wars by bleeding onto the stones. The peace between families who carry this promise has never once been broken—even if their names and clans have faded and their descendants have traded swords for spades. Eternity is what you promised her, and if you wish for time itself to know that or any other pledge, this is where those oaths should be made."

When the Wolf stole his bloodmate and parted from the company, he was heady with the wine of excitement. He carried Morigan as quickly as he had on their first night in Eod, and they were down the Sisters' summit in an instant. Morigan's laugh at his careless speed made his pulse thump like the tail he owned in his second skin.

*Where are you taking us*? asked Morigan as they swooshed into the woods. She could have picked at his mind, but that would have ruined the surprise, and she enjoyed the playfulness of her ignorance.

*Not far*, he replied mysteriously. *Close your eyes. Feel my heart, and remember when I first held you like this. I shall never forget.*

In his elation, it took mere leaps to cross the regions of Alabion. Morigan shut her eyes and nuzzled into the scented stubble of his neck. She waited to see where the wolf-carriage would deliver her. All this was so familiar to Morigan: the cradle of warmth and strength, the fluttering of winds that could not touch this safety, and the thundering and huff of the monstrous machine of beast and man that was her bloodmate. As the Wolf had suggested, as it had that dreamy night in Eod, her lover's engine soon swayed her into a bliss of near sleep.

*Open your eyes, my Fawn*, he said sometime later.

Groggily, she slipped to a stand. She held onto what she could of his huge fingers, and they explored the ruins the Wolf had discovered. Winter was a banished ghost to the evening—a feeble specter that ruffled the snowy trees and left a decorative glitter upon the broken stones and ancient pillars. In many spots, no chill could be seen or felt at all. Thriving ivy wound up nearby pillars and created tickling snake-nests for them to step over as they walked toward a deteriorated, rectangular space amid the small ruin. Further eschewing the winter, the plants on these vines bloomed with milky, luminescent flowers that might have fallen from the full, radiant moon above. How sweet the blossoms' nectar smelled to the Wolf and his bloodmate too with her half-wolf senses. She paused, dipped to pluck a flower, and inhaled its loveliness. The shadow standing over Morigan found that her sweetness overpowered any of nature's perfumes. The Wolf growled impatiently.

Morigan glanced to the handsome shadow. *What is it, my Wolf? You are pacing in my heart. What troubles you? Are you nervous?*

*No...yes.*

*You should not be. We were destined to come here. You have hunted a Fate this eve.* She smiled and cast her eyes over the ivy and stone and remembered a vision of this moment—or one soon to come.

*You know this place?* he asked.

*I do. I have seen it before.*

Without explanation, Morigan kissed his hand and rose. She kept the flower and slid it beside her ear. Now she led the Wolf. Destiny charged her blood like lightning. Her body hummed with eagerness, and it sweat from the hot beast of fire in her chest. In time and with guidance, her Wolf would decipher his imbroglio. A stone altar ahead pulled her. They stared at its surface—so old the elements had polished it to glass. In the moonlight, though, sparkled lines and etchings of stories and names carved into the monument. Other tales and persons were grooved into the surrounding looming pillars, none of which time had beaten. The pillars and the altar would be there forever. She must have mouthed the word "forever" while caressing the glassy tomb of history and listening to the whispers of ancient warlords and lovers who had pledged eternal promises on this spot. Then came the Wolf's red and hungry mouth to her ear. His kiss muffled these voices.

*Beyond blood and love, I must challenge myself to think of new ways to pledge my devotion to you,* he confessed, and he pulled back her silky hair to paint her neck with his tongue and lips.

*Which is why we are here. You wish to write our story on these eternal stones of promise.*

*Yes. Our names and our love. The story of a lonely wolf and a maiden fair. We have what we have made together,* Siogtine, *your blade.* He squatted, and his huge hand glided down her chest and rested against the metal at her waist. *I do not think myself a boastful man, but I want the world to hear my roar. I would carve our love into these stones. I shall share our truth with*

*Talwyn, who will undoubtedly glorify it into a spectacle. But I care not. I shall tell any person who asks how and why you are mine and I am yours. I would visit these stones every hundred years we spend together and add to our tale.*

*A noble wish*, said Morigan. *But that is not the only reason why you have come to this place.* She turned in his arms and studied his beauty.

*Is...is it not?* he asked.

*You know you cannot keep this dream of me forever. Do not fear losing the virgin Fawn you first chased. She has been hunted, claimed, and eaten. I have eaten her. I am your mate. I am a woman and a warrior, and one day, if we are blessed, I shall be a mother.*

The Wolf blushed, yet he could not remove his prowling hands from her slight waist or stop himself from huffing her flower petal and forest scent. She was not chaste with her affection either as she ran her fingers up and down the granite and fur of his chest.

*The hunt must end one day, and the feast must begin.* She smiled. It was as sharp and dangerous as the charm he wielded. *Do you really think we came here just to scribble on stones? So you could profess what I already know? We shall do those things, I suppose. But I have a purpose on this night too, my Wolf. I have seen the wet glory of our bodies pressing into one another in dreams. I am done with dreams. We shall not have many moments to ourselves in the days and years ahead. We shall not have the time to show how deep and hot our need flows. I am tired of waiting. Tell me you are the same. Say you want me.*

She spoke true. His beast could not discern the rusty perfume of fertility upon her—only the dizzy pollen of her seduction. His man could not think of any reasons why this should not be. How white the moon burned. It could not have been brighter or more arousing to the Wolf. All the world appeared ready for their union. Morigan's heart pounded as lustily as did an elk's before he sank his teeth into its flesh. The Wolf would never ravage her like that—even though she filled his stomach and loins with a scorching hunger. What scraps of clothing he wore began to tighten over his expanding desire.

As much an animal as he, Morigan helped him discard them and then took the veined organ of his passion in both hands. They shuddered, and their emotions—roars of fire and bursts of light—flowed back and forth between them. He gasped out a response.

"I do...I ache...I hunger."

"Good, Wolf." She laughed and stroked his meat.

It was a symphony of unrestrained cries—a lust that conquered fear, death, and reason. Their bodies were copper and ivory instruments ashine with sweat. The Wolf could not simply plunder his mate. She was clay that needed softening, and for hourglasses he coaxed her open with kisses and thick fingers. Upon the ancient slab, he laid her down. He loosened every knot from her neck to the tautness held in her strong hourglass hips. He moved to her silky, soft buttocks and down to the tiny toes of her feet, which he nibbled on as greedily as he did the rest of her white, luscious skin. In turn, Morigan fearlessly explored him, as he was her clay to soften too—harder clay, though, that required rougher force to make it yield. So she slapped his muscled, hairy canyons, tenderly bit his chest and nipples, and slipped spit-wet fingers into places of pleasure quite new to her ancient lover—ones she remembered from the naughtiest tomes in Thackery's tower. She teased his manhood with tongue and hand. At times, they twisted together like contortionists into a figure eight of limbs. He moaned and licked at her pink, quivering secret as she swallowed down part of his sword—a magik trick that its immensity fit into her beauteous mouth. Once the Wolf found a birthmark on the underside of one of his Fawn's gloriously full breasts. He worshipped the magnificent imperfection as if it were a line of Holy Scripture. He mumbled poetry between the kisses, licks, and wolfish bites he gave. Many times, he sprayed his seed, and she wet his fingers and beard with the drippings of her ecstasy. Wantonly, they used these essences as lubrication for further pleasure, and not once did they feel shame at their animal acts, their sinful reek, or their oiled skins of sweat and lust. As much as they came, their passion only rose. Fires and starlight within them consumed their senses with spots and fevers. When at last Morigan seemed ready, tender, and able to accept his full and throbbing weight, it was she who laid the Wolf down on dirt and snow. It was she who would wear the crown and conquer. The vision of her lowering herself with her breasts as high and white as the moon, the parted sigh of pleasure on her temptress's mouth, and the teeth-baring hiss as they finally slid into their lock and key of flesh would be a fantasy for the Wolf in all the ages yet to come.

*My Wolf...*

*My Fawn...*

Roaring now and riding the waves inside each other, they were unsure of fingers, faces, and voices. The Wolf and Morigan came again—and again—before finding their panting, barking rhythm. In a whirl of time, heat, and starry spins, she rode him. She returned his bites, which were sometimes bloody and slightly fanged but never deep. She rolled with him but was never bruised or scuffed by the ground, as his arms always shielded her. Never had Morigan felt so physically and emotionally full inside. The Wolf could also not recall having been so deeply planted and so utterly connected while communing through flesh. Their wholeness was a wine neither could stop drinking.

When finally their passion ebbed, they found themselves far from the altar in the melting snow of the forest nearby. Morigan was entwined in the Wolf's great limbs and warm from his furnace. They stank so strongly of each other's scents that their reek lost its offense and was all they knew. Day had come. Last they checked, it had been evening. Neither lover really had words—only smiles, gasps, and kisses to explain his or her bliss. Eventually, the Wolf rose to an elbow, spooned some ice in his palm, and melted it to water to feed his Fawn. She drank from his hand, and the sensuous sight tugged at his raw loins. While watching her untapped sensuality, his desire stilled. He gazed upon her in dawning wonder, and he saw her as a woman, wife, friend, lover, and teacher. Morigan's star pulsed as calming as ever within him—perhaps brighter than before. She'd lost none of her virtue, and for that, he felt humbled.

*Are you hungry?* he asked.

*I should be.* She grinned, and her hand wandered the path of fur to his groin. *I suppose I'm starving, come to think of it. Mostly for this, though some other meat would do.*

They laughed and tumbled and kissed. They did not start the cycle of lovemaking again, as they did not have another day to spare. They'd left their companions alone with three conniving witches, and they had new dangers in the East to pursue. As this was their feast, famine would now follow. Once this hourglass ended, they would be a man and woman of purpose. The lovers they'd been last night would have to wait until another sliver of time could be stolen. They each went for a long pee in the bushes, winced, and laughed from how sore they'd made themselves. Meeting again at the altar, they shared final lingering kisses and gropes. Then the Wolf swept Morigan up and took her to the various piles of her clothing and wares. He paused to study his glorious mate while she dressed.

*I meant what I said, my Fawn. I would like to write our tales before we leave. I would like us to visit this place again and again. Hopefully forever.*

Forever. She pondered the bronze and naked mountain—the sum of all things noble, wild, and honorable that Geadhain had borne. She would want and fight for nothing less. Eternity seemed too short a time to spend with him.

XI

Eean returned nude and slightly older than Elemech, who was startled neither by the change nor by the man her sister carried in her arms like a slumbering prince. Ealasyd was either with Mouse or off chasing grubs and faeries somewhere. Maybe she was even with the changeling, who'd hurried away to show his thought-to-be darling Elemech's gift. Deeply under Dream's waters, the drunken scholar did not wake as Eean laid Thackery on the pallet beside him, and no one bothered her while she changed into her threadbare yet comfortable blue kirtle and skirts.

"You look a bit more yourself," said Elemech as she lounged by her pool. She drank from one of the ever-flowing pitchers of mead. "I've never liked it when there are two of you younglings around. It's dizzying."

Eean came to sit beside her sister and noticed she seemed quite drunk. Pulling up her skirt, she dipped her feet in the icy, fathomless waters as her sister had done.

Elemech passed the pitcher without Eean's needing to ask. "Quite a few bargains you made this evening." She snorted.

"Only two, dear sister." Eean sighed and swigged a bit of drink. Then she pointed to Thackery in his swaddling of sheets. His angular middle-aged face wore a chiseled frown, and his salt-and-pepper beard pronounced his handsomeness even in the dimness. "He paid his dues with all the blood and sorrow life's given him. The Green Mother decided how many years, not I. She must believe he is worthy to have granted him so many."

"And...my daughter? You practically passed her to Brutus's son in a gown of virgin white," snapped Elemech.

"A bit late for sentimentality, isn't it?" quipped Eean. "Before the soldiers go off to war, it is always nice to stop in a port of call to find...inspiration. Morigan is a warrior and a woman, and she has urges just the same as her mate. I gave them nothing they did not want. I told the Wolf only of the Stones of Time—where he could record his tale for all the ages. Morigan I'm certain had other ideas for their time alone."

Elemech rested her head on her sister's shoulder, and the eldest stroked her hair and kissed her head with tenderness.

"Even I had my hands in the pie tonight," muttered Elemech. "I didn't poke it as much as you, though. Or Ealasyd."

Eean looked down. "Oh?"

"I think she's done worse than any of our games tonight." Elemech's frown went deadly cold. "She gave a choice to the dead man's daughter. A dark choice. I think she will do it. I believe she will let him in."

"Do you really fear the Gray Man that much, Sister?"

"I do," said Elemech, and she shivered.

# XVI

# HAND OF DOOM

I

*Queen Lila and her lover stand high upon rock. Winds ruffle her ear-drums, and thick clouds drape the sunlight in a drifting white curtain that parts now and again to allow golden spots to land upon a fertile, unformed prairie. She is nearly lulled into the comfort of her companion's warm, hard body, which presses around her in an embrace. Then she realizes his temperature, smell of iron shavings and sweat, and hirsuteness feel utterly wrong against her flesh.*

*"You are not Magnus," she hisses, and she tries to twist away.*

*The man doesn't let her go. His hands clasp her wrists and painfully pull her arms across her stomach in opposite directions. In this Dream, she does not have her sorcery to call upon, and she screams at her helplessness— a weakness unfelt since her days with the Arhad, or her assault by her husband. As much as she thrashes, she cannot escape her captor's heavily tanned, thick limbs. Dark, hot, and unyielding as sun-cooked copper shackles are they. Her captor laughs—a drum of a sound—at her attempts. He holds her against his great strength and whispers to her. All she can do is recoil slightly from the stink of his strange breath. It's as if he has sucked on metal coins.*

422

*"I would have saved us all," he says. "If only people had seen the wisdom of what I offered. The prosperity of a realm without the Kings' whims to rule it. I would have broken the yoke of the true oppressors."*

*"Taroch," she gasps.*

*Although the warlord lived before her time, there are few beings—ghosts or otherwise—who have ever challenged the Kings, and Magnus's descriptions of Taroch's cultivated, cruel voice and copper skin betray him. The warlord's ghost manipulates the Dream, and he is before her. They are close enough to kiss. Forthwith, his ancient tribal charisma paralyzes her. He has sleek braids and a groomed beard—dark-blond hair peeks from his opened shirt. His gaze is much like hers but more golden than amber. The warlord is a keg of muscle, and his bombastic presence emanates the air of a giant. He is not wholly of man. Still, she does not know what starry blood has mingled itself into his makeup. What is it that makes him shimmer and entice like a scattering of gemstones glittering in a pool of sunlight? Richness oozes from him. It is seductive and as subtle as the lick he gives his thin lips while he appraises his captive—pleased by some part of her. He wears the loose, starkly crimson tunic of a Sorsettan. Even his clothes are made to allure one to sin and desire. She is enraptured now.*

*"Yes," he says, and he rubs her face roughly and sensuously with his hands. "You are like me. Not like them. We are kindred beings. Outcasts of the divine. We must work so much harder than they do to leave our marks on this world. For we are not born into greatness but become it. I was nothing—a sheepherder in the lands you see beneath us. Lands that would one day hold the city named and dedicated to my defeat." The spirit laughs and then flashes like the flip of a coin from handsome royal to grimacing brute. He shakes her. "Men worshipped me once. True adulation. They saw what my mortality had achieved—until the Kings ruined their love of me and sold me as a tyrant. Why should I help you with your revenge? Why should I give you anything?"*

*Lila is not aware of having asked this vengeful wraith for his service. She is a passenger to her dark motives—asleep when she is awake. Even in dreams such as this, her intentions are unclear. Taroch calms and caresses her anew.*

*"Nobodies. We are nobodies together. You can change that. I see it. You can make my name live again. You can make the world see my glory, and since it would not take my mercy, it can have my hate. The Pale Lady came to me too in my pit of oblivion. She woke me from the long sleep. She told me*

*your fair hand would rebirth my greatness. You don't need Magnus anymore. I shall be your partner in sin. Let our black wedding be grand, wicked, and full of doom."*

"*Pale Lady? What wedding?" exclaims Lila.*

*The warlord interrupts her. A hunger is within Taroch—a need come from abandonment and festered into a lust for all things gold and precious. She is powerless as he kisses her with his iron-and-silver-tanged mouth. Memories are returning to her now and the mist of days past taking shape. A promise. In one memory, a black shadow is lurking over her. Sometimes it is whispering, and more than once she answers it back. Did she meet the shadow first in the hospices of Eod? Did she sense it as a chill in the corner or as a reflection of something wetly black, churning, and grand in the eyes of a dying wretch on his hospital cot? Aye. She believes that is where the darkness found her. For where else would the Pale Lady—Death—lurk but around the beds of those slipping into the abyss? Death's promise wriggles into her head like maggots—its insinuations of ruin and doom.*

*No! This is not I! I am no monster! she rails, and she pushes Taroch's probing lust out of her mouth. He falls apart into a cloud of hissing insects. Flies, dust, and locusts thicken the air. She is choking as if Taroch's tongue has detached and crawled down her esophagus. When she sees what she had ejected—the glistening, bilious stew of white grubs and retch splashing over her fingers—she is nauseated. She vomits further from the sight and stench. How can this be so real? she wonders deliriously. She falls and dashes her knees on rock, and that pain is as real as it could be. It fills her consciousness with spectacular stars. Spinning, spewing, weeping, and chewed at by buzzing scavengers, Lila collapses into ruin. She is at the shrieking limit of her sanity when the hospice shadow abruptly displays its dark reverence before her sight. It is grotesquely gargantuan and manifest, this monolith of ash, dust, maggots, black slops of oil, and clattering bones. Death is all she can see, smell, or taste on the river of her vomit. Death covers the earth, sky, and sun of the dreamscape. She is so small, shivering, and brittle. She could be one of its wormy discharges—a maggot and nothing grander.*

**"Remember your duty,"** *says Death.* **"Do not fail me."**

*As a warning, or simply to stress her maggoty insignificance, the ebon mountain of rot falls upon Lila. She is washed in decay and drowned in death.*

## II

Erik needed to hold the queen until her screaming ended. Every night since boarding the cargo vessel and since that dastardly arm joined them, nightmares had plagued the queen. The only curative for her thrashing fits seemed to be Erik's strong arms to restrain her until the wave of terror ebbed away. An instant always came right after the fear evaporated when Lila's golden eyes reflected all the warmth and light of a woman whom he would cross oceans, swords, and lines of virtue for. That beauty lingered only for an instant. Then the cold mistress, the Queen of Sorrows, reclaimed her body and reached for her grisly relic as a child would reach for her favorite teddy to ward off the monsters. Then she paid him not a speck of attention more unless a meal or duty was required from him. More than once, he had caught her caressing her face with Taroch's withered fingers, and he felt certain the relic contributed to her madness. He wanted to throw the unholy thing overboard and end this dark quest before it ruined them completely. Alas, she never parted with the arm of her new lover, and her gradual insanity quashed his own secret desire for her. Ultimately, however, he had his honor and his promise to Magnus.

After settling the queen in the cabin's only bed—he had a blanket and some creaking boards that sufficed for a soldier's needs—he spent the morning watching the icy shoreline of the Northlands through a frosted portal. Though not of an artistic temperament, he nonetheless could feel inspiration in the mist-rolling hills of snow, the vales of glittering trees, the black, fatted mammals bleating on rocks, and the flocks of birds as grand and shrill as the winds that rocked the waves. He regretted he'd never explored all their frozen valleys and lakes of glass. He would not on this adventure either. Perhaps he could once the war ended. *Which war?* he asked himself with bitter humor.

For there were two threats to Eod and Geadhain, and Menos was only the first. Should his queen's mission succeed and Menos fall, Brutus would be the next—and true—trial for Geadhain. Dour as an old hangman, he frowned for the people of Sorsetta that the queen had thrown as bait for the mad king's jaws. She'd sent no aid or soldiers—just a thin suggestion of danger to the Keeper of Gorgonath. She'd left thousands to die so she could clandestinely chase whatever madness she pursued. Quick deaths he wished for every man, woman, and child in Sorsetta. Any end seemed preferable to a hollow, black-eyed existence.

The freighter swayed onward, and Erik watched the sunrise break over the Northlands. He enjoyed the sparkling sight for a moment and then went to fetch the morning meal. Had he known his honor would be reduced so fast and so far to that of a courier and errand boy for a deranged sorceress, he would have turned his back to the mission when Lila offered him the chance—or so he liked to believe. He sulked and left the cabin. The queen stayed swaddled in the bedclothes and stared into an empty corner of the sparse chamber while caressing Taroch's pruned arm.

Once up in the biting winter air and surrounded by the shouts of happy men, he sighed. He was glad to be free of the queen's lonely company. He walked among the tied and tarp-covered crates, and he hailed hatted and bundled mariners, people he knew in passing who were genial and asked how he—John, the name under which he traveled—and the Lady Siobhan were doing. "Lady Siobhan's doing very well. Still not faring so kindly with the waves," he lied.

She'd not been up to see the sky since they'd caught the freighter by chance. It had stalled to repair a broken rudder on a shore many spans up the Feordhan from where the entity had tossed them. (He dismissed the chill flash of that encounter as it resurfaced.) The *Fleet Otter* and its captain and crew were good salt-of-the-earth people. All had homes and families in the smaller fiefs of Central Geadhain that they saw only seasonally but loved year-round. They had no ambitions or interest in the politics and wars of higher men. Nonetheless, as Erik strode around helping with rigging and chatting about the banalities of the weather, the occasional whisper of war, mad kings, and fleets of crowes disrupted the day's pleasantness.

"My sister in Fairfarm sent a letter warning me of any southern voyages. I told her we'd be sticking to the Upper Feordhan," said a tanned, nearly toothless man. His name—Jack—was the same as his occupation.

Rigorously, he smoked his pipe while talking to his mate and coiling rope. Erik paused to hear them speak.

"A dam. A damned dam," continued Jack. "Made of metal and magik."

"Right more of the mad king's lunacy, I say," replied his fellow sailor. "What's the good of an Immoral, anyhow, when we has no need to be ruled or kept safe, and they be causing more buggering than blessings? I say get rid of them. Both. I has no sides, and no one wins in war, but maybe Menos and that Iron bitch will do the deed. Not right. Not pretty. Certainly done, though. We has no need for legends—only technomagik and the sweat and thinking of men."

"*Immortal*, you idiot." Jack laughed.

"I ain't a schoolmaster, and I never been schooled."

"That much is for certain."

The sailors cackled themselves into coughs, and Erik and his dark cloud of thoughts left when they asked him why he stood there with his thumb up his arse. As part of the inner circle of power, Erik rarely heard the genuine opinions of those who paid taxes and tilled the land. It was not the first time in this voyage that people had spoken of dissatisfaction with his kingfather or the Immortals in general. With so many advances in technomagik, the great miracles of the Kings faded increasingly into irrelevance. Men and their short lives did not appreciate that these advances had come only because of the Kings and their safe harbors of thought and culture. A generational rift was growing. On one side were those who appreciated the old order for what it had nurtured, while on the other were those who enjoyed the fruits without understanding the seeds that had sowed them. One small caveat was that the people still did not widely believe Magnus had been defeated. A great fog of mystery shrouded Magnus's fate, and the gossip hounds could not pierce it—and would not chance their reputations with the darkest rumors of his demise lest he return. At least the lips of the palace appeared sealed, and most soldiers who'd made it back from Mor'Keth possessed too much honor or terror ever to speak of what they'd seen.

Those tongues could not be held forever, though. Secrets and whispers had already leaked out. Erik grasped at the hope Magnus lived. *I wish you were here, Kingfather, for all your works are decaying into the dust of the desert from which you raised them. I hope, however foolishly, that you live still, and will carry us through to one last age of wonders.*

Erik stopped at the ship's railing and glared into the dawn. Although the sun didn't answer his question about the kingfather, the uplifting, crimson aurora reminded him that light—and hope—always rose anew. One had only to wait for it.

He hurried to find the second mate, check their course, and get some food for his queen. As miserable as she appeared, she should eat, and he needed his strength too. For beyond this period of darkness, the sun would rise again, and life would soldier on. Preferably, Magnus would be with them then, since Geadhain would be a sad, bitter mother without him.

### III

Unexpectedly, the queen greeted Erik as he stepped into the cabin. She was even kind. "Oh. You're back. You were gone such a while I nearly started to sleep again." She hugged Taroch's arm for comfort. "Such horrid dreams."

As the queen had become less herself and more repugnant, so too had Erik discovered many new and less pleasant characteristics within himself—including impudence. "Perhaps it's that grotesque thing to which you cling. It poisons your head," he said with as much politeness as he could stomach. He threw a wax-papered parcel on the bed. "Food. You should eat." He appraised her sunken eyes and frazzled hair. "Maybe use the lavatory too when you have a chance. In another morning, we shall arrive as close to the Iron Valley as this ship will pass."

The *Fleet Otter* was en route to trade the goods of Central Geadhain with a settlement around the far northern bend of the Feordhan. Valholom, the place was called—a name as Northern sounding as he'd ever heard. However, he and the Lady Siobhan were not to be taken that far. They were to be left on the nearest deserted shore to Menos, where Kor'Keth weakened into a rock-and-boulder beach outside the Iron Valley. While Erik brooded and scowled unwittingly at the queen, she was at least eating and had placed down her ghastly lover to get at the food. Perhaps her separation from the object restored some of her nobility.

"I know you think I am horrible," she mumbled, crumbs falling sloppily about. "I am, I suppose. However, this is what war and loss do to a person. I warned you before you stepped on this road with me."

She had. This was true. Erik came to her bedside and sat. "I do not think you are horrible," he said. "I think you are lost."

"I agree," she whispered, and she put down the stale biscuit she held. With more sadness than bitterness, she went on. "I have been very lost without Magnus. Each day passes without his coldness, and still I shiver more. I cannot reconcile myself to being alone. A thousand years of wholeness replaced by..." The word she sought choked her. "I'm starting to wonder what it all means. If I was ever really free in choosing my life. My husband even—loving him was no choice." She glanced at Erik. "I do have you, though. I have chosen you. You are something to hold on to."

"My queen."

"Lila." She mixed a laugh and a sigh together. "Call me Lila. That is what Magnus called me when he found me. When my days were darkest."

Gently, Erik took the queen's hands. "What he will call you once more."

The queen caressed the warrior's cheek as she would a son's—as if she were mourning his father's passing. "He is dead, Erik. If not dead, then in a torment no man—immortal or of earthly flesh—can endure. My dreams...I shall tell you so you may lay your hope to rest. In some of the dreams that suffocate me while I sleep, I have seen what Brutus did to him before he died. Atrocities of sin. Sacrileges of brother to brother. Rape, savagery, and defilements never before witnessed in time. I would spare myself a bit of pain if I knew these were only my worst imaginings, but I believe they are the cries of his ghost—a flutter of horror that echoes in the shell of the one with whom he shared his blood. If by some slim and impossible chance he lives..." She shook her head and took her hand away. "If he lived, I would feel him. Feel something. My insides are hollow, so he is dead. We should accept that. Brutus will join him in eternity too once we have dealt with Menos."

As quickly as that, their moment ended, and she snatched up the withered limb.

"I would like to know what you intend to do," Erik said mutinously.

"It is better you do not," replied the queen.

She would say no more. He could not stay to watch her fondle the remains of the dead warlord, which seemed almost to glow when she petted it. He left the revolting pair for cold winds and fresher space. She could stay in the dark where she was determined to belong.

IV

Though pulled back and forth in an emotional tug-of-war over his queen—love, lust, loathing, pity, and remorse—Erik realized he'd been drawn too deeply into her spell to think on his own. This was not what Magnus would have wanted for him. He would not declare the King's death—not until he beheld the beautiful corpse with his own weeping eyes.

As soon as he stepped on the deck, all these troubles blew away with the blustery wind. It was a gay and strange day, with a soft storm borne on a few black clouds amid a sea of sunshine. The strong, fickle winds saw to it that many hands were needed to batten down the ship. At once, Erik put his broad back to work.

In the evening when the storm had subsided, the tired sailors gathered on deck for some well-earned warmed ale. They passed pipes and raised cheers and reminisced about the lives awaiting them elsewhere. When the circle looked to Erik for a few words, he froze before replying.

"I...I am thankful for this voyage. For our fortune in finding you when we were stranded," he said, and smiled.

"Here, here!" cried Jack, and he nearly slipped off his crate from liquor or excitement.

The rest of the crew joined in the cheer. When they had calmed, the captain, a lean and leathery fox of the sea, glanced at Erik. "You have an angler's silence to you and the strength of a Fairfarm ox," the captain said gruffly. "It's a shame you cannot stay longer. The pleasure of meeting has been ours, and I speak for all these old goats. Should you ever choose to leave the employment of your noble lady and be without a land or title to hold, the *Fleet Otter*—or any seaworthy vessel—would be glad to have you."

*A fine dream,* mused Erik. *To sail sea and river and blow wherever the wind sees fit to lead.* It was not a dream for him, however—not now. The sea fox tipped his hat and raised his mug. He had read the man's pause perfectly. "Once the world has settled into its new shape, perhaps," he suggested. "She still has much settling to do. That's why I prefer the water for now. It's where her chaos is ever the same and her mood always moody."

"Speaking of moody, how is that fine lass with whom you share your cabin? Staying safe and warm, eh? Perhaps a bit of tonic this morning to ease her seasickness?" Jack winked.

Erik flushed at the implication. It also dawned upon him that he hadn't attended to the queen once that day other than to deliver her breakfast. Surely he should check up on her.

"His mistress," said the sea fox, and he partook in a short laugh with the rest of his crew. "Not like you lot and your unclean minds would think. She is a real lady. I get that sense of her. A noble, I would say. Where have you come from again? Southreach, was it?"

"Yes," said Erik. Quite gradually, he'd learned to tell a lie without even a tingle of disappointment. "Lady Siobhan has family east of Menos, which is where we are headed. She will stay there until the storms of war have passed."

"Wise," agreed the captain. "We shall stay away for the season as well and pray our loved ones have taken our advice to stay out of the path of Iron tyrants and mad kings. What else can men do but hide from the forces that be rain and thunder?"

*A glum way to end the day*, thought Erik. Still, he wanted a bit of rest before they reached the Iron Valley, which the cartographer and nest-watcher claimed would be on the morrow. He bade the sailors good night, good fortune, and good sleeps, and then he slowly wandered down the stairs into the hold. If his pace was lazy and he held onto the knob to his cabin for sands, it was because he floated—a little drunk—in dreamy waves. Something about the captain's offer made his vision flutter with imaginings of himself at a wheel, wind in his hair, and gulls crying in his ears. Erik was not a dreamer or a planner or one who looked to tomorrow with any great expectation. At that moment, he realized he'd never really envisioned a future that did not center on his duties to his kingfather. That day, however, he'd found a possible future of his own—a blue bride and master. A commitment and love whose only control over him would be how passionately she filled his vessel's sails with her song.

V

In the morning, Erik and the queen hopped into a dinghy with Jack and the sea fox, who felt he owed the travelers a send-off for the lady's generous fare. They rowed to the tumbling, water-slogged quarry of the Iron Valley's beachfront. The sun shone brightly and the farewells between the three men were also golden. The queen stayed somber, silent, and as uncommonly pale as she had become of late. Thankfully, her severed friend was trundled out of sight in a bundle under her arm. Standing in the water and watching the dinghy slowly recede into the sunrise, Erik waved a final time to the sailors and drew this scene in his memory. This would be his last dawn before the darkness, he felt.

"Why are we standing here?" asked his relentless mistress.

He turned and splashed toward the shore. Once through the wettest, rockiest shallows and onto dry land, they paused on the beach so the queen could decide on their direction. To their left rose a topple of ancient boulders and massive stone slats. *The warped spine of a dead giant*, thought Erik. This was Kor'Keth as it had fallen hundreds of years ago after the earthquake. A dense forest to their right sprawled and climbed to green, prickling heights of pine. They looked back to the Iron Valley. Only because the day was so blue and bright, Erik thought he saw the black spire of Menos beneath a threatening, purple cloud beyond. The queen must have noticed it as well, as she too stared in that direction.

"If you haven't guessed by now, we are headed to the Iron Mines," said the queen, and she unwrapped her piece of Taroch. "All will be made clear once we arrive there. I promise."

With that, she began to walk in the direction of the Iron Valley. Erik marched quietly along behind her. Soon the woods enfolded them in cool darkness, and there was nothing to speak of for two persons feeling sick with dread. Sweet birdsongs and the rustle and waft of pines reminded Erik of life's wonder and of his mission to destroy this glory. Bitterly, he stamped his qualms into the dirt where his honor lay. He would finish his task as a weapon. He would do this for the queen and for the love of his kingfather, but there would be no more services for her come the morrow. *You might ruin yourself, my queen, but I shall not follow you off the cliff of doom. I care too much for this world—and my soul. I shall save you if you can be saved.*

*Still, I shall not corrupt myself beyond the dark deed you plan, and I shall save myself first.*

Bold, dark promises did he swear. These vows he would never have taken or contemplated as a loyal son of Magnus. If the queen needed shelter later, he might still take her to Carthac. With equal uncertainty, he might walk away and wash his hands of the sins he was sure she meant to commit. He imagined himself hopping on the nearest northbound boat and discovering the joys of being a frontiersman. A peculiar sensation stirred within him. It was a whirl of fear and thrill—the rush of rebellion.

That day they stopped only to relieve themselves and eat the rations the *Fleet Otter*'s crew had given them. Night cast sly gray shadows from stars that hid in invisible clouds. It was in that silvery, white-outlined dark that Erik noticed the forest's sickness—the crumpled bushes and fallen pines. Decay seemed the fitting description, for he spotted black, unnaturally withered trails in the tall verdure and smelled mossy rot in the split logs they bypassed. In a few more sands, limestone claimed the trees.

The echo of their scuffling feet announced the travelers to the waiting heap of broken towers—the ziggurat of blackness that was the mouth of the Iron Mines. From somewhere in Erik's memory stirred a nightmarish scene of riding with Magnus through a crevasse in Kor'Khul.

*"Do you see the stain?" asks Magnus. He pulls out his gleaming sword and points at glimmers in the dunes that Brigada trots past. "Two tribes fought here. Those are their weapons in the sand. Still, after hundreds of years. I would say no warrior of either side lived. Not one."*

*Erik doesn't have to look far to see this stain. Underneath his puffing, bothered mount, the sand is as gray and fine as graveyard dust. In the high rock-walled valley, the moonlight fails to reach them. It is as though they have been cast in a black silk veil, and the wind is as chilly as the angriest of Magnus's tempers. When Erik studies the shadows, which seem almost painted on, they seem so deep and thick that he loses himself to their folds and lurches with vertigo. So he looks straight ahead to the taunting shimmer of moonlight that is a gateway out of the great crack—these two black hands of stone that feel ready to close and crush them like flies—and he tries to be bold while shivering.*

*"Caedentriae," mutters the king.*

*The king does not explain this word, and he tells their small party to spur their horses and hurry through. When they are out of the groove of darkness and cold, Erik takes a gasp of freedom. He has escaped from something—a ghost or a presence. He has survived a graze with the other side.*

As Erik and Lila walked up to the Iron Mines, he felt that forgotten shiver again. It was as if watchers were everywhere—a coliseum of shades cheering on the rasping breeze. What could Lila possibly hope to summon in this malevolent place besides more evil?

The queen stopped before a crooked upright well that belched moldering gas in their faces. Great stones appeared to have been thrown or dragged away from the collapsed timber-framed entrance. The clean, chalky fractures amid the soot indicated a recent upheaval. *Stranger and more wicked by the speck,* thought Erik. Something seemed to have made a path for them and wanted them to go on. The voice upon Taroch's Rest perhaps? Was it here? Clenched and trembling, Erik glanced around for a dark figure spying on them from atop a rock. He looked for someone highlighted in the moonlight but spotted nothing.

"We must go down," said the queen.

Erik hoped the woman possessed the barest sense to conjure them a light. Maybe she would in a speck, but for now she walked into the dark curtain. Without question, she would leave him there, and he quickly stepped into oblivion himself and then fumbled in the musty tunnel until he found a hand that thankfully was not Taroch's. In fact, the warlord's limb made for a ghastly torch with its subtle green pulse. For once, its repulsiveness had a purpose besides inducing nausea.

Even if Erik had stayed and scoured the toppled shadows of the Iron Valley, he would never have seen the darkest among them—a figment of black with a sliver of white. Once the queen and her champion were deep into the nightmare, the shadow slunk over the tumbled land and followed them into the mines.

VI

By the Kings, the air smelled unholy. Erik didn't think one could distill evil into attar. However, in the Iron Mines, as dust untouched by men or mice feet for centuries whirled from their passage, he tasted every nasty flavor in the greasy ash that blew upon him and slithered its way into his mouth—charcoal, singed fat, and the zinc bitterness of powdered bones. Onward they shuffled through precarious buckled tunnels that did not threaten them with dust or noise. The utter stillness was more unnerving that the crashings of a collapse would have been. Skeletons scowled at them from ash banks and were stretched to leering and heinous distortions from the fell light of Taroch's arm. Once, Erik saw two bony hands reaching out of their heaps and clasped together. They had been killed while either praying or being pulled to safety. *Romantic or horrific?* he wondered. *Probably both.* He knew the story of the Iron Mines—at least all of it one needed to hear. Tens of thousands had been crushed to death under rock by technomagikal greed. Erik was not as versed in this history as the queen, however, and after a while she spoke jarringly in the soundlessness.

"Thackery was a wise man," she said. "When we became friends, he told me of his flight to Eod. You would not know this, but he flew others out of the Iron City before—and after—he left it himself. He braved the stony path above us, the winds, and the dire footholds of the Iron Valley. He knew all there is to know about this magnificent grave."

*Magnificent.* It was not the word Erik would have used.

The queen continued and grew excited by her own tale. "Do you know why the mountain fell? Many know of the toll and a few know of the aftershock in Menos. Almost none is old enough to know the science behind the disaster, and Menos has done much to see that minds and books forget. Thackery's curse—the curse of his whole family—is being too clever. They dig and dig until they unbury a truth. At times, they pull up something that really should be left as is. So Thackery knew what should not be known. When we go a little deeper, then you will too."

*A little deeper? How far into this abyss can we go?* Erik wondered. As a man of the salt forests—a dry, inhospitable place honeycombed with caves and pitfalls—Erik possessed a sense of depth and navigation. Apparently, the queen did as well—or some diabolical intuition guided her. She never once paused to consider which path to take. He wondered whether her certainty in this maze was another sign of their damnation. What voices led her? What being had prepared this road for their coming? Even without Thackery Thule's genius, he could still unravel a few threads in this mystery. Cold visions came upon him in the dark of a bone-raking whisper, his flesh scuttling with maggots and weevils, and the gurgling of his body as it rotted from within, was squeezed in the vise of a hand surely as large as the mountain atop them, and then tossed away. *Go east. Finish what you have begun.* Death must have been the queen's shepherd. Death wanted her to complete a task. He could not imagine that Death would want to bring life and verdure to this crypt. The queen had come to commit an atrocity.

Where was Death now? In panting terror, he looked around, but he noted only dust, ash, and gloom. Death would be here somewhere. It had rolled out the carpet of welcome. Hesitantly, he considered telling the queen of the powers with which she bargained and of the shadow that must be trailing them. When he called her name, though, her green, sneering countenance turned to face him, and this challenged most of his bravery.

"What?" she hissed.

"You...should consider what you are doing. One last time."

"No." She shook the glowing arm at him. "You should consider your place. And your promises. I shall not keep you to your word, if you have lost your honor and wish to flee. I shall come to no great harm. The souls of the lost want me here. I can feel them."

As she closed her eyes, he felt a breeze—the first he had felt since entering the tunnel. It was not natural wind, however, and as it picked up force, its icy, wet kiss wriggled right under Erik's clothing. A billow of debris whirled within it and surged with the hints of wailing faces. Erik shielded himself and screamed as the blast passed through him.

A speck later, the fright was over. The wind had howled off. The queen laughed maniacally at his fear, and she continued cackling as she carried on walking. She abandoned him in the dark with the skeletons and their ghosts. At the risk of becoming one of them and unsure of which way his legs would take him, Erik ran—toward the mad sorceress, as it turned out.

VII

These were the longest hourglasses of Erik's life. Magnus had once told him the legend of a man cursed by an ancient witch. He was doomed forever to push a rock up a hill, only to have the stone tumble down again when he'd reached the top. Somewhere on Geadhain, the man still labored with his rock—although the witch herself was long dead. Erik's tale also included a witch and a cursed man. The rock was his attachment to the woman whom he followed in the dark. This affection of his was so twisted with wounded, unrequited love, honor for the dead, and a crippled sense of duty that it was akin to a narcotic. No matter the speeches he gave himself or his surges of willpower, he could not wean himself off Lila. Truly, he did not know whether he loved her or wanted to end her compassionately. His feelings had become this loathsome.

They went deeper into the flesh of Geadhain. Erik's inner darkness made bearable the surrounding shadows and rising whispers. Indeed, voices and presences circled the abandonment now. They flicked their serpent tongues into his ears and caressed the flesh under his armor with dry fingers. Malevolence surrounded them like the pressure one felt when climbing to great heights. Their progress followed a different trajectory, though, and it was always downhill.

Ruins of the past rose up out of the dark and receded back into it—the remnants of an underground society that had once flourished here. Whatever relics they kicked and disturbed were stunningly well preserved. Tools and shattered carts were lightly rusted when they should be corroded. The garments of the skeletal damned fluttered in tatters, but logically the moths and mites should have eaten the fabrics to dust centuries ago.

The travelers entered two grand caverns. A tin-roofed settlement of smashed houses cluttered each. Around the settlements stood stalled carriages with opened doors piled in sand—the signs of a great and failed escape. In one settlement, Erik thought he saw footprints, large and small, surrounding a torn-apart wagon—although he could have been mistaken.

Death had kindly cleared more obstructions for them, and soon they slogged through dripping and recently drained tunnels. The mud was rank and black as potash, and they became so grimed that only Taroch's hideous arm was visible without much squinting. Doom. Doom. Doom. Erik could hear the drums of darkness—and the drumming of his terror—and he'd numbed himself into a death march. He would not break down and have the queen and her spirits laugh at him again.

Lately, he'd been discovering many independent parts of himself, but freethinking would not serve him now—not until the queen gave the spirits the blood they demanded. In these dank hollows, he sought to be the weapon he had been for Magnus, and he drew strength from the simplicity of that role. Distantly in his mind, so far away as to be no more than a mere impression, there gleamed a picture of sweet, salty winds and the thrill of heaving waves. Without quite realizing it, Erik held on to that tiny light as the world became darker and darker.

To the deepest dark they came at last. They strode into a resonant limestone cathedral of a space that should have been chattering with bats—if there had been living things in the mines. As with the sopping passages they'd traversed before, the whole of the massive chamber had been emptied of a tremendous quantity of water. Erik could tell that from the miring, knee-deep silt into which their boots plunged. Creeping, cold logic told Erik where all the water had disappeared to and whence arose the uncanny reverence this hollow church demanded. The crevasse.

Only short steps away, the ground suddenly ended. One slip on this treacherous mud and he or the queen would career into the next world. Water and muck sloughed into the fissure and fell into a slurping, hungry vacuum of darkness. Erik felt that if he were to toss a stone and listen, no sound would come. Ever. The chasm was a gateway to darkness, and in the foggy shadows above the descent, as Taroch's light shone there, every angry horror of the Iron Mines eddied and was nearly given shape. In the haze drifted a ghostly freak show—floating sticklike figures pronged in thorns. Moray eels of shadow swam up from the abyss, and their lumpy tails and fins glided against the tenebrous mist. He gazed upon something with a gigantic tumor of a head and felt it look back at him with a dozen jellied eyes. He felt it press itself with squiggling fingers against the quivering veil between life and death. He quickly ended his fixation. Whatever wrongs had corrupted the mine and captured its souls had begun on this site.

He nearly went no farther. The queen, though, smiled and walked ahead. "Here is where the pride of Menos nearly doomed it," she declared. "And where that pride will come full circle to complete that destruction. I thought of how to protect Magnus's achievement, and while peace was always his way, without him here to negotiate with the Iron monsters, peace will never work. I had a dream one night of Menos simply falling. Tumbling like a black house of cards. The sight...was glorious. I believe it was a divine vision. When I awoke, I recalled suddenly and clearly Thackery's tale. Of how the smallest spark of truefire lit the vein inside the Iron Valley, which magnified the wrath of the fault line. Two disasters—the first begetting the second and greater one. I remembered how that flicker of flame nearly brought the Iron City to its foundations. After that, my goal was clear."

Near the edge of the chasm and that slippery death Erik envisioned, they stopped. The queen turned and held Taroch's arm like a sword. It shone as a green and ghoulish brand of starlight. Erik shielded his eyes and heard the spirits in the pit wail in delight. The queen's pronouncement rang over the noise. "I have power but not enough to ensure Menos will never rise again after its second fall. Taroch, mighty Taroch! He could transform water into gold, loaves of bread to silver, and air to fire to ice. He was a sorcerer of legend. They say he was not wholly mortal—that he was born partly of a common woman and partly of a force descended from above. Seeing his dead flesh thrive with magik still, I know this is true. Taroch will do what I cannot. He has told me. He will have his chance to rule West and East but only through the preservation of one and the devastation of the other." She was hunched now and grinning with dark, delirious lust. She stepped back from Erik. "The channel of truefire is still there. You see? Still inside the fault we behold. Even if the vein of truefire is now empty, Taroch can mix the air and muck that clots it into a new blood...to fill a greater vein. A thick and throbbing vein that leads all the way to the black, iron heart of our enemies. Imagine, Erik, how an explosion of that magnitude would agitate the fault. One pebble to set off the truefire, and the whole range of Kor'Keth would bury Menos's sinful history so deep that tomorrow's children would have only fables to remind them of why they should never behave like the doomed and damned of the Iron City."

Erik saw the truth now. She was not simply mad but possessed. Somehow, her grief had become an open window into her soul, and the whispers of spirits, Death, and a remorseless warlord had all taken their turns slipping through. She was not herself. She had not known her actions for however long this evil had picked at her wounded heart. Erik reached for the queen.

"No!" she screamed, and she smote him with the sword of Taroch's limb, which drove him into the mud like a hammer of stone. Groaning and helpless, he could only cry her name—Lila—as she spoke an ancient word that summoned thunder and made the spirits keen. Then she threw her dazzling relic into the pit. Erik expected a flash of foul magik, but an orange fireside heat and radiance dispelled the chamber's darkness.

The queen whimpered and swayed as if to faint. She would go either back into the mud or forward into the sun that was rising from below. Either way, she needed her sword. Erik dug himself and his honor out of the mud and lunged to her side. Miraculously, he caught the queen before she fell to her demise. In his arms, she trembled and wept. She seemed to loathe what she had done.

Lights splayed gloriously around the cavern. This was a wonder, considering the damage the sight foretold. The truefire had been reborn. From below, magik rumbled and plumed forth gusts of fiery brightness and wind. Any moment now, a fragment of mud or stone would dislodge at just the right velocity to spark the cavern into a spectacle of flame—a river of explosions and earthquakes that would course all the way to Menos. The Iron City was doomed, and they were too.

"You must go," whispered the queen to him tearfully.

"My queen." She pressed her fingers to his lips for silence. "Lila," he continued. He spoke in a whisper as well, for even a bold voice might end their lives early. "Where would I go? I am spans under the mountains. They will fall upon me before I ever see the day. You have damned us both."

Sorrow contorted her face, and she tried hard not to sob. "I never wanted this. I do not know what took hold of me. I have been so angry inside since Magnus turned on me. Since losing him in Zioch. I know he was not himself...but I have never forgiven him."

"Nor should you. No man should have touched you as he did. I would have killed him. If it had been possible. If you had let me."

They held their breath together in a beat that said more than any words.

"I was ready to die, then and now," she whispered. "Though not for you to follow me to the grave."

"I would follow you anywhere," he confessed.

In the glimmer between life and death, unholy flames sweltered their skins, and all blurred into a heated dream. The two saw each other truly without titles or pasts. They were two hopeless souls shackled to madness, obsession with their king, and fear of losing him and being alone. What it all meant, or could mean, was meaningless. They would be dead in a speck. Erik brushed away some of Lila's filthy hair and finger-painted her cheeks with his large, muddy hands—as he had done many years ago in a stable in a moment as precarious as this one. This was not the drawn passion before a kiss but an exchange of loyalty, compassion, and friendship deeper than lust. They might have simply held one another and wept while the fires consumed their embrace. However, there came a voice.

**"Well done, fleshling. I can see why the maggots call you a queen. In the cold, moonless worlds I rule, where my worshippers skin themselves in my honor, you could be a high priestess of my glory."**

Erik clapped a hand over the queen's mouth to stop her from screaming, and they clung to each other and slowly turned to the speaker. Death was not what they had expected. They had imagined something more initially intimidating than a shriveled, sunken-cheeked elder sporting hardly a tooth or spot of hair and dressed in tattered, once-fancy pajamas. If they hadn't been so terrified, they might have recognized the flesh the Dreamer wore. However, it was old and ruined now. Death hovered majestically atop the filth. Its vessel's gnarled feet dragged in the air, and ethereal strings held up its body. As Erik and Lila beheld this trembling being, they could feel with their souls the screaming, spinning vortex housed within its decrepit body. They saw the starry dark of space spinning in the vessel's eyes—as clear a glimpse of Death's vastness as mortals would ever see. They would fall into that darkness—but not today.

**"In your honor, for the army you have raised, I shall give you the same blessing I do to the darkest daughters of Xalloreth. I shall give you a reprieve from my hand, so you might go forth and lead more into my embrace. See, fleshlings, how merciful a master I can be? See this, and serve me well with your tiny lives."**

Was this mercy? The army they'd raised? What despicable evil had the queen's madness driven her to commit? In their horror, neither could say.

**"Since you cling to her soul, manling, you may go too,"** said Death. **"Protect my servant."**

Death waved them away as the nuisances they now were to her. Once dismissed, they found themselves gripped by a great hand of darkness, crushed into a maggoty paste, and thrown on putrid wind a hundred spans in a single speck. When their flesh reformed, they were vomiting upon the stony beach where the *Fleet Otter* had landed. Yet there was no time to compose themselves, for the world was about to heave with a sickness far greater than theirs.

Boom! Boom! Boom!

Three gongs announced the end of the world—or at least of the part of the world on which they stood. The detonations that followed were not as loud, since each of the two stumbling witnesses was deaf after the first. Each eruption blew clouds of stone and fire into the dawn. Instantly, the whole of Kor'Keth's spine was obscured in blackness, and a monstrous snake of smoke gobbled up more of the mountains. So much soil and stone flared that the whole of the West deformed into a whirling brown cauldron.

They felt more explosions, though their ears still rang too badly to hear them. Surely they coughed from all the ash and bled from the rain of scorching clods and shrapnel, but these were minor concerns for these summoners of doom. They did not shriek in delirious denial. For they knew well the damage and their hand in it. All around them was its evidence—a wall of twisting, mushrooming destruction where mountains had stood since Geadhain was a blushing green lass. They had ruined the Green Mother. They were servants to Death herself. Their sin had stained the world.

## VIII

Death stood at the tear between life and unlife and waited until the fires finally surged and bits of her vessel's flesh began to flake off. If she stayed to watch further, she would lose more of her body. At this rate, the vessel would not have long to serve her, as she'd been forced to manipulate him like an angry puppeteer using a stiff puppet. Hollowing him out would have been ideal. However, the maggot would not relinquish his soul. The contemptible thing refused to die.

Death stepped through the passageways of eternity and out onto a great, rocky hill surrounded by sparse pines. Before her, a valley of green rolled along and then met with the menacing slate mound of the Iron Valley. She watched the landmarks fall without interest. All things were meant to die—even stone. The manling's spirit inside cried as it often did. Hopefully, her next vessel would not bleat as childishly. Gradually, the flashing clouds settled to a fog of ash, and Death moved from the mount. She wanted to walk among the ruin and to breathe in the decay of her new kingdom.

She took a step and was in a black city. It was blacker than it had ever been and sweet with the wails of children and the screeching of dying animals, breaking machines, and shattered men. What a glorious aria it was. All of man's accomplishments here had fallen. Death saw an ebon, glassy tower broken and bent on itself like a snapped sword. She noted hundreds of small, birdlike ships lying in smoking lodes or smoldering in the wreckage of imploded houses. She glanced to the wall made of unassailable iron. It had been cracked in places like a cheap ceramic cup. When she'd surveyed enough of the ruination from this one spot, she walked through the city of the dead. She wandered and touched those who pleaded for life. She crushed their souls and tossed them into the void. A spark of her Will remained inside each empty vessel. That sliver of her grace made the blessed corpses moan and lurch to unlife. Corpses stumbled to their knees. In the absence of limbs, they wriggled like hideous grubs. The rising dead finished off those whom the catastrophe had not. A few of the least chewed remains were then brought to Death's feet, and she sat on a smoky pile that passed for a throne. She infused these new offerings with her gift. Before long, the whole slag heap of a city echoed with screams and crawled with reborn—faster, more violent versions than any Menosian master could hope to run from. Not many fled quickly enough to save themselves, and Death's army swelled indiscriminately with babes, geriatrics, masters, slaves, whores, murderers, and the sadly misplaced innocents of Menos. When night fell, a whole city of the dead groaned Death's thousand names into the rolling, thick stew of ash and misery that had become the Iron City. Death had her army. It was time for a new vessel.

## IX

The never-ending smog in the east buried Erik and Lila deeply in shame and gloom, and their souls felt as dirty as their encrusted garments. Day to noon to dusk went by, and the clouds only darkened. Erik wondered whether they would ever clear or whether the shroud was permanent. For as long as they were to live—forever in Lila's case—the land would remember their crime. Cartographers might even name the disaster after their disgrace—Queen's Folly. *Likely something crueler*, thought Erik. He doubted, though, that he would be more than a footnote to these events. Soldiers never were.

*I should have stopped her. I should have been stronger. I should have been the man who—*

"Magnus?" cried the queen suddenly. She bolted off her rock and looked to the stars in the south, as if the voice in her head and winter in her heart came from the heavens. "Magnus?" she gasped.

Erik stumbled from his perch and fell before the queen. She was slowly moving her lips but saying nothing. She was conversing in her head. *Can it be?* he thought. He waited and waited. Finally, she shrieked and fell into a swoon. He caught her and lowered her to the ground. She would not speak but for small gasping sobs.

"What? What happened?" Erik demanded. "Is he alive? He is! He must be!"

The queen paused in her grieving, touched their foreheads together, and wept more quietly. "He is free. Yes. He was not dead—although nearly so, and held there. All my dreams were true. And he knows, Erik. We cannot hide our truths from the other. Magnus has seen what we have done. He...*despises* me. A...monster, he called me! Daughter of Death." She sobbed again as though racked with pain. She composed herself and took a deep breath. "Our king has declared me an enemy of Eod and an enemy of life. He told me he never wishes to see you or I again."

All Erik's armor of pride and love broke then, and he sobbed.

# XVII

# A NOT SO ORDINARY DAY

Adore woke to the roo-doo-doo of a clockwork cock. She cursed the bloody machine, hauled herself to the bed's edge, and rubbed the sleep from her eyes until her apartment came into focus. About a year ago, the folk in her neighborhood had pitched in for the obstreperous annoyance. She'd voted for and given coin toward its purchase, so she could hardly complain. Admittedly, the device did the trick. It woke the workers and servants of District Twenty-Two and got them on their way on time, even if it was an annoyance on days without work. She considered a day without work and smiled.

After a few more irritating roo-doo-doos, she got up and crossed the creaking floor to a burnished basin sink, old and worn but clean. A circular window quartered in iron trim gave her something to stare out while she washed last night's dishes, wiped down the buckled oak countertop, and filled a kettle for the stove.

As he did every morning, old Master Jenkins waved to her from his window across the way. He looked like a friendly mad technomagikal engineer— unruly white beard and spectacles. He was usually wearing a posh vest and carrying a pocket-chronex on a chain. As with the iron cock, she'd grown used to this constant in her routine. After he disappeared from the window, she stared for a spell at the facade of the elegant black building opposite hers. Its chimneys puffed morning smoke into Menos's purple haze of a sky. Then she let her attention wander to the other windows and enjoyed the peep show of life.

Families, old dames, and bachelors such as Jenkins moved around in their fishbowls. A few who caught her gazing nodded or hailed her with a polite flip of their hands. One hearty-bodied gentleman she'd spied before was doing chest exercises upon the floor, pumping himself up and down, and gleaming with an attractive kind of sweat along the canyons of his back. Aadore made a pleased "hm." *Close your curtains if you don't want the whole neighborhood to see you*, she thought. The man possessed no such humility, though, and often strode about nude after his morning bath, so she assumed he wanted an audience. What was his name? She felt she should remember it, seeing as he'd once asked her to the pub. Derek? Dennis? Sands later, she was dumping her unfinished tea down the sink, and he swaggered his dewy and naked body past his window. Curtis, she remembered, as if triggered by the hypnotic metronome of his swinging member. Had she seen him without his clothes prior to his invitation, she might not have declined.

*Only one man you need to worry about today*, she thought. *Sean.*

Her brother was coming home after nine years away, during which time only letters had told of his incredible life outside Menos. She would finally be able to lay eyes upon the lad—although he would be a "lad" no longer, she assumed. He was probably a handsome young fellow by now and stiff competition for Curtis in D Twenty-Two. She hoped he wouldn't be doing what soldiers usually did when on break from their duties: drinking and whoring. At least, she hoped not the latter and not here. There simply wasn't room enough for another boarder—even a temporary one.

While taking a distracted bath, Aadore took stock of her humble holdings. It was no more than a square room with a single bed, a kitchen, and an open-concept lavatory in one corner, for which she should probably buy a standing screen. She pondered what other changes would be realistic within her slim budget. Sean would have a military stipend to contribute as well, so she determined it would be best to put the matter aside until they'd had a chance to look at their funds together. What a pleasant thought—togetherness. It curled the corners of her mouth into a smile.

With a little melancholy, she summoned the memory of her united family: mother, father, young Sean, and a scrappy, shaggy dog they'd adopted. It was a happy memory, despite the passing of her parents. They'd each gone peacefully and suddenly. Father had keeled over while polishing the master of El's shoes. There was a certain irony in the fact that he'd literally worked himself to death. Aadore could smile at this, having come from a line of servants and yes-men. Mother had gone within a few weeks after Father. Aadore had found her cold and gray in the afternoon after she'd missed her at the estate. The Els had been kind in granting Aadore a leave for her bereavement. A whole week, they'd given her.

Although he wrote, Sean couldn't attend either burial. She remembered going to the funeral in the company of a couple of maids and gents from the estate and then spending the days in her flat sipping wine and reading. She must have cried, though she found it hard to remember now. Summoning sadness required effort when one's life wasn't all that terrible—at least not as terrible as it could be. Surely, the Els had been good to the Brennochs. They'd employed her father, her mother, her, and even her brother, in a sense. His chances of being accepted into the ironguard would have been slim without Moreth's endorsement.

At the moment, she was once again enjoying paid time away from work —not for a funeral but so that the Lady El could accompany her husband in the West. Thus, even in the violent City of Iron, even as what the West would call a beaten-minded slave, Aadore was short on regrets. Under the skin, Menos was not so different from any other place to live. Perhaps its darkness made the lights that shone here and there across the city dazzle that much brighter. She had a job she did not dread. She lived in a modest neighborhood of laborers and serfs. Thanks be to the El's generosity and the funds of her parents' estate, she owned her own home—deed and all. There was little more a Menosian woman could want, other than a wealthy husband. She preferred books to suitors, though, and the Lady El had been even more gracious in lending her handmaiden as many books as she requested from her grand library. Aadore wondered whether Sean too might want some books to read, since there was not much in the way of entertainment at her home. She recalled his having read spooky tales of Alabion and the occasional adventure story. However, his tastes had likely changed since those distant years.

When she started feeling like a waterlogged raisin, she stopped her daydreaming and got out of the lukewarm bath. She whistled and sang while she dressed for the day. Once ready, she checked herself in her vanity.

She possessed a highland woman's comeliness: dark hair, bold brows, and a strong and slightly frowning mouth. She usually found these features crude and ugly for a woman. Today, she felt herself to be glowing and decided to top off her shoulder-jutting blazer and caged skirt ensemble with a few accessories: a lady's hat hung in a lace veil, and in her hand, she held her fanciest umbrella. She posed before the mirror and blew herself a kiss. She felt quite ridiculous. Even as the skies rumbled, the world outside her window darkened, and rain began pelting the window, Aadore's smile did not diminish. After almost a decade away, Sean was coming home. There was only one more sleep now. She didn't see how the predictable misery of Menosian weather could ruin that most magnificent gift.

II

The weather was more bark than bite. There was plenty of thunder and lightning, but only a smattering of rain found its way down the black buildings that walled in the street. What scarce, toxic precipitation there was trickled—sometimes in thick globs—out of eaves troughs, onto the cement walkways, and in congealed streams into the gutters. The runoff Aadore sidestepped reminded her of the pretty messes the Lady El left on her palette when working on a studio piece. Color was all around Menos, if one looked beyond the gray. Aadore used her umbrella as a walking stick and remarked silently on the lovely twists of magenta in the skies that day. *That color reminds me of a flower, though I cannot say what kind. I believe Master El gave his lady some of that very color one day.* Moreth was a gallant master and oft filled his lady's boudoir with rare flowers, gemstones, and treasures—things taken from lands far away and with names that tangled the tongue.

"Aadore!" A deep voice interrupted her thoughts.

She turned to the caller. Other hustling folk were in the street with their heads down and hats on to the weather—except one fool, who flagged her with his bowler.

"Curtis?" she said. Seeing him in his clothes was a bit of a shock.

He must have run to catch up, as he was a bit breathless as he approached her. As he did, he straightened his sandy hair, pulled back his broad shoulders, combed out his mustache, and quickly popped his hat back on his head when he realized rain was getting into his eyes. He seemed dressier than Aadore remembered. He was as dapper as the fellows with their cravats and top hats passing them in the street—valets for masters.

"Did you get a new job?" she asked.

"I did," he replied. "Second courier for the Third Chair himself."

Aadore hoped the veil hid her sneer. She'd met his employer before during dinners hosted at the El estate. The man made her skin itch from filth. As if the Iron sage's unwashed appearance, unrestrained flatulence, tendency to snort while he ate, and greasy jowls were not repulsive enough, the man's opinions were despicable and his treatment of slaves and lesser vassals reprehensible—even for a Menosian. Or had the Els spoiled her and corrupted her perception with their benevolence?

"We share opinions on that," replied Curtis, shrewdly noticing her sneer. "'Never question the coin, especially when it's good,' as we say in the Iron City. Come. Allow me to escort you down the way."

Aadore took Curtis's arm, and they began to walk.

"Congratulations," said Aadore.

"Thank you."

All things considered—the thunder, the poisonous and occasionally hail-size excretions pinging onto the metal shingles of the surrounding buildings, and the disheveled criers ringing their bells and caroling about the war on the White City—it was a rather perfect morning for Aadore. It made a wonderful music in her head and heart. Goodness, was she ever happy today. Curtis noticed her smiling.

"I'd like to think your cheer has something to do with me."

Aadore considered the rest of the man attached to the firm, large arm into which hers was linked. Without glancing at him, she drew his face in her mind. It was a bit soft and puppyish, with wide eyes and long lashes. He had a confidence, though, that had allowed him to risk rejection not once but twice. Her smile deepened.

"It might," she replied. "You certainly have my attention."

Curtis leaned over and whispered hotly, "I should hope I have caught your attention after all these weeks of exerting myself for your approval. For a while now, I couldn't say who the buxom woman was watching me from on high. I never saw more than her breasts, which were suitable enough for certain...recreations. Until this morning. You lingered a bit longer than normal, and I caught that unmistakable strong chin of yours. Your mouth too is remarkable in its beauteous scowl. I don't think I've known a woman who can look so dour and so alluring."

Aadore felt mortified—wan then flushed, anxious, and excited. A lewd confession, however, was the least of what could unnerve an Iron mistress's handmaiden. She replied coolly. "How do you know you have not misplaced your efforts? There is Ms. Browne in the suite above me or even Master Hainsbury in the suite below. He's well known to have an attachment for his departed wife's bustiers and undergarments."

Curtis stopped and beheld her. In his eyes was a shine of self-assurance. "I know what I've seen, and you know what you've seen. The question now is whether you would like to see more."

*Oh my. Oh my*, she thought. What a scandalous young man. She was surely many years his senior. He was twenty-five at best, and she was thirty-seven. This was certainly better than reading one of Lady Beatrice's soppy romances, though. Her mouth spoke before her mind could think of any contrivance to halt it. "I would," she replied. "I would indeed."

"Tomorrow night? I have some errands to run for my new employer. Seems the council is going to be quite busy today. I can only imagine whose body will be in the gutter by Tensday."

She sighed with heartfelt disappointment. "Tomorrow my little brother returns from his posting after far too long away. We are each other's only family. The rest of the scattered Brennoch clan live like hill people of the earliest ages—sheep farmers, herders, and foragers. Somewhere around Meadowvale. It's not even a town. I believe it's just in the hills." She turned up her nose with snobbery. "I've never, ever met them. I would not send him to those estranged folk. He needs his sister and the Iron City's culture. I've even saved up to treat him to a phantograph show. I had the whole week to myself to prepare, and I've left things to the last sand. Now I have a million and one things to shop for before he arrives. What do young men even like these days?"

Curtis gave her a particular grin. After a moment, they laughed.

"Well, he sounds like a very lucky man to have such a doting woman to care for him," said Curtis. "I should like the same treatment myself one day."

"You will have it," said Aadore.

Another gleaming, sensual stare he cast her way, and then they strolled onward. They wandered past the tall rows of black, looming manses. Formerly the estates of failed or defamed masters, they had been retrofitted into apartments for the not-quite poor. The two chatted as they sauntered along and nodded to any ironguard standing along the walkways. Here in D Twenty-Two, the citizens' taxes were not simply stolen for the insatiable avarice of the Iron rulers. A measure of expense and attention was paid to maintaining certain infrastructure: a lean martial force, criers, and even cus-todial workers. In general, the streets were as clean of criminals and garbage as one could find in Menos.

Outside D Twenty-Two, even in some of its adjacent neighborhoods, it would not be advisable to walk in broad daylight without a burly friend and a pistol. What was peace ever but an illusion? *A social construct to fence out the dark desires of men*, reflected Aadore. In Menos, one knew where to find civility and barbarity. The lines were rarely crossed or confused. There was more hon-esty in that order than Aadore believed one would see anywhere in Geadhain— though all that could change if Magnus and his Nine Laws ever found their way East. She was not a spiteful woman, but it would be easier if the Immortal King were dead, as went one of the rumors, and people were left to rule people.

She knew she was ruining her perfect morning by brooding over the war, this threat to the Menosian order she held so dear. Thankfully, Curtis distracted her with a question.

"Sorry. What was that?" she asked.

"Oh, I asked why your brother was on leave so close to the eve of out-right war. Seems a bit odd, no?"

*More war talk after all.* Somehow, the topic surfaced at any and all times. War had invaded the Menosian consciousness—she supposed that could

451

not have been avoided. She also had no answer for Curtis. Details had been scarce in her brother's letters. Almost too scarce. *No*, she thought forcefully. *The war will come and go just like the storm of fire and ice. Another disaster for the historians and other important people to resolve. I am not one of them, and Sean, a mere soldier, is not either. We are both servants to these great powers, and we should not concern ourselves with their movements. That he is coming home and that he and I shall be together is the sum of what is important.*

Aadore shared none of her thoughts with Curtis, and he assumed rightly that she did not wish to reply. The rain let up, and orange scabs appeared in the clouds—sunlight trying its damnedest to squeeze through the firmament. With the signs of real day came quite a bit of quick heat, and they were soon fanning themselves with their hats. Eventually, they came to an open gate positioned between two black metal booths. Men, women, and small carriages flowed one way—mostly out into the great noisy causeway cluttered with speeding vehicles and shouting persons. A few pistol shots cracked in the sky, but the ironguards at the gates barely flinched.

"I'll see you to a carriage," suggested Curtis, and he smiled unevenly. "I wouldn't suggest walking around too much. Gunshots already. It seems as if it's going to be one of those days."

III

The day passed eventfully for Aadore. The city seemed in a bit of an uproar. The tension between East and West thickened the already smoky air. As Curtis had advised, she took carriages to the markets beneath the Iron Wall. Being streetwise and sensing the agitation—and desperation—of the day, she decided to hire a mercenary as an escort. Soon after, a man who called himself Skar accompanied her as she wandered. He wore a patched suit that tested its seams with his size, carried a holster that looked as if it held a safari rifle, and was as chewed in the face as his name implied. She doubted she would have much trouble with him around. Aadore and her companion shopped all over for food and necessities for her brother. Her scavenger hunt took her through the tumbledown market stalls and to the quainter ateliers in the dingy-windowed neighborhoods nearby. She hoped to find a certain gift for her brother there that had eluded her: fragrance.

When she was twelve summers old and her brother was barely walking, they'd been welcomed along with their parents and a few other choice servants of the El estate for a summer repose on the north bank of the Feordhan with the Lady El and Moreth. The Lady El had favored them when they were children. Perhaps this had been because she and Moreth had no children of their own.

She recalled that the vacation had not been in the ideal spot—very windy and exposed and on a beach without much sand. The looming, shadowy pines had seemed as if they were prickled giant monsters. However, the blue, rugged water had been beautiful to stare at, like a cerulean snake that rode the world's back. They had tried to play in the water, but it had been too cold to stand in for long. The Lady El had gently laughed at them for their stubborn attempts to swim. Most of the time, Moreth had been away somewhere. Aadore had possessed no idea where he camped at night or why he went with many armed men and seemed to return with few.

Of that splendid memory, the smell of pines and the salty, scraped-earth waft of ocean were two scents she'd never found again in Menos, which had plenty of smells. That memory had held Sean in thrall too. They'd talked about it many a time. She wanted to surprise him with the things he missed most, such as his favorite corn-and-flax bread, that ghastly felsalted beef that always conjured a fart, and these special fragrances from their childhood. She and Skar found the first few treats quickly. The scents, however, took until the evening to track down. Even then, they weren't exact matches, but overly astringent mockeries of the natural scents. *That will have to do*, she thought with a sigh, and she stepped out of the latest atelier and into the warm purple dusk of Menos.

"My children! My people of Iron!"

The call must have resounded from an enchanted horn—possibly a grand spell of far-speaking. It startled Aadore. She recognized the voice of the speaker, Gloriatrix, and she was even more frightened. Skar earned his crowns by catching the basket Aadore nearly dropped and then slipping it back on her arm.

CHRISTIAN A. BROWN

A crinkle of static could be detected in the echoing oration that followed and a prepared calm in the intonations. It was as if this speech had been previously recorded. Masters, slaves, servants, and mercenaries—all the various shades between gray and black that composed the Menosian populace—halted and hushed at the sound of the Iron Queen's voice. Carriages rolled to a stop, and masters leaned their groomed heads out into the filthy air with expressions of interest instead of disgust. In humid silk-laden chambers, pleasure maidens and lads paused their sensual theatrics and listened with their clients to the booming voice of the divine that shuddered through the walls. Elsewhere, people garbed in pitch used this rapture of the citizenry to slip with the greatest of ease upon their intended victims. They too listened with appreciation, though, while cutting red lines across the throats of their marks. All the way up and down the grimed ebon streets, Aadore saw displays of solemn fealty. Her countrymen's love for their nation stirred her. She felt proud to be a child of the Iron City. If she had come from a weaker nation, the queen's speech would almost certainly have made her cry. However, neither she nor her countrymen suffered from the mawkishness of the West.

"Too long have we held our ground and our silence in the East. Too long have the Immortal overlords of this world caged our ambition. Brutus, one of these half-men, has gone mad! He has destroyed his own creation and quite possibly the other rabid animal of his kind. If they have not ended each other, then one or both will return and seek to enforce their ancient order of Immortal over mortal. The greater over the lesser, the strong over the weak: this is the order we have lived by. The order we were once scorned for by these very half-men, who simply did not want to be reminded of their hubris for they rule the same way.

"The truth of rule, my children, is that rulers rarely differ. We are all the same in some important respects. We all must separate wheat from chaff. We all must make decisions that damn or please thousands. At least I, as a Menosian woman, know the sting of these laws, for I have lived through them myself. I have watched my husband executed for treason. Had I been queen then, I would have sentenced him with no greater mercy. I am mortal. I know pain, obedience, and many lessons the half-men will never know because they cannot. They are not mortal. They are not the same as we are.

"After I bring my black whip down upon Eod's lambs and after I have taught them they were no freer before than now, I believe they will one day thank us for our intervention. So welcome them into your manors, businesses, and lives when we return with them in chains. Rejoice, people of Iron, for this is a joyous day. We have begun a war against tyranny. A war of liberty. You will hear from me again once this new dawn begins. We shall celebrate the end of the Immortal Age together."

"Hear, hear!" cried Skar.

Beside her, the great man quivered. It was the most emotion he'd shown all day. A swell of shouts joined Skar's, and he saluted with his fists to his chest like a member of the ironguard.

In another few beats, whatever patriotism had erupted took a backseat to industry, and slaves were pulled along for not listening, coitus resumed in the brothels, and folk began disappointedly discovering the various bodies stashed in closets or alleyways. *Who will clean this up?* they wondered. Life could pause but never be stopped. This was the essential principle of Menos. Like a malignant growth, it would endure. It would overpower all who did not agree with its expansion. While Aadore might have needed a mercenary to watch over her purse and welfare that day, she felt quite safe. There was nothing in the world the spirit of her people and their queen would not conquer. It was better to be part of the wave than of the village it devours. She wished her queen well and hoped for a swift end to the bloodshed and a quick adoption of Eod's people into her society. However, in all honesty, she believed Gloriatrix would succeed without something as sentimental and useless as the prayers of her people.

IV

Skar stayed with Aadore for the remainder of the afternoon. He even softened a little after the queen's speech. He opened doors for her and helped her bring her wares to her flat. She'd stopped at a few more stores prior to ending her shopping trip and was quite encumbered with goods, including an awkward rectangular privacy screen for the lavatory area.

Once upstairs and settled, Aadore worried that Skar was expecting a payment other than her crowns, but he stayed only for tea, some tinned fish, and a few nibbles of the bread and butter she offered him. They had a fine bit of conversation as well when Skar learned her brother was a soldier. As soon as that became known, Skar went on about his years in the ironguard, during which he'd accumulated his oft-broken nose, the pattern of scars upon his face, and his nickname. Aadore and the mercenary parted with a handshake, and he gave her a list of the taverns and spots where he could best be recruited again. As he was walking down the hallway, he turned back. "Give him a warrior's homecoming," said Skar. "A fat and hearty feast will do. Trust me. Soldiers don't get much but slop on the front lines. Don't drown him in kindness, though. It's always hard for those who spend their lives fighting to come back to a different pace of life. Trading sword for table knife, as it were. Be patient as well, since he might not adjust as quickly as you want."

"I shall. Thank you." Aadore smiled.

"Do smile more often too," said Skar, and he gave her a chipped-tooth grin of his own. "You're quite pretty when you do."

Aadore blushed as she closed the door. She leaned against the wood and pondered. What a week of surprises and delightful encounters this had been—and Sean was not even home yet.

V

That night Aadore couldn't sleep, and she squirmed in her bed like a worm until finally getting up before dawn to make an early cup of tea and watch the purple light of dawn rise. Curtis wasn't in his fishbowl that morning. He must indeed be as busy with missives as yesterday he'd suspected he would be, and her day felt out of sorts without his glistening flesh. Since she'd been a servant all her life, she tidied her apartment in a blitz and barely cracked a sweat. She then read to pass the time. Alas, no words on any page interested her, and the pile of books grew by her bedside until she tidied them too. When she finally consulted her chronex, she saw it was time to leave for Queen's Station and meet her brother.

She threw on her coat, examined her flat, and ensured everything was in order. There were two chairs and a quaint table laid with lace upon which a few glass oil burners and some plated foodstuff were displayed. She hoped the silver toppers would thwart the mice for a few hourglasses. It was generally not a clever idea to leave food outside of hermetically sealed containers. The adventurer's fleece bedroll she'd purchased had been placed alongside her bed. She had no idea how tall Sean was, and it seemed foolish to invest in real furniture until he arrived. *A boy...no, a man and a soldier,* she thought, *would ideally like to pick how he dressed and where he slept.* She adjusted the lavatory screen one last time. She was still unconvinced it would offer much privacy and dissatisfied with the feathery pattern on the panels. She hoped Sean would like the comforts she had for him. They weren't too fussy, which was in line with Skar's advice.

She realized then that a hue of anxiety colored her excitement. She and Sean had been apart for almost a decade. She knew little of her brother or his mysterious deployment in the West. She knew a memory of Sean—a ghost—and not the man he'd become. Who was she to him, and how would she have changed in his eyes? The soft purr of the eternally cycling sands of her chronex was like the sound of crawling spider legs. It caught her ear and gave her pause. How she heard its susurration above all the bombast of the Iron City was a miracle come from years of keeping time and arranging duties. Stranger or brother, someone was coming to live with her. She'd make it work either way. That was what Menosians did—survive, conquer, and adapt. Aadore locked up her flat and hurried to the station.

VI

With the streets swimming in dawn's aubergine shadows—the perfect cover for assassins, deviants, and muggers—Aadore traveled once more by carriage. The coachman went by way of the Evernight Gardens, and she had a rolling peek at her mistress's estate—the steepled, spiked roof, the outdoor arcades of iron, the sculpted hedges, and the glaring white flowers. Such ostentation prepared her for the sight of Queen's Station and its grand steps, upon which she'd often stood while awaiting packages sent from afar to her mistress She'd never been inside. Usually, couriers met her at the spot where she was today deposited. She paid the coachman a bit absently—and possibly too much—and stepped out.

Carriages reined to hairless undead steeds crossed in scars and stitched with metal plates formed a line along the road, and before her lay a wide slate plaza. It was sparklingly clean. Truly, not a flutter of refuse and no more than foot traffic were permitted in this hub before Queen's Station itself. The great disparities of Menosian living could be seen in the crowd through which she pressed. There were silk and satin masters with their tidy valets, and urchins combed to respectability and holding signs that offered themselves and their time for sale. Some acted as porters to the valets and their masters. Others spit shined boots or negotiated at the ear of certain masters for deviances she did not care to understand.

The air was a dizzying confusion of sweat, perfume, industrial grease, and smoke. Aadore produced a kerchief to hold over her mouth as she walked across the plaza, and she came to steps hewn for the feet of titanic forces. The stone here gleamed an absolute black as if mined from the night sky. *What incredible opulence*, she thought. She couldn't place the material, though. Everything from there on was made of that rock. The steps preceded a courthouse, foreboding and grand as a temple of doomsday worship. Above the dark edifice, the slowly gyrating swarm of ebon ships astonished her.

This was the single most breathtaking sight in Menos besides the Crucible. They were twins really—two masterpieces of man's ingenuity that could possibly never be trumped. In Eod she knew they had advancements, but caution, ethics, and other sophisms reined them. Eodians could not create this kind of monument. It was too grotesque. It defied good taste and decency. She was impressed as she strode deep into its shadow, which was darker and colder than a winter's night. She lost track of the ships from her vantage point and gave up wondering whether one held her brother. The rest of her climb was uneventful except for the ironguard beating a man. The man being beaten dropped a bit of change in the assault, and she was quick to snatch it off the steps before the urchins swept in to claim it. It was a great and lucky day indeed. She had the highest hopes and renewed expectations for her reunion.

At the top of the steps, near one of the many pillar-framed and guarded arches, an ironguard asked for her papers. He gave her a small inquisition before allowing her into the station. She passed through without being dragged off like the gentleman from a few sands before, and she used her fair-gotten gains to purchase a bit of taffy from a vendor in a slapdash, questionable stand just inside the entrance. The candy tasted more sour than sweet, and its chewiness made for a vexing diversion while she found her way.

The station was equally strange and disorienting—a hodgepodge of religious grandeur and utterly bewildering technomagik. The great metal ceiling stood so high and black it could not be seen but rather was heard as an echo overhead that caught and threw back all the raucousness of the station like a cathedral's roof. Aided by the soft white gaslights of the place—some on wiry lampposts and others attached in caged sconces to walls—she eked out further details such as the frescoes of wailing faces hammered into the metal trim at the bases of walls and the subtle ornamentation of the clawed feet of the wrought-iron-and-oak benches. Often the benches were set in blocks like pews. Each block of seats faced a dangerous-looking office barricaded with chain-link fence. She noticed numbers and letters posted on the plaques along the fences outside these curious stations. They contained designations such as gate A 1, B 3, and C 5.

Within Queen's Station, there dazzled as much hullaballoo as without—crowds, arguments, merchants such as the taffy peddler, and shadier fellows selling wares from their coats. A musician occasionally caught her ear with a tune. Most everything, though, sounded meek because of the roar of skycarriages, bleating horns, and magnified voices rattling off flight patterns and mechanical concerns in codes. The voices of these hidden conductors startled Aadore whenever they blasted from little boxes of black mesh attached to the pillars that kept the whole station from falling down.

She knew to expect her brother at Gate S 3, which she spotted just up ahead. She took a seat on one of the least occupied benches in the waiting pen with about ten sands to spare, according to her chronex.

Aadore placed her unfinished taffy in its wrapper. The thing had fused into a brown, rubbery blob and refused to be ingested. She tried to sit without looking anxious. A number of ironguards patrolled this gate—more than she'd seen at Queen's Station. When she took count of the others like herself—servants and working folk—she noticed hardly another person of her stature. A young mother attended her infant with near matricidal disinterest. She scowled and ignored its whimpers and stunted arms, which reached for her from a basket she'd placed on the floor. She pushed the basket farther away with a toe as Aadore watched. Nearby, an eager young husband clutched a bouquet of wilted flowers that were the best Menosian horticulture for sale in the station. She envisioned his wife throwing them in the trash when she arrived or possibly over the wailing child of that wretched, scowling mother, who'd finally decided to discard her baby. *It's not right to bring life into a difficult world if you aren't ready to care for it*, Aadore thought. She could not bear children herself. She cocked her head as the mother glanced her way.

Aside from these two civilians, she sat among soldiers wearing taut, collarless uniforms—the handsome ones they wore when not in their iron shells. *Must be flights exclusively for the military lads and ladies*, she decided. Who, then, was *that*? She wondered at the enormous fellow bundled like an Arhadian widow in black scarves and a voluminous coat. Down the bench from her, he rested. He rocked slightly, smelled of harsh cologne doused over fearful, sharp sweat, and clutched his right forearm with a leather-fingered fist. The nursed limb seemed strange somehow—shorter, maybe. She stared while trying to decide what was wrong with it.

"What, you fuking fool? What are you looking at?" he hissed.

The man's low-brim hat did not hide so much of his face that she missed the snarl on his porcine features, and his supercilious tone was unforgettable. Horgot, the Iron sage. Aadore apologized and glanced to her hands. She was certain the master would not recognize another's servant. They were all faceless to him. *But I remember you*, she thought. Once she'd controlled her pulse, she gave the master the occasional surreptitious glance—the kind servants made frequently to one another behind their masters' backs. She amused herself by deliberating on this repulsive coincidence. This was a charming mystery, and that was her favorite genre next to romance.

*All right*, she thought. *An apparently incognito Iron sage on a military flight to somewhere.* Why wouldn't he simply take one of the off-charter crowes from the Crucible? Why debase himself with a near civilian-class passage? It would seem the master was trying to sneak away. From what?

Perhaps the council had turned again. Perhaps one of the snakes in the basket had bit its fellows, and he had been denounced and marked for murder. If that were the case, though, she found it quite stupid to use a military channel for his escape. Horgot's flight had to have been sanctioned, then—at least under some measure of agreement from the council. She wondered what she could safely extract from Curtis on the matter. His busy day could have revolved around the Iron sage's current feint. Furthermore, she'd be sure to let the story casually pass from her lips to Beatrice. Sometimes it was better to let someone else solve a mystery—especially one involving an Iron sage.

"Aadore?"

The voice was quiet but deep and longing. She did not recognize it as her brother's, since Sean had always been a songbird. She did not want to acknowledge the black-bearded, gangly soldier who stood before her with a face so starved, peaked, and hollow she could cut herself just glancing at him. That was why she had looked away from the gate as he emerged— pretended she did not know this tall specter while he limped his way over to the bench where she sat. He used a cane. He'd never even handled a cane before. By all that was merciful, she could tell he'd seen things, her brother. He'd been burned by a fire from the inside out, and the shadow that remained around his deep-brown eyes was the tear-smudged ash of despair.

"Sean?" she asked.

It was truly a question, for her most dreadful reality was before her—a stranger wearing her brother's skin. The soldier slumped and dropped his pack to the bench. Sitting appeared to be an agonizing process. He hissed, winced, and fumbled one leg a bit as he settled. It looked stiff. "Yes, Aadore. It is I."

Queen's Station spoke for them. It bleated, shouted, and clanged its cacophonous order. A blond woman met the gentleman in waiting with his sad, droopy flowers. Her hair was quite short, which only brought out her handsome features. The happiness Aadore had been denied seemed to have found that pair instead, and his sweetheart told him his miserable bouquet was lovely, kissed him, and took his arm as they strolled away. The next round of travelers was ordered to form a line before the gate. The bench shifted tectonically when the disguised Iron sage removed his weight from

461

it, and the siblings were nudged closer. They touched shoulders and then at last, hands.

Sean breathed the longest sigh and watched the huge swaddled fellow walk to the inhospitable barricade of glass, iron, and wire. He thought perhaps he should have stayed on the other side of that fence and never come home. It would have been less cruel for his sister not to see him at all than to see him broken.

"I'm so sorry, Brother," whispered Aadore. He could tell she was holding in her tears. She hated to cry. "You're just...much older than I remembered. Thinner too."

"And crippled." He tapped his cane against his shin, and it rapped hollowly as if on wood. "A prosthetic."

"What? I mean...why couldn't they—"

"Graft me a new one?" Sean's laugh was bitter and short. "Seems magik doesn't work so well on the Brennochs. Think back, Aadore, on how we were never taken to the physician. Never patched up from a scrape beyond what bandages and hedge medicine Mother used. I think they knew, our parents. The bastards. They knew there was something wrong with me—with us, maybe. Fleshcrafting doesn't work, and now I have this fuking anchor on my body. Indeed, no sorcery at all seems to affect me, and believe me...they tried."

Aadore knew the stabbed-from-the-inside look when someone hid terrible pain. Her mistress did it often, and most Menosians were practiced in the art. She could see something rear in Sean's memory then—a terrible agony. The fire that had burned out his innocence. She dared not ask what it was—not now and not here.

"Let's...get you home," she said. "You can tell me all about your time away. I do want to hear, Sean. I want you to tell me. I've made us a lovely meal, and I have a place for you to sleep."

Aadore squeezed her brother's large, thin hand. His bones were sharp.

"Just a drink will do," replied Sean.

He grunted from the pain of standing, collected his pack, and began to walk on ahead. He left her behind. She wanted to weep at the accusations about her parents and the intimations of what Sean had suffered through these last many years. He'd been lying to her in letters, it seemed, or keeping from her the heinous truth. Had those letters even been written by him? She wondered this with a sinking feeling. What was all that talk about trying things on him? She leaped up and raced after him. "Sean, please."

Destruction began most subtly—an oddly howling wind and a scent too sharp and sour. In this instance, all of Menos knew the onset of doom from the slow, angry groan and the rumbling and rising of pistons within the earth. If Geadhain were ever to produce a scream from its soul beneath the immeasurable tons of shifting earth, then this sound building to a trembling, teeth-chattering hum would have been it. Aadore reached her brother, and they held each other close in the rudely shivering station. Huge curved panels dropped off the columns and dashed on the ground like dinner plates. The tiles under their boots cracked like eggshells and warned of a fall into a rumbling abyss. Even the wretched mother and Horgot—beside the others in the line—fell against the wire fence and clung to the mesh, each other, and the babe in his or her basket. The storm under the soil rose until the benches were sliding. A few fell into small splits that had appeared. When it all stopped for an instant, there was a jarring stillness in the dusty shadows, and the screams of the confused and mildly wounded blistered the air. Aadore believed they would be all right, and she grinned to her brother like a miner in the dark.

Boom! Boom! Boom!

Three detonations destroyed Aadore's hearing. The sudden throbbing deafness granted her a vacant clarity. It created for her a silent, moving phantograph of her city's doom. She could feel but not hear herself screaming as her knees bent and her body thrashed. Regardless of his disability, Sean had a foothold in the upheaval. His bony grip stopped her from being thrown into the cracks opening all around that swallowed like quicksand people, benches, poles, metal beams, tiles, and earth itself. Queen's Station had become a quagmire and a storm in one with the perilous, swirling ground and the split colonnades and girders smashing down like lightning-struck trees.

Sean backed them away. They stumbled from the sinkhole that neither the Iron sage nor the young mother had escaped quickly enough. The mother was waist-deep in an anthill of detritus when Aadore looked. The shrieking woman threw her child—basket and all—with what at first seemed love and then revealed itself to be selfishness: she meant to use her hands to claw for survival.

Aadore did not see the woman's death. Instead, she stumbled with her brother. They reached, tripped, and risked themselves on a conveyor belt of doom to save the Menosian child cast into the rubble. They did not ask why or pause, for it was in both their hearts to act. Aadore caught the blanket in which the child was swaddled, and it unrolled like a towel. Sean managed to break the fatal cartwheeling of the naked infant—a boy—with the curved handle of his cane and dragged him nearer until Aadore could gather the child in her arms.

When she stood, deaf and delirious, she did not think to save anyone else. They did not reach for the hand of Horgot, who wailed curses as he shat himself and was compressed into a paste of turds, fat, and screaming rage—the essence of his being. The Third Chair vanished along with all of Gate S in an explosive burp and a flourishing furl of wire. One of the great columns added its crumbling mass to his grave and ripped with it a swath of the ceiling. With that card pulled, the whole of Queen's Station surrendered. Beams in place for a hundred years and bolted with magik, feliron, and the sorrow of slaves moaned with all the misery of their creation and dropped into the shuddering, erupting cauldron of death.

When the sublime shock faded, Aadore became aware of her limbs again. She realized she was alive. That reality did not match the world around her, though. The brimstone and soot cloud peeled the ashy skin from her face and made it an agony even to open her eyes. She felt the hand of her brother, though, and she heard—or imagined in her humming head—the mewl of the young life they'd saved. Sean started to lead them. How her one-legged brother blindly dragged them through this afterlife, she would never know. He must have walked in death before. He must have kissed the Pale Lady herself, taken her maggoty tongue into his mouth, and made love to her rotting body to have the courage to steer through this damnation. She saw men and metal twisted into ruin. New pillars rose from this fire-crackling purgatory. They were planted in mounds of shapeless trash and lavished in blood and soiled remnants—scented and sauced in a buttery charcoal reek and a crimson-black glaze. She felt she might never again eat meat. Although she could hear once more, all there was to hear, besides the babe's cries, was the flapping of hot wind and the dusty settling of whatever apocalypse had undone the Iron City. There were no sounds of life. It was as if they were all that remained of their people. She wouldn't think it. She couldn't.

But lo, the ashen veil gave way to bleary smoke, and what should have been a blessing of sight warped into a revelation of horror. For Sean had lead them from the heart of the collapsed building to the steps of Queen's Station. The steps were unrecognizable, still glowing orange with infernal heat, and piled in fractured plates and rods of igneous material. They'd come to a height to view the city, and all that lay beneath them was a pitted, fiery staircase, an entrance to the billowing furnace their great civilization had become. This was unlike the scarring brought by the storm of fire and ice. This was a reckoning. By the iron of their souls alone, Sean and Aadore did not quake or weep. Their fortune still astonished her.

"How? How are we alive?" gasped Aadore.

"We cannot be the only ones," replied Sean. "I shall not accept it."

Ripping off what remained of his shirt, he salvaged enough scorched material to make a child's sling and fixed his sister with a truss. The child would not stop crying until she gave him a finger to suckle—a trick she'd seen Mother use on Sean when he was young. When she turned to Sean, she saw the complex lattice of scars upon her brother's naked torso—wounds from an older horror than this. The strongest weapons came from toil and beating and burning metal. He was no different, and she warmed with pride at the story of survival told on his flesh. They held hands and faced the smoldering light and black clouds of what should have been dawn. Finally, all drifted to a whistling sadness.

It was in that calm that the sound of screams came to them. The two walked down the steps fearlessly. They were ready to see who and what remained

# XVIII

# SHADOWS OVER EOD

I

"Are you praying?" whispered Rowena.

She could not think what else the Voice could be so deeply engaged in as he hunched at Maggie's side, held her hands, and clenched his eyes shut in thought. Rowena had memories of the medicine workers of the Arhad practicing similar meditations when they communed with the ancient spirits of sand, wind, and fallen warriors. She did not believe in their sorcery and had less faith in Alastair's power to heal Maggie, if indeed that was his intent. Whatever state he'd entered, it was far away from the grated, lightless kennel into which they had been thrown. The arrangements were more rudimentary than in their prior cell—not that it made any difference when Menos was about to obliterate the nation for which she held her secrets.

Earlier, she'd been delivered another blow to the head for an outburst and did not recall herself being loaded onto the *Morgana*—aside from flashes of black metal and echoes of boots on plated floors that came to her in swoons. She couldn't tell where they'd ended up. The meshing of their metal cage was loose enough only for air and not for sight. Echoes and teases of flickering light from somewhere beyond their confinement made her suspect their cage was in a cargo hold. *We're just waiting to die now. An old horse they can't yet*

466

*be bothered to put down. Galivad, I do hope you and your foolishly bright songs somehow survive this end. I shall try too.* Determined to live, Rowena fished up the pride of that weak, filthy girl—the *khek*—once lost in the desert. That was the girl who would not die even as brutal heat cracked her lips and skin and her eyes dried up like nuts. Rowena and that shade of her past were always close. As much of a woman as she had grown into, the *khek* lived beneath her strong skin. Rowena was not nearly ready to die—not until she saw that silly man one more time and did everything she could to save Eod.

She called to Alastair loudly. "If you're not praying, I hope you're figuring out a way to get us out of this cage."

"I was praying," muttered Alastair. He kissed Maggie's hands and laid them over her breast. She looked like the proper corpse the Iron marshal had nearly made her.

"I did not think you were the religious sort," said Rowena. He shrugged. "Who even is there to pray to?" she continued. "The spirits of legend, the great beasts, and the sorcerer kings are all dead, forgotten, or do not care for our tiny lives. We have only two Immortals who would hear us. One is missing; the other is mad. Prayers will not save Maggie. Her Fate is ours to mend."

"The oldest powers might be forgotten, but they have not left us," warned Alastair with a threatening twinkle to his stare. After a cold laugh, he added, "You are right, though, sword. They are not listening. They do not care."

Snap! The immense black bird they rode in, made to rule the skies as a warship tore through the ocean, was suddenly pitched downward by a powerful gust of wind. Up the cage bounced. They were almost hovering like a carnival ride the queen had once forced Rowena to ride in Fairfarm. Then the cords tying their prison to the floor of the hold broke. There came a terrible heave and a flailing leather snake—a binding—whipped into the cage and lashed her hand as the ship dropped. The three prisoners fell into a tangle. They woke Maggie with their elbows and knees, and they held tight. Without its restraints, their cell was rolling end over end like a die. In the toss, there was some screaming, quite a bit of bruising, and finally a crash.

"I think one of your 'powers' might have heard you," wheezed Rowena.

One square corner of the cage had been dashed right off. The cube leaned on its points against a few better-secured crates, and they'd been poured out onto a stippled metal deck. They were free. Possibly not for long, though,

467

for shouting sounded in the hold with some soon-to-be-flogged Menosian pleading he had only stepped away for a sand.

*Charazance, you dastardly fox,* thought Alastair. She had bided her time, waited for all the gamblers at the table to expose their tells, and stalled until the pot brimmed with coin before laying down her cards. Alastair snatched Maggie and Rowena and began running from the wreckage and the noises of Menosian pursuers. They were in a hold. It was quite mundane after all their suffocation in Menosian culture. The tall steel ceilings banded in bolted struts hummed. The orchestral chamber muffled their footsteps. The hold's most devious details and evils were likely hidden in the crates they ran past. Maggie's rude resuscitation gave her pep, and she could match her limping pace to the fleetness of her companions. It pleased Alastair to no end that under her scars, scabs, and blood-knitted hair, her fire and perseverance had not been snuffed. Even in their peril, he took a speck to turn and squeeze her hand before continuing.

Where was Charazance's next miracle? *Come on, then. You haven't popped open the cage just so we can be caught again. There must be another trail...a hatch...a ladder.*

A panel.

Scoundrels like him always knew where to hide. He had a nose for holes as good as any rat's. Few people in their frenzy of running and dashing behind crates would ever have looked up and recognized the importance of one of the roof's loose panels. A common mind would not have thought to use the crates as mighty stairs. The escapees would have to make a climb, and there was a risk they would be seen and shot. The dice were hot, though, and his mistress was plundering the table. Alastair threw himself on Charazance's mercy and urged the women up.

"I don't see anything!" hissed Rowena.

"It's there. An exit," he insisted. "An access, I wager. I cannot say whether it's a vent or a crawl space, but it will take us away from here."

Rowena tried to make out what he was describing.

"I trust you," rasped Maggie. They were her first words since the torture.

That gave Rowena faith in the rogue as well. There were now several more Menosians shouting in the hold. Rowena grabbed the corner of the nearest box and started climbing. Maggie followed. Fear slowed time to a crawl. Rowena felt each trickle of beaded sweat and thud of her heart. These brought forth bursts of desperate strength. She was a strong woman, and with that power intensified, Rowena quickly came first to the top of the mountain of crates. Fate still smiled upon them, and although she could see black men moving like little ants down in the maze of shipping containers, the ironguards' shouts echoed distantly, and fiery holes didn't fill her body. They hadn't been spotted. *Amazing*, she thought.

"Open the damned thing!" whispered Alastair as he flopped himself atop their pinnacle.

Maggie pulled herself up as well. Rowena was impressed. Where the poor woman got her energy was a mystery. Turning her attention to the plate, Rowena noticed it appeared to have fallen partially open. It was like a half-raised skycarriage ramp. *Well, this is strange*, she thought, and she gave it the slightest pull. That was all it took to lower the piece of plate just enough for the three to tread up it and into an air shaft beating with fans. The plate even had a handle, so Rowena was able to pull shut the ramp.

Everything that had just happened appeared worthy of several drinks and a stern suspension of disbelief. Their escape had been extraordinary.

Rowena mumbled to the faceless shadows around her. "How did we—"

"Luck," said Alastair, and he grinned so widely she could hear it in his voice. "Seems she is finally on our side."

## II

*I shall return, my lamblings. In a day. In a week. I hope no longer. I shall find us a new home. Have faith in your mother and be strong,* Elissandra told her children. Then she gave each a kiss on the cheek. From the way Elineth winced at her kiss, Elissandra felt the age for coddling her son was nearly done. *We are all growing up and getting old,* she mused, and she left the children to read the few books they'd brought with them from the Iron City.

She closed the door to their quarters. In the rustic chambers beyond— wooden furniture, brass lamps, a log-framed hearth, and a cast-iron stove—a plump old man waited for her. "How are the children?" he asked earnestly.

"Fine." She struggled to conjure his name. "Fine, Herschel. Do see they are entertained. They enjoy...unusual games. Do play along."

"It's Hansel, and I certainly shall," he said, and he beamed.

Throughout the majority of his caregiving days, the silly oaf would likely be locked in the cellar or prey to another of her lamblings' unpleasant jokes. She'd taken the piece of Hansel's mind that would care, however, and filled the emptiness with memories of Elineth, Tessariel, and herself—a cousin thrice removed. Elissandra maintained no particular malice toward the man. He'd simply been the first in Gloamhollow to answer his door to an old lady with her two large cats. Above all, she had to know her children would be safe, and he was the key to that assurance. She would leave him some coins for his troubles later—though Menosian crowns would surely have depreciated steeply by the time of her return. Eod's Fates were bound for the archivists too if she did not add a dash of lightning to her step. Elissandra shocked her faux cousin as she reached up into the air and tore open a glimmering black slit. He was flabbergasted still more when she widened it and strode through. Elissandra could erase that memory as well, or Tessariel could work on her skills doing so should the man's astonishment persist into annoyance.

She had all Geadhain to cross and hourglasses in which to do it. She'd seen the future in a vision so overpowering its revelations seemed inevitabilities. She knew that come dawn, Menos would be a pit of death, darkness, and ruin, and that there was only a meager chance Eod too would not fall. The Fates were now silent, as if no future remained.

III

"Are we ready?" asked Lowe.

The queen of Eod stood on the ivy-twined balcony overseeing the red sunrise of war. In the weeks since her acceptance of this duty—and curse—Leonitis believed Lowe had become as much a royal as any ever crowned. He did not know whether after Magnus's loss, the real queen could have shown the same majesty and confidence this charwoman had found within herself. Throughout the streets of Eod, Lowe's speeches continued to rouse the peasantry. "We are Geadhain's hope! We are the keepers of tomorrow!"

Beholding the woman before him, Leonitis failed to separate the royalty from the ruse, so masterfully had Lowe knitted herself into the illusion. He wondered whether she could ever return to being a mistress of the kitchen. Stirring from his daydream, Leonitis realized he'd been gazing at her and had yet to respond. "Yes," he replied and saluted with a fist. "The ward is up."

Magik shimmered over Eod's white houses and silver towers. It was as though the city were contained within a glass clamshell. The sunshine made it through the pearly haze but not without a little refraction, and the whole of Eod's heavens lit up like a starscape no matter the hourglass of day. *Beautiful*, Lowe thought. *A white shield of hope against the blackness of Menos.*

"Gorijen calls it a witch wall." Leonitis walked up the steps to join her at the railing. "Ominous for such a lovely sight—though as long as it protects our city, I see no harm in how it is named."

"We did this, my hammer," she whispered. "We did what our king and queen—bless and preserve them—could not. I hope it is enough."

"I believe it will be."

They smiled and savored the sweetness of peace—the bustling city, glimmering clouds, and cries of Eod's white birds who knew nothing of war. This would be their memory for which to fight.

"We should go to the east wall," said Lowe. "I shall not leave our people without their leader. We shall face the Iron skies together."

Leonitis did not question the conviction in every word she uttered. Ardently, he too believed in these words. Here stood the leader who would hold off the Iron City. The Lion bowed with grace and honor until she told him to rise. As they moved into the cool chamber past the balcony, they seemed as unflappable as stone beings. Even when the door to the queen's quarters burst open, they simply moved into formation. Lowe went behind her hammer, while the weapon of his borrowed legend was drawn.

It was only Rasputhane looking flustered. Leonitis flung back his mighty hammer, and the queen stepped out.

"My queen!" exclaimed the spymaster. "My queen! Word from Menos. Well, from Fairfarm to Riverton to Taroch's Arm and farther. I can see no corner of the map where this news will not reach, and it already spreads on pigeons and far-speaking stones like wildfire!"

"What news? What are you on about? Calm yourself!" boomed Leonitis.

"Menos," he blurted. "The Iron City has fallen."

"Fallen?" muttered Lowe.

"Fallen?" echoed her hammer, and he gaped in shock.

Bolts of doubt, horror, delight, and astonishment stormed their hearts. Queen Lowelia required a seat, and Leonitis needed the back of his queen's seat for balance.

"Fallen," said the hammer again.

Each time he uttered the word, it felt no more believable. Menos, with its bones of feliron, fallen? Even the notion that such a civilization could be physically destroyed seemed untenable. Moreover, the spirit of the Menosians was just as obdurate. Menos could not fall. Not any of these three had truly desired that fate for the wicked city and its people. They had wanted a military defeat, perhaps—a humiliating loss to send the dogs back into their kennels to lick their wounds and plot for another thousand years. Never annihilation, though. Magnus would never have committed or ordered this destruction. *Who then?* Leonitis wondered.

"The queen," whispered Lowe. "She said that she would strike at Menos. Was this her strike?"

There were no gasps. There were only dry swallows of this bitter lump of truth. The not-present queen had committed genocide. Lowe wondered whether it was really doom on that scale. "Tell us," she commanded, and she closed the door Rasputhane had left open. "Tell us what you know."

At the moment, only a hodgepodge of facts was known. An indeterminate but epic disaster had struck the Iron City early that morning and leveled all Kor'Keth's northeast range from the Iron Valley to the eastern front. Tremors had been felt to Fairfarm and Blackforge, and scouting parties in those regions warned against investigating the scope of decimation due to the spans of impenetrable ash—a cloud so dark no wind or light could break it apart. Ghastly cries came forth from the realm, and yet not a soul from within the fiefdoms of Menos or the Iron City itself had been heard from since the reckoning.

"I can't believe what she's done." Lowe gritted her teeth in disgust. "I killed a rat myself, and I shall never forget that wickedness...my wickedness. I had every intent of blasting Menos's crowes from the sky...but this..." She looked tearfully to her listeners. "What is the penance for the murder of thousands? Or hundreds of thousands? Each of us has silently signed Queen Lila's damned contract with our own blood!"

"We don't know the extent of the damage. We don't know that the queen did this," countered Rasputhane. He said this with a kitten's aggression and could not stop clenching his hands.

"We know," said Lowe in a grim and final tone.

Queen Lowe lay back in her seat. She felt as tired as all the old women in the world, and she pondered the unholy crime. The three suffered mightily behind their clenched expressions—three solemn generals who had been complicit to the darkest doom.

Eventually, Leonitis asked, "Does it mean...is the war over?"

Queen Lowe and Leonitis looked to Rasputhane, whose own gaze was now focused on the whitish, wavering skies beyond the balcony doors and a fleck of blackness in the distance. Three flecks, actually, that were moving in tandem. He knew instinctively they were not birds. Suddenly white, he said, "No. The war is not over."

## IV

Once through the panel, the three escapees found themselves in a restrictive ventilation network. Sometimes, the tunnels narrowed so much they shuffled on hands and knees while staring into each other's arses. At other points of intersection, the metal crawlway opened to four-cornered spaces with great fans that sucked at their clothing. In these boxed hurricanes, they clung to each other like mountaineers atop a blustering peak and grunted along to the next intersection. The going was never easy, and they did not seem to know where they were headed. Rowena assumed this given the Voice's "hms" and bemused "ah-has." These could barely be heard over the whooping thrum in the tunnels whenever he picked a direction. While crawling through yet another impossibly small space, she pulled on Maggie's leg, and Maggie tugged on their leader's leg so they might stop.

"Do you have any idea where you are headed?" Rowena whispered.

"No. Not at all," said Alastair.

"Well, should we not..." Rowena felt challenged to come up with her own plot.

"Exactly," said Alastair. "Best to just keep our chain gang moving. If we are always moving, something is bound to happen."

Although his reply sounded annoyingly glib, Rowena could make no counterargument. Every now and then, as they quietly crossed grates that dropped into iron hallways and rooms, the noise dimmed, and they could hear what was happening below—marches of ironguards, frantic engineers, and barked orders to find assassins and prisoners. This revealed, among other things, that they were not the only concern aboard the *Morgana*. Thus, being quiet little mice and staying in motion as Alastair proposed seemed the best and only course. Rowena could not help but listen for mention of Galivad. Even his death would be news, but she always came away without a hope or grief to nurse. Had Beatrice eaten him? Galivad had certainly made it sound as if the Menosian would. Rowena's contemplations condensed to a diamond of resolve, and if Galivad was indeed dead by the lady of El's hand then Rowena would be the sword of judgment to end the woman.

Lost in her brooding, Rowena had no idea how long or far their wriggling had taken them when suddenly the thrumming fan music that numbed her hearing ceased, and the sounds of echoing voices replaced it. Alastair stopped their progress momentarily, and when they resumed, they did so with stealth. Noises teased them from another tall junction farther along. Reaching that junction became an exercise in dread and patience. They moved one hand and one knee at a time across a desert. They were not wrong to be cautious, though, for when they approached a chamber of fans—all eerily stalled and still—they saw they were not alone. The instruments of a skilled trade—some tools, a belt, and a worker's ladder—were all piled together at the shaft's exit. Beyond, Rowena could just make out a shadow in the soft light of the metal room. A man.

His back was to them, and they continued slinking out of the tunnel. After pawing around the ladder like cats, they unfurled their aching bodies without a gasp. Strides ahead, the man fidgeted with something like the tripod that phantographers used for their captures. This was a very strange place—and occasion—to take any sort of phantograph, though.

Perhaps the three-legged support was needed to steady one's hand for another purpose. The wafting voices came again, and they were much more resonant. The bodies of their owners were closer—perhaps right below. At the sound of one speaker's voice, Rowena froze. Galivad. She froze again at the others—Beatrice, Moreth, and the Iron Queen. It appeared they were arguing.

"He's not a pet; he's a prisoner," declared the Iron Queen. "Give him to the Iron marshals and be done with it."

"No," replied the Lady El.

"Beatrice!" exclaimed Moreth.

A shivering pause fell, and Rowena imagined the Iron Queen turning people into blocks of ice with her stare, and then Her Dark Majesty said, "Excuse me?"

"I do not fear death," interrupted Galivad boldly and deeply. His words touched Rowena.

"But you should, watchmaster," threatened the Iron Queen. "If not your own demise, then the death of all you value. The death of Eod. Behold the Immortal King's city—the white stain that has existed since time immemorial to insult the struggles of man with its arrogance. Behold as I wipe that stain clean. What is that? That shimmer? Gustavius! Report!"

He was alive. Galivad was alive. *Alive, alive, alive.* So too was Eod for the moment, and yet that felt less important to Rowena's pounding heart. The glimmer of joy she felt for Galivad's survival sparkled like the metal rod that the man—whom they tiptoed toward—slotted into his support. By the Kings, it was a gun. A Menosian hunting rifle—the kind used for sporting herds and the hulks of Alabion.

Below, the Iron Queen shouted. "No more dallying or strategizing. We have built an apocalypse into these ships. Now bring down the fire. The quickest way through a closed door is with a bomb. Blast the bloody thing! All of it. We shall raid the ruins of Eod. Why is it so damned hot? The air should be fixed by now."

As it turned out, neither the malfunctioning ventilation system nor Eod's defenses was the Iron Queen's biggest problem. Here priming his rifle was an assassin ready to kill Gloriatrix and perhaps all the wicked flock gathered on the command deck of the *Morgana*. Galivad could easily be among those doomed in the crossfire. In sands or specks, the bullets would begin. Unless Rowena or one of her companions acted now, they might not reach the assassin in time to stop him from shooting whoever. Quickly, she deliberated the advantages of letting the assassin do his work, and yet every potential blessing came with the caveat that Galivad—who sounded as if he was close to the Iron Queen—could also die.

The assassin pressed the nozzle of his rifle against the mesh that caged the fan. Rowena heard the scrape against the metal. He was ready and wait- ing now only for a cue or a word. The creeping trio watched him tense his shoulders. His finger would twitch soon.

"Damn," said Rowena, for she knew what her body was going to do.

The assassin heard her, as did her companions, but none reacted fast enough to stall Rowena's charge. The large woman stomped across the metal floor and alerted everyone who had half an ear to the commo- tion. She was not in a place of reason but burning in the flames of a fire much hotter than rage. Like a rumbling, fiery train did she come upon the assassin—a helmless man concealed in the cloth uniform of a Menosian soldier. He had scarcely turned and released his rifle ere she slammed her weight and fists into him. They tumbled. The assassin possessed a body trained for quickness and rediscovered his martial finesse after being ambushed. Fists and knees flew into Rowena, but she was a brawler and a brute—a stone woman. She spit out some blood and the tooth he'd cost her and beat whatever she saw with her flint knuckles. The assassin made the understandable error of kicking his short-haired, muscled foe in the groin, and she smiled, grabbed his leg, and twisted the limb until it made a brutal snap. The assassin wailed, and Rowena's monster hands went for the man's throat.

This was less a battle than a tavern brawl, and Alastair and Maggie watched dizzily. A speck later, the combatants tripped and vanished while they held each other in a dark lover's tangle. Rushing over to investigate, Maggie and Alastair discovered an open hatch in one corner of the chamber with a ladder leading down. They peeked down and saw that the wrestling pair had fallen onto a feliron floor polished to the richness of black marble. Rowena had landed atop the assassin, and although she groaned in pain, it seemed she would live. On the other hand, the would-be murderer appeared crumpled and dead. Perhaps this was his life's only virtuous moment—inadvertently saving Rowena. Faces surrounded Rowena, and hands pointed accusations and blue-tipped rifles. Almost at once, the Iron Queen's cold purple eyes looked to the peering shapes in the ceiling.

"Come down slowly, and we might not shoot you before you reach the floor," she said.

## V

Elissandra fell into the hot sands of Kor'Khul. Her steps into Dream were getting sloppier. Her body was breaking down like a worn sponge. She was missing a hand and surely all of one ear now. Without a mirror, she wasn't entirely sure of the extent of her deformities. Elissandra touched her head with the only five fingers she still owned and was happy to discover a face intact in all other regards—although part of her scalp felt curiously smooth. She did not suffer from vanity, though, and had held onto more of herself than any Dreamwalker—aside from the great Morigan—should have on a journey this exhausting.

She had one more step—a leap, actually. For this would be a hazardous bound into moving matter and then a hobble to find the Iron Queen afterward. Could she do it? Could she reach Gloria in time? Doom painted itself beautifully on the horizon. There the city of Eod shone as a pearl wrapped in starlight. Three grand shadows eclipsed it. The shadows were tilted ovoid moons of nightmare black with ruffling feathers tipped in molten power.

By the Kings, the Sisters, and all the ancient glories of the world, Gloriatrix had outdone herself. She'd created legends—horrific legends, but bringers of awe and eminence just the same. The Furies would evoke an unholy cleansing. Their glowing spines were slowly flushing forward into an angry porcupine's stance, and the tips of those enormous lances or—Kings forbid—the lances themselves would launch upon Eod. Nothing would live. Nothing could live in such incineration. Perhaps Gloriatrix still operated under the delusion that there would be pillaging, riches, and fresh slaves afterward. In reality, there would be ash. The Everfair King's valley of light would be a crater as dark as Menos, which she knew by now had suffered the fate shown to her in her vision. Death for death. Doom for doom. Damnation for the world. Even she, a twisted former Iron sage, grieved for the wretchedness of what was foretold.

*One more step*, she thought.

Elissandra stumbled from the dune that was trying to eat her waist, reached up with the smooth stub of the missing hand, swore, and used her other to rip open a gateway to Dream.

VI

Gloriatrix sat on her simple iron throne on the glittering bridge of the *Morgana*. She surveyed her new queendom, and its sinfully elegant architecture rather enthralled her—the metal dais from which she presided and the broad encircling steps that led downward from her roost. The panorama of the wasted desert of Kor'Khul and the clouds the vessel tore through were displayed on a tinted portal as grand as the moving phantograph she had once watched as a child on a great screen in Menos. On the platforms descending from her throne, engineers sat at their mechanically chattering, unearthly consoles. These resembled insect chrysalides strung in black crystal secretions, and they were beautiful and ghastly to behold. The dark and starched-uniformed people fiddling with these bizarre instruments all worked, quiet members of her hive, and spoke only when their tempered-glass screens could not divine what information they required. So much of this techno-magikal brilliance came from the unknown frontier of advancement. They were miracles of the modern age—each a wonder that would not have existed without her as the muse.

Whimsical thoughts of her three black monstrosities ascending past the burning shield that surrounded Geadhain teased the Iron Queen's austerity into a smile. She was oh so happy, even if, in the darkest closet of her heart where she kept the starved prisoner of her emotions, she was a little sad that Gabriel, Sorren, and Vortigern weren't there to share this moment. Only she had survived. Her wretch of a brother, she realized, had scattered her mirth into a thousand uncollectible pieces. Perhaps he wasn't in Alabion and instead he'd fled to the City of Wonders, which in an hourglass would be the City of Cinders. Good. Thackery could die in the flames along with the freedom he'd chosen to trade for his family's pride.

An Iron marshal strode up the steps to Gloriatrix. He wore rubbers and a bib as if coming from an interrogation. Anxiously, he whispered to the guards present, who then passed the words to the Iron lord nearest Gloriatrix. None of the secret-bearers seemed to want to break the news the marshal had brought to their queen. Iron Lord Gustavius, the last to hear, was one of the Iron Queen's chosen aides. He was a favorite of hers for his weathered, unkind face, chopped gray hair, gloomy nature, and artless words—they shared too a deep history of which they rarely spoke. Sometimes, she thought of him as one of the gargoyles at the Blackbriar Estate animated by magik. He even drawled his words in a long, labored way as would a stone man. She was surprised he held his tongue.

"Spit it out," demanded Gloriatrix.

"I would not want to trouble you," said the Iron lord.

"Trouble me."

"Yes, my Queen," said Gustavius, and he gave a short salute—a backward fist to his breast—in caricature of Eod and symbolic of a dagger being plunged into an enemy's heart. "The Iron marshal has told me that the three detainees from Eod have escaped. However, we are not sure of the details."

The Iron Queen's moods were indecipherable, and her silence crept out like a slow poison. Finally, she glanced at the Iron marshal. "Were the prisoners in your care?" she asked.

"Indeed, my Queen," he said, and he bowed.

Gloriatrix waved at the man. "Take him somewhere quiet, shoot him, and throw him into the desert."

With the judgment made, no amount of the Iron marshal's pleading would sway her. A pair of ironguards wrestled the marshal from the Iron Queen's presence. Gustavius waited until the screaming man was off the bridge before considering another address. When all was quiet but for the music of the consoles and hiss of the tremendous winds tickling the black hide of the *Morgana*, he asked, "Is that all, my Queen?"

"Are you looking for them?"

"Certainly."

"Then there is nothing more to be said. No more failures to reprimand for the time being."

"Yes, my Queen."

Gloriatrix returned to watching the skies and land unfold. Complications and incompetence were all part of the road to victory. Every success came through a gauntlet of strife and failures, and her taking of Geadhain was a trial only begun. Once Magnus had been unseated, there would still remain the threat of his mad brother in the South. However, she was prepared to test her Furies against the black magik of Brutus and quite sure she would plant the flag of victory into his ruined corpse. A dark star was soon coming, and she would be the queen that it foretold. She would sit upon the world's throne. Many people would try to stop this divine ascension—the Kings, the nations that did not share her vision, and Horgot and his loyalists. Thanks be to Elissandra for warning her of the Iron sage's treachery. A whole garden of rotten fruit stank in Menos, from what she'd heard. Elissandra had taken care of a bit of pruning herself with Septimus, and three of Horgot's assassins had been caught when the manifests, transfers, and personnel dossiers of those come to Fort Havok had been examined. Spies were easy to spot once the spectacles were placed on and one knew where to look. At present, there would be few if any infiltrators left in her tightly fisted organization.

"Any word from the dogs in Menos?" she asked.

An hourglass ago, a far-speaking communication had been sent to Horgot and his conspirators. It had let him know that the Iron Queen knew what he had done, and that he should beg for the mercy he wasn't likely to receive.

"No," replied Gustavius. "Actually, we are encountering a few issues with our communications equipment. An interference."

"Interference?"

"We have been unable to reach Horgot—or anyone else for that matter—since this morning. The engineers are checking our channels and stones. They believe it is an effect of our distance or altitude—perhaps another variable of this rather new technomagik."

"Fix it," she said, and she fanned herself. She could see the hair matting at Gustavius's temples too. "We shall need to contact the Iron City once Eod is ours. I promised the people as much in my preemptive victory speech. It's feeling more and more like the desert in here, but the desert should be out there. Fix that as well."

"Men are working on both problems as we speak," Gustavius assured her.

The Iron Queen made a disgruntled snort. Here she was flying the skies with a salvo of doom in the most advanced vessel ever constructed. She was about to subdue the oldest kingdom in history, and she couldn't tell her countrymen of the moment when they should praise her name. For all the inventions of technomagik, the brightest minds still fumbled to crack the walnut of how to talk over far distances. Men could live past their years, quell the elements to peace, capture images on paper, glass, and screens, and do infinite wonders more, and yet people still relied on pigeons and magik stones to most accurately deliver messages. How ludicrously barbaric. She knew the reason for it—ethereal static. The sages of East and West agreed. It was an effect whereby Geadhain's atmosphere ran with invisible currents of power that disrupted the consistency of magik. Maintaining sorcery over great distances, therefore, was a feat left to the Immortals and departed sorcerer kings. A tremendous amount of power was needed to create even the short spurts of dialogue from a far-speaking stone, and the magik was spent right after.

Not much of a convenience in an age of conveniences. Perhaps her war could solve that problem too. Kill the Immortals, and surely some of Geadhain's magik would die. Maybe a bit of that static would fizzle. Though she wasn't a metascientist, this was just about the only untested theory that remained. As more of her role in the new world arranged itself, she considered that she was to be less a ruthless queen and more a revolutionary industrialist. *Gloriatrix, queen of tomorrow, bringer of the age of progress.*

Dawn celebrated her glory, and amid the swirling sands and clouds, a dot of white appeared—Eod. She clutched her chair and waited for the pearl on the horizon to grow. In moments, Geadhain's new dawn would begin with some darkness and doom. However, the light would come after. *What a queer sentiment hope is,* she thought, *to possess me now.*

Moreth, Beatrice, and the shackled watchmaster of Eod appeared quite suddenly before her. Their interruption disgusted her in her moment of exultation. "What is it? Have you come to watch the new dawn with me?" she asked.

"Yes," said Moreth a little unsteadily.

The Iron Queen sneered at the watchmaster, who stood behind the white ghost of the Lady El. "Why is he here? So whole still?"

Beatrice's husband tugged on his wife to answer, but the woman was quiet.

"He's not a pet. He's a prisoner," said the Iron Queen. "Give him to the Iron marshals and be done with it."

"No," replied Beatrice.

"Beatrice!" exclaimed Moreth.

Gloriatrix leaned toward the bold woman. "Excuse me?"

"I do not fear death," declared the watchmaster, and he strode out from behind Beatrice's protection.

The Lady El had been shielding him, realized Gloriatrix. However, she could spit poison at that later. In truth, the watchmaster's impudence amused her.

She laughed. "But you should, watchmaster. If not your own demise, then the death of all you value. The death of Eod." The Iron Queen stood and pointed to the *Morgana*'s glass eye to the outside. There the red mountains of Kor'Keth manifested around the glowing, sprawling nest that was Eod. "Behold the Immortal King's city—the white stain that has existed since time immemorial to insult the struggles of man with its arrogance. Behold as I wipe that stain clean. What is that? That shimmer? Gustavius! Report!"

While Gustavius ran off like a flaming man, Gloriatrix stomped around her dais. She was too furious to cast threats or questions to the ill-mannered masters and their well-treated prisoner of war. Sands passed. She glared at the shivering dome around Eod and waited for Gustavius to return from his huddles with terrified engineers and people throwing their arms up in dismay.

At last, she shouted, "No more dallying or strategizing. We have built an apocalypse into these ships. Now bring down the fire. The quickest way through a closed door is with a bomb. Blast the bloody thing! All of it. We shall raid the ruins of Eod. Why is it so damned hot? The air should be fixed by now!"

People took their seats, tapped on screens, and twisted dials. Gustavius hurried back to his post, and all the grim dignitaries to this disaster watched the window and felt—with dread or pleasure—the vibration of the *Morgana* as her grotesque artillery primed itself. Eod turned black from the shadows of the Furies that hung over it. In a speck, the city would be a smoldering pit. Gloriatrix restrained herself and pondered how great a decimation to execute. The city still possessed valuables to submit to her new empire. If she crushed their shield and leveled half the place into ash, she presumed that would send a firm message about the cost of resistance. Here and now, the age of Immortals would end, and a Black Queen would create history. Gloriatrix and those around her were queasy from anticipation.

"Are we ready?" asked the Iron Queen once the hull had stopped shuddering.

Gustavius nodded. The sudden sound of heavy scuffling overhead stole the moment of her command to fire. She roared for someone to discover the cause of the noise. A speck later, they all saw a jumble of shapes fall out of the ceiling and crash onto the bridge. When the Iron Queen and her company reached the offenders, one appeared already dead from the drop, and ironguards surrounded the other. With her spider's sense of a tremble in the web, Gloriatrix felt the presence of the two timid, peering souls up the ladder hole from where the tumblers now lay. She gave them fair warning.

"Come down slowly, and we might not shoot you before you reach the floor," she said.

The two shadows wisely descended into the circle of their captors. Gloriatrix remembered them as the prisoners she'd met briefly prior to their escape.

"You have come just in time to watch the fall of an empire," said the Iron Queen.

Gloriatrix snapped her fingers, and the reclaimed prisoners were rounded up at rifle point and then steered back up the many levels to her seat of power. Gloriatrix sat on her throne, took a breath, and prepared to watch the world burn. Rowena was behind her. The sword looked around, and her helplessness horrified her. This could not be Eod's end or the end of the woeful man who wept and reached through his chains for her hand.

"Iron Queen," she said bravely. "Please. I know this is not the way. There can be peace. Only moments ago, we stopped a man who was to kill you. Our people can be allies if one meaningful step is taken. Does our kindness mean nothing?"

"It means you missed your chance," replied Gloriatrix. "I shall not squander mine."

She turned away from Rowena, unaffected by her plea. The time had come for a toast to the dawn of a Kingless age. She raised her hand. "Fi—"

"Gloria! Stop!" cried a woman.

The Iron Queen rolled her eyes and hissed. *Really?* What was this farcical circus of objections ruining her moment of glory? She leaped off her throne and turned to the woman hobbling up the black stairs, whose voice and insolent use of her shortened name she recognized as Elissandra's. Something seemed peculiar about the Iron sage once she stumbled into the inner circle. The queen saw her handless limb, the vacancy where an ear would be, and the side of her head half-bald as if in some voguish fashion. The lisping of the word "stop" seemed frightfully discordant too. When Elissandra anxiously grimaced, Gloriatrix noted the woman was missing several teeth. Had Elissandra always appeared so frightfully mauled? Gloriatrix should have remembered that much. Gloriatrix understood then that magik had corrupted her own memories—and Elissandra's flesh. "What...happened to you?" the Iron Queen asked.

Elissandra shook her head and grabbed the Iron Queen with her only hand. "A price. I paid a price to reach you, and I am glad I have. You must stop this war at once."

"Stop? Why?" Gloriatrix cast off Elissandra's grip and backed away from the circle of watchers. Stabbed by this apparent betrayal, she spit, "How dare you of all people make such a demand of me? More pleading for more mercy. What fools you all are to think others' appeals can influence me. I am Menos! I am Iron! I have no husband! No sons! No love but for the children and pride of the Iron City!"

With a foreboding sorrow, Elissandra said, "Then you have no love at all. Nothing for which to fight. The Iron City has been destroyed."

Wondrously the Mistress of Mysteries billowed with a silver light that shone and stirred through her clothing and hair. She swept her hand toward the great glass portal on the bridge. Eod was clouded over in gray. As if a fog had lifted, the view cleared to a vision much bleaker—a black city drenched in smoke. Shadows lurked in the toppled remains of dark houses. There were so many dark houses and cracked streets. None could identify the disaster until they spotted the split ebony tower—the indestructible yet rent Crucible. It gleamed for a moment in the dullness.

The vision vanished, as did the light from Elissandra. The great armor of the Iron Queen weakened, and she could not hold herself up in the shock. As she dropped, Gustavius—more agile than his age suggested—dipped under the Iron Queen like a gallant lover and carried her to her iron seat. Much of the vinegar had drained from Gloriatrix's veins. The Iron Queen could not speak. She did not ask whether the vision was falsified or still to be told, for her spider's mind had woven the threads of Menos's silence into the tapestry of reality. The Iron City was no more.

Gone. Dark forces had claimed it, as no other power could lay such waste. Had it been Magnus's magik? No. He was too noble ever to bring this bounty of death. Had it been the sorcery of his mad brother? How could Brutus's power reach so far? If not the brothers, then whom else could she blame for the hollow animal that screamed in her guts? She searched for the target of her hate but was lost in a black whirlpool that drowned her only deeper. Someone, anyone, must be blamed.

"Gloria," the white witch said gently.

Elissandra knelt before the shaking queen, and the women spoke silently from one mind to the other with the barest movements of mouths and eyes.

*Now you see you have been fighting the wrong war*, mind-whispered Elissandra. *You have been carrying the hate of a nation as a substitute for your own suffering. Because you do not want to face the darkness—the loneliness you would otherwise bear. Some sins can be forgiven; most of ours cannot. All we can do is live for our children and hope they have better lives and make more honorable choices than we have made.*

Gloria clutched Elissa's arm. She dug with desperation and shouted back to the woman in her head. *I cannot. I know no other way but the hard iron road. I have no children to save.*

*You do*, countered Elissa. *Your son. I felt in that vision the presence of the cold, unnatural power that took him. I feel it has now taken Menos. If you must fight for one thing, fight for your child and for the lives of the lost lambs on this vessel or those still in the darkness of the Iron City. Do you think you can go no lower? Do you think you cannot lose more of your soul? Damnation does not happen in a day. You are close, though, Gloria. You are close to damning not only yourself but also the world. Magnus could be the only ally strong enough to face the Black Star and the forces that ride with it.* Then Elissa shared the most crippling truth as she patted the Iron Queen's cheek. What else were any of them but children wanting comfort after all? *The Black Queen is not you, Gloria. However, she is coming, and she will make your games resemble finger paintings when compared with her wicked masterpieces. I have played in the darkness long enough. I have overindulged that side of my nature. It is time for you to come out into the light too. If you will not resemble something white—which I don't think will ever suit you—then be a shade of gray. Do not doom us all.*

The Iron Queen's claws went deeper as the caged misery of her heart bled out. *How? How would I even begin?*

*Begin with allies. Begin with peace before the* real *war. Even if you keep your empty hunger for power afterward, we must change our roles for this season of war. The enemy of my enemy is my friend. You have no friends, except for the strangeness of whatever we call our connection. You have no city. Consider that deeply and wisely.*

Consider Elissandra's words deeply and wisely the Iron Queen did—along with all the evils and wounds in her soul. This was to be a great contemplation, and the maimed witch left her so she might dreamily stare out into the vista of fragile peace.

Elissandra was no hero. She'd done this duty for her children. No matter the selfishness of that spark, she sensed all creatures who were not merciless black queens could find the essence of this warmth as well—at least once or twice in their lives. She hoped and kept faith that Gloria would not disappoint her.

When it came, Gloriatrix's response was another thread of this chaos. "Lower our arms," she declared in full voice to show that her leadership had not faltered. "We shall meet with the delegates of the City of Wonders. We shall see whether the oldest wounds can be healed for the sake of East and West. The might of Menos will be needed to stand against the mad king, and

Eod's grace will go far in rebuilding the Iron City. You four are no longer prisoners but our emissaries in these talks. Remember this as the kindness for which you asked, sword of the queen."

"I shall," promised Rowena.

While Rowena believed not a note of the Iron Queen's sincerity or wishes for peace, she could not argue with the woman's firm conviction for whatever new inglorious scheme she now plotted. For now, at least, Rowena and her companions were no longer prisoners. For now, at least, there was peace.

# XIX

# FIRE AGAINST FLAME

## I

The mad king's army was moving and blowing in like a season of sick warmth over Gorgonath's emerald hillocks. A push of hot, sticky air from the north tired the grass and battled the creeping winter, which always rose from the south. On the dark northern breezes, the silent Faithful, most sensitive to the cries of the Green Mother, tasted ash and smelled charcoal, metal, and blackened fat. They knew a fiery, foul army was coming to crush all that had stood since the lands were young. Despite this sure doom, Gorgonath's forces watched the north. They were pensive and quite without fear. This was a strength Beauregard could not claim for himself. He passed the nights pacing the Ancient Wall and wondering whether he would ever see his mother again or even live to kiss a girl.

Once the mad king's advance had been proclaimed to all of Gorgonath, the populace began to move. Those who would not fight—including Amara, who was too holy to be risked—retreated to the Silent Peaks. Those who would battle gathered at the mountain base in the grand plaza before the city's gate, where travelers would park their vehicles. There were no wagons or carriages there now, though, aside from those that served to cart payloads of weaponry or supplies. Instead, orderly tents and small fires filled the area. In these encampments, with the whispering militia and silent Faithful, Beauregard and his father now lived. When they had daylight with which to work, he and his father drilled with the soldiers. He took lessons on close combat, and his litheness seemed to serve him well.

"Good work, lad. Fast as an angry cricket," claimed Nithan, and he clapped.

Devlin called off their wrestling after having been unable to pin his eel of a son, and the two sweaty men walked over to the old fellow watching them from his seat near a struggling fresh campfire. Nithan offered them water, some tepid bean stew, and bread. They sat and chatted about everything and nothing while the sun and the remainder of the army rose. The three men were now fast friends. Nithan's words always rang kind and with wisdom, and his moderate grayness, hearty frame, pipe-smoking habit, and red cheeks (just like those of his children and wife) made him feel like an older relative to Beauregard and Devlin.

After breakfast, Beauregard and Devlin splashed themselves—a soldier's bath—and threw on clean jerkins. Nithan waited for them with two horses, a cart, and an ox on the road into Gorgonath. Among the chores of each and every day, with or without war, waste was collected and taken to the Silent Peaks. There it was added to other organic mulch and repurposed into rich fertilizer. Before being given one of the shifts for the duty, Beauregard hadn't thought of how the city, which possessed no apparent technomagiks for handling waste, could maintain such cleanliness. Now he was familiar with the Sorsettans and their beliefs in the recycling of all things—finding uses for what was considered useless in society.

*They really find a reason for every bug, leaf, and turd. Amazing,* mused Beauregard, and the colorful city jostled up and down to the beat of the ox he drove. Beauregard tried not to imagine the pastel towers and their vines enflamed. The reality, though, viciously imposed itself. *We are not defenseless,* he willed to the world without realizing he'd identified the Sorsettans as his countrymen. Just a hand away in a reinforced pouch on his hip and still tingling through the leather lay the wonderstone—his miracle.

Amara had called him a man the day he had been blessed with the gift, and it was true. Wars, mad kings, and miracles were his concerns—the kinds of worries any young lad would swap for a girl or some coin. However, he was a child no more, and thus childish things had to be placed in the closet, where he might go one day to remember them wistfully.

Beauregard would not and could not return to being the boy whose grandest dream was to sing as a minstrel in Eod. Even the long wandering life of a true bard that Amara had imagined for him seemed remote—at least today. Only when the mad king was repelled could his own adventures begin.

The Sorsettans were not without hope. In order for the mad king to penetrate the city, it would take a wave of force, and the people had more than prayers to protect Gorgonath. By what he'd seen, the Faithful were dervishes in battle. Each man was worth two or three of the Sun King's mindless vessels. At range, the army fought with crossbows and darts tipped in the black poisons of deep-sea predators. They would thin even half-dead attackers with their brutal paralytics before the Ancient Wall was ever threatened.

The Sorsettans also harbored a secret weapon no mad king would expect from peaceful farmers and monks—explosives. Through an alchemy Beauregard would need a more scientific education to grasp, gases that came from the congealed pits of organic refuse and excrement could be captured, condensed to liquid, bottled, and then used in small doses to light lanterns and fires. Recently, small doses had not been the order of business, and the whole of the Faithful's keep—all the persons unskilled in martial disciplines, including the elderly, disabled, and young—had been tasked with churning out tempered vials filled with this fluid. These were then wicked like candles and wrapped in flammable coatings. It was a rather ingenious idea credited to Amara, who surprised everyone as a capable warmaster. She would fight fire with flame and see whose wrath burned hotter. The flames of the Sorsettan incendiaries exploded on contact, shattered stone like ceramic, and lingered in a skin of flaming oil. These advantages meant that even with the strongest fire retardants, the Sun King's army would still be vulnerable.

So Beauregard's daily shite haul served this new industry too. At the gates of the Silent Peaks monastery, the faintly farting copper pots—lidded and rubber-sealed against most of the stink—would be traded for crates full of Sorsettan Thunder. Beauregard had coined the term once he'd heard the booming tests from well down the mountain. Thereafter, the phrase had stuck in the people's vernacular. He was not sure how the term had spread, but it had likely passed from Nithan to Eloa to all the folk taken in by her loquaciousness. Regardless, he wasn't affronted at having his hand in history. Indeed, he felt rather proud.

As the oxen and horses rode up the last trail of rock, Beauregard smiled and waved to the folk standing outside Gorgonath's sanctum. Seeing Eloa and Amara amid the flock of multicolored laborers, the men hopped off their seats and saddles to greet them as the cart rolled to a stop. They then aided the workers in removing pots and adding boxes. Every hand appeared well trained in the duty, and in a few quick sands, the cargo was ready.

The Sorsettan crew members flew off into the keep on their wings of fuchsia, teal, and autumn. Meanwhile, the five of them lingered. Eloa and Nithan chased each other around like a fox and hen. They giggled and traded kisses. Evidently, they'd missed each other.

Amara thrust a note at Beauregard. "Love always endures," it read.

The three who were not trysting leaned on the cart's lip and enjoyed the bright, cool day. A stardust of frost made the keep and mountains shimmer. Still there fell no snow, but Beauregard was told winter never came to that in Gorgonath. Rather, it blew up the channel of the Feordhan and skipped the city entirely. The legend said that the snow would come to Gorgonath only when the people had lost their love for the Green Mother. Beauregard believed that meant never.

"It does," agreed the young man.

Amara didn't mind his speaking these days when no one was around. Amara passed a second paper in a speck. "Would you mind fetching some felsalted beef? Strength for the people on the front lines."

"Of course," said Beauregard.

Eagerly, he hopped to his feet and dashed into the keep. Devlin grinned at his son's energy and willingness to commit himself to a cause. One always hoped the best for one's offspring, and he dared to tempt disappointment by thinking Beauregard could become a man of lordly caliber. A note was slipped into his hand.

"He has a powerful spirit. The Green Mother favors him."

"As do I." Devlin sighed. "I wish I had told him sooner about how precious he is to me. I feel as if I have lost years of love."

Amara touched his hand, and it felt like a spark. Her owlish gaze held him so completely he did not sense her next note until she pressed it urgently into his other palm.

"What else have you not told him?"

As if she'd burned him, Devlin leaped and stepped back from the Keeper. "How do you know?" he whispered.

She shook her head and gestured with her hands up. Amara called for peace and approached the hunter. She conjured another note. It was almost magik how fast and unseen her fingers moved when writing, dispensing, or disposing of her communications. Frowning and hesitant, Devlin claimed her message.

"I don't read souls. I hear secrets. I know the sound of a truth when it is kept scratching inside one's heart. Your heart has been scratching since we met."

Devlin imagined a little rodent in his heart clawing to get out. Devlin's sorrows made him slump, and he shuffled back to the cart to sit and pout. Amara's shadow came too. In a moment, he felt ready to tell her of the birth, of his reluctance as a father, and of the years of passive resentment he'd inflicted on the boy. The Keeper stalled his confession with a touch. Somehow, the prestidigitator had given him more paper to hold, which he knew to read.

"I am not the one you need to tell."

*Kings be damned.* Her wisdom stung. The Keeper claimed her note and then took Devlin's hand. They made a strange sight when Beauregard appeared. He was huffing with a young stallion's exuberance, two sacks slung on his shoulder.

"Don't you two look gloomy," he chuffed. "We haven't lost yet, and I think the Sun King is in for a rude surprise."

*A rude surprise indeed,* thought Devlin.

## II

Often Devlin awoke in the night to find Beauregard gone. By now, he knew where to find him. Using his hunter's eyes and a borrowed spyglass, he could see the boy's lonely shade atop the Ancient Wall. There his son paced and haunted the balcony of one of the two gatehouse towers as grand as the staffs of giant immortals driven into the land. He knew Beauregard's restlessness drove him there. That night, however, Devlin was just as afflicted. He waited in his bedroll, and once Beauregard had slunk off, he gave casual chase.

Faithful were about, and they were more ghostly than the shadow he followed. The warrior monks, though, never objected to folk's wandering at this hourglass. From the encampment, Devlin strode all the way down the crunching stone road—which did not betray him to his son—and toward an accommodating arch beside the Ancient Wall's gates. As he'd rarely been this close to the fortification, he took a fleeting interest in how the two immense sheets of rock worked to seal the city and how they had even been placed into position ages before. It had to be magik. However, the rumbling he remembered from when the gates closed spoke of gears—technomagik, at least. Soon another mystery distracted Devlin. Torchlight ruffled an ante-chamber with a stairway so old that dust ingrained the stone in a chalky whiteness. A few more Faithful stood within, beside the archway, and under the stairs, and they seemed nearly invisible in the dimness. One faded specter noticed Devlin and pointed upward as if Beauregard could have gone elsewhere. Devlin waved a cordial thanks and climbed.

What a long climb it was up these tower steps against a strong, cool breeze. His son's youth kept him farther and farther ahead. As Devlin ascended, he required many pauses and used these breaks to decide how to confess his secrets to his son. By the time he'd reached the top, he still had no answer. However, he was quite weary, and he hoped exhaustion would make for easier truth telling. Leaving the windy stairwell behind, he strode out onto a long crenelated balcony. Beauregard's far-off figure gleamed as a sliver wet in moonlight, and he took his time to reach the lad. They met at the edge of the watchtower, and he joined his son—also placing his hands on the stone and staring over the land. The boy noticed him but did not turn. For all the boy's cheerfulness, he held an innate twinge of melancholy in his soul.

"I wanted to talk," Devlin admitted. "Before Brutus comes."

"Which will not be long," noted Beauregard. Oddly and like an animal, he tilted his head. "I have been coming up here when it's quiet and dark and practicing the silence the Faithful preach. While I do not think I shall ever master it, all people can hear and feel many things if the nights are calm enough and they listen with all their hearts. I think I can hear the mad king coming and feel the heat of his sins on the wind."

Perhaps Beauregard could sense these portents. Nothing about Beauregard would surprise Devlin, as fast and unrestrainedly as the boy had grown. He prayed Beauregard would maintain that capacity to listen compassionately once he learned the truth.

"Let's say all does not end well," said Devlin. "I want us to part as two honorable men should without the messiness of lies."

"Lies?"

Devlin nodded shamefully. "Lies. Or truths that have never been said, which is almost the same."

"I'm listening."

He was listening, and still Devlin could not speak. Finally, Beauregard turned to face his father. Devlin was shivering, and his face froze into a grimace as he tried to hold in his tears.

"Oh, Father," he whispered and held him in his arms.

With that, the large fellow fell apart like a rusted bicycle. He retched out painful moans and clung to his child as though their roles had been reversed. After twenty-two years of unrequited coldness, did he even deserve forgiveness? Why now, when life or death was drawn in the sand, did he find his feelings? What a terrible father he'd been to accept a child only to abandon him. He'd treated Beauregard as though he were the product of a mistake—like a mess he'd begrudgingly been forced to clean. He'd never beaten his boy, though he might well have been kinder to strike with fists and not absence. Now and then, he'd given the lad a slap for his unwillingness to be a man by his standards. Yet in these weeks together, Beauregard had revealed himself to be twice any man when it mattered. Mayhap the boy's rebelliousness had been a shadow of his father's cruelty, for children learn and do as they see. Regardless, he could have been kinder and less wasteful with this gift of fatherhood. For being a father was a gift, and Devlin felt like the dumbest of fools for not having valued that treasure sooner.

Beauregard was too clever and too old a soul for such a young man. He let his father's contrition ebb and then forced the man to look upon him. "I know, Father. For years, I've known," he said.

"What? Known?"

"I know I am not your son."

The words set Devlin's lip trembling again. "How?"

Beauregard smiled easily. Devlin could not understand the boy's strength. "You and Mother, when you argue, it's like two kingfishers over a trout. I don't think either of you know just how loud you can be. More than once, you hissed that I was 'her' son, and you didn't mean Mother. That's passion, though. That's love—how the two of you argue. I know you two have loved me. Still, as I became leanness to your largeness and smoothness to your great bearded self, I figured that more than our personalities were different."

"I never meant those words I said to your mother!" declared Devlin, abruptly roaring with his bearish voice. "You are my son. You will always be my son!"

"I know, and you are my father," said Beauregard. His gentleness calmed the bear. "Blood is only one tie. We have made others—as men and friends. I shall never have another father as you have been to me. I too am sorry that we stood so far apart for so long and that it took disaster to throw us together. I am very glad, though, we are at last together."

Devlin sniffled and crushed his son in a hug. "That we are. That we are."

The tears ran out, and they were themselves again—the friends this journey had molded them into and not strangers drowning in the past. However, one ghost called to Beauregard.

"My mother. The one who bore me—not the woman I love. Who was she?" he asked.

Devlin would hide nothing from here on. "Tabitha's sister. She is dead, and I am sad to say it. You came into our care before that dark event. We couldn't say no. Well, I tried, but you've heard your mother when she gets a bone between her teeth. Your mother and I were not blessed with children. Belle—that was her sister—had one more than she could handle."

"One more? I have a brother? Or sister?"

"Yes. A brother."

"Tell me. Please."

Devlin did. He told his son the tale of a wanton songstress—a woman with the blood of Alabion whose very voice could enchant people and animals to bliss. She was a woman torn between her freedom and children but not wholly irresponsible. She'd entrusted her second son—the most precious, declared Devlin—to the care of her sister, Tabitha. The whole truth came out into the air, the world, and stars above, which twinkled perhaps a little brighter for the love of which they heard. Mayhap a twinkle or two was a tear as well for what was to come.

### III

At dawn, the sun rose as a crimson shimmer with a thin line of darkness spreading low over the horizon. The strange earthbound storm rumbled unpleasantly. Scouts watching knew this dark force of nature was at last the mad king's army soiling the air with fire and smoke. In their spyglasses, the stoic Faithful could see the most heinous, twisted shapes. It was good they'd trained so hard not to use their voices, for the first instinct of all who beheld what marched toward Gorgonath was to scream. They tremblingly wrote their notes to one another, and from watchtowers to road to encampment to the Silent Peaks, the message reached then rang as harshly as the gong that clanged early in the morning grayness. "The Sun King has come."

Men leaped from their bedrolls and stumbled into leather armor. They grabbed cudgels, pole arms, war staffs, and a lesser number of slings and bows. As the Sorsettans weren't inherent warmongers or smiths, the best they could manufacture for their protection were hardened hides, sticks, and things to hurl. Beauregard caught many people fumbling from nerves. His own hands stayed steady, and his mind remained a pool of calm water. Charitably, he helped his fellow soldiers pick up their arms and buckle their chest pieces. He gave them his charming grin or hummed a tune to stir their courage. Each time, his cheer worked like a tonic against sorrow. Even after the revealed secrets regarding his unusual mother, he chose not to consider this effect anything extraordinary.

People collapsed the tents. They drew wagons down the long road, hacked the lumber into bunkers, and soaked the wood. All Gorgonath's defenders understood they were not the only ones who would use fire. Once the barriers stood in concentric half circles about the gate to form the lines of defense if the mad king breached Gorgonath, people assumed their places. The soldiers remaining behind these barricades in the inner bailey of Gorgonath might never see the fires and doom on the other side.

Beauregard and his father were not among those potentially fortunate people. Being hunters and skilled with bows, they had been assigned to the jutting barbican atop the gate between the two towers. It resembled a jaw-bone of stone teeth, thought Beauregard, and it would take a good dash to reach it.

"Good luck, lad," said Nithan, interrupting the young man's stare.

Beauregard turned, clasped hands with the fellow, and shared in a back-slapping embrace. His father made similar partings, and they said no more lest they tempt the Fates with farewells. Nithan strode to his post near a wall of crumpled wood. He stood tall as an old shepherd—with a spear rather than a cane—beside a grungy huddle of soldiers. If this was to be Beauregard's last vision of the man, it was a proud one, and it would serve his memory well.

Father and son hurried along then. They had tarried to the point that people were already to their posts, and the watchtowers echoed empty when they arrived. This made for a haunting, lonely ascent to a midway landing that led into the fortress atop the wall. They entered a vaulted and gray cor-ridor with narrow windows and slits of light that one would find in a church. In here, activity and noise abounded.

Faithful crisscrossed the floor, split open crates, counted quivers, and delicately carried unusual nests with straw and tender fabrics. Within the nests rested orbs that looked like glass eggs but were sling bullets filled with the volatilities cooked up in the Silent Peaks. Beauregard hadn't seen this brand of artillery and again felt impressed by the deranged genius displayed by Amara when she was forced to protect her people. Amara—both the lion and the lamb. He hoped her gamble for all their fates paid off. *I still have a trick up my sleeve too*, he thought, and he touched his tingling pouch and its wonder.

Devlin knew where to go, and he took them up a side stairway and onto the ramparts. A red and harsh sun temporarily blinded them. Sight seemed unnecessary to sense the danger, and they smelled an ashy pother gusting in from the north—a wind of death and flame. How soon the end had come and how hard the bite of reality. The lad wished he could be afraid but was instead drawn to the edge of the battlement. A Faithful stood frozen and staring. Beauregard grabbed the immobile man's spyglass to see what so frightened him.

Beauregard received his answer. Under the crimson-and-smoke sunrise shambled hordes of monster-men. They were horrors stitched of golden slag and man flesh sutured to bladed, pronged, and clubbed weaponry. He saw red-eyed men of charcoal carrying staffs of glowing embers. He saw dead ash-black knights thundering in on soulless steeds. Agog at this army of nightmares that had once been men, Beauregard lost his breath and courage. Come dusk, his walking black corpse might be among the army's rank and file.

The lad was abreast of the conflict in Zioch when the Everfair King and Brutus had clashed in a war of ice and fire. This explained the bizarre elements he and his father had encountered in Mor'Khul. Once, somewhere in the frantic mists of preparation for this battle, Amara had shared her insights on paper. She believed Brutus had called upon a primal power of the Green Mother to conquer his brother's cold.

"A wyrm," she'd written. "The true essence of heat and the greatest of its kind. Ignifax, if he must be captured in words—the father of fire. The Keepers say no other flame could melt the ice of the Everfair King's power. Still, I do not think the mad king would bring this chained beast here, as that flame would destroy the flesh he wanted to reap. I doubt he even has the power to unleash it again in its true majesty so soon. To draw upon its power, perhaps. To use it as a furnace for unholy magiks. But an actual summons would require the power or sacrifice of a thousand sorcerers. It would require a wonderstone greater even than yours." She frowned as his lips mumbled to her words, then quickly snatched and disposed of the note and handed him a written apology. "I have said too much. Only the closest children of the Green Mother know of this talk of wyrms and stones and sacrifice."

Around him, Amara always appeared to be loose-lipped with the "forbidden lore" of her sect. He felt a flash of irreverent happiness then as he realized they were good friends. His good friend appeared to be correct at the moment, and he saw no writhing, titanic coils of scale and fire. That was how he figured a wyrm would look, though really, he had no idea. Thus, the worst of Brutus's grunt hadn't been brought to Gorgonath, which meant their chances of survival were increasing.

*Wait,* he thought. What was that great shadow? That furnace seething such smoke into the day at the rear of the hideous host? At first, Beauregard's balls withered and his guts sank, for he thought he saw a wormy shape. This wasn't entirely misconstrued, for a shadow coiled and moved in the haze. It was not a creature with scales or fire, though. He needed to adjust the spyglass to see better, but even then what filled the glass seemed incomprehensible. A tarry earthworm as broad as the Feordhan? A massive turd flecked with undigested rice? All the equivalencies of which he could think possessed the same nauseating blend of rot, death, and squiggling things. Nothing could have prepared him for what he saw then as he slowly swept the spyglass lens along the massive thing—a skull, a black branch of an arm, half legs, rib cages, burned swords, slick horse heads, and every other scorched and mutilated part of an animal or warrior. What was this atrocity? Bodies? Sticky resin and remains scraped from the oven of doom after the Kings' conflict?

Beauregard thought he saw a second enormous snake wriggling behind the first, at which point he passed the spyglass to his father in time to slap his knees and vomit. Devlin didn't need or want to see what would soon be upon them, and he passed it back to its owner. Then he rubbed his son's back and took the lad to sit beneath the parapet. Sands of precious time passed before either felt as if he could speak.

"Battle is never pretty, Son," said Devlin. "I am glad to see a bit of fear in you after all your songs and careless joy today. I would have worried, otherwise. Only a fool does not fear death."

"Death?" Beauregard shivered. "We shall have no escape from that. He's using the dead again, Father. Not the ones who are mostly dead but the truly dead and gone. They've been...mixed..."

Mentioning the squirming, mingled tubes of mortal offal, even trying to construe their details again beyond the sheer length of the fatty behemoths, made for a sickening contemplation. Beauregard began to gag again.

"Worms," Beauregard managed. "Deathworms."

"I don't know what those are, but I shall soon enough." Devlin clasped his son by the back of his neck. "Focus, Beauregard. Get a bit of that strength back, and hold on to some of that fear. That sickness in your belly, that agitation and terror, it might burn your insides, but it will keep you alive. Hold on to that edge. Choke that fear down just like you did your sick. Can you do that?"

"I...I think so," he said.

"Good. That's the right brew, lad."

Devlin helped his boy stand.

"Thank you, Father," said Beauregard.

"Anything for you, my son," replied the great man.

His son noticed now that Devlin had regained nearly all the size and presence he'd lost in the Summerlands. In that moment, he looked as magnificent a father as any boy could wish for.

"Now, let's drive this madman away," said Devlin with such burning conviction that Beauregard almost believed it could be done.

IV

As the mad king, Brutus did not play by the rules of honorable warfare. So the Immortal's conquest lacked any notion of civility or reason. As the defenders of Gorgonath awaited the red storm of Brutus's army, they expected the storm to slow and for the army to arrange itself from the messy rows of foot soldiers, red-eyed sorcerers, and cavalry. They waited for an emissary to ride forth and ask for their surrender. But in this war, there would be no etiquette, no rules.

They were not prepared for this. They'd forgotten Brutus was not a king of order—not anymore. He wanted only one thing: their bodies. Apparently, he would take them dead or living. Parley was unnecessary. When the dark wave neared to within a span, all in the inner bailey were forced to inhale the greasy bonfire stench of countless burned dead. However, those on the ground were spared from the retching terror of what the souls in the Ancient Wall faced.

From the Ancient Wall, people witnessed the fullness of their enemy and doom. It was a black river of desecration wending through the highlands, clouds of cinders and smoke above, and outside the gates a thousand clamoring damned. Maybe more. However, that was not the evilest of what

Brutus brought with him, for the deathworms—a name that quickly stuck—claimed that privilege.

Reason was raped at the sight of it. The mind cackled when trying to fathom what putrescent things had been mashed, and tarred together into a colossal land-bearing snake. Courage fell like the tears of the weak, and the deathworms blared foghorn cries that rattled every bone and stone in Gorgonath. Some of the Faithful lost their bravery through their throats as Beauregard had while watching the sloppy serpents of mortal garbage slither their way toward the city. Occasionally and carelessly, the behemoths crushed the damned in their approach. Two deathworms had been bred from the battlefield in Mor'Keth. Each had been created for smashing the Ancient Wall of Gorgonath—of this there was no doubt.

Somewhere high above it all, as soon as the deathworms' gurgle echoed, Amara prayed with the others for an unlikely victory. Brutus, a speck in the dark field that spanned before the Ancient Wall, made a command over the voices droning his name. The mad king's animal bark came louder than all the pandemonium and his deathworms' mewling on the plains.

"Doom!" he roared.

With that, the wave crashed down on Gorgonath. For Beauregard, the battle was a haze. Too many shrieks, explosions, whirs, and clangs all occurred in a hurricane of delirium. He might have been dreaming. Several times, the smoke clotted so dense and full of muffled cries he believed himself dead. He lost his father once and then again. Somehow, they always found one another as sooty demons in the fog and greeted each other with grunts. Details were unclear in the blood-haze, and all the lad knew at various points when reason surfaced was that the battle was going terribly for him and his new countrymen. The Faithful had not considered that Brutus would bring two great colossi of death to be his hammers to the stones of Gorgonath. They had not known such nightmares could even be bred. Who but a dark seer would have seen that future?

Brutus unleashed his pets immediately. Suddenly, the rotting snakes were upon the gates and shuddering the ground like earthquakes. Sorsettan Thunder was being hurled from slings, hands, and even in entire crates over the Ancient Wall. The defenders did whatever it took to stop the deathworms as they slammed themselves into the city's stone doors. What splattering hunks flew off the deathworms did little to dissipate their masses. Hollowed in places like cheese, the gargantuas smoldered, reeked, and wailed, but they could not be stopped or even slowed. Many crates of Sorsettan Thunder thrown by the hysterical defenders missed their targets and demolished sections of the Ancient Wall instead. Fulgurous chaos descended upon the battlefield, and the world lit up like a festival of terrors with smoke, fireworks, and spins of centrifugal force. In a speck, it was raining nothing so commonplace as water but sizzling splats of gore, stone, and metal that Beauregard darted to avoid. More bombs, deathworm wails, and moaning shadows rose from the mist of war.

Then Beauregard's smoke-demon father appeared beside him once more, and with no grunts this time, he threw the young man down the tilting deck of the ramparts. The ramparts were ruined in a way most dire, and they cried stone screeches over the deathworms and other ear-murdering sounds. Beauregard was too deaf to understand any of it and had an instant of peace in the bleary shaft he thought might be one of the watchtowers.

"Father, what—"

Crack! Crash! Boom!

Another of Devlin's tackles saved Beauregard's life, and the two rolled as wrestlers would down the stairs. Fate blessed them, and they struck a wall instead of falling until their necks broke. They had a moment to untangle and collect themselves— although it was hard to do much other than scream, wave their hands in the dimness, and hope something came through their ringing heads. *Ow! Own! Ow!* Beauregard's father harped, and after a speck the lad added some consonants and understood the word "down." Down? What was down? The lad solved the riddle as a tremor tossed the tower and threw a powdery avalanche their way. By the Kings, the Ancient Gate had been breached. The wall was falling.

Beauregard thought of the deathworms sprawling their flaming, bleating carcasses on Gorgonath's door. He thought of the deathworms simply lying there until their weight or the explosions from the incendiaries their fall triggered blew the primordial stones into dust. What horrific despair to know all their readiness and resolve had been for naught and would be undone in a single feint. *Not all. Not yet,* he remembered, for he still had the wonderstone.

Disaster met the two at every step. They found crushed and dying Faithful amid the collapse. They helped a man up only to have him sputter out a bloody end in their arms.

At the base of the watchtower, the smoke, sweat, piss, and dew of blood had formed into a fog of death through which played a mighty song of battle. Indeed, the Ancient Wall lay sundered, and Brutus's horde had poured into the inner bailey. The arch leading from the watchtower had caved in atop many fleeing and crushed Faithful. They crept carefully, climbed the rubble, and peered into the horror through a fingernail of a gap leading to the outside.

Everything appeared as bad as it could be. The flickering rot of the deathworms, quite disassembled into slag in this final death, puffed a smokestack of blackness beside their hideaway. The whole area billowed with ruin. They saw no sign of walls through the smoky curtain, and the spillage of glowing, fractured stones all about the courtyard confirmed the worst. Brutus's horde flooded Gorgonath with clattering men glued with metal and blackened sorcerers who left embers and craters in their wake. Many barricades had toppled. Only the most distant and desperate defenses remained near the great road leading upward—the same road Brutus would march to pillage the fleshly treasures of the Silent Peaks. Amara, Eloa, and all the people and children in hiding were certain to die.

Hopelessly angry, Beauregard watched the dark knights spear men he'd broken bread with yesterday. He watched the red-eyed sorcerers set folk whom he knew to be fathers aflame. He felt like the slowest creature in the world trapped within amber while all else moved. They would not win. There was no chance. No one could stand against the monster that was Brutus.

As if calling a dark spirit's name, his gaze found the mad king—a bronze and nearly nude giant. A black mane obscured the giant's face, and he had more muscles and savagery than any beast the young man had ever known his father to hunt. Beauregard needed no more than a glimpse of the Immortal to recoil from him. It was like staring into a fire pit and knowing what that heat would do if one spread one's arms and leaped. The giant's footsteps could well be the drums and explosions that shook the battlefield he calmly walked, so in tune with the destruction was he. He threw aside barricades and men as if they were dollhouse playthings.

503

"Brutus," Beauregard whispered. He was fixated.

"Yes," hissed his father. "Not one king but two. Look!"

In his entrancement, Beauregard had missed the second Immortal. Behind the mad king and being dragged unkindly through the slop was a man of ice and shadow. Stripped to basic decency, wearing a cage over his head that would be found in a torturer's dungeon, and burdened with a disproportionate weight of chains for so slender a man, King Magnus walked with astonishing pride. Against Beauregard's every expectation and understanding of torment, the man's posture spoke of a Will that would not bend to Brutus's violence. His soul would not debase itself by acknowledging his tormentors at all, and that included the skinny damned who herded him with pikes fused into their arms or pulled on his chains. Even under the iron restraints, soot, and blood, the man radiated beauty and power.

*The king. The king is alive*, thought Beauregard. A butterfly of hope flapped within, even though he was not a royalist.

"I know what we must do," said Beauregard.

"What? Do? What can we do?" exclaimed his father. "The battle is done. Sorsetta is lost."

"No."

Beauregard brimmed with rash designs. How he wished he could explain the torrent of urges and theories in his head—all these signs and lessons learned on their long journey. *A wonderstone in lesser tongues*, Beauregard recalled. *The rarest mineral on Geadhain. It is said to have the power to grant miracles, break any magik, or cast out any evil.*

Many fates and probabilities assaulted Beauregard. Amara's wisdom. The one and only person Brutus feared, here and now and in their presence. Belle, his birth mother, and her queer gifts, explained to him only the night before. Indeed, his whole strange and sacred travel into the mystery of the South with his father.

Tangled paths arrived at this singular junction of clear opportunity—there would never be another so perfectly aligned. They would have to act fast, and even for a lyrical soul like Beauregard, words became cumbersome tools to express the sublime synchronicity of this moment. Beauregard tried to share the storm raging in his head and came off gasping and confused.

There was a magik he had not counted on, though—the bonds of father and son. Devlin surmised what brewed in the young man's head.

"You...want to free him," said Devlin in slow amazement.

"It is what I must do," declared Beauregard. "I have never known something so entirely with my heart."

Father and son were shaking. Quite likely, they cried through their makeup of grime. In the smoke and doom, though, neither could tell. Devlin grabbed his child and held him. As a true father, friend, and companion, he did not stir the sands with doubt. He did not try to reason with his son. He did what fathers should. He gave a choice and chance to the child who would succeed him in the chain of life. Devlin pressed a kiss to his son's forehead and then began scrambling away over the rubble toward the mad king.

"What are you doing?" cried Beauregard, but his soul already knew.

"I am giving you your future," called his father.

Devlin left his child in the dark to complete a legendary task. *Be brave. Be strong. I love you, my son.* Were there more instants, he would have whispered these adorations. The time for his own heroic deeds had come, though. He had a hunter's unusually keen eyes, and he spotted the untouched crates of Sorsettan Thunder to the left of the ruin from which he crawled. He ran to the crates and danced over bodies both Sorsettan and monster—more of the former than the latter.

He worried not about the mindless hordes of the Sun King all around him. The monsters barely noticed his movement, so concentrated were they on their march ahead. Such slow-witted legions were a weakness of the mad king's army. Devlin hoped the champions of tomorrow would learn to exploit that—for these champions would fight one dark mind in several bodies, and that mind was blind and drunk on its own magnificence. That was how he, as a hunter, understood how to goad the mad king away from his brother. Brutus was a careless, rampaging animal—a bull who would charge if provoked.

Once with spiritual intuition, he turned and saw his nimble child slinking down the rockslide of the tower and then vanishing like a stalking wolf into the smoke. *Good. Now run, run, run. You still have a ways to go, my son.*

Devlin did too, and he did not look again to know his son's fate. He relied on the Green Mother to preserve Beauregard. She had entrusted the lad with this holy mission. He felt blessed that he, a faithless man, had found true conviction on this journey. By the time he had reached the cover of the crates and ducked behind them to assess the state of the battle, the Sorsettan army looked nearly destroyed. All the barricades, save for a stubborn few, had fallen. At the cost of nearly all the Faithful and their militia, Brutus's herd had been thinned, and Devlin had a speck before his last fellow citizens were doomed. These were his people as much as those in Willowholme. Perhaps they were even more worthy of his fealty, for they'd brought him the gift of truth and peace. Those were things a person needed before the end. Devlin was not afraid. Reckless and bold, he stood and summoned the rabid king with the loudest scream he could muster. "Brutus, you cur! You coward! You shite! King of nothing! King of rapists and pedophiles! King of illness and sin! King of weakness!"

At the sound of his name, the black lion turned his head. Then he was striding through smoke and flame toward Devlin measuredly and plod-dingly. He was hunting the offender. In haste, Devlin fumbled through his pockets for the flint he'd been using to light the incendiaries on the ramparts. Praise the Green Mother, he found it. It was another miracle that added to his burgeoning faith. With his fist, Devlin shattered the lid of a wooden box, grabbed the nearest sloshing cocktail, and lit the strip of rag that flopped out of its end. He smelled the king first—a musk so thick it could be spread into a black butter of filth, sex, animal sweat, and armpit funk. Next came the laugh of a thundercloud—a primeval force so much greater than his pitiful self.

Devlin looked up into the face of horror, and it stood while pouring its breath and stench over him. The mad king was dizzying to conceive. He was all hair, stink, and blood and too much strength to contain in a skin. His power wriggled and moved within him like a nest of serpents.

"What would you hope to do with that?" demanded the Immortal.

Devlin laughed back. "Not much. Slow you down, perhaps. My son will do the real work."

The king twitched—the glimmer of an animal's rage. In the next moment, either Devlin dropped the incendiary into the crates on his own, or the swat of the Immortal loosed his grip on it. He wasn't quite sure.

Boom!

Devlin was thrown high and far, which saved him from the worst of the blast—the bit that would have killed him instantly. However, he was not spared the flash that seared off most of his clothing and face, and he was not spared from landing on broken wood that speared him. In his twisted throes of death, though—propped on a crucifix of ruin—he had a lovely view of the end. His pain vanished. His body had no idea what to worry about or fix when everything was broken. Pleasantly, Devlin saw a shadow prancing in the kiln of flames he'd made. The Immortal would be busy for a while.

He tried to find his son in the chaos. It was a difficult feat, as all flowed slowly and peacefully in the haze in which he drifted. Before the white mist overcame his senses and before he listened to crystalline chimes and whispers telling him to go elsewhere, he managed to turn the cotton puff of his head—as light as a dream—toward the last stand of the Sorsettans. While the mad king occupied himself with the flames, the defenders had made some progress. Perhaps because of the king's distraction, the whole black army—except for the red-eyed sorcerers—had stalled like sleeping puppets without their guiding hands, and the straggling, bloodied Faithful seized this moment to bash and slice the monsters.

*Good for them. But I don't care about that. Where is my boy? Where is Beauregard?*

The whispering lights directed Devlin to a clump of frozen damned. He traveled outside his flesh, and soft hands or the wings of a thousand doves carried him. Blissfully and tenderly, he watched his son slip out of the fog. Beauregard looked filthy and was sobbing. He surely understood the explosion and its cost. Beauregard, brave Beauregard, though, did not stop even to think about his duty. He did not hesitate to call his magik, despite never having used sorcery before. Devlin couldn't say how magik worked, but he thought it required belief and wonder, of which his son had a well full—enough to sate all Geadhain's thirst. Into that well, his son tapped.

Perhaps he found there a spark of his unfamiliar mother and her enchanting songs or perhaps a deep and golden vein of his own. Floating in the veil of death, where secrets are truths, Devlin witnessed the unfiltered beauty of his son's soul. He watched his child sing his magik—his pain, fear, love, and devotion—to the crystal he held aloft like a hero's blade. Devlin gloried as the magik wove together in threads from the star that was Beauregard into the

507

star of the wonderstone, which then roared into a great sword of righteous, fuming brilliance. Then his boy brought the blade down upon the iron cage on Magnus's head.

There echoed a sundering, thundering crack. It was as if Geadhain had split to her core. The ageless stones in Gorgonath trembled, but Devlin did not feel the quake. His spirit flesh tingled from the sudden shriek, though, as cold and angry as all the years of the Long Winter funneled into a single cry. "Brutus!"

A howl whirled within the all-consuming maelstrom of light his son had summoned, blue and frosty with filaments of its own might. Winter had been unleashed. Magnus was free.

After that, Devlin knew his son was safe. The whispers promised him so. Now he could go, and he let the whispers take him.

# XX

# SACRIFICE

I

Mouse made it quite far on her own. She went down the cliff a second time without rest and through the enchanted woodland of unseen, laughing creatures. She could hear, if not see, the mischievous things. Where she wandered now, the winter had lost its warmth. The wolves no longer pranced with deer but chased and chewed upon them, and the trees had transformed into a thicket. Without the Wolf's hands to clear the path, she was thrashed and torn in sands. Each step punched through a skin of ice like a plate of glass. Although freezing, she sweat from exhaustion as though in a fever.

The moon shone, and the branches had not yet knitted their black blanket over the sky. She could at least see a little. When she failed, as it seemed certain she would, her companions should be able to spot her corpse without much effort. *No. No dying. No giving up. Move, woman*! However, her body grew resistant to her coaching. It slowed and slowed, and the woods rose in darkness. She heard the hungry howling of stalkers. She assumed she'd entered the outermost region of the Pitch Dark. Going as deep as she needed to go would be impossible without her companions, but they would never assist her if they knew what she planned to do.

Not despairingly but rather limply, she fell into ice or a tree. Either way, it was hard and grating. She felt she should call for aid. Perhaps the Wolf would hear her. If she wanted to live, if she wanted to stay awake and not fall into the eternal, numbing bed of a winter grave, she needed to call out. Mouse nearly wheezed the Wolf's name and then stopped. The thought of something else struck her—three others who might aid her without question.

"Mouseling, your lust for retribution glows with the fullness of a witch's moon," she recalled. "Such beautiful hate you water in your soul's garden. Should you wish to satisfy that darkness, to call upon the shadows and wrath of Geadhain, say our names but once and with true and black desire. We shall come."

"Mmmgnna...Malbleth...Meeg," she mumbled.

It was spoken with the spirit if not the gusto of a true plea. The cold had set in to a chill that banished the shivers and made her eyes as heavy as stone shutters. She wondered whether her gibberish had reached anyone. She realized how stupid she'd been not to call for the Wolf. Alas, these were the regrets of the damned, and she began to slide and then fall down the dark well inside her head.

Crunch. Crunch. Footsteps. Shadows fell over her.

"The Mouseling called," cooed Meag.

"She looks rather tired. Perhaps we should let her sleep," suggested Malabeth.

Mouse moaned her objection.

"Don't be so cruel," said the eldest. "Grab an arm, each of you. I'll take the feet."

The shadows shuffled around Mouse, and she was lifted. She saw spinning suggestions of three pale, grinning faces, ebony hair, and crimson clothing. The women's hands gouged like knives against her flesh.

"Before we set off, there is the matter of price," said Morgana.

"Indeed, Sister," agreed the witches.

Mouse's arms were dropped, and her body slapped on ice.

"What awful nursemaids you two can be," chastised Morgana, who still gripped the Mouseling's legs. "She is a black and full flower of pain. She will pay us our due and bring us something for our stew. Won't you?"

"I...shall," gasped Mouse. "Please...take me. Take me."

Beyond these words, Mouse could not direct the Furies. It was no matter. The red witches were keen to the heart's unsaid desires. They knew where the Mouseling wanted to be taken. They did not have to be told. Whistling and chatting about all things bloody and foul, the red witches and their charge vanished into the Pitch Dark.

## II

"Magnus!" cried Morigan.

A normal man's reaction to his lover's shouting a name other than his own after a night of exquisite copulation would be jealousy or injured pride. However, the Wolf stopped mid-climb and brazenly hung off the sun-and-snow-shimmered rocks of the Sisters' aerie with one arm. He allowed the woman who had been slumbering against his chest to collect herself. She appeared quite befuddled by where her Dreams had taken her. He felt it had been a river deep and far. He'd hardly sensed her light in him while she slept. A moment's pause did not bring her relief and only wrinkled her beauty in worry.

*My Wolf*, she whispered and shivered from dread. *I wandered many places while we traveled. I saw many things—all damning but none of them clear. I saw a city of ancient stones with a grand wall, houses of pretty colors, and the mad—I am sorry—Brutus assailing it with his army.*

*His army? I thought his forces were ruined*, replied the Wolf.

*Enough to stop him from taking Geadhain or Eod but not whatever city I saw. He did not take the city, though. Bravery and sacrifice stopped him. A beautiful boy. His heart is like a star. He sang. There was a flash of light and then a winter I think was Magnus. He is free!* She frowned. *But then the mists become murky and the portents all grim. I saw Eod under a black cloud, and I do not know what this means or whether it was an end. And Mouse! A dagger, a full moon, and blood frozen in the snow. I have seen this once before, and I must stop it!*

*I do not like any of these portents*, the Wolf growled.

*I do not either.*

Busily Fate spun away, and threads snapped. Morigan sensed she was missing a pattern in the great weave. She became angry at this incomplete awareness and the truths being held from her, the Daughter of Fate. Mouse, a dagger, and a full moon. *Find out*, she Willed her silver servants. *Find me nectar. Find me truth.*

The Wolf flinched from the shudder of her magik as it passed through him and into the world. He waited. She lay still for only a speck until her spirit returned into the body he held. "Merciful Kings, no!" she screamed.

Morigan became hysterical and squirmed in his embrace. She would never escape him, but she seemed unafraid of being dropped.

"The moon! Last night's moon was full!" she screamed.

There was so much more to tell her beloved, for the bees had brought their mistress a feast of Dreams of what had taken place the previous night with the Sisters and their pack. Thackery had stolen some years. Adam had bargained with Elemech. The most ominous Fate, though, was Mouse's. She had been given the key she sought to the door of darkness. It had come in the form of a whisper from the most innocent—and somehow most harmful—of the Sisters Three.

"There is a place where power can be found," the Sister had said. "Where the stones have known worship since this forest was a child. They speak the oldest tongue, these stones. It's the language of sacrifice. It was here that the Faithful would come and welcome the Dreamers into this world. Here, the earliest covenants between soil and star were made. One can make those covenants still, Mouseling. One who bears the mark, who has the flesh of a vessel, and who has a Will—a dying Will—strong enough to wake the stars."

Instead of continuing to resist her bloodmate, Morigan pressed into the Wolf with her flesh and Will and passed memories. The Wolf's eyes swelled as he partook of what she knew.

"Is it too late?" he whispered.

"No. I don't care. We must see," said Morigan.

He climbed down the cliff. Rappelling in drops, he took grand leaps as if using a rope. The Wolf hurried, although the outcome was already written in blood.

Mouse was dead.

✳ ✳ ✳

III

The witches laid Mouse into a snowdrift as downy and white as a nest of feathers. It even made tickling puffs as they placed her. Her skin had lost all feeling some while before, except for the gouging of the red witches' claws. Now a small fire rekindled within her flesh. Awakened by this magik, Mouse suddenly perceived for a watery-eyed moment the three women crouched around her. For a flash, they were hideous, rotten-mouthed, and decayed. At their backs loomed woods as dark as their expressions.

"As far as we shall take you," said the paunchy witch. "But we gave you a bit of breath to keep you going now."

"It won't last long, Malabeth," teased the sister who quite resembled Elemech but was haggard and not haunted. "You really should have died back when we found you."

"Go on, then, before you do," said the witch with the wisest and wicked-est stare.

"Die, that is," said all three.

Like three gruesome owls waiting for a rodent to move, the red witches perched in the snow, tilted their heads, and watched Mouse find her feet. She looked around and saw the ivory tips of buried ruins and, farther off, the lesser buried dimpling in the snow where she and her companions had made a campfire in nights gone by. Would they hate her for her choice? Would they understand if she failed? She found it difficult to glance upon the stone altar. The snow had not found it or mysteriously decided to avoid it since Morigan had cleared its glassy ebon surface. *A blackness come from many offerings of blood*, she thought.

"Reminisce later. We are hungry," said Malabeth.

When Mouse turned to thank them, there were no women in the snow—not even markings to show anyone had been present. She turned around, and the altar beckoned with a wink of moonlight off its blackness and a sweeping gust of snow. Her moment, her destiny, had arrived. There were a million ways in which this could go horribly wrong. Were Talwyn here to lecture her on the process of conjuring a Dreamer, he would warn her she might not be a fitting vessel for the power she wished to invite. Still, Ealasyd had mentioned suitable flesh, and if Sorren—that filthmonger and moral excrement of a man—could house a Dreamer, then she, as his niece, should be able to as well. Her instincts told her that the blood mattered most in this ancient formula. Blood—the true currency of the old world. It was what all these forces traded in and valued. She needed to know and see the mystery herself. To do that, she needed to take a single deadly test.

"A vessel," Morigan had said. "A host in which something else is kept. No—in which something sleeps. When it wakes, it is a nightmare. I have seen this thing. I have sensed it in others before. In Sorren. And something similar, only blacker, in the mad king."

The night after her father's death, when her companions believed she was asleep, the seer's whispered confession had kept her wide-awake. She hoped Morigan would not blame herself now if all that remained was her body for them to bury. Warm with sweet melancholy, she knew the Wolf would pick her a grave beside her father.

Holding on to that image, she felt at peace. When she lay atop the stone of sacrifice, she felt still and open to the arms of oblivion, as had all the offerings in all the other ages that had lain there. The moon's somber white eye was upon her as she undid her blouse and exposed her breasts to the cold. She had scars there as well as lower from her more enthusiastic clientele in the pleasure houses, and thinking of their despicable acts made invoking a rite of blood and death so much easier.

Like a conjurer of the mind, she called forth all the dark terrors and shining stars of her past. The delight of hearing Adelaide's giggle. A vision of her father's yellow smile. An image of a man who had viciously raped her. The face of her evil grandmother as Menos tumbled with fire and ice. The Wolf in his kindest moments. Memories of her great-uncle's wisdom and teacherly tone. A flash of Morigan snarling as she leaped into the fire that Aghna had become. A true friend Morigan was, she realized. Once Mouse had dived into the currents, there seemed no end to the stream of memories. What a grand life she'd lived—a life as full of darkness as it was of light. She regretted nothing, aside from how powerless she'd been when it came to saving her father. If the Dreamers would hear her and if they could feel pity in their distant way, she would have justice for her father—and all the fathers of Geadhain, if she could. Now she grasped how delicate and magikal the ties of family could be. To Mouse, this act was not an end but a leap of faith.

Mouse touched the iron marker on her neck and asked the Gray Man to hear her painful tale. She told him his sacrifice was ready. She cried with unrestrained and sobbing grief. She wept as she never had before, and she took her iron dagger from its sheath. Above her, the white eye of the moon glowed as if she'd caught its attention, and she glared back with her furious Will.

Then she plunged the blade into her chest.

## IV

Morigan and the Wolf arrived at the ruins of the Ancients—he'd torn through the worst of the Pitch Dark without a scratch. The weather came on thickly and wept snow. The Wolf set Morigan loose from his arms, and she dashed through the storm toward the altar. As a killer of the ages, the Wolf knew the dark shape ahead and that the pink trails on the altar were Mouse and her frozen blood. In fact, he could see the tautly set corpse through the veil of winter. Slowly, he walked forward. He was heavy with this loss and aware too of musky, metallic, and oiled scents borne on the winds. Therefore, he came to Morigan more perplexed than grieved, and he could not match his blood-mate's stunned, quivering anger. For a great long while, Morigan had nothing to say and no tears to give. She could only fall against her lover, clasp the gray, icy hand of her friend, and wish for this nightmare to dispel itself. Finally, she turned, reached out to touch the frosted metal embedded in her friend's heart, and then traced the crimson veins on the rock and in the snow. There wasn't much blood, or the stone had drunk it up. Morigan returned her caressing fingers to her friend's blue lips. Out of decency, she tried to pull Mouse's blouse shut and shutter the eternal gazing of her eyes. The woman's clothing and skin were frozen, though. Her friend had become a statue. Morigan sobbed.

*You warned me, my Wolf,* whispered Morigan. *Once you said it was your curse to watch the world die. Now it is my curse too. Mouse. Someday Thackery, Adam, and Talwyn. I should not grow close to anyone ever. I cannot bear these losses as you do. I cannot see them as natural and simply thank the Green Mother for the time we have shared. I still see it as something stolen, which I resent. I hate our world for being so cruel that this is how Fionna, who might well have been my dearest friend, leaves us. It is disgusting. Not her choice to die, to seek power in an unfair world—that was brave. But this...she deserved so much more.*

*My Fawn, there is no peace to find in Mouse's end. All I feel in you and in myself is sadness.*

The Wolf spoke his heart's truth. The fire beast did not pace or thump his tail in her chest but keened. Soon her bloodmate sang the same tune. He wept a few tears and howled, which expressed his pain better. Morigan also surrendered to the beast in her blood and howled for the soul that had left their pack. She remembered her fellow prisoner, friend, and sister on this journey. Each memory drove a knife into her and ripped more noise from her throat. Together, she and the Wolf sang their bestial elegy. While they grieved, the Wolf willingly ignored the intruders he'd earlier detected. Then one of them interrupted their mourning.

"How very tragic," mocked Augustus.

Bound in a heavy winter cloak, leathers, and a scarf as he was, it was only the knotty twist of Augustus's lean and deformed countenance that made him recognizable to the Wolf. Emerging with the Broker from a whirl of snow, Augustus brandished an ironguard's rifle. However, there was no trace of a Menosian guard. He seemed to have flawless aim with his single, glaring eye. Half the meat-porridge of his jaw curled to show some teeth—a smile.

"Let me tell you what I think," suggested Augustus. "We've been damned on the journey here. Lost everything except for each other and a rifle. My men too and that should-be-abortion that is my half brother. My honor as well, which you probably didn't think I had anyway. Pride too. That has been the cost of chasing a dog and his bitch into the shitehole of Geadhain. Do pardon, my friend," he said to the Broker. "I know this is your home." The Broker nodded his forgiveness. "Good thing he has such a honed nose," continued Augustus. "Followed you better than any bloodhound all the way here until the trail ran out. We were camping just over the wall there when your fool friend appeared, flashed her tits to the moon, and offed herself like a virgin sacrifice to the slave kings of yore. My friend smelled all the blood, but we missed the show. Shame. I would have liked to put a bullet between those anthills instead of a knife."

Augustus shifted his rifle. "I have learned to hunt and kill the worst of what Alabion has thrown at me. I daresay there is not much I fear now. Not even you—the monster who burned me. I am sure the man who lit the match is around here somewhere, and I'll deal with him next. My shame began back then in the fire, and it will be remedied today. An eye for an eye, or lives for a life. As I haven't forgotten how fast you are, and I have no intention of returning to my lands when there are other realms to stalk, I don't much give a fuk for Gloriatrix's instructions. It's hard to see in this blasted whiteness, but I think I have a good shot now."

*A good shot? At what?* wondered the Wolf. He made as wide a target as a house when immobile...unless Augustus meant someone smaller and less visible in bad weather. Morigan.

The Wolf spun in time to save her from a barrage of blue-fire bullets, but many gouged his shoulder, upper back, and spine. From his previous experiences of having been shot, the Wolf recalled that the injuries would bleed, bruise, and eventually spit the bullets out like slivers. That could take a day or so, though, and time was not their friend right now. Hunkered down behind the altar and safe for an instant, he hissed to his bloodmate. *Go! Get away from here! I shall tear these beasts to shreds and come for you when the murder is done!*

However, Morigan was a wolf as well—prideful and furious. She shook her quite intractable—and bleeding—mate. *I shall not! I shall not leave our friend's body to these scavengers! I shall rip and tear them too!*

"I do like a hunt!" called Augustus. "I was top shot at the Chasing of the Hart, though I shan't be keeping this beast's head. There won't be much of it. She'll be as pretty as a mincemeat pie."

Augustus's rifle sang his threat, and a bullet scraped the Wolf's hand, which had gripped the side of the altar since he'd dropped. He cursed and licked his bloody knuckles. They needed to do something. They could not argue any longer.

Whoosh!

A sudden wind seemingly conjured from the Everfair King himself came blustering through the ruins. It threw all the whiteness into a shearing blind of ice. The wind forced the bloodmates to cling to each other and sent Augustus into a shrieking fit.

Clank!

Over the howling wind, the Wolf's ears caught the bounce of a dagger off the stone altar. Next, all present heard and felt the silvery sound waves sliding like splinters of fire and ice into their flesh. Beings of light and magik played rich, pleasing, and chilling music on crystal instruments. It evoked a drunken delight—a thrill of remembered starscapes, youthful adventures, romance, good wine, and falling asleep in the arms of a lover.

The music that wasn't quite music also flooded the senses with dark impressions of moonlight and wolves and of faery tales in which witches ate children and women threw themselves from cliffs when their husbands died in wars. A wind, a presence of storytelling, mystery, and shadow, had entered the world.

Drawn by a lunar pull, they each looked up, and against whatever impossibility, they saw the white sphere of the sun ringed in darkness. It was an eclipse unnaturally reversed. Only for a speck did it appear, and then it vanished with the wind and ethereal orchestra.

"Enough of you," said Mouse.

As though she'd materialized from a gust of snow, the corpse on the altar suddenly stood before Augustus. She seemed decidedly alive and snatched the rifle from the startled lord and tossed it into the winter dunes. However mortal she appeared, though, she possessed a sheen and a silver and foreign stare. She looked at Augustus as if he were the lowliest of creatures. What beheld him, whether mortal or master from beyond, the minuscule tyrant could not tell.

"I know where you belong," said she without mercy or joy. "The red witches will enjoy your meats."

Mouse, or what passed for her, touched the master of Blackmore. There arose a misty scattering of silver light that faded with Augustus's scream. Ruthlessly, the vengeful risen woman looked for the other sinner—the one whom the red witches would most savor. Unfortunately, the slick monster had fled. His escape would be no more than an inconvenience to her. She could find him now. Perhaps not as effortlessly as Morigan could, but she could do almost anything if she woke the Dreamer inside her flesh and asked.

"Mouse?" cried Morigan.

Mouse turned. "Mostly," she replied, and she laced up her bloody shirt over an unmarked breastbone. "I have business to finish with the Broker. I made him a promise long ago. Wait for me."

A flock of snow doves fluttered in, and faster than a spark—faster even than the Wolf could see—their once-dead companion disappeared.

V

*Death is the longest sleep Mouse has known. On and on, she goes floating down a black river without a course or paddle. She is not sad, because she does not understand the nature of sadness. She does not dream, because there are no hopes to fulfill or hidden quandaries to solve. There is a current and shadows and no more with which to concern herself. If she holds onto a raft in the river to nowhere, it is a pyre of the anger that cast her into death. She might have forgotten the "what," "why," or "how" of her grief and her name, even, and yet the rage of whatever is not remembered has branded her soul. It makes her spirit shine in the flowing dark. This alone defines her in nonexistence. This Will is a beacon of wonder for those mighty beings who can see in the blackest blackness.*

**"Traveler,"** *says the Gray Man.*

*Like that, the darkness ripples to gray, and a voice pulls her elsewhere. His words are shivers—not sounds. He is an outline in the mists that well and pour about her ghost like the fog over a smoky battlefield. Nothing is clear in this space. Not her body or the twists in this nonexistence that coax thoughts of snakes, moons, and ocean waves. Here there is a swaying tranquility. She could be in a gray, breezy field or upon a gray sea that rocks a gray boat. She can remember herself at last and not only her anger.*

*"I have come for power," she says.*

*The Gray Man seems to be smiling. However, she cannot tell but for the tickling of the tingles that are his words.* **"Worthy warrior, little Mouse, how far you have traveled to offer yourself. Customarily, we make the offers. We seek our vessels. I am...amused."** *The grayness shudders. She feels it is a laugh.* **"I believe you will show me great amusement. I believe your tale is grander than you know. How brightly you living ones shine for such tiny stars, and you are among the brightest my ancient sight hath seen. Come,**

CHRISTIAN A. BROWN

*little Mouse. My warrior. My poet. Show me the sins and glory of the waking. Make me drunk on their tales. Sing with me their songs. Dance with me their dances. Say the words. Make the vow. Invite me into your soul."*

*"Come," she shouts into eternity. "Enter me."*

*The Dreamer fills her in a gulp of wonder—a breath so large that even fleshless, she stretches precariously. She cannot hope to contain this greatness. Can she? This wistful gust that is the Dreamer meanders across vistas of stars, moons, and other worlds. He is music, and he is the wind. In her mind, she sees flashes of many floating rocks, wonders, and people in the void through which he blows. Can she call them that? People? Some beings are monstrous and horned. Others are pale and glowing. Most she cannot distinguish the ecology of bizarre, prickling, shambling, striding, slimy, elegant, radiant, grisly things that are the animals or more intelligent beings within the tree of stars. How the Gray Man loves the music the waking weave with their tongues, throat flutes, and snouts! How he adores the crack of purple lightning on desolate worlds! He chases the tails of comets and listens to the fluttering of grass on distant plains. Every wind and every willow is an instrument. Every babe born and elderly sigh of parting is a note on his sheet music. The Dreamer's love of the art of life is cataclysmic. It breaks her mind into pieces to try to fathom this delight. He is a bard to the cosmos and a highwayman of time and space. He is the epicure of creation. Now he is inside her and settled, and she no more feels herself stretched to breaking.*

***"Wake,"*** *commands the voice within her soul.*

She did.

Abruptly, he cast her into a winter morning. She awoke unfettered as though from a deep and welcome sleep. She recalled all the wandering and ethereal peace of her talk with the Gray Man. Without a doubt, that Dream pleased her more than did the grimacing, metal-mouthed monster—the Broker, the Jabberwok—and the tremendously mutilated man pointing a flame-tipped rifle in her general direction. At her companions, she realized, and she grasped the whole of the scene.

She grasped so much more than that as well. In a euphoria of heat—the Dreamer's presence—the bard of the cosmos infused her with every detail of the repulsive stories of these men. She knew their tales as wholly as she knew her own. She knew Augustus's great book of sins and abuses, and the

520

full docket of the Broker's crimes against men, boys, women, and animals came to her in a sickening rush. Mouse knew of three ravenous judges who would find fair sentences for the sinners. She owed the red witches a meal.

*May I? May I punish them?* she asked the Dreamer, and felt a shrug of acceptance that she hadn't initiated spasm her body. Sleepily and almost yawning at the intruders, Mouse slipped off her stone bed.

## VI

Mouse knew where Augustus was going, and she imagined the three shadows cackling and readying their sickles. Though she would have liked to visit longer with her friends, she was focused on the second sinner who had dashed through the forest. Silly, wretched monster to think he could escape a being that skipped through stars like a flat stone over a lake. She couldn't tell who was the girl born on Geadhain and who skipped the stars. None of that mattered at the moment.

A tiny skip, and Mouse appeared deep in the forest. She was amid a copse of black pines fluffy with snow. Nearby, the Broker blundered through white banks and bush. He had not seen her and shrieked when he did. In his fear, the animal seized his reason, and he hunched and snarled at Mouse. "What! What did you do? To my...my friend?"

"More than a friend," said Mouse. Her voice was hollow, and her head rang with the gory, masochistic intercourse the two wretches performed together at night. "I'll take you to him."

"Back!" hissed the Broker.

While she stood her ground and grinned, the Broker's stare inked over, and his posture bristled with bone. He began to change. Mouse laughed at his burgeoning monstrousness. She was utterly fearless. Even the Dreamer received his fill of the amusement he sought and flooded her with tingling heat. They let the Broker split his clothes, warp, and thrash into his lumbering, hideous true self—his mashed-up mockery of crocodile and bat and of animal rage and horror. They allowed him to blare, snort, and then pound the forest in a path of stomping doom meant to end her life. She found his grotesque proportions, tusks, and tiny wings more freakishly amusing than she remembered—like a curiosity at a circus show. Ultimately, when the Broker's batty nostrils came so close that snot flew upon Mouse's face, she and the Dreamer were done with this game. They waved and bid farewell.

"Good-bye," they said.

Gently, in keeping with the Dreamer's temperament, there came a cosmic laugh. It was an echoing of bells and wind, and then a gust of flurries plucked up the Broker and carried him away. Vengeance had been served. The dish, though, felt cold and unfulfilling.

She wanted more; she wanted Aghna. Alas, the Dreamer exercised the pull of the chains she'd willingly placed about her neck. *No. No*, he said in his wordless way like lightning bolts to her bones that radiated meaning. *That was an interesting song. However, we have my whims to entertain.*

Amid a whirl and a blur, Mouse returned to the altar and her companions whom she'd left for only a sand. Astonished, they beheld their resurrected friend. Then Morigan rushed ahead, threw her arms around Mouse, and wept with happiness. As soon as they made contact, the strangest thing happened. The ecstasy of the Dreamer rose so hotly in Mouse's body that her mind floated off in a whirl of thoughts, stars, and passions into the waves of thunder the Dreamer rode around the universe. Geadhain and its green dot on the black map to which she now had access looked a dim and pedestrian place to linger when she had all of creation to gallivant across. Mouse left her body temporarily so her master might speak.

**"Daughter,"** said the Wanderer. **"Of all of my children in the great black sea, you are the most precious. I have waited for this moment. To hold you, as the waking do. To feel the flesh of my flesh. I am here. I am with you."**

"You!" cried Morigan.

She pulled herself and the vessel apart and glared in reprimand at the entity that wore her friend. It was a miracle she could see through the queer radiance. The pulsing shadow that filled Mouse's flesh was haloed in blinding light. Merely by stepping into reality, the Dreamer's presence caused whispers and waves in the air around him. Morigan sensed hints of his secrets and his trips and philanthropy toward the living and lesser. She felt racked with all the anxieties and tensions of a girl meeting her truant father for the first time.

"What do you want?" asked Morigan.

The Dreamer came nearer and caressed his daughter's cheek with a starry hand. ***"To hear your music. To sing a song together. I have ever been the watchful moon and sad starlight in the sky, envious of the flesh that could hold what we cannot. Not all those who Dream believe themselves above their creations. I see how we are shaped by life and not merely the shapers. I long for the beauty I see and so rarely touch. I shall see this tale through until its end, which even then is only a beginning."***

The Dreamer kissed his child's head then, and through his lips he passed feeling as overwhelming and sweeping as a tide of flame. Morigan soared through a million worlds alongside a comet and sprays of stars. She witnessed more mysteries in that speck than her dreams or fantasies would ever contain. Entire worlds shone like gemstones beneath the sea. Alien ecologies dominated by thunderheads and walked by beings charged with lightning. The queerest realm like a less-gray Menos where people lived in cement towers and rode self-propelled carriages on wheels.

Through every fantastic voyage, of which there seemed to be no end, a presence, a cosmic wind, rode with her. It glowed with a child's joy. It was her father, and he was love. He was creation's patron, curator, poet, and greatest admirer. Flying with him, she understood her father with the utmost profundity. She knew he had never truly been distant—only hindered by the rules of flesh. Finally, he'd broken that barrier to touch and love something of his own. Of his many children in many worlds—he did not hide from the truth-seeking stingers of her bees—she was indeed the most cherished. For she was the one who could walk between the worlds. It was Morigan to whom he could speak and with whom he would never feel alone.

***"A touch for now is all I shall take. If I do not sleep, this vessel will suffer,"*** said the Dreamer. ***"You are never alone, my child."***

Morigan understood.

Lightly she drifted back into the shadows and away from the shine of the Dreamer. Again she could see clearly in a land more familiar to her than the wonderscapes her father roamed. During Morigan's journey, the Wolf had crept up to his bloodmate and placed a hand upon her. His fire beast in her belly grumbled protectively. Morigan took her bloodmate's hand and her father's too and squeezed both. That was all the introduction she would make between the two. The dark light simply faded, and the Dreamer returned to his sleep.

Mouse returned to her body with a grunt. After traveling the starry ocean of eternity, the cruel shell of mortality felt like such an ugly experience. How bland and cold the world seemed. Then she glanced at the two persons who held her, and she thought perhaps it wasn't all bad. Mouse hadn't been spared any of the Dreamer's secrets, and she knew the connections between her master and her friend. Leaning into Morigan, she whispered to her sister with the greatest care. "I guess we're family now."

"We always were," replied Morigan.

Mouse laughed. The whole day was absurd and delightful. Somewhere in Mouse's flesh, the Dreamer chuckled in his sleep. Tighter and tighter, the two women embraced. After a moment, the Wolf threw himself into the mix. Once he had finished crushing the ladies, he ruffled Mouse's hair as a troublesome brother would. He noticed a stark-white streak near her ear.

"A price," he whispered and brought the matter to their attention. "You will undo yourself if you call upon him too much or too greatly. I would not play with any more magik for a while—if indeed we can even call your miracles that."

Mouse grumbled, tried to hide the streak by pushing it behind her ear, and thereafter struggled to stay upset. In one day, she'd cheated the Pale Lady, filled herself with the power of a lord of creation—a good one too, as that could have gone either way—and vanquished two villains. It was not a bad day for a worthy warrior. Was that what she was? The Dreamer seemed to think so. She smiled. Aghna still needed her due—and a fate worse than the red witches' stewpot. There also remained the threat of a wicked Black Queen who would soon put Geadhain on the dinner table. However, there were those who would defend the Green Mother. Some men and women would scream and thrash against the darkness.

She'd sought the Dreamer to feed her darkness, and she hadn't believed that mission would ever bring her light. Nonetheless, there she stood—no longer powerless and not corrupted by power either. It was quite a messy trip she'd taken to get there down a road of blood and pain. However, all her trials showed that if one only persevered, if one never surrendered wholly to weakness, and if one believed in the strength that came with surrendering to others, then all obstacles would fall.

Still, her vengeance was not forgotten. It had only been postponed. Before she met the white wolf again, she would learn the limits of her contract with the Gray Man, as Aghna was a vessel older and cannier than she was. Aghna could wait. Vortigern was dead, and there would be no bringing him back—or at least her Dreamer had yet to show her how to invoke that miracle. She assumed her father would be happier to see her move on.

*I am a better woman. I am a stronger woman, Father. Not only with power but because I know I can control my hate. I know it will not destroy me. Be patient. I shall avenge you. First I must save the world.*

Spontaneously, Mouse laughed while walking along with her companions. Morigan and the Wolf smiled at this sunshine finally within their dark friend, and they knew the storm of her sorrow had at last started to blow over.

### VII

Left behind, the rest of their company had been scanning the forest like dreary widows when the three finally returned. The Wolf carried both women in his arm sling—as he had Thackery and Talwyn before—and their friends greeted them with joyous shouts. They tried their best to topple the Wolf with their embraces. There seemed no end to the glee, for in a speck, the three returnees realized the dauntingly handsome, somber-browed fellow with a hawk's sapphire stare and peppery ebon hair was Thackery Thule.

"Look at you! Look at you!" cried Morigan, and she poked at the man.

The sage blushed, mumbled about his reversal of the sands of life being no big deal, and fended her off with lean arms that she remembered from her visions. Eventually, Morigan let him be. Needing to tend to her pack before dealing with the Sisters, she took Talwyn into a confidence to tell him of his brother's passing. Morigan could feel he was upset and deeply wounded, even though he made light of the matter. "It's for the best," he said.

Apart from the merry company, the Sisters Three watched the party's interaction from under the veil of vines at the cave's entrance. Ealasyd's brightness burned away their gloomy stealth, and the youngling ran into the laughter and hugs and looked for any place to insert herself.

"I'm so glad you're alive," she said, and grinned at Mouse. "I got in mighty big trouble for saying something I don't even remember!"

Mouse bowed to shake the girl's hand. "I thank you for your words, wise witch. You have done greater deeds than you could know."

"Oh, that's lovely!" replied Ealasyd.

Flighty as a butterfly, Ealasyd slipped away and wandered over to the Wolf. She asked him about the redness on his back. "Scratches," he replied, but she'd already moved somewhere else with another question, the answer to which she was not likely to hear.

Soon Eean came out in the sun, sat on a frosty rock, and took in the happiness of the company. She neither contributed to nor inhibited their play. The serious Sister stayed in the darkness and was unwilling to be merry. While the companions shared their extraordinary tales, the Wolf often spied Elemech watching. The stink of her worry wafted to him, and he noticed her staring at Mouse—or, more accurately, at the divine being slumbering inside her.

*She is scared of the Dreamer*, he whispered.

*Who?* asked Morigan.

*Your mother.* He shook his braided mane. All this familial drama was still a surprise. *It is an unusual dread. Not the fear of a stag being chased. That odor cannot be mistaken. But it is a fear.* He sniffed deeply and caught winey, rosy aromas mulched with Elemech's sweat. *Ha! Love. Damnable as it is. She has affection for the Dreamer and has no idea what to do with herself.*

*We were all afraid of love. Once.* Morigan pulled him tighter, and they kissed. *And look at us now.*

*Yes. Look at us.*

The Wolf smiled through their kiss, and they ended it quickly. Then they and the others joined the wise Sister around her rock and discussed where next their journey would take them. It was another road and another tale but one step closer to the end.

# XXI

# ALLIANCE OF THE DAMNED

I

Dawn yawned on the horizon and washed the sliver roofs of Eod in orange flame. The view from the ivory balcony of the king's chamber struck Beauregard as a wonder that he never, even as the mooniest youth, would have thought to see. A book's worth of miracles and glorious horrors had he witnessed this season, which felt as long as the twenty-two years of his life combined. Inside, regret paced the chambers of his soul—a restless mourner crying Devlin's name. In counting the deeds and dooms wrought and survived, he would have loved for his father to stand with him and gawk at this white and silver city with a veil of pearl magik protecting its great preciousness and beauty.

"Have you ever seen so much splendor or richness?" Devlin might have said. "Behold the afterlife, boy, and call yourself a ghost, for we have truly moved beyond the pale!"

*Boy*, he mused. He was no more one of those. Willowholme and his time there had faded to an innocence he would never reclaim. Now he'd become a sword, the right hand of an Immortal and champion of the City of Wonders.

Already the bards crafted uproarious distortions of his ascension—tales in which he had smote a deathworm with a sword of light and clashed with

Brutus's claws until the villain fled. Epic prose emerged of him unchaining and carrying the King. After riding through the white gates of Eod—sharing the saddle with Magnus—his adoration as a hero had started instantaneously, and he'd been heaped with many titles: the savior of Sorsetta, the hand of justice, and the spellsong. The last was the king's favorite. As usual, the truth was a simpler, sadder tale.

*Amid the absolute sunshine called from his soul, there wavers his father's face. His limbs and torso are like an unfinished watercolor and bleed off into the brilliance. A ghost. Beauregard knows this is the essence of Devlin before his father travels elsewhere. He wants to shout a farewell, but his soul is screaming magik, and the Everfair King's now unbridled power comes with its own furious shout. "Brutus!"*

*With that, a magik much grander than his light rips through him and into the mist. Beauregard cannot see, sense, or hear but for the dazzling winter currents: sapphire bolts, ivory threads, and flapping, cawing, claw-shaped winds that roar and rend as would rabid monsters. All this great arctic storm flows from the one whose chains have been broken. As the unleashed tide of the imprisoned Immortal washes through Gorgonath, Beauregard wonders how he, at its epicenter, is not instantly eradicated by it and turned into a puff of frosty ash. The king's cry is violent, but it has announced the target of his retribution. The king's power is apocalyptic but knows where and whom to harm. Soon Beauregard will learn the Immortal is so noble that, even when he has been stripped to something less than a skinned animal, Magnus would never ruin innocence or life. Thus, while in the midst of the Long Winter reborn, all Gorgonath is merely star-dusted in ice and blinded in snow. Perhaps not the entirety of the city is as privileged as those in the inner bailey. They cling arm in arm and gape at the white hurricane and its kaleidoscope of blues and golds— this beautiful spinning disaster.*

*There is a smaller red distraction in the borealis—the site of Brutus's punishment by fire. On that spot, the king's merciful storm is far from kind, and the pitted Ancient Wall is catapulted with lashes of lightning and meteors of black ice. Not even the Ancient Wall, however, suffers much more destruction than Brutus's horde has already inflicted.*

*When the storm has finally calmed, glassy wax monsters of Brutus's horde decorate the inner bailey. The creatures are frozen so deeply they snap off as the wandering, wonder-drunk crowd of Sorsettan defenders poke at them. Beauregard awakes from his journey into the light. In the past, on certain solstices and celebrations, he has gotten drunk on the honey mead of Willowholme, and today his head is much more sore and dizzy than on the mornings that followed those revelries. As he tumbles, a man catches him with hands that shiver him with electric chill. This is the Everfair King's grip. On and off, Beauregard blinks at the extraordinarily beautiful and mournful figure who holds him.*

*"What a miracle for us to meet." Fingers of ice caress his forehead and then the star on his cheek. The king's whispering continues. "A birthmark. Just like the one true star of the North, as your mother said. I did not forget her words. Come, my liberator. Gentle soul. Noble soul. Your powerful magik has weakened you. Rest, my knight."*

"Are you thinking about him?" asked the king.

Magnus could exercise supreme lightness or stone heaviness, depending upon which aspect of his presence he wished to project. That day, he manifested like a silent white cat of the North and was within strides of Beauregard before the young man noticed him. Once he had been noticed, though, it was impossible not to pay absolute attention.

Magnus was dressed casually for a king in a brigand's silk shirt and simple white pants. Nothing about his proud demeanor was threatening. Still, no matter what clothing the king chose or how approachable and kind his words were, Beauregard—and others—could not break from the magnetism of his presence. Magnus had witnessed nations rise and fall. He'd walked the world through ice, fire, and dust, and these experiences and elements had forged him. In his stare stormed the dread and authority of the Long Winter. Beauregard had seen the king in his icier temperaments gaze at a person with such scorn that he shivered. Only the Iron Queen appeared immune from this effect. In the king's heart burned a sense of righteousness as unquenchable as the Age of Fire. However, the Season of Dust expressed itself most plainly in his sultry, sand-smoothed charisma.

Beauregard was fairly convinced he liked girls. The king's beauty, though, played strange tricks with his own longings—the shock of night that was Magnus's hair, the gemstone eyes through which he gazed, and the pale, admirable body as smooth as a woman's and somehow as hale as a man's. He brought with him a cloud of fragrance of oils and flowers so exotic they could not be placed. No wonder people tied themselves up in knots before the king. Even Beauregard usually failed to stop himself from staring.

That day, at least, he remembered his formalities—or believed he had done so properly. He swept back his cape and bowed. "My king." He required a speck getting down and then up again. The armor and regalia—a silver and ivory breastplate, reinforced leggings, and bracers—were still rather cumbersome for a novice warrior.

"Only bow if I have asked you for service," King Magnus said, and he smiled. "Your knees will be raw and sore if they hit stone every time I address you."

Beauregard puffed. "So many rules. So much decorum I have yet to master."

"You do not need to worry about decorum around me, Beauregard," said the king with a particular sadness. "Together we have been through what destroys most people."

One of the white scars that crossed Magnus's lips often went unnoticed but pronounced itself in the daylight. It was a reminder of his brother's torture and the iron mask—of the wounds that not even eternal flesh seemed to mend. The king and his new spellsong were old friends to pain. They'd met after crawling across a metaphorical, though almost literal, field of broken glass and doom. They were kindred. They had each lost what was most vital to them—love. As much as Magnus had once cared for Erik, he felt endeared to this boy more. They each understood what could be taken. They knew the cost of justice.

If Magnus had not been king, he would have thrown the lad's uncomfortable regalia and every ounce of decorum into the abyss of frivolity where it belonged. What mattered more than court and civilities were the families, friendships, and relations between people. Had he been in possession of this wisdom thousands of years before, the City of Wonders would be a civilization of poets, lovers, and troubadours—a realm without all this technomagik and progress to confuse the relationships that modern advancements were designed to protect.

*The more we achieve, the further we are removed from our values,* the king thought. *I would take it back if I could. Back to Brutus and the wilds. Back to teaching people how to use their tongues for the joy of communication and the community in their souls. Where has all that simple beauty gone?*

As Magnus brooded, a slithering frost threaded over the balusters and under Beauregard's feet. He knew his master's moods and their effect on the environment. He stepped out of the chill.

"My king?" he asked.

Magnus looked down at the glittering railing. "I do often drift off into one mood or another. Thank you for bearing them out." He turned and smote Beauregard with his winter stare. "Your father. I had asked about your father."

"I...indeed," replied Beauregard. "I think of him often. I think of that day in Gorgonath."

"The people are all safe thanks to you and Devlin. Thousands upon thousands. I hope that gives you comfort."

"It does, though it does not bring him life."

"No."

"No."

The men glanced away and gazed out over the city.

"Your mother," said Magnus brightly and abruptly. "Have you had any news?"

"I have." Beauregard chuckled. "A letter the other day from Bainsbury. She is doing well and rather insistent I get on with the details about how I now walk with the king. She speaks of you as if the stars align in your passage." *Which they very well might,* mused the spellsong. He paused. "She asked about my father, whom I have been suspicious in not mentioning past Gorgonath. I haven't told her all our tale. Not yet. News such as that should be delivered in person."

"I shall find some time for you to take a leave and stay with her for a while," said the king. Magnus reached and placed a cold hand upon Beauregard's shoulder. Framing the question delicately, he asked, "What of your other secret?"

"The watchmaster?" Beauregard shrugged.

When he and Galivad had first encountered each other during the initial round of greetings and war salons held in the grand Chamber of Echoes, Beauregard had recognized his brother by the name imparted to him by Devlin, the face, and mannerisms of the fellow. However, the thought of talking with him there and then and in the meetings that followed had paralyzed him and developed into something of a burr in his boot. Moreover, he had yet to tell Tabitha about Devlin, and he felt he should wait until that visit home to learn more about his original parent and his brother—now a watchmaster of Eod—before speaking to Galivad himself with a head half full of notions.

"I still don't know how you knew," said Beauregard.

The king smiled as he explained. "If you watch people as deeply as I do, you can always tell when they are hiding secrets. In the face and eyes, there is a tightness and a clenching to hold the truth. You are quite masterful with your guile for such a young man. Nonetheless, I could see the tension when you and Galivad were in confines together. Yours was a specific discomfiture. A frustration that only blood can bring. For there is a thread that can never be cut between blood. Between brothers..."

"Yes. You would know of that, my king," said Beauregard.

"I would." The king paused. "I shall not press, and I would never intervene with your choices. However, I shall say you should keep in your judgment that family is all we have. It is what defines us."

"Do you still believe that after what Brutus has done?" asked the spellsong.

He had perhaps overstepped his bounds. Few walls existed between this green youth and the ageless king, though. After their nakedness at Gorgonath and the sacrifices made and understood as they held each other like children in an apocalypse, disagreement between them required effort.

"I shall ride the river of love and hate to its head," declared Magnus. "I shall purify Brutus of his demons before he is judged. One cannot condemn the insane for his or her actions. I do hate him with all my heart. Every speck, though, I long for the closeness only he and I can share. Every moment of my existence is a dance between disgust and yearning. I have sealed him out again." Magnus tapped his chest. "Out of my soul. His dark passenger has taken too much of him. Sadly, he is my brother no more."

Even the full font of Magnus's winter could not destroy his Immortal brother back in Gorgonath. Having escaped the deluge of arctic death that poured from Magnus, Brutus had somehow vanished. The wild man was not to be forgotten, though. The mad king and his dark whisperer were sure to return with whatever ghastly, swarming horde of dead, burned, and ravaged souls they needed to wash their stain across Geadhain. A bleak quiet came over the men.

"I believe you will have the reckoning you desire." Beauregard clapped his cold master's back. They truly had forgone all rules between a king and his servant. "I am no seer, so I cannot tell whether it will be a trial to end with a hanging or not."

"Seers. Yes," considered Magnus. "Rowena told me of the one good deed my wife set into motion while I was gone. Of this strange child of the moon named Morigan Lostarot. Living right here in Eod. She is a gift of such power. She is a key in all this. One of many. The great work we make cannot be held together by just one thread. All are necessary for the material's strength. We must meet her eventually. At least we must learn how her quest with Thackery fares."

"Do you trust Alastair to fulfill his agreement?" asked Beauregard.

Beauregard had met the man, but he honestly struggled to recall when. Everything about Alastair—even remembrances—felt smudged and obscured. From the Voice's crafty smirks to the flippancy with which he treated an affair such as the Immortal Kings' devastating feud, Beauregard had developed a spontaneous distaste for the fellow. Even when shaking the man's hand—in the Chamber of Echoes, he now remembered—Beauregard's fingertips had felt greasy afterward. It was as though the snake oil from which Alastair made his trade rubbed off on the palms of others. Still, the shadowbroker claimed to be able to track the heroes in the East, and he was the only resource they had to rely upon for this matter.

"Trust? Hardly," said the king, and he elbowed his frowning companion. "Something in his eyes I strangely cannot read. A familiarity. No matter. From what Rasputhane tells me, he is quite esteemed among his order. The nearest to a leader the Watchers allow. I do not think him honorable, but I do think he can be trusted for this task. He speaks of this young seer and her friends as if he knows them personally. I suspect he has an angle in this dark game we all play. Therefore, we should watch him, as the master watches the servant he thinks might be stealing. Wait to catch the sneak in the act with the lady's jewelry in a bag."

"He'll clean out the silverware too," said Beauregard.

The men laughed. How grand that felt after a week of sullen talks. Still more of those were to come, unfortunately. Always an early riser, Gloriatrix would be waiting. Beauregard fumbled in a small pouch at his waist and pulled out a fine crystal-and-silver chronex.

"I suppose it's time." Beauregard sighed.

Surely the king wanted to entertain these bouts of political bickering no more. The king echoed his sigh with one of his own. Stepping closer to Beauregard, Magnus confided in a whisper, "You know I detest her demands as much as she detests making them. The Iron Queen would rather take than ask, and I can see her silently appraising the value of Eod. Which stones can be broken, sold, and reconstituted in the new, more hideous Iron City she envisions. I shall try to teach her as I would any of nature's corrupted souls the value of light and mercy—two lessons I suspect will roll off her iron flesh. However, it is my duty to try. Once this conflict with my brother has ended and Brutus meets his justice, the snake we have invited into our garden will strike. I know this. Be that as it may, the Iron Queen commands the greatest technomagikal armada that has ever flown over Geadhain, and she has come to us with a plea—however disingenuous—for our aid in ending this war and rebuilding the Iron City."

"She did not come here for diplomacy. She came here to destroy the City of Wonders," spit Beauregard.

In his short life with Magnus and this country, he'd come to love it as much as he had Gorgonath. He felt munificence for every land, people, and wonder in his life. Certainly, his father's passing and the trials of his journey had stimulated this spiritual largesse. Despite his valor and morality, talking about tyrants such as Gloriatrix made him uproariously uncontrolled and angry.

With a touch as light as mist, the king eased the wrinkles from Beauregard's handsome, hate-wrung forehead with a single stroke of chill. In the young man, he saw the same delight in and honor of creation that inspired him to face a life of endless days.

"I know," replied Magnus. "You know I do. What's more, it is the depth with which you care for my city, its lives, and all the lives beyond that will allow us to outwit the Iron Queen in whatever she plots. It is not faery tale or parable, though while darkness is eternal, so too will light always triumph.

There are constants in our world. The sun rises and sets, love blooms and fades, and children are born and die. I have watched so many of these cycles that all I see are movements of gray. No—silver. For all these great movements shine. You understand that beauty. Its essence. I have seen you call forth the wonder in your own heart—a magik conjured through sacrifice. I say this as a true and meaningful honor, Beauregard, but I have never seen or known so noble a child of Geadhain. Consider that from someone as old as I am. With all my memories and champions come and gone, you are a man ready for knighthood, roaring in his blood with chivalry. Trial after trial Geadhain threw at you. Tests of bravery. Challenges of wit and survival. Finally, the choice to balance life, death, and love. You conquered them all. So however dark and horrid a wind Gloriatrix might blow, you and I shall stand and laugh at her fury."

A tear had crept down Magnus's cheek. He wiped it off, and as it froze, he flicked it over the balcony. Then a stiff wind blew up, and thunder rumbled in the pristine sky.

"I thought I had a son, once. A knight," grumbled Magnus. "A man I could trust with my kingdom. Yet he and the woman whom he was charged to protect signed their souls to darkness when faced with no lesser a choice than you made in an instant. I cannot tell you how deeply their betrayals have wounded me. Lila's especially. A thousand years of love thrown into the fires of hate. I hope she loathes herself as much as I loathe her. As much as I loathe myself. For I too have done unspeakable things to her. Things I was a fool to believe even a thousand years of love could heal. As for Erithitek—he did what I have seen weak men do countless times. He cannot truly be blamed. It was Lila's wind to which he bent. I think the man loves her." Magnus laughed, and lightning flickered above them in sudden black clouds. "She is too strong to love him back. She will snap him first." He shook his head. "I thought I knew her as well as I knew my brother. I thought she would preserve the life and kingdom I created. In another handful of lifetimes, I might understand what she has done and what we have done to each other. Then perhaps we might forgive the other...but now to me she is no better than the Iron Queen. A queen of ashes is what she has become."

Magnus's face set into a sneer, and the dark clouds flickered on high. It would rain in a speck, and violently. Beauregard took the king's hand, which had become a fist, and the thunder and graying skies cleared.

"Do you know where they are?" he asked.

"No," spit Magnus. "Better they never return. I seek only my brother now, and every Eye in Eod and beyond hunts him. No one must ever know what Lila has done. It is to our benefit that Menos is so toxic in its dealings it has enemies in every direction that would sabotage its city. Should the Iron Queen ever learn—"

"She will not," assured Beauregard. He thought a little and then added, "I do pity the mater who must play a role for which she was never born."

"If the queen was known to be absent, it would lead to suspicions," said Magnus. "The mater served Eod better than the real queen in my absence. The mater is merely wearing a mask, as we all must do—except for us, here and now. I know not through what Fates I was blessed with the sincerity of your companionship at so dark an hourglass, but I would trade it for nothing."

The two men watched the day rise over the wonder of Geadhain—her red, ancient humps, the coarse breath of her desert, and the great golden eye of her light. They stayed until Gloriatrix and her ghoulish cabinet, which included that strange witch woman who was missing some hair, teeth, and a hand, assuredly fumed at their tardiness. What greater moment could there be, however, than this sunrise? This communal, primitive pleasure of heat and light warming the flesh and soul? Despite the gulf that should exist between man and king, mortal and Immortal, they stood together as true kindred. They were not brothers and not quite friends either. They were men determined to see beauty preserved until its inevitable, graceful end. They were the defenders of Geadhain and knights of the Green Mother. They would fight and die for her honor. What had passed had been a skirmish. Next would be the war with Brutus and the Black Queen—the war of all wars.

Both men gazed so sternly upon the horizon, imagined and real, they failed to heed the bold green bird that fluttered down and perched on the railing until it pecked at the king's hand. Magnus loved the Green Mother's feathered children. They had been his playmates when Brutus was not, and once he'd paid this creature his attention, he noticed it had a special charm. Its white tufts and the long black feathers mixed into its emerald plumage were those of a species he had not seen since—

"Alabion!" he cried.

The bird was cleverer than even a trained, caged animal should be. It pecked again at his hand and then hopped around so they could see a note tied with ribbon to its leg. With haste, the king claimed and unfurled the missive from the unflinching bird. He read the message with Beauregard. Their faces cycled from shock to dread before settling on wonder. The miracle messenger flew away and vanished like a sparkling emerald into the sunshine. Magnus incinerated the note with a burst of cold flame and then scattered its ashes over the balcony. He was smiling slightly. "Hope, at last," he said.

Beauregard nodded. They knew then what must be done.

# XXII

# NEW DAWN, NEW DUTY

I

*All roads come; all roads go.*
*A threadbare cloak no means to show.*
*However far I wander, I cannot stop the song.*
*Green, so green, and ever singing*
*To the Fairest Mother's tune.*
*A pit of the feet*
*On the stony drums of the longest walk,*
*A pat of the beat—of hunger*
*Or rain—on my weary head.*
*Might find some warmth, or straw, or bread.*
*Might find a lass to pass the night.*
*Might find a cove that glimmers bright.*
*In moonlight where the oldest rule*
*From throne of rock*
*And starry pool,*
*I find my humility,*
*Bend to knee,*
*Give prayer to the lords of antiquity.*

*Up on the road once more,*
*With a song and drums of rock and wind.*
*The longest road,*
*The oldest song,*
*It never ends;*
*Not even when I die.*
"The Traveler's Song"—Kericot

F or much of the day, Thackery recited Kericot's poem in his head. He remembered an enchanting bard he'd once heard singing it in a tavern back when he was a young man in Menos. What an out-of-sorts, jaunty number it had made for at the time, considering all the gloom and smoke in which the bard had performed. It had been some middle-class tavern for masters and their whores, witchroot peddlers, and assassins to parley in as he recalled. Curiously, the singer manifested no more tangibly than that recollection—though Thackery remembered the bard's voice as exquisite and husky. This preoccupation with the tune and its singer bothered Thackery all through the morning's travel, and he didn't notice much of the progress the company made. Alabion was relinquishing the holdings of her kingdom. The great green and bark towers had surrendered to pines of normal proportions, and the claustrophobic growth had given way to pleasant gardens of snowy, copse-ringed fields spotted with rocks and icy wading pools.

Conversation remained sparse between company members. Like Thackery, they pondered various dreams, omens, and burdens. An ally walked with them no more, and his sadness was still an ache they each carried. They'd learned the identity of their enemy but not yet her nature. That quest would take them into the lands that time and nature abhorred so greatly that no elements there worked in balance—into the dreaded chaos of Pandemonia.

Thackery was mostly ignorant of the place. He knew only that it was a water-divided continent many weeks' of sailing to the east. How they were to cross the channels that divided the two lands became an issue of concern for later. Whenever worries emerged about a Black Queen, a Black Star, or heading into a realm where the elements were broken and where even, according to Talwyn, Morigan's magik might not work, he pushed them into the drawer that was growing rather stuffed with concerns. Besides, the bard in that dingy memory seemed enough to occupy him at the present.

"Sh!" said the Wolf suddenly.

A flash of his hand stressed the need for caution. As practiced and careful as assassins, they assumed hunches, crept through the snow, and used the trees for concealment. A clearing lay not far off, and they saw hints of silver and movement within the space. Voices too came through the flecked winter air. Too shocked to hold his gasp, Thackery recognized one of men speaking. He'd been mulling over the husky voice—not crooning on this occasion—for the bulk of his morning.

"The Voice!" he said loudly. "That's his voice! Alastair or whatever his name is!"

"Alastair? Here?" exclaimed Mouse.

Much to Adam's chagrin, Mouse dashed ahead and disappeared through the trees. Adam called after her and was plainly heard through the agency of the magik stone Elemech had given him—a sliver of rock from the Sisters' aerie fashioned into a twine necklace. The magik did nothing to stop Mouse.

"Fionna! Come back!" he called, and he took off after her.

Morigan then rose from her crouch, since her stealth was now quite spoiled. She strode to catch up with the headstrong members of their pack, and she and her bloodmate came to a parting of the forest. Amid the bushes and rocks trundled in snowy coats spread a clearing. Within, balanced on delicate spider legs of metal, stood a grand skycarriage of Eod with dozens of shining portals along its bow—a ship for many passengers.

On the glass steps of the vessel, two men sat and regarded each other disdainfully. One gentleman was the foxy Voice most of them knew. The second was lean and quite white. The proper fellow seemed a bit like Vortigern in his poise and stature and was quite possibly a lord or at least a Menosian man of means. Apart from this initial resemblance, the fellow held himself more austerely than Vortigern had, and his expression seemed most comfortable as a scowl. A bowler cap rested on his knee, and he tapped the end of an embellished cane off the stairway. Upon spotting the man and catching his unmistakable waft of blood—a stink set beneath the skin from years of killing—Caenith growled and swelled with veiny intimidation.

"Impressive," said Moreth. "I heard you were an animal. Now, though, I see you are so much more."

"Do leash him, please," said Alastair, and he rose.

"What are you doing here?" asked Mouse. "How did you even find us?"

"My dear, mighty Mouse," Alastair replied patronizingly, and he strode down into the snow and gave her a dramatic, insincere embrace.

He did not explain that craftily slipped into her garments during their last meeting had been an abundance of witchneedles—the magik of which had certainly helped him track her. He didn't have to explain this. Mouse's mind quickly deciphered his coyness. She would do a thorough search of her garments as soon as she was alone.

"The King of Eod received your message," said Alastair.

Next, he approached Morigan and the Wolf. To each of them, he bowed with an unexpected and sincere respect.

"That was not our message," replied Morigan. "Thackery had the idea to send word of our progress to Eod. I am glad the message traveled fast and far. I am glad the King of Eod is well enough to receive our words."

They'd made a last request of the Sisters to send a missive to King Magnus and Queen Lila recounting their discoveries. Thackery had written a colorful letter. He had sketched the heights and failures of their journey and given it to the Sisters to deliver through whatever messengers they might use.

"Indeed," said Alastair. "That is why we have come—to bring you to Pandemonia so your quest may continue. The sands pour ever on, and time is our worst enemy in this war. Please come aboard. The flight to Pandemonia is a long one."

"Come aboard?" The Wolf gathered phlegm and spit. "With him? I know that smell now. It is the blood paint of the House of El. Why does a silver dove of Eod fly with a deathmonger of Menos? Has the whole world gone mad?"

"What a lively and angry beast," said Moreth. His waxy mask tensed into quite a hideous grin. "You will need a guide where you are going, and I know those lands better than even the greatest trackers in Pandemonia. Even you, with all your...delightful barbarity, will struggle. Pandemonia is twice the monster you might be. Why am I here to help? Yes. I can see the stupefaction

CHRISTIAN A. BROWN

dripping from each of your faces. From the state of you savages, I would not expect you to know of affairs occurring in civilized realms. The East and the West are allies, united against the mad king and the dark forces he has conspired with to ruin Menos. We are all together. Friends."

Shrugging theatrically, Moreth cackled as madly as a lunatic eating broken glass, and he clacked up the stairs into the skycarriage. An ironguard and a Silver watchman stood on each side of the portal and looked uneasy.

"The journey is long, and we shall have much time to talk," promised Alastair. "Everything is not as strange as it might seem—though all is quite... unknown."

Into the skycarriage the Voice swept as well. The companions remained outside frowning, shuffling, and grimacing as they tried to resolve the concept of Eod and Menos, with all their fundamental resentment of one another, as allies. Eventually, Thackery attained whatever resolution he needed to move on, and he climbed aboard the vessel. He was too intrigued by how Alastair could be the same bard in his memory from years ago and yet untouched by age since that time. Another Immortal? Another pilgrim to the Sisters? He must know.

Mouse followed him next, and Adam went with her. Talwyn gave a nervous shrug to the bloodmates and hurried up the steps. Morigan and the Wolf remained outside in the winter. They passed thoughts, fears, starshine, and fire-wolf rumblings into the other.

*The world is sicker than I knew,* said the Wolf.

*It is just change, my Wolf. Change is never to be feared. Shall we see what changes the East will bring? I would be lying if I said this hunt with you has been anything but extraordinary.*

The Wolf smiled, sharp and handsome, and his fire flared within Morigan. *A hunt,* he thought, and the wilds of the East now thrilled him. It was a new land to conquer with his bloodmate—further mysteries to chase and devour. Perhaps they would play this game forever. He certainly hoped so.

*When this is done, we hunt and chase and roam. We are free from Fate and bound only to each other,* he said.

*I swear to you,* she promised.

542

With her dainty hand in his great one, they walked onto the skycarriage and bid farewell to the secrets and sorrows of Alabion. They decided on no more sorrows or suffering. They were the hunters of Fate—recalcitrant children made to break the laws and defy the most ancient of beings and orders. To the shivering guards they passed, the bloodmates' mischievous expressions seemed to imply a need to be careful of what one wished for. If the makers wanted chaos, then chaos they would bring. No Dreamer or design would be safe from their hunt.

# EPILOGUE

The woods trembled in dread that day. Groves drowned more with shade than sunlight, and there were few tweets and grumbles from the many denizens of the wood. The ice-patched streams Eean crossed throughout her foraging appeared blocked with rafts of twigs, leaves, and often a dead, rotting animal or two. She was without her sister's foresight, yet she sensed these jutting obstructions were omens of chaos. Therefore, rather than tend to the hunt for fragments of Fate for little Ealasyd, she followed this trail of destiny.

She began to tread through steaming black mulch of thawed greenery gone to waste. What a rotten trail it was, Eean quickly discovered. She used her cane to lift away the gooey brown serpents that had once been vines. She gently kicked more astonishingly decomposed carcasses out of her path, and she sighed at these beasts' suffering. A visitor had come to Alabion—a lady whose passage wilted life and made footsteps (or potholes) of blubbery maggots. These too Eean dodged with her nimble steps. In her adult flesh, Eean became the fastest ranger in this realm, and locating the defiler took only sands. Soon she'd circled around the Pitch Dark, forded an angry rapid that winter could not freeze or tame, and ended up somewhere east of the white groves atop the changeling city. The pale trees glowed distantly above, and the tree line dipped and ran into a valley.

She contemplated what awaited her and then descended. The snow melted, the trees flopped like rotten cornstalks, and she slogged down a hill of black slop. She was filthy when she reached the bottom, and she huffed in disapproval. The source of this ruin lay ahead. She saw the vessel moving next to the most atrophied trees in the forest, which had turned gelatinous in texture and buzzed with flies. An ebon-splattered geriatric fellow moved amid the quagmire. He was digging, from what she could tell.

She waved her hand before her nose to help disperse the spoiled apple-and-manure stink and went forward a little. She stopped when she stood close enough to see the vessel better. Already, a grave toll had been extracted from him. He looked more bones than skin and more scalp than hair. He had as many spots and as much beauty as a toad. As the vessel turned from the pit in which he labored, he growled at her to stay her distance. She noted that his teeth had all fallen out. That did not prevent his mistress from forcing her dry, echoing speech through his gummy hole of a mouth. ***"You cannot stop me, Sister of the woods,"*** said Death in her voice of shivers, spiders in the ears, and scratching leaves upon stone. ***"I shall have this vessel."***

Eean had not come to interfere. With narrowed and moody eyes, she watched the vessel finish exhuming items from the grave—two arms, a pair of legs, a torso, a heart, and at last a head. Eean knew to whom the body parts belonged. Nonetheless, she merely observed and frowned. She would not intervene in this desecration.

When the vessel had finished his work, he removed himself from the grave. The act shattered one of his brittle shins, and he slumped to a knee. As the vessel needed to touch the dismembered remains anyway, his failing at this moment and his inability to be operated further did not matter to his mistress. There existed a certain delectable irony, thought Eean, in how this man who had once played with the strings and hearts of the living had been transformed into a puppet.

"What she wills, she wills," whispered Eean.

Sorren finished his final task. Dark clouds splotched the heavens, and brilliant whips of lightning suddenly lashed the sky. Thunder wailed, and a great screeching, pulling wind came forth. However, Eean could not be moved. She was not dashed about like the uprooted trees and animal corpses that circled in the air. The jets of black mud going off around the area like geysers did not strike her. Eean pulled tight her shawl and leaned on her staff. She waited for the door to eternity to shut itself. Raising the dead and reinstating the soul within its cage of flesh was a messy evocation—an affront to all nature's laws. She scowled at the perversion and at the howling rage from both the Green Mother and the spirit being beaten back into his body. He must have agreed to come back. He must have agreed to whatever unfair terms the Pale Lady had proposed, for the desecration calmed. Once the leaves and debris had settled, the naked and gray-skinned man in whom Death resided—still as ghastly and handsome as before—stepped over the husk of the last vessel and toward Eean.

*"I came for the girl-maggot of this bloodline. I see, though, that you filled her already,"* said Death. *"I should thank you for your interference. This vessel honors me with its anguish and rot."*

"If you have what you seek, leave our lands," said Eean.

The Dreamer hesitated, and the land hushed with an unearthly calm. It was a beat in which the wind and all creatures of Alabion fell quiet—the contemplativeness of Death. Canny Eean fathomed a few of Death's workings—how, on her secret abacus of bones, she calculated the measure of keeping the meddlesome presence before her alive. Every creature would pass into Death's embrace eventually, even the Sisters Three. When that sand came, the Dreamer would give them no lenience. Death was as merciless as her dark mother, Zionae, was—only leagues more dangerous, because Death was not insane. No—death was an element as passionate and single-minded in her rationale as a plague. Death represented a single shade of color: black. Death became the last paint on the picture and the only stroke that mattered, for hers was what finished each and every picture in creation. Eean wondered whether it was her turn to be painted. Was this her time? Without her Sisters, her magik might not be enough to defend herself—and her claim to existence—against the fury of one who slept beyond.

"Awfully quiet when it was so noisy here not long ago," croaked someone behind her.

"Ruined our meal, it did," said another.

In a rustle of crimson, Morgana—chewing what was certainly a finger—stepped alongside her almost-twin in the muck.

"You should not be here, Dreamer," said Morgana. "These are our woods. We bring death here. Not you."

"Go," all four witches hissed, united.

A Sister and a trio of shadows were not adversaries Death felt like testing with her new vessel. She frowned and then crumbled into a whirl of ashes that twirled away into the sky. Eean kept her thanks from the shadows for coming to her aid. They were Alabion's wrath. They had their own principles of rage, punishment, and violence that they heeded. Moreover, it would be as vainglorious as congratulating oneself, for these shadows were only her Sisters' and her natures separated and given form. Or had she confused the hierarchy of this arrangement?

"Your time is almost up," warned Morgana, and she strode off. "The Green Mother is angry. The Green Mother trembles in rage. She will not suffer your games, these Dreamers, or their fools anymore. The season of temperance has ended. We move ahead, my shadow, into the season of blood."

"Wait. What about that one? He smells delightfully wicked," whispered Malabeth.

"Leave him be," snapped Meag, with her eye for fats and flavors. "He is a collection of stale bones, and the meat is quite spoiled. Not even good for stock."

The shadows faded.

Once they'd left, Eean wandered to the shivering, broken creature who'd endured Death's abuse. By whatever stubborn miracle, he squeezed out faint breaths. Sorren deserved no mercy, but Eean had in her heart the compassion at least to attend to a creature for its final heartbeats so it would not die alone. So she squatted and watched the wretch wheeze slower and slower. It was the tempo of an end that she knew so well. "Do not fear the darkness," she murmured. "Something grand or wondrously horrible comes after. But only if you do not linger or become lost."

Sorren's single blue eye suddenly gleamed like a wishing star in the muck. He clung to life. Sorren whispered for Eean to come close, and though his lips only moved and he drooled into the mud, the Sister heard him plainly.

*My mother...my brother*, he said.

*What of them? They are no more a worry of yours. Close your eyes, and go into the dark.*

*No.*

*Yes.*

*I shall not.*

Mayhap he was not simply being petulant. Was there was a reason for Sorren's resistance—some desire that bound him to a body that could not speak or move? At their ends, men reminisced about lost glory, lost women, and lost pride. However, this soul worried for the woman who'd delivered him into Geadhain and the brother he'd devoted his adulthood to loathing and punishing in the vilest ways. How different this seemed from his last plea before the dark, which had been all selfishness and envy. At the doorway to damnation, had he discovered something genuine? A sliver of true soul? A meaning beyond self-idolatry and gratifications? Eean found herself intrigued. Eean felt compelled to hear the rest of what he might say.

*I must*, he began.

She leaned nearer and listened to his secret whispers and confession. After passing on his truths, the winds of his Fate would go in one of two directions. Either Eean would walk on and leave him for the winter to freeze and the beasts to frolic over his bones, or the Green Mother would compel her to offer him a bargain. Unlike what her shadow Morgana had proclaimed, it seemed Geadhain was not yet spent of mercy. The rush of divinity entered the Sister. She felt the Green Mother's grace as a rapturous shiver in the woods, the cold kiss of a breeze, and sudden flurries. She felt it as the ripple of a grand mystery in the clouds and the bursting smell of raw wet soil piercing the reek of the dead swamp in which she and her supplicant remained.

She had her answer. Perhaps he would find his salvation. "*Siogtine* (Penance)," she said.

At that, Sorren's toothless mouth flinched into what smile he could wring from himself, and Eean slung him upon her oaken back and carried him into the trees.

—*Fin*—